Pilgrim

Mitchell Lüthi

SENTINEL
CREATIVES

Book Cover by Rune Hrafnagaldur

1st edition 2023

For mom and dad.

"Tainting the air, on a scirocco day, the carcase of a hound, all loathsome, lay in Nazareth's narrow street. Wayfarers hurried past covering mouth and nostrils, and at last, when purer air they reached, in Eastern style they cursed the dog, and the dog's owners' ancestors, and theirs who, bound to care for public cleanliness yet left the nuisance there to poison all around. Then, that same way, there came 'Isa, the son of Mary, of great fame for mighty deeds performed in Allah's Name. He said, 'How lovely are its teeth, so sharp, and white as pearls': then went his way."

— J. E. Hanauer

"Rat!" he found breath to whisper, shaking. "Are you afraid?"

"Afraid?" murmured the Rat, his eyes shining with unutterable love. "Afraid! Of him? O, never, never! And yet--and yet-- O, Mole, I am afraid!"

— Kenneth Grahame, The Wind in the Willows

1

She has many names, as all great cities do. *Aelia Capitlonia, Shalem, al-Quds, Bayt al-Maqdis.*

Jerusalem.

The name itself is a promise, a proclamation: that this is the city of peace. Within her narrow streets, a kaleidoscope of colour and smells riot. A profundity of voices fill the vaulted spaces, their words scrawling through the air, echoing between tapering walls and arched corridors. Swathes of early light conjure up the city, bringing the substantiality of her being into existence. To those who know her past, who understand the contradiction embedded within her name, there is a heaviness to her presence, and yet, still, they long for her.

She awakens from the cobwebbed depths of a fevered dream, her eyes wide and luminous, for a moment vivid with the nightmare architecture of her dreams. The shadows disperse as she stirs, but they linger at the edges of her smile—beneath the domed rooftops and crenellated walls, within the ingresses and niches, the crooked façades where men with faces to match the cracked stone live and breathe and play out the city's contradictions in an irregular symmetry.

Their smiles conceal a fear they all share: of transgression.

Not of the violation itself.

But of having transgressed—and been seen to do so.

There is no moral accounting that can absolve them from the sin of what they have done. The truth that lies at the heart of their own contradiction: that they have come to Jerusalem to kill in the name of God, to violate His most sacred laws in His name. And if not to kill, then to rut like pigs in her lavish dominion, engorged and engorging themselves upon her ample offerings. There is no paucity of gold and silver in God's kingdom. It pays for the frankincense and myrrh that mask the smell on bone-dry days when the blood spilt into every crevice curdles in a reek that fills the gutters, rising up the lime-washed walls and bright stucco casements. Whorls and skeins in the stone laid bare. Patterns thought random, unveiled—now, their origins known.

But the incense and gorging, the violent distractions, cannot hide another fitful truth left unspoken by all who reside within her walls: that she would give herself willingly to whichever suitor claimed her next and had the strength to hold her. That this is a city born of a confusion of truths, and in such a place, lies pass as easily as truths on the tongues of saints and priests, mad men and lepers.

The three doomed men, a Hospitaller and two Templars from Antioch, waited at the foot of the gallows while their crimes were read out to the watching crowd. They had broken the king's peace with Nur ad-Din, and now not even the protection of Rome would see their necks spared.

Dietmar recognised one of the men, a Saxon from Odenwald, who had ridden east, first to fight for God, and then for land. They had rolled dice together in the gambling halls of Malcuisinat and shared a bottle of sweet wine from a Venetian barge docked in Jaffa. The man's temper had flared with the drink, revealing a sharp tongue and a sour mood. Nevertheless, they had parted ways amicably enough, with Dietmar's purse all the heavier for the man's drunkenness.

The other two were strangers to him.

They squatted in the shade in their dirty gambesons, talking quietly amongst themselves while their sins were recounted. By their sand-washed skin and oily hair, they hadn't been afforded the opportunity to bathe since their capture. Dietmar searched their faces for signs of guilt, some trace of remorse, or regret, or even fear. Despite their filth, the fetid stench no doubt emanating from their boots and stained vests, they held their heads high. They even laughed at a joke shared by one of the Templars, their teeth showing like hyenas from behind cracked lips.

We have done no wrong, those smiles seemed to say. *We are God's warriors and shall reap our reward.* Never mind the temporal laws they had violated, the oaths they had broken when they rode out from Kerak to hunt Syrian convoys on the road to Egypt.

Has it come to this again?

He thought of the last time he had seen Christian men reject the will of the king, and of the fortress in the sand they had all died in. They had met their fate with their heads held high, too. Proud, foolish men. But theirs had been a rebellion encompassing both the spirit and the mind. They had not only aimed to defy the temporal laws governing all Franks in Outremer but also to *break away from them*, to establish an independent, sovereign dominion beyond the laws of Amalric and Nur ad-Din. In doing so, they had declared themselves heretics and iconoclasts. To go against Jerusalem was to go against God.

That had been different, Dietmar decided, watching the knights below as they were urged to their feet.

"An unfortunate twist of fate, don't you think?" Gelmiro, the man at Dietmar's side, took a sip of his wine and squinted down at the square from their terraced balcony. "I wonder if these men would have come to

Jerusalem if they had known that they would eventually hang for fulfilling their oaths?"

Dietmar shrugged. "They swore fealty to the king."

"And chastity. Yet you'll find a Templar's mantle hanging from the doors of every brothel in the Levant. Should we hang them too?"

Dietmar sighed, recognising the trap for what it was.

He shook his head.

"So, what's the difference?"

"The difference," Dietmar said, turning to appraise his companion, "is that Nur ad-Din has it in him to sack Jerusalem, whereas the whores do not."

Gelmiro laughed and patted Dietmar's arm. "Wouldn't that be a more pleasing prospect? An army of whores, wielding swords like cocks as they storm the Temple Mount. Our brave knights powerless to stop them for fear of killing the bastards they'd pumped into their bellies."

Dietmar choked on his wine and shook his head. "God's teeth. Are all Iberians as coarse as you?"

"Are all Germans as genteel?"

"No."

"Then yes."

Dietmar shook his head again but smiled this time. He'd mistaken Gelmiro for a turcopole or Seljuk when they first met. The Patriarch's secretary dressed like a local, donning the silk burnous and slippers, perfuming himself with saffron and musk. His short black beard resembled that of a Syrian, and his swarthy complexion stood out among the Franks of the king's court. Dietmar had greeted him in clumsy Arabic, raising an embarrassed eyebrow at Gelmiro's lengthy reply in kind, before the secretary's face had broken into a grin, and he revealed himself to be a sevillano from Al-Andalus; "too barbaric to be an Arab."

Dietmar watched his friend while he drank. Gelmiro's foolishness sometimes caused him to forget that he was a powerful man, one that had the ear of the Patriarch and more. His vulgarian ways were disarming, and Dietmar often let his guard down after a few of Gelmiro's quips. But that was probably the point. Gelmiro's mind was always at work, constantly seeking an advantage. Each smile that graced his face was calculated, every coarse word intended to shock and disarm so that whatever followed would be more palatable—usually, a favour involving a risk only the truly desperate would consider.

In nature and temperament, as well as in appearance, they couldn't have been more different.

Dietmar stood a full hand taller than his companion, his broad shoulders and thick chest filling out the tunic he wore. His hair, left long in the style favoured by his countrymen, hung past his neck. He had started shaving when he noticed the first flecks of grey in his beard but had then decided to let it be. He was no longer a young man. Those years when the boldest took advantage of their agile limbs and courage to leave their mark on the world had been spent forging the legacies of other great men—and taking their coin for the effort. But soon, those years would be behind him as well.

His hazel eyes swept over the throng below, taking in the panoply of skin and linen, tunics and *khalats*, the variations of brown and white, dust and bone. Such a condensed array of individuals—lords and noble, landowners and merchants, shoulder-to-shoulder with waifs and labourers—was unthinkable back home. But here, where men's fortunes rose and fell with the sun, the distinction was less obvious. The crowd shifted on the uneven grots, their attention divided between the words of the Marshall and the sharp elbows of their neighbours.

"I will miss our conversations, sevillano," Dietmar said, raising his cup to sip from but then deciding against it, leaving it on the table instead.

The vintage was too heavy for him, the heady mix of tannins left a bitter aftertaste and stained his teeth. He had grown to prefer the local *vinellos*, watered down as they were.

"I will miss your miserable company too, *seigneur*. Whose wise counsel will I elect to ignore with you gone?"

"You have enough greys in your beard to seek your own counsel now," said Dietmar, his tone becoming serious. "And I have my affairs back home to attend to."

"Seven years is a long time."

"Aye," replied Dietmar.

It was.

Seven years since he'd handed custodianship of his land to the church. Seven years since he had last laid eyes on the black forests of Zwingenberg and breathed its cool air. Seven years since he had stood in the glade where his wife and son were buried.

Gelmiro seemed to hesitate, as if he were building himself up to something, like a dog about to beg for scraps. Dietmar braced himself.

Here it comes.

He had known there would be a proposition from the secretary—their enjoinders were rarely free from the web of plots and intrigues Gelmiro had entangled himself in. At his most cynical, Dietmar often wondered if he wasn't just another piece in a game Gelmiro was playing, a means to an end.

But perhaps that was his conscience reflecting a dark thought of his own: that he, too, was using Gelmiro. His relationship with the secretary had proven most profitable, contributing a significant amount of coin to pay off his debts during the seven years he had spent in the Levant. In him, Gelmiro had found a willing sword and a reliable ally. Someone whose presence as a *chevalier* elevated situations beyond that of mere sell-swords. And, more importantly, someone whose loyalty was assured.

Dietmar glanced at his friend, expecting to see the knowing grin that usually preceded any discussion involving money and violence. But there was something almost apologetic about the look on the Iberian's face.

"What is it?" he asked quietly.

The crowd roared below as the Marshall finished reading out the convictions. Now, the knights were ushered up the gallows steps toward the waiting hangman, like a lion in its cage, starved to make space for these breakers of the peace.

"It is a minor thing," Gelmiro said, fidgeting with his ring.

"Not so minor as to spare me a priest's hesitation. I have seen that watchful look on you before. It usually means trouble. Spit it out."

Gelmiro placed his cup on the table beside Dietmar's and straightened his back. "You would find yourself in the Patriarch's favour if you were to escort a relic of His Holiness to a chapel in Naples on your way home."

"That… is a minor thing."

Gelmiro took a breath. "Against the wishes of King Amalric."

"Fuck no."

"Dietmar, please. There is much to be gained here. An offer from the Patriarch is not to be rejected out of hand."

"Forget it."

The Iberian raised his hands in exasperation. "Be reasonable. Rome wishes to see this done."

"Yeah?"

"The highest authority."

Dietmar waved a hand at the men on the gallows, their nooses being slipped over their heads and tightened around their necks. "Tell that to them."

Gelmiro picked up his cup, drained it, and refilled it from the flagon. His hands were shaking. "I sometimes forget there's no love lost between you Germans and the Pope. This petty feuding is not worth your time, not with so much at stake."

"Politics," Dietmar said. He didn't concern himself with man's obsession with power; that was Gelmiro's job.

"Everything is politics."

"Not everything. Keeping this head on its shoulders, for one. And the rest of my body out of the charnel pits of Mamilla, for another. There's no politics in that."

Gelmiro gave him an exasperated look. "Then forget about the politics. Think about what might be in it for you. The Church has the power to forgive the debts against your land and grant you absolution for years to come."

"What use is that if I am dead?"

"There's more." Gelmiro stared into his cup, swilling the wine as they listened to a priest performing last rites below.

"Do this," he drained the cup and left it beside the flagon. "And there is a chance your boy will see heaven."

Dietmar stared at him, his anger rising. "Bastard."

"Peace, friend," said Gelmiro with a placatory gesture, though he shrunk back in the face of Dietmar's glare. He waited for Dietmar's nod before continuing. "I am a bastard. Everyone from Murcia to Cairo knows this. But I am not a liar, not with you, anyway. My master will petition Alexander III to absolve the sins of your child, and so he will be granted God's grace. I will see it done. You have my word."

"Sins," Dietmar growled. What crimes had his child committed that the murderous knights below had not done a thousand times and more? Even with the hangman's noose around their necks, they were granted absolution by the ink of a papal bull and penance by the words of a priest. His son's only crime had been to die before he was christened and to break his mother's heart when he had.

“It is possible,” said Gelmiro softly. He could see the anger boiling behind Dietmar’s eyes, waiting to spill over into action. He had broken his friend’s trust in this, he knew—using his boy’s fate like a bargaining chip, like coin, or secrets, or lies. Just another tool to get what he wanted. He was better than that, he wanted to say. Only he knew he wasn’t.

“There is precedent,” he offered instead. He was giving his friend a chance, and if helping him helped himself, surely there was no shame in that? “The Holy Innocents. Unbaptised Jews who received the Beatific Vision without fulfilling the sacrament.”

“Their baptism was one of blood,” said Dietmar, shaking his head. “To die for your faith is to enter God’s grace. It is not the same.”

“No, no it is not.” Gelmiro conceded. “I am merely suggesting that there are more ways than one to cleanse the soul of original sin. If the Pope can grant remission to all who march behind the cross, perhaps he can find a way to grant absolution to your boy. At the very least, you will have God’s highest representative on earth petitioning for his soul. That must count for something?”

Dietmar grunted, mulling it over. It was a good deal, he had to admit. But that only made him suspicious.

“The king and your master, they are still at odds?”

Gelmiro winced. “Things have been… bitter between Amalric and the Patriarch. My master is eager to see relations between them settle so that the business of running the kingdom can continue in earnest. But…” He waved his hand noncommittally.

“Perhaps something the Patriarch should have considered before forcing Amalric to leave his wife? Divorce will do that to a man, make him bitter.”

“He had no choice in the matter.” Gelmiro sighed. “It was the baronage who decided it was time for Agnes of Courtenay to go. But I’ll admit that was poorly done. Now Amalric is eyeing the Church’s properties and wondering if he shouldn’t divorce us from our rentals in exchange. Of course, it was his new wife's idea to begin with. Sometimes I think God is mocking us."

Dietmar chuckled. "It'd be a shame if the Church were to be deprived of her rentals. That's what? Half the city?"

"You laugh, but it would be a catastrophe." Gelmiro dusted off the sleeves of his burnous and leaned against the balcony, sweeping the gathered crowd with his bead-like eyes. They were dark in his skull but missed nothing. "The Patriarch's income from those properties is substantial. Without it, the Church would surely flounder, and the city along with it."

Dietmar frowned as his gaze shifted toward a pair of fellahin urchins watching the platform below. Their rags were no cleaner than those of the condemned, though they had committed no crimes to earn their inequity.

"And how much of that income goes to alms, I wonder?" Dietmar looked away from the scene, gazing out over the city. "I see the Patriarch has begun work on restoring the old walls of the Sepulchre. And the masons are already talking about the profits they'll make from his new tower in the Quarter."

"Important work," Gelmiro replied. "This city flourishes off the back of the pilgrim trade. The holy sites must be maintained, old ones restored—"

"New ones invented."

"Indeed." Gelmiro winked. "So I would prefer if the Patriarch's name, or mine for that matter, were never mentioned. It might give Amalric the pretext he needs to snatch up the last privileges of the Church. There is nothing the Court could do; he would have his 'just cause'."

"Aye, he would," Dietmar agreed, leaning against the railing beside Gelmiro, steepling his fingers as he thought things through. He had originally planned to secure passage from Jaffa before returning home to his own lands at a leisurely pace, perhaps visiting old friends along the way.

This changes things.

"If we were discovered—"

"Don't be."

"But if we were…" Dietmar's voice trailed off.

"Then you will be on your own. My master won't intervene. He cannot afford the risk. I will do what I can unofficially, but…"

"We'll hang."

Gelmiro nodded. "That's the short of it. If they catch you in the desert, I suspect they'll forego the trial and bring back your heads. Regardless, it's a risk worth the reward, yes? I see your eyes, old friend, you are tempted."

Dietmar snorted. "Why does Amalric care what the Pope does with his relics?"

"*Politics*," said Gelmiro, a smile peeking through his beard.

"If I'm to risk my neck for this, I'd rather know why."

"So, you'll do it?"

"Aye, you knew I would, you sly weasel."

"I suspected. There was as good a chance you'd fling me off the balcony instead."

"I still might," said Dietmar. "I haven't made up my mind about that yet."

Gelmiro chuckled, then raised his hand, staring into his palm.

Down below, the crowd roared into life, cheering as the priest descended from the gallows' steps. Knight killing was a bitter business, but that didn't stop them from enjoying the show.

Gelmiro waved his hand with a delicate flourish, moving his fingers like the wings of a starling. Like them, the starling did not belong here. It was an intruder, an interloper in the land of nightjars and sparrows. Only through violence had it managed to impose itself, fashioning the natural order around its presence. And like them, only violence could dislodge it.

"Eleza Ephium could cure the sick with a single touch." Gelmiro turned his hand over and then dropped it by his side. "Leprosy, pox, rot… All cured. Sadly, through an irony crueller than that which has befallen our rampaging friends below, he could not heal himself. He eventually succumbed, drawing his last breath in some poor house in Cyprus, where he'd spent his final moments helping the weak and infirm. For that, he was made a saint. His hand, preserved by God's will and not a little care, is said to have retained some of its miraculous properties."

"What's that to the King?"

Gelmiro swayed his head, bobbing it like one of the court's preening peacocks. "I suppose you'll find out soon enough. The King's boy, young Baldwin. They say he is a leper."

Dietmar sighed. He had heard the whispers, impossible to avoid in a city steeped in courtly gossip. He'd paid them little heed; such things were as unlikely to be true as they were dangerous to know. Even a lie could get your throat cut if it were the wrong lie. "Poor bastard," Dietmar muttered. He was as good as dead already. "How old is he now? Ten? Twelve?"

Too young to have truly lived, to have even known what it was that he was losing.

"Old enough to understand his fate," Gelmiro replied, fidgeting with his ring as he voiced his thoughts. "If the boy is to one day rule, he will require an advantage—or at least the appearance of one. Even if the hand does nothing, the court has yet to confirm Amalric's line of succession… They won't accept the boy if they think him weak."

"So, it is politics," Dietmar growled.

Gelmiro nodded. "We must be cautious. If his father were to catch wind of our plans, the Patriarch would disavow any involvement, and we would both face the hangman's noose. I don't need to tell you, but that fate would not befit my neck. Nor yours. I would much prefer to see us grow old and drunk together. You in your cold, dark castle across the Rhine, and me sipping wine in God's Kingdom."

"So why move it?" Dietmar swiped lazily at a fly hovering near his cup. The sun was warm against his skin, and it felt good to be in it, even if it was to witness a hanging.

From his spot on the terrace, he could just make out the gardens adorning the inner walls of the city. Neatly trimmed rose hedges followed the walkways, which cut between the carnations and jasmine rows. The pathways culminated in a fountain in the middle of the yard, surrounded by tall cedars and wide-limbed lemon trees.

On the other side of the garden, away from the living quarters, lay the stables and livestock markets. All manner of birds rested in hocks, waiting to be bought for food, or their eggs, or their songs. Pigs wallowed in the mud closer to St. Stephen's Gate. Nobody cared for their songs.

Dietmar could see as far as Mount Montjorie, where the Christian kings had camped the eve before taking Jerusalem. They'd stripped the forests bare to fuel their siege, leaving behind a gnarled mound.

Behind him was their prize—the peaks of the Holy Sepulchre, the very heart of Christendom. Men had waded in blood up to their knees and bridle reins to secure it. Some of that blood had never been washed away, even long after the men who spilt it had gone to meet their God.

"The Church's needs are greater," Gelmiro stated plainly. "Our time here as Christians is drawing to a close, my friend. Rome sees it, even if others do not. Nur ad-Din has united the Saracens to the north and east, while the foetid corpse of the Fatamid Empire sealed our fate when it was swallowed whole by Nur ad-Din's lieutenant, the Wolf of Damascus. We are surrounded, and no help will come. Rome would see her holy relics safe or destroyed before they fall into enemy hands."

"What would you have done if I refused?"

As if there was ever a chance.

Gelmiro rolled his eyes. "I could piss off this balcony and find another knight with a debt to pay off. Shall I?"

Dietmar shook his head. "No, save your piss. I'll do it."

Gelmiro grinned, raising his cup to pour more wine. "*Alhamdulillah*," he said, "I haven't had enough drink for a proper piss yet anyway."

The gambling knight from Odenwald died badly. His neck didn't snap with the drop, so he just hung there, choking as his feet kicked out and his face turned black. A sergeant-at-arms finally ended his suffering, pulling on his boots until the life left him. The others died quickly.

***

When Dietmar first laid eyes on the bone-white walls of Jerusalem, he had been struck by awe. Now, this was a city of God, he had thought, and known well then why others regarded it as the centre of the world. He had seen other great cities in his travels: the jewel at the end of the Bosporos River, the place the Northmen had called *Milkagard*, and the Greeks' Constantinople: New Rome. He had walked beneath towering walls and prayed within grand temples, but none compared to Jerusalem.

In his youth, Dietmar often daydreamed about riding east to wage war in the Holy Land, defending the legacy of the moribund Roman Empire against the young civilisation of Arabs. To him, Outremer possessed only two qualities: it was a place of great feats and a place of great men. He would listen intently to the stories told by the pilgrims returning from Jerusalem, Antioch, Galilee, and other lands across the Middle Sea. They spoke of marauding Turks from the East, vicious Franks gone mad with greed who stalked the hills of Nazareth like hungry ghouls, and of the fringes of New Rome where men stole noble women from the Peloponnese to trade for gold and relics. Myths and legends became truth to his ears, as they often did in the ears of the young, and he listened with rapt attention as an old *rotten* described a ghostly "white-clad knight" who struck first in every battle against the heathens and led the armies of Christendom to victory in the Levant.

The world grew through these stories. The empty places on the map were slowly populated by distant kingdoms and ancient cities, inhabited by men who lived, and fought, and died beneath different stars. Dietmar's wonder only grew as he heard of the excesses of the Greeks, their tongues eager to please but treachery never far away.

They serve themselves first and then God, he was told. *They are not like us.*

When Conrad III raised his banners and sent envoys throughout the kingdom, Dietmar was still too young to answer the call. He watched the German king float down the Danube from the shore beside his brother and father. Some fifty-thousand men followed the king to bring Nur ad-Din to heel and Edessa back into the fold.

When Dietmar announced that he would one day join his countrymen in Outremer, his father laughed.

"Leave dying in the sand to the second sons," he said, gripping Dietmar's shoulder tightly and then glancing at his brother, Huldrych. "There, at least, they may prove their worth."

Conrad's mighty host returned in fragments, humbled by the storms in Choirobacchoi, then by the Sultan of Rum and his vengeful Turks, and finally in Damascus, where the combined armies of France and Germany were repelled, forcing them into a disorderly retreat before heading home.

Other than fulfilling his pilgrimage vows, Conrad had achieved nothing.

The king turned his mind to other problems—depleted coffers and barbarian tribes to the north. The Empire's fascination with the wars in the East dwindled, if not disappeared entirely. Each spring, new waves of men and women would venture east, only to return with stories to share the following winter. The scales of power in Outremer had changed—the Fatamid Empire was no more; Egypt was ripe for the conquest. The race for Cairo had begun.

But by then, Dietmar's attentions had turned elsewhere.

The world had grown more complex for him. As he matured, he learned about duty, the importance of leaving a legacy, and the value of certainty—traits instilled in him by his vigilant father. His place, it was made clear, was by Rudolph's side, not in chimeric dreams. Faraway lands were just that—markings on a map for him to wonder at, but no more.

When he met Enneleyn, his childhood dreams of ghostly knights had faded away, replaced by the joys of family, the prospect of raising a child, and the creation of a home for them. Suddenly, the world seemed less complicated again. However, those idyllic days were not destined to last.

Standing in Jerusalem that first morning had felt like awakening from a dream—a dream that had been equal parts good and bad before it had slipped into a nightmare that had nearly consumed him.

A city of God, he'd thought. He'd hoped.

But now, he hated it. The heady scent of saffron and cloves had disguised the rot when he first arrived from Jaffa after crossing the Middle Sea. Smiling faces had greeted him from the barbican of St. Stephen's Gate, where the first Christian martyr had been condemned as a blasphemer and then stoned to death. Those friendly faces had promised him much and welcomed him as a friend.

He hadn't noticed their broken teeth, their tombstone grins.

It wasn't just the people that unnerved him. The city was old, its history violent. The scars of the past were etched into its stone—the Holy Sepulchre, where Christian men had tortured Orthodox priests to relinquish the shard of the True Cross; the streets and houses where warrior-pilgrims had ruthlessly slaughtered anything that moved and pillaged what remained. In a certain light, Dietmar could almost see remnants of bloodstains on the platform leading to the Temple Mount, where countless Muslims had perished—trampled by the mob, caught in the frenzy, or falling from the steps as they tried to escape.

The violence had ceased only when the stench became unbearable. And that smell had never truly left. It stained all who entered the city, seeping into their skin like wet into walls, until one could see it reflected in the eyes of every person encountered; in the fervour of the fellahin; the resentment of the Jews; and the prideful arrogance of the Franks.

Over time, his nose became attuned to the odour creeping up from the sewers the Romans had built, like old meat gone grey and wet. It had taken him longer to notice the liars' tongues behind the crooked smiles, their wolfish grins.

Homo homini lupus est. The proverb matched the black beast on his coat of arms, all teeth and claws and a blood-red tongue. As a child, he had thought it a fearsome sight. But now he knew it for what it was. A warning: *Man is a wolf to man.*

2

Razin and Tomas were waiting for Dietmar at the top of the Roman Cardo, haggling with fruit vendors beneath the old pillars. Razin glanced up at his approach and motioned toward Tomas, who was still deep in negotiations with a short, grey-haired man behind the stall.

"I have yet to see a man more reluctant to part with his coin than your priest."

Dietmar offered a thin smile. If Tomas had ever truly been a priest, he would have been defrocked long ago. "I have seen him search for change in the collection box at St. John's. Still, rather a miser than a spendthrift, no?"

Tomas pointed to a basket filled with strange, pinkish bulbs and snapped his fingers. "What are these over here? They look like swollen radishes."

The vendor sighed into the cloth of his hood and lifted a tray of thinly sliced wedges from behind the stand. By his pained expression, it was clear he'd been entertaining Tomas for some time now.

"These are Carthaginian Apples from Ifriqiya," the vendor explained, offering the tray forward. "They were brought here at great cost to me and are considered a delicacy even in Mahdiya."

"The Devil's fruit, no doubt," said Tomas, biting into one anyway. Red juice ran from his mouth as he chewed, staining his lips bright pink.

"And you, seigneur?" inquired the vendor, noticing Dietmar as he offered the tray.

Dietmar waved it away, opting instead to choose the three ripest-looking apples from their basket. He handed one to Razin, another to Tomas, and tossed the vendor a coin before Tomas could object.

"For your time," he said with a wink to the merchant.

The vendor plucked the silver out of the air, disappearing it down the sleeve of his robes. He gave Tomas a triumphant grin and nodded his thanks to Dietmar, who was already turning away from the stall.

"Getting fleeced by the merchants of Cardo," Tomas grumbled, hastening to catch up with Dietmar and Razin. "No wonder your estate floundered. They say only a poor man knows what to do with a rich man's money. I could have gotten twice as much for half what you paid Yesha."

"And one day, when the street rats at the bottom of David Street decide to stick a knife between your ribs, Yesha will only pause long enough to step over your body and maybe check your pockets." Dietmar tossed his apple in the air and deftly caught it again. "Besides, my accounts are in good order. Or they will be soon enough."

"Not with Adelman hovering over them," said Razin. "Your bookkeep has never seen a dinar he couldn't skim off the top."

"He was my father's man," said Dietmar.

"He probably stole from him too."

Tomas took a bite from his apple. "So, what did the weasel want?"

"Is it not enough for an old friend to want to say his goodbyes?"

Tomas scoffed, spitting out bits of fleshy pulp and wiping his mouth. "His goodbyes? That little shit would trade away the last shards of the True Cross if there was something in it for him."

Razin nodded, stepping aside as a merchant and his two-wheeled cart rumbled past. His gaze followed the vendor's progress down the cobbled road until the cart disappeared into one of the covered markets ahead. "Men like us don't last long in the games Gelmiro plays. And when we die, we die bad deaths."

"Important men die all the time in the east," added Tomas sagely. The words had become an unofficial mantra among those who called Jerusalem home. If it wasn't by treachery and murder, then it was in battle or worse—a slip in the ancient corridors of the city or a fall from the steps to a miserable death, unremarkable but for its banality. And sometimes, like the knights that morning, it was the king's justice and a rope.

I will take a mediocre death, Dietmar thought to himself.

Interesting deaths were for the young and brave, for those with eyes blazing with ambition and the conviction that typifies all youth. An invincibility that only begins to wane when those twilight years appear on the horizon. But more than that, interesting deaths were never quick, Dietmar found. And seldom painless.

He would rather not linger when his time came.

Stretching his legs, he glanced at Tomas. "Then we are lucky we are not important men."

Tomas snorted but held his tongue, chewing on his fruit instead.

They left the Cardo behind, stepping onto St. Stephen's Street and following it toward the Patriarch's Quarter. When they reached the top of the Street of Herbs, the lively cries of vendors blended with the sounds of craftsmen in their workshops. The groan of cramp-iron being bent around stone; fine chisels chipping away at marble and limestone to create trinkets and keepsakes for the pilgrims who flooded the city; precious rocks polished smooth and scraped down until they shone.

Short-bearded Syrians rubbed shoulders with dark-haired Greeks and pale-eyed Latins. The air hummed with a hundred voices, a desultory murmur of a dozen languages all beneath the vaulted ceiling of the covered market. They manoeuvred through the uneven grots, where shadows and piles of accumulated filth threatened to spill onto the road from holes leading to the depths of the city.

A second Jerusalem, Dietmar thought as they picked their way through the crowded street. He had ventured into the sewers once as a favour to Gelmiro when he first entered the secretary's employ. He'd been tasked with tracking down a debtor—some down-on-his-luck lump who had opted to flee rather than repaying his debts.

Dietmar had expected the filth and detritus, perhaps some vagrants eking out a living in the small places of the world, scavengers who shied away from the light of his torch when he came close.

When he had thought there no end to the winding tunnels, they had opened up into a cavernous chamber beneath one of the city's ancient pools. There, he had seen something he *hadn't* expected: a thriving subterranean metropolis, complete with a bazaar to rival those of Malcuisinat and the market streets above.

He had stood there gawping at the lip of the tunnel until a merchant caught sight of him and hobbled over, unveiling his offerings with a flourish. Dietmar had recoiled when he saw the vendor's wares—fingers strung together on a string, dangled like a macabre fishing line.

When he eventually emerged from the tunnels, Gelmiro was waiting for him, a wide grin adorning his face. Dietmar had sworn at him, called him a bastard and threatened to beat the shit-eating grin off his face, but Gelmiro had simply tossed another coin purse at him before he could make good on his promises.

A meat market, he'd thought. Some cannibalistic enterprise that had somehow survived in the holiest of cities. But it was not, as Gelmiro explained. It turned out that Dietmar had stumbled upon a relic market—one of the oldest in the city. *Beneath* the city, away from prying eyes. Such places offered a range of sacred limbs and bones to those unbothered by matters of certification or origin.

Dietmar eyed one of the shadowed corridors and caught sight of a figure moving inside, beckoning him with an outstretched hand.

Not today, bone-monger, Dietmar thought, looking away.

Broad arched entrances opened up ahead of him, revealing the openings to each shop, divided by a series of transverse arcades. The stalls were narrow but deep enough to accommodate the workshops where the craftsmen created their wares. Above the shops, wooden galleries were supported by stone corbels, serving as sleeping quarters for the craftsmen and shopkeepers.

Each doorway bore the marks of ownership: the inverted T of the Templars and the SCA ANNA of the Abbey of St. Anna, who vied for rent from the shops.

Fishmongers, forced to the stalls nearest the entrance, barked out prices, dragging Dietmar's eyes to their catch with enthusiastic waves. Gilt-headed sea bream, catfish, and carp lay on wooden boards, their scales glistening in the streams of light pouring through holes in the ceiling. They already looked a day past their selling date, and his nose twitched at the smell.

A man noticed Dietmar's gaze and called him over, his hands stained with fish guts as he wiped them on his apron. Dietmar shook his head and continued walking deeper into the market, away from the fishmongers and their stink.

As they moved away from the scent of sea and iron, Tomas engaged in haggling over a piece of ginger with a spice vendor while Dietmar and Razin watched the guards playing dice in front of a nearby shop.

"You'd take my whole hand for this spindly stick of ginger?" Tomas made a chopping motion for the unimpressed vendor. He dropped the stick of ginger and crossed his arms, waiting for the shopkeep to lower his price. And so it went.

"Tomas was right," said Dietmar, watching as a dark-skinned guard bearing the Templar's cross on his breast gathered up all the coins, laughed at his cursing opponents, and pocketed his spoils.

Razin raised a brow, his thin face expressing nothing more than his usual suspicion. "Gelmiro wanted something? Even now that you are set to leave?"

"Aye. It is because I am leaving that he wants me."

Razin blinked at that. "Why?"

Dietmar shrugged. "Easier for him to wash his hands of me once it's done. Less chance of it coming back to bite him in the arse."

Tomas rejoined them, proudly holding up the stick of ginger. His smile faded when he saw the looks on Dietmar and Razin's faces.

Somewhere nearby, a dog began to bark.

"Who died?" Tomas asked, taking another bite from his apple and then tossing the remains on the floor for the rats to fight over.

Razin scratched his neatly shaped beard and glanced meaningfully at Dietmar.

May as well, Dietmar thought, bracing to announce the change of plans. Tomas was like a grumpy old mule when he didn't get his way, and the news was bound to set him off. "We'll be making a small detour on our way to Zwingenberg," he began slowly, carefully watching Tomas's face to measure his response. "We need to visit the basilica in Naples, where we are to deliver a relic on behalf of the Church."

"That doesn't sound so bad," said Tomas. The barest flicker of a smile appeared behind his red beard. "They make good wine in Campania, and their women are friendly. We can spend a day there after we dock."

Dietmar looked uncomfortable.

Then he told them the rest.

"Bastard!" said Tomas, shaking his head when he had finished.

Dietmar winced. "Who? Me or Gelmiro?" He looked to Razin for support, but it was not forthcoming.

"The both of you!" Tomas snarled. "What's to become of our gentle stroll to Jaffa? Our leisurely voyage across the Mediterranean? There'll be no sipping wine and feasting on honeyed figs, basking in the sun. Not if Amalric sends his butchers after us!"

Dietmar grunted.

"And another thing," Dietmar continued, raising his hands to placate Tomas before he could protest. "We won't be taking a ship from Jaffa. In fact, we won't be travelling from any of Jerusalem's ports at all."

Tomas's brow furrowed in fury. "Then how do you propose we leave?"

This will do it, Dietmar thought.

He took a deep breath, trying to choose his words carefully. "Instead, we will take the Pilgrim's Road to Antioch. Gelmiro has arranged for us to receive assistance from his contacts there, who will help us travel to Messina and then Salerno."

"Antioch?" Tomas almost howled. "But that will take weeks! We'll be broiling in the sun, our feet turned to blisters, and our tongues like sand in our mouths."

Dietmar held up a hand, trying to calm his friend. "The King's dogs would sniff us out in Jaffa or Acre. Better we take a path less travelled, a route that is not so closely watched. A mule will spare your feet, and we'll have ample water to muddy your tongue."

Razin drew a small knife from his belt and started peeling his apple. "Less common or no, they will catch us in the sands if word reaches their ears before we reach Antioch. How do you plan on keeping ahead of them if they catch wind of our departure?"

"We will have time," said Dietmar. He inhaled a breath of cinnamon and cloves, rosemary and saffron, and faintly beneath, the grey rot of the old city. "Amalric intends to convene the *Haute Coure* to decide on the matter of Salah al-Din and his raids from Egypt. According to Gelmiro, it is already a foregone conclusion: Jerusalem must show her strength or suffer for her weakness later."

Razin licked a piece of fruit from his blade, pondering Dietmar's words. "They plan to ride against Saladin?"

"Aye," Dietmar confirmed. "They've been spoiling for a fight ever since he tried to take Montreal."

"When that fight comes, it would be better if we are not in it."

Dietmar grunted. He had heard of this vizier-turned-conqueror and the vast armies at his disposal. They said he was a learned man, zealous. That he was a greater strategist than even Nur ad-Din, who had united all of Syria. Such men brought dangerous times with them.

I have done my Christian duty and more. He would not have a scimitar sheathed in his belly, not when he was so close to fulfilling his goals, not when he had a chance to reclaim his boy.

"We will make our excuses and depart shortly after the forces mustered by the Haute Coure. With any luck, we'll be in Antioch before they return."

"A fine plan," said Tomas, with only a little humour. "Now, let's hope that weasel Gelmiro can keep his mouth shut long enough for us to leave the city, eh?"

"He'll feel my hands around his neck if he doesn't," Dietmar replied, forcing a smile.

Trusting in one hope was risky enough, but now two? It seemed like they were pushing their luck.

They moved deeper into the market, where the scent of candlewax and the sound of woodcarvers filled the air. A man selling bundles of firewood hissed out prices, his robes soaked with sweat.

"Ten bezants for the conquerors' wood! Wood from Nablus, ten bezants!"

"There are no more forests in Nablus," Tomas called as they walked past.

The wood merchant patted his brow with a cloth, leaning over his table and gesturing toward Tomas. "Come, take a look! The last wood from Nablus. Cedar from Mount Lebanus." His face was as thin and angular as the carp on the tables behind them. His thick lips parted in an unfriendly smile. "Pine from Hebron. For twenty bezants, I'll even offer you kindling from the very last beam of wood used in the siege of Jerusalem!"

Tomas cackled, dismissing the vendor with a wave of his hand.

Next, they came upon a stall selling candles. The seller, with hands scarred by his craft, watched them from behind his workbench. The scent of animal musk emanated from the shop in the back.

Candles crowded the table, their tapered wicks long and limp, hanging over their sides like fishing lines still to be cut. Tall ceremonial candles stood alongside cheaper-looking wax squares. Some were roughly carved into shapes, vaguely resembling the holy sites scattered throughout the city. There, the Temple on the Mount, David's Tower, and perhaps the Virgin Mother—or possibly an ass.

Dietmar pointed to a thick column of tallow with the five-folded cross carved across its width. "How much?"

The merchant appraised Dietmar, calculating how much he could extract from the Frank before replying: "One bezant."

Dietmar handed the seller his coin and picked up the candle. He would light it in the Lord's Temple before they departed the city, leaving it with his prayers at the top of the Temple Mount.

He perused a crate of musty scrolls claiming provenance in the time of Heraclius. Then, he examined the work of a carver who swore the wood he used came from the very cart Paul rode into Jerusalem. And if not the cart, then from the same tree at least, *please seigneur, it's true.*

Dietmar had it in mind to buy something to take home, a keepsake of his time in the Holy Land to go with all the scars, but nothing in the Street of Herbs caught his eye. He briefly contemplated visiting the *Ruga Palmariorum* for a palm branch when a voice cried out from one of the stalls.

"*Chevalier! Mon ami!*"

A potbellied Frenchman with round eyes and hairy ears stared at him from across the lane. Dietmar's gaze shifted to the vendor's table, noticing an array of fresh fruit: apples, lemons, plums, and jars of figs.

"*Non, merci!*" he said with an apologetic smile. No sooner had he looked away than he felt a firm tug at his sleeve. The little Frenchman stood beside him, staring up at him.

"I am not here for fruit," Dietmar stated firmly, the apple feeling like a hot coal in his hand.

"Fruit would only turn to ash in your mouth, chevalier."

"What?"

Cheeky bastard.

He tried pushing past the merchant, but the little man only smiled and stepped in his way.

"Have you not seen the vapours rising from Satan's furnace?" The Frenchman blinked at him with grey eyes gone red at the edges. "Cinders! Cinders! That is all you will find if you feast from the fruit on its shores!"

"Then don't sell me fruit from its shores. Get out of my way."

The merchant remained unmoved. "Soon, all fruit will come from its shores, which will cover the world!"

"You're mad."

The barking dog let out a strangled yip and fell silent.

"What's he saying?" Tomas appeared at Dietmar's side, joining in the curious gaze of the onlookers.

"Something about the Dead Sea," Dietmar murmured.

"The Sea of Devils!" the madman exclaimed, pointing a knobbly finger at Tomas. "It is the mouth of Hell. The birds won't fly over it any longer, haven't you seen? They know the truth!"

"I have seen it," a voice called out from the crowd, belonging to a long-haired Georgian with yellow teeth. The man beside him shook his head, another Georgian. They started arguing.

The mad Frenchman took this as his cue, addressing the gathering crowd instead of Dietmar.

"Old Tirus, the blind serpent lurks beneath its waters, belching black plumes of smoke as if he were the Devil's chimney." The merchant waved his hands in the air, imitating the path of a serpent through the sea. "Soon, he will come ashore to wrap his coils around our city. Then we will all be damned!"

Tomas and a few others laughed, but the atmosphere grew sombre as more people fell silent.

"And who can deny the foul stench seeping into our homes each night? Rotten fumes from those putrid waters!" The merchant turned back to Dietmar, his hooked nose like a beak on his face. "Can you smell it, Chevalier?"

"Aye," Dietmar admitted before he could stop himself. There was no denying it, anyway. And he'd rather be called a fool than a liar.

"You see!" the vendor bellowed, raising his hands in triumph. "It is the smell of flesh cooked in the fires of Hell, no natural odour. Because it is against nature, the laws do not apply! If you doubt my words, throw iron upon its waters—it will float, as if to confound God himself!"

"And a feather?" asked Tomas, with only a half-hearted chuckle. "What happens to a feather?"

"It sinks!"

"What?"

"It sinks! To the bottom!"

"Don't be a fool, man."

"The Englishman doubts me! Is it because the crown of England rests upon a Norman head?"

The little merchant gave Tomas a mock bow, waving his hands in a sarcastic flourish, and then lowered an imaginary crown upon his oily brown head.

The guards, tired of their games, had taken a keen interest in the unfolding events. After a few quiet words, the turcopole and his comrades rose from their seats and began making their way toward the Frenchman.

Time to leave.

Dietmar had endured run-ins with the Templars and their enforcers before and had hoped to avoid them altogether before returning home.

Undeterred, the would-be oracle continued his speech, now raising his voice like a priest in sermon.

"Only the faithful shall be spared!" he cried. "They will pass through the poisoned waters of Satan's Sea like the River Jordan, unscathed and unblemished by its putridity! Only those damned, those sons of Moabites and bastards of Ammon, shall fall to the serpent's coils."

The little man spun on his feet, turning to stare Dietmar straight in the eye. "Chevalier! Do you believe?"

Dietmar frowned, feeling the gaze of the crowd upon him. A pair of Hospitallers had appeared at the bottom of the street and were in an intense conversation with the guards.

The Frenchman grinned. "Ho! But it is not enough to believe!"

"We should go," said a voice beside his ear. Razin.

"Yes!" The Frenchman hissed, his voice like the cooking pans of Malcuisinat, the spit from his mouth like oil. "Run, now, Chevalier. While you can. But know that Satan's tide will rise like the waters of Güstrom and drown you wherever you are!"

Dietmar paused.

Güstrom was near his home.

"What do you know of me, *blaireau*?" His discomfort turned into anger. *How does this little mad bastard know of Güstrom?* He looked up, past the merchant, searching the throng for familiar faces, eyes that would give away the trick, the joke he had been made the butt of.

Güstrom, where his mother had died.

The merchant laughed, carrying on his tirade. Now speaking in French, "*Si je ne peux pas influencer les cieux, je soulèverai l'enfer*," then in German, "***In des Teufles Küche kommen.***" His eyes widened, as if seeing Dietmar for the first time. He shook his head, like a mother disappointed by a child that wouldn't learn.

It looked like he might cry. "Where are you going, Chevalier?"

The guards began to push their way through the crowd, urged on by the two Hospitallers behind them. The dog had started to bark again.

"Leave him," said Razin, shouldering Dietmar forward as the crowd dispersed. Nobody wanted to be on the other end of a Hospitaller's baton, or worse—their questions.

Dietmar fixed his eyes on the little merchant, whose scoffing face had transformed into bewilderment and confusion. He clung to the nearest passer-by, speaking rapidly in French, only to be shoved away. He tried the next person and the next, but nobody wanted to be near him.

Dietmar watched him until he disappeared amidst the crowd, like a tusk of stone swallowed by the sea.

When Dietmar blinked again, he found himself standing outside the Street of Herbs, breathing in fresh air and gazing into the sun. Razin gently nudged him forward, steering him away from the stream of people pouring out of the covered market.

"That crazy little bastard," said Tomas, shaking his head as they crossed Temple Street. Dietmar nodded silently, his thoughts fixed on the Frenchman's final words: *Quo Vadis?*

He looked up and saw they were passing beneath Iscariot's Arch, from where Judas was said to have hanged himself.

He looked away. That's enough death for one day, he thought, trailing behind Tomas and Razin.

When Dietmar took a bite from his apple, it didn't turn to ash or cinders in his mouth as the Frenchman had predicted.

It was rotten.

3

A steward led Dietmar through the palace gardens and into a grand, barrel-vaulted twin hall, where servants hurried between narrow columns, carrying wine and refreshments for the thirsty mouths outside. Dietmar had visited the king's hall once before, being introduced to the court as a minor nobleman from the Holy Roman Empire. The king had given a brief nod of recognition before turning his attention elsewhere. Just another German in Jerusalem.

Then it had been the heart of winter. Torches had blazed from wall-mounted sconces, while iron braziers with hot coals had dotted the space like haystacks after harvest. Today, the hall basked in natural light streaming through open doors and windows, its only occupants fleeting.

Dietmar paused to admire the marble fresco behind the king's seat, empty now as the court convened outside. Silver-gilded filigree adorned the edges of the fresco, shaped like acanthus leaves that swirled outward in the style of the old Corinthians. The mosaic itself was resplendent, even in the dim light filtering through the wheel windows on either side of the hall.

Roots and vines, bearing all manner of fruit from the Garden of Paradise, twirled around the stoic face of an angel, his head adorned with a halo of gold lintel. The angel gazed down at Amalric's throne, a watchful guardian. Or perhaps it was disappointment etched upon those seraphic features?

Jerusalem still stood, but the scavengers had begun to circle. Whose name would be remembered when future generations spoke of her fall? Amalric's rule had begun with successes against Nur ad-Din and his lieutenants, but later years had been marred by controversies—both personal and diplomatic. His relations with the Greeks had soured, and his campaign in Egypt had ended a bathetic failure. And now, the vultures in his own camp were snapping at his heels, urging him to act, to gamble, so that they could feed.

Dietmar did not envy the head that wore the crown. Less so now that he knew of the malady that ailed the king's son. Not for the first time, he wondered whether he was doing the right thing. Even if the relic—this hand—afforded Baldwin no respite from his suffering, was it not a father's duty to try? Would it not offer some small comfort, whether real or perceived, to simply sit in the presence of the relic?

Damn it, he thought, banishing the idea before guilt could overwhelm him.

The steward guided him past the fresco and through a groin-vaulted corridor on the other side of the hall. They walked along a passage framed by Romanesque pillars and conchoid niches that interlocked like the fingers of a folded hand.

Dietmar heard voices ahead and followed the steward into a spacious courtyard overlooked by terraces and a small domed tower. He paused on the descending steps, listening to the low susurrus punctuated by louder caws, like crows amongst querulous bitterns. The Court. A nervous anticipation filled him. This had never been his place—the false pleasantries, the preening cocks in their linen shirts and khalats, the perfidious words spoken with a deceitful smile. In that, his brother had been more like their father than he, though neither Rudolph nor Huldrych would have admitted it—another stubborn irony.

He briefly wondered what his brother was doing at that moment: cutting his way through the Moors, grinning from ear to ear in that wolfish way of his. Or perhaps he was lost in one of those dark moods that would take him, turning him distant for days on end. Even then, his brother was better suited to the vulgarities of court than he was.

But I am here, and he is not.

Dietmar took a deep breath, steeling himself, and descended the stairs.

It seemed that all the nobility of Jerusalem had answered the seneschal's summons and were now gathered in the king's palace to convene the Haute Coure. Some four hundred nobles occupied the benches in the courtyard, arranged in rows that formed a slight U shape around the central fountain. Three straight aisles divided the rows.

The seneschal's chair, little more than a stool with a leather seat, sat at the front of the benches. To his right was the king's seat, and to his left were the judges' bench and tables.

Dietmar was directed to a spot near the front, just behind the benches reserved for the most prominent members of the Frankish nobility. As a mere *burgesse*, Dietmar was entitled to a vote along with the other chevaliers and minor noblemen, but they typically aligned their votes with their liege lords, so it was more of a technical freedom than anything else.

However, the liege lords held enough power to challenge even the king when united, and they often did.

Dietmar nodded his thanks to the steward, who quickly disappeared back into the hall to fetch more wine. He considered taking his seat for a moment but opted to stand in the shade beneath the terraces instead.

Beside him, a familiar face leaned against a pillar. Arne, a Dane from the lakeside principality of Farum, with whom Dietmar shared a stable. He was tall and well-built, like most of the men from the north. His long blonde hair flowed down to his shoulders. He greeted Dietmar with a smile and then nodded toward the judges' benches.

"Reynald nearly tore Jocelyn of Novara's head off this morning," Arne said. "The young pup told the court he wasn't going to pay what he owed John Gerierr for all his sheep that died, and Reynald nearly leapt over his bench at him. I've never seen a man change his mind so swiftly or come so close to pissing himself without following through."

Dietmar laughed with him and turned his gaze to Reynald Grenier. The Count of Sidon was widely regarded as one of the fairest minds in Outremer, and his contributions to Amalric's *Assise sur la ligece*—the laws of the kingdom—were rumoured to be as significant, if not greater, than those made by the king and his favoured jurors. Reynald's sharp eyes peered out from beneath thick, bushy eyebrows, long since turned grey. His broad shoulders marked him as a warrior, his ink-stained fingers as a scholar, and the slight red sheen in his cheeks as a drinker. Few men so typified the Franks in the east as Reynald did, and the stories of his exploits, both in battle and in the drinking halls, were legend.

He sat beside Geldemar of Tiberiad, a notorious philanderer whose many dalliances with the married women of the court meant he'd had to become adept with the blade, and Theobald Tabor, a quiet drunkard who preferred his books to company.

The seneschal's voice boomed across the courtyard like a mason's hammer. "Now hearing the matter between his lordships Ser Baldwin and Ser Conrad!"

Dietmar turned his gaze to the noblemen in question and watched with mild disinterest as they addressed the court on the matter of a contractual dispute his father would have relished. *Form and function!* Rudolph always used to say. *The details, son. That is what distinguishes noblemen from mere chattel. Pay them great heed.* Though both Dietmar and Huldrych were present, his father's lessons had always been meant for him alone.

He looked away from the proceedings and let his eyes drift over the gathered faces—some in rapt attention, their eyes fixed on the trial, while others quietly conversed or sank deeper into their cups.

There sat the Archbishop of Tyre and Chancellor of Jerusalem, his pig-like eyes creased as he leaned forward to hear the whispered words of Odo of St. Amad. On the other end of the bench, Eschiva of Bures and her son Hugh sat quiet and still, missing nothing. The Patriarch of Jerusalem, dressed in all the pomp and frill his office afforded, sat far from the king's seat, surrounded by his many advisors. Dietmar did not count Gelmiro among their number, but he had always been of better use where no one could see him.

The king himself reclined on a gilded chair with ornate armrests fashioned in the shape of twin lion heads, their oversized canines bared in a rictus roar. Amalric had been handsome in his younger years, with sparkling eyes and an aquiline nose, his long blonde hair pushed back. Now, he was a fat man with a thick beard to hide his jowls and a drooping nose that made him appear a vulture to those he deigned to look upon.

A practised eye might have discerned more from the ebb and flow of the court—the shifting allegiances, the dominant factions, and who currently held the king's favour. But Dietmar had no such eye, being neither a man of the court nor one inclined to find much fascination in its intrigues. Even back home, he had shown little interest in the affairs of the halls of power. That had always been his brother's domain until their father's passing left Dietmar with the lion's share of the estate. Any hope Huldrych had of elevating his position in Barbarossa's court died along with him. Huldrych sold what goods he had soon after, ignoring Dietmar's pleas for him to stay, and travelled south to find his fortune fighting the Moors in the Kingdom of Navarre. The last Dietmar had heard, his brother was carving out a little fiefdom of his own in the service of Alfonso VIII.

And here I am, in the court of a fat king and his vultures.

He had never envisioned crossing the Middle Sea or imagined that he'd end up fighting off Saracen raiders—men who looked and spoke in the same tongue as the eastern Christians he'd been tasked to protect.

Once his youthful fancies had been drilled out of him by his father, his ambitions had seldom extended beyond the edges of Odenwald. He had been content to see to the complaints of his serfs, keeping the wild forests at bay, and to paying his dues to Emperor Frederick Barbarossa. The happiest moment of his life came when Ennelyn told him she was expecting. Then, nine months later, even that moment was eclipsed by another.

Enneleyn gave birth to a son on the first day of Spring. They named him Rudi, after his father, and opened their doors and wine cellars to anyone who would share in the good news.

But something was wrong with their child.

Dietmar had been the first to notice.

Rudi struggled to breathe, and each ragged breath he took was laboured and tight. They watched in horror as his condition worsened. None of the physicians they consulted could offer a cure, only palliatives to soothe the boy into fitful sleep.

A week after Dietmar had first noticed the problem, Rudi was dead.

The best days of Dietmar's life turned into the worst—another symmetry, a vicious, ugly symmetry. And then his days grew darker still. Enneleyn fell, breaking her neck in a fall down the rain-soaked stairs. Dietmar was shattered, his world crumbling before his eyes.

He was left alone in a home filled with empty rooms, haunted by memories. As the silent months passed, his properties fell into ruin. First, the bridge connecting his homestead and lands to the town of Bensheim collapsed. Unable to afford its repair, Dietmar lost his rentals to the abbey across the river. When he couldn't pay Barbarossa's taxes, he was forced to take out a loan from the moneylenders in Heidelberg. Unable to repay that debt, he turned to the usurers in Bensheim and eventually to the Church.

All the while, his thoughts wavered between the bottle and despair, sinking him further into his own ruin. Until one day, a grim-faced Adelman appeared at his door and warned him that unless something changed, his father's home and the resting place of his wife and son would soon become the property of another.

So he had taken out a mortgage against his lands and then taken up the Church's offer of Absolution—a guarantee to all those who fought for God in His Kingdom. The real incentive, however, had been the Church's decree that any interest due from *crucesignati* would be frozen while they were in the service of Jerusalem.

Seven years had passed since then, and in that time, he had fought for lords and kings, princesses and merchants, the Pope, and more. He had raised enough to secure his lands and return home. Gelmiro's offer to forgive his debt would make him a wealthy man, but that wasn't why he had accepted it. If there was even a chance for Rudi's soul to bask in the light of God, he would take it, regardless of the cost.

The noblemen's bickering and fighting, the intrigue of the court, even the fate of kingdoms seemed as nothing when compared to this. He almost wanted to laugh at the foolishness of it all.

Arne saw his smile and thought he was still on about Reynald.

"He will give this one a short hearing too." The Dane motioned to one of the pages for more wine. Then he nodded to Ser Conrad, a young man with the beginnings of his first beard. "In matters of property, the sins of the father are inherited by the son. *Land!* My German friend, that is what the law is concerned with."

Dietmar nodded and turned his attention to Reynald as he questioned the young heir.

The Count of Sidon stared down at the defendant, like a mountain bear who had just spotted an intruder in his territory and was about to dispatch them with a flick of its paw.

"Do you deny the existence of the agreement betwixt your father and Ser Baldwin?"

Conrad shook his head, his long brown curls cut in the style of those south of the Urals. "No, ser. The contract is true. Only you have highlighted the problem in your question: it was between my father and Baldwin. It is no business of mine."

"Is there a copy of this contract that the court might examine?" Reynald inquired.

"Yes, my lord." Ser Baldwin raised a hand, sending a steward forward to deliver a tightly rolled scroll into Reynald's outstretched fingers.

Reynald unravelled the scroll and scrutinised it before looking pointedly at Conrad. "This is the same contract?"

"I do not contest the provenance of the agreement."

Reynald nodded, then ran a stained finger down the page. He nodded again and handed the contract to Geldemar. The philanderer barely looked at it before passing it to Theobald.

Then Reynald cleared his throat. If the seneschal's voice was like a mason's hammer, then the Count of Sidon's was the breaking of the walls of Jericho.

"The contract stands!" he declared. "If you dislike the obligations arising from your father's dealings, then you must pay your way out. Until then, honour the agreement! Next!"

Conrad looked shocked. "But, ser, this is—"

"I said *next!*"

The young lord sat down, complaining bitterly to anyone who would hear him. A sixth sense made him look back at the benches, his words fading when he saw Reynald's expression. The Count of Sidon leaned forward, his hands like big meaty hammers before him. "If you do not like my judgment, feel free to say so now. Invoke your right to judicial combat and be the first in the kingdom to do so. How about it, boy? Meet an old man in the field and test the truth of your claim against the truth of my sword."

Conrad stuttered, his head held low. "N-no, my lord."

Reynald snorted, tugging at his beard with an ink-stained hand. "I didn't think so. Now, who's next?"

Dietmar and Arne shared a quiet chuckle at the young noble's misery. It wasn't every day they witnessed the smug and powerful being put in their place, and Reynald was in fine form. Better yet, he was fearless.

"A good thing Reynald counts a swordsman like Geldemar among his friends," Arne remarked. "He must have made his fair share of powerful enemies. A whippersnapper like Conrad is just the type to try do something stupid about it."

"Aye," Dietmar agreed. "But the old bear can look after himself. You heard what he did at Banias? He cut a bloody swathe through Nur ad-Din's men to get to Humphrey of Toron, that dumb bastard. If it were a choice between him and a dark shadow in an alleyway, I'd still bet on him."

The courtyard fell quiet as the seneschal rose from his seat, his deep voice no longer as impressive now that Reynald had spat thunder from his bench.

"Now deciding on the matter of Ser Hadley of Ramla; absent and not represented; marked as violator of the Assise sur la ligece. His punishment is to be determined by the Haute Coure."

The seneschal sat back down, but the courtyard remained silent. Not even the scraping of the scribes' quills could break the stillness. Violating the Assise sur la ligece was as good as throwing one's life away. The noble in question had lost all rights to trial and had been deemed guilty almost solely by accusation alone.

Hadley's lands would be seized, and he would be cast out of Jerusalem if he managed to avoid execution.

The Assise sur la ligece was among the most sacred laws of the kingdom—a guarantee of the property rights of the baronage and their vassals. If anyone took another's property without just cause, the entire noble class would align against them, regardless of allegiances or family ties.

Ser Hadley had anticipated his sentence and fled to Tripoli, where rumours suggested he had been reduced to begging for scraps at his cousin's table. Every noble in the court knew that fate could befall them if they erred. Witnessing one of their own fall so far might have been humbling for some, but Dietmar knew it wouldn't last. They would be at each other's throats for Hadley's land the moment his sentence was decided.

Beasts.

But not even beasts were so treacherous.

Dietmar couldn't help but compare the Haute Coure to the grand German court he had visited with his brother. How different it had seemed to the energy that ran through matters here. Huldrych had gone willingly, he begrudgingly. Together they had sat beneath the sloping domed roof of the *Hofgericht* and listened to the Emperor's lords deliver judgments upon thieves, murderers, rapists, and traitors.

There had been little fire in those judges, none of the vim and vigour of Reynald or the cruel charm of Theobald. Those lords had simply fulfilled their duty, dispensing the law in case after case in a dull monotone, ruining lives and serving justice with each stroke of the quill. There was no sense of urgency, of *opportunity*.

Perhaps that was the way of empires. Once the foundations settled and certainty of continued existence replaced the chaos… Great personalities became subdued by the endless tide of checks and balances, papers upon papers until all that remained was the system and the husks of men who governed it.

A man could rise amidst a bit of chaos, Dietmar had found. He could show his worth and be rewarded for it. Men like Gelmiro, who had clawed their way up from the dirt. Not so in the heart of empire, where certainty was valued over wit and ambition.

Perhaps it wasn't politics he disliked after all, but rather the endless bureaucracy of empire that he had witnessed back home. Maybe that was why so many young men and second sons flocked to the Holy Land, where a man could still determine his own worth, where chaos and disorder still reigned supreme.

Reynald licked his lips, signalling the servants for more wine. Geldemar and Theobald had since sat up beside him. This was no minor dispute, no failure of service or squabbling youngsters. The recognition and enforcement of the Assise sur la ligece kept the king in check and his barons honest. If that were to ever change, Jerusalem would collapse from within long before the scimitar and crescent moon could knock a single stone from her walls.

Reynald took a sip from his goblet, now freshly filled, and cleared his throat. "Ser Hadley of Ramla has been accused of, with force and violence, taking upon the lands of Amarius Barisan. I understand that there was some prior disagreement and dispute and that Amarius failed to fulfil an obligation owed to Hadley?"

A short, bearded man in a grey tunic stood up from his bench and nodded. Then, seeing Reynald's expression, he added, "Aye, ser, there was."

Reynald sighed, shaking his head. He glanced at the king, who remained motionless, offering neither a word nor gesture to ease Reynald's mind.

"Nevertheless," the Count of Sidon continued, addressing the gathered nobles. "Hadley acted without the court's say-so and, in doing so, broke the Assise sur la ligece. There can be no excuse. I see he has already taken it upon himself to carry out the first part of his sentence. And so it shall be. His lands are forfeit—his properties and any remaining credit shall be distributed among his existing creditors. Ser Hadley of Ramla, now of nothing, loses the rights of Frankish nobility in Jerusalem. May he never return."

"Ser Hadley of Nothing," Dietmar repeated quietly as Reynald and his fellow judges rose from the bench. "Surely a man of his position should have known better? Why ride against Amarius at all? He knew the price of breaking Amalric's ligece."

"I heard it was his son who did it," said Arne, turning his broad face to look at Dietmar. "They were feuding over Amarius's daughter. The girl had been promised to the Hadley boy, but after witnessing his vicious temper, she begged her father to break off the engagement. He did. When the son heard, he rode out in the night and knocked down Amarius's gate, forcing him and his household to flee.

"So the father must suffer for the sins of the son." Another irregular symmetry, Dietmar thought, recalling the contract Ser Conrad's father had agreed to and he was now being forced to maintain. There was symmetry in everything.

Arne exchanged his empty goblet for a new one, before returning his attention to Dietmar. "Reynald would have hanged him. That boy has been before the court three times already. Even the old bear has his limits."

Dietmar raised an eyebrow and turned to watch the old man stroll into the aisles to take his place amongst the gathered nobles. Reynald was a fair man, though not known for his patience.

But it was to Hadley's sacrifice that his thoughts drifted. The man had given up everything so that his son might live. There was honour in that, even if it meant living as a dog.

Dietmar felt his gaze settle on the fat king. Amalric was stroking his beard, staring into his goblet as his advisors rattled away in his ear. What would Amalric be willing to do to keep his leper son on the throne?

Anything.

Dietmar knew it the moment the thought crossed his mind.

They wouldn't be so different in that, a king and a chevalier. Only for Dietmar to succeed, Amalric would have to fail. The Hand of Saint Ephium would need to leave the city. Another cruel irony gifted by God, who knew how to make men suffer if nothing else.

Then the seneschal's voice boomed again, and the matter of Salah al-Din was brought to the floor.

4

Aimery of Lusignan addressed the court with the confidence of a man who knew his position was secure. The son of a Poitieran noble, he had been involved in a failed revolt against his liege lord, forcing him to flee his lands. With the rebellion crushed and his future in doubt, Aimery had followed the path of his warrior sires and made for Jerusalem, where he had found favour in Amalric's court.

His fortunes had risen considerably when Agnes of Courtenay became his patron, funding his ventures and introducing him to powerful circles. They had risen further still when he married Eschiva, daughter of Baldwin of Ibelin, cementing his place as a man of import.

He strutted across the marble courtyard, his thick golden-brown mane framing his square jaw and sharp, near-yellow eyes. He had eschewed the orientalised style of the lesser nobles, preferring a simple linen shirt and breeches. A green cloak, so finely woven it seemed as smoke on his trail, was his one concession to court fashion.

To Dietmar, Aimery resembled one of the kings of old—tall, handsome, fierce and proud. Not like the fat king reclining in his chair, his belly turned to butter, his breasts like a woman's. But for all King Amalric's faults, he had ruled wisely—as wisely as any man could have in his position, while Aimery had turned Judas and betrayed his own lord.

Dietmar had overheard Tomas and Adelman gossiping about Aimery, claiming that his brothers had murdered the Earl of Salisbury using a blade gifted to them by Aimery before he fled to Jerusalem. Such rumours were hostile things, but the Lord of Lusignan's silence on the matter did make Dietmar wonder.

Aimery came to a stop beside the seneschal's chair and smiled warmly at his audience. When he spoke, his voice was like mulled wine to their ears.

"Honoured friends," he began, his hand raised in a simple greeting. "Would that I were here to bring you better tidings—to tell you that the days of peace will continue and that our greatest concern remains the shipping of wine and cheese to fill our bellies and wood to fill our hearths!"

A few laughs greeted his words, and some of the nobles raised their cups, but there was a subtle tension in the courtyard now. Everyone had heard of Saladin's growing brazenness, and the threat to the kingdom was becoming tangible.

"I will speak plainly," Aimery continued, touching the seneschal's shoulder with an easy familiarity while the diminutive Miles of Plancy appeared like a bald rat next to his cutting figure. "Our enemies have flourished while we have slumbered in our winter halls. Nur ad-Din's unification of Aleppo and Mosul, along with his conquest of Edessa and Banias, means a united Seljuk Empire now stands at our doorstep. The eyes of its master are now fixed on Outremer and its most precious prize: Jerusalem."

"While we have occupied ourselves with petty rivalries, our defences have fallen into disrepair. Our swords have dulled, and our arms have weakened. If the forces of Islam were to march upon us now, we would surely fall."

Aimery turned to Amalric's seat, acknowledging the king for the first time—last, after the seneschal, after his audience. His voice dripped with sweetness as he ingratiated himself with his master. "If not for the efforts of our noble liege, we might have already perished. Was it not he who took the war to Egypt and enlisted the aid of Constantinople? Was it not he who negotiated the peace with the Saracens?"

A murmur of agreement spread through the courtyard, a soft chorus of approval. Amalric blinked once, regarding the strutting Lord of Lusignan with something bordering on contempt. He knew the words carried a double meaning: Amalric had indeed saved the kingdom, but he had also allowed its defences to crumble. He had sallied forth against the Fatamid Empire but failed to seize Egypt and keep his Greek allies honest.

The king of Jerusalem harboured no love for Aimery of Lusignan whose patron, Agnes of Courtenay, had once been his wife. Some said she had taken the young noble as her lover.

With a flick of his wrists, Amalric silenced his chirping advisors. Taking a deep sip from his silver goblet, he allowed wine to trickle down his beard and into the ruffles of his tunic. Then, he nodded to Aimery. "Say your piece. You have my ear."

The king's voice, usually marked by a stammer, was now smooth and cold. Dietmar wondered at the fury that could cure such an impediment, if only for a moment.

Aimery bowed graciously, his smile fixed. He knew the game he played and played it well.

"We now stand at a crossroad," Aimery proclaimed, turning to the open courtyard with his back to the king. "Like our fathers who crossed the Taurus Mountains, we have a choice: whether to stay or to go? Whether we remain the masters of God's Kingdom or to be mere chattel, to be laid open by Saracen blades?"

"Stay!" a young nobleman called, slamming his empty cup against his bench. His face flushed with drink, he had the mood of the nobles with him.

"Oh! We stay!" shouted another, to cheers from the crowd.

Aimery's smile widened. "You have my heart, friends! But it will not be so easy. While the tide of Nur ad-Din rises, another threat appears to bite at our heels: the dog, Saladin!"

A chorus of boos greeted Aimery's pronouncement, and two knights from Poitiers barked like mad dogs, showing their teeth.

Dietmar glanced around the benches, staring at the once-dignified nobles. The court's atmosphere had transformed—gone was the solemness of before, replaced by the easy mood of a mummers show, with Aimery as its hero.

He looked back to the Lord of Lusignan.

Oily bastard, he thought, though he couldn't deny Aimery's talent for showmanship. Aimery laughed, extending his hand and pointing to the barking knights with enthusiasm, joining in with the clapping crowd.

Arne turned to give Dietmar a sour look. "I know those knights," he said. "They came across with Aimery from Poitiers."

They're from his household, then. Dietmar glanced at the barking knights.

"They bark like mutts because their master told them to," he said, looking back at the Dane. It was all part of the show, just like everything else.

Arne grinned. "And they call the Saracen a dog!"

Aimery's voice suddenly softened, and his barking hounds fell silent on cue.

"A dog must still be disciplined if it is to heel at its master's feet," he said, the crowd straining to hear. Then, louder, "The dog must know the whip if it is to obey! Saladin has forgotten the whip, and so he snarls at us, building up the courage to bite."

"What must be done?" one of the Poitiers knights called out, and other voices joined in until the whole court was up in a roaring clangour.

Aimery smiled, his golden eyes gleaming with triumph. They would do anything for him now.

When their calls subsided, silent anticipation settled upon the Royal Palace. Not even the songbirds at the king's ear dared break it. Aimery let the moment linger, slowly pacing the courtyard, his head down in thought.

"We must show our strength," he declared, turning on his feet to face them once more. "We must gather our arms beneath the One True Cross and make an example of Saladin while he and his master are still at odds. We can take him now, strike down this mangy desert dog. But only if we act swiftly. What say you?"

The courtyard swelled with the eruption of the nobles, their cheers and cries for war bouncing off the stone walls like a howling wind. The Poitiers knights banged their cups against their seats, and others joined in, adding to the roar.

Even Arne was swept up by Aimery's appeal and cried "Deus lo vult!" while raising his hands in salute, as if Aimery were a long-lost Roman emperor and not some upstart young lord seeking to bloody his sword.

And have us bloodied in turn.

Are we so foolish as this? To run toward death at the first sound of honeyed words?

Dietmar chuckled inwardly. Of course, they were. That was precisely how they'd come to be in Jerusalem in the first place. *Honeyed words and faith,* that was all it took to rile up the forces of Christendom.

But not all men were so easily convinced.

He spared Amalric a glance and saw that the king's face remained unchanged, with nary an eyebrow raised to betray his emotions. Amalric wouldn't have risen so high if the lines on his face were as easy to read as a palimpsest. Or perhaps Dietmar simply lacked the ability to decipher it. Still, he thought he glimpsed the white of Amalric's knuckles before the king unclenched his fists and called for more wine.

Miles of Plancy waited until the cheers subsided before rising from his seat, only to be greeted by a renewed roar as soon as he stood.

"A vote!" he called out, attempting to make his voice heard over the clamour of the other nobles. "We must vote on Aimery's proposal."

Aimery didn't bother trying to restore order. He knew the will of the crowd would not be stifled; it could only be directed one way or another. He laughed at the seneschal's feeble efforts, clasping his hands before him and bowing to the benches.

Dietmar thought he looked like a lion then, with his golden eyes and flowing mane, his teeth bared back. And around him, a court of fools, laughing hyenas who would follow whoever wielded the biggest sword, whoever's bite proved sharpest.

"Silence!" Reynald suddenly roared, slamming his fist against his seat and rising to glare at those around him. He waited until not even a breath stirred in the crowded courtyard before turning his gaze to the seneschal. His glare had softened, but only just. "Perhaps it would be wise to hear from other parties before calling a vote," Reynald declared. "Aimery's words ring true, but he is one man, and to decide our fates on the say-so of one man would be… imprudent."

Miles of Plancy widened his eyes at Reynald's words, embarrassed. Or perhaps he was imagining the bear of Sidon smashing his bald head in like an egg?

"Of course, of course, my lord," the seneschal replied. "We will open the court and hear from all interested parties. Forgive my hastiness."

Reynald nodded slowly, wrinkling his mouth in disdain, and then sat back down to engage in a hushed conversation with Theobald of Tabor.

While the Count of Sidon may have missed the hateful glare Aimery cast his way, Geldemar of Tiberiad did not. The swordsman-cum-judge rapped his cup against his seat, catching Aimery's eye, and then smiled at him, a fox to a lion.

Aimery blinked first.

By the time order had returned to the court, the seneschal was ready to call the first witness. The Patriarch of Alexandria had abandoned his post when Saladin seized control of Egypt, displacing the existing hierarchy like a pike thrown into a pool of carp.

The Patriarch told the court of the horrors that had befallen the Christians who remained, describing churches torn to the ground and others that still stood, only to be converted into Muslim places of worship. His recollection stirred something in the audience, his words falling on sympathetic ears. Discontented voices soon rose in disgust as he detailed the plight of Christians in Saladin's Egypt. If he were to be believed, they were being dragged from their homes and thrown into the sea. If he were to be believed, the once great churches of Alexandria now served as temples to Allah.

Never mind that they had been Muslim houses of worship before the Christians came. Never mind that they had done the same to the mosques in Jerusalem, and worse.

Aimery no longer needed his Poitiers knights to sway the crowd's sentiment; they followed his lead willingly now.

"Bastard heathens," Arne muttered, crossing himself as the Patriarch concluded his testimony. "We should have broken their backs when we had the chance."

When would that have been? Dietmar wanted to ask. When barely a handful of knights and peasants had stumbled their way into Jerusalem? God had smiled on them that day, but if they had tried their luck any further, they would have all died in the sands. Every attempt after had ended in failure. Perhaps God's will extended only as far as Jerusalem and the other great cities were not meant for them? Such thoughts were best kept to oneself, and Dietmar maintained his silence, nodding in agreement with Arne's words.

With his testimony complete, the Patriarch rose from the seneschal's seat and slowly made his way back to his bench along the aisle. The gold on his fingers caught the midday sun, and Dietmar wondered how much truth had passed the Patriarch's lips, how much had he really lost?

Next, Odo of St. Amad, the Master of the Templars, informed them of the threat Saladin posed to the routes connecting Jerusalem to Hebron and to the eastern towns of Jericho and Amman. According to the knight, the Kurd was both the greatest threat to Christian security and also powerless in the face of Templar steel. It was precisely the sort of existential threat coupled with bravado that Dietmar had come to expect from the Order, whose fortunes were inextricably tied to their ability to conduct violence and expand the limits of their domain.

Odo's words were, Dietmar thought, less well received. Everyone knew of the Templar's interests in the south, and of their growing estates, and their voracious appetite for more. Odo had grown rich, and his beady, black eyes were always on the lookout for more profit.

Finally, long after the sun had reached its zenith, when renewed calls for a vote were being voiced by tired nobles, Jobert of Syria took to the front of the court. He swept down the aisle, his black mantle billowing behind him. He waved away the offered seat, sending the seneschal scurrying beneath the gallery with a pointed flick of his head, and came to a stand between Amalric's chair and the judges' empty benches, where Aimery of Lusignan was now hovering.

The Master of the Hospitallers fixed a lingering gaze upon Aimery and then bowed to the king. When he turned to the court, his words were sharp and cutting.

"What miserable curs you all are to fall for such tricks!"

Gasps erupted from the crowd, and someone even laughed. Dietmar thought it might have been Geldemar.

"Did we not learn our lesson in Banias," Jobert continued, "When Nur ad-Din washed us away like the tide? Or in Egypt, where not even the combined arms of Komnenos and Outremer could dislodge Saladin from his throne? Bah!"

His words were met with silence.

The knight lord strode across the open square, sweeping the benches with his hard stare, and then turned to look at Aimery once more.

The Hospitaller was tall and cadaverous, with a wispy beard and heavy-set features. His gaunt face was marked by the scars he'd earned campaigning against Nur ad-Din in Syria the decade before. He had lost a finger to a Seljuk blade in Harenc but taken the head of the *faris* in return.

Jobert was no friend to the king. They often clashed over the crimes of certain knights within his order, and each time the knight lord fell back on the protection offered by the *Pie postulatio voluntatis*, the Papal bull recognising the sovereignty of his Order, much to Amalric's frustration.

To be usurped of authority in your own kingdom. Dietmar could understand the king's annoyance. The knightly orders proved an effective weapon when their aims aligned with the king's, but more often than not, they became thorns in his side.

Still, the Master was no fool and had grown weary of endless conflict and its costs. His predecessor, Gilbert d' Aissailly, had been deposed while still alive due to his lavish spending.

Jobert would not see the same thing repeated.

"Do you think the fate of your father is lost on us?" Jobert said, his expression softening as the whites of his teeth showed under his top lip. "No man deserves to live out his last days in a Saracen cell. To die in one! Your desire for vengeance is as natural as God's grace. But do not mistake your anger for wisdom. You would see the whole kingdom devoured to sate your lust for vengeance."

A murmur spread through the court, the gaze of every noble fixed on Aimery.

Dietmar thought he saw the king smile into his wine.

The Poitiers lord smiled too, but it was a cruel thing, his upper lip curled in a leonine snarl.

"You deny the threat to Jerusalem?" Aimery stepped forward, his body turned toward the crowd, ever the showman.

Deftly done, Dietmar thought. Aimery had side-stepped Jobert's first thrust—his father's death in the hands of Saracen goalers—and instead appealed to the fears of the audience: a skilful parry and riposte.

Jobert's eyes narrowed. "There can be no denial. The threat is indeed great. Only, it is your—"

"This knight of the cloth," Aimery continued before Jobert could finish, "would have us cower in our homes, waiting for the dog and his master to tear down our doors and feast upon our flesh! Where is the honour in that, I ask? Where is the *wisdom*?"

"Coward!" one of the Poitiers knights shouted before being dragged back to his seat by his neighbour. This was not a matter for the crowd.

Jobert growled, standing straight as Aimery began circling him on the courtyard floor. The Hospitaller towered over the Frenchman, but he was all bone and sinew, gangly-looking next to this young nobleman who looked like a king.

"I call for prudence," Jobert declared to the court. "We are not so strong that we can amble into the desert and recover from another loss at the hands of its master."

"Hah!" Aimery laughed now. "So it is our arms that you doubt? You do not think our brave knights are fit to task? Perhaps that is why you fill your ranks with so many turcopoles?"

Jobert's mouth tightened, his hands clenched at his sides. "They are good Christian men."

The crowd murmured again, and there was laughter from the back seats. The Hospitaller's face reddened. He was not used to being mocked. Shaking his head, he glared into the aisles before fixing his gaze upon Aimery, who smiled back at him. Jobert knew he had been outmatched.

"Heed my words," Jobert said, his dark eyes like empty sockets in his skull. "When Saladin sinks his teeth into your neck, you will find that he is no mere dog, but a wolf… and that his teeth are long and many. Then you will realise that this task has been folly and your life ended too soon. And for what? Vain pride? For that, you will condemn us all? Bah!"

Aimery watched as the Master strode back toward his bench, but the young lord wasn't content to leave it at that. "Go ring your bell, Hospitaller," he called out, mimicking the motion with his hand. Once, twice… and then he clenched his fist, twisting the gesture into something vulgar.

Dietmar winced, feeling the tension ripple through those who recognised the insult around him. Aimery had invoked a dispute from the Hospitallers' history, when they had clashed with the Patriarch over land and money. They had rung their bells during his sermons to fluster the poor man. It was a shameful memory, not befitting of the noble order. But the gesture had taken on another meaning.

Wanker.

Jobert slowed his steps, and for a moment, Dietmar thought he might turn and confront the lord. But the moment passed, and Jobert of Syria returned to his seat with no blood spilt.

"Vote!" a voice called, and then another, and another until the seneschal reappeared from beneath the gallery to order proceedings.

"If all are satisfied," Miles said when the noise had subsided, "we shall proceed with a vote on Aimery of Lusignan's proposal."

He glanced nervously toward Reynald to see if he had any objections. The gruff old lord simply crossed his arms and leaned back in his seat, his silence serving as his reply.

"Very well," Miles continued. "Seeking a majority, we shall begin with a hand vote. If there is any doubt, we will settle matters by ballot. All those in favour of Aimery's proposal to address the problem of Saladin head-on, the details to be determined by the King's Council, raise your hands."

A sea of hands shot up, leaving no doubt as to the court's will. Dietmar looked around, seeing even Reynald and Geldemar's hands raised in support of the motion. When he turned his gaze to the king, he saw Amalric's hand raised as well.

The mood of the Frankish nobles was a fickle thing, so it may have been from a sense of shrewd self-preservation that they voted. Or maybe Gelmiro had been right: Jerusalem had to show her strength now or suffer for it later.

"Those against," Miles called out.

Barely a dozen hands went up, mostly from those loyal to Jobert of Syria or from those who harboured enough disdain for Aimery to vote against their own interests.

"The motion is passed," Miles declared, patting his sweating forehead with a cloth. He waved his free hand toward Aimery, but the lord brushed past him, his lips curled back to show his teeth.

"Ho there!" Aimery called out, marching across the courtyard. "I didn't see your hand raised either way. Are you not fit to vote?"

With a groan, Dietmar realised the words were meant for him.

He hesitated, frozen in place as he watched the lord bear down on him.

Shit.

"Well?" Aimery barked, coming to a stand before the front row. The other nobles had turned to stare, and he could hear Arne shuffling along the pillar beside him to create more space.

Dietmar cleared his throat. "I did not think it right to vote on a fate I will not share in."

Aimery raised an eyebrow. "You won't be joining us in the defence of Jerusalem?"

"I am returning home," Dietmar replied, opening his palms. "My lands need their master. I have been here seven years. You must forgive me if I choose not to spend another."

This seemed to satisfy Aimery, who nodded, his expression softening somewhat. "What is your name, chevalier?"

Where are you going?

The same question Paul had asked the Christ when they met along the Appian Way. He thought of the Dead Sea spitting fire, a tumultuous shape shifting beneath its black waves. The rotten fruit in his mouth and the mad Frenchman's hacking laughter.

"Dietmar of Zwingenberg," he said, meeting Aimery's yellow eyes.

"A German!" Aimery laughed, and something nasty appeared in his stare. "Your emperor entreats with the Kurdish dog even while he snaps at our heels. Is that why you are leaving? You would rather get rich off Muslim coin than help your fellow Christians?"

Dietmar tensed, feeling anger stir within him at Lusignan's words. He would not be made an example of, not like Jobert.

"My emperor's business is his own," he replied firmly. "I have fought for God in His Kingdom, and I have fought well, longer than most."

"Until the first real challenge presented itself," Aimery mocked, waving his hand dismissively at Dietmar. "But isn't that the way with you Germans? Loyal only to your own."

Odo of St. Amad reappeared on the courtyard floor, prowling behind his lord like a caged lion.

Aimery's words went quiet, almost a whisper. "Or perhaps it is cowardice?"

The voice in the back of Dietmar's mind, the one that warned him when he had drunk enough or when he had spent too much time rolling dice—the voice he often ignored—urged him not to draw the knife on his belt and stab the bastard lord so full of holes his wine spilt from his belly across the yard. This time, he listened. But only just.

Aimery noticed Dietmar's hand hovering over the blade and bared his teeth again. But before he could goad him on, King Amalric stirred from his seat, his pendulous gut hanging like a saddle bag from his torso.

"Go sit your arse down, Aimery," he said. "You will have your w-war. Let the German go home to f-fuck his wife and raise his bastards. He's had enough of God's Kingdom, and I've had enough of your voice."

Aimery held Dietmar's gaze a moment longer, then snorted and turned to the king.

"My Liege," he said, bowing so low it could only be mocking. With that, he strode out of the courtyard, leaving his seat empty. The court soon followed.

5

Dietmar arrived back at his rooms just before nightfall. He had purchased a smallholding in the northeast of the city, in what was now known as the Syrian Quarter. The property had come cheap but with ample space for his small household and a pleasant enough view.

His neighbours, a collection of Eastern Christians from Oultrejourdain, Orthodox Greeks, Syrians, and down-on-their-luck Franks, kept to themselves, which suited Dietmar just fine. He nodded in greeting to the old, grey-haired man who liked to watch passers-by from the front steps of the neighbouring dwelling and wondered what would become of him when the Saracens finally arrived.

He'll still be here, nodding to the faris lords like nothing's changed.

Would anything truly change?

Did it really matter who ruled Jerusalem? He thought of the blood that had been spilt to capture the city, the blood that had been shed afterwards, and the blood that would flow to keep it.

That mattered.

But to old men on their steps, he imagined it mattered less. The shifting of rulers was simply a marker of the passing of time, and they would likely be content to smile at whoever ascended the steps as long as they were left in peace.

Razin and Adelman were waiting for him in the dining room, which they had converted into Adelman's office. The price of wood being what it was, homecooked meals were a luxury few could afford. They mostly ate greasy hot food from Malcuisinat or the other market streets that dotted the city, leaving the dining room and kitchen unused.

Adelman was hunched over one of his ledgers, surrounded by piles of notes and papers stacked nearly as high as his head on the table. Razin sat on the seat opposite, reclining in a cushioned chair, his feet up on the table. He was focused on a small block of cedar wood he had purchased at the market, using the same blade that had sliced his apple to whittle away at it. He looked up as Dietmar entered.

"So, it is decided then?" Razin asked, gently blowing away the dust from his carving.

"Aye. Aimery will have his way. There is to be war."

"A costly business," said Adelman, peering over his books. His dark brows creased for a moment, coming together like two prickly slugs, and then he returned to his ledger.

"Costly and foolish," Razin added. "Saladin will have entrenched his position since displacing the Fatamid Caliph, turning Egypt into his fortress. And if his master comes to his aid, then there is no hope at all."

Dietmar settled into a chair and began unlacing his boots. "They say there is no love between Saladin and Nur ad-Din. They believe he will not come."

He had stayed a while after the vote, listening to the nobles—still high on the fumes of Aimery's speech—plot and scheme the quickest route to Cairo.

As if they had not tried it all before.

And then against the rotting corpse of the Fatamids, too weak and slovenly to swipe at the Franks biting chunks of meat from their haunches. But even then, the Franks had failed. Now they faced an entirely different beast—a nimble and cunning opponent with enough men to punish any failures.

They will open up the corridor to Jerusalem.

Every man lost in this futile endeavour will be one defender less on the city walls when Nur ad-Din and Saladin come for us.

For them, Dietmar reminded himself. By then, he would be long gone.

Razin glanced up from his carving, fixing his gaze on Dietmar. "He will come. It is hard to imagine after so short a time here—yes, seven years, I know. But that is not enough to understand. Nur ad-Din has lived and breathed this war his entire life. There is nothing he desires more than the restoration of the Holy Land. *Nothing*. His every move has been toward that end. He will not sacrifice the chance because of some bad blood with his lieutenant."

"Jobert of the Hospitallers said as much," Dietmar admitted, slipping off his boots and leaning back in his chair. "They will not ride south with Aimery and his host."

"Then what chance they had is halved," said Razin, returning to his whittling. "That skeleton knight and his men have made the difference more times than I can count. Jerusalem's allies grow few indeed."

"A costly business," Adelman repeated, setting aside his quill and rubbing his tired eyes. The bookkeep dressed like a cleric, donning long, dusty robes that had turned yellow at the edges and a black hood he wore even in Jerusalem's sweltering summer months. He wore his thinning grey hair behind his ears, which had begun sprouting unruly hairs of their own.

"We will need to sell this property before word of this war spreads," Adelman sighed. "And even then, I cannot promise we will make our money back. These new pilgrims from Normandy are a miserly bunch—everyone says so. They'd rather spend their coin on rentals than make investments! We will have to sweeten the deal. Perhaps Talbert can offer us a rate on his stables to forward to any prospective buyers?"

"There is no 'we'," Razin said, not looking up. "It is not our coin that was spent."

Adelman brushed off the comment, wiping his nose with a cloth from his pocket. He blew into it before letting out another drawn-out sigh. The warmer clime disagreed with his humours, and he spent near as many hours sneezing as he did complaining about it.

"There will need to be coin for replenishments for our journey," Adelman continued. "Horse feed, the last rent owed to the stables, our own accommodation once we've—*if* we manage to sell this place. Then there is the matter of the silver needed for our passage from Antioch and again from Messina." Adelman shook his head, barely holding back another sigh. His lips went thin at the thought of all the expenses. "And that's to say nothing of the journey home!"

"Gelmiro has offered to cover a portion of our costs," said Dietmar. "He understands the strain this journey will put on our finances. He will also loan us a guard to escort us part of the way."

"More mouths to feed," muttered Adelman. "We will be spent before we reach Germany!"

"Dietmar has the coin," said Razin. He turned the wood over in his palm to inspect. Wood the same colour as his hand, Dietmar thought.

There had been no dark-skinned men in Odenwald growing up. And for all Dietmar knew, there still weren't any. In one of his stern lectures, his father had spun tales of eastern men who rode to war on skinny horses and fired arrows from the saddle. They had listened wide-eyed as he recounted tales of godless savages—men who ate their own dead and sired with their sisters, their only purpose to breed and feed.

But even then, Dietmar had suspected his father fibbed. His words carried with them the air of authority only age could bring, but Rudolph had never answered the call to defend Jerusalem, nor had he ventured east himself. His stories were secondhand, gathered from the mouths of others, from the men who traded tales of their wounds for coin in the taverns. They quickly learned that the truth wasn't worth as much as a good story.

Still, when Dietmar had encountered his first Syrian in Adrianople, he couldn't help but pause and stare until the merchant took notice. As the vendor barked out his prices, Dietmar had realised that all men were the same, and the only colour that mattered was the colour of your coin.

To live and die for bits of silver and gold.

To kill for it, as he had.

Upon his arrival in the city, Dietmar had taken any job he could find. Was he any different from the bastards and cutthroats he had encountered over the years? He contented himself with the knowledge that his actions were merely a means to an end—a way to save his land and legacy. But perhaps every bastard had their reasons too? Maybe each man had a tale to excuse the butchering and violence? Such thoughts made it harder for Dietmar to do what he needed —knowing that the man standing before him had his motivations, no less valuable than his own, made it harder to kill them. And so Dietmar spent little time contemplating such things. The other bastards didn't, so they wouldn't hesitate when the time came.

Adelman grunted wearily as he rose from his seat. It was getting dark quickly, and he needed the light to work. He lit a pair of candles beneath the window and then turned to the metal sconce, filled with more candles, at the centre of the table.

He lit them one by one, slow and methodical like everything he did, then blew out the taper. "When we get home," he said, settling back in his chair, "we will need enough coin to see to the repairs of your estate.

Those monks have a keen eye for business, but I wouldn't trust them to have kept things in good repair while we were gone."

Dietmar nodded in agreement. Then, when he saw Razin's expression, he shook his head before his friend could speak. Adelman would retire after their journey home, and Razin would assume responsibility for managing the accounts. With his sharp mind for algebra, he was already double-checking Adelman's work when the old man went to bed—which seemed to be happening earlier and earlier each night, though he slept in late.

If Adelman noticed the lines through his work and the new figures appearing in the margins in another hand, he hadn't said so, and Dietmar was content to spare him the humiliation. He would broach the topic of Adelman's retirement once they had passed the Rhine.

"We will cross that bridge when we get to it," said Dietmar, waving his hand to close the matter.

"The bridge!" Adelman groaned softly, prompting an eye roll from Razin. "You don't think it's still in ruins?" Adelman wiped his nose nervously. "Surely, by now, the Church's masons have seen to it. Why, if they haven't, it'll mean—"

"I'm sure it's fine," said Dietmar, trying not to grind his teeth. "Knowing Abbot Albert, he would have prioritised securing the lost revenues after its collapse."

"It has been seven years," Razin added, wiping down his carving with a finger.

That seemed to settle Adelman somewhat. He blew his nose again and returned to his books. Dietmar and Razin exchanged a wearied glance, then Razin fixed his attentions on completing his carving while Dietmar watched.

He whistled softly under his breath as he whittled at the wood, cutting thin pieces with deft slices of the blade. Dietmar found comfort in the slow, certain monotony of the task after a day of listening to rich men squabble.

Still, his thoughts loomed out from the peace, no longer caught between distractions.

They took him to a dark, cold place. They always did. A place that was never far away, despite his best efforts to keep distant from his own horror.

Something curdled inside of him, then the darkness unfurled in a tranche of memories that nearly shook him physically.

Ennelyn's hand on the small of his back.

Her soft words to calm him when his brother had stormed from his household.

And then, Rudi.

He felt suddenly claustrophobic, and the cold feeling only grew, until it felt like someone had dragged a wet cloth over his skin.

He is here, Dietmar realised, in this cold.

The sound of Razin's carving formed a rhythmic staccato to his ruminations.

What have I agreed to, he wondered hazily, his thoughts slowing to a trickle. *To make an enemy of a king and condemn a prince to a life of suffering?*

His eyes had started to droop by the time his friend finished his carving.

Razin smiled a smile of self-satisfaction and placed the figure on the table, clearing the last of the dust away so Dietmar could see.

He had carved a lion.

***

The next morning, Dietmar rose early to wash at the bathhouses near St. Anne's. He had taken to the hygiene habits of the locals reluctantly at first but then with more enthusiasm—washing twice a week whenever time and coin allowed. Tomas, on the other hand, required more encouragement, and it was only when Dietmar commented on his musky odour that he would do something about it.

That morning, Tomas stirred from his sleep to join Dietmar of his own accord. He would make an exception for the Temple Mount, which Dietmar had suggested they visit after the bathhouse.

Razin made his usual excuses, and Dietmar thought it best to leave Adelman to sleep. The old man tended to be sharp-tongued and ill-tempered in the early hours, making for poor company until well past noon.

Razin was still cursing at the bookkeep's snoring when Dietmar and Tomas stepped out onto the street.

A cool breeze swept in from the Judean Mountains, whistling through the near-empty roads. Dietmar was grateful for the padded vest he wore beneath his tunic to ward off the chill.

"God's breath," Tomas muttered, huddling deeper into his hood. "If I had known a winter day would make an appearance this far into summer, I might have stayed in bed."

"The walk will unfreeze our bones," said Dietmar distractedly. He had slept poorly, his dreams plagued by apparitions from his past. He glanced at Tomas and forced a smile. "But not if you shuffle along like an old mule. Come on."

Tomas grumbled something under his breath but quickened his pace.

Fingers of light cut across the city, poking holes in the shadows and sending the rats scurrying for their burrows. In ages past, the breaking of dawn would have been accompanied by the Muslim call to prayer, but that tradition ended when the Franks conquered Jerusalem.

The Syrian Quarter had another name, too, from before the settlers from Oultrejourdain and Europe had arrived to fill the empty houses. It had been the Jewish Quarter first. *Juiverie*. There had been no Jacobite churches in the Quarter then. And no empty houses either.

The Jews and Muslims who resided there had been driven out and forbidden from returning. Some had still come back, of course, either as converts or in secret. Dietmar knew of a few Jewish families living near David's Tower. Dyers by trade, they paid a hefty tax for their faith, but in return, they were allowed to do business in the city.

Not everyone could afford the religious tax, however. Most commoners kept their faith to themselves, and Dietmar didn't pry, though he suspected Islam and Judaism were the unofficial religions of large parts of Jerusalem.

So, it had come as no surprise to Dietmar when Tomas nervously informed him that Razin was a worshipper of Allah.

Tomas had woken early one morning for a piss, he'd said. But those still being the early days in Dietmar's household, he'd stumbled into the wrong room, thinking it were the privy. He had found Razin prostrated on the floor, his knees resting on a small rug pointed south toward Mecca.

Razin had looked up at his arrival, a note of alarm on his face when he saw Tomas by his door. But Tomas, by his own words, had simply shrugged, asked him where the pisser was, and then left him to his business.

God was God, he'd told Dietmar at the end of the story. He had watched Dietmar carefully to see his response, his words as much a test as an explanation for Razin's reluctance to partake in some of the more holy festivities offered to the Christians of the city.

God is God, Dietmar had agreed. Then he'd told Tomas he didn't care who any of them worshipped so long as it wasn't money or wine. Tomas had chuckled at that and told him the only other thing he worshipped besides God was a woman's thighs and what lay between them.

In truth, that had surprised Dietmar more than the revelation about Razin's faith. It was only then that he realised no man of God could curse in as many tongues as Tomas did and that the hooded figure he'd taken for a travelling monk was more a drunk and a beggar than a priest. But by then, it was already too late, Tomas had settled into his rooms, and besides, Dietmar had started to quite like the musky-smelling fellow.

God is God.

An abstraction. An answer—but vague and distant. When had he stopped believing? Had he? Before Ennelyn and Rudi, his faith had been a simple matter, but without them... He had stopped thinking about faith in terms of some naïve duality—of belief and disbelief, zealot and iconoclast. To him, it was a dance of contradictions, a delicate tapestry woven from threads of doubt and conviction to create a web that defied any such febrile categorisation. Faith without doubt was less interesting to him than a faith that embraced the vast spectrum between fervent devotion and cynicism.

Still, he envied the doubtless faithful, who had found God—that elusive spectral cypher. Those men and women who had not had their conviction shaken as he had.

Now, it felt like God was with him still, only waiting in the next room. All it would take was for him to open the door.

So why hadn't he?

Some feeling, a perplexing, uncanny urge he couldn't explain, prevented him. And so he left God waiting, knowing that the door swung both ways.

"The season is changing," said Dietmar, turning his thoughts away from such ineffable things. "There will be cold days ahead on the road to Antioch."

"And a pox on Gelmiro for suggesting such a thing." Tomas crossed himself as they passed a cripple on the streets but ignored the beggar's plea for alms.

"I do not mean it," said Tomas with a sigh after seeing the look Dietmar was giving him. "But I trust your friend even less than I like the idea of marching out into the hills like merry pilgrims. Shall we sing while we walk, I wonder? Or shall we be silent like the Carthusians?"

"Neither," Dietmar responded with a slight smile. "But I would rather walk in silence than hear you sing."

"If the king catches us, I will sing him a pretty little song about a weasel and a hand."

"He won't catch us."

"But then, who will hear my song?"

Dietmar chuckled as they moved onto Jehoshaphat Street, joining the growing stream of foot traffic heading east. Travellers would be making their way from Jehoshaphat's Gate that morning to visit the sacred sites in the valley or ascend the road to Bethany and the Mount of Olives.

Tomas crossed himself again as they passed Lazar House, muttering a quiet prayer and quickening his pace.

Dietmar wondered if his friend ever crossed himself out of awe and wonder or if it was solely driven by fear and disgust? Then he decided it was not a fair comparison at all. Not in a city where horrors lurked in every corner. He glanced up at the sick house.

"They are closer to God," he said. "Spare them the pity you would not grant a beggar."

A pair of knights of St. Lazarus appeared on the balcony above, their green crosses on their tabards marking them out as doomed men.

"It is only because they are nearer to death," said Tomas, eyeing the knights warily.

The two men leaned against the balcony, exchanging words as they watched the street below. If not for their tabards, Dietmar would have found them unremarkable. They were tall and strong, showing no visible signs of the Lazarian mark. Most likely, they had been drawn from the ranks of the holy militant orders in the city, perhaps the Hospitallers, who frequently attended to the sick.

One of the knights laughed. It was a warm, hearty sound that echoed down the street.

"You wouldn't guess he had a foot in the grave," said Tomas.

"What would you have him do?" asked Dietmar, letting his irritation creep into his voice. "Mope about until they burn his body? Hide away until the rot takes him?"

Tomas made a sound that suggested he thought that was precisely what the knight should do, but upon seeing Dietmar's expression, he kept his silence.

They skirted around the entrance to the sick house, staying well away from its open doors and the shrouded figures lingering on its steps. Pale individuals watched them from the shadows, their eyes rinsed of colour, replaced by a sickly yellow hue.

Dietmar thought of the boy then. They would call him the Leper Prince when word of his condition got out, when his tutor's secrecy failed, or his ailment became apparent to even the inexpert eye. Would he hide away in the shadows of a leper colony, ruling through his advisors who smelt like incense and linen from all the time spent in his rooms? Or would he bare his diseased face to the world and rule as a king might until his body finally failed him?

For the second time in as many days, Dietmar found himself questioning his task. Was it hypocrisy to save the soul of his son while condemning another to suffer? If this hand of a Saint could alleviate Baldwin's affliction and give him the mind to rule, should he not do all in his power to deny Gelmiro and the Church? But life was fleeting… and the king's son would find God's grace—that was guaranteed by a life of suffering, was it not? Rudi faced an eternity of cold darkness.

And besides, he was his son.

Dietmar had a father's duty. Surely God could understand that, couldn't He? But Dietmar wasn't so sure. When the time had come, God had been willing to sacrifice His own son for the sake of humanity.

Another strange symmetry, he thought.

Tomas noticed Dietmar's troubled expression but mistook it as worry about the forthcoming journey. He pulled his hood tighter and offered him a half-reassuring smile.

"Men older than Adelman used to take the Pilgrim's Road before ships to Jaffa were a common thing. And the king has better things to do than to follow us fools into the desert."

"It is a long walk," Dietmar mused.

"Not if you're riding in the back of a cart like I plan to. You would, too, if you saw the size of the thorns along the way to Nablus."

Dietmar shook his head, letting his friend's banter distract him from his thoughts. "No thorns from atop Theseus's saddle. But you'll have to endure the worst of Adelman's snores and sneezes beside him on the cart. You know what the open air does to that nose of his."

Tomas pursed his lower lip, his bushy velvet brows knitting together. "Perhaps I will walk after all, like St. Anthony through the desert, leaving you all to follow my footprints!"

With that, he skipped ahead of Dietmar and broke into a jog, disappearing around the corner opposite St. Anne's.

Dietmar followed.

The bathhouses were deserted at that early hour, and Dietmar took his time lowering himself into the warm waters of the first open pool he found.

The baths reminded him of those of the *caravanserais* he had frequented in Constantinople, with their vaulted ceilings allowing streams of sunlight to cascade in from above and walls adorned with intricate mosaics.

He scrubbed his skin with a hard soap that smelt of olives and berries, ridding himself of the dust and grime he had acquired since his last visit.

If only it was so easy to wash away the memories.

Would he be willing to forget the last seven years if he could? Wallowing in those warm waters, he decided that he might.

When he was done, he submerged his head fully beneath the waters, only coming back up for breath when his lungs started to burn.

By the time he and Tomas finally left for the Temple on the Mount, his skin was taut and wrinkled, and Tomas no longer stunk of musk.

The sun had reached its zenith when they reached the *Templum Domini*, and clear blue skies greeted them from the foot of its steps. A brisk wind cut through the north-facing gardens that enveloped the plateau, offering some reprieve to their backs as they ascended.

Tomas's robes clung to his sweaty form, and Dietmar barely managed to conceal his mirth at his friend's complaints.

"Wash *before* we go, he says, so that we can be clean for the church. Only to make us trek across half the city under the midday sun! Clean? Hah!"

Tomas wiped his forehead with his sleeve. "Might as well leave my clothes out to dry and enter the temple as naked as I am in the eyes of God. Like Jesus the babe, only with a belly."

Dietmar smirked. "The temple guard will cut your balls off if they see them hanging anywhere near the Dome."

"Better not then," said Tomas. "I like fiddling with my balls too much to become an eunuch."

Dietmar rolled his eyes and continued toward the great leaden dome at the centre of the plateau, not bothering to wait for Tomas to catch up.

The Dome of the Rock stood as a circular structure, its walls rising sharply at the corners, topped with a flat tiled roof. About a third of the way across, a majestic grey dome bulged upwards, towering over the rest of the building. Roman-styled pillars had been built around its walls, forming an intricate nest of stone and marble.

At its pinnacle, the glistening golden cross caught the sun's rays.

On the northern approach to the temple, another garden unfolded, featuring lush pine and cedar trees, embraced by a vine-covered marble colonnade. Across from the temple, the Templars had constructed various storage facilities, granaries, stables, and even baths to serve the Templars Palace, which shared the Mount with the Dome.

Dietmar had thought about visiting the Church of the Holy Sepulchre, joining the throngs of devoted faithful in its bustling halls, giving thanks to God beneath the figure of Christ in mosaic and the altar of his holy prophets. But when he paid his dinar to the Augustinian canon overseeing the church and stepped inside, he was glad he hadn't.

In truth, he had always felt closer to the presence of something extraordinary in the echoing chambers of the Temple.

Perhaps it was its proximity to so many holy things—the cradle of Jesus hidden within its alcoves, the cavern within the rock where Jesus was said to have retired when he grew tired of the mocking of the Jews, and where he had listened to his disciples' confessions.

There was an unmistakable presence beneath the curved ceiling that comforted Dietmar. But deep down, it also terrified him.

Men kill for this, too, he thought. That feeling. Even if they didn't understand it, they yearned for it. Something that suggests there is more to life than just the temporal—that the promises of priests and kings, imams and rabbis, hold true. For if they don't, what else is there?

Moving slowly beneath the crenellated arches, Dietmar marvelled at the marble frescoes that covered the walls. Biblical scenes were woven seamlessly with ornate designs, delicate flowers, and exotic animals. The warm gaze of St. Nicholas, standing upon a marble plinth near the centre of the Dome, was embraced by the blooming Lily of the Valley.

Inscriptions in Latin and Greek, verses from scripture, and promises made by Christian kings spiralled across the ceiling amidst vibrant frescoes, their intricacy surpassing even that of the bathhouse. The smooth marble flagstones gave way to unevenness mere steps from the entrance, transforming into a sea of jagged paving where masons had attempted to conceal the cave-like floor.

Their efforts had been to no avail, as the protruding stone stubbornly persisted behind the chipped marble, an eyesore in the Temple of the Lord. An iron grille had been installed by the monks in an attempt to dissuade pilgrims from removing fragments of the rock, but to Dietmar, it only detracted from the beauty of the place.

Lighting his candle from the large copper-plated candelabra beneath St. Nicholas's altar, Dietmar embarked on his circuit of the temple. Tomas had vanished into one of the niches, claiming to pray, though Dietmar suspected he was simply taking his noonday nap. Either way, he was thankful for the peace. He hadn't had much of it since arriving in Jerusalem.

When he reached the rock peeking out from beneath the broken marble, he placed his candle on a wide iron sconce already filled with half a dozen other flickering candles and knelt down to pray.

Christians revered the temple for its connection to Christ and the divine intervention that spared Isaac's life when God commanded his sacrifice.

But he had heard other stories about the temple, too. Stories not mentioned by the monks residing in the nearby abbey and tending to the church grounds.

In one of the city's various drinking holes, Dietmar had once pondered aloud why the rock beneath the Temple's floor was covered by marble. A young Venetian with curly dark hair had chuckled in response.

"It is said to hide the footprints," the Venetian had shared.

"Footprints?" Dietmar had asked, bemused.

"Footprints of the Prophet Muhammad and hoofprints of his winged horse," came the reply. "This was once a Muslim temple before the Jews and Christians arrived. Didn't you know?"

"Oh?"

"Look for yourself," the man had said. "There's even a mark from when Gabriel pushed the rock back down when it tried to follow him to Heaven."

Dietmar had looked, but most of the stone was veiled beneath the marble cover, and the monks didn't take kindly to visitors clambering over the iron grille. He had thought about discussing it with Razin but had not yet found the courage to broach the topic of his friend's faith. And so his curiosity went unsated.

When Dietmar finished his prayer and opened his eyes, he thought he heard a sound, like hooves and horses, but it was only the stables nearby.

***

When Dietmar and Tomas returned home, a pale-faced Adelman met them at the door.

"We've had a message," he said, casting wary glances in both directions before hurriedly ushering them inside.

"What is it?" asked Dietmar.

"Speak, man!" Tomas demanded, losing his patience.

Adelman wiped his nose and then his sweaty brow. "It was from Gelmiro," he said. "I fear he has been discovered. He says we are to leave the city at once, before it's too late."

6

"What else did he say?" Dietmar wanted to shake the wide-eyed Adelman but somehow managed to restrain himself.

"The g-guard," Adelman stammered, his voice trembling. "The guard will meet us by the North Gate. The relic will be delivered to us th-there."

"Is that all?" Tomas asked, his gaze darting down the passage behind Adelman. "Where is Razin?"

The old man gathered himself, straightening his back and taking a deep breath. "He's gone to rouse Talbert and the horses. He wants us to leave as soon as it gets dark." He knitted his brow. "What is to become of the sale? Who will buy the property at this late hour?"

"There will be no sale," stated Dietmar, already striding toward his room. "Come. Get your things. We'll have to meet Razin at the stables and make do with the coin we have."

Adelman hastened to follow, his sandals clicking against the stone floor. "We have some credit with the bakers on Temple Street. They will still be up preparing tomorrow's bread. And Alvaro at the pools can fill enough flagons and waterskins that we won't run out. But I will need to tell him now if we are to leave tonight. Perhaps with the coin we had set aside for rent, we will have enough extra for beef and horse feed?"

"Do it," said Dietmar. "Go. We'll collect you with the cart at the old pools. Make sure the bakers don't skimp on the loaves. And get some apples if you can." Dietmar paused, remembering the mad Frenchman and his ashen fruit. "Forget the apples."

"Water, bread, meat," Adelman repeated, scurrying back down the passage toward the door.

"And no apples!"

Dietmar dragged a heavy burlap sack out from under his bed and began packing his few belongings. He swiftly added a spare pair of breeches, sturdy leather riding boots, a thick blanket, and a tightly rolled map of the old city to the sack.

Christ's bones, Dietmar swore silently to himself. How had their plans been discovered already? Whose treacherous lips would need sewing?

We need more time.

Once he finished packing, he put on his padded shirt and started strapping on his greaves.

"Help me with this," he said as Tomas appeared at his door.

Together, they lowered the hauberk over Dietmar's head and buckled on his rerebraces.

Dietmar watched as the Englishman's nimble fingers secured the last of his buckles. "You can still avoid this, you know. I won't think any less of you. Our path will be about as far from a leisurely voyage as it gets, and the men pursuing us mean us harm." He paused, making sure Tomas understood the weight of his words, and then continued, "There's a good chance we won't make it to Antioch."

"Then they can bury us in the desert." Tomas tugged at his scruffy red beard, eyeing the buckles, and gestured for Dietmar to turn around. "My prior always said there'd be no Christian burial for me when I'm gone. Not for a drunkard blasphemer, *no, no*. But maybe he'll say a prayer for me when he hears I died in the service of the Pope? That might impress the old Benedictine if nothing else."

"Perhaps he can spare a prayer for me while he's busy with yours." Dietmar stretched his arms, feeling the fit of the braces against his mail. He'd acquired them in Constantinople, after noticing the splint rerebraces worn by the city guards. They fit snuggly against his hauberk, and though they were tight, they had saved him from countless scars in battle.

"I always thought I'd die in my forests, an old man," he said, lowering his arms and gazing at his hands. "Or brought down by a boar I'd misjudged, a tusk in my heart, still laughing at my foolishness."

Not alone, here in the sand.

But he wasn't alone.

"Delightful," muttered Tomas, shaking his head.

Dietmar smiled. "You'll change your mind once you see the lowlands. It does something to you. I can't explain it. Trees as tall as city walls, rivers flowing as wide as the Old Cardo. And everywhere there is life! The forests teem with it, and the rivers too. It wouldn't be such a bad place to die."

"I'd prefer to meet my end sitting in front of a crackling hearth, my belly full of wine."

"Aye, that wouldn't be so bad either."

"Not so bad?" Tomas wagged his finger. "In Jerusalem, only a king can afford to die in front of his hearth. Imagine that! The kind of death every peasant in England anticipates, and here it's a privilege reserved for a few. Hah!"

Tomas tested the last buckle, then stepped back to look him over. Satisfied, he retrieved Dietmar's tabard from the floor and brushed off the dust. The yellow fabric had seen better days, and there were some stains that wouldn't come out. But the black wolf of Zwingenberg looked as fearsome as ever, its gaping maw showing white teeth as sharp as swords, its single red eye the colour of blood.

"Razin won't stay here either," Tomas remarked. "He's had enough of the city. I think he hates it, or what it has become, anyway. Too many memories. And there's nothing for him in Ramla, not after they took his family's lands. So he'll follow you. Which leaves me alone in this stinking city. What would I do in Jerusalem by myself?"

"Fiddle with your balls," said Dietmar, raising his arms so Tomas could lower the tabard over his head.

He rolled his shoulders, feeling the weight of the mail settle upon them, then secured his sword to his belt.

Tomas handed him his shield. "I can do that from the back of our cart, where there's no Temple guard to cut them off."

Dietmar chuckled, leaning his trigon shield against his leg and pulling on his gloves. "You are a filthy cretin, Tomas. But I'll be glad to have you with me all the same. And with a bit of luck, I'll get to see my forests, and you'll get your hearth, and the both of us a belly full of wine."

Tomas grinned at that, but his smile faltered. "What do you think will happen to Gelmiro?"

"Suddenly fond of the weasel, are you?" asked Dietmar.

"They'll hang him, won't they? For plotting against the king or some such thing?"

"They might." Dietmar picked up his sack and hoisted it over his shoulder. "But there's a good chance he's already vanished into a hole somewhere. Gelmiro is…"

"A weasel?"

"Aye. If he had the time to warn us, it's probably because he's already safe and sound, well beyond the city walls… where we should be heading too if we don't fancy the end of a rope."

Dietmar ushered Tomas out of his room, turning to take one last look around before leaving.

A small bed beneath a narrow window. Dusty floors and cold stone walls. It had been his home for seven years.

No, not my home.

A place of waiting, that was all.

A home spoke of comfort and warmth, of love and commitment. He had experienced that once, and this was not it.

Triumphs and regrets swirled through his thoughts: his campaigns of blood and sand, the princes and barons he'd bled for, the angry letters he'd written by candlelight to his brother, the letters he'd received in return. This room, his time here, it had been a place between—between his old life and the new.

He was glad to see the back of it.

Satisfied that he hadn't forgotten anything, he closed the door and followed Tomas into the night.

They piled their things onto two handcarts and pushed them through the Quarter, taking care not to rush along the cobbled roads flanked by looming edifices to either side of them. When gloats of shadows pooled too deeply to safely traverse, Dietmar lit an oil lamp, sending dirty light chasing after the darkness. They walked in silence, and Tomas frequently glanced over his shoulder, nearly toppling his cart. Afterwards, he became more watchful of the road ahead.

Dietmar's thoughts dwelled on Gelmiro's fate, and he felt a pang of guilt as he wondered if his friend would betray them. If it came down to choosing between his own neck and the necks of his friends, Dietmar wasn't sure Gelmiro had it in him to make the right choice. Deep down, Dietmar had always known this, and Gelmiro hadn't pretended otherwise, openly admitting his self-centred nature. It was Dietmar who had considered him a friend. And now he'd risked all of their lives for his own selfish gain.

Dietmar said a quiet prayer for the safety of the little Iberian, hoping he would prove to be as resourceful as Tomas believed him to be.

The main thoroughfares were empty, the commoners and nobles alike gathering closer to the markets and the Street of Bad Cooking for their supper. Still, they kept to the narrow alleyways, keeping their heads down as they walked. A pair of greasy Franks observed them as they trundled past St. Anne's, but their eyes had returned to their game by the time they reached the corner, leaving them unbothered.

At night, the city was an altogether different prospect. The narrow alleyways seemed filled with menace. Shadowy corridors and niches that stood straight and tall in the light of day, now at odds with their own geometry, curving in on themselves impossibly. Each bark of a dog rebounded off the walls a thousand times, ringing through the streets like a hellhound had been let loose in the city.

They moved as swiftly as the cobbled lanes allowed, shambling past the vacant, hunched dwellings with their small, watchful windows that looked like eyes.

When they reached the Old Pools, a pale moon had risen, casting long shadows across the water. The morning's cool breeze had dissipated, leaving the pool's surface calm as glass, rippling only when a passerby drew water from it.

They collected Adelman from the Roman pumps. His cart was laden with bread loaves, dried meat, and waterskins. A stocky fellow with scars on his face and straw-coloured hair helped them fill the other carts with more skins, and then they were on their way again.

They followed the *Via Dolorosa* to the walls, taking the longer route past the gardens until the stables finally appeared ahead.

"Wait here," Dietmar instructed, leaving his cart with Tomas and Adelman. If the king's men lay in ambush, there was no point in them all walking into it. Would Gelmiro's betrayal have extended as far as the stables they used?

If the little weasel has betrayed us at all.

It was funny how easily he came to think of his friend as traitor. Sad. But you didn't live long in the East if your trust in others was unwavering.

The stables loomed dark, shielded from the moon's light in this secluded corner of the city walls. Dietmar paused in the middle of the empty yard, straining his ears for the sound of Talbert and Razin attending to the horses.

The night was eerily quiet, without even the sound of rats scurrying between their holes to break the silence.

Dietmar flinched at a sound to his left, his hand moving instinctively to his sword.

He hesitated.

It was only a horse stomping its hooves against the dirt floor, blowing hot breath against its stall.

Damnit.

He was getting twitchy.

He glanced toward the nearest stable door, squinting into the inky blackness before raising his hands at the shadow moving off the wall.

"Peace, friend," he said, seeing the glint of steel and a familiar silhouette.

Razin sheathed his knife and stepped forward, nodding in greeting to Dietmar.

"Your stablemaster is nowhere to be found," Razin informed him.

Dietmar motioned for Tomas and Adelman to join them. "Talbert is a drunk. What about the horses?"

"Saddled and fit," said Razin. He opened the stable doors, revealing three horses waiting within their stalls. "But I could not attach Comus to the cart alone. That beast has a foul temper. It would be better if we found another."

"Never mind that now," Dietmar said, a smile forming on his face as he approached a shadowed figure in one of the stalls. A towering warhorse of nearly eighteen hands.

"Theseus," he said warmly.

The horse shook its head from side to side when it saw him and moved forward in the stall.

Dietmar reached out with a hand, running it through the destrier's thick black mane and then patted his neck affectionately. It had been a while since he had ridden. Too long. That would be remedied now, at least.

"Come, help with the cart," he said when Tomas and Adelman arrived outside the stalls. "We have a long journey ahead, and Comus is already in one of his moods."

With their combined efforts, they managed to attach the grumpy Percheron to the cart without losing any fingers in the process. They loaded the back of the wagon with supplies and their belongings. Once Tomas and Adelman were safely seated at the front, Dietmar and Razin mounted their own horses and led them into the yard.

Razin rode his Arabian beside Theseus, his smaller grey mount positioned a head lower. A cold smile appeared on his thin lips as he spoke. "So, German. We are to outrun the King's men, after all. With a wagon full of water, a drunkard priest with no wine, and an old man with his books. I must say, I don't favour our chances."

Dietmar glanced at his friend, noticing the glimmer of mail beneath Razin's linen shirt. His long dark hair had been pushed back and hidden beneath a fine cotton wrap that hung to his shoulders like a hood. He looked like a *faris* lord, and would have been but for the coming of the Franks to Palestine.

Why doesn't he stay?

He would have his lands returned to him when Nur ad-Din's men flooded Jerusalem. The life he had been born for. But instead, he would risk everything in the dirt and sand, all so Dietmar *might* have a chance at salvation for his son.

He added another thing to the list of things men killed and died for: gold, God, and brotherhood.

Dietmar turned in his saddle, waving Tomas and the cart forward. "Gelmiro will not have warned us in one breath only to betray us in the next." He looked back at Razin. "Come, let us trust in our sevillano one last time. He has seen us well in the past. And anyway, if you think Tomas hasn't secreted some wine onto the back of that cart, then you don't know him at all."

Another rare smile cut across Razin's face, and he prodded his horse up beside the cart.

"I think you have the truth of it," he called back to Dietmar. "You haven't replaced all our water with cheap wine, have you, Tomas?"

"Heh." Tomas grinned, folding the reins over his knuckles. "Not with cheap wine, no."

Adelman shot Tomas a sharp look from his seat, then peered into the back of the cart, grumbling about expenses.

"Relax, old man," said Tomas with a sigh. "There's no wine back there. And if there is, it's not from our coin. No, no, leave it be. That's for my sacrament. You wouldn't deny me that?"

With Tomas and Adelman still bickering, the cart rolled out of the yard and headed west.

Gelmiro's guard met them beneath the barbican of St. Stephen's Gate, emerging from the shadows like wraiths.

"Woah there," said a tall, hardy-looking man with flinty eyes and a serpent's mouth. "Are you friends of Gelmiro's?"

“Aye,” said Dietmar after exchanging a glance with Razin. If they had been betrayed, lying now wouldn’t save them. Still, his hand rested on his sword.

“Are *you*?” he asked, his eyes quickly sweeping over the assembled men. A dozen of them, all clad in unmarked tabards over mail shirts. They carried an assortment of weapons: swords, spears, and even a few crossbows. Dietmar recognised one of the guards—a young dark-haired man Gelmiro had set to squire for him.

Achard, he thought. Or maybe Amice? It didn’t matter. The boy had strange eyes that lingered too long and a malign manner that Dietmar had taken a disliking to. He’d hoped to work it out of the boy but had dismissed him when he saw he needed watching around women.

Dietmar gave the former squire a curt nod, relaxing slightly. Not the sort of company he would have chosen, but seeing a familiar face went some way toward calming his nerves.

“We’re friends of his coin, ye.” The captain strolled forward, extending his hand to Dietmar. “Geoff from Anjou. Me and these lads will see you and your precious cargo safe and sound.” His gaze flicked to the cart, and Dietmar knew he’d have to keep an eye on him, too, just like the squire.

Bloody Gelmiro, he thought.

“Is that it then?” Geoff took in the contents of the cart with a quick glance, then turned his attention back to Dietmar. “I was expecting something more… ostentatious.”

The mercenary saw his look and showed his teeth. Yellow, even in the dark. “Oh, don’t you worry, ser. We know what you’re carrying, and we want no part in it. We’re in the job of protecting, after all. It wouldn’t look good for our future prospects if we started flinching. And it wouldn’t be good for our necks if we stole from the Church neither.”

Dietmar grunted, handing Geoff his reins before dismounting. He didn't like the look of the ragged band, but it was too late to change his mind now.

Bloody Gelmiro.

"We were told we would receive delivery here tonight. You haven't seen another driver? Scared him off, perhaps?"

Geoff shook his head. "No, ser. We've been quiet as mice, on our best behaviour we have."

"What's happened to Gelmiro?"

"Couldn't say. Got a message from him just like you, I imagine. Plus, a bag of silver for our trouble, of course. And the promise of more once we reach Gibelet."

Dietmar paused. "You're not taking us to Antioch?"

"No, ser. Gibelet is as far as we go. After that, you're on your own. But that's Chevalier country. You'll be safe so long as you keep to the road. Lord Raymond leaves his thieves to wither until they're nothing more than husks. Says it's a warning. Well, it works. They've long since stopped trying their luck."

Dietmar stared past the captain toward the barbican and open gate. The guard post stood empty, and he saw no sign of the gatekeep.

"They've been paid to leave us be," Geoff explained, following his stare to the empty watchhouse.

"For how long?" Dietmar felt his nerves settle just a little more. If Gelmiro had been captured or their plans discovered, the city gates would be barred, and men bearing the five-folded cross would patrol the streets.

Geoff shrugged. "As long as we need. But I'd prefer to put as much road between us and the city by morning if we can, though."

"You and me both," Dietmar said, taking back Theseus's reins and casting a glance at the dark streets behind them. "But for now, we wait."

***

Tomas fidgeted with his hood, glaring irritably at Adelman while he blew his nose.

"If Gabriel's horn were ever found missing, Heaven's angels could use that trumpet on the end of your face instead."

"I cannot help it," said Adelman miserably, wiping his nose. "My humours, they—"

"Yes, yes, your confounded humours. We know." Tomas rapped his knuckles against his wooden seat impatiently and turned to Dietmar, who stood by the cart, watching the road.

"We could be waiting here until Judgment Day. Why not send one of us to see where our relic's gotten to?"

"Off you go then," said Dietmar, not looking up.

"Right," said Tomas, not moving from his seat. "We don't know where it's coming from, do we?"

Dietmar winked at him and then waved for both Tomas and Adelman to be quiet, tilting his head to listen to the sounds of the city. He could hear the pigs rustling in their pens nearby and the soft pecking of hens in their hocks, not yet asleep. But then… Yes, he hadn't been mistaken—the slow grate of wheels on stone.

Dietmar squinted down the eastern road toward Herod's Gate and watched silently as a small cart, led by a pair of dusty mules, emerged from the gloom.

The cart rolled up beside the barbican, where a gruff, bearded man, who looked like he could have been the third mule with his buck teeth and long nose, pulled the cart to a halt.

"To Antioch?" the man asked, his pitch-black eyes fixed on Dietmar.

"Aye." Dietmar met his stare and then pointed to the mules. "But those aren't coming with us. They'll only slow us down once the road gets rough, and if we're being followed—"

The driver flicked his reins, rolling forward before Dietmar could finish.

"To Antioch!" he called back over his shoulder, passing through the gates.

Dietmar let out a long sigh and shook his head in response to Tomas's bemused expression. Adelman was already snoring beside the Englishman, his haggard snorts as loud as bells.

"To Antioch," Dietmar repeated to himself.

And so they left Jerusalem to the sound of pealing bells.

7

They took the north road to Nablus, riding through the night until the shadowy veil of the Kidron Valley was to their backs and only dense hills lay ahead. Their path led them through low fields and withered orchards, between scattered clumps of twisted thorny hedgerows and over stone-packed soil flattened by the countless feet that had travelled the road before them. By day, pilgrims swarmed the route, making their way to holy sites in Sapphoris and Nazareth, journeying as far as the Sea of Galilee and Mount Tabor. But at night, the road was empty, and they made good time.

So it was that when dawn finally broke, they found themselves moving through the sloping hills of Old Samaria, with the peaks of the Temple Mount and Mount Zion appearing as mere specks in the distance.

Razin rode alongside Dietmar at the head of the caravan, listening to Tomas pester the relic keeper with questions. The two shared a love for drink, and when Tomas noticed Nicolo sipping surreptitiously from a wineskin, he left Adelman with Comus's reins and joined the Italian on his cart.

"How do we even know you have the relic?" Tomas asked, handing Nicolo the skin. "You could have a box full of wine back there, and we'd be none the wiser. Not that I'd complain, mind you. Only, I imagine some of our company might not be as forgiving as I."

Razin blinked. None of them had actually seen the relic. All they had was this Keeper's word that it was there.

But what kind of madman would traipse across the desert with an empty cart and only his ugly mules?

The same kind of madman who would drag an amputated limb across the desert, he thought cynically.

The horse-faced Nicolo leaned forward in his seat, lowering his wool chaperon further over his head to give him some shade. "The *ex corpore sanctus Ephium* is not for the eyes of gawping Benedictines. And I wouldn't sit for weeks on this accursed wagon for wine, even it were good wine!"

"So it *is* back there," Tomas said. "I wonder, how long has it been sitting in that musty box?"

Nicolo looked at him and counted under his breath before grunting. "Nearly one hundred years. And before that, in the reliquary of the Church of Saint Lazarus in Cyprus."

"Rotting away, then?"

The old man shot him a sharp look, but then his shoulders slumped, and he nodded. "It's kept well enough for what it is, mind you. Better than most, I'd say. The Keepers of the *scriniarius* have been careful, but…" He waved a hand. "Such things are not meant to survive beyond death."

Tomas leaned closer to Nicolo, a conspiratorial smile on his face. "Does it do what they say it does?"

Nicolo grunted. "Stink? A little."

"No, no." Tomas snatched the wineskin back and took a draught, then wiped his lips against his sleeves. "Does it heal, man? That's what I want to know!" He scratched at his sweaty brow and leaned back in his seat. "I remember there were some old bones shoved in a reliquary in Seeon when I visited. The monks told me it was the bones of a saint and charged me a pfennig to see it. I could touch it for two. So I did. But when my crooked back still hurt, I made sure to pick my coin out from their pockets on my way out. Sneaky bastards."

Geoff rode up beside the cart, showing his ugly teeth and gesturing to Tomas for the wineskin. He took a sip and nodded. "I once stood before the bones of Saint Guillaume, and they didn't stop my arse from itching neither. Maybe it only heals big things, is that it, scrini? Maybe you should pop open that box and let Amice have a look. He's got something big protruding from the end of his—"

"It's *scriniarius*," Nicolo growled. "And it's not for the likes of you. You had better keep away from that box if you know what's best for you. Nothing good will come from poking around in there, ho ho! I promise you that!"

Razin turned in his saddle, slowing Riba so he could peer at the wooden cask on the back of Nicolo's cart.

It was a small thing, unassuming in size and decoration, not like the gilded monstrosities he was used to seeing paraded around the streets of Jerusalem. The dark wood of the box appeared as though it had been lacquered with rich oil left on for too long, and it was framed by a trim of dull iron.

He was no stranger to the veneration of relics—and had heard and read of blessings associated with them, justified by the *hadiths*. Still, the reverence with which the Christians in Jerusalem treated them bordered on the obscene.

And yet the note in Nicolo's voice seemed closer to fear than reverence.

"You speak as if it is a thing cursed?" he said, turning his gaze to the Keeper.

The scriniarius snorted, and one of his mules—the larger of the pair, with black ears and near-human eyes—nipped at Riba as it passed by.

"Easy, Balaam." Nicolo raised his whip in threat, and the mule *hawed*, lowering its ears.

"Your Balaam is a foul beast," said Razin, shaking his head at Nicolo.

The mule seemed to hear him and *hawed* again, twitching its long black ears as it ambled forward.

"Oh, he's not so bad," said Nicolo. "It's Silensus you have to watch out for. He'll bite your fingers off and spit them out before you've even blinked. Then you'll have to scrounge about the weeds for your poor digits—unless he decides to swallow them, that is. He's a dark heart, that one."

Razin gently nudged Riba forward, careful to keep a distance from the mules, but curious to hear more from Nicolo. The Italian waited until Razin drew near, then handed Tomas the reins and leaned back on the hard wooden seat, taking a sip from the wineskin.

"You asked if this charge of mine, bestowed by the Church no less, is a cursed thing. How can a creation of God be cursed, I ask in return."

Razin resisted the urge to smile. He had engaged in many such conversations in the bazaars of Damascus growing up. The Latins, for all their military prowess, were sorely lacking in matters of theology. Razin was not a vain man, but he struggled not to feel like an adult correcting the clumsy attempts of a child in such discussions.

Leaning forward in his saddle, he rested his arms on the saddle horn and motioned to Nicolo. "To say that a thing of God's cannot be cursed implies one of two things. Either there are no evil things, or evil things do not come from God. But if they do not come from God, then where do they come from?"

Nicolo absentmindedly picked at his gums with a dirty nail and smiled as the answer came to him.

"The Devil."

"*Iblis* cannot create," Razin explained patiently, like his uncle had when instructing him on the *kalām*. "He cannot create any more than you or

I. Creation is the prerogative of God and God alone. So, either we must conclude the impossible: that there are no evil things, or accept that even a thing of God's might be cursed."

Nicolo sighed, reclaiming the reins from the grinning Tomas. He shook his head at Razin. "You Arabs are too neat with your words for my liking, but… I see the logic in your argument, even after half a skin of wine. You won't get me to say God cursed the hand, though! Not even after a full skin!"

"What's… wrong with it?" Tomas glanced back at the box, crossing himself when it rattled along to the bumpy road.

"There's nothing wrong with it!" Nicolo snapped. "Look, I've already said more than I should have. This wine, God! I shouldn't drink in the sun. I shouldn't drink in the morning!"

Tomas opened his hands. "Well, now you've told us a little, you may as well tell us the rest."

"Damned a bit, damned all the way, is that right?" Nicolo snorted, and the sound was a little like Balaam's braying.

"I suppose it'll keep the more curious amongst you from trying your luck. You'll have heard the story of Ephium then?"

"Only what Gelmiro's told us," replied Tomas.

"I fancy he only told you the good bits, that right?" Nicolo snorted once again.

Haw.

"It's true that Ephium had a healer's touch. They used to say he was a descendant of Midas, blessed where the king was cursed. I don't know much about all that. Only, when all's said and done, he couldn't heal himself." The old man tugged at the reins, slowing his mules over the uneven road. "For a man who favours helping the sick above all else, that's as good as a curse, don't you think?"

Razin pondered Nicolo's words carefully. It seemed a strange way to view the world, at odds with what he had learned as a student of *Ash'arjya*.

"Being unable to help others when one possesses the power to do so would be more of a curse," he said. "No, it seems to me Ephium did as he should have, fulfilling the responsibilities that came with his talents."

"Maybe," Nicolo replied, giving Razin a sidelong glance. "But it's what came after his death that makes me believe he was cursed anyway."

The cart jolted and swayed, the wheels chipped by rocks along the uneven road. After a moment, the road smoothed out, and the cart resumed its gentle rocking motion. Nicolo gestured for more wine, consuming the last drops before tossing the empty skin into the back of the cart beside the box.

"Something's attached itself to that rotting hand," he slurred slightly. "I wouldn't normally believe such a thing, but even the Patriarch refuses to be near it. I think that's why he sent it away. He can't stomach being in the city with it."

Razin frowned. "But what about its healing properties?"

"It has those, too," said Nicolo gruffly. "Open that box, and you'll feel your pain fall off your back like it wasn't there to begin with. But get too close—if you *touch* the hand, why, you'll damn yourself."

"What… happens?" asked Razin, curious now despite his reservations.

Nicolo made the sign of the cross in one lazy, perfunctory motion. "Whatever killed Ephium will take you too."

"Is it a plague?" Tomas asked, giving the box a nervous glance. "The rot?"

"I wouldn't know," Nicolo admitted. "I've never seen it happen myself, only heard the stories."

Razin let out an audible sigh. "Stories spun to deter restless hands from a century-old relic. No wonder it kept so well."

Of course, he thought, shaking his head at his own naivety. He should have foreseen such a mundane conclusion the moment Nicolo opened his mouth.

"Believe what you want," said Nicolo, his voice suddenly sharp and clear. "I've witnessed things during my time with the Church, let me tell you. And these stories don't come from nothing! You would be wise to heed my warning, freely given, and not to mock the truth I tell you."

"I meant no offence," Razin replied, offering a soft bow of his head. "I have no interest in the contents of your box, Keeper. My only concern lies in its safe delivery."

Nicolo smiled, his buck teeth like *meleke* blocks in a mouth too small for them. They were very white, Razin thought.

"A curious mind should never have to apologise," said Nicolo. "It is only the actions of the curious that concern me, and even then, only when they come within my little orbit."

The Keeper let out a yawn, pulling his chaperon over his eyes and handing the reins to Tomas. He looked at Razin from under his hood. "I can trust you not to open the box while I take my morning nap, eh? I've drunk too much by half and spoken too much by a lot."

Razin tilted his head, slowing Riba to a trot as the cart continued its rumbling journey ahead. In the distance, he could just make out the faint contours of Mounts Ebal and Gerizim.

***

Razin al-Did Ibram al-Ramla was raised in the shadow of Mount Qasioun, in the city of the Gardens and the Moon.

In Damascus.

When his father fell fighting the *Ifranj* at Edessa, Razin's mother sent him to live with his uncle, Abdul Mushrie al-Ramla. He'd been little more than a boy then, still wild with the anger of his loss. But more than anything else, he'd needed guidance.

His uncle, who had no children of his own, took on the responsibility of Razin's education with great zeal, filling the gaps left by Razin's limited education in Ramla. Mushrie started him on the Greeks and gradually worked his way through the wisdom of the ancients before moving on to the teachings of al-Farabi and Ibn Ba Jjah.

Within those scholarly texts, Razin found a purpose, even amidst his search for meaning. As his interest in philosophy grew, so did his fascination with theology.

Night after night, Mushrie and Razin would engage in spirited debates on matters of faith, freedom, and war. His uncle welcomed these disagreements, relishing the intellectual discourse his young nephew provided while also cautioning Razin to be mindful of his questioning nature. In the spirit of the Prophet, differences of opinion were a blessing, but that didn't mean they would be to everyone's liking.

It was a lesson Razin would learn the hard way years later when his eyes were charcoaled black by the fists of an older boy near the Roman street. Razin had raised a question about *ijmā*, a fundamental tenant of Sunni pragmatism. The question had not been well received.

Years later, Razin knew that the boy had taught him a lesson better learned from the fist than the sword. Still, the lesson could have been less… thorough. After that, he reserved his more controversial opinions for the ears of his uncle and his closest friends: Ibn al Hasan, the older boy who had taught him that first lesson, and 'Iweyz, a member of the Emir's personal harem, who took an interest in Razin after overhearing his debates with a scribe outside the palace.

She had seen something in that bony-kneed youth who wouldn't back down. And Razin, unaccustomed to the attention of women, especially one of such grace and charm from the palace, quickly became infatuated with her.

His first experience with the Franks came some years later.

He and his uncle had been sitting in the orchards, engrossed in a discussion about Abū al-Barakāt al-Baghdadi's critique of Aristotle, when news of the Frankish siege reached their ears. Fear gripped Razin then, and his apprehension heightened when he witnessed the armies of the Ifranj kings appearing alongside the river, clad in silver armour and white mantles.

The Christian army had surged against the city's walls like a relentless tide, all fury and pride and wrath... but the walls stood firm, fortified by the unwavering faith of those who resided within.

On the third day of the deafening sounds of war, a voice rose above the chaos, capturing Razin's attention.

It was the voice of Nur ad-Din, resonating like honey in his ears. The sultan preached the cause of holy war, calling for vengeance and the reclamation of the Holy Land for the devout. His words found willing hearts, including Razin's.

In that moment, all of Mushrie's reason and pragmatism had been forgotten, the logic of his mind abandoned for the passions of his heart. When the Franks were finally repelled from the city gates, their campaign in ruins, Razin knew he wanted to fight for Nur ad-Din. For Islam.

When he was old enough, Razin left his uncle and his books and joined the Jihad against the Ifranj. He fought in skirmishes along the River Jordan, raiding Christian settlements and convoys, bloodying his sword in minor battles. Eventually, he joined Nur ad-Din's muster at the fortress of Hisn al-Akrad.

There he had hoped to meet wizened warriors, men like his uncle with whom he could discuss philosophy and law, debate the *kalām* and *ijmā*. He had thought to find warriors of like mind in the army being mustered. Or better yet, of difference: scholars in mail who could challenge his ideas, dispel his foolish notions, and sharpen his mind to a razor's edge.

He had been disappointed.

Nur ad-Din's camp was filled with drunkards and brawlers, women who coupled with soldiers for coin, and lutes that played sickening rhythms into the night. In his dark tent, amidst the revelling ifiranj and their harlots, Razin discovered something else. It was a small thing at first, barely worth thinking about, but it had grown over the years, a seed nurtured by every broken vow and promise he bore witness to, every heinous act of mindless savagery and wanton violence, every contradiction in his pursuit of God and the truth. That something was doubt, and it had been his constant companion ever since.

The following morning, the Franks had soundly thrashed them.

And they had deserved it.

Razin narrowly escaped from Hisn Al-Akrad with his life, struck by a Templar's blow to the back of his head mere moments into the battle. When he regained consciousness, the fighting was already over, and vultures had descended from the skies to feast upon the fallen.

He'd often wondered whether that blow had spared his life—if rising earlier would have led him to be trampled like so many others. Perhaps it was akin to Hasan's fists on the Roman road—a small misery that later saved him from even greater suffering.

From Al-Akrad, Razin rode to Ramla, hoping to see something of his family home, but he did not recognise it anymore. The men and women who lived there were strangers to him, even those he had known in his youth before his mother sent him away. He visited his mother's grave but didn't linger. Instead, he continued his southward journey, intending to reach Alexandria and engage in discussions and debates with the Shi'ite Fatamids. But the Wolf had already emerged there by the time he arrived, and with him, more war and killing.

Razin would have celebrated Saladin once. By all accounts, he was everything they said he was: devout, learned, funny when he needed to be, ruthless when necessary. Some said Saladin was in Damascus when it was besieged all those years ago and that hearing Nur ad-Din's words had ignited the fire that drove him against the Franks, like they had Razin's.

But Razin's ideas were no longer what they once were. They had been tempered by war and experience and by the philosophies of As-Suhrawardi, who believed that all religions were revelations of the same truth. Holy war was not compatible with such an idea.

So it was with that in mind that he took the road to Jerusalem. There, in the city of God, he had found fellowship with men he would have dismissed as infidels in his youth and as barbarians in his later years. They were still both of those things, that much hadn't changed, but they were also more besides.

***

They rode through the foothills of Old Samaria for two days, following the road toward the growing peaks of Ebal and Gerizim. The thick gorse and shrubbery covering their surrounds offered little shade against the sun, so they wrapped their heads in cloth like the Bedouins and ensured their mounts were well watered.

They quickened their pace when the wind turned suddenly warm, and they saw a dark smudge creeping over the ridge of Mount Ebal—a sandstorm that would soon break over Samaria. They hoped to be in Nablus before it did.

On the third day, they came upon a strange sight.

A man stood in stocks beneath an old pine tree on the corner of the road. In truth, two strange sights met them as they crossed into the foothills beneath Mount Ebal. Trees didn't grow long enough to become old in

Outremer, and those that had survived first the Fatamid, then Seljuk, and then Latins axes, were usually hidden away on some peak, too high up to be worth anyone's while.

And yet, here one stood, its long yellowing branches offering the first bit of shade in three days.

As they approached, the man in stocks looked up and offered a sheepish grin. His hair and beard had been shorn. Fresh welts marred his skin where the blade had cut too closely during his recent shaving. A sign hung around his neck. Written upon it in bold lettering were the words:

Leave him

Dietmar slowed to a halt in front of the stocks and waved at the others to do the same. The man watched them, his eyes swivelling to each of their faces, never quite meeting their eyes. Tomas clambered down from his seat and made his way to the back of Adelman's cart. He retrieved a waterskin and unfastened its seal, then approached the man cautiously.

"Hold," said Dietmar, raising a hand. He shifted on Theseus's saddle, leaning an arm on the saddle horn and peering down at the prisoner.

"Why are you here, brigand?"

"Give me a drink, and I'll tell you," the man replied.

Dietmar shook his head. "Tell me your crimes, and we'll decide on your drink."

"Then you'll never know."

Dietmar let out a sigh and turned to Tomas. "Give him some water. But only enough to wet his lips and loosen his tongue."

Tomas held out the skin but hesitated. "What is your name?"

"Paul."

"Tilt your head, Paul."

The brigand who was Paul chuckled and turned his head up to sip from the skin like a calf suckling at its mother's teat.

"Why are you here?" Dietmar repeated. "Come, you've had your drink. Tell us."

Paul licked his lips and blinked away the water that Tomas had splashed on his face, then smiled up at Dietmar.

"I poisoned the well."

Dietmar growled, stiffening in his saddle. "Which well?"

Razin sensed the growing unease among the rest of the company and urged Riba forward to stand beside Dietmar. Their horses required more water than they could easily carry, and if the few water sources along their route were compromised, they would face an almost insurmountable problem.

"Which well?" Dietmar repeated sharply, his patience wearing thin. It wouldn't be long before the German dismounted, and the man in stocks would find himself with fewer teeth to smile with.

Geoff and his men murmured among themselves, exchanging looks that typically preceded violence.

"Where are you from?" asked Razin, changing tact. Any answer beaten out of Paul was not going to be worth trusting. If he could get him to talk, perhaps he would tell them freely. If not, there was always Dietmar and his fists.

"Balata," said the brigand.

"Why did you poison the well, Paul of Balata?"

"To kill the thing inside it."

Razin hesitated.

"What thing?"

Geoff and his men fell silent, and even Balaam managed to quiet his incessant braying, allowing the uncomfortable stillness to settle.

"What thing?" Dietmar repeated. He dismounted Theseus and took a slow step toward the man in stocks. "Tell us. And no fibs. I'll know if you're lying."

Paul laughed. It was a wretched sound, Razin thought. And dry, like sand washing bone, setting his teeth on edge. After his laughter subsided, Paul shook his head—a strange sight with it in stocks. It reminded Razin of a pig caught in a gate, wriggling to get out.

"They thought I lied when I told them the thing had taken their dogs," said Paul. "And then when their children went missing, they looked at me as though I were the one responsible."

Dietmar crouched down in front of Paul. "Did you?"

"No!"

"Then you had better tell us what happened to them."

Paul sighed, his smile fading now that he knew that nothing he said would satisfy this knight, whose big hands had curled into hammers by his side.

"I'm telling the truth, and God take me if I lie!"

"Speak then," said Razin impatiently. "And may God take you anyway."

Paul shifted his weight, transferring it to his other leg, and curled his lips. "The custodian told me his bucket was stuck, that he couldn't get water for his service."

"What custodian?" Razin asked. "Which well is this?"

"Jacob's Well."

Dietmar snorted dismissively. "You expect us to believe that a creature lurks at the bottom of the well where Christ once drank, stealing children?"

"It is the truth!"

"Carry on," Razin urged, hiding his relief. Jacob's Well was on the outskirts of Nablus, but there were many other springs from which they could fill their skins before reaching it.

Rather the Christ's well than ours, he thought glibly.

Paul moved his gaze to Razin, still not meeting his eyes, but slowing their restless twitching long enough for Razin to see their slightly distorted shape, with pupils appearing more oblong than round.

"I yanked the rope myself, pulled it hard as I could, but the old custodian was right. I thought it must have snagged on a rock coming up, so I tied a rope around my waist and lowered myself down to fetch it. But it was no rock at the bottom of that stinking well." Paul shivered, his hands clenching in their posts, dirty nails cutting into his palms. "When I reached the bucket, I pulled at it in the dark, but it wouldn't budge. Then I heard something stirring beneath my feet, moving in the water. I let out a cry, yelling for that damned custodian to pull me back up. And then I saw it. A red eye blinked at me from the darkness. Before I could get away, a head as large as a horse lifted itself from the water, and I knew I was going to die. But then Charibert pulled me up, and I was still alive."

Razin detected no dishonesty in Paul's voice as he spoke, all while his strange brown eyes danced disconcertedly in his head.

He is mad.

That was the only explanation.

"What was it?" Tomas asked in a hushed voice.

"They didn't believe me," Paul continued. "Thought I was making excuses not to work, that I'd been drinking and lost my wits. Not even Charibert, who heard that slopping sound when he pulled me out the well. Or if he believed me, he wouldn't speak of it. Either way, I was the only one to do anything about it when those children went missing.

"I threw dead things down there first to foul the water, so no one would use the well. But I think I was only feeding the beast. Then I took a solid block of aconite. Shepherds use it to keep predators away from their flocks. When Jesof found it missing, he knew it was me who took it. And now here I stand, waiting for that storm to come and strip away my skin, all for doing what's right."

"So you tell us," said Dietmar, rising to his feet. "Did you succeed then in your task at least? Did you kill it?"

Paul spat at the ground and shook his head. "If it's dead, it died at the bottom of that well, and we won't know of it until its body rots and it does to the water what I set out to do myself."

"There is some justice in that," said Dietmar. "If you are telling the truth."

"I am."

"We will see when we pass Nablus." Dietmar looked away from the brigand, his eyes resting on the shoulder of Mount Ebal, where the dark shadow was making its way down the slopes. "We will take shelter from the storm there and then have a look at your beast at the bottom of the well. If I see a red eye staring back at me, I'll petition for your release."

"Why not free me before?" Paul pleaded, his eyes fluttering in panic. "Chain me if you like, only don't leave me to be caught in that. I will perish, surely. Would you have that on your conscience?"

"You broke the King's law," said Dietmar, turning his back to Paul and striding to his horse. "I will not do the same. If your cause is just, no harm will come to you."

Dietmar mounted his horse, giving Tomas a look that said he should do the same. He ignored Paul's further pleas, guiding Theseus back onto the road and motioning for Adelman and Nicolo's carts to move forward.

Razin rested in the shade a while longer, watching as the company made their slow march toward the mountains. The coming sandstorm looked like a brown cloud now, its tufts fully concealing the rocky slopes of Mount Ebal. It would be fierce when it hit, engulfing the land in a howling tide of sand and grit. As Razin watched, it seemed to quicken, moving swiftly down the hillside.

He briefly felt a twinge of sympathy for Paul, but it quickly faded. Even if there was some beast lurking at the bottom of Jacob's Well, there were better ways to go about killing it than poisoning the water supply. The man's eyes had unsettled him, too, their constant twitching and strange shape enough to put him ill at ease.

He glanced back at the stocks to catch one last look at the brigand but instead caught his breath.

The stocks were gone, and so was the tree.

Before he could call out to the others, movement caught his eye on the road behind them.

Riders. Coming quick.

8

"Riders!" Razin called. "On the road!"

Dietmar swung around, rising in his saddle to get a clear view over the heads of the company. Razin was racing toward him, pushing his Arabian on, his one arm pointing back the way they had come. Figures emerged on the road behind him, silhouettes storming toward the pine tree.

No... not the pine tree. Dietmar let out a soft gasp. It was gone. And Paul of Balata with it. In their place were a few clumps of wiry bushes with white thorns and bulbous shapes that looked like fingers.

Magic?

Something Arcane?

Or a trick?

"We don't have time," Razin urged, seeing his confusion. He reined in beside him, swiftly turning his horse while drawing his sword. Sand and stone shot up where Riba's hooves met the road, the sound giving life to a hot wind that swept through the hills.

"We must meet them or be overrun by their charge," Razin declared. He barked out a curse in Arabic and motioned Riba forward. He glanced back at Dietmar, his face set. "Come, German!"

Dietmar snapped out of his daze, tearing his gaze away from the empty foliage. He looked at Nicolo and Tomas, who were still frozen on their cart. "Go!" he yelled, stirring into motion. He had wasted precious moments befuddled by the absent tree and missing Paul.

The riders were closing in, swallowing up the road with every second.

Where had they come from?

"Keep moving!" Dietmar roared. "Make for Nablus. We'll hold them off." He drew his own sword and waved it at Adelman, who needed no further prompting. The old man flicked the reins, urging Comus forward with haste.

"We must face them," Razin repeated, raising his voice for Geoff and his men.

The mercenary captain tilted his head, studying the growing silhouettes, his brow knitted.

"I won't fight the King's men if that's them," he said. "If we beat them now, they'll only hang us when we return home."

Amice, the squire, nodded from the saddle beside his.

Dietmar's frustration grew. "Then what good are you?" he growled, swivelling his gaze to confront the mercenary. "Have you not been paid? Or was the coin not enough to cure your cowardice? Come now, what will it take? Another bag of silver, or perhaps only gold can cure your yellow liver?"

Geoff flashed his rotten teeth in a crooked grin, then spat into the sand. His hand hovered over his sword, his calloused fingers twitching with anticipation. Dietmar thought he might lunge for him then.

Try me, you cutthroat bastard.

But before he could say anything more, Amice drew his blade and scowled. "Saracens."

"Bah!" Geoff glared at Dietmar but then turned his horse and called out to the rest of the company.

"You hear that, boys? Cunting Saracens mean to part us from our coin! On our own cunting road! I've got five denarii for each of their heads. Gosse, I don't want to see you lurking at the back, you spindly bastard. Move it!"

Geoff dug his boots into his destrier, an unpleasant beast with sharp ears that looked like horns. He joined his men as they formed a narrow line on the road. There was just enough space to ride five or maybe six abreast where the road flattened out near the hill's base.

Dietmar noticed the ugly grins spreading across the faces of the mercenary band, like a pack of ragged foxes. He followed their gazes down the road and soon realised why. The approaching riders were only half their number. With surprise on their side, they might have been able to take the company, crashing into their rear and cutting through Geoff's guard in a bloody assault. But not anymore.

Dietmar pressed Theseus forward, moving into a trot to join Geoff's men. He turned at a cry from behind and saw Tomas scrambling out of his cart, his robes billowing in the wind.

The storm!

It was upon them already.

So fast?

Again, he thought of magic.

A towering wall of swirling sand and debris raced across the road like a tremendous wave. It rose high enough to hide the sun, casting a long shadow that engulfed everything between the foothills. A ferocious wind came with it, tugging at Dietmar's tabard and pulling at the heavy hauberk beneath it. Some of the hardy bushes that lined the road were uprooted, as if plucked out of the sand by a hidden hand and devoured by the mouth of the storm.

Nicolo stood shouting into the wind just ahead of the storm, hastily covering the heads of his mules with cloth sacks. Balaam's panicked braying was like a tolling bell, each cry bringing the dark cloud closer. Adelman had sought refuge under his cart, his eyes wide with fear as he watched the approaching wall of grit.

Tomas called out again, landing on his feet beside the cart and pointing at something on Dietmar's right. There was a look of alarm on his face, but Dietmar couldn't make out his words over the howling wind.

"Shit," Dietmar muttered, quickly turning to see more riders bursting onto the road. They were behind Geoff and his men, leaving only Dietmar between them and the carts. He counted three riders, with a possible fourth and fifth breaking through the foliage behind them.

The men wore mail shirts beneath coats of hardened leather, which covered the flanks of their mounts too. Dietmar's eyes shifted to their shields, round in the style of the eastern empires but bereft of any markings indicating their allegiance. They'd be Nur ad-Din's men then, not keen on breaking the peace with Amalric. Their faces were hidden by the long nose-guards of their cone helms and the mail coifs that covered everything but their eyes.

The first rider glared at him and barked something in Arabic, his mail aventail flapping in the wind. Then, his gaze shifted upward, widening at the sight of the approaching storm. Dietmar was certain he heard the rider curse in French but didn't hesitate long enough to wonder at it.

He charged forward, Theseus responding to his command with an instinct no training could ever replicate. Though it had been some time since their last ride, the warhorse knew its trade, swiftly reacting to every subtle nudge of Dietmar's knees and heels with a speed that would have put a viper to shame.

The rider with the aventail attempted to turn his horse, but another warrior pushed his way onto the road, leaving no room for manoeuvring. He twisted awkwardly on his mount, desperately trying to bring his shield around to face the German knight.

Dietmar swung at him hard, leaning forward in his saddle to channel the full weight of Theseus into the blow. Too late the man tried to raise his sword to meet him.

Dietmar's blade cleaved through the warrior's hardened coat, tearing through the leather and mail to bite at the flesh and bone beneath. Blood sprayed from the open wound, drenching Dietmar in a crimson mist as he rode past.

Dietmar licked his lips before he realised his mistake, then spat the blood onto the sand, swiftly turning to face the remaining riders.

He must have appeared as some blood-soaked barbarian then, his face and hair covered in gore—a devil in the sand.

To them, I will be, he thought, urging Theseus forward once more.

The aventail man gargled something, dropping his sword as he tumbled from his horse, only to be trampled by the rider behind him. His head split open like a Carthaginian apple. Pink juice and brain stained the ground around his shattered helm. The second warrior urged his horse onward, even as its hooves crushed the fallen rider, reducing him to a pulpy mess of gristle and broken mail. Once clear of the carnage, the rider raised his curved sword and charged.

Then the sandstorm hit.

Dietmar braced in his saddle and dropped his linen wrap over his eyes just as the tide of screaming dirt swept over him. Grains of sand bit into his exposed neck, raking him like searing needles until he tilted his head forward and hunched his shoulders for protection. Thorns rattled against his rerebraces, embedding themselves between the rings of his hauberk. Through the thin fabric of his *keffiyeh*, he strained to make out shadows moving around him—some stumbling across the road, others riding on.

There!

He lashed out with his sword and was rewarded with a cry, followed by a deep sound like a bovine in distress. He swung out again, and the sound abruptly ceased.

From his left, a horseless figure lunged at him, grabbing at Theseus's reins. Dietmar caught a glimpse of a face through the haze and instinctively flinched. The eyes behind the cracked helm were the same as the man whose brains had been spilt out over the road.

Dietmar batted him away, first with a forceful kick from his boot and then with the tip of his sword. The figure vanished into the storm. Another shadow darted around Theseus's legs, moving too swiftly for Dietmar to strike at. He thought he heard a grunting sound, like famished pigs finally let loose at the feeding trough. Following the sound with his eyes, he peered into the haze but saw only flittering shadows.

There is something wrong with this storm.

Dietmar snapped his head to the left, squinting as more bestial noises echoed through the wind—grunts and mawwing sounds like a bear scraping through foliage, followed by a chomping sound, like something were feasting. Unease stirred in Dietmar's stomach now that the adrenaline of combat had started to subside. He flinched at a rattling sound behind him, hunching further in his saddle and forcing Theseus forward without daring to look back to see what it was.

Something brushed against his knee, and he swung out instinctively with his sword, but it met only empty air.

We are not alone.

Dread washed over Dietmar at the realisation.

A riderless mount charged past, narrowly avoiding a collision with him. The horse frothed at the mouth, its eyes rolling wildly in its head. Moments later, the haze momentarily lifted, revealing the horse's rider standing just ahead.

The man's armour had been reduced to tattered rags, with little more than strips of hardboiled leather hanging from his waist like the old Roman *baltea*. His attention was fixed on something shifting in the darkness, just beyond Dietmar's field of vision. The warrior lifted his sword, taking a hesitant step back.

When Dietmar blinked, the man's head was gone. A mist of blood lingered in the air like a halo where it had once been. Dietmar thought he glimpsed a large shape moving behind the headless body, too massive to be a rider and horse, but it vanished beneath another veil of dust.

Theseus suddenly bucked beneath him, kicking out at a small figure trying to cut at his hooves.

Not cut, Dietmar realised with a pang of disgust. *Bite*. At first, he thought it was a snake, but then he saw the long fingers and a crooked grin of tiny white teeth. They were as sharp as knives, and Theseus whinnied in pain as they sunk into the flesh just above his front hoof.

Before Dietmar could lean down and strike at the wicked thing, his horse reared up on its hind legs and sent him tumbling onto the road. He rolled in the sand, scrambling to his knees as he tried to regain his footing, but then something hit him on the head.

"Wake up, German." Dietmar felt a hand on his arm and then a gentle squeeze. "Your journey is not done yet."

He opened his eyes, blinking away sand and spitting out the remnants that clung to his lips before remembering the events that saw him on his arse. He reached out for his sword, feeling the warmth of the earth, then the cold hilt against his fingers, and finally, the reassuring grip of the leather handle in his palm.

"Easy, friend," said Razin, kneeling beside him. His hand rested on Dietmar's arm, just beneath his rerebrace. There was a strange look on his face, not of worry. Dietmar knew all about that expression; Razin wore it like a permanent mask more days than not. This was different, more… severe.

Memories of the headless man and the shadow in the sand flooded back. Panic gripped him, and he quickly looked down at the rest of his body, half-expecting to see a severed limb or his guts hanging out from his belly. But he was whole, with nothing more than dirt and grime covering his stained colours. He let out a relieved sigh and pulled himself into a sitting position.

The remnants of the storm still lingered in the air, motes of sand suspended like tendrils of a morning mist. The wind had covered the road in sand and uprooted most of the dry shrubs that lined it. The hills looked barren now that they had been plundered. Ugly and empty, their soil churned like a field before the first seeding.

"What of our men?" Dietmar asked, glancing back to see Tomas soothing Nicolo's mules. They had managed to pull the cart some way forward, veering off the road in their panic. The cart now sat at an awkward angle, caught on the slope of what must be an old drainage ditch. The scriniarius was a few paces away, kneeling beside Theseus and tending to the horse's hoof. Adelman remained where Dietmar had last seen him, huddled beneath his cart, his grey hair standing on end like a frightened cat.

Razin handed him a waterskin and motioned for him to drink. Dietmar washed the taste of blood and sand from his mouth with the first sip, spitting it out before taking a deeper drink. The cool water soothed his parched throat. He must have been shouting during the storm, though if he had, he couldn't remember.

"Two of Geoff's mercenaries," said Razin, watching him drink. "The Genoan and the Hungarian. One with a broken neck and the other slain by a blade. They died quickly."

"And in return?" Dietmar handed back the skin and accepted Razin's outstretched hand, allowing himself to be pulled to his feet.

"Geoff and his men killed two. I took down another. When the storm hit, Riba panicked and carried me into the hills. I may have killed another there." Razin tucked the skin back into the folds of his burnous. "I could not see in the dust. I may have only wounded him. But this is no place to be wounded. He won't trouble us again."

As Dietmar stood up, he had a clearer view of the storm's aftermath. It was more severe than he'd first thought. The land around them had been reshaped, with new hills forming where there had been none before and old ones vanishing entirely. An open plain stretched out to the east, revealed now that vegetation had been uprooted from the soil. There must have been a parallel path somewhere there, an old Roman side road or shepherd's trail the raiders had used to ambush them. Dietmar glanced back at the main road, but it had been swallowed by the sand, leaving no trace behind.

"So, nearly half their number then, with the rider I killed," Dietmar said, brushing off his rerebraces and plucking thorns from his mail. "They won't be so bold to try again. Not in broad daylight, anyway. We will need to have a care when night comes, though." Dietmar paused, giving Razin a long look. He scratched at the cleft in his chin and let out a sound that was somewhere between a sigh and a grunt.

"There was… something else in that storm. Besides the men and horses."

It bit a man's head clean off.

What beast?

If a beast at all?

Razin blinked, his eyes red from the sand.

"Did you not hear it?" Dietmar continued, searching for any flicker of recognition in Razin's eyes. "A sound, like bulls in the rut, bellowing and grunting like they were to be bred. And then... there was the thing that bit Theseus." He hesitated, aware of how his words might sound. "A snake, I thought when I first glimpsed it, but it had bony hands and teeth like a shark. Its eyes were milky white, as if blind, yet it saw me clearly. Theseus threw me off before I could kill it. Then there is another matter: Paul and his tree..."

"Gone," Razin confirmed. He hadn't laughed at Dietmar's story. He hadn't even scoffed, as Dietmar had half-hoped he would, his doubt and mockery precluding any consideration of the implausible. No, he had nodded.

At least I'm not alone in this madness, Dietmar thought.

"There was a foulness to that wind," Razin said softly, as if speaking too loud might summon it back. "I did not hear what you heard. But I felt... something. Like I was being watched. A presence beside me in the darkness, silent and eerie. And now... tell me, my friend. Do these hills look like the ones we came through?"

"The storm must've—"

"And I can no longer see Mount Ebal and Gerizim."

"What?" Dietmar frowned and looked to the north.

It was true. The distant peaks, which had grown with each day of their journey, were gone. Dietmar scanned the horizon, hoping he'd been mistaken, that their remade surrounds had disorientated him. The land appeared flatter, somehow. And not just because all the undergrowth had been torn up. The once soaring hills of Samaria were little more than molehills now... if they were the same hills at all. The unsettling feeling that had plagued him amidst the shadows in the sandstorm returned, crawling up from the depths of his stomach like Paul's creature from the well.

Another trick?

Paul and the tree disappearing was one thing, but entire mountains?

Dietmar flinched at a loud bark behind him, like one of the fang-mawed beasts of the king's menagerie rattling against its cage. When he turned, he saw that it was only Balaam braying at Tomas.

"You see," said Razin, with that intense gaze of his. "This is not the same land we came into. We have been tricked."

Dietmar shook his head, understanding but not wanting to.

"We are in *another place*," said Razin, a note of panic entering his voice.

"Hush yourself, please, my friend," Dietmar whispered urgently, placing a hand on Razin's shoulder and scanning the surroundings for prying ears. Two of Geoff's men were nearby, sorting through the belongings of the dead raiders. One of them howled out a haggard laugh at something the other had said, and then they were both laughing.

"That is not something to be said out loud," said Dietmar. "It is impossible besides."

"It can't be true," Razin agreed.

"See." Dietmar took a breath. *There was a logical explanation, after all.*

"But it is true!" Razin finished. "Look, German. Look and tell me we are still on the path to Nablus. Don't you see? There's no road here!" He kicked the dirt with his boot, digging deeper and pointing at the sand. "There is nothing here. Not by the Romans, nor by anyone else after. How is that possible?"

Dietmar stared at the small mound of dirt at Razin's feet and then looked up at a call from Geoff.

"We will talk of this later," he said, not waiting for Razin's reply. He left his friend with the mound of dirt and marched across the loose sand toward the mercenary. It wouldn't be long before others shared Razin's doubts, and he would need an answer for them when those questions came. He spared a glance at the empty space where the mountains once stood but quickly blinked away. He would need answers for himself too.

Geoff stood over one of the bodies with Amice, sharing a flask. The two of them wore the same smug looks, their teeth blackened by whatever they were drinking. It was probably the same thing that had turned Geoff's grin to rot, but that was his business.

"Maybe not *cunting* Saracens after all, eh?" Geoff nodded to Amice, gesturing toward the fallen warrior. "Show him, lad. You're the one who gutted him anyway. Poor bastard."

The squire blocked one nostril with his thumb and blew snot out the other, then crouched next to the body and lifted the corpse's head, cradling it in his hands. Flies swarmed around a wound in the man's chest, the blood already congealing where Amice's sword had ended his life. The flies stirred in agitation before settling back down.

"Never killed a knight afore," said Amice conversationally. He tugged at the dead man's mail coif, pulling it down beneath his chin. "Thinking I might get to enjoy it. They die just like any other men, who woulda thought? This one shit himself when he fell. I heard it, even in the wind."

"Quiet, boy," Geoff snarled. "He is still your better, even dead. Even with shit in his britches."

"I won't shit myself when I go," said Amice, but fell silent when he caught the glare from Geoff.

As Amice removed the cone helm from the warrior's head, long blonde hair cascaded onto the sand, framing a broad face with high cheekbones and thin lips. The brilliant blue of the dead man's stare had dulled in death, but the eyes were unmistakable.

"The Poitiers knight," Dietmar snarled.

Geoff gave him a look. "You recognise him, then?"

"Aye, he was in Amalric's court, barking like a dog for his master, Aimery of Lusignan."

"Agnes of Courtenay's bedwarmer?"

"The king would have your tongue if he ever heard you say that."

"The king isn't here, and thank the Christ for that." Geoff prodded the knight's leg with his boot, curling his upper lip. "Sad luck this, going out dressed as a Muhammad worshipper, with a bastard's blade in his belly. Why'd he do that, do you reckon?"

Dietmar blinked, recalling Aimery's impassioned words to the court, how he had prowled like a lion before the fountain, demanding vengeance and war. "They're stirring up the locals, raiding Christian caravans to provoke a response. But this far north…."

Geoff gave him an empty look.

"Politics," Dietmar muttered, scanning the body. The Poitiers knight's heavy jaw hung slightly ajar, showing the whites of his teeth beneath his upper lip. His beard, a shade darker than his hair, was neatly trimmed even three days' ride from Jerusalem. Dietmar thought of Aimery then and briefly wondered if all men from Poitiers were so well groomed.

Another thought wormed its way into his mind, confusing things further. Aimery already had his war with Saladin. Surely, he would not be so foolish as to invite conflict with Nur ad-Din too? Did his hubris run that deep?

"What do we do with the bodies?" Amice dropped the knight's head unceremoniously and rose to his feet, dusting off his hands.

"Bury them with our boys," said Geoff. "They're Christian men. Maybe not *good* Christian men, but then neither are our lot. No point leaving them to rot in the sun. We're not savages."

"Is that all of them?" Dietmar began counting the dead. The man he'd ridden down was still where he had left him, his broken head buried beneath the sand. Another lay near Adelman's cart, a crossbow bolt sticking out of his chest. Then there was the Poitiers knight at Dietmar's feet. Geoff's dead mercenaries lay side by side, their faces hidden beneath their wraps.

"I count three of Aimery's men," said Dietmar. "Razin took one off the road, but he may have survived."

"That's all of 'em," said Geoff. "There would have been more, but that damned storm came between us and our prey, ain't that right, boy?"

Amice bared his teeth. They'd be as rotten as his master's in no time at all.

"There was another," said Dietmar, thinking of the riderless horse and its wild, rolling eyes and the warrior in tattered armour. "He lost his head."

Or something took it.

Geoff frowned. "I promised the lads I'd pay them for every head, but no one took me quite at my word. Haven't seen any heads lying around neither. And I doubt those shitting thieves would have stuck around long enough to retrieve their dead, do you?"

"No, maybe not," Dietmar replied.

It had been dark. Perhaps he'd been mistaken.

But to be so mistaken? Even in the midst of swirling shadows and that clawing darkness, he had seen something… something that did not belong.

Dietmar snapped his head around at a cry of alarm, his sword already half-drawn before his eyes settled on the source of the commotion—the scriniarius.

"It's gone!" Nicolo bellowed from beside his cart, his hands open at his sides. "They've taken it!"

"Taken what, you daft old fool?" Geoff stormed toward him, gesturing for him to be quiet, with Amice hurrying after. "Do you want every damned Saracen south of Damascus to know we're about? What did they take?"

Dietmar groaned, staring at the empty back of the cart.

He already knew.

"So, we have been betrayed after all." Razin sat rubbing his chin while he watched Dietmar's pacing. "But not in the way we expected, yes? What interest does Aimery have in this relic?"

Dietmar came to a stop beside a distraught Nicolo, who was busy taking comfort from his mules, running his hands through their hardy coats while murmuring a Latin prayer. Silensus nibbled at the Keeper's hair, chewing thoughtfully, his large ears perked as if listening intently.

"He might use it as leverage," Dietmar speculated. "If he knows why Amalric wants it, he may plan to use it to improve his position at court or to gain leverage over Baldwin when he ascends the throne one day."

"Then why the show?" asked Tomas. He had pulled Adelman out from under his cart and was brushing off the old man's tunic. "Why attack us like Syrian raiders if not to cause more trouble with Nur ad-Din?"

"Amalric's *ligece*," said Dietmar with a sigh. Seeing Tomas's look, he explained. "Aimery would hang if it were discovered he'd stolen from fellow Christians, from the Church, no less. He might be a lord and even have Agnes's ear—"

"And she his cock," murmured Geoff.

"But he would face the gallows all the same, and that's before the Church gets involved."

Nicolo stopped his prayer, looking up with his red eyes. "He will be excommunicated for this."

"Aye," Dietmar grunted. *The oily bastard.*

Tomas gave Adelman's tunic one final pat before scratching his forehead. "What about us? Those who lost the relic in the first place? Won't we be condemned as well?"

"We bloody well won't," said Geoff. He clapped his hands and signalled to his men. "Come on, lads, look lively! One of you needs to find us some lovely tracks to follow. Leave them, Eudes. We'll bury that lot later. And you can stop pilfering through their things, Hemnar. Don't think I didn't see you. Now, I've got a bag of coin for whoever finds me those cunting thieves' trail."

Adelman flinched at Geoff's booming voice, shrinking away as he strode past.

"We should go back," he stammered, dabbing at his nose. "If we… if we tell Amalric what happened, maybe… maybe—"

"Maybe what?" asked Razin, raising an eyebrow. "Do you think he will forgive us our part in all this? No, bookkeep, the moment we took the relic from the city against his wishes, we defied him. Worse yet, our actions bode poorly for his son. To him, we are no different from Aimery and his knights. He would hang us the moment we stepped foot in Jerusalem."

Adelman let out a soft whimper. "What do we do then?

"There's nothing for it," Dietmar declared. "We must recover the hand and continue on our path to Antioch as planned. Those knights can't have gotten far, and they will have wounded among them."

Tomas spat at the dirt, getting some of it on his robes. He wiped it off with his sleeve. "A pox on Gelmiro for giving us away, and to that bastard Frenchman of all people. A pox!" He locked eyes with Dietmar. "And this time, I mean it!"

Dietmar didn't argue with his friend. His doubts about Gelmiro's loyalty still lingered, but voicing them served no purpose. To what end? If he saw the hand safe to Naples, he would have the Church's favour, and with it, the chance to redeem his son's soul. That mattered.

Gelmiro would face the consequences of his actions eventually, Judas or not.

But even if they somehow managed to reclaim the hand, they had other pressing concerns to deal with. Razin was right. This didn't look like the path to Nablus. Dietmar swept his gaze across the plains stretching out beneath the foothills, looking for any markers or points of orientation but found nothing save vast expanses of empty sand.

There *was* a subtle haze on the horizon, Dietmar thought. A sheen from the sun's reflection that allayed his misgivings somewhat. He'd seen something similar after a storm on the Middle Sea. It had to do with the air, the captain had told him when he'd voiced his concerns about the missing coast. The burly Venetian had pulled out a compass and dragged it across the map in his quarters, showing him their route. They were as close to land as they'd ever been, he said. It was just the horizon that looked nearer after the storm. It was a trick, nothing more.

And this will be too, Dietmar concluded. Only, there were other things to consider here, so many leagues from the Middle Sea. The disappearance of the road, the strange sounds in the storm… the presence Razin had described.

He'd felt it too.

And then there was whatever had bitten Theseus. Some wicked desert creature stirred up by the storm? What else could it be?

Something else, he thought, his mind drifting beyond the world of reason, conjuring a word from a chthonic place within him:

Demon.

"Ho there!" Geoff's voice called out, jolting Dietmar from his thoughts.

The mercenary captain stood on a small ridge that hadn't existed before the storm. Its steep slope was slightly ribbed, like the coast after the tide receded. Like the trail behind a great desert serpent, Dietmar thought darkly.

Eudes, the bald and bearded mercenary with a crossbow, knelt beside Geoff, his gaze fixed on something atop the ridge.

Dietmar and Razin hastened up the hill, with Tomas and Adelman huffing behind them, leaving Nicolo with the mules. As they reached the ridge's top, Dietmar paused, taking in the sight before him. There was a trail leading from the rise across the plateau, but that wasn't what drew his attention. The sand was covered with hundreds of smooth pebbles, forming lines that stretched into the distance. The stones, no larger than thumbnails, were as dark as coal, making them stark against the dune.

"Strange, eh?" said Geoff, watching Dietmar's reaction. "Looks like they've been planted like a crop. They're all in lines, seeded for the harvest."

Dietmar tilted his head and saw that the mercenary was right. The stones rested in straight rows, with roughly equal distances between them. He picked one off the ground, turning it over in his hand as Tomas surmounted the ridge.

"What?" the Englishman gasped, sucking in a lungful of air and wiping the sweat from his brow. Adelman sat down in their shadow, his face pale. He took the waterskin Razin offered and wet his brow, then poured more down the front of his tunic before returning it to Razin.

"Where did this come from?" Tomas asked, regaining his breath. He glanced at Geoff, who shrugged. "Must've been here all along, and then the storm uncovered it again for us lucky folk."

Tomas muttered under his breath, fingering the wisp of red hair on his chin as he scanned the stone field. He seemed about to voice his thoughts when Eudes stood up and nodded to Geoff. "I figure four or five horses and someone on foot."

"You sure?" said Geoff.

"Ye. The storm would have blown away any animal tracks, so whatever's left is—"

"From those buggering knights. All right, Eudes. Fair is fair. I'll add a bag of coin to your tally once we reach Gibelet."

"Not before?"

Geoff curled his lip. "Ask again, and you'll get half a purse. How's that? Now, go find the others. We gotta get these carts over the hill and find our relic. The quicker we get going, the quicker you'll get your coin."

Eudes gave Geoff an old Roman salute, cackling as he slid down the hill.

"Cheeky bastard," muttered Geoff, shaking his head. He knelt down to retrieve a stone of his own, examining it before flicking it into the sand. Then he turned to Dietmar.

"Best get your horse, chevalier. Looks like we have our route."

9

It was nearing mid-afternoon by the time they pushed the carts over the ridge. Geoff had proposed abandoning them and leaving them with the mules, but Nicolo wouldn't hear of it, folding his arms across his chest and leaning back in his seat with a set look on his face. After a brief debate, Dietmar had conceded that the Keeper had a point. They couldn't afford to leave the water stored in the carts behind, especially if their journey through the desert stretched beyond a single day. And so, the carts came, and the mules, too.

Though there was no discernible road on the plateau, the ground through the stone field was firm, allowing them to travel without issue, making good time beneath the afternoon sun. Dietmar rode alongside Tomas, who had taken Comus's reins while Adelman dozed in the back of the cart. They had already tried to wake the bookkeep twice, but his snores persisted, seemingly growing louder with each attempt.

Tomas sat quietly, his usually talkative mouth set in a tight line. Each time Dietmar thought he might say something, he hesitated and leaned back into silence. His eyes were fixed on the path ahead, never moving from it, not even to glance at the stone field.

After a while, Dietmar guided Theseus closer to the cart, speaking softly so that only Tomas could hear. "You know something about this place, don't you? I can see it in the way you've been watching the road, avoiding it as if you were Lot's wife. What is it?"

Tomas shook his head, a soft curse escaping his lips. "It's silly," he said. "Just a story."

Dietmar furrowed his brow, recalling the Keeper's words about stories seldom coming from nothing. Perhaps Tomas knew of some allegory or tale that could shed light on their current predicament. What had happened to them.

Had he already accepted Razin's theory that they were somehow in a different place?

But where?

He had an idea. A place that presented itself, a word that appeared without hesitancy in his mind. But he would not contemplate the thought and pushed it aside.

"Tell me," he told Tomas.

Tomas sighed, finally lifting his eyes to stare at the rocks surrounding them.

"There is a story outside of the Bible about the Christ."

"There are many."

"This one paints the Christ in a… less than flattering light." Tomas fidgeted with the reins, wrapping the leather over his knuckles like he'd seen Nicolo do. The pause grew, and Dietmar began to think Tomas might choose not to share the story. But then, with a resigned expression, he began. "The story goes that Jesus was walking on the road to Bethlehem when he encountered a farmer toiling in his field. Out of curiosity, Jesus asked the farmer what he was planting. The man, tired from his labours, ignored the Christ, for he did not know who had asked. So, Jesus asked again, 'Ser, what is it you are planting?'

'Pebbles,' cried the farmer, tired of being bothered.

The Christ frowned at this and then asked again, a final time, 'Ser, what do you plant? I would know.' The farmer glared up from his seed rows and told him again, 'Pebbles! Pebbles! Pebbles!'

The Christ said nothing to this, for there was nothing to say, and carried on his journey to Bethlehem. When he was gone, the farmer looked to his field and saw that his seeds had all turned into tiny grey pebbles, leaving him with nothing for the harvest."

"Hah!" Adelman barked from behind Tomas's seat, startling both Dietmar and Tomas. They hadn't noticed his snores had stopped. "It wasn't pebbles but eyes!"

Dietmar looked back at the bookkeep, who was still lying on his side. "Eyes?"

"Eyes!"

"Why would it be eyes?"

"You're not making any sense," said Tomas.

Adelman laughed again, muttering about eyes and peas before his loud snores filled the back of the cart once more.

Dietmar straightened in his saddle, putting Adelman's strange words out of mind.

Stories were a second history in Outremer. They shaped places and their people, flittering from the mouths of fellahin to the ears of Greeks and Syrians, proliferating and changing to match the context and beliefs of their speaker and listener. Dietmar had learned to interpret these tales since coming to the Levant, understanding the underlying messages they conveyed. These stories were coloured by the perceived truth of its teller; here a man suffers for his stubbornness, or is rewarded for kindness; here a man learns that factfulness and truthfulness are not always the same or that a lie well-meant can be as harmful as a truth poorly told.

The thought that these stories could be true, that they held a literal meaning, unsettled him. He didn't doubt that many of those native to the Levant, whose own histories and families were as deeply rooted in the soil as the stories they told, believed the tales as they were presented. But there was a part of Dietmar, a condescending, arrogant part that could not be dislodged, that thought of the stories as no more than quaint oddities.

For them to *be true* and not simply the form structured around a simple message, a means to convey some deeper truth…

He tried not to let his discomfort show when he looked at Tomas again. "Do you think this is that same field from the story?"

"What else could it be?"

"Well, we're not on the road to Bethlehem, for starters." Dietmar pointed to the nearest stone. "And these stones are black, not grey."

"Heh. A minor detail that might have been lost in its retelling," said Tomas, though he did not seem convinced. He fell silent for a while until Dietmar thought he was done talking. But then Tomas spoke again, his voice laced with concern. "I have heard some of Geoff's men talking. They say we are no longer on the road to Nablus. That we are lost since the storm."

Dietmar cast a sideways glance at the mercenaries riding alongside them. Amice and a tall Norman with a face like a fistfight. He had seen them talking too, the quiet conversations and nervous gestures. Soon, he would need to address their growing unease, even as his own doubts began to loom.

"How can we be lost?" Dietmar asked. "We haven't moved until now."

"I don't know," Tomas conceded, rubbing his chin. "But there is something strange about this place. Can't you feel it? And this hill… Even Adelman has noticed it, and he barely knows whether it's night or day most of the time."

Dietmar raised a hand to try placate his anxious friend, but Tomas continued, his voice going shrill. "Where are all the bushes? Everything is so barren here. There were never any trees, I know, but if this is Samaria, then I do not recognise it!"

"Easy, friend," said Dietmar when Tomas paused for a breath. "I have questions too. But we must have a care not to panic or to stir up fear in the others." He nodded toward Geoff, riding at the front of the company. "If we are to find Ephium's hand and reclaim it, we need level-headedness. We need Geoff and his men by our side."

Tomas reached into his robes and retrieved a skin, taking a deep swig from it. He wiped his lips, stained with red after he finished.

"Besides," said Dietmar, holding out his hand for the flask. "If we walk where the Christ walked, then that's no bad thing, is it?"

Tomas snorted, passing him the wineskin. "You forget where the Christ's path led him, friend. At least we already know our Judas."

"Aye," said Dietmar, taking a sip. He spat it back out and made a face. The warm wine tasted like piss.

The landscape underwent a gradual transformation as the sun descended. At first, the changes were subtle, barely noticeable. The sturdy sand beneath their feet darkened, assuming an ashen grey hue. Small rocky outcrops emerged along their path, adorned with sprouting roots and weeds. The previously flat plain became uneven, marked by shallow dips and grooves that hinted at the presence of a long-dried riverbed.

As they continued their journey, the gaps between the pebbles grew wider until there were none left at all. Instead, larger rocky formations dotted their path, and Dietmar's gaze was drawn to peculiar flowers adorning their peaks. The flowers boasted broad petals, vibrant red, with tips blackened as if scorched by fire. A curious contrast amongst all the grey.

The hills converged further down, merging into a single solid wall of rock and hardened sand. More of those strange flowers hung from the cracks in the ravine and grew all along its floor. When they reached the bottom of the slope, Geoff rode back to Dietmar, signalling for the company to halt.

"What is it?" asked Adelman, stirring from his sleep. He blinked leadenly and sat up to stretch his arms.

"We're about to find out," said Dietmar, nudging Theseus forward to meet Geoff and his ugly horse.

Through conversations with Geoff and his men, Dietmar had learned that the mercenaries had joined Gelmiro's employ during the Antioch riots a few years ago. A ship full of Greeks had arrived at the port, refused to pay the levy—on account of not having received payment for services rendered in one of Amalric's campaigns—and somehow managed to rile up the local populace in a slew of ugly skirmishes that lasted a week.

The violence had spilt over from the docks to threaten the Church's properties in the city, forcing Gelmiro's hand. He had hired several bands, including Geoff and his men, to tackle the docks while the city guard contained the conflict. Geoff and his men had apparently distinguished themselves, earning a permanent place on Gelmiro's payroll.

The mercenary looked unsettled, and for once, his yellow teeth were hidden behind his chapped lips.

"My boys are not liking this," he said to Dietmar. "They've already been mouthing off behind my back. They think I can't hear them, but I've got an ear like a pig that knows it's for the slaughter. *That's right, Liso! Now shut your filthy mouth!*" Geoff's glare pierced a swarthy Italian a few paces away before he turned back to Dietmar, shaking his head. "At first, I thought it was just the usual gossiping. They're like a bunch of old whores when they're bored. But now I think they might be right."

"What is it?" said Dietmar, echoing Adelman's words.

Do I even want to know?

A part of him yearned to ignore the commotion and turn his horse back the way they'd come. But there was nothing back there for him to return to.

Geoff spurred his horse, gesturing for Dietmar to follow as he rode toward the front of the company. They approached a widening ravine, its walls growing taller as the ground dipped to form a steep slope. Here, the flowers thrived like wild weeds, sprouting from every crevice and crack, obscuring the ground beneath.

"Yeah," said Geoff when Dietmar saw what was at the bottom of the gully. "Imagine our thirsty axes not stumbling upon this lot, eh? Makes me wonder just how close we are to Nablus."

A forest?

Here?

A thick grove of trees dominated the far end of the slope, extending across the wide throat of the ravine. Pines and cedars grew beside clumps of green conifers and stout-looking oaks, their flush limbs stretched outward with the fearlessness of those who hadn't come to know the axe. The trees stood taller than any Dietmar had encountered since arriving in Outremer, reminiscent of the towering giants of his homeland. A blanket of pine needles and cones covered the floor, and Dietmar saw the faint outlines of what looked like ruins nestled away in the shadows of the forest.

It's not possible.

And yet, there it stood, as deep and tall as any of the forests back home.

"The tracks go in there," Eudes announced, appearing on the slope ahead of them. Dietmar hadn't even noticed him ascending, his eyes so fixed on the forest. *It doesn't make any sense.* That much wood would be worth more than all his lands in Germany. That no Christian king or Seljuk sultan had harvested them was unimaginable.

Geoff sucked on his teeth, his gaze fixed on the towering trees. He turned his horse to face the rest of the company, some of whom were murmuring anxiously among themselves but fell silent upon seeing his stern expression.

"Who wants to be made a rich man? There's a bag in it for whoever spots those thieving shits first!" The mercenaries sat expressionless on their horses, watching him in silence. Most of the company had travelled between Jerusalem and Nablus on more than one occasion, and none of them had seen anything like this. The presence of the forest unnerved them, a sentiment Dietmar couldn't blame them for—he felt the same unease.

Geoff tried a different tact, rising on his stirrups. "Right. There's coin in it, for sure, but it's more than that. Gelmiro wants to see that relic delivered safe and sound. And in my book, he's as good as the Pope himself. That means we're doing God's work here. We are His faithful servants, are we not, Amice? Are we not?

The squire crossed himself, a yellow grin on his lips. "Amen, captain. We certainly are."

"Right," said Geoff with a wicked smile. "Then into the *cunting* forest we go!"

They edged slowly into the woods, their eyes darting between shadows, searching for any sign of the knights. A weighty stillness enveloped the world at the base of the ravine, a silence that made Dietmar want to be silent in turn. Only the slow rhythm of their horses' hooves and the occasional braying of Balaam disturbed the tranquillity, and even those sounds seemed muted.

Like Orpheus on his descent into the Underworld.

Would he find Ennelyn at the heart of the forest?

Or his son?

Orpheus had found his wife waiting for him and bargained with Hades and Persephone for her release. But Dietmar had no sweet songs to soften the Devil's heart, only his love. Perhaps he would be forced to remain so that they might go free? He would take that bargain and be glad for it.

When the trees grew too thick, they left the carts behind with a jittery Adelman assigned as their guardian. The old man would probably hide under his cart again the moment they were gone.

Better a coward with the carts than within our midst.

Eudes led the company, his gaze fixed on the tracks, his crossbow resting across his knees. Geoff followed closely behind him, accompanied by Amice and Liso, the curly-haired Italian. Dietmar and the rest trailed behind.

They moved in near silence, unwilling to break the hush of the forest, with the exception of Eudes, and then only to point them in the right direction.

Dietmar tried counting the trees they passed but soon gave up. He let his eyes fall on the nearest pine—a towering giant with healthy branches and bark the colour of leather. It reminded him of the woods back home and the vast hills above his estate covered by them. A sea of lush, impenetrable green that only offered tentative glimpses at the hidden world within. Enneleyn would guide him through those trees, dragging him away from his bickering father and brother—those heated voices—and into a sanctuary meant for them alone.

Something caught his attention at the base of the tree, and he slowed to look. The bark had been stripped from the lower portion of the trunk, peeled away like the skin of an apple, leaving behind unsightly brown scars. He glanced at the neighbouring trees and noticed the same pattern repeated.

There were other markings too. Deep grooves cut into the limbs of an ancient, yellowing cedar; a young pine uprooted and left to decay on the forest floor.

The sight of the skinned trees reminded Dietmar of the stable doors where Talbert's cats used to scratch themselves after hunting rats. Their little bodies had worn away the wood until Talbert hammered in a few nails to deter them.

As for the deep grooves and torn-up pine… he thought of the silhouette he had glimpsed in the storm, too big to be a horse.

It had taken that man's head.

Some chthonic beast.

But what had become of the rest of the body?

He tried not to fixate on the memory, dismissing it as nothing more than a shadow in a storm of shadows.

It could have been anything.

Or nothing.

Yet, no matter how hard he tried, the shadow refused to release its grip on his mind. He rode with his hand resting on his sword, vigilantly observing the gaps between the trees.

The first sign of the ruins they'd seen from the slope was a lone pillar jutting out at an angle from the earth, half-buried. It looked Roman in origin: a Corinthian with deep channels running up its shaft, culminating in a delicate floral capital befitting a king's palace.

Next, they came upon a pair of marble flagstones partially submerged within the sprawling roots of a towering pine. They had since lost whatever colour they might have had and bore the faces of unrecognisable figures—long lost nobles of Rome or heroes, or just rich men who sought immortality in stone—either way, long forgotten.

A little further ahead, they reached the largest of the ruins. It looked like it might have been a temple once or perhaps the home of a wealthy statesman. A broad portico stretched between a row of Corinthian columns.

Who would live here?

In this forest of the underworld?

To the Romans or Greeks or whoever had built this place, the feeling must have been more profound, closer to their deities who roamed among them.

Oracles or priests, Dietmar mused, staring past the portico.

The temple itself was expansive and deep, consisting of four chambers before the rest of the structure vanished behind a maze of overgrown roots and trees. Or perhaps it was closer to an administrative building, he thought. Like those that lined the streets of Constantinople, with enough room to fit the long queues and the thousands of ledgers needed to run the city.

The temple's gabled roof remained intact, with only a scattering of broken tiles on the flagstone floor in front of the portico. It probably still leaked when it rained, but only if the water managed to penetrate the dense canopy above.

Eudes dismounted, leading his horse across the flagstones and then kneeling beside a chipped block of marble up ahead. Dietmar thought he saw a stain spread upon it, dark and wet. The tracker ran a finger through it, lifted it to his nose, and then nodded to Geoff.

"They're in there," said Geoff softly. He waved at his men to dismount. "Looks like they've got a wounded one after all, so well done to your Syriano, eh." He gave Razin a wink and then dropped from his horse, walking it toward the nearest tree, tethering the reins to a low-hanging branch.

Razin didn't respond. He had heard worse during his time among the Franks and seen worse in their dens of gambling and drinking. Men like

Geoff were as common as dirt in God's Kingdom. Dietmar sometimes wondered at that—how Jerusalem seemed to attract such villains. Shouldn't a sacred place inspire men to greatness? To rise above their baser instincts?

He thought of his own time in Jerusalem, living life as little better than a sword-for-hire. The only difference between himself and Geoff, really, was that people addressed him as "ser" when filling his purse with coin and called Geoff "bastard" when he wasn't listening. Was that all there was between them? Breeding?

They might call me bastard, too.

He dismounted Theseus, taking his shield from his horse and gazing at its faded crest. His father would turn in his grave if he knew what had become of his eldest son. He'd turn again when he heard of the debts Dietmar had incurred. Rudolph had always been proud, even when humility would have served him better. He'd never asked for help, not in all his years raising Dietmar and Huldrych, not even after their mother died. They had dragged her bloated body from the lake not a week before Dietmar's fourth birthday. She had been missing for three days, and rumours had already spread among the staff. *Rudolph's buried her. She's finally escaped the brute.* Everyone claimed Dietmar was too young to remember, but he did. He'd seen her green skin and swollen features, the empty sockets where her eyes had been—eaten by the fish.

Huldrych had been spared the scene, being safely ensconced in his nursemaid's arms and whisked away before he could make sense of the commotion. He'd only been a year then, but Rudolph wouldn't look at him after their mother's death. It was his eyes, Dietmar thought. They looked just like hers.

But that was all of their mother to be found in Huldrych. The coldness and hardness that defined their father were manifested in Huldrych so that he became a reflection of the man he despised. Dietmar could only watch as they tore into each other night after night until Huldrych stopped taking the bait. Then they sat in silence, which was even worse.

Despite his faults, Rudolph had managed to raise them both while steering his estate through drought, famines, and the Emperor's tax. And he'd done more than just survive. He'd prospered.

Only for Dietmar to throw it all away, caught in his grief.

What would Enneleyn say if she saw him now, traipsing through the strange trees on the other side of the world? Her green eyes would sparkle with amusement at the company he was in.

"Two donkeys make you an ass, too," she'd say, her gentle, cruel words from a voice as beautiful to him as birdsong. Then she would smile to show she didn't mean it and take his hand in her own. The stories he'd have to share with her! Of audiences with kings, mad dashes across the desert, backstabbing merchants and fiendish priests, of strange women who danced like snakes with coal-black eyes and lips as red as… Some stories were not meant for his wife's ears.

Enneleyn's cheeky smile faded as he struggled to remember his boy's face. He recalled the feeling when he'd first held him and the sound of his laughter, his cries in the early hours—he even missed that—just the sound of his voice.

Dietmar frowned, still staring at his shield.

He couldn't remember Rudi's face.

"Come, German," said Razin, fastening Riba's reins to the same tree as Theseus and gesturing toward the temple. "We shall be like the Greeks in the temples of Troy, searching for the hero Aeneas."

Dietmar blinked away from his shield and slipped an arm through its straps. He had never read Homer, although he had heard Razin talk of his stories often enough. "Did they find Aeneas? Those Greeks?"

Razin pursed his lips, subtly shaking his head. “Better we are like Shahrazad, then, searching for a way to keep her husband from killing her.”

“Did she?”

Razin chuckled. “It is a long story, my friend.”

Dietmar felt himself relax a little, laughing with Razin even though he had missed the joke.

Geoff signalled his men to silence as Dietmar and Razin joined them on the portico steps. He glanced over his shoulder. “In there?”

“Aye,” said Dietmar with a nod from Razin by his side. Tomas and Nicolo appeared, each wielding a club the scriniarius had retrieved from the back of his cart.

Geoff fingered his gums with a dirty nail, his eyes sweeping across the company. There were fourteen men, including Dietmar. More than enough to overpower Aimery’s knights. But that was in an open fight. The temple offered a different challenge entirely. A man could disappear in its shadows, hide away in the dark places only to lash out at the unwary. Here, numerical advantage held less sway, and Geoff was well aware of it.

The mercenary captain grumbled something to Amice, sending the boy sauntering through the doors ahead.

“Right,” said Geoff, watching him go before addressing the rest of the company. “There’s no point delaying. Night will be here soon, and I’d like to be out of these shit woods when it comes.” He drew his sword, and Dietmar saw the glint of steel dusters on his other hand.

A proper villain.

“I’ll only say this once,” Geoff continued, “Don’t go wandering off on your own in there. I won’t come looking for you, understand? In you go then, this cunting temple isn’t gonna sack itself.”

10

Dietmar inhaled deeply as he stepped inside, taking in the essence of the place as he stared into the gloom. The first thing he noticed was the sheer size of the flagstones—each as wide and tall as a man. Their transportation would have been a monumental task, and he'd seen no marble quarries on their route. The ravine they had traversed only had more of that ashen grey stone.

Light blossomed to his left as Eudes lit a torch he'd taken off the wall. Dietmar took another torch from a nearby sconce, lighting it off Eudes's before holding it up to look at the rest of the chamber.

The room unfolded, revealing its true size, and Dietmar found himself squinting to discern its details. A row of empty stone niches covered the walls to either side of the chamber, like the enclaves of a crypt, small cavities one atop another, waiting to be filled.

By what?

Dietmar moved further into the room, noticing the twin pillars that framed the door on the opposite end. Thick shadows veiled their capitals, obscuring their actual form. Unlike the Roman colonnade outside, these pillars were hewn from a lighter stone, possessing an off-white hue reminiscent of bone. Their mason had lacked the finesse of the Roman builders too. His hand had been heavy against the stone, leaving uneven slopes and asymmetrical ridges along their shafts. Symbols and faded lettering worn away by the years covered their bases. The foreign marks stirred no recognition in Dietmar. They may have been Egyptian or Babylonian for all he knew.

Razin paused to examine the pillars, his head tilted back to see if he could make out the heads of one of their capitals. The neck of the column grew narrow, carved thin to elevate the roughly hewn forms cut into the top. Snakes, he thought at first, staring at the coiling shapes wrapped around the headstone. Their thick, muscular bodies intertwined like the fingers of a clasped hand, forming a spiralling wreath that disappeared into the gloomy ceiling. Razin's eyes narrowed as he noticed the ragged teeth jutting out from one of the stone-serpent's jaws in place of fangs and then the faint line of a crest or dorsal fin on its back. Not a brood of vipers then, he thought.

He stood there, blinking into the murky ceiling, until Dietmar called at him to follow.

The next room was wider still and had a faint musky odour. A line of marble-topped slabs lay in its centre. The flagstones had been replaced. Or rather, the floor had remained bare, revealing the rough stone from the temple's foundations, left open and exposed. A series of grooves had been cut into the stone floor, connecting the slabs.

Dietmar had visited a catacomb before. The first time, to see his grandfather's bones in the Darmundstat crypt. They had been stacked like kindling for a fire, his grandfather's leering skull sitting upon his wide, empty ribcage. Dietmar had flinched at the sight, but his father's hand had rested on his shoulder, forcing him to look.

The second time had been to see Enneleyn's body after her fall. She had been covered by a linen shroud, her precious lips pressed against the thin cloth, forming subtle slopes against the fabric. They wouldn't bury her in the vaults after… after… Dietmar blinked. He couldn't remember. He had stood there hopelessly, bargaining with himself and with God… perhaps even the Devil, so that she might suck in a breath and fill her lungs with life again. His prayers had fallen on deaf ears, leaving him alone in the stony air of the crypt until the priests had led him out.

Geoff stalked toward the nearest slab, kneeling to examine the grooves in the stone beneath it. In the light of his torch, it looked like a fungus had sprouted within the shallow channels. He scratched at it with a nail and rubbed the dark residue between his fingers, frowning.

"It's blood," said Razin softly, though his voice carried over the stillness of the chamber. Geoff's expression twisted into a snarl as he wiped his fingers against his breeches. "So, this is a pagan house," he growled, rising to his feet and spitting at the slab. The flame of his torch seemed to diminish at his words, retreating from the inky darkness surrounding them. Geoff remained unperturbed. "Must've been from when the Romans were still fucking each other half to death in the name of their wine god. We'll have to burn this place when we leave, of course, as faithful servants of the Lord." He dusted off his hands, showing his yellow teeth again. "Then, on our way back, we'll secure the forest and carve out kingdoms for ourselves with the timber. How does that sound, lads? Our reward for honest toil."

His men exchanged wary glances.

They didn't want to come back.

The company moved deeper into the temple, leaving the slabs and ancient blood behind. There must have been an opening ahead because a gentle breeze stirred, causing their torches to flicker and tugging at their hoods and cowls.

Dietmar trailed behind Geoff and Eudes. When he glanced back, he noticed that the company had instinctively drawn closer together, huddled like a school of fish, seeking comfort from one another, even if they would never admit it.

Gradually, the room expanded, its straight walls curling outward until they walked through the centre of a vast rotunda. Dietmar gazed upward, searching for the domed ceiling, but found only darkness. As he looked down again, he realised that the walls had vanished, extending beyond the reach of their torchlight. He briefly wondered at the trick of the eye that made the temple appear so much smaller from the outside. But then, he'd only seen the portico and colonnade, and they had walked far… well beyond the antechamber visible from the front.

More pillars loomed before them, eliciting dark murmurs from Geoff's men. And this time, their captain's furious glares weren't enough to silence them.

"What's this?" hissed Liso, waving his torch at Geoff, then joining the others in scrutinising the columns. Like the ones flanking the chamber's entrance, these pillars had been hewn from an off-white stone bordering on yellow. Chains dangled from the shafts of the three columns, nailed into the rock at approximately head height. Each chain was as thick as Dietmar's arms, and iron collars were affixed to their ends, large enough for a horse or perhaps even a bull. Dust coated the manacles, and Dietmar noticed more dark, fungus-like residue smeared on the collars.

Their size perplexed Dietmar. He thought of all the beasts large enough to fill the iron collars, but none would require more than rope to secure, surely?

"Scared the godless men who fucked in these halls are still here, Liso?" Geoff sneered, marching past the columns and kicking one of the collars with his boot. It bounced across the hard floor, scraping against the stone before settling on the other side of the pillar.

"They were not godless," Razin murmured, his gaze set on the nearest column. He approached it, his eyes tracing the markings at its base. He reached out with a hand, running his fingers over the simple geometric shapes intermingled with the scrawling text. When his touch reached the first letters, he turned back to Dietmar. "Their sin was that they worshipped many gods, not none."

Geoff scoffed from ahead. "Too few, too many. If you don't believe in my God, you're godless in my books. I don't care if you have fifty bull-headed…" His words trailed off as his eyes narrowed, scanning the company. "Where's Eudes?"

Dietmar looked around, searching the faces of Geoff's men, now gathered at the base of the third column, but Eudes's bald head was not among them.

"He was just here," Hemnar, a towering Swede, said. "Maybe he went for a piss?"

Geoff shook his head. "I told you lot not to wander, didn't I say? If you need to go, piss where you walk. I'm not following you into this pagan crypt. Eudes! I hope you heard that, you greedy cunt!"

Dietmar swivelled his head, catching a glimpse of movement in the darkness to his right. Geoff had noticed it too. "Come on, Eudes!" he called, striding toward the spot. "Put your cock away. I won't ask a second time."

The shadows danced beneath the glow of the torchlight, undulating like the tide. A gust of cool air crept through the chamber, whistling through a narrow passage or shaft, leaving their torches flickering. Dietmar said a hasty prayer to Saint Lucia, tightening his grip on the torch, and took a slow step toward the farthest pillar, where he had last seen Eudes.

The column loomed over him like a jagged tooth embedded in the hard stone. That familiar sensation gripped him again, tugging at his mind, exerting a subtle pressure that slowed his thoughts. This time, he recognised it. It was the same thing he'd felt when he prayed on the Temple Mount—an impossible presence that both soothed and terrified him. Like God was near.

He took a shuffling step forward, his eyes darting over the markings on the stone shaft. There was a pattern to it, he realised: the baser geometric shapes filled the lower portion in rows, while the markings grew more sophisticated as they ascended. Whatever it was, it had been written in more than one language over many years.

One of the runes caught his eye, a simple motif amongst the scrawling text. A hieroglyph, he thought. It depicted a man in side-profile, perhaps a king? He sat resting upon his haunches with his legs crossed in front of him. One hand was raised, two fingers pointing toward the heavens, while the other hand gestured downward, toward the ground beneath his feet.

He took another step and paused, a twisted feeling in the pit of his stomach.

Something had cracked beneath his boot.

Dietmar stumbled back, his torch held out as he stared at the ground. Piles of animal bones lay strewn across the floor, so thick in places that he couldn't see the rock beneath. Some had been stacked in small heaps, like those in an ossuary—tiny offerings to a god whose name had long since passed from the minds of men. Sheep heads lay beside horse skulls and the remains of long-dead reptiles. A mound of tiny humanoid ribcages must have come from monkeys traded in the markets, brought to the Holy Land by foreign merchants.

It looked as though the bones had been… gnawed clean. He realised with a start that many of them had been snapped open, their marrow sucked out before being discarded. Some beast had made this temple its lair.

"We should leave," said Razin, coming up beside him, his lips contorted in disgust.

"The hand," said Dietmar, staring at the bare skull of what might have been a wild cat in its former life. Captured by death-worshippers and left to rot beneath the shrouded cupola. They hadn't fucked in here. They'd feasted.

"All the same," Razin insisted. Geoff was crunching through the bones now, calling for Eudes in ever louder tones. "We should leave. We can wait for those knights in the forest or track their trail beyond the temple. This… is not a good place."

Geoff gave a satisfied grunt, spotting Eudes's silhouette in the gloom and striding toward him. "Where's your torch, you daft bastard? Put your cock away and come here. What did I say about wandering off? Now here I am doing the thing I said I wouldn't do just to find your sorry arse… Eudes?"

Geoff halted in his tracks, squinting at the figure on the edge of the light. He glanced back at Dietmar, motioning him forward, before tossing his torch across the bone carpet. The torch bounced, scattering remains as it skidded to a halt. Its flame licked at the bones, briefly sparking as it ignited on some residual fat that had survived the marrow-eater's administrations.

From the corner of his eye, Dietmar saw something move out of the light—matted hair, like that of a dog or a lion, after gorging itself on a carcass, blood and gore staining its dark, tangled coat. He dropped his torch, allowing it to roll to his feet as he unsheathed his sword.

They were being watched.

"Eudes?" Geoff called out. A figure stood amidst the splintered bones. The flame of Geoff's torch spluttered against a warm wind that breathed through the chamber, sending shadows stretching across the floor. The man stood with his back turned, his head hidden. He wore a mail hauberk and a dirt and blood-stained tabard of royal blue. Something rested in his hand, but Dietmar couldn't make it out in the gloom.

"It's not him," Dietmar said when he saw the mane of hair hanging to the figure's shoulders. All the same, there was something strangely familiar about him.

"*Tu vas bien?*" Dietmar called out, thinking it might be the other Poitiers knight. Geoff's men spread across the temple floor, their eyes fixed on the dark recesses of the chamber, sensing a trap.

"Where the fuck is Eudes?" Geoff grumbled as Dietmar stepped beside him.

Dietmar ignored him, advancing slowly toward the knight. Bones crumbled beneath his boots, turning to dust against his soles. The wind stirred once more, tousling the knight's hair. Dietmar paused, watching the motionless figure. Unless he held a hidden blade, the knight appeared unarmed, standing as immobile as stone—a fourth pillar in the chamber.

"*Homme de Poitiers?*" Dietmar tried again, inching closer. When the knight remained silent, Geoff hacked up a gob of spit and marched toward him.

"Enough of this," Geoff declared, reaching out with a hand to spin the knight around. "Where the fuck is—"

The question died on his lips, replaced by a soft groan as he met the empty stare of the man before him. Empty because his eyes had been gouged out. Rivulets of dried blood stained the knight's cheeks like tears, intermingling with his dirty beard. The skin around his empty sockets was frayed and torn, as if an oversized knife had been used to extract his eyes. His eyelids fluttered briefly, quivering like the wings of a fly caught in a web. Swollen and bruised, they hung loosely like the torn seams of a doll.

"Christ, man!" Geoff exclaimed, stumbling back.

Dietmar crossed himself instinctively and then took another step toward the man, frowning. The knight's long hair had grown filthy, and his beard was rugged and unkempt, yet beneath all the blood and bruises, Dietmar recognised the same square jaw and proud features.

"Aimery," he whispered, naming the lord of Lusignan. The nobleman had come to claim the hand himself.

Aimery's face twitched, and he turned his head in response to the sound of Dietmar's voice, some fragment of sanity stirring in recognition of his name.

"What happened here?" said Dietmar.

Aimery opened his mouth, his once-perfect white teeth now stained red, chipped like ruins. Blood and spit trickled from his lips, frothing at the corners of his mouth. A soft, gargled croak was his only reply.

"They've taken his *cunting* tongue," Geoff declared loudly. He raised his sword and peered over Aimery's shoulder, scanning the murky corners of the temple.

"Who?" asked Tomas from a little way behind, his voice trembling. "What happened to him?"

Nicolo let out a bark and pointed at Aimery, gesturing to the object still clutched within his bloodied fingers.

"He has the hand," Geoff announced, following Nicolo's stare. He beckoned to Amice. "Go get it will you, lad? Come on, move yourself. I'll keep an eye on this one while you take it."

The squire nodded but remained motionless.

Geoff growled, turning to his other men. "Hemnar?"

"Go get it yourself," said Hemnar, curling his lips and shaking his head. "I heard what the Keeper said about touching it. And now look what's happened to this git: his eyes 'ave rotten in his skull. His tongue has fallen from his mouth. You get it."

"No, no, look at his fingers," said Razin. "He did this to himself."

Even in the flickering torches, Dietmar could see the blood staining Aimery's fingers, reaching up to his knuckles. His nails were caked in gore, bits of dried flesh and remnants of when he had pierced his own brain with his fingers, turning him into something... less.

"But why?" Tomas's voice still quivered. His eyes widened, flinching at the sound of Dietmar's footsteps crunching over the bones.

If no one else would claim the hand, then he would do it himself.

Aimery cocked his head at Dietmar's approach, his lips parting slowly, giving the illusion of a smile.

"He's gone mad," said Razin. "Or else a *marid* has taken him. He will not leave this place now, but we must."

Whatever else Razin said faded into the background, like a dull hum, as Dietmar extended his hand toward Aimery's, reaching for the relic nestled in his grip. It was a wretched thing, dry and calloused. With its flaky, greyish flesh, it looked like the limb of a leper. He was suddenly glad for his gloves, but even as the thought crossed his mind, he found himself removing them, discarding them to the ground.

Why?

He heard Tomas call his name in warning, but his movements no longer felt his to control. His arm rose, his hand open, his fingers outstretched. He watched, a witness to his own actions but not a party to them. Then he plucked St. Ephium's hand from Aimery's grasp, blinking as the relic touched his bare skin.

Tomas called out to him again, but his voice seemed distant, and a low hum now filled Dietmar's ears, drowning out the rest. He winced as the buzz grew louder, like a wicked wasp droning in his skull, rattling against his eardrums from within. The hairs on the back of his neck stood on end, and a prickling sensation spread across his skin where he held the relic, like ants burrowing into his hand and fingers. He wanted to let go, to fling it into the shadows of the chamber, but a voice in the back of his head told him not to. It wasn't the same voice that warned him when to stop drinking or advised him against drawing his knife on foolish lords. This voice was… different. He didn't recognise it. But the strange realisation evaporated as quickly as it had emerged, swallowed by the rattling drone.

His hand trembled as he gazed down at the relic. The greyish skin felt as smooth as it appeared, like marble against his itching palm. Impossibly cold. The black-nailed thumb was slightly bent from being carried loosely in Aimery's saddlebag. Dietmar gently pushed it back into place, knowing this to be the right thing to do without knowing why.

A bead of sweat trickled down his forehead, and through the din, he heard Tomas calling him once more, shouting this time. Dietmar turned to face his friend and saw that his eyes were wide, caught between a moment of grief and terror.

Dietmar gagged the moment the stench hit him mid-breath. It was like the grey meat of the sewers, an open casket laid bare in a piss-stained cloister, the charnel pits in the sun. The world rushed back to him with that horrible breath, flooding his senses and throbbing within his head. The droning sound abruptly ceased, but a worse sound replaced it. Men were screaming behind him. He was screaming, and he couldn't stop.

A shape flickered in the corner of his vision, shifting within the darkness.

"Christ preserve us!" Tomas cried. "Jesu, please!"

A lion, Dietmar thought at first. Impossibly large, standing so tall that he had to tilt his head to look at it. Its dark coat was matted and stained, smeared with blood and shit like a dog that had been rolling around in dead things to hide its scent. Giant footpads scraped against the floor, black claws clicking upon the stone as the creature moved behind Aimery.

Dietmar felt his mind start to fray. And then he knew he had gone mad when he caught sight of the creature's teats—no, not teats. Breasts, like those of a woman, but covered in a thin layer of fur upon its chest. They were shapely and firm, with nipples protruding through the hair. Hardened, as if in arousal.

What?

Fuck.

No.

There was a blur of movement, a flash so swift that Dietmar nearly missed it. A forepaw, as wide as his chest, swiped at Aimery, vicious claws like knives slicing through his hauberk and into his waist. The beast pulled the lord toward it, sliding him across the floor in a single motion. Aimery went without a sound, his limp form hoisted into the air by leonine claws, his head lolling to the side.

Glowing eyes, shimmering like pools of molten gold, peered down at the lord, drawing him closer to a face that was more human than beast. The hair on its face was sparser and lighter. A sharp, aristocratic nose sniffed at the knight, and a long black tongue emerged from behind its lips, which peeled back to reveal a mouth filled with jagged teeth.

For a fleeting moment, it seemed as if Aimery had come to his senses. He writhed in the creature's grip, rattling out a garbled moan while attempting to dislodge himself from the hooks that pierced his side. His struggling only made it worse, and his entrails started to spill from one of the wounds in his belly. He vomited blood, splashing it all across the beast's face while it watched him.

The creature extended its jaws, cracking them open like a sealed tomb. They widened further and further, snakelike, until a gaping throat, a cave mouth, spanned across its face. Aimery let out another feeble cry, sensing without seeing the horror that awaited him. And then, he was gone, his cry cut short as he was thrust deep into the beast's gaping maw. The creature wolfed him down in three voracious gulps, its throat expanding to accommodate his girth, until Aimery disappeared into its belly.

Dietmar gulped down air and realised he hadn't stopped screaming since the creature had stepped into the light. His throat was raw. He glanced down and saw a stain covering the front of his breeches. He'd pissed himself too.

Hemnar, the big Northman, was the first to snap out of his paralysis. Perhaps it was because his people were closer to the old religions and their ancient gods that something in his blood stirred at the sight of this horror, propelling him into action like his Viking ancestors.

He hopped forward, taking three long strides and throwing his weight behind his spear, releasing it with a howl on his lips. The spear flew true, whistling as it carved through the air. It hit the beast just above its left breast, where its heart would be if it were any mortal thing.

The sound was like steel against stone, and Dietmar watched in disbelief as the spearhead cracked upon impact, falling to the ground with a dull clatter. It hadn't even pierced the creature's skin.

Hemnar's mistake became apparent too late—he had gotten too close.

The beast pounced like a cat, propelled by massive hindlegs. Lighter patches on its back unfurled into vulture-like wings. Flapping once, the creature surged forward with impossible speed for its size. Hemnar didn't even have time to scream. The beast crushed his body beneath its front paws, tearing through his armour and causing a sickening spray of blood to spurt up its fur. Hemnar's head burst like an apple dropped from a cart, leaving only his lower jaw remaining after the weight of the beast descended upon it.

"*RUN!*" Geoff screamed, spittle flying from between his crooked yellow teeth. It wasn't a command. It was all there was.

Dietmar spun on his heels, charging through the bones, kicking them aside as he raced back the way they'd come. Tomas and Nicolo were already passing the third pillar, with Razin a few steps behind. Amice stumbled to his left, but not enough to trip and fall… *to be another body between me and the beast*. Dietmar felt a pang of shame at the thought, and he grabbed Amice's sleeve, helping him regain his stride.

He could hear the beast behind them, gorging itself on Hemnar's carcass.

CRACK. PHHLP. SHLLLP.

He didn't dare look back as he ran, knowing that as long as he could hear the creature devouring Hemnar

—the eating stopped.

A thunderous sound, like a bull charging across a field, filled his ears. He swung around just in time to see the creature hurtling toward him, its golden eyes filled with mirth or glee or hunger or lust.

He couldn't think of a prayer, so he just hoped to God for forgiveness as he raised his shield, still clutching Saint Ephium's hand. He closed his eyes, awaiting his gruesome fate. But the creature leapt past him, swiping at Liso with its massive paw. The Italian cried out, his legs breaking before he hit the ground and went sprawling across the bones. Dietmar thought he'd be surely eaten, but the creature—the demon, for that is what it must be—didn't pursue him further. It left Liso on the floor to sob, his calls for help were ignored while everyone sought their own survival.

The beast bounded ahead toward the first pillar, leaping over their heads with ease, only to lash out at anyone who attempted to pass. When Amice tried to go back the other way, the demon bellowed, the sound like a lion's roar and a woman's scream. Amice froze in his tracks, hands raised in surrender.

The creature emitted another bone-chilling roar when Geoff attempted to sprint through the pillars, bounding toward him with mammoth strides, but it stopped when Geoff turned back and joined the others.

The beast was shepherding them or perhaps guarding them until its hunger returned, keeping a watchful eye to feast upon their marrow one by one.

"What do you want?!" Tomas screamed, his voice so close to breaking that Dietmar wondered how he'd even managed to get the words out. A large stain covered the front of his robes, and he had long since dropped his club.

The demon prowled between the pillars, its claws unsheathed, clicking against the stone floor like the talons of a carrion bird. Dietmar strained to comprehend the full enormity of the creature. It stood as tall as an elephant but longer and just as wide. A serpentine tail curled behind it, swishing through the air like a forked tongue. The demon's face was undoubtedly human, with pronounced cheekbones like those of a Greek statue and a jaw so sharp Dietmar thought it could cut skin.

Tomas screamed again, nearly at the end of his wits, repeating the question over and over until Nicolo placed a calming hand on his shoulder. Geoff and Amice appeared to be summoning their courage for another attempt to break free, encouraging others to join them.

"It can't get all of us," Dietmar heard Geoff say.

But it could.

The beast ceased its prowling, turning its gaze toward them and gradually inching closer.

And then, it spoke:

... EBERU BALATU KEZERU REDITUM SILUM ...

The words resonated like great sandstones grinding against each other, like the voice of the desert and all its misery. Harsh notes that no mortal should ever hear from a mouth that should never speak. Dietmar resisted the urge to scream again.

"It is the Devil's tongue!" Nicolo cried, dropping to his knees and repeatedly crossing himself. He clutched his club and pointed it accusingly at the creature. "Demon! You will not claim my soul. I am promised to the Lord, and no fiend of Hell shall have power over me."

The creature watched him, its golden eyes narrowing as he spoke. Its forked tongue darted from its mouth, hovering in the air as if to taste the words.

"Quiet!" Dietmar commanded, the beast's gaze turning to him. Its pupils were like those of a cat's—thin black slits floating within amber pools. Dietmar locked eyes with the beast, sensing the malevolent intelligence behind its razor-sharp features—an ancient face, as old as the temple they stood in, or perhaps even older.

"It's listening to us," he said softly.

The beast tilted its head at Dietmar's words, its lips curling to reveal the rows of shark-like teeth nestled within its red gums. It was smiling. The beast scratched at the floor, idly brushing away brittle bones. Once the spot was clear, it lowered itself to its haunches and watched them, sitting like a cat in the sun.

Dietmar flinched at the sound of the creature's voice when it spoke again, but this time, he understood the words, if not the sequence they were ordered in.

… FLESH THINGS BE WELL RECEIVED ACCEPTED DELICIOUS TASTY RUNTING OFFERINGS THE DARK CORRIDORS WITHOUT PRIESTS EMPTY COLD BEREFT …

The beast's voice carried a lilting hiss, each word accompanied by a soft purr from the depths of its throat.

… PESKY FLESHLINGS FALLEN THROUGH TOTTERING TWIRLING SLIDING THE WORLD THREAD WELCOME WELCOME QUESTIONS YOU MUST SOLVE PROBLEMS SOLUTIONS YOU PROVIDE TO SAY GOODBYES …

Its tail twitched behind it, gently sweeping across the dusty floor as the creature maintained its unwavering gaze.

"What… what is it saying?" Tomas broke the silence, his voice sounding frail and wispy after the lion-limb's deep draw.

It took Dietmar several moments to piece together what he'd just heard, each passing moment punctuated by the demon's sandstone breath. Then, it clicked.

"It wants us to solve a problem," Dietmar realised.

"A riddle!" Razin exclaimed incredulously.

Nicolo turned to look at him, his hands shaking at his sides. "Or what?"

"What do you *think*?" Geoff growled. "It will eat us. So, how many questions then, demon?"

... ONE ... said the beast, staring down at its footpads. It sheathed its black talons and then slowly unsheathed them again, leaving thin grooves in the stone beneath its feet.

"But we are many," said Dietmar. "Surely, you cannot pin all our hopes on a single riddle?"

I am talking to a demon.

The thing that ate Hemnar and Aimery.

And I am talking to it.

The beast looked up from its paws, a low growl stirring in its chest. ... MANY QUESTIONS SEGMENTED PARTS ONE ANSWER GIVE IT TO ME TRUST OR CHOOSE BUT FAIL TO PICK NO ANSWER TOOTH AND CLAW ...

"I will not," Nicolo declared, suddenly brave. He leaned on his club like a cane and rose to his feet, his hands trembling as he spoke. "I will not be the plaything of a demon! Go back to where you came from, this is the Lord's land, and we are His people! *Sub tuum praesidium confugimus, Sancto Dei Geni*—"

Nicolo's prayer was cut short by Tomas, who clasped his hand over the Keeper's mouth, letting only a muffled curse escape his fingers. Nicolo looked like he'd fight him off for a moment, but then his shoulders slumped, and he lowered his head in surrender.

The creature watched the scene unfold with bored curiosity, its eyes flicking between Nicolo, Tomas, and finally settling on Dietmar, where they lingered, fixed on the hand of St. Ephium still firmly in his grip. It turned its attention back to Nicolo, its black tongue sliding between its sharp teeth like a snake through coral.

... KEEPER KEEPER DO YOU KNOW WHERE YOU ARE ...

Nicolo pushed aside Tomas's hand. "Tell me!"

The creature made another sound, a deep rumbling purr that made its whole body shake. Dietmar braced himself, half-expecting the beast to lunge at them again. But it wasn't preparing for another attack. It was laughing.

"Where are we?" Dietmar stepped forward, momentarily forgetting his fear.

The creature growled, showing its teeth. ... PROBLEMS TO SOLVE SOLUTIONS GIVEN FAIL OR DO NOT FAIL CHOICE TO MAKE ...

"Give us the *cunting* riddle then," said Geoff. "I've had enough of this standing here, waiting to die. Let's hear it before I pass from old age."

The lion-thing rose from its haunches, its talons cutting into the stone as it stood. It flicked aside the cavernous remains of a horse with a swipe of its paw and emitted another low rumble from deep within its chest.

... AS YOU WISH ... it said.

... A BEAST THAT WEARS TWO FACES ...

... BEARS TWO TONGUES ...

... EACH WORD A FORKED PATH ...

... AND FLIES NORTH BUT NEVER SOUTH ...

A silence enveloped the temple as they waited for more. Then Geoff kicked at a bone with his boot and scoffed. "Is that it?"

"How long do we have?" asked Tomas.

The creature blinked. ... NOT LONG ...

When it said nothing else, they huddled in little groups to discuss the riddle. Tomas and Nicolo immediately began to argue, while Geoff and his men were more concerned with how they'd tackle the demon if they failed to find the answer. Liso's cries of pain had ceased when he fell unconscious, either due to shock or someone taking matters into their own hands.

"It can't be a coin." Tomas sighed in frustration. "What coin has two tongues and flies?"

"Then what?" Nicolo waved his hands. "A bird? But what if it's some hell-fiend we don't know of? What then? A *thing* with two faces and two tongues? That doesn't sound like one of the Lord's creations, does it? It might be a hellspawn!"

"It wouldn't ask us that." Tomas glanced back at the creature. "Would it?"

Nicolo scowled. "It is a demon itself! Who knows what it will and won't do? Treachery runs in its veins as thick as oil. Perhaps even if we get it right, it kills us anyway? I wouldn't put it past—"

"Enough," said Dietmar. "We won't get anywhere talking about it. Come, think!" He looked at their faces and then raised a brow. "Where is Razin?"

He felt the cold hand of fear on his chest as he wondered if his friend had fallen to the beast in its mad charge. But Razin stood near the chains of the third pillar, his eyes closed in thought.

"Razin?" said Dietmar, approaching. His friend's lips moved rapidly, repeating something like a prayer. Dietmar paused, listening to the unfamiliar words and recognising them as Arabic. He understood enough now to know that Razin was at prayer but not to Christ.

"Friend," he said, gently touching his shoulder. "We need your wits."

Razin opened his eyes, blinking slowly when he saw Dietmar's face. He frowned. "Nicolo is right. Treachery runs through the *ifrit*'s veins like wine through a king's. It will kill us no matter what answer we give."

"We must still try," said Dietmar, guiding his friend back toward Tomas and Nicolo. "I will not despair in this pagan ruin. Not in front of a demon or ifrit or whatever it is. I will not give it that."

Nicolo had taken to his knees and was using his club to scribble markings on the dusty floor. He wiped his brow and flicked away a bead of sweat hanging from his bulbous nose. The Keeper was not used to such physical exertion, and his breathing had only just returned to normal.

"Maybe a snake?" he said, looking up at Tomas. "I've heard stories about twin-headed snakes with split tongues. Might be that?"

Tomas shook his head. "But does a snake fly north? Unless it's been ensnared by a falcon's talons, I don't think so."

Nicolo contemplated for a moment, tapping his lips. "No, no, not that then… What do you think?"

Tomas shrugged. "That we're going to get eaten by this poxxing thing, and I hope its belly rots when it gets me."

The beast stirred between the pillars, stretching its forelegs and arching its back. Its tail curled around its neck, scratching its face, satisfying an itch while it cleaned off some of Aimery's blood.

"We haven't the time," Dietmar urged, panic stirring in his chest. He wouldn't be buried here, in this tomb, his bones gnawed upon for all ages. "Razin—"

"I do not know," said Razin. He seemed resigned to their fate, ready for whatever came next. Geoff and his men had reached agreement on some plan and were slowly fanning out around the pillars. They'd run for it the moment the creature pounced, trusting in their numbers to spare at least some of them from the fate that befell Aimery and Hemnar.

"So, we have nothing?" Nicolo asked grimly. "No answer?"

The creature unfurled its wings, stretching them fully between the pillars. They were a light grey, with thick feathers as long as Dietmar's arm. Darker fur grew along the ridges of their radiuses, which terminated in sharp, hooked claws like a bat's.

Nicolo bobbed his head excitedly, *hawing* like Balaam as he pointed toward the creature and rose to his feet. "I know! I know!"

"What is it, man?" said Dietmar, but the scriniarius ignored him, marching confidently toward the creature.

... YOU HAVE YOUR REPLY? ... said the beast, gazing down its sharp nose at Nicolo. Its wings extended into the gloom, beyond the reach of their torches. With a single powerful flap, the beast could be in the clouds. Free. And yet it lurked in the shadows of this temple, lost to the world. Dietmar wondered at that, but not for long.

"We do," Nicolo declared, resting his club on his shoulder and tapping his nose with his free hand.

"What are you doing?" Tomas called out. "Come back here, you fool!"

Nicolo waved Tomas away, flicking his fingers dismissively. From his voice, Dietmar could tell he was smiling.

"The answer," he said, "oh, demon from Hell... is *you*. You are the beast in the riddle."

The creature blinked lazily, tilting its head to stare at the Keeper. A curious expression settled on its face.

"The face of a lion and a woman," Nicolo continued, "Two tongues—one in your mouth and the other, your tail, which licks the air like a snake's tongue. And wings! Wings to carry you north instead of south."

The creature purred in delight, its stained teeth forming a jagged smile that stretched to its golden eyes. The slow rumble Dietmar recognised as laughter filled its chest again, making his heart race. The demon unsheathed its razor-sharp talons.

... NO ...

Nicolo's grin began to fade. "It's you! What else could it be? Please... another chance, then? One more, demon." The Keeper took a step back, nearly stumbling as his foot brushed against the crooked spine of a sheep's carcass. He glanced over his shoulder, meeting Dietmar's gaze. "Help."

The creature lunged forward, its mighty wings propelling it off the pillars. Bones and dust and sand sprayed across the floor, swept away by the force of its wingbeats. Nicolo screamed out, then swung his club in a final act of defiance. The blow landed cleanly, connecting with the thing's narrow chin, but the club merely bounced off it, like a stone skipping over water. The impact jolted Nicolo, causing the club to slip from his grasp and fall to the ground.

Before the Keeper could react, the beast was on him. Its hooked talons tore through his tunic, disembowelling him with a flick of its paw. Teeth like broken blades appeared from behind its lips and tore into Nicolo's shoulder, slicing down to the bone. When the creature withdrew its head, Nicolo's arm was gone. Blood fountained from the severed stump, drenching the demon in gore as it swallowed the limb.

Nicolo gazed upon his spilt entrails, his head swaying from shock and blood loss. A soft moan escaped his lips, but it quickly choked in his throat.

Haw.

In the span of a single breath, Dietmar witnessed the end of Nicolo's life. The creature swept him up in its jaws, forcefully thrusting him down its throat without chewing, using its paw to press him inward. It forced the old man down so hard that it seemed like its throat might tear, but then it expanded, like it had before, widening until there was enough space to swallow. Blood and saliva dripped from its lips, cascading down its throat and mingling with its matted coat. Dietmar watched as Nicolo's silhouette descended into the creature's gullet until it disappeared into its belly.

He flinched when something brushed against his shoulder and nearly lunged at it with his sword, only to realise it was Razin. His face had turned ashen, but there was a fire in his eyes now.

"Come, German!" he said, the resignation of before forgotten. "Unless you want to die in this pagan ruin after all?"

He didn't pause for Dietmar's reply, racing toward the shadows to the left of the furthermost pillar. Dietmar followed, seeing Geoff and his men dispersing like a plague of rats, a cat thrown in their midst.

The beast didn't waste time digesting Nicolo, springing forth from between the pillars to pursue its prey. Its horrific mouth bore a gory grin, and Dietmar thought he caught glimpses of Nicolo's fingers wedged between its teeth before blinking away. Somewhere behind him, Liso had started screaming again. He called for help, pleading for someone to save him. As his friends vanished into the shadows, Liso's cries grew increasingly desperate and panicked. Dietmar wanted to block them out, but he forced himself to listen to the man's final moments until the screams abruptly ceased, replaced by the sickening sound of the beast glutting itself on Liso's paralysed corpse.

Tomas stumbled into Dietmar's path, emerging from the shadows alongside Geoff, Amice, and two other men. More screams followed them, and Dietmar saw the beast stalking toward one of Geoff's band, a Dane cornered against the far wall. The man threw his torch at the creature trying to duck past it. But the demon was too quick. It slapped aside the torch and caught the Northman between its teeth. The torch flickered out before Dietmar could witness the man's fate.

They rushed past the last pillar, skipping over the chains and collar Geoff had kicked away earlier. Geoff's men split into three groups, each taking a different path toward the entrance. When Dietmar looked over his shoulder, he could make out their torches bobbing in the dark, the light framing their terrified faces. Every so often, a torch blinked out. Sometimes it was accompanied by a scream, mostly not.

By the time they reached the marble-topped altars, Dietmar couldn't see any more torches. Another piercing scream echoed through the chamber, followed by a low growl that drew nearer. Dietmar hurriedly guided their way between the slabs, clutching his own torch tightly. He'd considered throwing it into the temple and going without it, but the darkness around them was so thick they'd never find their way out again. And besides, if the demon had managed without light before they'd come, it probably didn't need fire to see.

Tomas gasped as a shadow darted beside them, but it was only one of Geoff's men. His tabard was stained with blood, but he appeared unscathed. He slipped in behind Geoff without a word, his eyes wide and staring.

At last, the door before the antechamber loomed ahead, seemingly larger and wider than Dietmar remembered. But surely too small for the beast? He remembered the uprooted trees and stripped trunks outside and felt a black pall cover his thoughts: they would find little safety in the forest.

So, that was it? They would be chased into the night only to be picked off one by one until they were none? Dietmar ground his teeth, gripping Saint Ephium's hand tighter in his own. He had failed. His son would stay in the cold, outside of God's Grace. But what of himself? Consumed by a devil? What waited for him at the bottom of the beast's belly? Would he, too, be damned?

The stink of wet fur and blood filled his nostrils again, just before the beat of the beast's wings drowned out the rest of his thoughts. The creature swept overhead, landing with a crack of splintering stone in front of the door. It extended its sharp talons and turned to face them.

Dietmar slowed in his steps, his mind racing as he searched for a solution to this impossible problem.

Why had the creature spared Aimery for so long?

He felt Tomas's hand on his shoulder, his voice telling him to run back into the temple the way they'd come. He ignored him.

Aimery had gone mad. He'd torn out *his own* eyes and tongue. But he'd been alive… until… until Dietmar had taken Saint Ephium's hand from him. The beast's eyes had lingered on it too. Was it out of curiosity or something else?

He gazed down at the cold relic in his hand, the burning sensation having faded to a subtle tingling, little more than an itch. He returned his gaze to the beast—what had Razin called it? The 'ifrit'? Its eyes were on him again, watching with barely veiled interest—catlike—as he sheathed his sword and raised the relic in his sword-hand.

"Is this what you want?" he called out, approaching the beast with his hand extended.

Tomas called behind him, running forward to pull him back. Dietmar pushed him away. Every fibre of his being was telling him to run, to cower in some dark corner of the temple until the beast was gone. But it would never be gone, though, would it? This was its lair, and it would find them all… unless…

"Come, take it then if this is what you want?"

The creature snarled, its face contorting in an ugly sneer. It didn't pounce, though, or charge across the floor to tear him limb from limb like it had done to the others. Dietmar feigned throwing the hand, stopping just before its release. The demon flinched, shuffling back closer to the door. There was another look on its face now—uncertainty.

"It fears the holy!" Tomas cried. "God's grace, it fears its own damnation!"

"Shut it," Geoff growled, already moving into step behind Dietmer. Amice and the other survivors followed suit, leaving Tomas and Razin to take up the rear.

"Is that it?" said Dietmar, staring at the demon. He took another step forward, bolder this time. "Do you fear your own damnation? Do you fear God's touch?"

The demon shifted uncomfortably on its haunches, visibly edging further away from the door. Saliva dripped from its mouth in streams, mixing with the blood in its fur. It still wanted to eat them, but it wouldn't come any closer. That's why it'd leapt over him to tackle poor Liso—it didn't want to be near the hand.

As they closed the distance, the demon rose to its feet and moved away from the door, leaving it exposed.

"Quickly," Dietmar urged, ushering the small band forward. He let Geoff and Amice lead the way, positioning himself as a guard between their path and the beast. It was licking one of its paws, watching him with its piercing golden eyes. It could crush Dietmar with a single leap, reducing him to nothing more than a stain beneath its paw. But it didn't.

"Who knew such a small thing could cause even a demon to pause," Dietmar said, meeting its stare. He braced himself when the beast lowered its paw, its tongue flicking out from behind its teeth. He half-expected it to speak again, to curse him in its sandstone tongue. Instead, the demon rose to its feet and silently retreated into the shadows of its lair without casting a backward glance.

Dietmar wasn't sure, but he thought he heard the faint rumble of its laughter as it disappeared into the gloom.

11

They burst from the temple as if the Devil himself were chasing them—which he might well have been—their pace unrelenting until they had passed the colonnade and reached the safety of the marble flagstones. Dietmar was thankful once again that he'd not discarded his torch. Night had fallen while they were inside, and it was near as dark in the forest as it was in the demon's lair.

Adelman emerged from behind one of the carts, his gaze fixed on the bloodstained tabards worn by Geoff's men. He glanced past them, scanning the forest with a furrowed brow. "What has happened?" he asked, confusion etched on his face. "Where are the others?"

"There are no others," Geoff snapped, swiftly releasing his horse's reins from the tree where it was tethered.

Tomas shook his head. "Gone to the belly of the beast, God spare them."

"God spare 'em," Amice echoed, clambering onto his horse.

Adelman crossed himself clumsily, watching Tomas as he went to comfort the mules. Balaam and Silensus bumped their heads against his open palms, whinnying softly before looking into the trees. If Dietmar didn't know any better, he would have thought the animals were aware of their master's tragic end. They turned their sorrowful eyes back to Tomas, their ears drooping against their heads.

"Why are we here?" Tomas asked suddenly, his figure dishevelled, shoulders slumped, and fiery red hair clinging to his sweat-drenched forehead. His robes were dirtied and torn at the knees from his earlier fall. His knuckles were white from clenching his hands.

When nobody answered, he asked again.

"I don't know," said Dietmar. A pitch darkness was descending over the sky above them, a howling wind soughing through the forest.

"Is this Hell?" Tomas wondered aloud, crossing himself. One hand rested on Balaam's neck as he stared at Dietmar. Tear lines traced through the grime on his cheeks, his skin pale as milk beneath.

"I don't know," Dietmar repeated. He gazed around him, taking in the pale faces and empty stares of the last remnants of their company. They were looking to him for answers—answers that he didn't have. And if he did know? If he could tell them that they were all damned, would that make it any better? He tried to meet Tomas's gaze, but his friend blinked and looked away.

"If this is Hell, then I would know it," said Tomas, staring into his hands. "Then I can make amends, seek forgiveness for my life of sin. Maybe—"

"Enough," Geoff growled. He dug into his saddle bags to retrieve a flask and then drank deeply. "That's not how it works," he said, wiping dark liquor from his lips. "If this is Hell, then we're in it. Tough. Best get used to the idea. The damned don't get to make amends."

Dietmar tilted his head, listening to the howling wind as it rustled through the trees. It sounded like a voice in pain. A creeping dread spread through him, like venom from sharp fangs was seeping into his veins. Images of Nicolo flashed before his eyes—wide-eyed and terrified, pleading for his life.

Before he was eaten.

Swallowed whole by a mouth with teeth.

He blinked and shook his head, Tomas's voice bringing him back.

"What?" he said, turning to his friend.

"Where do we go now?"

"I don't know," Dietmar admitted, and then louder for all to hear, "But we keep moving." He opened the bejewelled case at the back of Nicolo's cart and gently placed the hand inside, resting it on a bed of red velvet. His eyes lingered on it for a moment, like the creature's had with those golden orbs. He shook his head and closed the lid. There would be time for mourning and reflection later. But first, they had to put this accursed forest behind them.

"Leave them," said Dietmar when he saw Adelman untethering the other horses. Their riders would never return to claim them; the horses would only slow them down. He caught Adelman's expression and sighed. "Fine, untether them, but they have to find their own way."

"What about the carts?" Tomas asked, moving to help Adelman with the horses, limping across the pine needle floor but pausing to look at Dietmar.

"We take them," said Dietmar. Theseus greeted him with a low whinny, shaking his head and stomping the ground impatiently. He wanted to ride. Nicolo had bandaged the wound above his front hoof with linen from his own headwrap, and the horse appeared to be moving without discomfort.

"They'll slow us down," said Geoff, already mounted on his ugly mare.

"We'll need the water," Razin spoke up from his perch atop Riba. He watched the woods with calm detachment and then glanced at Geoff. "That might be all there is in this place. Best we guard it."

"Wherever this damned place is," Geoff spat. He signalled to Amice and the surviving mercenaries. "You heard him. Watch the water, lads. It might be all we get for a while, so treat it precious like, you hear? Right. Now, let's get the fuck out of this forest."

They retraced their tracks through the dense forest, taking it in turns to ride at the front and rear. Without Eudes's keen eyes, Dietmar worried they might get lost in the sea of trees, but Balaam and Silensus dragged them forward, not stopping even when Tomas pulled at their reins. Some instinct drove them, and Dietmar was content to let them guide the way.

The carts rattled and bumped over thick roots and branches, but their journey went without event. And before long, they found themselves on the edge of the tree line. They must have looked a strange sight, Dietmar thought, as they emerged from the forest. A handful of bloodied, wary men, followed by a half-dozen riderless horses, their eyes still searching for their masters. Whatever instinct propelled the mules had motivated them to leave the forest, too, though others had remained, waiting for riders who would never return.

Dietmar stroked Theseus's neck, running his fingers gently through the horse's mane, before turning his attention to his palm. The lingering tingling sensation persisted, though it had faded since he had returned the hand to its box. He turned it over, staring at his knuckles while he wondered at Nicolo's warning.

I shouldn't have touched it. Cursed or not, such a thing might still hold the ill humours that had killed Ephium.

Did I have a choice?

His movements had not been his own. Something had compelled him to reach for the hand, to touch it.

"We need a place to camp," said Geoff as they peeled past the last trees. The ravine rose above them, its tall walls black against the starless sky. "I won't go riding into God-knows-what in the dark. Not after that." The mercenary sucked on his teeth, shaking his head. For a moment, he looked aged, doubt etched into his greying brows and thin lips. "I need to think.

I need to sleep. And I need someplace quiet to take a shit without having to worry I'll be eaten the moment I drop my breeches."

Dietmar turned in his saddle, facing the tired and frightened faces behind him. Tomas had taken to talking to Nicolo's mules, distracting himself with stories while he rode. Adelman had asked about what they'd seen in the temple—about what had happened, but no one was willing to speak of it. He rode in a daze, his hands barely gripping Comus's reins as he watched the shocked figures that were all that remained of the company.

Amice and the three other survivors from Geoff's guard kept together, speaking softly among themselves when they did, and then only in Provençal. Guiscard, the tallest of the four, with a crooked nose and a thief's missing ear, met Dietmar's gaze with cold eyes and snarled something to the others.

They blame him, Dietmar realised. They hold him responsible for all the blood and death that had met them in the temple.

And why shouldn't they?

He had led them down this treacherous path—and if the blame did not fall at his feet, then Gelmiro's. But the Iberian was not here. And he was.

Only Razin seemed at ease. He rode a short distance ahead, scouting the path into the ravine, his head tilted back to look at its walls, scanning the rock for any signs of movement. He had named the demon in the temple… Perhaps he knew where they were? Dietmar decided he would have questions for Razin later, once they'd found a place to settle for the night.

"At the top of the ravine," Dietmar suggested when he realised Geoff was still awaiting a response. "In one of those outcrops we passed coming in. Then, you can squat in peace, and we can all make sense of what we've seen."

"Or try," Geoff muttered, kicking his horse forward.

As they reached the mouth of the ravine, the first stars began to appear above. But no moon. The sky was empty of its radiance.

Even the moon shies away from this place.

"These are not the same stars we slept under last night," said Razin.

"No," Dietmar agreed, glancing up at them. They covered the firmament like pinpricks in a black shroud, allowing faint light to seep in from the other side. In places, they were so densely clustered that he had to avert his gaze, blinking down at the rocky outcrop they'd chosen for their camp.

The strange flowers that blanketed the ravine had multiplied, covering every inch of soil along their path. Tomas had to stop Silensus from eating them, not knowing what they would do to the mule's stomach, but the beast was stubborn and chewed at clumps while it walked.

The outcrop itself was nothing more than an elevated mound crowned with grey boulders that offered enough space to guide the horses. They manoeuvred the carts into a clearing between the largest boulders and tethered their mounts to the wagons. The remaining horses were left to roam freely, though Tomas ensured they were watered and enlisted Adelman's help in grooming them.

They were all more diligent in their duties, Dietmar noticed. Seeing to them with a fastidiousness they had not shown before. They were looking for distractions.

And so am I, he thought, seeing to Theseus—anything to divert their minds from what they'd seen in that tomb of teeth.

They made a small fire in the hollow beneath the rocks, taking turns to keep watch while Adelman and Tomas prepared the meal.

Guiscard and Jehan, a pot-bellied Norman with eyes like black Antwerp beads, ate first and then took the watch. The rest of the company rested on their blankets around the fire, waiting for their dinner. Dietmar sat with his back to the night, listening to Tomas and Adelman bicker over whether the meat was ready.

More distractions.

"This isn't horsemeat," said Tomas, slapping Adelman's hand away. "It needs to sit a while, searing over the fire until it's just right. Then, a dash of black pepper, a pinch of salt, and just the right amount of honey. Fit for a king!"

"I know it's not horsemeat," Adelman grumbled, rubbing his hand where Tomas had swatted him. "I'm the one who paid for it. More than its worth, probably. But where else could I have gone at that hour?"

Odilo, the third of Geoff's men, a dark-haired Lombard, rose from his blanket and crouched by the fire. He sniffed once, then stuck his hand out and plucked one of the still-steaming chunks of meat from the metal plate.

Tomas snorted. "If you want uncooked meat, suit yourself. It'll be your arse shitting rocks tonight, not mine."

Odilo smiled, his teeth surprisingly white and square for one of Geoff's company. "I won't have it ruined with honey. If kings like it sweet, that's their business. But I'm not a king."

"You had me fooled," said Tomas, slapping Adelman's hand once again.

Odilo hissed as he singed his tongue on the meat but let out a satisfied grunt before crawling back to his blanket beside Geoff and Amice to eat.

"I'll have one sweet," said Amice from over the fire. "Already fucked a knight with my knife today, so I fancy I might try eating like a king and see how that fits me."

Geoff laughed darkly from where he lay. "See that it fits you poorly, you cheeky bastard. We've got enough kings here, and I won't bow my head to a cutthroat from Troyes."

Dietmar looked up as Razin appeared at the mouth of the recess, shifting closer to the fire to make room for him.

"Anything?" he asked as Razin sat down.

Razin shook his head, holding his hands out to warm over the fire. "I went as far as the first pebbles of the flat field and then back toward the trees, but I did not see anyone." He paused, frowning. "… or anything. We will be safe here tonight, I think. But tomorrow, we must find water. We had enough to reach Nablus, further now that our numbers have fallen. Still, we will have to fill our skins before finding the road to Antioch again."

His words were matter-of-fact, as if the brutal deaths of a few hours ago were no more than a question of logistics. Dietmar had always envied that about his friend—how easily Razin could forget the blood and chaos of battle. It was a skill he had yet to acquire.

But this was not a war.

That thing in the temple—whether it was a demon, a god, or something else entirely—could not be so easily dismissed.

Yet to contemplate the beast, to consider it for what it might have been, was not something Dietmar was ready to do.

A God.

The casual blasphemy stirred in his mind like a candle in the gloom.

It is no such thing. He shook his head at himself, annoyed by his own thoughts.

"Where will we go?" Tomas asked, offering Dietmar a piece of meat on a small wooden plate and another to Razin.

"North," said Dietmar, grateful for the change of topic. "Then west if we find nothing. Then south and east until we find our way back to civilisation."

"Anywhere but that forest," said Odilo, still chewing on a mouthful of greasy meat.

"Aye. Not there." Dietmar took a piece of bread from Tomas's outstretched hand and broke it in two, handing half to Razin.

They ate in silence for a while, lost in their thoughts, until a cold wind swept through the hollow, spraying them all with dust and ash from the fire. Before Dietmar could curse, Razin raised a fat-stained finger, motioning for quiet. Another gust of wind blew across the mound, slipping into every crack and crevice on its way across the plain. Then, on the edge of the wind, barely audible over the crackling fire, Dietmar heard it—a voice.

He crossed himself as it grew louder, his other hand reaching for his sword on the blanket beside him. He wondered briefly if God would be welcoming to him now that he came driven by fear.

"What the fuck is that?" said Geoff, rising to his knees. Amice, still chewing beside him, had drawn one of his knives and held it ready.

The wind stirred again, and this time Dietmar could hear the voice clearly—a woman's, singing a wordless song into the night, a mournful dirge. Another voice joined hers, deeper and masculine but equally filled with sorrow. They sang together as the wind blew, but their voices never met in perfect harmony, dancing like lovers out of sync. The song was only sadder for it, until it slowly faded with the wind, each voice going its separate way.

"Sumerian demons," said Razin when only the wind remained.

"Those… those were demons too?" Tomas blinked, wiping away the wetness in his eyes. "Why were they so sad?"

"Their curse is to know love," Razin answered softly. They were all listening now. "But to never feel the embrace of the one they love. Nor the warmth of their kiss or the taste of their lips. They are doomed to be apart forever, hearing only the sound of their lover's voice on the wind."

"You named that demon in the temple, too," said Dietmar, watching his friend carefully. "Ifrit, you called it. How did you know its name?"

"I did not," said Razin, shaking his head and meeting Dietmar's stare. He paused, some internal battle going on behind his fierce dark eyes. Then he sighed. "I still do not. Ifrit is not its name but rather what it is. It is one among the jinn, but its true home is Jahannam, where it should be left in chains."

"Jinn?" said Dietmar, not understanding.

Razin flicked the last gristle from his meat into the fire and wiped his fingers on a cloth at his belt before continuing. "According to hadith, such beings serve Iblis—the Devil—in his struggle against man and God."

"There are more of them?"

Razin nodded slowly. "Indeed, but not all of them mean us harm. My people used to worship those who did not serve the Devil. We captured their souls in talismans and charms to harness their protective powers. Some were revered like gods. We carved great idols in their names, erected temples to attract their favour." He waved his hand dismissively. "But that was before the coming of the Prophet. Under Tawhid, such practices are forbidden. We know now there is only one God, and it is to Him we must turn for aid."

"Where did they come from?" Tomas asked, his eyes wide.

"You will not believe me," Razin replied. "And if you do, you will wish I hadn't told you."

Dietmar snorted. "Better to know an ugly truth, is it not?"

Razin turned to him, and there was a flicker of uncertainty on his face. "Not always."

Dietmar held his gaze for a moment before Razin shrugged and stared back into the fire. He tossed a dry twig into the flames, then continued. "They have always been here. But those we see—the ifrits, rassad, *ûs*, marids, and so on—they are the descendants of the first men."

"Men?" scoffed Geoff, looking around the campfire. Amice and Odilo joined him in a contemptuous chuckle, but the others remained still, their eyes fixed on Razin.

"Go on," urged Tomas, huddling deeper into his hood.

Razin threw the last of the kindling into the flame and dusted off his palms before proceeding. "It is said that when Adam and Hawah were cast from Paradise, they were flung from different gates. Adam was thrown from the Gate of Penitence, while Hawah, the Gate of Mercy. They were separated by a great distance and wandered the earth for nearly two hundred years before they were finally reunited at 'Arafat."

During that time, perhaps through loneliness, perhaps out of nothing more than base lust, Hawah bore many offspring from the seed of devils, and Adam begot many children with female jinn. It is their children that prey upon the souls of men, tricking us into misdeeds or the worship of false gods—like the *mušrikūn*, *Quraysh*, and other tribes before the coming of the Prophet."

"Heathens," Geoff muttered, his smile now gone. "So, you expect me to believe that the blood of Adam runs in that *thing*'s veins? That Eudes and Hemnar and Liso died because the first man couldn't keep his cock out of something monstrous?"

If Dietmar had blinked, he would have missed it, but there was a flicker of uncertainty on Razin's face, another rare moment of hesitation.

Even you are lost here.

"I offer a possible explanation," said Razin slowly. "That is all. Whether you choose to believe, that is for you to decide. There are… other possibilities. Those embraced by the old religions—that these entities are gods and we are their creations."

Dietmar took a bite from his bread and washed it down with some wine Tomas had passed around. "These first religions," he said, handing back Tomas's wineskin. "They were like the *Wenden* to the north of my home, yes? Tree worshippers who venerated mad gods and made oaths to demons." He stared into the fire, remembering the hollow looks in the eyes of the knights who had ridden north instead of east, who had fought in the black forests against men who only knew hatred. Those who had made it home had been mere shadows, plagued by nightmares and fits of fear. When he had listened to their stories, he had known that they were not like the tales his father had told him and Huldrych growing up. These were true, and if not true in fact, then they were still the truest things to have ever happened to the men that told them. Experience was funny like that, sometimes. It might not have been actual demons stalking the woods, hunting them, but those men had seen and felt something he couldn't deny. Something he wouldn't dare deny after the temple.

He brushed away the crumbs from his lap and leaned back on his blanket, resting on his elbows. "I have heard tales of *Svetovid*, a four-headed god of war whom the Wends spill blood for. They say he rides with them, driving them into a rage that only human blood can quench. They attack our towns, burn our churches, kill our men, rape our women, and enslave our children. Fighting against them is as worthy as our wars in the Holy Land in the eyes of God, so says the Pope."

Razin shifted beside Dietmar, settling more comfortably on the blanket. "The mušrikūn believed in God. They even accepted that His name was Allah. They were not like your worshippers of Wodin or Svetovid or the gods of the Pharos."

"So, how were they different?"

"Sounds like the same blaspheming shite to me," said Geoff, chewing on his meat. "Who cares what name they give him?"

Dietmar silenced him with a look and waited for Razin to continue. To discuss such things openly was as much as an admission to Islam, and he could see the inner turmoil raging inside his friend.

"We are far from the walls of Jerusalem," said Dietmar softly. "No man will deny you your faith here. And if they try, they will only add me to their list of enemies."

Razin showed his teeth in another one of his rare smiles and then gave him a brief nod. "The mušrikūn worshipped Allah, yes, but it was not the

Allah of Islam. They were guilty of what we call *iftirā ʿalā llāh*: of falsely ascribing things to God. They understood the *nature* of God, but they were misguided, believing that He had partners… children. Who could be worthy of consorting with God? Only another god, they thought. And so they contradicted themselves, worshipping others between us and God—other deities they believed to be intercessors. They thought that by worshipping God's angels, they could draw closer to Him. But in treating those deities as gods themselves, they could not be considered Muslims and were rejected."

"But you do not reject the Christ?" Tomas asked.

Razin shrugged, folding his legs beneath him and staring into the fire as he spoke. "As-Suhrawardi writes that the great religions are all revelations of the same truth. Allah, in His wisdom, saw that there are too many people speaking too many tongues for one truth to be revealed in one place at one time. And so there have been many revelations. You believe in the same God as I do, revealed through your own prophet."

"The Christ is not a prophet," said Tomas sharply.

Razin raised a hand, looking up from the fire. "I meant no offence, friend. But if you did not believe as you do, then you would be a Muslim or a Jew and see the Christ differently. It is no cause for conflict."

"Tell that to the Pope," said Odilo, wiping his greasy hands against his mouth. "If it's no cause for conflict, then why the fuck have we been fighting you lot, eh? It's no game for us, either. I haven't seen Pavia in ten years. I don't know if I'll even recognise it when I do."

"It's 'cause war makes men rich," said Amice. "Or dead. In which case, it doesn't matter if'n you're rich or poor, you shit yourself all the same. Like that pretty knight I put down."

"Shut it, lad," snarled Geoff.

"It's true," said Amice, licking blood off his knife. "Why else would they have us here, fighting over this dirt? You think what's-his-name, *Parinakas*—"

"Emperor Doukas," Dietmar corrected, looking at the former squire in a new light. Not just a knife in the dark, then. He had some smarts to boot.

"Doukas, yeah." Amice nodded, scratching at his chin. He had thin lips and smooth, hairless skin, even after days in the desert. He gave Odilo an ugly look. "You think it's not in his interests to keep the Turks and Syrians busy in the Holy Land? Before we came, all eyes were on him and his. Now they leave the Romei alone and send their armies to fight over Outremer. And what about the Church? Every knight worth his salt mortgaged his lands to pay for his expenses and came across the sea to fight for God. I wager the Church's lands have tripled since Pope Urban sent our fathers and theirs to die here."

"More," said Tomas darkly.

Odilo grunted. "What about the Arabs and Seljuks then? Didn't the Fatamids fight for God before Saladin drove them out of Egypt?"

"They fought for power, too," said Razin. "It was power that made the Shia elders recognise Saladin, a Sunni, as their rightful ruler. And it will be power that drives him into conflict with Jerusalem. Not God. I do not doubt his faith—who am I to doubt the words of a stranger? Only, I would not be surprised if Jerusalem has only survived this long because the Wolf of Damascus likes to keep something between himself and Nur ad-Din. He will only move against the city when his path against his master is secured, not before."

"Bah!" barked Geoff, rising to his feet and stepping over Amice's boots. He unbuckled his belt as he walked. "What does it matter what those kings and sultans do or why they fight? It didn't matter when it was our faces in the shit, and it doesn't matter now. We won't be a part of it, not here beneath these stars that none of us know, listening to *cunting* demons singing in the wind."

He pushed past Dietmar and strode into the night, calling for Guiscard and Jehan. He laughed at something Guiscard said, and then his silhouette disappeared, leaving the night silent once again.

"He's right," said Razin once the stillness had grown deep. He tossed the last bit of his bread to Dietmar and lay back on his blanket, gazing up at the rocky overhang. "Politics has no place here. There are no kings or sultans, only men and their demons."

Dietmar frowned, tearing off a piece of bread and then looking down at Razin. "You said that the beast in the temple should be chained in *Jahannam*. Where is Jahannam?"

Razin blinked back at him. "Jahannam is Hell."

12

Tomas groaned, his eyes snapping open to stare at the stone overhang where he had been sleeping. Of course he needed to piss now, after all Razin's talk of demons and Hell, after seeing one of the Devil's own in the temple and hearing their songs on the wind. If that is what they even were? Demons? The creature had spoken to them, sure enough. But wasn't it the Devil's practice to tempt man into sin? He didn't see how a *riddle of all things* could accomplish that.

It was, he decided, the strangest experience of his life. And also the worst. He would never forget Nicolo's wide eyes staring back at them, his last plea for help… then that giant mouth opening to swallow the little Italian… the running and screaming and pissing—he'd pissed himself but felt no shame. The others had too.

And now he needed to piss again.

He lay still for a moment, hoping the feeling would pass. When it didn't, he swore beneath his breath and got up from his bedroll.

Jehan and Guiscard were sitting by the fire, feeding it from the dried roots and foliage that covered the rock face. Jehan gave him a nod and then whispered something to Guiscard, who turned to stare at Tomas over his shoulder. The Norman had a nose like an eagle's beak, so crooked and bent Tomas wondered if it were any use at all. And only one ear! It stuck out from under his oily black hair like a mushroom. Razin had said it was because he was a thief and a bad one at that. When Tomas had asked how he'd known, Razin had tugged at his one ear and laughed, then told him good thieves don't get caught.

Very funny, Tomas thought, shaking his head as he stepped over the slumbering bodies around the fire. They all looked so peaceful now, mere hours after the horrors they'd survived. But as he picked his way between them, he realised that wasn't true. When he looked closer, he saw that Dietmar was grinding his teeth, a sheen of sweat on his brow. Razin's fists were tightly clenched against his chest, his lips moving. It looked like he was shivering, caught in the midst of some fevered dream.

I'll have to wake them, Tomas decided. *But first, a quiet piss.*

"Don't go wandering far," came a voice from the shadows. Amice emerged from behind one of the boulders, his ugly face in an ugly grin, clearly delighted by the flinch he'd elicited from Tomas.

"I won't," said Tomas, resolving to be braver or at least to hide his fear better. His father had been full of vim and vigour and more courage than any man he'd ever known, so how had he ended up a coward? Had he inherited it from his mother? Was that even a woman's trait? He wasn't sure. He certainly hadn't learned it from her. Meggy had ushered him out from between her legs and through the door in what felt like the blink of an eye. It had been another cold Durham morning, with frost clinging to cobwebs and the morning dew yet to be evaporated by the sun.

"Go follow your father," she'd said, waving him through the door.

"Where?" he'd asked.

But she'd already turned her back on him, busy with his siblings, who were making their best effort to weave between her legs and follow him out. The door slammed shut a moment later, leaving him staring at their small house with its dark windows at the bottom of the street.

He hadn't really known his father back then. In truth, he had never really known the man at all. All he had of him were the stories told by others and a faint memory—an impression of hands, fingers moving in a slow, rhythmic beat against his palms in a gesture, beckoning almost.

He followed the stories.

They led him across England—from Durham to York, into the moors, where he laboured in the Churchyard and learned his letters until his teachers tired of him and he was left looking at yet another closed door. From there, he marched south, toward the bigger cities, until he found himself in the grimy streets of London. It was there he discovered tales of the *Begging Friar* and the *People's March* to the Levant—a pilgrimage his father had embarked on long before the armies of the Pope had stirred to save the Christians in the east.

The first crucesignati had followed Peter the Hermit from Picardy north through the Rhineland into western Germany, where he had raised his flock. Then, with a song on their lips and little more than pitchforks and woodaxes in their hands, they marched east. While the Pope had declared that the armies of Christ would leave for Constantinople on the day of the Feast of Assumption, Peter the Hermit and his ragtag group of clergy, peasants, women, children, and elderly had already embarked on their journey five months earlier, with Tomas's father among them.

In London, Tomas resolved to follow in his father's footsteps, chasing the stories of the man east and to wherever else they may take him—he had already heard tales of a Christian kingdom existing beyond the realm of Outremer, ruled over by a wise and just king, far from the reach of the squabbling Romei and Syrians and Turks.

He thought, somehow, in his foolish youth, that it *might* be him, this mythical king. It might be his father.

In Cambrai, Tomas heard tell of a band of one thousand peasants led east by a holy goose and nanny goat. The beasts had been taken by the holy spirit, he was told, filled with the implacable will to lead a pilgrimage to the Holy Land. Intrigued, he followed their path until the village of *Audignies*, where a sad old man revealed a darker truth. It was not the Holy Spirit that had influenced the animals, but rather the Devil himself. The man had pointed to the sprawling, dark forest behind him and shaken his head. The pilgrimage had come to a horrific end amidst the boughs of those ancient trees—though exactly how the old man wouldn't say.

From Audignies, Tomas walked for a week until he reached Lorraine. There he heard tell of another holy goose leading a poor woman through the city streets until she finally fell to her knees at the foot of the Church's altar and declared herself for God and Jerusalem.

"Even the birds are for Jerusalem!" said the priest who recounted the tale, taking the coin Tomas had offered for a true history of the People's March. Tomas had berated him for trivialising Christian seriousness with such vulgar fables and then told him what he had learned about the fate of the goat and goose disciples from Cambrai, leaving the wide-eyed storyteller behind.

If he could hear my stories now!

Tomas trudged into the dark, lifting his robes to relieve himself.

I've already pissed on myself once today, he thought as he stared up at the sky. It was like looking into a sea of floating torches, each star a blazing, blinking light large enough to put the North Star to shame. And there were so many of them! He'd never seen a night sky quite like it. Wherever he looked, the heavens greeted him with their radiant glow, allowing him to see as far as the ridge of the ravine, even without the presence of the moon. Beyond that, he knew, was the forest's domain and the beast in its temple.

"Poxxing demon," he murmured. Had he really followed his father's path across the world only to be damned to Hell and eaten by a Godless beast? Perhaps that had been his old man's fate as well.

William had bounced from Cologne to Worms, then followed the Rhine eastward toward the Taurus Mountains, where he fought against the Turks and pagans before finally reaching New Rome upon the River: Constantinople. A bemused Alexios had welcomed the ragged band of warrior pilgrims into the city before quickly shipping them across the river to fight his enemies for him. That'd ended poorly.

Tomas's father had been one of the few survivors of the ill-conceived occupation and subsequent siege of the fortress Xerigordo. It was a Greek—Tomas's namesake—who had dragged William from the ruins and carried him to the waiting ships sent by the Romei to rescue them.

Sometime later, William had reappeared in Durham, sired a few children with his mother, and vanished once again. This time, for good. Tomas thought his father might have returned to the Holy Land to finally enter Jerusalem all those years later. But the truth, he knew, was likely less romantic. William had probably died somewhere, succumbing to his final breaths in a muddy ditch or languishing in some poorhouse like Saint Ephium.

Or perhaps he had fallen to Hell, too, like his son. He thought of that gesture once again, that fleeting movement of his father's hands—the only memory of the man he had that was truly his own.

Tomas dropped his robes and blinked up at the sky one last time. It appeared closer here, as though he stood beneath the towering roof of one of the magnificent cathedrals he'd seen in France. Only, the space between the stars *really was* like the sea. It shimmered and swirled, moving gently behind the radiant lights, with varying hues of midnight blue and black fading into one another. He thought he caught a glimpse of a shape moving within that infinite void—none that he could fully describe, staring into all those stars strained his eyes—but he was given the impression of a great form moving behind them, swimming through the sea of night. When he blinked again, the shape was gone, and the swirling pools behind the stars had calmed.

Frowning, he continued to gaze at the sky for a moment longer before returning to awaken Dietmar and Razin from their slumber.

The next day they came upon an oasis and more besides. People.

13

Jehan was the first to spot it, rising in his saddle to stare at the blur nestled between the two hills on the horizon. They had been riding for half a day, heading north, past the stone field and the slope where they had been ambushed the previous afternoon. By midday, they found themselves amidst steep hills much closer in kind to those of old Samaria. The company began to relax, their mood shifting as they rode farther from the temple. Even Dietmar found himself easing into the idea that they might not be so lost after all.

"*Veder*!" Jehan called, his paunch slumping over his belt as he turned to wave excitedly. "Look, *cavaller*! Water!"

Dietmar shielded his eyes with a hand and squinted at the haze, blinking as he tried to make out what Jehan had seen. The slopes curled around a flat basin in the distance, forming a valley dotted by scattered bedrock and clusters of bushes with yellow-tipped leaves.

"More blasted trees," muttered Geoff, curling his lips in disdain. "We're not going there. I don't care if it's the waters of Paradise that gives them life. I won't go."

"Easy, boy," Dietmar said softly, patting Theseus gently before leading him up the slope for a better view. Razin nudged his own grey mount up the hillock to join him, the nimble Arabian navigating the landscape with ease. The blurry outlines became clearer from their vantage point, and Dietmar was able to make out the bending silhouettes of palms thickly clustered between the hills. Light shimmered off a flat pan in the centre of the trees, like the sun from his chainmail.

"If this is Hell, it's not what I expected," Dietmar commented as Razin came to a rest beside him.

The lack of fiery pits and eternal pain had not disappointed him, but still… there were demons here.

"What do you see?" called Tomas from his seat. Balaam and Silensus were slowly dragging the cart leftward, heading toward a small bush covered with hoary red bulbs. Tomas tugged at their reins, but to no avail.

"Trees," Dietmar called back. "But only a few, not like before. These are—" He paused, his eyes narrowing as he caught movement at the foot of the tallest hill. Razin had noticed it, too, and leaned forward to stare. Together, they watched as the movement grew bolder until the outlines of horses and their wagons became visible, making their way along the ridge toward the shade of the trees.

"A caravan," said Razin, just as Jehan and Guiscard reached the same conclusion, chattering excitedly in Provençal and pointing toward the figures in the distance. More figures emerged, tiny specks of white and yellow and red beneath the hills, but all converging toward the trees.

"A strange sort of Hell," remarked Dietmar, turning Theseus back down the slope.

Razin grunted, watching the figures a moment longer. "It would not be Hell if it were not populated by the damned."

The caravan, it turned out, was not just one but three separate trains moving toward the palms. The distances between them had appeared smaller from the slope, but as Dietmar and the remains of his company neared the closest caravan, he saw that the other two were barely within hailing distance. They rode nearer to the hills, coming toward the hollowed-out basin from the north.

Riders from the nearest convoy peeled off from the carts when they spotted their approach, eyeing them wearily from behind their headwraps and mail coifs. Amice waved at them, opening his hand in friendship while he gripped one of his knives behind his back.

"Peace, friends," Geoff called out, riding a little ahead. "We are of Christ but would break bread with any we find in this strange land."

The first of the riders pulled down his mail coif, revealing a bearded mouth and the olive skin of a Turcopole. He raised an eyebrow at a *haw* from Balaam, then looked past Geoff at the small column of riders and riderless horses behind him. Raising his other brow, he asked, "Where are you from, and where are you headed, friends?"

"Jerusalem," said Dietmar, coming up alongside Geoff. "And we make for Nablus, and then Antioch. We were no more than a day's ride from Nablus when the storm…."

The rider nodded, waving his hand in a wide gesture. "It dragged us from our path too. We are heading to Arsuf, but we cannot find the road. My master's tongue grows sharper with each hour that we are lost."

Geoff shifted in his saddle, exchanging a meaningful glance with Dietmar before leaning forward. "Have you… seen anything?"

A beast of carrion.

Those wings and talons. How could a God look thusly?

Dietmar shook the images from his head and watched the turcopole closely. The rider seemed to notice Guiscard and Jehan's bloody tabards for the first time, misunderstanding Geoff's meaning. "Raiders?" he asked, looking pointedly at Guiscard's stained colours. "We have travelled unmolested, but these are troubling times indeed if Saracen raiders ride so close to the Pilgrim's Road."

Dietmar nodded, urging Tomas and Adelman forward before turning back to the rider. "Aye, we were attacked. But not by Syrians. They were Frankish raiders looking to settle old scores from Jerusalem. They won't be harrying us again."

"Franks?"

"Buried in the sand behind us now."

But not all.

The headless man had gone someplace… else.

"You haven't seen anything else, then?" asked Geoff. His ugly horse lumbered forward a pace, sniffing at the Turcopole's mount. "No beasts or their spoor in this damned place? Or anything… odd?"

"Nothing," said the rider, distracted by a call from his caravan. A fat man stood on the back of one of the wagons, sticking his head out from behind the canvas to bellow at his servant. The rider let out a frustrated sigh and then looked apologetically at Dietmar. "My master requires my attentions. But come, join us. I would hear of your travels and the Franks who attacked you. We are headed the same way for now. Why not share our path a time?"

The rider's name was Samael. His master, a fat dyer from Tiberias with the name of Levi, welcomed them into their convoy with a jovial clap of his hands. "Good to have some more swords around! Our convoy should bristle like a Romei porcupine, ha ha!" The skin around his neck wobbled as he spoke, swollen like a toad's. "Our Samael and Erasmus know their way around a blade, but they're no men-at-arms." He gave Dietmar a knowing look. "Between you and me, I think they'd flee at the first sign of Saracens, eh, Samael? Isn't that right?"

Samael pursed his lips, exchanging a pained glance with Dietmar. "No, master."

Levi chuckled, his body shaking as he rocked on his heels. He wiped his mouth, closing the gaping wet chasm with the back of his hand, then nudged open the canvas door of the wagon with a shoulder.

"Come, my little lambs, meet our new escort," he beckoned, clicking his pudgy fingers into the darkness, then turned to eye the heraldry on Dietmar's tabard. "With any luck, that's the only wolf among your number, eh? These fragile flowers aren't for the plucking!"

"Hear that, Amice?" said Geoff, winking at the squire. "I'll cut your balls off if you touch good ser Levi's daughters. Keep your filthy hands to yourself."

Amice snarled, his mouth a knife wound across his face. But then he laughed, his eyes creasing as Levi's flowers timidly emerged from the wagon.

"Enough, lad," Geoff said with a snort, barely able to contain his own grin.

If Levi's two daughters were flowers, they had long since wilted. Their thick locks were tightly wound in buns atop their heads, mimicking the courtly fashion. But this only accentuated their heavy brows and strong, sharp chins. They had inherited their father's thick neck and round nose, but their freckles seemed to be a trait from their mother, adorning their faces in splotches.

"How do you do," said Dietmar, ignoring Geoff and Amice's suppressed laughter. The girls smiled back at him, fluttering their lashes like hummingbirds. Their father clicked his tongue and pushed them back behind the flaps, then wagged a finger at Dietmar. "I won't have you wooing them, knight. Not them, my pride and joy. I won't have my lambs taken by a wolf and his cross."

Dietmar blinked, then inclined his head. Levi's jovial demeanour had given way to iron, if only for a moment. "Your daughters have nothing to fear from me, on my word as a knight."

The dyer looked nonplussed by the oath, shaking his head.

"I have had a wife," Dietmar continued, "and shall have no more."

Levi clicked his tongue again, and a moment of understanding past between them—one not defined by their differences but by shared horror. The flint in his eyes diminished, giving way to something softer once more. "My condolences, knight. One is enough for most men. My precious would haunt me from the grave if I ever chose to pursue another after her passing. She haunts me enough while still in the land of the living, ha ha! Her and my sweet petals."

Dietmar lifted his head to survey the other three wagons in Levi's caravan. They were large, two-horse wagons with closed canvas canopies, hiding the contents within. A ragged band of drivers had taken the pause to water the horses and to check the fastenings of the coverings. They cast veiled glances at Dietmar and his companions, conversing quietly among themselves as they moved about.

"Mordants and fabrics," Levi answered before Dietmar could ask. "We had some cured meats too, but my little flowers ate those on the first night. *Kevashim r'avim*! Ha ha! Ah, but the good folk of Arsuf have a liking for my linen, so here we are."

Levi laughed again, his broad shoulders heaving with his booming voice. "Have to get there first, though. Don't we?" His shoulders sagged slightly as his laughter faded. He glanced over his meaty arm toward the darkness of his wagon and then frowned at Dietmar. "I'm not sure my little lambs are made for travel. And I'm certainly not made for listening to their constant voices neither. But come, let's see what we can hear from those gathering amidst the palms. Maybe they've seen a road we haven't yet come upon? Or perhaps I can find a couple of *Yehudi* brave enough to marry my daughters, ha ha!"

Dietmar met Levi's grin with a smile of his own, then turned his attention to the distant silhouettes making their way toward the trees, tracing their path. He couldn't make out any ruins or temples from where he sat, and the figures moving beneath the ridges didn't look like the damned either. He glanced back at Levi, the dyer's wet eyes rolling at the sound of his daughters' voices in the wagon behind him. If Hell for Levi was a journey with his two girls, then that wasn't so bad a thing.

***

"Their mother's waiting for us in Tiberias," Levi said, walking alongside the wagon. "She thought it'd be 'valuable' if Sara and Miriam saw what their *Abba* does. She thought they'd treat what they have more preciously if they knew what went into filling their bellies with puddings and tarts. She was wrong, of course. And I told her as much, but…" Levi shrugged, parsing his hands toward the line of wagons. "I think she just wanted them out of her hair, a little peace and quiet while we put ourselves at risk. When the storm hit, I thought they might realise the dangers that dog my steps, but before the dust had even settled, I heard their shrill voices—bless them—already complaining. Perhaps some of your men could entertain them with stories of their exploits? Put some fear into their little hearts, eh? Mind you, not too much. I'd never hear the end of it."

"You saw nothing in the storm? No men or riders… or anything else?" Dietmar walked Theseus by the reins, keeping pace with Levi as the wagons rumbled over the sand beside them. Clusters of grass dotted the ground, growing around patches of dark rock and stone. Hardy, grey bushes stood like sentinels across the basin, growing taller as they approached the oasis.

"Sand and more sand. Oh… and even more sand, ha ha!" Levi's chin wobbled as he appraised Dietmar. "I'd quite like to know how your men bloodied themselves too. I'm starting to suspect it's not a story for my girls, eh?"

"They wouldn't believe it if I told them," said Dietmar, leading Theseus around a mound of tall grass. He watched Tomas and Adelman's carts as they rolled past. He could feel Levi's eyes upon him as he walked. His curiosity was piqued.

"We were set upon by raiders from Jerusalem. That much is true," Dietmar explained. "They took something from us and vanished into the storm. We tracked them from the dunes into a ravine, which led us to an ancient forest with towering trees as grand as David's Tower."

"Trees? In Samaria?" Levi snorted. "You're right. My daughters wouldn't believe you."

"Aye, but that's not the worst of it. We found an old temple in that forest—a Roman ruin, or maybe something from before. The raiders had disappeared inside, so we followed them and finally took back what was ours. But... some beast now calls that temple its home. Or maybe it'd always been its home? The Romans might've built the walls around the demon to house it... and then worship it."

Levi crinkled his brow, half-smiling, unsure if Dietmar was serious or not.

"It hunted us," Dietmar continued. "It killed half our number and whatever was left of the knights who stole from us."

"A lion, perhaps? One of the last—"

Dietmar laughed loud enough for Tomas to turn back on his cart and stare.

"That was no lion," said Dietmar when he was done laughing. "Though it had some of the makings of one: claws as sharp as Simeon's sword, paws as thick and heavy as a mason's hammer, a cavernous mouth... but mere beasts have no malice or hatred in their eyes when you stare into them. No, madness is the realm of man and demon, and I assure you, it was a demon as surely as I am here walking with you now."

Wherever we are.

Levi cast a nervous glance over his shoulder, as if the demon might be on their heels even now. He wiped his eyes with his palms and frowned. "How did you manage to escape then? If this *mazzikin* is as cunning and cruel as you say?"

Mazzikin... ifrit... demon... so many names for horror.

"It let us go," Dietmar replied after a brief pause. He wondered how much to share with Levi. The dyer had an honest face, but so did all the best liars. "We... bargained with it, promised not to return while it ate its fill on our dead."

Levi shook his head. "A bargain with a demon, my friend. This is no tale for my girls."

"No, I suppose not. But it is the truth." Dietmar said, watching as Samael and Geoff entered the shade of the first palm trees. Riders from the other caravans cautiously approached, calling out to each other in various languages—French, German, Arabic. Dietmar turned back to Levi, seeing the doubt writ upon his round face. "Ask your Samael how it is he came to be lost. He may not realise it, but he must suspect something. We are no longer in Samaria, not since the storm."

Levi grunted, quickening his pace across the sand. He cast a backward glance at Dietmar. "I do not think you lie, knight. But let's first hear the news from the other caravans, eh? Perhaps before I tell my daughters we have lost ourselves in a place filled with demons. I can already hear their shrill voices in my head. I'd prefer they didn't grow any louder."

***

The shimmering basin that Dietmar had seen from the slope revealed itself as a tranquil oasis of water nestled amidst the palms.

"I don't see any river," said Razin, walking beside Dietmar and Tomas. "It must be filled by an underground reservoir."

"Or the Devil's piss," said Tomas.

Dietmar chuckled. "Does that look like piss to you?"

Tomas shook his head. The water was clear and deep, its bottom hidden from view. Small pebbles, similar to the ones they had encountered on the plain, covered the wet soil surrounding the basin. Veins of pondweed and creeping reeds grew in the shallows alongside water lilies and white-flowering crowfoots. Horses from one of the caravans were already wading into the pool, their riders standing by in the shallows, filling their waterskins.

Geoff and Amice stood near the sandbank, kicking at pebbles while keeping a watchful eye on the riders from the last caravan as they passed between the trees. They rode smaller horses, like Razin's, and wore long-sleeved chemises beneath coats of studded leather, turban-wrapped helmets, and quilted aketons.

Their shields were round.

"*Saracens*," snarled Geoff, motioning to Guiscard and Jehan, who were tending to their horses. Samael was already fingering the hilt of his sword, whispering to Levi as he watched the Syrian riders nervously.

"Let's settle down," said Levi, still untethering the horses from his wagon. "I won't have blood spilt in front of my girls unless it is absolutely necessary. Besides, they don't look interested in a fight, do they?"

Guards from the Syrian convoy came to a halt on the other side of the pool. One of them, a short, stubby figure with a long beard and a bright red turban, raised a hand and inclined his head in greeting. Levi returned the gesture, speaking quietly from the corner of his mouth while he waved. "They're likely just as lost as we are. Let's not bloody the only water we've come upon, eh?"

"You look after yours; I'll look after mine," said Geoff. He turned away from the rider, making eye contact with Levi before shrugging. "But we won't start anything, not unless we're provoked. How's that?" He flashed his yellow teeth when Levi nodded and turned back to monitor the Syrian convoy.

"It'd be a poor fight for us anyway," said Dietmar, counting the warriors riding alongside the Syrian convoy. He'd counted ten already, and more were emerging from the trees behind them. Unlike their own caravans, the Syrians did not have carts or wagons. Instead, they had loaded crates and panniers onto nearly a dozen sturdy horses, resembling Dietmar's destrier more than the Arabian foals. Robed figures walked alongside, shouting in Arabic when the horses strayed.

Just how big was that storm? Dietmar wondered. For it to have dragged in a Syrian caravan, it must have stretched far indeed.

Dietmar turned at a curse from Tomas and watched as he tried to coax the now unharnessed mules toward the pool. Balaam brayed, showing his block teeth and stomping the sand with his front hooves, refusing to budge.

"Stubborn bloody donkeys!" Tomas exclaimed. "Don't come hawing at me when you're thirsty later, then. It'll be your own damned fault."

The riderless horses that had followed them from the forest splashed into the pool, quenching their thirst and finding relief from the heat in the cool shallows. Some ventured further in, wading deeper until the water reached their necks. Dietmar looked down at his own dusty vestments and sand-washed skin. It'd take more than water to wash the filth that coated him. After the temple, he felt dirty inside too.

I'll need to rinse my soul, he thought.

Samael and another guard from Levi's caravan led their own mounts to drink while Levi and his daughters watched from the shade of a nearby palm. Guiscard and Odilo were busy talking to a man from one of the other caravans near the shallows. From the looks on their faces, there was no good news.

"Let's find out what he knows," said Dietmar, leading his horse toward the reeds. "At worst, we'll learn which way they've already explored and isn't worth following ourselves."

Amice chortled. "If you think that's the worst he could tell us, you weren't in that buggered temple with us when the mad thing got loose and ate half our faces off."

"Shut it, lad," said Geoff.

But the boy was right.

"They don't know shit either," said Guiscard at their approach. The big Frenchman thumbed his lips, scratching at a scar on his mouth. "Tell 'em what you told me, Anjier."

Anjier, a guard from the second convoy, took a sip from his waterskin and studied Dietmar while he drank. He stood tall, like Guiscard, but their similarities ended there. Anjier had narrow shoulders where the Frenchman's were broad as a bull, and a weak chin with a small mouth that gave him the appearance of a petulant child. He blinked his heavy-lidded eyes at Dietmar, then motioned toward the carts of his own caravan. One particular wagon stood out—it was larger than the rest, adorned with gilded accents and silk blue curtains. A glimpse of a face peered out from behind the curtains before quickly retreating.

Royalty, Dietmar thought.

It didn't mean anything to him. Some lord or lady lost out here with the rest of them. They wouldn't be afforded any privileges. Not from him.

Anjier corked his waterskin and disappeared it into the folds of his burnous. "We were three days on the road to Jerusalem when the storm hit. The moment it cleared, I knew something wasn't right. I couldn't see the mountains anymore, for one. Then, when night fell, I didn't know any of the stars either. 'Course, I couldn't admit that to the little princess. Her mother'd cut my balls off if I scared her. Still, she started asking questions I couldn't answer. It wasn't long before we all knew we were lost, even her."

"Where are you from?" Dietmar uncorked his waterskin and made his way toward the pool, leaving Geoff in charge of Theseus. He gestured for Anjier to join him.

"Galilee," said Anjier, following him onto the soft sand around the basin. "We are escorting the Lady Marie to Jerusalem to join her mother, the Lady Eschiva. Then I'm taking my coin and heading for Jaffa and home. I've had enough of the East, I reckon. I'll join my father in his fields in *Guérande* a while and then see what *Nantes* has to offer."

"There's always room for a man and his sword in Nantes," Dietmar said. He had spent some time in the city as a boy, visiting his cousins and drinking enough wine to sink a ship when he wasn't out riding with them. Brawls were a common occurrence, moving from one tavern to another like a relentless tide that only subsided with the morning light when sober minds prevailed. "A man with experience could charge what he wishes and get it too." He knelt by the basin, splashing at the shallows with his hand. The water was cool, kept chill by the shade of the palms and the deep underground reservoir it came from.

"I'll be glad to be rid of this place," Anjier confessed.

"Aye," said Dietmar. "It spits you out after a time, like a piece of chewed-up bone."

"Your man mentioned that you're also heading home?"

Dietmar nodded. "Once we reach Antioch."

"Seems a strange route you're taking. Why not cross from Jaffa or Acre?"

Dietmar lowered his skin into the water, filling it as he watched Adelman lead Comus into the pool. The big Percheron plucked a clump of riverweed and began chewing on it while Adelman fussed over him.

"We have business in Nablus," Dietmar explained, glancing up at Anjier. He liked the Norman. He was blunt and to the point, with a carefree attitude that reminded him a little of Gelmiro. He decided to tell him a little more. "We are not without enemies in Jerusalem. Some would have seen our journey cut short. They might've stopped us in Jaffa. We thought the road might serve us best."

"And how's that going for you?" Anjier coughed into his hand and wiped his mouth, frowning at his palm.

"Ho!" called Adelman, splashing in the water and waving. "Look, in the reeds!"

Dietmar rose to his feet and followed Adelman's extended hand into a dense thicket of river reeds and pondweed. A shape lay concealed within the stalks, covered in silt and grime.

"What is it?" Anjier winced as he coughed again and took another sip from his skin to soothe his throat.

"I don't know." Dietmar took a step toward the foliage, raising his waterskin to drink from. Anjier hacked out another cough behind him, and he paused. It sounded wet, like it came from deep in his lungs. He knew that kind of cough; it usually ended in a gargle. He hesitated, lowering his waterskin without taking a sip and turned back to look at Anjier.

The Norman was staring into his hands.

They were covered in blood.

"Don't drink the water!" Dietmar roared, flinging his waterskin into the shallows. It sank with a hollow *plop*, disappearing into the murky depths. Dietmar waved at Adelman. "Get out! Get out!"

Now Anjier was coughing up his lungs, his blue eyes turning red and swollen as he gasped for breath. Others had started coughing too, and Dietmar saw the same scene unfold on the other side of the bank, where the Syrian convoy was resting. Men clawed at their throats, falling into the shallows to drown and die. One of the horses reared up, kicking its hooves in panic, blood frothing at its mouth.

Dietmar looked away, shielding his face from the spray caused by the dying mount's frightened throes. His eyes caught on something in the reeds, floating out from between the stalks now that the water had been disturbed. It was a sign—a wooden board with stained words, black ink dripping into the water.

He had seen it before.

Leave him

What?

"Get out of the water, you fool!" Tomas stormed toward the shallows, lifting the hem of his robes to wade in before Razin pulled him back, shaking his head.

Adelman yanked pitifully at Comus's reins. The horse had gone too deep, nearly up to its neck. The Percheron's nostrils flared as it pushed through the mud and weed.

It's too late, Dietmar thought. *It will have drunk its fill already.*

But he couldn't bring himself to tell Adelman to abandon the horse.

Comus whinnied in pain and stopped where it stood, still shoulder-deep in the water. Then it heaved itself forward, managing another step before hesitating, as if its hooves had caught on something beneath the surface. The water around it rippled, rolling out in a small tide, like an air bubble in the underground reservoir had finally been expelled.

Balaam let out a loud *haw*, causing Dietmar to flinch as he watched the horse struggle. Comus stared at the water around him, turning his great head from side to side, breathing in huge lungfuls of air.

Another wave swept over the shimmering waters toward the shoreline. Adelman let out a cry and dropped Comus's reins, half-running, half-swimming back to the shore. A shadow moved over the pool, following the wave like the tail-end of a lash.

Not a shadow, Dietmar realised. Something oily and long, moving impossibly fast.

There was something in the water.

Adelman cried out again, half-collapsing in the shallows, dragged down by his wet clothes. He stared back at the frothing waters around Comus, frozen in fear by the bubbling pool.

"Fuck," said Dietmar, crossing himself before striding into the water to retrieve Adelman. Water flooded his boots, squelching between his toes as he marched out. It felt warm against his skin, like the dozens of bodies in it had left some of their own heat in the chilled pool. Balaam was *hawing* incessantly now, his voice a panicked

haw haw haw

Dietmar sniffed the air, his brows knitting together as he waded into the basin. It smelled like smoke. Like ash and cinder. He thought of the mad Frenchman in the Street of Herbs and his raving rant about Old Tirus puffing smoke into the world. He had said they would all be damned, that the great serpent would wrap its body around the city, and eventually the world...

—where are you going, Chevalier?

The words appeared in his mind like a soft whisper, spoken in a voice he didn't recognise. He frowned, shaking his head. It was the same voice that had told him not to toss the hand aside in the temple before the demon emerged. It was laughing.

He had forgotten.

But now he remembered.

He ground his teeth and splashed toward Adelman, ignoring the mocking laughter that lingered in the back of his mind.

Comus grunted loudly, the sound like a broken horn. The horse managed another slow step forward and then stopped, swaying in the mud.

Dietmar blinked.

The water surrounding the horse began to steam, vapours rising like fumes from a boiling pot.

Get out! Get out! Get out!

Tomas shouted something from the shore, but before Dietmar could turn, the water around Comus exploded.

Smoke and water erupted from the basin, revealing a shimmering black body with coils as wide as Dietmar was tall. The oily appendages, dripping with water and slime from the depths, wrapped themselves around Comus and began to constrict.

Another devil.

Dietmar nearly pissed himself again when he saw the head of the beast.

It slid out of the water like a blade from its sheath, rising slowly to stare at the thrashing equine in its coils. Red eyes glowed from the top of its serpentine skull, as bright as torches in the noonday sun. Serrated scales covered its flat face, and a row of jagged gills flared at its neck. A long black tongue slithered out from its mouth, mingling with the billowing smoke that continued to pour forth like a furnace in full blaze.

The snake tasted the air.

Comus gave another desperate kick, one last attempt at breaking free from the serpent's grasp, but the creature's grip was so tight that the motion barely registered in the water.

A demon in the water.

Old Tirus.

It will eat us all.

But only if we let it.

Dietmar snapped his eyes away from the beast and grabbed the moaning Adelman by the shoulder, hauling him up from his knees. There were enough dead men here already, and Dietmar was determined not to add to their number.

"Lean against me," he urged, pulling Adelman by the waist. The old man complied, his grey head rocking on his shoulders like a puppet, his wide eyes still on the serpent.

Anjier lay in a heap near the reeds on the sandbank while other bodies—horses and men—lay scattered in the shallows, their faces purple and bloodied. Razin and Tomas were calling for Dietmar, imploring him to get out of the water.

Where else am I going to go? Back toward the giant snake that could eat him whole in one bite? He glanced back at Comus, half-carrying Adelman over his shoulder while he lumbered up the bank. The water surrounding the serpent had turned red with blood and bubbled like the hot springs beneath the caravanserais in Constantinople.

The snake had its jaws firmly wrapped around Comus's head, its massive fangs sunk deep into the horse's neck, spilling its lifeblood across the basin. A crooked fin protruded from the serpent's back, like a malformed vulture's wing. It fluttered as the creature fed, momentarily rising out of the water, stretching its membranous webbed flap.

This fucking thing better not fly.

But there was only one wing. Crooked and bent.

For a second, Dietmar thought about wading back into the pool to strike the beast while it was encumbered, to stick his sword into one of its great glowing eyes and avenge Comus and Anjier and Paul of Balata.

I would die here.

Then who would avenge me?

The serpent twisted in the water, forcing Comus deeper into its gaping maw, its massive scales undulating as it devoured the horse.

Dietmar felt a hand on his arm, and then another as Razin and Geoff lifted Adelman's weight from him.

"Another *cunting* demon," snarled Geoff as he helped them back onto the sand. "And this one's poisoned the only water we've found in this damned place."

"No," said Dietmar, brushing away their hands to stand alone. He sucked in a deep breath, his gaze fixed on Tomas guiding Adelman toward their carts. Then, he turned his attention back to the basin. "Paul did this. He poisoned the well: Jacob's Well." He pointed to the sign still floating near the reeds. The shape entwined by the weeds and mud had come undone, loosened by the waves. It hung out in the water.

A body.

Bloated and green, with a shorn head and scars that covered its skin.

Geoff growled, muttering something about devilry, and shook his head. "How'd he get here? And Jacob's Well? We're a long way from Nablus, I thought we'd all agreed?"

"I don't know," replied Dietmar. His eyes followed the serpent's writhing form as it swallowed the last remnants of Comus. He could just make out the shape of the massive Percheron as it made its way down the snake's digestive tract, motionless as it passed from one end to the other. Dietmar's lips curled as an idea formed. "What if this is the other end of Jacob's Well?"

Geoff stared at him blankly.

"This water comes from somewhere, doesn't it?" Dietmar continued.

"An underground reservoir," said Razin.

Dietmar nodded. "What if that reservoir feeds into this basin and the well? Maybe into more places besides? Paul warned us about the beast in the well. What else could that be?"

"For fuck's sake," said Geoff. "You think we can just follow the reservoir, and it'll lead us to Nablus, then?"

“It is not so simple,” said Razin, pausing to think. “We are not on the same plane as Nablus. But perhaps the well is like a bridge, and the *Falak* found it?”

“Falak?” Dietmar put a hand on his sword. It looked like the creature, this ‘Falak’, was done with Comus. If it were anything like the ifrit in the temple, it would be far from satisfied.

“Later,” said Razin, watching the serpent move toward the body of one of Anjier’s caravan. It showed no interest in savouring the corpse, instead swallowing it whole before moving on to the next.

Dietmar followed Razin and Geoff back to their horses, mercifully untouched by the toxic waters of the oasis. Tomas had shoved Adelman onto the back of his cart and was busy attaching Balaam and Silensus to their straps. The mules had known something was wrong. They’d sensed the evil in the water.

The Syrian caravan had already departed, leaving their dead where they lay. Anjier’s convoy lay in the sands and shallows, resting beneath the palms peacefully, as though in sleep. Only the blood and vomit that covered their mouths gave it away.

“I believe you!” called Levi, clambering onto his own wagon. “Come, knight! We will wait for you, but we must leave this place. Your Tomas was right. It is the Devil’s piss in there.”

14

"God's teeth, is every corner of this place inhabited by another *cunting* thing that wants to eat us?" Geoff scowled at the sky, slumping in his saddle as they rode away from the oasis.

Tomas crossed himself, sparing Adelman a glance as he made the motions with his hand. The old man lay shivering in the back of the cart, sniffing and snorting into the sleeve of his damp tunic.

"That was a bad bit o' business," said Amice. "Woulda come pretty close to seeing if I shit myself when I go there, eh, Geoff? Those lads from the other caravan didn't make much of a mess, though, did they? They just crumpled in on themselves like they were going to sleep." He had been halfway through his first sip of water when Anjier started choking. Geoff had shoved his fingers down the back of his throat so hard it looked like he'd blacked out for a minute. But then the captain's dirty fingers had forced the water up from his stomach, along with the remnants of his breakfast. Dried flecks of vomit still covered the neckline of Amice's greying tabard.

Geoff scratched his chin, peering between the hills they were moving into.

"You can count your luck I only had to finger your throat," he said, glancing back from the slopes. "If it'd been that serpent coiling around you, you can bet that pretty knife of yours I would have left without a second thought. You can carve yourself out of that one's belly, like Jonah."

"I reckon you and Odilo would have come to my rescue. Ain't that right, Odilo?"

The Pavian shook his head.

Amice chortled. "Don't be shy. I know you wouldn't leave your good mate to be eaten."

"Like we left the others?" Odilo snapped.

Amice sighed. "Don't be such a blackheart. What's with you Pavians? Always in a dreary mood. No time for laughter back home? Or is that why you won't laugh, because you miss your home?"

"Aye," Odilo replied sharply. "I miss home, and I miss the quiet, but most of all, I miss not *being fucking eaten by fucking demons*, you cunt."

"Woah, woah." Amice raised his hands, his lips pulled back in a servil's grin. "No need for that. We're all friends here, aren't we? Looking after each other and all, like Geoff when he tugged at my tonsils. I'd have done the same for you, you know?"

Odilo snorted. "Sure you would have. And checked my pockets while you were at it."

"Watch it," Amice warned, still smiling. There was a glint in his eyes now. His hand inched closer to the knife at his belt.

"Whatever," said Odilo, not meeting Amice's stare.

Dietmar listened to their squabbling a little while longer until Amice's veiled threats became too much for Geoff. He barked at Amice to shut up and sent him to ride at the back of the convoy with Jehan. Dietmar shook his head and urged Theseus forward, passing Levi's wagon and the other carts with their ashen-faced drivers.

"So, Hell, then?" said Dietmar, riding up alongside Razin.

His friend nodded once, then let out a long breath as his eyes swept the slopes on either side of them.

"It is Hell or someplace in-between." He rested a hand on his saddle horn and gave Dietmar a sideways glance. "The body in the basin…"

"It was Paul, wasn't it?"

Razin nodded.

"How?" Dietmar stared up at the dark slopes and then brought his eyes back to Razin, who remained sitting quietly.

He doesn't know either, he realised.

Of course he doesn't. How could he?

"It was witchcraft, wasn't it?"

His friend regarded him for another long moment and then sighed. "It might have been a *qareen*, which is magic of a sort."

"A qareen?" said Dietmar, testing the word. "Another one of your jinn?"

"Of a kind. It is a reflection—of a person, of a thing."

"Why was it there?"

"In Samaria?"

Dietmar nodded.

"Perhaps to warn us." Razin made a sweeping gesture with his hand to show that he was speculating. "Perhaps we witnessed an echo of something from the past, a memory in time stirred by the storm. The qareen is not meant to occupy our plane."

Dietmar stared at him.

His friend looked uncomfortable. These were things seldom spoken of, he could tell, even among the Muslims. The existence of such things raised questions, ones that might survive answers given by any but the most skilled theologian.

"You said it is not meant for this plane," said Dietmar. "But if not ours…"

Razin gave him a helpless shrug and shook his head. "You think to divine where we are by learning where the qareen came from, but it is not so simple. What we saw on that road, this Paul in his stocks, might have been nothing more than an echo. A voice from *Barzakh.* If he is there—in the lowest depths of Jahannam, would you think we are there too? No, my friend. There are horrors here, but I am not yet convinced that this is truly Hell."

"But you have some idea?" Dietmar searched his friend's face for an answer, some suggestion that there *was* an answer. But Razin's face offered nothing.

"There are… other realms," Razin finally spoke after a pause. "Places that exist between the material and spiritual kingdoms: Araf, Malakut… others that reside between Heaven and Hell."

Dietmar cast another glance up at the grey sky beyond the surrounding slopes.

Neither Heaven nor Hell.

He squared his shoulders and looked back at the ragged convoy navigating the hills.

Tired, scared eyes met his own.

"How do we get home?" he asked, turning to Razin. "*Can* we get home?"

"I don't know," came the sombre reply.

"What about that snake?" Dietmar pressed, unwilling to let his friend retreat from the conversation. "The *Falak*, you called it? How did it come to be in Nablus and here? There must be a way, surely?"

"You said it yourself." Razin tilted his head. "The reservoir must feed into Jacob's Well somehow. Otherwise, the Falak has found a way to tunnel between places, burrowing through the planes where the boundaries are thinnest. If it has found a way to cross the *as-Sirāt*, then even the domain of Heaven is in peril, and all that lies between." Razin saw his expression and sighed. "We were fortunate, if you can even call it that. The Falak is a mighty beast, one that might challenge the order of things. What you saw in that pool was but a glimpse of its true nature. Given enough time, it will grow and grow until not even the heavens and the seven hells can contain it. Then it will consume the bridge between the planes and cast us all into its fiery stomach to writhe upon the hot coals that simmer in its belly."

Dietmar raised an eyebrow, watching his friend's face turn from solemn to dark, his sharp features contorting with worry. What Razin had described was not unfamiliar to him. Old Tirus, Leviathan, Falak, the Norse *Jormungandr*—these were the serpents that would end the world. He'd sometimes wondered how so many tales could share so many characteristics if there were not some truth to them. Or perhaps it was man's fears, reflected in myths of his own making, a mirror of his own instincts and intuitions, compounding the fears he already felt for God's less noble creations. He'd often thought the snake had gotten a raw deal ever since it appeared in the Garden of Eden to tempt Adam and Eve, an unfortunate legacy handed down from the great Deceiver himself. But now that he'd seen the beast with his own eyes, well, maybe man's instincts had been right all along.

"Might we follow it?" he asked, straightening in his saddle. The sloping hills were beginning to level out around them, and more rocky outcrops dotted the landscape, forming in the gullies like sores on a leper's skin.

Razin shook his head, his eyes fixed on something in the distance.

"Why not?" persisted Dietmar. "If it has discovered a way to reach Nablus, can we not follow one of its tunnels?"

"And risk emerging in one of the Seven Hells?" Razin spat at the sand. "Or worse, appear before the gates of Jannah before our appointed time? Without passing the bridge of as-Sirāt and having our deeds in life considered? No, German, we will not follow the Falak through the tunnels. To do so would risk much more than our lives."

And what if it is in there, waiting for us?

Dietmar sighed. He doubted Tomas or Adelman would be willing, let alone Levi and his daughters.

"Look," said Razin, pointing toward one of the gullies. The gilded wagon from Anjier's convoy was just ahead, emerging from behind an outcrop of grey sandstone rocks. It slowed as one of its drivers noticed them and came to a standstill in the thick sand. A shadow peered out from behind the curtains. This time it didn't disappear when it saw them watching.

Dietmar waved, and after a moment, the drivers waved back.

"Great," snarled Geoff coming up beside them. "More mouths to feed."

***

The Lady Marie of Galilee was a few years older than Levi's brats at most. She had fair hair and skin as light as butter, with eyes that matched the bright blue of the curtains draped across the windows of her wagon. A tall man with heavyset features and eyes like flint hovered over her protectively when she stepped out into the sand. They, along with their two drivers, were the sole survivors from Anjier's convoy.

The man's name was Arcadius, a Romei hailing from Constantinople and the girl's bodyguard. He wore the heraldry of Marie's house—red towers on a field of yellow—displayed over his shirt of lamellar plate. A bucket helm with slanted eye slots rested by his side, while the head of a formidable war axe pressed against the sand in his other hand.

Arcadius's sharp eyes were constantly on the move, searching for threats amongst this new convoy, settling more often than once on Amice's smirking features. Fair enough, Dietmar thought, though Arcadius returned his greeting warmly enough.

"We will join you," said the Romei once they had finished with introductions.

"If you will have us," the Lady Marie added, placing her small hand on Arcadius's arm. Mousy thing though she was, she carried herself with solemn dignity. Dietmar thought it would be hard to say no to her.

Arcadius inclined his head, revealing white specks among the red hair surrounding his crown. When he looked up, Dietmar noticed the deep lines etched into his weathered face. He was old enough to be his ward's father, or father's father. Still, his broad shoulders and deep chest hinted at a strength that hadn't waned with age, and Dietmar didn't envy the man who came between him and his charge.

"You are most welcome to join us," said Dietmar. "We would not deny you something that costs us so little but brings much comfort in a place like this. We have some water and fodder for your horses, and if Adelman ever rouses from the back of his cart, perhaps he can manage to find some bread as well."

The Lady Marie smiled, and Dietmar felt his heart grow just a little warmer for it. "You have our thanks, noble sers," she replied. "We have water and feed enough for our Drax and Alexei, but I do not think we could say no to your charity if you have bread to spare."

Amice leaned forward in his saddle, resting his elbows while he stared at the Lady Marie. "I'll share my bread with the Lady if she likes." He showed his teeth, that knife-wound smile of his taking on a predatory glint. "Some of my honeyed meat, too, if she has a liking for it, which I suspect she does... Wouldn't want her to starve. It wouldn't be... *civil*."

Arcadius growled, slowly raising the axe by his side. "I don't like your tone, little man. If you so much as look at the Lady Marie in a way I find displeasing, I'll do something we both won't like, but you more than me, I promise you that."

Amice's mouth was a thin line, his eyes fixed on the axe head pointed at him. "That's a big axe. Heavy… slow. Think you're quicker with it than I am with my—"

"Shut your mouth, boy!" Geoff barked, cutting off Amice before he could finish. He shook his head, offering an apologetic gesture to Arcadius and the Lady Marie. "He's got a loose pair of lips, but I'll see to him, don't you worry. You won't have any trouble from us, on my word."

"See that you do," Arcadius grunted. He let the axe fall to his side, still glaring at Amice. He held his stare a moment longer and then pivoted on his heels to guide the Lady Marie back toward their wagon.

"Don't mind old 'Dius," the Lady Marie called over her shoulder. "He's a big old grumpy bear, but he's grateful for your hospitality. As am I."

Dietmar smiled again as she clambered back up the steps to her wagon, her bodyguard never more than a step behind. He *was* like a bear, he thought, watching Arcadius's towering frame stoop to cross beneath the carriage door, his massive arms sweeping the Lady into the dark confines within. Or like a big midwife, fussing over the child in her care.

They made for a rag-tag bunch—a knight, remnants of a mercenary band, a drunkard priest, a recalcitrant Muslim, a bookkeep half-scared out of his wits, a dyer's caravan, and now a Lady and her guard. Not the company he would have chosen to traverse this 'place in-between', as Razin had called it—purgatory, surely? But God had a funny sense of humour, and if not God, then the whims of fate. And who was he to question either? If God had seen it fit to damn them, then He'd seen it fit to offer them a weapon against the denizens of Hell, too.

The hand.

Dietmar carried it with him, safely tucked in a bag by his side, ready to confront any new horror that crossed their path.

We won't be such easy prey the next time.

He nodded at Razin, who was discussing the terrain ahead. "The ground… rocky… night… soon." Dietmar nodded again, not really listening. An unsettling feeling had stirred within him, and he thought he heard a distant voice calling his name.

It did not sound welcoming.

"Ho!" Razin snapped his fingers in front of Dietmar's face, clicking his tongue in irritation. "Are you with me, German? Now is not the time for daydreaming. Not if you ever want to make it home."

Dietmar blinked, grinning back at his friend. He nudged Theseus forward, following behind the Lady Marie's wagon. "Aye, I'm with you. Let's find a place to hunker down for the night. I'd rather we not wander into one of those singing demons when dusk falls."

Razin offered him his waterskin and a concerned look. "You look paler than usual, even for a German. How much of Paul's foul water did you swallow in your foolish gambit?"

Dietmar took the skin and shrugged, uncorking it. "I am tired, that's all. I need some sleep and perhaps a bit more of that honeyed meat if we have any left."

Razin watched him closely while he drank, then took back the skin, dropping it into the open mouth of one of his saddle bags. It seemed like he had something more to say, but before he could speak, Dietmar dug his heels into Theseus's flanks, pushing the horse to pick up speed. The urge to ride had suddenly gripped him, and he hooted back at Razin to join him as he raced through the sands.

***

"That solves that problem," said Geoff, staring down at the river from the top of the ridge.

"You think it's poisoned, too?" asked Tomas. "God's bones, Paul will have some answering for if he's fouled all the water. Dead or not."

Dietmar shook his head, dismounting from Theseus and walking closer to the edge of the ridge. "Whatever Paul did to that well, it won't be enough to foul a river, not of this size. But I doubt they're connected." He peered down the sharp rockface at the dark waters below—a vein coursing through cadaverous terrain—sand scarred by uneven steppes like ribs pressing up through skin. The river bent westward, splitting into two where the slopes turned dark, as if formed by volcanic ash and lava during the making of the world—or perhaps Hell itself was close, and they were walking atop it, separated only by a thin layer of stone and sand.

"I don't much like the look of it," said Tomas, leaving his cart to join Dietmar at the ridge. Adelman, now recovered from his stupor, was busy tending to Balaam's coat and engaging in quiet conversation with the mule. He put his head close to its mouth as if to listen to its reply. Dietmar thought he might have gone mad, but what could he do?

This is not a place for madness, he thought. And then, *it is the perfect place.*

"It'll do to fill our waterskins and washdown the horses," said Dietmar, looking down at the river. "But don't go wading in. And keep your wits about you. I've already had to pull Adelman out from one cursed mouth. I'd rather not have to do it again."

Tomas grunted. "You'd have to throw me in. I won't put a toe in that water, even if I ponk like the Devil's own."

"Which you do."

Tomas crossed himself and peered at the sweat patches under each of his arms before smiling thinly. "It's a comforting odour, don't you think? Means I'm still alive."

Dietmar laughed, turning from the ridge to clamber back upon his mount, leaving Tomas to his stink.

***

They followed the ridge toward the river, moving two-by-two and pausing only to help dislodge the carts when their heavy wheels got stuck in the sand. Veiny roots protruded from between the rocks along their path, thick and long like the tendrils of a mollusc's husk. The bulbs they sprouted from were as pale as bone, the skin of their bases so thin as to be nearly translucent in the sun. A yellow, slightly gelatinous substance filled their insides, like honey. Dietmar stared at them as they rode past, resisting the urge to itch when he noticed the honey-like goo was filled with thousands of tiny insectoid creatures. They coated the bulbs, too, like maggots. He thought he could hear the sound of a thousand wings, the droning buzz of their colonies, but the roar of the river below soon drowned it out.

Water spilt out from a black eye at the bottom of the ridge, thundering against the rocks in a plume of mist that cooled the air. The river foamed white where it hit the stone, frothing like a churning sea. As it flowed through the steppes, it gradually darkened, taking on an almost black hue that resembled the oozing of oil through the sand.

The ridge curved around the cave mouth so that their path down the slope deposited them a little more than a stone's throw from the river itself. A furry coat of moss grew along its nearest bank, as thick and long as a maiden's hair in places. Dietmar stared at a bushel bobbing in the water, flowing with the current. From above, it looked like a body resting in the river with just the tip of its head visible, while the rest was submerged beneath the murky waters.

He blinked, thinking of another body in the water a long time ago.

His mother.

He didn't let the thought linger.

There was no way of telling how deep the river ran. Its banks sloped gently at first, and the water took on a lighter hue here—brown, like the brackish waters of Lake Güstrom back home. But then the slopes disappeared entirely, dropping sharply like the walls of a canyon and making Dietmar think that the river ran very deep indeed.

For a fleeting moment, he thought he glimpsed something beneath the surface—pale skin and the impression of a webbed tail slicing through the roiling current. But he only caught the movement from the corner of his eye. When he turned his head to look directly, the shape had vanished, leaving behind only the frothing white crest of water surging over the black current.

"Something there?" asked Adelman from his place on the cart beside Tomas. His eyes had remained wide since the basin, and his snorts and sneezes had taken on an almost rhythmic pattern—like his humours had finally aligned, but now he had gotten used to the habit. Dietmar found it strangely reassuring—a piece of normality among the mess that he could cling to, like flotsam in a storm.

Dietmar shook his head. Even if he was sure of what he'd seen, he didn't think he'd have shared it with the old man. Sometimes it was better not knowing. He used to think the truth was always worth pursuing, worth understanding, no matter the cost. That was something instilled in him at an early age, probably as a response to all the lies his father had shared—knowingly or otherwise. Yet, even in Jerusalem, doubts had started to creep in. And now? How could it help to know that the things they had seen existed? Things rooted, not in biblical tales, nor even—though he wasn't sure—in Islam, but something before. What did it mean for the race of men that they shared their existence with the damned? What did it mean for his faith? Were they all just empty bags of meat spinning toward a pointless end in the pit of some fathomless being? He couldn't accept that.

But there was another possibility. One that Razin seemed to have accepted—that such things, such places, could only exist in parallel to the heavens, not in place of them. They occupied the other side of God's grace. This was a challenge they would have to overcome, that was all.

Levi poked his head out from the back of his wagon as it rolled to a stop. He knitted his brow, taking in the dark waters with a long sweeping stare before waving to Dietmar.

"Might be good fishing here if the water's clean, eh?"

"Might be," said Dietmar.

"Not that I'd eat anything that comes from this place." Levi laughed, but it sounded hollow and quickly subsided. "Imagine the things swimming around in that? No, not for me and mine!"

A tail and pale skin.

Some beast of the black water.

"Before long, we won't have a choice." Dietmar wondered how long their food would last. They'd packed for days, any longer and… "Else it'll be our own mounts, and that'll be a poor thing for us all."

Balaam let out a defiant *haw*, like the old mule disapproved of the idea.

Adelman descended from his cart, attempting to reassure the mule. "They won't be dining on either of you. That would be a foolish business," he declared, sneezing into his hand and wiping it on his tunic. He pushed back what remained of his hair and added with a mischievous grin, "Just listen to old Adelman. I'll keep you safe if you keep telling me your secrets, how's that?"

Madness, Dietmar thought again.

But at least he'd found some comfort in this place.

"Come on, back on your cart," Dietmar told Adelman, motioning for him to return. He looked to the others. "We'll follow the river a while and then find a spot to rest for the night, but not too close to the banks… Let's not have any surprises while we sleep."

"What then?" said Levi.

I don't know.

"North," he said, trying to force some certainty into his voice. The truth was, he didn't know any more than they did. How could he? All he had was a hope that they'd somehow appear back on God's green earth and no reason to hold that hope. But some things were best kept to yourself, just like the truth. Especially in a place where hope hung by such a fragile thread that even the lightest of winds could break it.

Levi shrugged, his chin wobbling as he observed Dietmar with those watchful eyes of his. He might have sensed his uncertainty, but if he did, he said nothing of it.

Good man, Dietmar thought.

"North then," Levi affirmed. "I'm with you, knight. We all are."

***

Tomas splashed in the cool water, wetting his feet and rinsing his hands before filling his waterskin to the brim. Once removed from the swollen, silt-covered riverbed, the water was crisp and clear and tasted as good as anything from the pumps in Jerusalem.

They'd been cautious at first, hesitant to come within a few feet of the brooding black river that carved its way across the steppes. Finally, they had settled beneath a copse of tall, leafless trees that looked more like stone than any living thing. Huge boughs, as wide as four carts abreast, with thick knobbled ends like elephant feet, grew all along their side of the river. The tree limbs stretched out over the water, their thirsty roots drinking from the inky depths. Lichen covered the bark, growing like a fungal skin up the trunks, thriving on the mist and spray where the roots met the flowing current.

Dietmar wasn't sure exactly how to explain it, but it felt *old* beneath the trees. Ancient. Like the air beneath the spidering branches was the same air it'd always been, stagnant beside the racing river. It made Dietmar think of home and his father's tomb… and his father's father's in the crypt. A breath in there felt like a kind of sacrilege, as if your presence alone had disrupted the careful order of things.

That's how it felt beneath the massive branches of those elephantid trees.

They lingered on the edge a while, watching the cloudy water churn against the banks. But none of them had the courage to stand on the shore and fill their skins. Then, finally, when the sun had started dipping behind the hills, Adelman proposed leading the two mules near the water to gauge their reaction. It was only after Balaam and Silensus had wandered up to the muddy shore that Dietmar thought about what the old man had suggested.

Then he remembered Balaam's panicked bleating at the basin and the stubborn mule's refusal to go with Tomas into the reservoir.

Could it be that they had some preternatural sense about these things? It wouldn't be the strangest thing that had happened, after all.

When Silensus dipped his russet head toward the water, his ears twitched back against his head, Dietmar found that he'd been holding his breath. He let it out with a snort but smiled when the mule began drinking from the river. No monstrous beast with scales for a hide appeared to pull the mule under, nor did it start frothing at the mouth like Comus in the pool.

After that, they all filled their skins and took turns leading their mounts to drink. Adelman stayed with the mules well after dark, watching the icy vein as it pulsed past their spot beneath the trees. He and the mules remained like that until Dietmar called at him to come away and join them by the fire. Safe by day, the river might be, but nights offered new threats.

"You are from Odenwald?" Arcadius handed Dietmar a small steel flask and gestured for him to drink, his attention shifting momentarily to his ward across the fire. She sat beside Levi and his two daughters, listening to Tomas as he fussed over their food.

Dietmar sniffed at the flask. It smelled of aniseed and berries, a hint of mint, and something sharper. He turned the flask over in his hand, admiring the intricate carvings skilfully etched into its side: a bear with two heads fending off the hounds at its feet; a rider with his lance emerging from a grove of pines; a crow perched above, watching the scene. It depicted a classic hunt, though the dual heads of the bear added a unique twist. The liquor within was smooth on his tongue, immediately warming his belly and lifting his spirits.

"Aye, Zwingenberg." He passed back the flask with a nod of thanks. "I hold some land there and a minor interest in the town. How do you know of it?"

"The Hunt," Arcadius said simply. He secured the flask's lid and turned his gaze back to Dietmar. "I rode with Walter of Saint-Omer, moving from one great hall to another in search of beasts worthy of his mantle. We stalked the woods of *Nibelungensteig* for your giant boars, spitting them on our spears. Then we hunted the wolves in your hills, but they proved too cunning, vanishing into the *mittelgebirge* the moment we caught sight of them."

Dietmar raised an eyebrow. "How come you to this, then?"

Arcadius snorted. "A lady's minder?"

"Aye, a bodyguard."

Arcadius smiled, reclining against the trunk of the strange tree they sat beneath. "No need to mince your words, chevalier. I know what it is I do. What better way to retire an old dog? The prince has grown weary of the hunt. He'd rather drink and feast and laugh and fuck his wife. There's no place for an old soldier like me in his court. I'm nothing more than a reminder of his youth and a strength he no longer has."

Dietmar stared over the fire at the Lady Marie, laughing with the other two girls. Her eyes gleamed with humour, and by the blush on Sara and Miriam's faces, Dietmar guessed that she had shared something less than ladylike.

Arcadius sighed, following Dietmar's eyes with his own. "Only thing is, setting me to watch her reminds me more of my own youth than anything else. She's got her father's wit, his eyes too. And only a little of her mother, thank God. Cold-blooded reptile. That's why she's been sent to Jerusalem. Chiva wants to squeeze all the warmth out of her so that she's just another harpy in that nest of the King's Court."

And if not a harpy, then prey for one.

There was no place for gentleness in Amalric's Court. The girl would have to learn quickly and become, at least on the surface, something else. But Dietmar didn't bother explaining this to Arcadius. He would already know.

"And what does her father say of it?" he asked.

Arcadius shrugged, flexing his scarred and swollen knuckles. Years of wielding his mighty axe had taken a toll on his hands, inflaming them with choleric blood and ill humours. "Walter sees the good in people," he said. "Even in Chiva. He trusts in God to see things right, and if that fails, in me to keep his daughter safe. But I can only protect her flesh, not her soul."

Dietmar nodded, acknowledging the truth in Arcadius's words. "There are still good men in Jerusalem," he said, his thoughts drifting to Gelmiro. He tried not to wince, wondering how the young sevillano had fared. It seemed unlikely that his path from Jerusalem had been as treacherous as theirs.

That weasel bastard will be hidden someplace safe and warm with a flagon of something expensive to keep his conscience numb.

He wondered briefly if Gelmiro had come to the King's Court ready-made or if he'd been fashioned by it like all the others.

"The King is an honourable man," Dietmar continued. "And his Court is not without men of worth: Reynald Grenier and Geldemar of Tiberiad are honest and loyal. Seek them out when you tire of the harpies."

Arcadius scratched at his beard, eyeing Dietmar with his black eyes, leaving the unspoken unsaid.

If they ever made it back onto the road to Antioch.

If they survived whatever horrors awaited them on their journey. Chiva and her harpies, the intrigues of the King's Court, would be a welcome relief after what they'd seen.

Dietmar looked up as Razin emerged from the shadows, appearing like a wraith from the darkness. He knelt beside the fire, plucking a piece of meat before Tomas could protest. When he'd finished eating, he washed his hands with water from his flask and dried them on the small cloth hanging from his belt.

"And?" Dietmar asked, growing impatient. Razin had been gone the better part of the evening, taking Riba into the hills to see what lay ahead. Even in the darkness, his eyes were sharp, the night offering little hindrance.

Razin wiped his lips clean and tilted his head. "There are lights on the other side of the river. About a day's ride west if we can find a way across."

Lights? Who could live in a place like this?

"What is it?" said Dietmar. "The lights?"

Razin pursed his lips, letting the cloth drop back to his belt, and then he said what Dietmar had already guessed at. "I think it is a village."

***

That night, they slept beneath the ancient trees that looked like elephant stumps and listened to songs sung by demons on the wind.

And Dietmar dreamed.

15

He knew it was a dream the moment he awoke in it and felt her hand clasped in his own. Enneleyn was alive and by his side, her lips forming that skew smile of hers he had come to obsess over.

"Come on," she said, dragging him forward. She wore a simple white dress that hung to her knees, the one she had worn in the privacy of her rooms, barely hiding her modesty. Her hair was platted back in a neat weave, pulled tight against her head, loose curls hanging to her ears. He smiled. They were in the forest. In *his* forest.

Home.

He followed after her, running barefoot beneath the trees, the grass and fallen leaves soft between his toes. It was early spring. He knew it by the smell of things. The air was rich and sweet, coloured by blossoming spores in the field that hugged the treeline. Apples hung from the limbs of a winding tree, its roots thick as pillars, growing deep into the earth. He plucked one as they passed and kept running.

"Where are we going?" he called, letting her pull him by the arm. She laughed, glancing back at him before letting go of his hand and dashing ahead. "You'll see!"

He followed the familiar path through his grounds, passing the old logger's house and the crumbling boundary wall that divided the forest. He followed her through the ruins of the old church and splashed in the shallows of a spring that fed into the lake, running beside its sun-kissed waters before chasing Enneleyn up a low slope back into the forest.

He was always a few steps behind her fleeting figure, no matter how fast he ran.

The trees grew thick and then thinned again, parting like the lips of a lover's kiss to reveal a glade nestled in the centre of the woods. Soft, pale light filtered through the canopy, casting long shadows that stretched like ethereal fingers across the grass. In the centre of the clearing stood a grey boulder, like a giant's back pressing up from the earth, its muscles rippling in the silver light. Beside the stone lay a mound of soil covering the forest debris. A small hole lay opposite it.

"Come, husband," said Enneleyn, turning to blink back at Dietmar. "Come and see your son."

He stumbled forward, his legs moving of their own accord, drawing him closer to the hole. A cold wind swept through the glade, swirling leaves in a mesmerising dance upon the ground. The once-sweet fragrance of flowers and ripe fruits turned acrid, and the sharp stench of something else tinged his nostrils. He tried to resist, to halt his steps, to pull away from the hole.

I'm not supposed to see.

I'm not supposed to know what's in there.

But he already did. This was the glade where he'd buried his wife and son.

His legs propelled him forward, driven by some inexorable force, until he stood beside the boulder. Up close, its surface was polished and shone like a pebble plucked from a pond. When the light touched it, it gleamed as though wet.

He paused, his gaze fixed on the shimmering reflection in the stone. It was like looking into a broken mirror. His body appeared misshapen, his arms elongated and thin, his chest sunken and hollow. The face staring back at him mirrored the gaunt features of the skeleton knight, Odo of St. Amad. And there was something else. In place of his chain hauberk, he wore a cloak of white, its long hood draped over his head. A green cross adorned his left breast.

"Look." He felt Enneleyn's hand on his back. Gentle. Reassuring. His eyes drew away from the stone, coming to a rest above the hole. It was a small thing: no wider than the spade that had dug it. But it was deep. Deeper than he remembered.

"You have to look," said Enneleyn in a voice that was not entirely her own.

He took a step forward, leaning over the hole to peer into the darkness below. Roots stuck out from the tightly packed soil, their tips cut by the spade that had unearthed the grave. Worms wriggled amidst the dirt, their pink bodies twisting in the shafts of sunlight. He moved closer, his head now fully over the hole. There would be a small wooden casket at the bottom. It would be rotten by now, and he hesitated, fearful of what he might see contained within. He took a deep breath.

I'm not supposed to see.

He blinked. The hole was empty.

"You see?" said Enneleyn in his ear, her voice taking on a subtle hiss, like a crackling fire.

"He is risen."

Dietmar jolted awake, gasping for breath, his head pounding like it'd been split in two by Arcadius's axe. His vest clung to his body, drenched in a clammy sweat that reeked of sour milk and eggs. Rolling onto his side, he fumbled around for his waterskin, remembering Enneleyn's face and how he'd reached for her in his dream.

She had been there.

Alive.

It wasn't the first time he'd dreamt of her, but this time felt… different. What did it mean? What good omen could be found in his son's empty grave?

His fingers itched, burning as if they'd been left to cook on the embers of last night's fire. Slowly, he opened his eyes, groaning at the surge of pain that accompanied the motion—at the light and colours that greeted him. He ran his tongue over his gums and teeth, tasting the metallic tang of iron and salt. His teeth felt swollen, larger, like they were meant for a bigger mouth than his own.

Finding the leather bottle, he mustered the strength to sit up, propping himself into a seated position to watch the black waters flow past the bank. Jehan and Guiscard walked alongside the river, regarding the choppy current as they strolled toward the camp. The last few stars still hung in the air behind them, glinting like precious stones in the void, like stones in black soil.

Then he remembered the empty hole. And Enneleyn's words:

He is risen.

Blasphemy.

He pushed the thought aside, forcibly banishing it from his mind, and took a deep breath. That hadn't been her. Just a figment in his shattered mind, a distorted reflection of what he'd seen and felt these past days. He clenched his jaw as another wave of pain flooded through him.

It wasn't just his head that hurt: every fibre of his being throbbed with discomfort, even his teeth. He flipped open the waterskin's lid and took a long sip, letting the cool water run down his mouth and neck. In his dream, he had worn the green cross, like a Lazarian. What would Tomas have to say about that?

Lowering the waterskin, he wiped his mouth with the back of his hand, flinching as a sharp pain shot through his gums. He stuck a finger into his mouth, digging at the back teeth, grunting like a pinned horse while he scraped at his gums. He felt something come loose, breaking off against his nail.

He frowned, staring down at his hand.

A broken tooth lay in his palm, its root coated in blood.

—there'll be no holy order for you

A voice.

Dietmar swung his head around. "Who's there? Who said that?"

Blood surged in his ears, pounding like the beat of a drum, drowning out all other sounds. Razin glanced up from his bedroll, his lips moving, but Dietmar could not hear his words.

Laughter. A hacking cough.

Inside his head.

He was going mad.

Something long and hidden stirred in the back of his mind, uncoiling like a snake to the sound of leather being stretched taut. He felt it brush against his consciousness, an alien presence resting beside his own, occupying a narrow corridor in his head. It settled.

—it's always the teeth that go first

Dietmar flinched.

The words were like ice, a frozen breath inside his head. Goose pimples covered his flesh.

—then the nails, then the hair, then...Well, I'll leave that for you to find out

Dietmar crossed himself, whispering the Lord's prayer as he repeated the motion. There was a demon inside his head. Or the Devil, speaking words to him like he had the Christ. It would try to tempt him, to lure him into its blaspheming ways, to make a heretic of him.

—*no, no, not a demon,* the voice sniggered,a hollow laugh echoing in Dietmar's mind. *I am nothing so... provincial. And you are far from the Christ. But not as far as some. Your Arab, for instance. Yes, a man who lives with the Devil's doubt on his shoulder. Sin! Or perhaps your priest? Little buggerer, yes, yes. Sin! But ho! It's the bookkeep who lives furthest from the Lord... the things I could tell you about him!*

"Shut up," Dietmar snarled, shaking his head in an attempt to rid himself of the voice. He could *feel* it, and when he closed his eyes, he could almost see it—a rotten thing curled up in the dark. Wet flesh, like a sore, covering its skin. An empty, boneless hide.

The voice sniggered.

—*yesss, you see me. Ugly as sin. Too ugly for a mother to love. Better I was drowned at birth, but here we are. Do you think your Enneleyn would have loved me? Could she have?*

"Shut. Up!" Dietmar barked, hurling his waterskin across the camp. It struck the tree Arcadius was sleeping under, landing on the ground near the Greek's head.

"Oi!" Arcadius's eyes snapped open, his lips curling like a snarling bear.

Dietmar ignored him, shaking his head as he let out a heavy sigh. He listened to the blood still ringing in his ears, waiting for the voice to taunt him again. But there was nothing.

Silence.

"German?" Razin's gaze bore into him, his brow furrowing like tightly woven rope. He rose from his bedroll and retrieved the waterskin Dietmar had flung across the camp. "You look like you have a fever." He offered the waterskin back to Dietmar and stared at the tooth still resting in his palm.

There is a voice in my head! The Devil! Dietmar formed the words in his mind.

He opened his mouth to speak.

Nothing.

Razin gave him another concerned look.

"I'm fine," Dietmar replied, closing his hand and pocketing the molar.

The lie came easily to his lips, replacing the words he had intended in the space of a breath. Had something stopped him from confessing to Razin, or had he changed his own mind? But worse:

The lie had felt good on his lips.

"Drink, friend. You must have inhaled more of Paul's foul water than you realise." Razin gestured to the skin. "Flush it out and hope that it passes in the sunlight. Otherwise…" He opened his hands and shrugged. "This is not a place to be sick."

"We'll throw him on the cart if we have to," said Tomas, joining Razin beside Dietmar. He peered down at Dietmar, frowning at the sight of the sweat-stained vest and glistening forehead. "Might even be worth tossing him in the river first."

Dietmar took a sip from his waterskin and set it down on his lap. "It was just a dream."

Tomas regarded him sceptically.

"Of home," Dietmar finished.

"No pox then?"

Dietmar snorted. The pain had begun to subside, leaving behind a cold stiffness. He pushed aside the waterskin and slowly got to his feet, stretching his back. Nodding at Tomas and Razin, he forced a smile. "See? All better. You're like a pair of midwives hovering over me. Go on. I'll be fine." He let his smile drop, suddenly conscious of the missing tooth in the back of his mouth. He prodded the empty socket with his tongue, tasting salt.

The words of the old scriniarius echoed in his mind as he watched Tomas and Razin return to their bedrolls.

Something has attached itself to Saint Ephium's hand.

Dietmar glanced down at the leather satchel beside his bedroll, the one now carrying the hand.

Had he damned himself by touching it? Was it truly so simple? The demon in the temple had recoiled from it—because it *was* holy, surely? Or… perhaps it had known to fear it, known that the hand was even worse than its own hellish existence. What could be so evil that even a demon feared it? He nudged the lip of the satchel open with his boot and peered inside.

The hand rested as it always had: grey, cold, and lifeless, its scarred knuckles and calloused flesh as wretched as the moment he'd first laid eyes on it. Dietmar's gaze lingered on it, half-expecting the voice to return.

Nothing.

When he looked up again, Arcadius was staring at him from beneath the tree. They held each other's gaze for a long, uneasy moment before Dietmar nodded once and made his way toward the river. Tomas was right; he needed a wash.

***

"Who built this?" said Dietmar.

A stone bridge stretched across the river, as wide as a Roman road, with three barrel arches through which the dark, bubbling water flowed. The bone-white stone used for the roadway and parapet matched that of the temple, setting Dietmar's teeth on edge. Carved faces adorned the spandrel walls between the arches, their mouths open in rictus grins, allowing water to pass through.

"Or *what* built this?" Tomas mused from his cart, a few paces ahead.

Dietmar's gaze lingered on the space beneath the contorted façades and then travelled along the series of reliefs he found there. He saw landscapes covered by strange creatures—winged serpents drifting through clouds that transformed into waves, snakes with monkey heads, and towers that rose like fingers toward the sky. Among them, a jagged rock clenched like a fist. The third panel showed the body of a whale stretched across a ragged coast, horned crabs feeding from its rotting body.

And then, a figure.

A man—tall and striking, in scale armour that looked like it was crafted from writhing eels. His long hair was tightly tied at the nape of his neck, interlaced with wire or gold. His braided beard was adorned with beads and rings, corded into tight strands that hung nearly to his chest.

He appeared in every panel of the relief. Each scene, Dietmar realised. The relief told a story, but of what?

Could this be the Devil? Dietmar pondered, staring at the figure. He recalled the motif in the temple, the image of the man crouched with his fingers pointed toward the heavens. Was this the same being? Some long-forgotten god from a dead pantheon?

A vast sea served as the backdrop for each panel, its churning waters extending to the horizon. Waves crashed against the coastal slopes and surged above towers and rocks, dwarfing the other beings depicted. Even within the relief, the sea conveyed an overwhelming sense of immensity, a boundless ocean that seemed to cover the world and more. In its surging waves, Dietmar glimpsed the silhouette of a titanic form breaching into the world from whatever unfathomable abyss it resided in. It grew larger in each panel of the relief, the spiked tendrils of its mammoth dorsal like a range of mountains erupting from the sea. But no matter how large it grew, the full extent of its gargantuan body never emerged, leaving its true scale to the viewer's imagination.

Leviathan, Dietmar thought. *An end of things.*

He felt his eyes drawn back to the tall figure striding across the relief, hand raised to the sky with fingers extended. Had he summoned the beast from the ocean? Or was he the only thing standing between them and the void?

"It looks like it'll take our weight," Razin remarked, nudging his horse forward to join Dietmar. They moved past the line of resting carts and wagons, arriving at the mouth of the bridge.

"It might," said Dietmar, finally tearing his eyes away from the relief. The images lingered in his mind's eye a moment before he blinked them away, focusing his gaze across the river. The opposite bank gently sloped, its grey sand turning dark and hard, rising into a line of hills that disappeared in the distance.

"We could always follow the river," said Tomas, standing on the cart to get a better look. "Find another place to cross up ahead."

"How much farther to the village?" Dietmar turned to Razin. "They must be close if they built this."

"Not far now. I spotted the lights from the top of that embankment." He pointed north toward a steep rise of black rock partially submerged in the water like a seawall. The ridge looked steep enough that they'd have to go around it with their carts.

"We cross," declared Dietmar, looking back at the bridge. The chipped blocks of the roadway looked well-worn, covered in mud and dust from past travellers. Water bubbled up near the mouth of the bridge, where it'd been built low near the muddy slopes. When the river rose with the rains, it'd be fully submerged.

Does it even rain here? Dietmar glanced at the sky. Not a single cloud in sight.

Tomas let out a sharp whistle, and Balaam and Silensus strained in their harnesses, pulling the cart toward the bridge. The mules, at least, seemed undaunted by the prospect of crossing. Dietmar relaxed slightly and then snorted. He'd never been one for superstition before, but here he was, putting his faith in a pair of donkeys.

"That makes me an ass, too," he muttered to himself.

Levi's wagons trundled past next, with Levi's head peeking out the back of the last of them. He gave Dietmar a wink and then turned back to stare at the river. The Lady Marie's followed, her surly drivers eyeing the swift current with unease, while the lady and her guard remained hidden behind the curtains.

Dietmar joined Geoff and Guiscard at the rear. The large Norman looked uncomfortable on his horse—too tall by half. His feet rested awkwardly, his back hunched. He shot Dietmar a dark look before clicking his tongue, urging his mount forward to ride alongside Amice and Jehan.

Geoff spat at the sand before showing Dietmar his teeth in an ugly smile. "Don't mind him. He's a sour prick if ever there was one."

Dietmar frowned. "I've barely spoken a word to the man. Why the offence?"

Leaning forward in his saddle, Geoff rummaged through his bag before sitting back up. He offered his flask to Dietmar, who waved it away.

"It's not a long line from following you under Gelmiro's employ to watching his friends get eaten by a demon," Geoff explained, taking a sip from his flask and swishing the black liquor around his mouth before spitting some out. "Hemnar was his mate. Eudes too. It's not so much blame as it is resentment. I wouldn't dwell on it. He'll have your back in a fight. I'll see to it."

Dietmar watched Guiscard crossing onto the bridge, his head down and his gaze avoiding the black water beneath him.

Another reason to watch my back, he thought. *Another bastard who has it in for me.*

"There are things I would have changed," Dietmar admitted, blinking back at Geoff. It was a futile gesture, he knew. Men like Guiscard, like

Geoff, cared nothing for what could have been. All they saw was what was and how to benefit from it, if benefit they could.

"Like going traipsing through that *cunting* forest," said Geoff. "God! It's a miracle any of us made it out." He stared into his flask, lost in his thoughts. Fatigue had aged the mercenary—dark rings beneath hooded eyes, sallow skin. He looked up from the flask and said, "Sometimes I dream that we're still in there, in that butcher's temple, trying to find a way out. Amice has to wake me up. The boy's got ears like a fox, so he knows when I'm caught in a dream, bless him."

Dreams can be woken from, Dietmar thought. But what of Nicolo and Hemnar and the others? What became of a man in Hell when he was eaten by a demon?

Geoff scratched at his chin, nodding toward the pouch. "I suppose we can thank your saint for that miracle, eh?"

"The demons fear God's grace," said Dietmar, tightening the string corded through the mouth of the bag.

—do they now?

The voice stirred in the back of his mind, brushing against his thoughts, sending a shiver down his spine.

—an interesting proposition. I wonder… Yesss, I suppose they do fear God's grace. But is that what they see in me, or is it something… else?

Dietmar ground his teeth and tried to ignore his new companion's cackling laughter. After a moment, the laughter faded, though he couldn't shake the feeling that the presence still lingered, watching his every move. Waiting.

Theseus put one hesitant hoof upon the bridge and then another, walking carefully behind the Lady Marie's wagon. Muddy prints covered the off-white stone, and Dietmar spotted animal prints among the spoor.

"Wolf?" he said, gesturing to Geoff, looking for a distraction.

Geoff squinted, studying the tracks, then shook his head. "Couldn't say. Wolves aren't common in Samaria, but then again, we're not in Samaria, are we?"

"Not unless Hell's bled into the Holy Land." Dietmar leaned down in his saddle to take a closer look, slowing Theseus in his tracks.

The footprints were wider than his hand again by half and looked more like those of a bear than any wolf he knew of. The prints followed alongside the parapet for a while before veering left into the centre of the bridge, disappearing under the mud and wagon tracks.

"Think it's fishing in these waters?" asked Geoff. "That'd be a brave beast if it were. Odilo swears he saw something in the river last night—another of those snakes, maybe, or something else."

Dietmar peered over the parapet. The current had worn away the stone, leaving its corners smooth. Sedge gathered at the base of the dividing column directly beneath him, and he saw small plantweeds and clumps of river moss growing from the exposed silt—a little ecosystem shielded from the barrelling current.

He pondered the elusive shape he thought he'd seen moving beneath the surface—a slender pale form darting beneath the waves. It had appeared more akin to a shark than a serpent, but it could have been his imagination playing tricks on him.

"Whatever it was, I don't fancy meeting it, nor the beast bold enough to hunt it."

Geoff took another swig from his flask, swilling the liquid in his mouth before swallowing loudly. "I don't mind telling you, but if I'd known what Gelmiro's coin was getting me into, I would have let Amice shove his knife into his neck and been done with it."

"Your men would still be alive if you had."

"Fuck them," said Geoff. He saw Dietmar's look and laughed. "A bunch of blackhearts and bastards. None of them got what they didn't deserve, that's for sure. It's me I'm worried about. I've got a missus back home and a couple of my own bastards to worry about. Who knows what'll become of them without a father figure in their little lives."

—they'll all fucking starve

Dietmar chewed on his lip as the voice echoed in his head, its haggard laugh making his teeth ache. He tightened his grip on his reins, his knuckles turning white.

—better that than living with him as their father, don't you think? More cut-throats in the world with him as sire. No, no, better they starve and die, ridding us of his line

"You all right?"

Dietmar blinked and saw that Geoff was staring at him, an expression closer to curiosity than concern on his face. He mustered a faint smile. "Aye, sorry, lost in my own thoughts." He clicked his back, massaging his neck while clearing his throat. "I think Razin's right. I must've inhaled a part of that basin when I went fishing for Adelman in it." What else could he say? That there was a voice in his head telling him strange things? Laughing at him? They'd think him mad… and there was a good chance they'd be right.

There is a demon in me.

He ignored the thought and took a deep breath.

Geoff shrugged, then offered him his flask again. "This'll burn up the poison in you, trust me."

Dietmar eyed the flask sceptically but eventually accepted it. "Why not?" he muttered, uncorking it and raising it to his lips. He nearly spat out the first sip but then drank deep, hoping to dull his troubled thoughts.

"That's it, lad, take your medicine." Geoff grinned. "Tastes good, don't it?"

Dietmar coughed into his hand and handed back the flask, shaking his head. His nose began to run, and he wiped it with the back of his hand. "It tastes like vinegar."

"Ah! You'll get used to it," Geoff chuckled. He raised the flask for another sip, then tilted it toward Dietmar. "To your health, son."

***

They left the river behind just as a fever-sweat took hold of Dietmar. Tomas and Adelman fussed over him until he snapped at them, and they reluctantly let him be. Slumped forward in his saddle, head held low, he decided to sweat it out on his feet, or rather, on the back of his horse. The thought of sleep filled him with apprehension, afraid of encountering Enneleyn again. The shadow of her face and the memory of her laughter always led him back to his son's empty grave. He didn't want to be transported back to that glade beside the stone of broken mirrors and wriggling worms. If it meant enduring the scorching sun until his fever subsided, he would do so.

I'll die in my saddle if I die, he thought. *Not lying on my back in a cart like an old man.*

The ashen rocks that covered the steppes gradually transitioned to grey stone and sand and then to dry grassland slopes dotted with bushes. More hills loomed ahead, and a faint glimmer of silver hinted at a river splitting through a forest.

As the sun began its final arc above the hills, Razin called the convoy to a halt. He motioned to Geoff and his men, pointing toward a thin line on the horizon.

Smoke.

They moved more cautiously then, keeping their eyes on the sprawling bushland that stretched across the steppes. Thorny carobs with long, juicy bulbs grew in densely packed rows alongside low-growing shrubs and needle bushes. The coarse, chest-high grass scratched at Dietmar's legs as they rode over it. Above them, the hills flattened into long plateaus with steep, rocky inclines, split by deep gullies and shadowy gorges. Dietmar thought he saw a dark shadow detach itself from the rockface, sweeping down toward the plain before disappearing behind the hills. He wiped the sweat from his eyes, hoping to catch another glimpse, but the skies remained empty, cloudless, and grey. He turned his attention back to the grassy plain and continued riding.

A little while later, they could all smell the smoke, and Dietmar worried that Razin might have been mistaken and that they were instead riding toward a bushfire in the hills.

The carts came to a stop at Razin's command, and the occupants descended into the tall grass, curious to see what Razin had spotted. Leaving Theseus with Adelman, Dietmar hobbled up the slope toward the rocky hillock where his friend stood.

Another valley sprawled before them, tucked in between two canyon walls and a grove of pines. The river they had seen from a distance wound its way through the valley, hemmed in by a thick wall of thorn bushes that covered the dell like a carpet. But it was the cluster of buildings that caught Dietmar's eyes.

A dozen thatch-roofed dwellings huddled together in a half-circle, encircled by a low stone wall that had collapsed in places. A pair of wooden towers flanked the gates of the stockade, though they too showed signs of disrepair, their rotted rooves laid bare like an open ribcage to show the rafters within. Muddy pigpens occupied the space behind the towers, with their occupants lounging about in the shade or sniffing around the feeding trough, awaiting their next meal. A handful of fishing nets hung from the far wall, like a spider's web stretching out toward the silver stream that ran alongside the settlement. A wooden walkway encompassed the boundary of the stockade, its thick planks covered by rotting posts where the walls had collapsed.

Plumes of grey smoke billowed from three of the dwellings, merging into a single column they'd seen from the river.

"Well, it's not abandoned," said Tomas.

"Is that a good thing?" Arcadius asked, his eyes narrowing as he scrutinised the village. He leaned forward, his broad shoulders hunching, gripping his fearsome axe tightly.

"Looks like we're about to find out," said Dietmar, his fever all but forgotten, as a figure dressed in long yellow robes emerged from one of the buildings. The figure hobbled across the yard, the train of its robe dragging behind it as it made its way toward the well at the village centre. The figure paused before the well and turned to look up into the hills, as if it knew that it was being watched. Its hooded head seemed to settle on their spot on the slope.

After a long moment, the figure waved.

Dietmar waved back.

16

The robed figure greeted them at the gates, his one hand raised in a gesture of welcome while the other remained concealed beneath his long yellow robes that hung like curtains to the floor. Hunched over a walking stick, he grinned up at the convoy.

Ugly bastard, Dietmar thought despite himself.

The elderly man had a crooked mouth and a narrow jaw. When he smiled, only one side of his teeth showed, and as his hood shifted, Dietmar caught a glimpse of scabbed skin on the left side of his face, like he'd been burned, leaving him with only one eye. Bandages swaddled the dry skin above his eyebrows in a tight bundle, making his head appear mishappen beneath the cowl.

The man's jaw twitched, grinding sideways like a goat chewing, and then he shot off a string of words in a language Dietmar didn't understand. By the pause that followed, he knew there had been a question in there somewhere.

"What's he saying?" asked Tomas. "Is he going to let us in or not?"

Dietmar glanced at Razin, hoping the words might be in some dialect of Arabic or Hijazi that he was familiar with, but his friend shrugged, shaking his head.

"It's Aramaic," said Levi, poking his head out from the back of his wagon. He studied the man for a moment before climbing down and closing the canvas behind him.

"Do you speak it?" asked Dietmar.

"A little," said Levi. He rolled up his sleeves, strolling toward the old man by the gate. "My *dohdah* in Caesarea knew the tongue. She used to speak it to me when I was knee-high, said we ought to know the old words. My lessons ended when she passed, *zekher tzadik livrakha*." He smiled sadly and cleared his throat. "But I'll see what I can remember."

Levi raised a hand to greet the old man, who bobbed his head in return. His skew mouth was caught in a frozen grin.

What reason does he have to smile in a place like this?

He didn't look lost like them. No, he lived here, in those hovels behind the stockade.

"Ask him where we are," Dietmar said, motioning Levi toward the old man. He leaned forward in his saddle, resting his arms on the saddle horn, feeling the stiffness and soreness in his back. The sweat-soaked gambeson against his skin had turned cool and clammy. He longed to lie down, but the thought of succumbing to his dreams chilled him more than his own cold sweat.

Levi translated quickly, in sharp cutting words that sounded like a mix of Hebrew and Greek to Dietmar's untrained ear. The man's grin somehow widened before he replied in kind, spitting out a sequence of harsh words. Then, without hesitation, he spun around on his heels and hobbled back through the gate, beckoning them to follow with animated waves.

"And?" Dietmar pressed.

Levi scratched at his neck, his fat chin wobbling as he stared after the old man. He licked his lips and turned to Dietmar. "He says his name is Teoma, and that we are in *Ladah*, his home. He offers us shelter, but we must earn it first. We can stay if we help him."

"Ladah?" Razin's posture stiffened, his forehead creasing with deep lines.

Levi nodded. "That's what he said."

"And he wants our help?" Geoff growled. "'Course he does, then him and his can slit our throats while we sleep."

Dietmar stared at the old man dragging his robes through the dirt. Despite his pronounced limp, barely alleviated by his walking stick, he moved quickly. He was headed toward the huts.

He opens his doors to strangers.

Here.

What power does he wield that we are not a threat?

"What kind of help?" Dietmar asked, turning his gaze back to the dyer.

"No idea." Levi shaded his eyes with a hand and looked up at the empty watchtowers on either side of the gate. "But it sounded like he believed it was in our best interests rather than his own. I wager these towers and walls are here for a reason. Rather we find out what that is from *inside*, don't you think?"

"I'd rather find out now," said Dietmar, turning in his saddle to stare back the way they'd come. They still had a few hours of daylight left, but the thought of spending another night exposed while some beast lurked nearby was far from appealing.

Geoff growled, growing impatient. "Oi! Old man!" He whistled through his fingers, kneeing his ugly horse through the gate. "Help you with what? Come on. We're not agreeing without knowing what we're getting ourselves into. I know you understand me, you shit. Don't play daft. Spit it out, or I'll show you how bronze knuckles work."

Teoma halted beside the well, leaning against his cane. He turned to face them, still grinning. With his narrow chin and crooked mouth, he resembled a mountain goat, the white tuft peeking out from beneath his lower lip.

He barked out a single word and then pointed at Dietmar, waving his hand in a flourish, a dry cackle on his lips. Then he motioned them to enter once again.

"What the fuck does that mean?" Geoff turned to Levi. "*Kaftar*? Is that what he said?"

Dietmar didn't wait for Levi's response. He was looking down at his tabard, at the crest affixed to the dirty yellow cloth, and the sharp white teeth and red eye Teoma had been pointing at.

It seemed Geoff was wrong.

There were wolves here, after all.

They moved into the settlement slowly, wary of the old man's vague warning but eager to put a wall between themselves and whatever else occupied the valley before nightfall. The bargain they'd struck with Teoma couldn't be worse than the things they'd seen already, could it?

The old cripple looks harmless enough, Dietmar thought. With his skew mouth and crooked back. But what horrors dwelt within the confines of the village? What made Teoma so bold as to invite strangers into his home?

As they passed through the gate, Dietmar nodded to Razin, but his friend seemed distant, his thoughts absorbed by something Teoma had said, bringing a mask down over his face like a portcullis to hide his thoughts. A skill he had honed during their time in Kerak, where he and Dietmar had first started selling their swords to men they might have once considered their lesser. Brutish, blood-soaked barons who had elevated themselves at the point of the blade and ruled in the same way. The mask had served him well then, but Dietmar had noticed the habit had never really slipped, even when the times had grown less lean, and they'd been able to pick whose coin they took.

"Ladah," Dietmar probed gently, studying Razin's expression, hoping to catch a glimpse of his true feelings—a clenched jaw, a furrowed brow, a deep breath.

Nothing.

Dietmar frowned. "It means something to you, doesn't it?"

Razin sighed, letting Riba pick his way across the dried mud yard of the village. The smell of pigs and manure mingled with another unpleasant odour—the stench of rotting fish. Dietmar looked up, his gaze drawn to a wooden building resembling a longhouse nestled against the wall. Nets hung from the open windows, covering the floor in piles. Inside, butcher's blades were displayed on hooks along the walls beside more nets in various states of disrepair. Trophies adorned the posts and windows, each one more unsettling than the last. The long snout of a river shark, the thick leathery hide of a crocodile, swollen and rotten, and other grotesque beasts better suited to the depths of a nightmare than any river. Dried husks with scaly appendages hung from the mouth of a serpentine creature, suspended by two long spikes, giving the illusion of movement. Another beside it reminded Dietmar of the shape he'd seen beneath the current, with its thin fin and pale skin. It bore a humanoid resemblance: forward-facing eyes—dried up orifices now—and stubby toes that stuck out from webbed limbs, like a bat.

When Razin finally spoke, his voice sounded tired and distant, as if he could detach himself from the meaning of his words.

"It means that we have crossed the threshold between the temporal world and Jahannam. That we are on one of the Seven Planes, or somewhere in between. It should not be possible, and yet…"

Dietmar's gaze shifted from the fishmonger's hall to Razin. He nodded toward the huts ahead. "The people who live here—"

"If they are even that."

"Aye. They are the damned, then?"

Razin shrugged. "Ladah is a place where those who rejected the Prophet's message are sent to dwell. They are the unbelievers, those who deny Allah. If this is not the second plane of Jahannam, then it is a mockery of it. We would do well to be wary either way."

Caught between demons and the damned, Dietmar thought. He blinked, wondering which of the two now occupied the space inside his head. A devil? Or... something else?

He took a deep breath, easing back in his saddle. The pain in his bones persisted, but the fever no longer consumed his every thought. His gaze scanned the huts until it settled on the one closest to the well. It was a primitive dwelling, barely more than a lean-to constructed with wattle, daub, and clay. A reed roof covered its cone-shaped structure.

His eyes caught sight of bone charms hanging from the doorway—tiny bird skulls and other indistinguishable objects with carved ugly letters. Within the dark interior, a pair of white eyes blinked back at him. Dietmar raised his hand in greeting and glimpsed more figures crowded inside. A tall figure stood over them, a guardian to the children sprawled on reed mats.

He blinked.

Their silhouettes appeared misshapen, with elongated heads that slanted like a serpent's. He squinted, attempting to discern the shape of their skulls, but they vanished as the door slammed shut. Moments later, the eyes reappeared at the window, a mere hole in the wall, watching intently.

Children, he thought.

In such a place? Did they doubt God too?

He curled his lip in distaste. How could they know any different when they had been misled? He saw something of his own son's suffering in theirs. It was unjust to be punished for something beyond their control—these children could not help what they had been taught any more than his Rudi could have helped dying unchristened.

How could it be a sin when there was no choice?

His mood darkened with the thought, aware that he was flirting with ideas that would have raised eyebrows among God-fearing Christians back home. But how did the Greeks and Eastern Christians reconcile their differences with the Church? They did not believe in original sin, and yet they were still Christian. Christian enough for the Pope to raise armies in their aid, at least. And what about Razin? As far as Dietmar knew, the Muslim faith did not hold to such views either. It seemed somehow wrong.

I should have drunk more of Geoff's disgusting drink, he thought as they passed through the huts. *To deaden my thoughts, if nothing else.*

Teoma waved the carts toward an enclosure behind the huts, located beside an open-roofed gallery that might have been a smithy. The remnants of a fire still smouldered in its pit, and a bellows pump stood as the most advanced tool within its walls. More bone charms dangled from the doorway, and a pair of pig skulls had been affixed to the wall, their yellow bones blackened by smoke and ash. Dietmar looked at them uncomfortably. These were a pagan's tools, not a Christian's.

"If these are the damned," Dietmar said, his eyes lingering on the runic markings etched into the smithy's doorpost, "would it not be better for us to leave this place? Do we not risk much sharing a place with them?"

Razin gave him a dark look. "There are far worse things than the damned in Jahannam, my friend. Besides, I do not think we count amongst the damned, yet we are here. Perhaps the same holds true for them. Let us not be too quick to judge."

Dietmar nodded, his eyes returning to his stained and dirtied tabard. The yellow fabric had been tainted by dried blood from the temple and the grime from the basin. The Zwingenberg Wolf was fading, its once-black pelt turning a shade of grey, its red eye dimming. Was that him, he wondered briefly. Slowly coming apart, fading as they moved further into Hell? He felt like it: his aching bones and tender mouth, and the voice…

"Levi will need to ask this Teoma what it is we face," said Razin, his gaze drifting to the heraldry on Dietmar's tabard. "If there is a devilish beast lurking, we must also be cautious of those who have survived encounters with it, for they may be just as dangerous. It is no small thing to survive in a land amongst the jinn." He blinked away, bringing Riba to a stop near the enclosure. Samael and one of Levi's guards were helping Sara and Miriam down from their wagon while their father talked to Teoma just a few steps away.

"There were tracks by the river," said Dietmar, glancing back over his shoulder. Someone had closed the gate behind them, though he hadn't seen anyone besides Teoma and the shadows in the hut. He looked up at the watchtowers, but they remained empty. "The beast that left them must have been as large as a horse. Perhaps even bigger." He rose in his saddle, standing on his stirrups before swinging his leg over and dismounting. "Geoff thinks it might have been fishing in the river. If it's already eaten, perhaps we have less to worry about?"

"Assuming there is only one," said Razin.

"Aye, and that."

Dietmar stretched his legs, staring around the makeshift stables. The ground consisted of a mix of compact mud and, by the faint smell, manure. Bales of reeds were stacked up to the ceiling, and unnetted rope was coiled from wall to wall. A long feeding trough, about knee-high, occupied the corner of the stables, but whatever beast had drank from it was long gone. The wooden trough had started to rot.

Like everything else in this God-forsaken place, Dietmar thought, peering into the trough. A thin skein of turgid water lingered at its bottom, festering with the tiny white eggs of the insects who had claimed it as their own.

Levi clapped his hands together loudly, startling the horses. It seemed he had reached an agreement with Teoma. The old man took a pair of shuffling steps into the yard and pointed toward the huts with his walking stick.

"They'll feed and water us," Levi announced, striding over to Dietmar with a self-satisfied grin. "And they have space for us to sleep, as long as we don't mind sharing."

"Did you ask him the way back to Jerusalem? To Antioch?"

Levi sighed, turning to Teoma and barking out the question in that strange alien tongue. The old man waved with his stick toward the hills and barked back.

"He says we must pass through the Sandmouth," Levi translated.

Teoma erupted into a loud, haggard laugh, almost cackling, as he pointed over the stockades with a gnarled finger.

"I do not like the sound of that laugh," said Dietmar.

Levi shook his head. "Nor I."

"What about their predator? This kaftar?"

Levi's smile faltered, and he cast a sidelong glance at Teoma. "He told me that it hunts the plains and snatches their children. It's been trying to get over their walls every night. It keeps them awake and leaves them exhausted when they should be out fishing and hunting. Tonight, we will stand guard while they sleep."

Teoma called to them from the yard, waving impatiently. One of the hut doors opened, and Dietmar caught sight of a girl emerging from the gloom to help the old man, supporting his weight against her shoulder. She couldn't have been much older than the Lady Marie or Levi's daughters.

As she guided Teoma across the threshold into the hut, the girl glanced back toward the stables. Her face had a heart-shaped contour, with prominent cheekbones and a sharp jaw. Her dark hair was filthy, as was the smock she wore—little more than rags. Even from a distance, Dietmar could discern the colour of her eyes—a light green shade, almost yellow in the light. Then she disappeared into the hut.

When Dietmar looked away, he noticed Amice watching her with an expression he'd seen once before. He caught Dietmar's eye and smiled, giving him a cold wink before turning away.

It made his skin crawl.

"It'll be a welcome change to eat something other than bread and stringy beef," Levi said, rubbing his hands together and nodding. "From what I gather, the river is teeming with fish and… other things. Best you don't look too closely at what's on your plate, eh?" He motioned to Samael and then marched off to gather his daughters. "We eat before nightfall," he called back over his shoulder. "Then they light the fires."

Dietmar and Razin exchanged a look and began making their way toward the huts. Dietmar picked up his pace when he saw Amice stalking across the yard.

There was a hunger in his eyes, but it wasn't for food.

Dietmar squeezed into the gloomy hut beside Razin and Amice, squatting down to sit on one of the reed mats on the floor, with a bead curtain hanging from the doorway of the larger room, concealing its contents. Dietmar could see the silhouettes of figures moving in the shadows, likely preparing their meal.

The old man's daughters? He wondered. *Or his wives?*

For all they knew, Teoma was the only man in the village—some strange and depraved patriarch.

Dietmar made room for Arcadius and the Lady Marie, shifting again to accommodate Levi and his daughters until they were all sitting elbow to elbow, and the room started to grow warm from their bodies.

"Where is our host?" said Arcadius. He grunted, trying to find room for his long legs, but stopped at a word from the Lady Marie.

"Patience, 'Dius," she said, staring into the gloom. "They will not have known to expect so many of us, if any at all."

"Eat sparingly," said Levi. He sat nearest the door, his face framed by a shard of light that reached into the room as far as his knees. He looked at his daughters, sitting to either side of him, and instructed them loud enough for all to hear. "The food they have will be meagre. These are impoverished people, and we are not so desperate that we must take all they have. They have shown us kindness by opening their homes to us; let us not take advantage of their hospitality."

"Yes, *Abba*," said the daughter to his left. Dietmar wasn't sure which was which anymore. He could barely remember their names, though the one to Levi's right was slightly larger and more homely looking. That was Miriam? She'd taken after her father and was well on her way to developing a third chin.

—pig

Dietmar twitched, his mind numbing as the thing that had attached itself to the hand and now to him spat its vitriol.

—it speaks poorly of the father that his kin are so fat. And what of the mother? Whoring herself like Babylon's heirs while her husband is away

He averted his gaze, his eyes falling upon Arcadius and the Lady Marie, engaged in a quiet conversation in the darkness.

—ah! The choleric knight and his barren ward. He carries an axe he cannot wield for a princess who will never breed. What a fine bodyguard he makes! Would she even be here if the Greek had not spilt his seed in her mother's belly? He cannot hold his axe nor his load, ha ha!

Dietmar blinked.

—do they not share the same stubborn chin? You see it now, don't you? Yesss. I wonder if he knows? She does, as surely as sin

Dietmar shook his head and looked up as Teoma emerged from behind the bead curtain, his crooked grin shining in the dimness. He barked a command, leaning against the wall and parting the curtain with his stick. The girl followed him out from the second room, her arms laden with wooden bowls. Her large eyes swiftly scanned the room before she lowered her gaze. She had a cleft lip, Dietmar realised. The skin above her front teeth had split, lending her mouth an almost cat-like quality. Not wanting to cause offence, he averted his gaze and accepted a bowl when she offered it. It was warm in his hands and far from the humble stew he'd been expecting. Thinly sliced pieces of white meat were accompanied by a hardboiled egg, mashed chickpeas, and glazed green beans. A thick wedge of buttered brown bread was slowly sinking into the mashed chickpeas.

Teoma watched the girl impatiently from the doorway, clicking his tongue while she handed out the bowls. He said something sharp when she finished, her hands bare, and then waved her back into the second room. She lingered a moment, standing over Arcadius and the Lady Marie. Teoma growled angrily, chastising her. The girl tensed at the words before swiftly making her way through the room toward the curtain, stepping over their legs to return to Teoma.

"She is a slave," said Levi, seeing Dietmar watching him expectantly. "Bound to Teoma and the village for a past crime."

"What crime?"

Levi glanced at Teoma, who was forcing himself into a gap beside Amice and Razin. Levi waited until the old man was seated before gesturing toward the second room and speaking in Aramaic.

Teoma rubbed his scarred face, scratching at the burned side of his mouth with his dirty nails.

"He says she has a wicked soul," said Levi after hearing his reply.

Teoma spoke again, motioning for Levi to translate.

"And that she is not to be trusted." Levi repeated a word back to Teoma, gesturing with his hands as he spoke, then turned to Dietmar. "He says she is a liar."

Dietmar frowned. "And that is enough to enslave her?"

"Whole peoples have been enslaved for less," Razin remarked.

"Aye, at the tip of the sword after war, not by their own kin."

"What's the difference?" asked Razin, chewing on a piece of bread. He tore off another chunk and dipped it into his mash before peeling the egg. "What does it matter if it were through war or trickery or treachery that one man enslaves another? The consequence is the same, is it not? One is forced to do the will of another."

"Would you trust a man you feared?" said Arcadius, stirring from his side of the hut. He peered into his own bowl, lifting a piece of white meat to his nose and sniffing at it. "Chicken," he said, popping it into his mouth and chewing. He let out a satisfied grunt and picked up another piece, waving it at Razin as he spoke. "You cannot build a home out of fear, nor a village, nor a city. I would not trust a man who thought he might best me and then set me to his own ends, in chains."

"Nor I," said Razin, nodding thoughtfully. "And yet the Egyptians built their empire on the backs of their kin. The Romans, too, from the Greeks whom they enslaved. Men who were spiritually their brothers."

"Perhaps that is why those empires never found true peace." Levi wiped up the last of his mash with the heel of his bread. "Think of the Romans. Even before their fall, any semblance of peace they found was at the expense of others—conquest and slaughter. And in exchange? Roads and servitude. But not peace. Instead of extending the open hand of fellowship, they brought a clenched fist and war."

"Would they have become empires if they had acted otherwise?" asked Razin.

"Are they empires now?" Levi smiled, taking a bite out of his bread, with gravy from the mash smearing his lips. "There are other ways to spread the light of civilisation than through the sword. The same is true for religion, although it seems your faith prefers the fist. The Christians, too."

Razin snorted, looking up. "Do not mistake the greed of men for the tenets of their faith, friend. We all have our warlords, and they are motivated by more than just God. As are we all. Young Amice claims that it is land and power that drive great men, and he is not entirely wrong." Amice chuckled from the gloom, looking away from the curtain behind which the girl had disappeared for the first time since they had sat down.

Razin continued. "But we are not great men. Yet here we are, doing their bidding. We serve the will of others—like slaves. Only we believe we do so by our own choosing. If we understood the true motivations of our masters, do you think we would still have come to God's Kingdom? Have we been tricked? Fooled into thinking we are doing God's work, or do we all secretly know the game that is being played and accept its rules, knowing that this shared purpose is its own reward? That striving toward an end is an end in itself? We scratch out a living, fighting men over God and land, but it is enough that we have someone to fight and someone to stand beside us when we fight. That is what motivates us."

We know we are being lied to, and yet we come here all the same.

Dietmar had once heard it said that to enslave a man was to control his body, but to deceive a man, to convince him to act upon a falsehood, was to enslave his spirit and mind.

"That is why the tribes of Jerusalem will ride out against the tribes of Damascus," he said softly. "Talk of peace will always give way to talk of war. It is in man's nature…Though, I wonder what motivates our generous host?" He glanced at Teoma and found the old man's eyes already on his, the half-grin still etched on his face. Teoma gestured toward

Dietmar's bowl, urging him to eat with a wave of his one hand. The other hand remained concealed beneath his robes. His walking stick rested across his knees. Its handle was shaped like a lamb's head, with square goat-like eyes charcoaled black.

Teoma motioned again, pointing to the bowl and nodding.

"Ask him if he is a Christian," said Dietmar.

Levi raised an eyebrow. "You know he isn't."

"Ask him anyway."

Teoma watched the exchange with the same stiff smile, his hazel eyes shifting between Levi and Dietmar and then back to Levi when the dyer began translating. Once Levi finished, Teoma stroked the white tuft beneath his lips for a moment and then burst into laughter, his smile widening further. He spoke quickly, as was his wont, gesturing with his hand and motioning first to the reed mats beneath them and then to the sky above. He laughed again, shaking his head.

"What did he say?" asked Dietmar.

Arcadius growled. "He is a pagan, man. What more do you need? Haven't you seen the bones hanging from their doors? What Christian does that?"

"God's people marked their doors in Exodus," said Dietmar. He raised his hand, quieting Arcadius before he could reply. He didn't expect Teoma to be a Christian, nor a Muslim, or a Jew. Still, he felt an urge to *know*, to understand this strange little man and his beliefs. Why? he wondered. He had never cared about what gods men worshipped before. Perhaps it was this place?

Or perhaps it was the voice that now occupied a corridor inside his head.

It didn't matter. He needed to understand.

He nodded to Levi. "Tell me."

Levi sighed, wiped his lips clean with his hands, and placed his empty bowl on the floor. "He asks, what God can be condemned by a man? I think he's referring to the Roman, Pilate. For the sacrifice of your Christ to have been valid—which it was, or else the stain of original sin would not have been cleansed by his death—Pilate must have had the authority to judge and sentence God." Levi scratched his chin, smearing grease on his face as a smile tugged at the corners of his mouth. "He makes a good point, don't you think?"

Amice sneered. "A Jew would think so."

Teoma rocked on his haunches, leaning forward and wagging his finger, speaking directly to Dietmar this time.

"He says that if it were true, if man could condemn and execute God, then man must hold dominion over God, if not in Heaven, then on earth." Levi paused, listening to Teoma as he continued, his head bobbing, his fingers moving in a constant motion.

"He says this inversion is...." Levi furrowed his brow and blinked at Teoma, who motioned for him to continue, nodding his head like a magpie.

"Is what?" Razin asked, leaving his food half-finished on his lap.

Levi cleared his throat. "He says it is blasphemous. That it defies the nature of God."

Arcadius barked out a laugh. "He calls us blasphemers after spouting that shite? If we hadn't broken bread with him, I'd knock his head in. Jesu preserve me, I still might."

The nature of God, Dietmar thought. It was Teoma's misunderstanding of the Christ that led him to such a peculiar conclusion. It was not God who was condemned by the Romans, but rather, man himself. There had been no inversion. It had not been God on trial, but man.

Ignoring Arcadius's booming laughter, Dietmar looked uncertainly at their host. "Are we in Hell?"

Arcadius fell silent as Levi translated, his scarred knuckles resting against his knees, his eyes fixed on the old man. Everyone was watching Teoma now, waiting anxiously for his response.

He could damn them all with a word.

Funny, that, Dietmar thought. They might have been in Hell for days already, but it wouldn't be until they knew for sure that they'd be truly damned—that their last bit of hope would be swallowed up whole. What then? Succumb to despair and suffering? Or would they try to find a way out, battling through the underworld until they were finally free? He looked at the gathered company. Who would be their Heracles? Would it be Arcadius, with his bad humours? Razin and the quiet doubt that seeped into his every thought? Or would it be left to him to guide them out?

Teoma laughed again, that ugly cackle.

"He says this is not Hell," translated Levi.

Dietmar felt the tension in the room ease, like gentle breath escaping from constricted lungs.

"Ladah is in Jahannam," said Razin sharply. "We have seen the beasts that dwell here, the monsters that feed even now from the flesh of our friends. He lies."

Levi parsed his hands. "Or perhaps this is not truly Ladah, eh? Perhaps it is just a name."

"Then he lies still."

Teoma wagged a wrinkled finger at Razin, leaning forward so that the hood of his robes nearly obscured his eyes. He brushed it back with his hand, revealing the same slanted elongated forehead that Dietmar had noticed among the villagers upon their arrival. He recalled the bandages on Teoma's head.

Not bandages, Dietmar realised. *But bindings.*

Teoma tugged his hood back into place and motioned to Levi.

"This is the land of the *meshakh*," Levi explained. "I am not familiar with that word… it is…." He turned to Teoma, scratching his chin as the old man elaborated.

"It is the place of the beginning, I think. Yes, the beginning. But there are many other… lands?" Levi said, struggling to find the right words. "We crossed into one of them when we walked through the Sandmouth."

"The storm?" asked Dietmar.

Levi nodded.

"And how do we get back home?"

Teoma leaned back against the wattle wall, gently twirling the head of his staff in his hand. He spoke softly.

"We must pass through the gate of the Daughters," said Levi. "There we will find the Sandmouth again and home."

"The Daughters?"

"We will know it when we see it."

Arcadius grumbled, pushing his bowl away and stretching his legs. "I don't trust this old goat. Why does he speak in riddles? And he blasphemes! Even if this is Hell, it is no Christian hell. Ask him which god he worships, who holds sway in this… place."

"Do you really want to know?" Levi straightened his back, glancing cautiously at the daughters sitting beside him. They didn't seem to be paying any attention to the conversation, wallowing in their bowls like

—pigs

Not now, Dietmar thought, pushing the voice away, closing his mind to it. He noticed more faces peering out from the second room, their sloping heads pressing against the curtain, their eyes fixed on Sara and Miriam as they ate.

There was hunger in those eyes.

We're eating their food.

He didn't see the slave girl from before among the onlookers. She must have been hidden away, disappeared into some corner until she was called upon to serve her master.

Levi and Teoma exchanged another flurry of words, going back and forth while their audience watched. Eventually, Levi pursed his lips, his brow deepening into a V.

"He's not making any sense." He sucked in his breath and then picked up a beanstalk from his bowl, chewing on its end while he stared at Teoma. "He says he worships something from before God."

Dietmar hesitated. "What came before God?"

"That's the thing." Levi bit off the end of the stalk and wagged the stem at Teoma like a finger. "The word he uses is the same as the word for God: *Elâhâ*. So he is merely repeating himself."

Teoma bobbed his head. "Elâhâ".

"See!" Levi dropped the beanstalk back into his bowl and shook his head. "He worships the God before God. What nonsense."

"A god from one of the old religions?" asked Razin. "From some extinct pantheon?"

"Could be," Levi acknowledged. "But why would it have the same name?"

Dietmar frowned, seeing the expression on Razin's face. There was uncertainty there, behind his usual mask.

"What else can you expect from a savage?" said Arcadius. He scooped up the last bit of mash from his bowl, eating it with his fingers while he stared at Teoma. Teoma grinned, unaware of the vehemence in the Greek's words. He looked again at Dietmar, pointing at his bowl and speaking rapidly.

"He wants you to eat," Levi said with a frustrated sigh. "Night is coming soon, and we must light the fires."

17

"There's something wrong with Adelman," said Tomas as they walked along the perimeter of the stockade. Torches throughout the village were being lit, casting an amber glow that spilt from rusted brass sconces riveted to rotten stakes. Squat iron braziers, worn and blackened by years of use, stood outside each dwelling, crackling like hearths. In the centre of the yard, a pyre had been lit, fuelled by a mixture of firewood, dry reed bales, and old wattle sheets sourced from the village's ample supply. Still, there was no moon, no stars, and for every torch and brazier lit, an inky blotch of swirling darkness gathered between them.

Night had swept across the valley like oil, plunging the huts into darkness. It came swiftly, like the blink of an eye, never to reopen. In that first moment of emptiness beneath the desolate sky, Dietmar had felt the black coal of despair flicker in his breast.

This is what it means to sit outside of God's grace, he had thought, unable to see even his own hands before him.

Then, a spark, the sound of flint scraping against stone, and Geoff's ugly grin.

Even here, in Ladah, a forsaken plane haunted by pagans and their godless beasts, there was light. The thought of his son being even further from God than himself darkened his mood, turning him irritable. The howling wind only worsened his spirits. It tore in from the northern hills and through the ravine, a high-pitched shriek that set his teeth on edge and gnawed at his resolve. The nets hanging from the palisades swayed and scraped against the wood, clicking and creaking like an *Erdhenne* spirit.

"There's something wrong with all of us," Dietmar snapped. He had hoped for a moment of solitude to sift through his thoughts and stretch his legs, but Tomas had followed him. And so, they walked the wooden walkway along the outskirts of the village, mindful of the protruding nails and splinters that lay like thorns.

He turned to his friend, raising his torch to cast a glow on Tomas's pale face.

"We're here, aren't we?" said Dietmar. "I'd say that's cause for concern."

Tomas nodded, unperturbed by his friend's tone. "But Adelman… all he does is talk to those damned mules. And when he's not talking to them, he's talking *about* them. Balaam this, Silensus that. He hasn't been right since you pulled him out of that basin… since Comus and that snake. I think he's losing his mind."

Dietmar clicked his tongue and glanced back at Tomas. His friend's face appeared sharp and drawn in the torchlight, his red hair and beard reflecting the flickering glow like the embers of some Greek titan banished to the underworld.

Dietmar sighed.

"If he finds comfort in the company of those donkeys, what of it? It's better than him wallowing inside his own head, getting lost in dark thoughts."

"He talks to them like they're human, as if they understand him."

"Don't they?"

Tomas snorted. "Perhaps when there's something in it for them, stubborn old bastards."

"Then they're in good company."

Dietmar let the silence settle while he mulled over his thoughts. He was fond of the old man but had let a distance form between them. He couldn't deny it.

He glanced at Tomas.

"Adelman should've taken his pension and settled into retirement long before we came to Jerusalem. He wouldn't hear of it, donkey that he is." He sighed. "It would've been good to spare him some of this misery."

"He feels a duty to you."

Dietmar nodded. He remembered Adelman's face the day the bookkeep had brought the news. His estate teetered on the edge of collapse, its coffers empty and its income depleted. The old man had approached Dietmar, speaking softly through the closed door, but his words had cut through Dietmar's drunken stupor like a searing knife.

There isn't anything left.

In a state of disarray, Dietmar had flung the door open, reeking of wine and vomit, glaring down at Adelman. But the old man hadn't flinched.

Dress yourself, Adelman had told him calmly. Then he'd turned on his heel and limped back to his chambers, where he'd patiently waited for Dietmar to finally appear an hour later.

It hadn't been the first time they had faced each other over the books, Dietmar from within a fog of drink and self-loathing, Adelman from within his deep chair, quietly concerned.

But this time had been different.

If something didn't change, he was going to lose it all—his home, his land, and perhaps even his title. He had stared down at Adelman's scrawling notes, trying to make sense of the figures presented to him. The mounting interest from the loans he'd taken out against his estate was becoming overwhelming, themselves enough to cripple him now that his rentals had dried up. Another column displayed a series of steadily growing numbers beneath the imperial eagle. The Emperor was planning another campaign into Italy and had demanded a tithe from all his lords, either in coin or in troops, of which Dietmar had neither.

We'll... we'll have to sell off half my land, Dietmar had slurred.

Adelman had let out a deep sigh and then leaned back into his seat to consider Dietmar over his steepled fingers. *There is another way*, he'd told him. *A way to save your lands and earn the coin to pay off all your debts. But it is a dangerous business, and you might never return.*

How?

If you fight as a crucesignati, if you fight for God, the Church will freeze the interest on your loans. That might give us enough time to raise the coin. We'll have to find a patron there, or you'll need to wet your sword for whoever can afford you. In the Holy Land, there are newly made men with deep purses looking to protect their lands... to expand.

Fight for God? Dietmar had asked in a quiet voice. God had only taken from him, left him hollow and alone. Why should he fight for him?

If you do not, a year will pass, maybe two, and then you will be forced to sell again and again until the land your father built is gone.

Dietmar had shrugged.

Adelman's next words had pierced through his indifference: *The land your wife and son are buried in.*

Dietmar had blinked at that and looked up from the ledgers to meet Adelman's gaze. In that moment, he had seen the pain in the old man's eyes. He had been close to Enneleyn in his own way. And she had taken kindly to him, the old bookkeep bustling about Dietmar's estate, a relic of his father's time to Dietmar, but a connection to his past for her, who had only briefly met the old lord of Zwingenberg and known even less of Huldrych. Much of what she'd learned about Dietmar's youth had come from Adelman's mouth, and it was to Adelman that they first announced their pregnancy.

When Rudi had died, Adelman had wept alongside them. When Enneleyn had followed, Dietmar didn't think the old man would long survive her. Her loss had broken his heart, and for a while, he had been little more than a spectre moving between the rooms while Dietmar drank himself into oblivion.

But Adelman had endured, his duty to Dietmar keeping him tethered to the world. He had done his best to manage Dietmar's estates while Dietmar spiralled deeper into despair and self-destruction. But there were limits to what Adelman could achieve.

It is the only way, Adelman had said, staring over his ledgers in that musty room, the stink of drink and sweat pouring off Dietmar like a miasma.

The following morning, Dietmar had risen early and cleared his rooms of wine and drink. Then he'd ridden to Bensheim and declared himself for the Church and God's army. Within a week, he was riding east to raise a fortune and secure his estate. Adelman had ridden with him.

"His duty to me has long since been fulfilled," said Dietmar, glancing at Tomas and then staring at the nearest huts. In truth, what Adelman had done had gone well beyond duty. He had saved Dietmar, brought him back from the bottom of the darkest well. Without Adelman's intervention, Dietmar knew he would have perished in those rooms filled with bottles and his own melancholia. His land would have been seized from under his corpse, and any chance his Rudi now had of being brought back to the light would never have come to be. Dietmar could never forget that.

And yet, I can barely look at him?

He had allowed the distance between them to grow. Perhaps he had even encouraged it. The sight of the old man reminded him of home and all that he had lost.

He needs me, Dietmar thought. *More now that he is close to madness.*

He resolved to be more attentive to the old man.

As they walked, figures retreated into the doorways of their hovels, their faces concealed in shadow, their watchful eyes gleaming in the light of the braziers. Dietmar tried not to stare, but he couldn't help catching glimpses of their strangely jutting skulls and peculiarly shaped heads from the corner of his eye. He knew these deformities were a result of ritualistic binding, though never before had he seen such pronounced features. A church in Elztal displayed a pair within its reliquary and rolled them out to the delight of gawping visitors whenever enough coin changed hands—the 'Forest Brides', *Transsilvani* sisters who had somehow found their resting place in Odenwald. The priests did not hesitate to invent tales around them, attributing their abnormalities to evil-craft or vanity. Dietmar had even heard one priest claim that their misshapen heads were the result of an exorcism, swelling in size as the Devil was expelled from their bodies.

"It's not just Adelman's talking that has me worried," said Tomas, shaking his head. He paused near the wall, holding his torch up to a bracket fixed on the stockade. The torch came to life with a hot breath, the oily rags disappearing in a ball of flame. Tomas grunted, lowering his arm and turning to Dietmar. "When I went to fetch him from the stables to eat, I could swear I heard another voice in there with him. At first, I thought it might be Odilo—he's taken a liking to the old man since the incident at the pond. But truth be told, I don't think Odilo is all there either."

"Perhaps they'll find some peace in each other's company then," said Dietmar, only half listening. He peered over the settlement's walls, staring into the dark beyond the flickering torches. The hills had disappeared into the night, hidden beneath the veil of darkness. He could only see as far as the near bank of the river, its silver surface reflecting the torchlight from the palisades.

Tomas shook his head. "When I stepped inside, there was no one else. Just Adelman and his mules."

Dietmar blinked at him.

"Could he be talking to himself?"

"I don't know," replied Tomas with a shrug, caught between unease and uncertainty. "It didn't *sound* like him. But then, who else?"

"Maybe the old man is right, and the mules do talk to him?"

Tomas snorted. "Then we're all mad."

—yes

The word slipped out from the door Dietmar had closed in his mind, from where the voice waited, its tendrils sunk deep into his brain like venom.

He cleared his throat, blinking. "I will speak to him. But in the morning, once we've seen off Ladah's beast."

"Between talking mules and Ladah's beast, I don't know what to be more worried about."

"The thing that is trying to eat us," said Dietmar, walking ahead.

Tomas looked over the stockade into the blackness beyond the river. He strained his eyes, hoping to catch a glimpse of the bottom of the ridge they had descended earlier in the day.

A shadow stirred, causing him to tense, but it was only the wind rustling through the trees. After a moment, Tomas gathered the hem of his robes in his fists and hurried after Dietmar.

They came to a stop before the village gates and watched Geoff as he inspected the bolts and lock. The mercenary captain kicked the gate once with the toe of his boot, then raised his flickering torch to face them.

"Nothing's getting through here," he declared confidently.

"It's the *over* that worries me," said Dietmar recalling the size of the prints he had seen on the bridge.

Geoff cupped his free hand to his mouth, staring up at the nearest watchtower. "Oi! Odilo! Stop fiddling with yourself, and let me see you!"

The Pavian's face emerged from beneath the thatched roof, his fiery curls and thick beard glowing red in the light of his torch.

"How's the view up there?" asked Geoff.

Odilo shook his head. "I can't see anything beyond the walls. It's as black as pitch from the river onward, like staring down the bottom of a well."

"Maybe I should send you and Jehan out there with some torches if you're not doing any good up there?"

"Maybe you should go yourself."

Geoff snorted. "You lead, I'll follow. How's that? Come on, get down. You're no use to anyone up there. And you too, Guiscard!" He glanced at the other tower and gestured to the figure peering down at him. "You two keep an eye on this gate. Nothing comes through, you hear?"

Odilo's head disappeared into the watchtower, followed by a slew of grumbled curses. Shortly after, the Pavian reappeared, a saddle bag slung over his shoulder and a torch held aloft. He tossed the torch from the watchtower and began descending the rickety ladder, taking the rungs two at a time.

Geoff deftly sidestepped the plummeting torch, watching it bounce off the dirt floor where he had been standing.

"You see what I have to put up with?" he said, shaking his head. A humourless grin played on his lips. "Your Gelmiro will have to empty his coffers once all of this is over. I want recompense, contractual damages, let's call it."

Tomas sniffed and wiped his nose with the sleeve of his robes. He seemed to have picked up Adelman's habit. "If you can coax him out of whatever hole he's disappeared down, the little weasel. I have some choice words for him as well."

"You'll have better luck parting the Patriarch from the One True Cross than finding Gelmiro when he doesn't want to be found," said Dietmar.

Geoff barked out a laugh. "That might be the only thing that covers my account too." He flashed another grin and stomped off toward the huts, still chuckling.

Dietmar and Tomas left the gate, following the walkway along the perimeter wall. It had fallen in on itself in places, its stakes collapsing like rotting teeth, leaving huge gaps in the boundary. Under Levi's guidance, Samael and some of the drivers were rolling reed bales along the walkway, attempting to fill the holes. Enos, a tall driver with dishevelled brown hair, broad shoulders, and a nose that looked like it'd been trampled on, forcefully wedged a sheet of wattle into place between the stakes. He dusted off his hands and regarded the stockade sceptically.

"It only needs to look secure," Samael remarked upon seeing Enos's expression. Levi's guard approached the breach, gently tugging at the woven lattice and securing it to the rest of the barricade with a loose rope. "A beast won't know what'll hold and what won't. We fill the gaps and move on."

"Aye, as you say," said Enos, looking doubtful. He retrieved another sheet from the stack and crouched on the walkway, jamming it into the gap between the stakes and the tall reed bales.

Dietmar and Tomas observed the process a few more times before continuing on, nodding at Samael as they passed him.

"Doing your part then?" said Dietmar, noticing Amice leaning against the stockade, picking at his nails with his knife.

The mercenary licked his lips, showing teeth that had already gone grey from Geoff's drink. "You know me, ser. Never one to shy away from duty. Nothing pleases me more than a good God-given day's work."

Dietmar saw Enos watching with a snarl on his lips, but the man refrained from voicing his bitterness and turned to assist Samael and the others with the reed bales. They dragged one over the sand onto the walkway and rolled it toward the next gap.

Dietmar turned around when the door of the nearest hovel slammed open, and a giant form filled its hatch.

"Go on!" Arcadius bellowed, buckling on his belt. He glared at Amice. "Go find your master, you jackal. And if I catch you skulking around this hut, I'll blacken your eyes. Go on! Get!"

Amice scowled and detached himself from the wall, like a rock spider, when the big Greek lumbered toward him. His eyes darted from Arcadius to the soft light in the hut behind him. The Lady Marie sat beside Levi's daughters under the dyer's watchful gaze. When Levi noticed him looking, he rose to his feet and closed the door.

Nobody likes a scavenger, Dietmar thought. But Amice was more than that. He was an opportunist with a dark heart. Not for the first time, Dietmar wished he had allowed the boy to stumble and fall in the temple.

Amice spun the knife in his palm, guiding the pommel hand to hand while he weighed his options. For a brief moment, it seemed as though he might stick around to challenge Arcadius, but when the bodyguard stepped onto the walkway, he spat on the floor and sheathed his knife.

"That's right," said Arcadius, watching his back disappear into the gloom. "That craven little bastard will gut us in our sleep if someone isn't keeping an eye on him. And do worse to our women."

"He's handy in a fight," said Dietmar. The words felt cold to his ears. A febrile justification he didn't believe himself. Better to have one less blade than be worried it'll one day end up in your back.

Arcadius made a face.

"So is a dog, until one day it turns on you, tears your throat out."

The big Greek had exchanged his sweaty tunic for his shirt of fine lamellar plate. The polished scales glistened in the glow of their torches, shifting subtly with the movements of its wearer. It made Dietmar think of the figure carved into the bridge, with its writhing armour of eels. But Arcadius was no dark god conspiring against the world. He wore his thoughts on his face, in the deep lines of his cheeks and the crinkles at the corner of his eyes for all to see.

"No sign of this fabled wolf then, huh?" Arcadius glanced between Dietmar and Tomas, both of whom shook their heads.

Arcadius grunted, the lines of his face like oak. His dark eyes gleamed in the torchlight. "It makes my palms itch to wait around like this. Ser Walter would have had us mounted and out on the steppes to hunt the thing down, not sitting here like chickens in a coop waiting for the fox to get in."

"In the dark?" Tomas looked dubious.

"Hah!" Arcadius grinned. "We hunted Carpathian bears by the light of the moon. I nearly lost my arm wrestling one after sticking my spear in its belly." Arcadius shifted on his feet, adjusting the plate on his shoulders. He stared beyond their heads into the landscape outside the stockade before refocusing on Tomas. "The hunt, Master Tomas! It ignites the fire within the soul. We can still go—take a few torches, Geoff and his men, enough to form a hunting party and then some. What say you?"

Anywhere else, Dietmar might have agreed. But he had seen the demon and its temple, Razin's Falak and its world-bridging pool. Venturing into the night to hunt some unknown beast was the last thing he wanted to do.

"This'll be no Carpathian," he said. "If it's a bear at all, it won't be one fit for a lord's mantle. You saw what awaited us in the pool. Everything here is some twisted perversion of itself." He looked askance, his eyes flicking to where Teoma sat on a seat in front of the pyre. The old man was shrouded in his hood, concealing his burned face and deformed features. His walking stick rested across his knees, the lamb's head turning in his palm. "Even the people," Dietmar whispered. "The way they bind their heads, forcing them into strange shapes... And why do they hide from us, lurking in shadow while Teoma and his slave attend us? It's as if they're waiting for something."

"For what?" said Tomas, his eyes wide.

"Nothing good," said Arcadius. He scratched at the grey in his beard, then snapped his head at a shout from the gate.

It is here.

Then a scream pierced the air.

The devil hath come.

"Good Christ," Tomas swore, turning to stare in the direction of the commotion. "What was that?"

But Dietmar was already in motion, his boots pounding against the walkway as he ran back in the direction they had come. He could hear Arcadius behind him. The heavy Greek's strides were like hammer blows against the wood, his breath like the bellows.

Ahead, torches flickered, and figures flitted through the shadows, converging near the gate. A sudden gust of wind enveloped them, causing their torches to sputter before settling once more.

Dietmar nearly stumbled, barely regaining his footing before looking up.

The gate was open.

Somebody let it in.

A small crowd had gathered around the base of the nearest watchtower, their eyes fixed on something on the ground. Dietmar pushed through, waving his torch to make room. His breath caught when he saw what they were looking at.

Samael was kneeling over the figure of Odilo. The Pavian lay sprawled out on his chest, a pool of blood surrounding his head. His hauberk and tabard were in tatters, and scattered chain rings littered the ground. They gleamed in the torchlight. But it was his face that had drawn the gasp from Dietmar.

It had been chewed off.

Cartilage and moist flesh glistened in the light. Exposed cheekbones jutted out like snowy ridges on a field of red. His face had been skinned from the upper lip to the hairline and from ear to ear. Chunks of flesh were missing from one cheek, revealing the flat peaks of his molars. Where Odilo's broad nose had once stood, a flat ridge was all that remained.

Samael flinched as Odilo emitted a hoarse moan and coughed up blood onto the sand.

He's still alive. God.

"Get me a blanket!" Samael pleaded, extending his hand toward the crowd.

"Jesus fucking Christ," said Enos.

"He's fucked," said Amice, peering over Geoff's shoulder.

"We need to get him inside." Samael looked around until his eyes settled on a stack of reed and wattle bales. "Build a litter for him, quickly!"

When no one stirred, Dietmar stepped forward and swept his torch around to face the gathering. "You heard him. Enos, get some rope from the stables. Erasmus and… What's your name? András? You and Bere, gather enough sheeting to make a litter for Odilo. We need to get him inside. Move it!"

"And close the fucking gate," Arcadius growled. "Or do you want that thing to come back and finish this poor bastard off?"

"The rest of you…" Dietmar looked down at Odilo, then at the large paw marks in the sand and blood. "Move in pairs. Jehan, go with Enos to the stables. And no man moves unarmed! If you've got steel, I want to see it in your hands. If you don't, stay with someone who does!"

Those with assigned tasks quickly moved to fulfil them, driven by a sense of purpose that temporarily pushed aside their fear. The remaining onlookers murmured amongst themselves as they stared down at Odilo's motionless body, their faces filled with concern.

"Where's Guiscard?" said Dietmar, staring at their faces. He saw Geoff, Amice, Samael, Tomas, Arcadius, and a pair of Levi's drivers. But no Guiscard.

"Fuck," said Arcadius. He took the torch from Tomas and headed toward a dark patch of dirt beneath the second watchtower. Dietmar had taken it for shadow at first, but when Arcadius's torch illuminated the area, the truth became apparent.

"More blood," said Samael.

"That's not all," Arcadius said, pointing his torch toward a set of tracks mixed with the blood. His eyes followed the trail, leading in the direction of the huts.

"It's in here with us," Dietmar breathed.

***

"I've done what I can," said Tomas. "But if he is to survive the night, he will need a favour from the Lord."

"Is he comfortable?" asked Dietmar, staring down at Odilo. Tomas had dressed his wounds, hiding the worst of the beast's attack under linen wraps. He'd applied a soothing balm mixed with honey to prevent against infection. Still, the wounds had started to seep, and a rotten stink hung over the Pavian, joining the clawing musk in Teoma's hut.

Tomas wrinkled his brow at the question. "If he ever wakes, he'll be in more pain than he's ever been in before. That poxxing hellhound did the Devil's work on him. But for now… he rests, a miracle in itself."

"One aided by your care, I have no doubt," said Dietmar. He touched his friend's arm gently and nodded his thanks before rising to his feet.

Tomas had administered to Odilo while Dietmar and the others searched for Guiscard and saw to the safety of the Lady Marie and Levi's daughters. Tomas had remained with the injured man alone, sharing soft words of comfort while he saw to his wounds. He would have made a good priest, Dietmar thought.

—buggerer, the voice whispered, laughing.

"Shut up," Dietmar snarled.

Tomas blinked at him.

"No, not you." He clenched his jaw and tried to shake the laughter out of his head. "It's…" He thought about telling Tomas about the voice rattling around inside his head—the one that mocked his friends and told him lies. It could only be the damned Saint Ephium himself. But when he saw Tomas's concerned expression, he decided against sharing the burden. "It's nothing," he said. "I'm tired, that's all. I think I still have some of that foetid water sloshing about inside of me."

"You do look pale," said Tomas.

"Aye. A few days rest, and I'll be back to my old self. But that won't be anytime soon."

"Not for any of us. I wonder—" Tomas began, but his train of thought was interrupted by Razin, who entered the hut and gave them a curt nod.

"I cannot find him," he said, making way for Geoff and Amice. "He must have snuck out of the gate after letting that *thing* in."

"You think it was the old man?" Dietmar frowned. The thought had crossed his mind too, but only briefly.

"Who else?" said Geoff. "The rest of the villagers vanish into their little holes the moment they catch sight of us. Only him and his girl-slave wander about." Geoff spared Odilo a glance, shaking his head. "I doubt this poor bastard suspected a thing. Probably let him waddle right up to the gate before realising what he was up to."

Amice snorted. "Dumb bastard."

"Watch your mouth, boy," Geoff warned, looking away from Odilo. "This could have been any one of us. Consider yourself lucky you're not lying here with your face torn off, breathing what might be your last."

Amice shrugged.

Cruel bastard.

"And no sign of the beast?" asked Dietmar.

"Nothing," Razin confirmed. "The tracks disappear somewhere between the stables and the fishing hut. Arcadius thinks it might have climbed back over the palisades with its… kill… with the Norman."

"He's fucked then," said Amice, ignoring Geoff's glare. "Hopefully, the beast eats its full and doesn't come back for more. But if it does, maybe we should leave some of those villagers outdoors to tempt it? Better them than us… those pagan savages. What about the girl? I could go find her, just say the word."

Dietmar tilted his head to stare at Amice until his former squire blinked and looked away.

"Only a suggestion," said Amice quietly.

"And a *cunting* thing to do." Geoff licked the corners of his mouth with his dark tongue and glanced out the doorway. His eyes narrowed. "Sounds like they found something."

A moment later, Dietmar heard it too. Excited voices calling to one another, their fear smothered by sudden bravado, emboldened by each other's presence. Someone was banging at the wattle shell of a hut with a piece of metal, summoning the rest of the company out from the hovels—Arcadius with his axe, Dietmar thought. Then the Greek's booming voice rose above the clangour, confirming it.

Dietmar spared Odilo and Tomas a final glance and then motioned toward the door. "Let's see what they've found."

***

What remained of the man that had been Guiscard was less a corpse than it was a mound of gristled offal, barely recognisable as human. They found the remains in one of the abandoned huts past the stables, partially concealed by a wall of rotting timber shafts reserved for the palisade. The right side of the hut had caved in, taking much of the roof down with it, leaving a large hole through which the beast had likely carried Guiscard to chew on in peace.

The remains were spread out on a reed mat in the centre of the hut, like it'd been left for them to discover. Samael had stumbled upon the gruesome scene first and left a pool of vomit at the door to mark his discovery.

"Poor bastard," muttered Geoff, positioning himself between Arcadius and Amice in an attempt to maintain order. The imposing Romei had snapped at Amice upon his arrival but fell silent when he beheld the horrific sight of Guiscard's remains.

"He'll have a Christian burial," said Dietmar, his stomach churning as he gazed into the macabre scene. The flickering light of his torch illuminated the grisly details, each moment spent staring revealing more of the unsettling truth. The *meat*—it felt strange to think of human remains in such a way, somehow wrong to reduce a man's being and existence to so banal a term.

But that is what it was. *Meat.* It reminded him of the ground-up beef prepared by the butchers of Malcuisinat using leftover cuts. His stomach rolled again.

"There's no sacred ground here," said Arcadius, thumbing the sharp edge of his axe with a gloved finger. "Just those blasphemers' dirt."

"Then we'll take his bones with us," said Dietmar. "To be buried back home in good Christian soil."

"Aye," said Geoff, nodding his assent. "He was a prickly shite in life, but I won't leave him here to rot with these pagans. Not if it's no skin off my back."

Razin entered the hut, stooping low and covering his mouth and nose with the tail of his keffiyeh as he approached the mound of flesh. His flickering torch settled inside the hut, away from the wind. The light revealed Guiscard's dirty grey tabard and undercoat, as well as his mail shirt and boots beside the carcass.

Dietmar frowned. The Norman had been stripped before he'd been eaten.

What kind of beast did that?

Razin eyed the garments warily before looking past them, through the hole in the hut and into the night. The stockade loomed ahead, its rotting posts lit by a pair of guttering torches.

"Anything?" grunted Arcadius. "I can't see in that pitch."

Razin swept the perimeter with a flick of his head, his sharp eyes taking in the walkway, gloomy palisades, and stacks of reed bales in quick succession. He paused on a shadowy patch just beyond the nearest torch and raised his hand to draw attention. Dietmar followed his line of sight, noticing something that didn't quite belong among the tightly packed bales.

Before Dietmar could speak, a pair of golden yellow orbs gleamed in the darkness, and one of the reed bales began to shift.

Arcadius let out a loud whoop and charged forward, nearly colliding with Razin as he dashed through the hut, heading for the opening on the other side.

"What are you doing!?" Arcadius roared, spinning around to glare at Razin, his axe held at the ready. "The beast is right there! We can kill it now and be done with it."

"Look," Razin said, his grip still firm on Arcadius's elbow, his other hand clutching the torch. He pointed it toward the enclosure.

Another shape emerged from between the reed bales, squeezing through a gap in the stockade where Enos had attempted to seal it earlier. It was the same opening that had been covered with wattle sheeting and rope.

"There's more of them there," Geoff growled, gesturing toward another section of the wall near the gate. Dietmar turned in time to see two long-limbed shadows scurrying away from the walkway, disappearing amidst the huts. A high-pitched rattle followed them, a series of whining snorts and grunts that sounded to him like laughter.

The devils are among us, and they are laughing at us.

"Hyena!" Razin barked, finally letting go of Arcadius's arm. "We must get to the stables before they eat through our mounts."

"If they don't eat us first." The big Greek shrugged Razin away and then took another step forward. He paused at the entrance of the hut, his eyes scanning the scene. More black and brown bodies were forcing their way into the settlement, snorting and whooping as they got past the palisades.

Hyenas, Razin had said. Dietmar had seen some once before, back in Amalric's menagerie. But those had been short, stocky beasts, no taller than his waist. A pair of them could rip the throat from a man, it was true, and children had been known to go missing when they strayed too close to hyena packs. Still, they could be fended off with shouts and fire, and if that failed, the sword.

"They're too big," Dietmar breathed. The one lurking amongst the reed bales rose to its full height, stepping into the orange glow cast by the torch. It stood almost as tall as the palisade, its elongated forelimbs elevating its broad chest above the nearby torchlight. Its hind legs appeared stunted in comparison, giving the beast a hunched posture, though from the knots of muscle rippling under the hyena's fur, Dietmar could tell it was lightning fast.

The creature stalked forward, moving fully into the light. Its features were broad and flat, like a wolf's snout had been clamped and compressed, beaten with a hammer until it looked closer to that of a lion's. Deep-set yellow eyes rested beneath a heavy brow. The eyes were close together, with only the narrow ridge at the top of its snout keeping them apart.

Like a monkey's eyes, Dietmar thought.

As the creature prowled out of the light, he was given the impression of thin lips in a feral grin and a long, grey tongue lolling from its mouth. Dark red, almost black, blood clung to the wiry hairs of its gore-soaked chest.

It had been feeding.

Dietmar's gaze shifted downward, and he recoiled in disgust. A long, black shaft protruded from between the coarse hair around the hyena's abdomen.

It was aroused.

He blinked, turning away, only to flinch at another scream. It was followed by a chorus of curses and panicked voices. Spheres of light emerged further along the walkway, illuminating the huts closest to the wall. The shouts grew more alarmed.

Someone roared a warning. There was a hollow *crump* of metal against bone, accompanied by yet another scream.

The rest of the company had found the beasts.

"We must go," Razin whispered urgently, pointing back toward the door. Dietmar nodded, then glanced around at a scratching, scraping sound nearby. One of the beasts was digging at the shell of the hut next door, trying to get in.

"*Quickly!*" Razin urged, moving toward the door. He cautiously peered outside, surveying both directions before slipping into the night. Dietmar and the others followed.

They left Guiscard's remains to rot. They didn't have a choice.

18

Ladah was in chaos.

Everywhere Dietmar looked, large, long-limbed creatures stalked the streets, loping between the hovels with shambolic strides that looked like something between a horse's gallop and a bear's shambling gait.

Razin nearly led them right into one as they crept behind the fishing hut. It materialised from out of the darkness like a hungry mouth, its round ears pressed flat against its head as its slobbering jaws opened to welcome them with a breath of carrion.

Razin reacted a split-second later, driving at it with his torch and slashing with his sword. The beast recoiled, its wide yellow eyes filled with surprise as fire caught its fur. Arcadius swung his axe, narrowly missing its head, and the creature scurried away, retreating into the shadows, still sniggering and whooping.

"The Lady Marie and then your Tomas," said Arcadius.

They were crouched against the walls of the pig pen, staring across the yard. Shadows flitted past the pyre as figures sought refuge near its flames, hoping the beasts would fear the fire. But the hyenas stalked them unafraid, chortling and snorting as they closed in. They'd seen two of the drivers fall prey to their jaws, devoured by the relentless creatures, and more continued to emerge.

Dietmar had counted a dozen so far already.

"Tomas is right there," he pointed to the hut closest to the well, a mere dozen yards away, its door still shut. Tomas would be inside, praying fervently while he listened to the shouts and screams. Had he seen the beasts yet, or just heard their grunts and mocking laughter?

Arcadius shook his head. "The Lady Marie first."

"We should see to the horses," said Razin. "Without them, we are stranded here."

"Ai. Fuck the Lady Marie and Tomas," said Geoff. He paled and moved a little away from Arcadius, who glared at him in response.

"Begging your pardon," Geoff quickly added, "but the Arab is right. These *cunting* things will eat the horses out from under our saddles if they get half the chance."

"They've left the pigs be." Dietmar glanced into the pen. The pigs remained undisturbed, lazily lounging near their feeding troughs, stirring only to wallow in the muck.

"There'd be an ungodly racket otherwise," he continued.

"They know they're safe." Razin joined Dietmar's side, squatting down and observing the pen. "Those things, those *kaftar*, have the taste for man now."

"Then why aren't they eating the pagans?" Geoff curled his lips, scratching his mouth. His torch was planted in the ground, and his sword rested loosely across his knees as he leaned back against the fence. "They could tear through those huts and gorge themselves on those pointy fucking heads, so why don't they?"

Razin untied his keffiyeh and wiped the sweat from his upper lip with the back of his hand. He pondered, "Could there be some bargain struck between the villagers with the beasts? Perhaps, those who live here give up any poor souls who pass through, and in turn, they are left in relative peace...."

"I'll kill them," Amice snarled, stabbing the ground with his knife.

Once.

Twice.

"Every fucking last one of them. And that old man I'll do at the end. Him and his girl."

Another beast bounded past their hiding spot, its claws scraping against the sand, its long strides carrying it toward the well. It slowed, then skidded to a halt and turned on its hindlegs. Dietmar ducked back down, certain they'd been discovered, but the creature's yellow eyes were fixed on something else.

"Is that... Enos?" Razin whispered.

Dietmar peered over the wooden fence just in time to see a figure clamber over the stone lip of the well, unaware that he had already been spotted. He pictured the mercenary hiding in the cold and wet while the hyenas ravaged the village, clinging to nothing but the bucket and its rope to keep afloat. All the while, his friends died.

You should have stayed there, you fool.

Dietmar winced as Enos dropped to the ground. He crouched against the well's grey walls and took in his surrounds. The driver had discarded his mail hauberk and now wore only a dirty grey gambeson, soaked through and clinging to his slender frame like a wet rag.

The hyena moved swiftly, its padded paws carrying it across the yard with a stealth that Dietmar would not have thought possible for a creature of its size. It hurtled past the pyre, the short mane of hair along its back and between its ears standing on end as it closed in on Enos. The beast's ears twitched once, then swung back against its skull like a lowered mast, its hackles already raised.

"Go on, you stupid bastard, get out of there," urged Geoff, his voice a low whisper.

We can't just leave him.

"No, wait," said Razin, dragging Dietmar back down when he made to rise.

"God's teeth, man," Dietmar snarled. "He'll die out there."

"*Look.*" Razin stuck his fingers out toward gloom, beyond the pyre. Dietmar squinted, trying to adjust his eyes and peer into the shadows between the huts. His heart sank when he saw the figures watching the hunt. Two black silhouettes, even larger than the one currently pursuing Enos.

"We can't help him," said Razin softly.

Enos seemed to have realised something was amiss. He crossed himself and glanced over the edge of the well.

The beast was just a few feet away now, its black lips peeling back to reveal its menacing teeth. Enos didn't hesitate. He sprung to his feet, but instead of retreating to the safety of the well, he made a desperate dash toward the watchtowers. Perhaps he thought there was safety to be found at the top of their ladders, or maybe his instinct for flight kicked in before he could do otherwise.

Either way, it was the wrong choice.

Enos's legs were stiff from treading water, and his soaked gambeson weighed him down, draining his energy even further. Before he could reach halfway across the yard, the hyena *thing* caught up to him.

It loomed over Enos like a bear over a wolfhound. The tall Galilean hardly reached up to its sloping shoulders. The beast loped beside Enos for a moment, its lips curling back to hack out more of that high-pitched laughter that made Dietmar want to claw his skin off. Then, when Enos tried to pivot away, breaking sharply to his right, the creature pounced.

It snapped at his near thigh, sweeping Enos's other leg out from under him like a lion catching a gazelle. The driver cried out as he hit the hard ground with a heavy thud, scrabbling to get back to his feet. Blood streamed from his wounded leg where the hyena's teeth had cut into him.

"We must go," said Razin softly from beside Dietmar. "Let us not waste his death by tarrying."

"We're not going to help him?" Geoff asked, looking on as the beast lumbered over Enos to fully straddled him with its girth. He wrinkled his mouth in disgust as the hyena's member emerged, fully engorged. "Disgusting animal."

"There's nothing we can do," said Arcadius. His arms were crossed over the shaft of his axe, cradling it against his chest. He nodded toward the walkway in the direction of the Lady Marie's hut.

Dietmar flinched at another cry from the yard. Enos had somehow managed to turn onto his back and was desperately swiping at the hyena with his knife. The beast barely twitched as the blade sliced through its dusty fawn-yellow fur. Enos tried to retrieve his knife, but the hyena snapped at his hand, nearly taking his fingers. The driver made one final attempt to escape, wriggling his way out from between the creature's legs, but he was only halfway out when a massive paw slammed down on his chest, pinning him in place.

He screamed.

Then, the hyena's jaws opened over his face and snapped at his head.

Dietmar refused to look away as Enos's struggle came to an end. His muscles still spasmed even as his head was torn from his neck, blood splattering across the dusty yard, forming a stream that flowed past the well. There was a *crack* as the creature's teeth ground into Enos's skull, bone giving way to force. Grey matter spilt from the beast's mouth.

The other hyenas, who had been watching from their spot between the huts, stalked toward the kill, eager to share in the spoils.

"Leave your torches," said Razin, dropping his own to the ground. "The kaftar are not afraid of fire, and we'll only draw them to us." He nodded when Dietmar and Geoff left theirs where they sat, then peered along the walkway. The glow of the torches from the palisades appeared stunted, diminished now that the wind was dying down.

Dietmar resisted the urge to look back. He could still hear the hyenas laughing over their meal, their sniggering like the exotic monkeys he had seen in the markets of Antioch and Messina. There was a tearing sound, then something wet, and the snap of bones being broken open.

He gritted his teeth and hurried forward, following Razin into the dark.

***

"Careful now," Arcadius cautioned, guiding the Lady Marie between the reed bales. Levi and his girls followed closely, with Geoff and Amice behind them, then Tomas and Dietmar. Razin moved like a shadow at the rear.

They'd hidden away in Teoma's hut after retrieving the Lady Marie. At first, Tomas had refused to open the door. He'd called them liars and deceivers, accused them of trickery until Arcadius had threatened to peel open the hut with his axe and beat the Englishman bloody. Then he'd opened the door quick enough.

Once inside, they had sat in frozen fear and listened to the beasts eat their way through the remainder of the company. Sometime before dawn, the sounds of slaughter and feasting had given way to what they took to be the deep snores of animals, now with full bellies.

Not long after, Odilo had succumbed to his wounds, breathing his last breaths as the first rays of sunlight pierced the window to the hovel.

An ugly death, Dietmar thought. Immense pain, fear, and in those last few moments of consciousness, the knowledge that his remains would probably be eaten.

Tomas had said some words over Odilo's lifeless body, and then Razin roused them. *If we are going to go, then it must be while they sleep.*

And so, they'd crept out into the morning, making for the stables and hoping to God they'd find their mounts in one piece.

The hyenas lay strewn about the settlement, their chests and faces drenched in crimson gore, their distended bellies a testament to the feast they had indulged in. Remnants of their macabre banquet lay scattered all around—an abandoned skull with its spinal cord exposed, a chewed limb bearing grotesque welts where the flesh had been savagely torn from the bone.

A putrid stink hung heavy in the air, forcing them to shield their faces with their hands, desperately trying to suppress the urge to retch.

Arcadius raised his axe threateningly toward one of the slumbering beasts near the fishing hut. Dietmar's gaze followed Arcadius's gesture, and he noticed Enos's knife still lodged in the creature's front leg. He felt anger then, but he quickly shook his head at Arcadius. If the beast stirred before it died and woke the others, there'd be no fighting their way out. Reluctantly, Arcadius acquiesced, but his knuckles were white against the shaft of his axe, his eyes red.

Dietmar offered a silent prayer of thanks when they finally reached the stables. They found Adelman inside, still tending to his mules, seemingly unfazed by their arrival. He muttered something about Balaam's feed before shuffling across the floor to whisper into Silensus's long drooping ears.

The survivors moved into the stables quietly and swiftly began packing the food and water they'd need to keep them alive once they left the settlement.

"I've told them to be quiet," said Adelman, his eyes pleading. "They'll listen. They know it's important."

Dietmar raised an eyebrow at a muted *haw* from Balaam. The mule swished its tail and blinked its large eyes at him. Did it really understand?

"They can't come," he said softly, studying the mule's face for any sign of understanding. When nothing happened, he shook his head and snorted. What had he expected? "They would only slow us down," he continued, turning to Adelman. "We'll take what water we can and our horses... but the mules."

Adelman remained silent, his gaze shifting between Silensus and Balaam as he tenderly stroked their coarse black manes.

Dietmar grunted. He wasn't sure Adelman understood—that he was fully there at all anymore. The events of the past few days seemed to have accelerated his decline. He passed by the old man, gently patting his shoulder, before joining Arcadius to help unpack the Lady Marie's wagon.

There would be time for an accounting later.

But when? Dietmar wondered. *When will be a good time? Or will we all die in this place before I find the right words?*

"And make sure you've got something warm," Arcadius was saying. The Lady Marie nodded once and disappeared into the wagon. She reappeared a moment later, holding a thick bundle of fur tightly secured by a leather belt. She gripped the fur by the silver buckle, while a small dagger in a wooden sheath was clasped in her other hand. Ruby-red gems shone from its hilt.

"That won't be much use," said Arcadius, blinking at the dagger. "Those beasts have pelts as thick as that little knife is short."

"It's not for them," said the Lady Marie. She glanced across the stable floor to where Amice and Geoff were busy with their horses.

Dietmar felt a flush of shame. That the Lady Marie's greatest concern, even amidst the horrors they faced, was the slimy squire he had allowed into their company was a stain on his own character and no one else's.

"It won't come to that," he assured her. He tugged open one of the waiting saddlebags, took a handful of waterskins from Arcadius, and packed them into the bag. Glancing up, he met the Lady Marie's sharp blue eyes. "If he comes so much as a foot from you—"

"I'll bury my axe in his neck." Arcadius closed the wagon doors with a quiet click and then hoisted a saddle bag over each shoulder. His face went red from the strain, but when Dietmar offered him a hand, Arcadius waved him away. He grabbed his axe from where it had been resting against the wagon's wheel and marched toward the horses on the other side of the stables.

The Lady Marie gave Dietmar a sad smile and hurried after her bodyguard. She walked with pride, her head held high, uncowed by what she had seen. Dietmar had no doubt she had the heart to fend off any threat, but heart wasn't always enough. You needed strength, and sometimes you needed Arcadius and his big fucking axe.

He wondered then at what the voice had told him… that Arcadius had shared her mother's bed. Could it be? A *cold-blooded reptile*, he'd called her… If anything, such familiarity made Dietmar suspicious, and they did share a chin, that much was clear.

And what if he had? What business is it of mine?

He chose to ignore the lecherous thing's gossip and moved out into the yard.

"God's bones," he murmured, seeing the baggage Levi was dragging down from a cart parked outside the makeshift stables. His daughters were already laden with more than they could comfortably carry.

"You'll have to make do with less," Dietmar said, shaking his head as he approached them. "We'll have a hard enough time getting the horses past those Devil's dogs without them being overburdened. Come on, water and food only. Leave the rest."

Levi looked down at him from the back of the cart, his hands still gripping a wooden box that he had been about to hand to Miriam. It bore a trader's mark Dietmar didn't recognise.

"These are Minna's favourite," said Levi, his voice not quite a plea but close to it. He clutched the box against his chest, and the little clasp holding it together came undone. Orange fabric spilled from the lid before Levi could slam it shut again—finely braided collars and tunics, silk shirts befitting of royalty. "She won't forgive me if I lose them."

Dietmar sighed. "There are worse things. Some of them are lurking just behind those huts." He rapped his knuckle against the side of the cart and gestured to the box. "Put it down, Levi. There will be more boxes, more carts, and more cloth, but not if we remain here."

"Please, *Abba*," pleaded Levi's smaller daughter, struggling to maintain her balance under the weight of the stacked boxes in her arms.

Levi let out a groan. Reluctantly, he returned the box to its place on the cart.

"Talk to me when we're out on the streets after your mother's wrath," he said.

Dietmar helped him down from the cart and then turned to stare out at the yard. He thought he caught a glimpse of yellow robes disappearing into the nearest hovel, but before he could follow it, a high-pitched snorting sound filled the air. Then laughter.

The hyenas had awoken.

"Fuck," said Dietmar.

"Fuck," Levi agreed.

***

"Get inside!" Dietmar bellowed when he caught sight of the first tawny head emerging between the huts. He pushed Levi toward the open doors and drew his sword.

The last of the morning gloom was rapidly departing, dragging back the shadows that had made the settlement their home that night. Shards of light stretched from the surrounding hills over the palisade walls, casting the landscape in an ephemeral glow. It was into one of those radiant beams of light that the hyena stepped.

Its spotted coat seemed to shine in the sun, the curls from its long shaggy pelt like a golden fleece at its chest. Its distended belly sagged, revealing patches of black skin beneath the sparser hairs on its underbelly.

Then Dietmar noticed it had the first makings of an erection. Its loins stirred as it lumbered lazily across the yard, its phallus swelling ominously with each step.

What kind of sick and twisted animal grew aroused at the prospect of feeding?

At the thought of death?

"Go on!" Dietmar shouted, brandishing his sword at the thing. He searched the ground for something to hurl at it. "Get out of here! Away!"

To his left, he noticed another hyena emerging from the smithy, lured out by the morning sun. Two more followed closely behind, jostling with each other to reach him first.

Dietmar gave them all one last sweeping glance and then stepped back into the stables, slamming the doors shut behind him.

They came in through the walls.

They tore through the old timber frame with claws like hatchets and banged at the wood until it split and their jagged teeth could fit through.

Bang. Bang. Bang. Shhft.

They used their jaws to widen the gaps and pulled the thin boards until gaping holes covered the walls and doors.

Bang.

The sound stopped.

Something heavy brushed against the doors.

Dietmar held his breath, his gaze shifting upward to the ceiling. The wooden boards beneath the thatch roof groaned, bending under the weight of something immense moving over it. Dust trickled down from the crossbeams. A sound like nails scratching against the reeds echoed through the air. It paused momentarily… then resumed.

Levi and his daughters stared at the ceiling, pale with fear as the sound grew louder. Sara whimpered softly, and Levi pulled her closer. Arcadius positioned himself in front of them, with the Lady Marie by his side. She clutched her dagger, poised for defence, while he raised his axe toward the ceiling.

"Stand behind me," he whispered, but she didn't move.

Geoff and Amice waited by the walls on the other side. They held their swords over their heads, ready to strike at whatever appeared through the holes. Tomas and Adelman sat with heads bowed in prayer, kneeling between the mules. They'd picked up staves somewhere on their dash to the stables, though they were little more than rotting wood.

Dietmar blinked. It looked as if the mules were at prayer, too, their ears pressed back, and heads lowered to the floor.

He made the sign of the cross and whispered a quick *Ave Maria*, then turned to face the door.

Facing him was Razin, his sword held horizontally at his shoulder, directed toward the largest hole. His lips moved in his own prayer.

—what good are prayers? the voice said softly, almost gently. *They brought you to this, didn't they?* Then it laughed and went quiet.

Everything went quiet.

Silence enveloped them. Each agonising moment lingered like seconds spent awaiting the gallows. They knew it wouldn't last. The hyenas would break in and eat them all.

And our bones will rot in this God-forsaken place.

Dietmar cautiously inched forward to peer through one of the holes in the door but snapped his head around at a sound from above.

The ceiling groaned.

And collapsed.

A pair of furry bodies crashed to the floor, all snapping teeth and gore-covered pelts. They landed upon the foul water trough, flattening it under their weight before swiftly regaining their footing.

The horses went mad, kicking against their stalls, eyes rolling with panic.

Arcadius was the first to react. He pulled the Lady Marie behind him and lunged at the nearest beast—a towering, slobbering creature with a torn ear and teeth the size of fingers. He swung his axe at its near shoulder, but the hyena sprung forward, sending the Greek sprawling before his blow could land.

Before it could snap at Arcadius's face, Geoff darted in and drove his sword into the creature's hindquarters. The beast screeched in pain, its short, bushy tail dropping between its legs as it turned to confront this new threat. Amice followed up with a slash to its flank, eliciting another pained yip, while Geoff poked at it again, attempting to herd it out one of the openings.

Dietmar heard the door groaning behind him and spun around just in time to see a black mouth tearing through the wood. More faces emerged from the walls, one after another, as the creatures outside clawed and scraped against the wooden structure, showering them with splinters and debris.

"Good Christ!" Tomas yelled, pointing to the wall behind him. More of the beasts were breaking through.

We don't have long left.

But he wouldn't go without taking a few hellhounds with him.

He swung his sword at the ugly face before him, catching the beast on its nose just as it recoiled from the opening. It howled in pain, its incessant chortling replaced by distressed yips. Another cry caught his attention, and he turned to witness a horrifying scene. Levi was barely holding onto his one girl

—the fat one

as she was being dragged away by the second hyena. The creature had already engulfed her legs in its jaws.

"God, please," Dietmar pleaded, stumbling toward them.

The beast shook its head from side to side, like a dog pulling at a bone from its master.

Levi desperately clung on, dragged across the stable floor, still grasping his daughter's flailing body.

Miriam let out a horrible shriek, and something tore inside of her.

"Abba!" she managed to squeak before the air escaped her lungs. She gasped and went limp in her father's arms. Then the hyena pulled once more, and the girl's body tore apart.

Levi stood there, gawping down at his dead daughter.

"Levi!" Dietmar yelled at him.

The dyer looked up stupidly and tried to say something. Then he knelt down, cradling Miriam's upper body and futilely trying to push her spilt entrails back into her, as if he could push the life back inside the broken girl.

But she was gone.

"Levi!" Dietmar yelled again, grabbing him by the shoulder and pushing him toward Tomas.

Tomas and Adelman reached out, gently assisting the bewildered Levi as they carefully lowered what remained of Miriam to the ground.

Sara started to cry.

Then the doors came apart.

"Come on, you bastards," bellowed Arcadius, hefting his axe.

Hyenas poured into the stables in a relentless stream of mangy fur and snapping teeth.

"Dietmar!" Tomas called from between the panicked mules. "The hand! The damned fear the holy! Show them!"

Geoff cursed and stumbled back as a massive hyena crashed through the wall.

"Show them!" Tomas urged. The Lady Marie peered out from behind Tomas's robes, her face pale as a sheet. Her hands trembled as she extended her tiny dagger before her, shaking like branches in a storm.

She doesn't deserve this fate.

None of us do.

He thought of Amice.

No, not even him.

Arcadius swung his axe in a vicious arc, striking out, again and again, to hold the stinking curs at bay.

But that wouldn't last.

He was already getting slower.

Dietmar glanced down at the pouch at his side and swiftly unfastened the drawstring.

It worked against the demon, he thought.

But at what price?

He heard Geoff cry out and made up his mind, quickly pulling the relic from its pouch and striding toward the fight.

Razin and Arcadius were locked in combat with three of the beasts while another two—the pair that had fallen through the roof—attempted to flank them.

Arcadius swung his axe with a throaty roar at the hyena trying to skirt around his left side. The hyena skittered away, just out of range of the Greek's wrath. Arcadius exhaled sharply as he caught sight of Dietmar.

But Dietmar didn't pause to meet his questioning look.

He stepped forward, extending the hand like some odious offering. The nearest of the monsters stalked forward, its hackles raised. It favoured one leg ever so slightly, blood still trickling from a wound inflicted by Razin when it had grown too bold.

It blinked its monkey eyes at Dietmar, then considered the hand.

But it did not stop.

It did not hesitate like the demon in the lair.

Dietmar swore and quickly stepped back, raising his sword alongside the hand to fend off the hyena's advance.

—stupid dog, the voice chortled. *It doesn't understand. How could it?*

The hyena sprung forward, taking the flat side of Dietmar's sword to the head when it snatched at the relic.

Dietmar barely avoided the second hyena's attack, nearly losing his balance as he kicked at it, almost losing his foot when its black mouth snapped just inches away from the leather of his boot.

—its little brain has already rotten away. How could my gift scare it?

"It is no gift," Dietmar snarled, slashing at the beast as he staggered back.

—ah, so you do talk after all

"Bah!" Dietmar dropped the hand back into its pouch and gripped his sword with both hands, raising his guard. He caught a glimpse of movement to his left—a blur of bloody fur and teeth shooting toward him. Before he could duck out of its way, the silver scales of Arcadius's lamellar plate filled his vision.

Then a hand shot out, pushing him aside.

He tumbled to the floor, scrabbling on his elbows to get back up. From his knees, he saw Arcadius lunge forward, his great axe swinging.

The blade struck the hyena behind its ears, slicing deep into its neck and spraying blood across the stable floor. The beast yelped in shock and pain as the axe reached bone. Before it could snap at the Greek or scuttle away, Arcadius unsheathed the axe from its neck and struck again. His face went red with the exertion, but he pulled the axe from the wet bloody mound of bone and meat and slammed it back a third time.

The hyena staggered forward and then collapsed, its neck severed from its spine.

Arcadius hadn't been able to behead the beast, even with his mammoth blows, but he'd done enough. He let out a triumphant roar, panting like a dog over the dead hyena until Razin pulled him back, taking his place at the front to allow the Greek to catch his breath.

They all flinched at a cry from outside the stables and looked to see a hunched figure stumbling through the yard. It was Teoma. He shouted and waved his cane at them between his unsteady strides. When he got nearer, Dietmar saw tears running down the cheek beneath his remaining eye.

Even if he could understand Aramaic, he doubted he would be able to decipher the words that the old man barked out amid his sobs.

Teoma hobbled between the hyenas unmolested, dragging his yellow robe through the dirt—the shepherd returning to his flock. The beasts peeled back at his appearance, seemingly as stunned by the demise of one of their own as the old man was. They retreated to watch from the openings they had created in the walls.

As he made his way past the shattered doors, Dietmar saw a strange thing happen.

The bleeding corpse on the floor twitched, and its massive paws began to move. He thought it was somehow still impossibly alive and was about to slam his sword into its skull when he realised it wasn't moving.

It was *changing*.

The hyena's forelimbs retracted toward its body, shortening as the mane that ran from its head to tail vanished, and the hair of its pelt disappeared entirely, leaving just a short black tuft above its ears. Its jaws collapsed in on themselves, narrowing with a sickening snap to reveal a bearded mouth with rotten brown teeth. With a loud cracking of bones, its back straightened and narrowed, revealing a chest covered in hair.

Human hair.

"God, what is this?" Dietmar breathed, blinking as the hyena disappeared.

A man now lay in its stead.

He was tall, with long unkempt hair and blood-caked nails. His skin had a deep umber hue. His shrunken and shrivelled penis was hidden beneath a mass of pubic hair. But however much he had changed, he had not healed. His head rested askew against the floor, only connected to his body by a flap of flesh as wide as a thumb.

When Dietmar looked into the man's eyes, he noticed the same eerie yellow glow that had been present in the hyena's gaze.

Arcadius spat on the ground and lifted his axe to examine the blood along its edge. He snarled. "It is a union with the Devil these men have made."

"And may the Devil take them," Dietmar muttered, watching Teoma as he dropped to his knees beside the body, still cursing at them in his ancient tongue. What were they to him, these creatures? His children? Or was he the intermediary between them and the Devil? The old man had welcomed them into their homes, broke bread with them… Dietmar remembered the faces lurking in the shadows while they ate. Those hungry eyes. How many times had this ritual been repeated? How many hapless travellers had fallen into the mouths of these beasts to fill their bellies?

God! Anger surged through him—not just at the betrayal and their plight but at the *wrongness* of it all. These *men* ate *men* and transformed their bodies—only God had that right.

Dietmar strode across the stable floor and halted in front of Teoma. The old man snarled something at him, rising to his feet in his dirty yellow robes. But Dietmar paid no attention to his ranting. With a swift motion, he raised his sword up in a flash of silver on yellow and then red. The sword sliced through Teoma's robes, splitting them from the brown-knotted rope at his waist to the neck of his hood. The old man howled in pain as the sword pierced his flesh, dropping his staff and collapsing in a heap at Dietmar's feet.

The hyenas lunged forward, poised to defend their master, but stopped when they saw the tip of Dietmar's sword levelled at his neck. They understood that, at least.

Dietmar frowned as the old man struggled in his robes, still spitting bile and venom from where he sat.

Vicious little bastard.

His robes peeled away where they'd been cut, splitting further at the seams to expose Teoma's pink skin. The tattered garment dropped off him like an old skin, a discarded husk, revealing his naked form resting upon a blood-soaked bundle of yellow fabric.

Dietmar's frown deepened.

He only had one arm and one leg.

And a tail.

"*Kill him!*" Arcadius barked upon seeing Teoma's naked form. "Heathen, blaspheming, godless, treacherous pagan. *Kill him!*"

"Wait!" cried Razin, joining Dietmar's side His burnous was torn, and his left arm covered in shallow cuts where his mail had been breached. He appeared shaken but unhurt. Razin studied Teoma for a moment before shaking his head. "This is no ordinary man. I have heard of such half-breed kinds before. Strike them once, and they may die like the rest of us. But strike him twice, and it would take a thousand blows to kill him." Razin motioned to Dietmar's blade and then to the discarded red-stained robes. "You have already struck him once."

Dietmar glanced at Razin. "Are you sure?"

"It is the way of his kind. Trust me."

"Kill it," growled Arcadius. "Or I'll do it myself, and we can test your theory against the edge of my axe."

"Hold on!" cried Tomas, hurrying out from between the mules. "Just hold on a second. Can't you see? Look!" He pointed to the yellow eyes peering from behind the wall. "The beasts are afraid we'll hurt him. That's why they haven't slaughtered us yet. But once you kill him…"

Dietmar sighed. "They'll wipe us out."

He stared down his sword at the old man. Uncovered, Teoma's head resembled a wrinkled egg, one side marred by scars and deep lines, while the other appeared smooth as silk. Dietmar briefly wondered how Teoma had managed to wield the walking staff with only one hand. His tail, perhaps? Had it held the cane beneath his robes while he used his remaining hand to wave them in? Only the fluffy white tuft of the tail was visible, but it seemed long enough.

He looked up from the old man to the hyenas prowling outside the stable, watching them through the broken walls. They had all gone perfectly quiet, with not even their agitated high-pitched laughs to grate his ears. Their round eyes were fixed on Teoma, occasionally shifting to Dietmar's sword but always returning to the old man. Was it fear? A dog's loyalty? Whatever it was, they felt a dire urge to protect the little demon.

Are we to have no justice, then? Is this little bastard going to live after causing so much death?

Dietmar felt the sudden urge to drive his sword into Teoma's bald head and be done with it. Damn the consequences. But he stayed his hand.

"He's right," Razin said, nodding in agreement with Tomas. "We could use him to get out."

"And then what?"

"We head north to find this Sandmouth."

"If he hasn't lied to us."

Razin shrugged. "He had no reason to lie. He thought we'd all be dead by sunrise."

"Aye." Dietmar made up his mind and motioned to Teoma. "Get up, you treacherous little lurch. We're not done with you yet."

Teoma bared his skew teeth at him defiantly, but complied when he was guided up by the tip of Dietmar's sword.

"Cover yourself," Dietmar commanded, pointing to the rags on the floor. "We don't need to see your filthy backside."

Teoma seemed to understand and bent down to gather what remained of his robes. He draped them over his body like a toga, ensuring that his tail and lower limb were hidden from view. He looked up at Dietmar, his hand by his staff, waiting for permission.

After a brief pause, Dietmar nodded, and the old man rose to his full hunched stature, his mouth set in a nasty snarl.

You're lucky to be alive, you miserable wretch.

Dietmar turned to look at the tired and frightened faces of the survivors behind him. Tomas stood beside Levi, supporting the grieving father by his shoulder, while Sara clung to Levi's waist. Their eyes held the same blank stare of loss. Geoff and Amice were covered in blood and cuts, their mail shirts reduced to tattered scraps of metal. The Lady Marie remained in her spot on the floor, still holding her dagger out before her, her small hands trembling.

"Get the horses," said Dietmar. "We're leaving."

After a brief pause, he nodded to Adelman. The old man stood where he had always stood, between Balaam and Silensus.

"The mules too."

19

They found the slave girl asleep behind a heap of old netting in the fishing hut. Dietmar had figured her for dead, eaten by an opportunistic hyena as soon as Teoma had fallen into their hands. But she was very much alive.

And by her catlike hiss at his approach, angry too.

He had decided they would bring her along. The other option was to leave her here in the hyena den to try her luck against a pack of hungry beasts. So, it wasn't any choice at all. But the girl, it turned out, didn't care what he thought. She hissed her feline hiss and swiped at his outstretched hand.

"Ouch!" Dietmar pulled his fingers back and looked at her. "Do you want to stay here?"

She stared at him.

Those eyes like golden light, flecked with shards of the sea.

"You can't stay here."

He reached for her again, but she flipped over the spool of rope like an acrobat and retreated further into the fishing hut.

"I don't think she likes you," said Tomas.

"I don't think I like her much either." Dietmar rubbed his hand where the girl had scratched him and swore beneath his breath. "Come on, then. Let's fish her out."

"And if she bites?"

"Bite her back."

"I don't like the sound of that." Tomas stared into the hut. "She looks dirty."

Dietmar laughed darkly. "Then don't get bitten."

In the end, it was Tomas who managed to coax her out. He spoke to her in a soft, soothing tone and opened his hands to show that he wasn't a threat—*not like that silly knight whose skin you've used as a scratching post.* The girl blinked at him, glanced at his hands and warm smile, and finally emerged from behind the nets of her own accord.

"Shit," Dietmar muttered, still nursing the knee she had kicked during his second failed attempt. "How'd you do that?"

Tomas winked at him. "I think she wanted to come with after all."

Dietmar rolled his eyes and then limped into the yard behind them.

***

They wheeled their carts out of Ladah later that morning, departing through the same gate they had entered by, but in far fewer number.

They rode north.

"Can you see them?" Tomas asked from his perch beside Adelman on the cart.

"Aye," Dietmar replied irritably. "For the thousandth time, they're still following us."

"And now?"

Dietmar glared at Tomas, then leaned back in his saddle to glance over his shoulder. His eyes scanned the expanse of long dry grass before finally resting on the two figures trailing behind them.

"And?" Tomas pressed.

"Yes," Dietmar sighed. "Like I said, they're still following us."

"They'll be with us until we give them back their master," said Geoff. He was seated in the back of Adelman's cart beside Teoma, his sword never more than a few inches from the old man's side.

"They're brothers," said Adelman with some certainty.

Dietmar looked at him. "Brothers? How do you know?"

"Cain and Abel," said Adelman as though it were obvious.

"Who told you that?" Dietmar raised an eyebrow but caught Tomas's eye and kept quiet.

Whatever their names, it was the same pair that had trailed them from the village and into the hills, long after the rest of the pack had fallen off.

Loyal as dogs, Dietmar thought.

But they were men.

Abominations, yes.

But men.

There had been a tense moment at the gate earlier when Teoma had called out to the corrupted beasts, those *men*, and incited them to action. The one-eared monstrosity from the stables had positioned itself in front of the first cart, blocking their path and causing poor Balaam and Silensus to panic. Dietmar had thought for sure it would attack, but whatever it was the old man had said wasn't enough. The beast had yielded the road when Amice pressed his knife against Teoma's throat, threatening to carve another mouth for him.

After that, Geoff had gagged Teoma and clipped him behind the ear for the trouble.

From the village, they had followed the river, riding alongside the pines growing in the shadow of the ravine. None of them wanted to linger near those trees that made the wind sound like a wailing scream when it passed through them, and Dietmar had breathed a quiet prayer when the forest finally gave way to overgrown plains and the hills they now found themselves in.

The hyenas trailing them had dwindled shortly after, and by the time they crossed between the first hills, only two remained.

Cain and Abel.

They trudged on, the rolling hills now growing rocky and steep so that their mounts strained and their journey slowed. On several occasions, they had to turn around, their path blocked by stiff inclines or ragged terrain no horse and cart could hope to traverse.

They saw signs of inhabitation along the river—more wooden huts and hovels, small rafts tied up against the current, and nets cast into the black waters. They gave the settlements a wide berth but couldn't avoid the ruins they stumbled upon sometime before midday.

It was little more than an outhouse, a small block building resting against the slope between the grey rocks. Dietmar didn't even notice it at first, but Razin's keen eyes caught sight of it, and he called them to a halt.

Fire had gutted the place in the past, leaving its walls without a roof. Where the door once hung, there was just a black hole—a shadowy slit leading inside.

"A demon lives here," Adelman said softly, in a voice that made Dietmar shiver.

"Shut up," Amice snapped, shooting him a cold glance from atop his mount. Geoff's ugly mare trailed behind, and he tugged at her reins.

"We should keep moving," said Razin.

"Back the other way?" Tomas eyed the edifice uncomfortably. He had been jumpy since the village, and with good reason. What they'd witnessed...

Dietmar shook off the memory and stared at the slope.

"We've come too far already," said Arcadius. He drove the second wagon, sitting with the former slave girl on the seat beside him to keep an eye on her. Levi and Sara sat in the back, lost to their own melancholy. The Lady Marie had tried in vain to console them but had given up when she saw her words were wasted on them. What did she know of such loss? Now she sat with them in silence, her sharp blue eyes scanning the hills.

"We could go past the village?" Tomas suggested, but by his tone, he didn't like the idea much.

Dietmar gazed up at the structure, trying to see into the room behind the absent door.

"There's no one there," he said, but even as he spoke the words, he knew that wasn't true. There was *something* there. Something ancient and old, watching them.

He didn't want it to come out.

A heavy silence settled over the hills, and Dietmar saw his friends looking at each other nervously. They all sensed it: a presence, something threatening emanating from the ruin on the slope. It was Razin who finally broke the silence, turning Riba around to face the path they had traversed.

"Look," he said, nodding down the path.

The two hyenas were watching them from the base of the hill. The gap between them and the wagons had widened, and the larger of the pair—the one with the torn ear Adelman had dubbed 'Cain'—paced across the path, but it did not draw closer.

"They seem... agitated?" said Dietmar, glancing to Razin.

Razin nodded, his gaze still fixed on the hyenas. "We have reached the edge of their territory. What lies beyond is the domain of another."

Geoff spat over the side of the cart and turned to the block building. "Or maybe something's got them spooked. Perhaps the drunken priest is right, and we should go back."

Arcadius growled in response. "We're not going past that damned village, or am I the only one who remembers what we found in the last one? *Lycaon's Curse*—the wolf men. I won't end up in the stomach of some devilish beast just because you're scared of an empty ruin. Now quit your quivering; you're not maids." With that, he snapped his reins and wheeled the cart forward.

It took a moment for Adelman to cajole the mules to follow, but soon his cart rolled forward as well, and they continued on their way between the hills.

Dietmar watched the carts bump along the stony path ahead of him.

Arcadius is right, he thought, urging Theseus forward. A mere feeling was nothing compared to what they had witnessed in Ladah—Lycaon's Curse, the *Wulfen*. He knew the medicae in Constantinople applied reason to such tales: these were simply afflictions of the mind, stories of men who went mad and stalked the graveyards at night. Their tongues grew long and dry because of malnourishment, their eyes sunken and grey because they only opened at night. It was a simple condition but, more importantly, a *human* one.

Those physicians dismissed the more fantastical claims travellers brought with them from over the Balkans as mere peasant superstition, folk tales not worthy of proper consideration. Dietmar himself had doubted the stories. Then, having heard of more than a fair number of *böxenwolf* brought to trial—men who dressed in wolf skins to rob and scare travellers in the rural outskirts of Germany—he had rejected the idea of wolf-men entirely.

Even his priest back home had railed against such beliefs. When rumours of man-eating wolves spread through Zwingenberg, flocks of villagers had fled to the larger towns, bringing their stories with them. The tales had transformed with each telling, until it was said that the beasts could take the form of man or woman to lure you into the forests, where the pack would set upon you, leaving nothing but bones. Father Sander had told a congregation, packed to the rafters with nervous townsfolk, in no uncertain terms that *man cannot transform himself*. Not in such a way. Only God had the power to bring about such a thing—and why would God curse a man to such a fate?

—for the crime of making him look the fool. Why else?

Dietmar cursed under his breath and dug his heels into Theseus's flanks harder than intended.

—just ask the Romei, Ephium continued conversationally. *Or do you think the gods cursed Lycaon for no reason at all? Oh no, ha! He fooled them as good as Eris or Laverna ever could and paid the price for it. Just ask him*

But Dietmar had stopped listening.

He called the company to a halt a second time when he saw that the hyenas still hadn't stirred from the bottom of the hill.

There's something wrong here, he thought, pressingly aware that they were no more than a dozen paces from the dwelling. *Cain and Abel know it too.*

He kept his eyes on Geoff while he spoke, but even from the corner of his eye, he couldn't help but notice the peculiar architecture of the ruin. It seemed to take up more space on the slope than it should, hinting at a sprawling complex hidden behind the dark corridor. But they had only been granted a glimpse of its entrance...

I could see it all if I went inside.

It's just a few paces away.

Dietmar pushed the thought aside and glanced back at the hyenas. Both of them were now pacing the rocky path, crisscrossing one another as they padded upon the dirt. They hadn't taken their eyes off Teoma.

Geoff was right. Something had them spooked.

"All right," he said, pointing to Teoma. "Let's leave him here."

"Here?" Geoff looked confused. "But what about those dogs?"

"They won't follow us any further. Not past that."

"It doesn't feel right," said Arcadius. He rubbed his chin and eyed Teoma. "Just leaving him after all that. Not after what he's done… Who's to say he won't just wander back to his little hovel and continue on as before once we're gone?"

"He probably will," said Dietmar. It didn't sit well with him either.

Is this really it?

Is this all there is for the cruel little bastards of the world?

"We could kill him," said Amice. His knife appeared in his hand, and he showed his teeth. "Let me do it."

A gust of wind rustled the grass and whispered through the stone door of the ruin. Dietmar felt his eyes drawn to it and couldn't help but stare. Weeds sprouted around its base, and the walls appeared seamless, as if hewn from a single stone. There were no visible mortar lines, no discernible connecting pieces between the walls, nothing to indicate it had been built at all, really. And yet here it was.

"Aye, let the little bastard have his way," Arcadius said with a shrug. "If there's anyone who deserves it, it's him."

"No!" Dietmar's voice rang out, his eyes tearing away from the slope. "How much further do you think we can stretch our luck? That we're here at all, alive, is a miracle on its own."

"Is it?" said Amice.

Dietmar ignored him. "Even if we manage to kill him—which might not be possible—then who's to say those creatures won't overcome their fear and come down on us like the hellhounds they are?"

"They'll catch my axe if they do," said Arcadius, but his heart wasn't in it.

"And when your arms tire?" Dietmar pressed, shaking his head. He pointed to Teoma. "Take him down. Leave him. He can make his own way home."

Geoff grumbled under his breath but reluctantly pulled the old man to his feet. "Up you get, you old shit," he muttered as he half-dragged, half-shoved Teoma toward the back of the cart. "Just know that if it were up to me, I'd walk you into that stone box up there and close you in nice and tight."

Teoma let out a muffled yelp from behind his rag, then Geoff pushed him off the lip of the cart. Teoma hit the ground with a thud and lay there, struggling within his robes.

"Oops," said Geoff, raising his hands and turning to Dietmar. He showed his teeth. "Happy?"

"I will be once we're out of these hills." Dietmar nudged his mount forward, leaving their treacherous host behind in the grass. He came within spitting distance of the ruin but kept his eyes fixed on the path ahead, even when he could have stared directly into the opening to see what was inside.

He didn't want to know.

***

A coal-black cloud stretched across the horizon, hanging like smoke over a burning city. Whenever the hills parted, they saw more of it, tapering off to the east and west but thickening ominously to the north.

The sky beneath glowed faintly, dark and shimmering.

When they summited the final hill, they paused to stare.

"The sea," Dietmar said.

Tomas wiped his brow and looked at the sky. "And a storm."

"It's some way away. Come, we'll cross out of the hills before it hits."

Tomas narrowed his eyes, scanning the distant line on the horizon. "I don't see any poxxing daughters. Or a Sandmouth."

"It might be across the sea."

"So, we'll cross?"

"Aye, if we must."

Tomas nodded, settling back in his seat and taking the reins from Adelman. With a gentle prompt, he urged the mules to move forward. "If we must, then."

20

It had been dark for the better part of an hour by the time they descended from the hills to set up camp. Tomas was prepared to settle for the first available patch of flat ground to throw down his bedroll, but Dietmar urged them to ride on, eager to increase the distance between themselves, the hyenas, and the ruins before bedding down for the night.

They picked a spot on the outskirts of an overgrown field, beneath a cluster of trees near the river. It wasn't much, but a thicket of thorny bushes sheltered their left flank while their vantage point beneath the starry night sky allowed them a clear view across the field.

Adelman handed out a piece of dry meat and stale bread to each of them, which they washed down with water and a small tot of wine Tomas had been keeping from them. They forsook a fire that night, not knowing who or what might be around to see it.

When it was Dietmar's turn to take the watch, Geoff moved to wake him, but Razin waved him away and quietly took his spot instead.

Leaving Dietmar to his sleep.

And to his dreams.

He was standing upon a bridge. *His* bridge, back home in Zwingenberg. Only, the water that ran through it was as black as pitch. It trickled like oil beneath the stone arches. When he looked up, there was no moon in the cloudless sky, though there were many stars. They formed constellations he did not recognise.

A figure materialised on the other side of the bridge, and he felt his hand move toward the sword at his belt. He was clad in a shirt of mail and his rerebraces from New Rome, but the tabard he wore was of the purest white. The cross of St. Lazarus rested on his chest above his heart.

Lazurian.

Leper.

Was that to be his fate?

As the figure halted in the centre of the bridge, Dietmar recognised him as his father, appearing as he did during his childhood. Rudolph's golden blond hair had not yet receded, and his face bore a sharp jawline and thin, unsympathetic lips that never seemed to offer a smile.

Not to him, anyway.

"Rudolph," he tried to say, but all that escaped his mouth was a garbled grunt. He opened his mouth to speak again and found that his teeth were gone, leaving only empty gums for his tongue to slide over.

He tasted iron.

"Is this what is left of your inheritance?" said Rudolph angrily, his lips curled with disdain.

Dietmar remained silent.

That was when he saw what lay on the other side of the bridge. It should have been a town: Bensheim. But it was something else.

The ruin from the slope.

He knew it for what it really was now.

A tomb.

The stars above shifted with the realisation, coming closer than they ever should, flaring brightly so that he had to shade his eyes.

When he looked again, the bridge was gone, and Dietmar found himself standing beside his father before the open black portal of the crypt.

"Come with me," said Rudolph, extending a hand to Dietmar. "There is no point in suffering any further. You want to see what is inside, don't you?"

Dietmar shook his head. He knew what was inside.

"Come, now," said his father, firmer this time. "You don't want to anger me, do you, Dietmar?"

Dietmar shook his head again but remained where he stood, not taking his father's outstretched hand.

Rudolph shuddered, his teeth showing from behind his thin red lips. A vein spread from his neck toward his temple. It pulsed as Rudolph spoke. "*Come with me you ungrateful bastard I should have drowned you at birth like your whoring mother and your bastard brother come with me now or I'll cut out your heart and fuck your corpse.*"

Dietmar blinked.

Rudolph was gone.

But something was emerging from the tomb.

Vines burst forth from the earth around the stone. Black roots with tendril-thin fingers spread across the mouth of the vault, their lifespan compressed to a matter of seconds: growing and dying, growing and dying, all while Dietmar watched.

A hot wind blew out from the tomb, chafing his skin and making his eyes water. It pulled at his tabard like unseen hands. He closed his eyes against the wind, and it stopped.

When he opened them again, the vines had vanished, leaving the stone as clean and smooth as it had ever been.

But there was something standing behind him. He could feel its presence.

Then a voice.

Enneleyn.

"Where is my child?"

Dietmar felt his stomach flip and the hair on his neck rise.

He couldn't turn around.

He didn't want to.

There was *something* wrong with her voice. It crackled and croaked, dry, like it came from a throat not meant for speaking.

She is dead.

Gone.

But the dead live with us still, in our thoughts and words.

But not like this.

"Where is he?" she repeated, her voice now whispering in his ear. He could feel her breath against his skin. It itched and burned. He needed to leave, to run. But he couldn't move, and his skin itched. It *fucking burned.*

"Christ, please!" he bellowed, finding the strength to take a single step forward, drawing closer to the tomb, toward the abyss of darkness. There was something inside now.

I'm not supposed to see.

A soft light blossomed from the burial vault, a corpulent glow no taller than his knee. Behind it, a stone slab was unveiled, covered in ancient script. Words that had not been read in a thousand years, in a language not uttered in living memory, flashed before Dietmar's eyes. He felt them form on his lips, his tongue effortlessly navigating the unfamiliar syllables.

This is the 39th tomb.

From the 9th year of the king.

The contents be disturbed at great peril.

And he be liable to He.

A God lives here.

Let him slumber.

No! He dragged his gaze away, staring up at the stars instead. They were in motion now, a shifting milieu of light. Or, no… Something *behind* them was moving. A colossal shape. It swelled in size until it engulfed the entire sky.

It.

Whatever it was.

"Give me your hand," Enneleyn whispered. "And then we can see. Then we can all see."

He felt her cold, leathery hand next to his own, touching his skin with an eerie tenderness. A whiff of tomb breath filled his nose, and he tried not to gag.

"Take it," she said, firmer now, commanding… desperate.

He shook his head and saw the shape in the heavens consume the stars, their lights blinking out one by one, like candles beneath a great tide.

If he took her hand, he would die. Or the thing waiting in the tomb would come out, and the world would end, and he would still die. He knew that.

A shiver ran down his spine as Enneleyn's cold hand enveloped his own, her grip tightening as she searched for a response from him. But he would not be tricked, keeping his hand limp by his side, leaving her to desperately paw at it with her cold, bony fingers.

"TAKE IT!"

He thrust her hand away, forcing it from his own with a terrified yell, and then found that he was lying on his back.

In the dark.

And someone was shouting at him.

The figure standing over him.

"Shut your bloody mouth, you ragged weasel," roared a voice from one of the bedrolls. Arcadius. A leg kicked out at the shadow standing over him and sent it staggering.

Amice, Dietmar thought, his eyes adjusting to the gloom.

"You're looking to stir again, are you?" Arcadius growled. "How could you see anything in this dark? Get away from him, or I'll knock your teeth out, you little shit."

"I swear to Christ, I saw it." Amice moved into a crouch over his own bedroll. He looked like a jackal ready to spring.

"Saw what?" came a sleepy voice to his side. Tomas.

Dietmar blinked and looked around the camp. Then, he groaned as he spotted the hand lying on the ground beside him, outside of its pouch. Memories of his dream flooded back—his father, Enneleyn, and… something that was neither of them.

But it was just a dream.

Amice spat at the ground and looked at Dietmar, his eyes wide. "I saw him talking to it, to the hand, while he slept. He held it up to his face as if it were an ear, and it *fucking moved!*"

"Bullshit," said Arcadius, though he gave the hand a nervous glance.

"I swear on my dead brothers, I did," Amice crossed himself and pointed at the hand. "That's the Devil's business, just like everything else in this place. We need to make a big fucking fire and burn it or throw it into that hole we saw in the hills."

Dietmar sat up on his bed roll and leaned over to retrieve the hand from the ground, feeling the same cold dead skin he'd felt in his dream. He returned it to its pouch and then looked up at the faces staring at him. The Lady Marie and Levi were stirring where they lay, wiping away the sleep in their eyes as they looked to the commotion while Sara continued to slumber peacefully between them. Razin's bedroll remained empty; he hadn't returned from his watch.

—*tell them!*

He wanted to.

He needed to.

There was something rotten inside of his head, and it was coming out. This was no saint; it turned his thoughts and dreams wretched and his heart cold.

"I..." he hesitated.

Then he thought of his son, and he knew he couldn't. That was why he was here, wasn't it? To bring his boy back from the darkness. But if he told them, what chance did he have? They would burn the hand or cast it out into the desert... Maybe even him with it.

Have I damned myself to save my boy?

So be it.

Dietmar let out the breath he'd been holding and shrugged. "I had a bad dream, that's all." He met Amice's milk-white eyes in the gloom. "I don't know what you saw, but—"

"We're here because of that *thing*," Amice snarled, stabbing the air with his finger, his gaze fixated on the hand in the dirt. "None of this woulda happened otherwise. It's cursed, like that dead Italian said it was. We should have listened."

"The hand saved us," said Tomas, sitting up and patting down his hair. "We all saw it. It kept the demon in the temple at bay

—*single-handedly.* Ephium barked out a laugh like it were a wet thing caught in his throat. *Lamussu won't have me near her, the filthy lion bitch. Oh, but what I wouldn't give to see inside her head, to nestle up among all her secrets! She was the consort of kings, you know, perhaps even to her savage gods. Why, I'd give up my left hand! Ha ha!No?* There was a sound like a sigh, like air escaping wet lungs. *Of course, it is a simpleton I find myself companion to. But perhaps you're not so simple as you appear? What's this?*

Ephium snorted, and then Dietmar felt something strange inside his head, like his mind was being forced through a sieve, strained and rinsed.

After a moment, he realised Ephium was grinning.

—I see you have your own secrets, little knight. Curious indeed… Why, you've hidden some even from yourself. But don't worry. I'm here now. Would you like to see them?

Dietmar clenched his jaw and forced himself to focus on anything but the voice ringing inside his head. Slowly but surely, he squeezed the corridor between him and Ephium shut.

It was getting harder. But then there was silence, at least in his mind anyway.

"It didn't help much with the hyenas," Arcadius was saying. The Greek had sat up on his bedroll and was rubbing his shoulder. He'd complained about a pain in it since they'd left Ladah. Since he'd brought the beast down with his axe. He lifted his arm uncomfortably, winced, and then nodded to Dietmar. "They didn't even blink when they saw it. Cain nearly bit your arm off too. What good is that?"

"Those were men," said Dietmar. "Cursed men, but men all the same."

He wasn't sure why that mattered, only that it seemed important. If the hand truly had been a blessed relic, what good would it have been against mere men?

Arcadius thought it over and then nodded. "Perhaps. If you say it fended off a demon, then I believe you." He looked sideways at Amice. "And even if I didn't, I'd take your word over the little bastard's any day."

"It's dark, lad," said Geoff, uncorking his flask and taking a sip. "You might have been mistaken. We've all seen things we wish we hadn't. It plays with our heads."

"I know what I saw," Amice insisted, though he sounded less confident about it now.

"Get some rest. Here, this'll help." Geoff passed his flask to Amice and stood up. "I'll take your watch. But don't let me come back to hear you've been stirring again, right?"

Amice nodded stiffly and then lay back down to nurse the flask.

Dietmar knew Amice wouldn't be getting any more sleep that night. And neither would he.

"*Who are you?*" he hissed, careful not to raise his voice. The question was for the one inside his head.

He saw images from his dream, the ancient corridors and yellow slabs of rock, a dark enclave and old stone. The inscription had been in no tongue he knew, and yet he had been able to read it with ease.

Ephium remained quiet. Watching in that way of his, a presence that couldn't be ignored.

As Dietmar lay his own head back down, he heard Ephium's voice inside his head. He was laughing.

21

Razin picked his way along the riverbank, moving silently from the copse of trees beyond their camp and into the cool night.

He wanted to walk a while before someone came to take his place on the watch, and he managed a few hours restless sleep. He should have waited until the morning to explore, but there was something about the river that drew him to it. It reminded him of the river where he had grown up. Not in colour or shape. Unlike the black vein splitting the field beside him, the *Baradā River* was crystal clear. It fed the orchards with water so pure that it seemed no matter where you looked, ripe fruit held your gaze.

He had spent many a youthful summer in the shade of those groves, debating with his uncle Mushrie and listening to his stories. When he grew older, he would swim in the river with the other children and follow them into the deeper water beneath the *Bab al-Faradis* bridge. There, they would play games, which usually devolved into mudslinging fights until the guards on the bridge or nearby farmers chased them away.

He had met his first love under that bridge. *Shuhadah*. But she had been promised to another, and Razin had little by way of prospects to tempt her family into changing their minds. So, it had been a few fleeting moments shared, her impossibly large eyes and quick hands beneath the water, but nothing more.

Still, it was Mushrie's stories that had stayed with him the longest. They had brought him comfort even when Damascus lay under siege, and it seemed the invaders from the west would add another city to their conquests.

The memory of that fateful morning when the Franks arrived remained etched in Razin's mind, as vivid as if it had happened only days ago. There had been a disturbance in the city—a cult of moon-worshippers had been exposed, and the Emir of Damascus's own son had been implicated in its practices.

Nur Ad-Din's lieutenants had unearthed the cult, and some had suggested that his naming of Emir's son had been a political move to better his position should anything ever happen to Unur. Nur Ad-Din's marriage to the governor's daughter in Aleppo the previous year had already showcased his unyielding ambition, leaving no doubt about the extent of his aspirations.

So, when morning broke, Razin had waited with bated breath for the violence to begin. Many had feared there would be bloodshed. It seemed inevitable that loyalists to Unur's son would clash with Nur Ad-Din's men—though the Seljuk ruler was still some days ride away with his *askars*—even as the Franks encroached upon the city walls. But there had been nothing. The streets had remained quiet.

And then the rumours started.

Unur knew of his son's blasphemies! The Emir belongs to the Moon Cult himself! The mušrikūn will sell the city to the Franks! There had been other things said, too. Less the words of wide-eyed waifs in the bazaar, spoken in hushed tones away from watching eyes. *They worship another One God; it is the other side of Allah that they see—this lunar cult.* Some said that the figure they worshipped was older than Allah, that it had a better claim to being the creator. But such things were only said after a furtive glance either way, with a finger raised to the lips.

When Razin had told his uncle what he had heard, Mushrie had berated him for gossiping like a woman and told him to wash the filth out from between his ears.

"But 'Iweyz says there are witnesses," Razin retorted. "That Unur and his son were seen with priests of this moon god. Unur's own harem says it is so!"

"And you would condemn a man on hearsay?" Mushrie considered him with one of his penetrating stares. It was the same look he gave Razin when he was about to point out a contradiction in his logic or some failing in his proofs.

Razin hesitated. "Uncle—"

"What did I tell you of the judgments of Karakash?"

Razin winced, seeing the fault his uncle had already identified.

Mushrie leaned back in his seat and sipped on sherbet water, waiting for his nephew's reply.

Razin droned out the expected response. "The impartial judge would render guilt on the innocent, so long as a party was punished."

Mushrie nodded, ignoring his student's tone. "And what happened when the miser called to him from the casket as he was carried to his grave, to be buried alive by his greedy cousins?"

"The judge said that he would not allow the evidence of his poor senses and the miser's bare word to weigh up against a crowd of witnesses who claimed that the miser was dead."

"Yes, and we know that the mourners were paid by the miser's cousins to say that he was dead so that they might inherit. But what became of the miser?"

Razin sighed. "He was buried alive, uncle."

"Just so," said Mushrie with a nod. He placed his bronze cup on the table and smiled. "So you see, the words of the many can be a fickle thing. Better not to rush to conclusions when other, simpler explanations are at hand. Be patient, my boy. The truth will reveal itself. But not if we bury the poor Emir alive."

Later that day, they had sat upon the rooftop of their home and watched the Franks prepare for the siege.

"Look," Mushrie said, pointing across the rows of tents that rose like pillars on the field before them. The occupiers had swept across the orchards, flattened the farms and fields, but they could not conquer the river.

A flock of cranes had risen as one from the Baradā, climbing to the skies to form a whirling spiral, mingling with the swifts and swallows already circling above the Frankish camp.

"Recall the birds who fought against the Abyssinians when they sought to conquer Mecca," Mushrie said. "Perhaps they will fight for us too?"

Razin watched the skies intently, hoping to see rocks dropped upon the Franks from up high, like in the *sura* Mushrie was referring to. When nothing happened, he looked away, disappointed.

"Perhaps we should build a totem to Hubal," he said, naming the pagan effigy in Mecca during the time of the Abyssinian invasion. "Maybe then they will fight for us."

At that, his uncle gave him a look he had never seen before, one that he was unlikely to forget. *Hurt*, like his mother's face when news of his father's death had come, and *anger*, like he had felt when he saw the first Christian flags appear beneath Mount Qasioun. It would have been better if Mushrie had clipped him behind the ears for his impudence, for his callous blasphemy. He'd half-expected that he would, but Mushrie never resorted to violence to discipline him. His words were enough.

When he met his uncle's eyes, he swore to himself never to speak in such a way again.

Mushrie steepled his fingers and looked at Razin like a teacher about to give an important lesson to a student who might not be ready to learn it.

"I know," said Razin, raising his hand in surrender. "I know, I know."

"We must not be like the Israelites who turned to *Baal* and *Ashtaroth* and only looked to Yahweh in times of trouble. Those so-called 'gods' cannot intercede. If we fall to their worship, if we are tricked, or our hubris leads us to their feet, then God may not intervene when we finally call on him for aid."

"Then why did God help the Meccans?" asked Razin, unable to help himself. "Were they not devotees of Hubal?"

"Because..." Mushrie unfolded his hands, setting them side by side on the small table they shared. "The Meccans knew then already that there was only one God. They were the people of God, even if they still had their idols and minor pantheons. They fought for God, and so God fought for them. But it takes time for old traditions to die out, for people to give up the continuity they find through the old beliefs. They look for connections to their ancestors, for legacy. Change takes time, even if people have already committed to it in their hearts. Those statues survived long after the belief in the gods they represented had gone."

Razin nodded at this, deep in thought.

Not long after the siege was lifted, he made up his mind.

He would fight for God too.

Razin paused to stare at the black waters coursing past him, remembering those moments with his uncle. Mushrie had only smiled sadly when he told him of his intentions. He had known for a while that Razin would leave him to fight, like his father had against the Franks. He had palmed his hands as if to say *what can I do?* And then hugged his nephew fiercely, promising to pray for his safe return home. That had been nearly twenty years ago.

Razin followed the current along the sandy bank. A thousand stars reflected off the river's inky surface, and yet the river itself seemed no lighter for it. Even the mirrored light seemed dimmer than it should, like a tepid candle shining out from behind dirty glass.

Shapes rose from the churning water, rocks obtruding like stony seracs, pressing back against the seething current. Half-buried sultans of stone, the unyielding emirs of natural architecture, submerged beneath a vein of the world.

There was no tranquillity here, Razin thought. And that was what he recognised about the river: there was a sense of restrained violence, a tension resting just beneath the surface. These could be the same waters that swallowed the world during Noah's flood.

Razin turned to look back the way he'd come, at the dark silhouettes of the hills they'd crossed the day before. Even those were not so different—they could have been the foothills at the base of Mount Qasioun.

He thought of the ruin they'd found and the sinking pit in his stomach when he'd stared past its doorway. Maybe that was not so different, either? The Mountain overlooking Damascus had its own sacred ruins, the birthplace of Abraham, for starters—another, the Cave of Blood, where Cain was said to have butchered his brother Abel.

Everything here was an inversion, twisted, as if to mock the truth Razin held dear. The brooding black river—a perverted mimicry of the Baradā. The rolling hills—a pale opposite to the reassuring peak of Mount Qasioun. The birthplace of Abraham, a place of hope… the black hole in the hills… something else.

When Teoma had told them that they were in Ladah, he had thought it madness. This could not be the second plane of Jahannam. Where were the *Zebani*, the guardians of Hell? And he had seen none of the *Ahl al-Nar*, who should have crowded the place like cockroaches.

Even now, he doubted.

But what if Teoma's invocation of the word was not in the same spirit as when Razin or any other good Muslim used it? A Ladah with other characteristics, those at odds with what he had been taught.

The idea was anathema to him. To court it was to invite the very thing that saw one condemned to Ladah in the first place: doubt. And yet, in the pursuit of the truth, he would be called to scrutinize every idea on its merits, at least if one was to refute it fully. Was that not the way of the *Al-Haqq*?

Even as he considered the question, he had his answer. It was *within* the tenets of Islam that he was to pursue the truth, question men and their ideas, forge new philosophies and sciences. To accept premises or conclusions that contradicted the word of Allah was to practice *shirk*. If Mushrie had heard the little jinn's claim—his implicit suggestion of an unpairing of Ladah and Jahannam—he would have called him a damned *mushrik* and told him not to foul their ears with his *al-kufr*.

The only explanation was that they *were* in Ladah, Hell. Or they were not, and this was not Hell, even if they called it Ladah. Jinn were not to be trusted, Razin knew. They could be capricious and mistruthful. The Prophet himself had warned that these ghuls were liars, but he had also said that they were not all evil. Instead, he had thought them closer to man, driven by their own ambitions, sometimes good, sometimes not. Teomas's had been decidedly evil, and it was only reluctantly that Razin had considered his words relating to the way back home of any use at all. It would take a far more duplicitous fellow than Teoma to have foreseen their survival, despite his best efforts to ensure otherwise and point them astray.

But then, who was Razin to know the mind of a jinn?

He rubbed his tired eyes and smiled to himself. This was not the hour for such questions, and he was certainly in no state of mind to entertain the thoughts spinning around in his head. Perhaps on the morrow, with a few hours sleep under his belt.

Yes, that would be better.

He turned on his heels, ready to make the short walk back to camp but hesitated. Had he left something behind? He looked down and saw his sword still in its sheath at his side, his *tathir* cloth hanging from his belt, his waterskin on a long leather thong across his chest. The rings of his mail shirt reflected even the faint starlight from beneath his burnous.

All in order.

Still, that feeling. Perhaps he'd left something in the forest? He turned toward the trees, taking one step and then another, until he was walking amongst the long-limbed ancients that grew along the shore. His boots crunched as he trod over dry leaves that covered the floor like an autumn carpet. A row of small trees rose to his right, chest high. Their branches were filled with scrumptious berries. He saw an apple tree ahead, its many branches heavy with a ripe harvest.

He frowned.

These had not been here before.

Why was he here?

To help me.

He spun on his feet, crunching the amber gold carpet beneath his heels, his sword already drawn.

"Who's there?"

Something scraped and scrabbled through the trees, scuttling like a dozen tiny legs moving over the leaves. He snapped his head around at a movement to his left. Even with his sharp eyes, he could hardly make out anything past the berry orchard. The weak light of the stars had not penetrated the thicket above.

Something made a sound in the dark.

I am here.

Razin held his sword toward the sound and looked for the source of the voice. He heard another soft scraping, like teeth on dry meat, and then he saw her.

A woman in a long-skirted white *jellaba* stood beneath one of the trees, her jet-black hair pouring from the hood of her silk burnous.

Razin blinked. She was beautiful beyond all compare. Her near-perfect oval face surrendered to a subtle cleft in her chin, a delicate blemish that only succeeded in making her appear more alluring. Her lips, a gentle pink the shade of a blossoming Damask rose, were parted ever so slightly in a suggestive smile. Above her sharp nose, wide eyes the colour of autumnal leaves blinked back at him from beneath thick lashes, made darker by the kohl that shadowed them. They hinted at innocence but at willingness too.

I would not have called out, but the forest is ripe with fruit… and I cannot reach.

The woman, the princess—for that is what she surely was—lifted her delicate hands to show the chains that confined her movement. Thin manacles bound her wrists, they themselves near as beautiful as the woman who bore them—fine latticed silver intertwined like the thread of a rope to form the restraints.

"Who—" Razin had to clear his throat. He blushed and tried to hide it, but she saw and smiled with those soft, perfect lips and fiery eyes, only making him blush harder.

"Who did this to you?" he said once he had gathered himself.

It was my father. Her voice was like the kiss of Spring. *He wishes to marry me off to the wicked King. Please, I would just like to taste the orchard's harvest one last time before I am locked in the King's rooms forever. Will you help me?*

Razin felt a sense of ease come over him, and he lowered his sword, then sheathed it. She *was* a princess… and would be a queen. Who was he to deny her?

"Princess," he said with a soft bow. "Tell me which fruits you desire. And if they are here, I shall pick them for you. If they are not, I will comb the forests of the world to find them and bring them back to you."

The princess laughed, and her eyes shone with pleasure. *I would rather you remain close*, she said, and he felt his face warm again. *Please, there are fruits just above my head. If you were to reach them for me, I would be in your debt, and you would be in my heart.*

Razin inclined his head and stepped forward. He felt clumsy before this great beauty, who, even in her chains, carried herself with grace.

She smelled like jasmine and honeycomb, he thought as he stood near her. He avoided her piercing stare, nervous he would embarrass himself by blushing again. He, a grown man brought to blushing youth by this woman! He peered into the branches. Before he could even react, she was up against him, her cool breath blowing sweetly on his neck.

The apple, she said in his ear.

He could feel her curves through the thin cotton of her jellaba, her breasts pressing ever so slightly against his chest. Her skin was warm and soft beneath.

His loins began to stir.

The apple nearly fell into his palm the moment he touched it, so ripe it was and willing. Now he met her gaze, letting her eyes that stared like beacons of night burrow into his own. Her scent was overpowering, a heady blend of fragrance that made his pulse quicken: jasmine and honeycomb, but something else beneath. A strong musk, though not unpleasant.

He placed the apple in her waiting hands, still held together by the band of silver chain.

"Come with me," he said, cupping her fingers around the apple, holding them gently in his own.

I am promised to another. The corners of her mouth rose, her lips parted further.

He wanted to kiss her.

"A wicked king, you said so yourself. Come with me, away from the wicked king and this wicked place."

You do not think it beautiful here? The princess frowned, her thin eyebrows curving above her blinking almond eyes, hurt.

He wanted to cry.

He thought of 'Iweyz then and the look of disappointment on her face when he had told her he was leaving.

He had thought his departure might stir something in her—words or actions that were more than the friendship they had formed. And for a brief second, an intake of breath, she had looked at him like he had always hoped she would.

But she was a consort to the Emir, and he was a boy.

The moment passed, and she hugged him goodbye.

Would he have stayed for her if she'd asked?

Razin blinked and said clumsily. "It would be more beautiful if you were without those chains."

So, free me.

"...and dress." Those words were not his own, he thought briefly, though he desired it all the same.

She smiled again, her eyes no longer the portals of innocence from before.

So, free me.

Razin tugged at the chain and saw that it was wrapped around the trunk of the apple tree they stood beneath. He stood back and drew his sword.

The princess moved to his side, her smooth curves nestling against his back, her scent filling his senses.

Free me.

He brought the sword down. It cut through the chain in a single stroke, parting the silver rings and letting them fall to the ground like a snake without its head. He smiled, breathing in the lavender and honeycomb musk, and turned to the princess, ready to claim his prize.

But she was gone.

He stared at the ground where she had stood a moment before. The apple he had plucked for her lay resting on the leaves. Even as he watched, it withered away, turning grey and rotten. He stepped back, flinching at a stink that punched his nostrils—it was her musk, but more potent than before, as if amplified by her absence. He recognised a vile note in the smell, like a dead thing dug up and wet. He blinked down and saw stains on his sleeves and chest where the princess had touched him.

Razin lifted his hand and sniffed at his sleeve. It stunk like rot. Like a grave-thing had rubbed itself against him, and he against it. He stumbled out from under the tree, blinking as his eyes watered and he tried not to gag.

As he wiped his face, he thought he saw something moving toward the river... Scuttling, like a white cadaverous spider through the undergrowth. But when he looked again properly, it was gone.

22

They broke camp just before dawn, after a quiet breakfast of stale bread and a few more scraps of dried meat. It had rained sometime during the night, soaking their bedrolls through to dampen their clothes. Their moods were sour, and what words passed between them were sharp.

Nobody felt like talking anyway, and they trudged along the river in silence, moving through more overgrown fields but seeing no sign of any farms.

By mid-morning, they had entered a swampy marshland infested with flies and gnats. A low fog hung over the place, obscuring their path and making it difficult to track a course for their carts.

Dietmar had just started to second-guess their route north when they came upon something unexpected.

A road.

And not some goat's path or huntsman's trail, but an actual mortar and limestone, brick and stone *road!* Dietmar whispered a quiet word of thanks to Saint Thomas and led Theseus out of the marshes.

"Who built this?" Tomas asked as the mules pulled his cart onto the road.

"Who cares?" Amice spat over his horse, swiping at a fly hovering by his ear. "It's a road, isn't it? Better than getting eaten alive in this swamp."

"Romans?" Geoff speculated, paying no attention to the squire.

"Here?" Tomas gave him a look that told him what he thought of that idea. "And I care, lad, because I'd quite like to know if the people who built it have any intention of *eating us alive* if we happen to find them on it."

Dietmar followed the stone thoroughfare with his gaze, tracing its course through the marshland until it curved alongside the river, disappearing into the thick foliage of the wetlands. Tufts of grass sprouted between the smooth grey paving stones, and sections of the road had crumbled with time. Whoever had constructed it had allowed it to fall into disrepair. Nevertheless, Amice was right—it was better than the swamp.

"What do you make of this?" Dietmar asked as Razin rode up beside him. Like the rest of them, his friend had spoken little since the morning.

"It's not Roman," Razin replied.

"No," Dietmar agreed.

"Whoever built this built the bridge too."

"And the temple?"

Razin shrugged, appearing distracted and weary. He hadn't slept either. Dietmar was about to ask what troubled him when Razin shook his head and pressed Riba forward. "I don't know who built it," he said. Then he was riding ahead of Dietmar, hunched forward in his saddle.

"He's been like that since I relieved him of the watch last night," Geoff said, scratching his chin and pulling at a grey hair in his beard. "Skittish. He told me to keep an eye on the water, then vanished. I didn't see him again until we broke camp, and then only when he came walking back out of those shitting woods nearby."

"What was in the water?"

Geoff shrugged. "Nothing that I saw. Doesn't mean there wasn't something, though. The Arab's got better eyes than me, even when I'm at my sober best."

Dietmar grunted and let his gaze settle on the river. He watched the frothing lip until a call from Arcadius stirred him. Then he clambered from his horse to help the Greek pull his cart out of the mud.

The marshland gave way to more overgrown fields and then to marshland again before the swampy waters receded, and they found themselves riding beneath a thick leafy canopy. Trees, unlike any Dietmar had ever seen, crowded them on both sides, with wide trunks and roots that seemed to grow upward rather than into the ground. Creeping vines hung from every branch, and a carpet of moss covered the floor beneath, encroaching onto the stone slabs of the road. The calls of strange birds echoed above the sound of the river, lost from sight behind the green wall that surrounded them.

There was no breeze to offer relief as they continued along the road, and the air beneath the canopy became hot and humid. Soon, sweat stained the backs of all the riders, their garments clinging uncomfortably to their bodies.

Dietmar walked alongside Arcadius's cart, leading Theseus by the reins to stretch his legs. The horse's tail swished behind him, warding off the persistent flies that had followed them out of the marshes.

Dietmar glanced past Arcadius to the former slave girl sitting quietly beside him. "Has she got a name?"

Arcadius wiped his forehead with a cloth, only to realise it was already drenched with sweat. He let out a frustrated groan. "If she does, she hasn't shared it with me. I haven't heard a word from her since we left that damned village."

"She's scared," said the Lady Marie from her seat behind him. She had unrolled her pelt and used it to cushion the hard wooden surface of the cart, creating a makeshift nest. Despite the heat, Sara had taken to curling up against her, finding comfort in her presence. The Lady Marie stroked her hair gently while she listened to the men talk.

Arcadius glanced at the girl, who sat on the edge of the seat, her eyes darting between the trees, branches, and the unfamiliar roots and ground cover. Her gaze moved swiftly, alert and observant, like a predator. Suddenly, she tensed, her attention focused on something above her.

In an instant, her hand shot out, snatching a fly out of the air in a blur of movement.

"She doesn't look scared," commented Arcadius dryly. He raised an eyebrow and crinkled his lips when he saw her discard the remains of her catch into her mouth. "Maybe a little starved and half-savage… but not scared."

Dietmar watched the girl chew, noticing the surprisingly white teeth behind her cleft lip. She hadn't had her head bound like the other villagers or Teoma.

So, she doesn't worship their gods?

Or perhaps, as a slave, she was deemed unworthy of such transformations? Dietmar wondered what she might have done to be considered evil by a creature that lured people into his village to be eaten.

A sin against gods that don't exist, he thought.

But what crime was worse than eating your fellow man?

He blinked, and then she was looking at him, staring holes into his face with those intense yellow eyes. After a moment, he looked away, unable to sustain the intensity of her stare. He slowed his pace until he was walking alongside Levi on the cart.

The dyer from Tiberias looked deflated. His face was drawn and pale. He hadn't been eating, and though it had only been a few days since Miriam was taken from him, he had lost weight in his cheeks and neck.

Dietmar had tried to console him, sharing his own experiences of loss, hoping to offer some comfort. But the words had felt hollow, even to his own ears.

Levi had seen his child *torn apart* in front of him. He had been holding onto her while she was split in two. How could anything compare?

Levi acknowledged his greeting with a subtle shift in his wallowing, a tilt of his head that might have been a greeting in return.

He needed a distraction, or he'd fall into the same despair that had taken Dietmar after Rudi and Enneleyn. And here, in this place… he would not survive it.

"Have you tried speaking to her?" Dietmar nodded to the girl, hoping to redirect Levi's attention.

Levi grunted, his eyes fixed on his hands in his lap.

"In Aramaic?" Dietmar pressed.

Finally, Levi looked up, wiping his mouth with a hand. A fly landed on his cheek, but he paid no attention to it, either unable to feel it or simply not caring.

"And what good will that do, eh?" He shook his head. The fly crawled slowly toward the corner of his mouth. "You think she can tell us more about her blasphemous gods? You want me to sit through more lectures about her pagan beliefs, like her master's? And then what? Tell me, knight. Do you think that when the rest of her village feasted on the dead, that she abstained? Or do you think she might not have been tempted to partake?"

"Hush now!" The Lady Marie glared at Levi. "Hasn't your daughter seen enough? Heard enough?"

"I'll ask you to mind your own business," said Levi, earning himself a hard stare from Arcadius. Undeterred, he continued. "Shouldn't she know if one among us is more beast than human? Look at her. *Look at her!*"

The Lady Marie flinched, quickly covering Sara's ears with her hands. Ignoring the girl's complaints, she snapped back at Levi, "Even if she did, what choice did she have? She was a captive! Would you condemn her for simply trying to survive?"

Levi snorted. "Simply trying… Nobody does anything they don't want to. Not even a slave."

"Listen to yourself," Dietmar said coldly. "It's not her you're angry with. It's Teoma. Don't let grief cloud your judgment, Levi."

"I should have killed the little imp when I had the chance." Levi sighed, finally slapping away the fly as it reached the corner of his mouth. "What do you want me to ask her?"

"If she has a name, for starters."

Levi nodded, leaning forward in his seat and calling out to the girl. When she didn't turn around, Arcadius nudged her by the elbow and pointed back with his thumb. It looked like she might ignore him too, but when the Greek made to poke her again, she twisted in her seat and stared at Levi.

There was an awkward pause, and Dietmar wondered if Levi had changed his mind. But then he started talking, quickly now that he had refamiliarised himself with the language.

After a moment, the girl shook her head.

Dietmar frowned. "What did you ask her?"

"What you told me to ask her," said Levi. He leaned back in his seat and palmed his hands.

"She doesn't have a name?"

"No, she doesn't."

Dietmar looked at the girl and shook his head, bemused. She was still staring at Levi, her golden-green eyes like gemstones.

"What should we call you then?" he wondered out loud.

"Just call her 'girl', like I've been doing," said Arcadius. "She responds to that… mostly."

"That won't do, 'Dius." The Lady Marie untangled Sara's limbs from her arm to fan her face with a hand. "How about… 'Ele', after the Greek goddess of freedom."

"That's a stupid name," said Arcadius. He flinched when the Lady Marie slapped his shoulder and raised a hand in surrender. "All right, it's better than 'girl'. But none of us are free… not here."

The Lady Marie nestled back against her pelt, wrinkling her brow. "How about… Sophia?"

"Tanit," said Levi quietly, sitting up and meeting the gazes that turned towards him. "She was the old Carthage goddess of the moon. She had a cat's mouth, too, I believe. And we need a moon, don't we?"

"That's settled then," Dietmar declared before the Lady Marie could object.

"Aye, it's a good name." Arcadius agreed, gently nudging Tanit between the ribs and pointing at her with a smile. "You are Tanit. All right?"

Tanit stared at him, blinking lazily, before turning her gaze back to the trees.

"What if she doesn't like it?" The Lady Marie pushed Sara's arm gently aside again but relented, allowing the girl to cuddle up against her.

"Tough," said Arcadius. "Which one of us had a say in how we were named anyway?"

"Tanit," said the Lady Marie, repeating the word under her breath. She glanced over her shoulder at the girl and nodded. "It will do."

Tanit, as she was now named, remained quiet on her seat. If she had any thoughts on her new name, she kept them to herself.

By the time anyone realised they had come upon another settlement, they were already in its midst. Dietmar tensed in his saddle as he scanned the small conical rooftops that peeked out from behind the trees on either side of the road. The structures were nearly invisible with their bamboo and reed walls. Ladders and ropes fashioned from knotted vines dangled from the branches above, and faint outlines of more dwellings could be seen in the canopy above the road.

Razin emerged from the trees just ahead, leading Riba by the reins, his sword held loosely in his other hand.

"There's no one here," he said, coming up beside Arcadius's cart.

The burly Greek had his axe resting across his lap, and he impatiently thumbed the shaft. "Abandoned?"

Razin glanced back at the forest and then gestured upward at the tree huts. "Unless they're all hidden in the branches. But I found no signs that anyone was here."

"It's better that way," said Dietmar. He drew Theseus forward and climbed the war horse's side, settling heavily in his saddle. "I'd rather we not see another soul than meet more cursed men like we found in Ladah. I'm sorely tempted to set fire to these squalid huts as is, but they'd take half the forest with them…even then…"

Tomas eyed the trees warily. "Where did they go?"

"To meet their dark gods, I hope." Arcadius tapped the blade of his axe one last time. Then he flicked his reins and whistled at his horses. "It's best we leave them to it. Come on."

***

The occupants of the village announced themselves with a soft buzzing sound and the rank stink of unwashed bodies.

—*death*, whispered the voice a moment before Dietmar saw the corpses. They hung from trees like rotten fruit on both sides of the road—a foetid orchard.

"Christ's teeth," Dietmar murmured, crossing himself as he gazed up at the dirty feet dangling from the branches. He counted a dozen bodies before he stopped counting.

It was an entire village's worth.

"What happened here?" Tomas asked, his voice muffled from behind his sleeve.

Geoff rode closer to the nearest trees and stared at the bodies suspended there. Among them were a woman and a child, possibly no older than ten. Someone had tied them to the branch they were laid upon, binding them with vines and… something else. A viscous white substance coated their remains. It looked like a form of resin or the thin silk of a cocoon. It hid their faces from view. Dietmar was grateful for that small mercy.

Why is it only in the wake of death that we find peace in this place? The thought was a gloomy one but no less glib than the realisation that, wherever they had found life, violence was never far behind.

Dietmar glanced back at the carts and saw the Lady Marie shielding Sara's eyes. Her own face was pale. She was hardly any older than the girl she sought to protect. Who would cover her eyes and hide her from the horrors of the forest?

"It's like some sort of webbing," Geoff remarked, reaching up to touch the legs of one of the figures. He scraped off a bit of the white substance and rubbed it between his fingers before turning to Dietmar. "Maybe we should burn this place after all."

"These are still fresh," said Amice from the other side of the road. He prodded a corpse hanging on the lower branches with his knife, only to swear as a swarm of insects emerged from where they had been nesting on the body.

He shooed away the flies, guiding his horse back from the agitated swarm.

"Must be a day old," he said. "Maybe less."

"Something must have got them in the night," said Arcadius.

"Rather them than us," Amice muttered, glancing back at the corpse. The flies swarmed over it like bees on a honeycomb, obscuring its features further.

Rather them than us.

Amice had said the same thing in Ladah after the boy had proposed using the villagers as bait. Was there nothing redeemable about him? Even here, looking at dead women and children, did he feel no pity?

"We should keep moving," said Razin. His brow was knitted together like two storm clouds, and his eyes darted toward the trees every few seconds. It looked like he was waiting for something. Dietmar had never seen him look so uneasy, not even in the temple.

"Is everything all right?" he asked softly, riding up beside his friend so that the others couldn't hear.

Razin dragged his eyes away from the trees just long enough to appraise Dietmar. He appeared… lost, but then his gaze hardened, and he pursed his lips. "I should ask you the same question, German."

Dietmar shook his head slowly, not following.

"Tomas told me about last night," Razin continued, still staring at him. "About you and the hand. About it… moving."

Dietmar snorted. "It was dark. I was still dreaming. I—"

Razin didn't let him finish. "Amice isn't the only one who has noticed. You've been acting strange, my friend. Sometimes, it's as if you're a thousand leagues away, in another world, seeing things none of us can see…listening to something none of us can hear."

"Nonsense."

Razin looked back at the trees and shrugged. "Maybe. But a mind is a fragile thing. Push it too hard, too quickly, and it will snap."

—he is distracting you

"In the right conditions, with enough time, we can handle almost anything. But this… If you broke, I would not blame you. None of us would."

—ask him where he was last night

"I'm fine," said Dietmar.

—liar

"I think I took in too much of the basin when I pulled the old man out. Perhaps a fever…"

–ask him what he found by the river. I can still smell her on him, all hot and wet like a maiden on her red moon. Delicious filth

Dietmar blinked.

–ASK HIM!

The words spilt from his mouth before he could stop himself, but as they came out, he realised he didn't want them to stop. "Geoff said you seemed off after he relieved you from your watch. That you disappeared a while… and this morning you have not been… yourself."

"Is there a question in there somewhere?"

Dietmar shrugged. He licked the inside of his mouth, feeling the empty spot where his tooth had come out.

"Did you… see something? Touch something?"

Razin snapped his head to stare at him, his eyes slightly widened. Was that… surprise? Disgust? Guilt?

"Touch something?"

"It is a simple question."

It was a while again before Razin next spoke, but when he did, his voice was calm. "No, my friend. I did not *see* or *touch* anything. I am sure that if I had, I would tell you, not so?"

"Aye," said Dietmar with a subtle nod.

Razin looked at him again and then shook his head. "Let us get out of this forest. It smells like death in here." He didn't wait for Dietmar to reply, clicking his tongue and urging his mount into a steady trot.

–he lies, said the voice once Razin had put some distance between them.

"I know," Dietmar replied.

They slipped out of the stinking forest sometime in the afternoon and emerged onto an open plain that extended all the way to the sea.

They rode for a while, swiping at the flies that followed them and perspiring in the humidity, until someone finally looked up from the road. And then they all froze in their tracks.

The storm clouds they'd seen from the hills had finally broken, sending forth a deluge over the broiling sea in the distance. Monstrous waves the size of small mountains crashed against the coast, pouring an inky-black tide far past the beaches inland. But it was the *colour* of the clouds that made Dietmar want to look away. They were sickly green and glowed with a soft luminescence that hinted at the unnatural and obscene.

The sea itself was so vast that he didn't know how they could ever cross it. To make things worse, there was no sign of the Daughters—whatever those were—or the Sandmouth.

He was just starting to despair when Geoff called out. He was pointing at a blur on the shoreline.

Something shone there in front of the sea, like a pearl against the black waves and horrible green horizon.

It was a city.

***

They'll never listen, said Balaam.

No, no, never, agreed Silensus, chewing on a stalk. *They think he's mad.*

"I'm not mad," said Adelman. He'd taken the reins from Tomas, who was napping in the back of the cart, sprawled out between the remaining waterskins.

Quite right, said Balaam. *We wouldn't talk to you if you were.*

No, no, we wouldn't. Silensus shook his head irritably, flicking his ears to ward off the flies.

"Perhaps if I speak to Tomas first?" Adelman glanced back at the Englishman, who was using his arm as a makeshift pillow against the last of the bread. "He might believe me?"

Balaam *hawed. And tell him what?*

"That the hand is—"

Leading us to Hell? Silensus snapped at a fly.

Balaam turned his grey head to look at Adelman. *Whispering in your friend's head?*

Even now, it talks to him, Silensus declared, casting a sidelong glance at Dietmar riding alongside Arcadius's wagon a few yards away. *Telling him its stories. And lies! Filth and filth!*

"You can hear it?" Adelman wrinkled his brow and patted down his hair, more out of habit than anything else. His mostly bald pate glistened with sweat, and he wiped it with his sleeve.

It is very loud, said Balaam, swishing his bushy tail to shoo away the flies. *I do not think it knows we listen.*

But we do, we do. Silensus brayed, a low nasal sound that Adelman had come to recognise as the mule's chuckle. *What good would these big ears be if we couldn't hear with them?*

Adelman found himself smiling at that. He'd first heard the mules talking to one another in the camp between the boulders that first night after the sandstorm. While the others listened to the song of the demons on the wind, Adelman had found himself standing behind the mules while they chatted, quite unaware that he was listening.

I hate it when they sing, Balaam complained. *How will we sleep with that racket?*

Always the same song, too, added Silensus. *So sad… but—*

Would be nice if they came up with something new once in a while.

Silensus had made a soft nasal bray at that, then noticed Adelman watching them. *It's the old man again. I wonder if he has any carrots for us.*

Or apples.

"No apples, I'm afraid," said Adelman and showed his empty palms.

Balaam had nearly kicked him in surprise, his brown eyes going wide in alarm. But Silensus had taken it in his stride. *Any carrots?*

"I can go look," offered Adelman. "But I can't promise anything."

Yes, yes, Silensus had said, showing his flat teeth in a strange sort of grin. *Wouldn't say no to a little square of sugar either, if you have any?*

Oh, oh, any sugar cubes? Balaam had recovered from his shock and was looking at Adelman's pockets eagerly. *Nicolo always used to have a block or two for us. Rest his soul.*

God bless him, said Silensus.

Then the two mules had lowered their head in what looked like prayer. After a moment, they'd raised their heads to stare at Adelman expectantly. They wanted their treats.

Adelman's smile faded as he stared over the backs of the two mules, their hooves plodding toward the city on the horizon. Black waves rose up in the sea behind it. Titanic mountains of water that made him think of the Great Flood. He couldn't help but imagine those colossal water mountains crashing over the beach, inundating the land. Their massive swells seemed poised to cover the world.

But they never seemed to pass the city, and it was only as they drew closer that he realised the magnitude of the towering walls and buildings before them. Pillars as tall as any he'd ever seen in Germany or Constantinople loomed above walls that put Jerusalem's to shame. Stony white edifices like the cliffs of a ravine appeared behind the pillars, block upon block of buildings the size and width of the mountains that sat astride Jerusalem. Bright domes shone out from between the buildings, each as vibrant and large as the dome of the Church of the Holy Sepulchre.

The Romans couldn't have built this.

He wondered briefly if any man could have at all.

"What are we going to do?" he said, half to himself and half to the mules pulling his cart.

"Hopefully, not get eaten," came a voice by his ear. Tomas had stirred from his nap.

23

"This is not like the village," Razin said firmly. "Once we pass through those gates, we won't be able to fight our way out. They will close like the seal of a tomb at our backs. The mouth of a hungry beast around us, with we in its belly."

Razin did not want to go into the city. He did not want to go *near* the city, but it seemed he was in the minority.

"These are not some savages in mud huts," Arcadius countered, standing beside Dietmar next to his cart. They had parked off the side of the road, in the last thicket of trees, before the land changed and man's hand became evident everywhere. *Ahqafs* covered the plain beneath the city walls—long winding sand tracts that had been irrigated into canals. Narrow strips of soil lay between each reservoir, abundant with green orchards and crops, wheat and vegetables that extended all the way up to the walls.

Arcadius waved his hand toward the city. "This is a *civilisation.* Men who eat men could not build such things." He glanced at Razin. "Just as men who enslave their brothers could not."

"Perhaps not," Razin replied, shielding his eyes with his hand. "But history is one long line of civilisations being conquered by savages. One need not look past the Levant and the coming of the Franks to see that."

He ignored Arcadius's growl and Geoff's chuckle. It hurt his eyes to stare at the city too long. In the heat of day, it appeared as little more than a haze in the distance—a burnished jewel of vestigial bronze—a stain. The storm looming behind it added a strange atmospheric presence, like a blossoming dome of lazuli blue rising from the sea to challenge the sun, to pull back the golden curtain.

"I would not sleep comfortably behind those walls," Razin said, turning his gaze from the city. "Nothing we have seen here has done anything but try to kill us. We should be mindful of that. A civilisation? Perhaps, but it is one that has managed to survive in this… place. A place such as this breeds cruel men, I think."

"We're running out of food," said Tomas. He sat on the back of Adelman's cart, rummaging through the remaining provisions of meat and bread. "A few days at most, then we'll be reduced to toenails and prayers."

Razin turned to Dietmar. "What do you think?"

Dietmar ran a hand through his hair. It had started to thin and grey almost overnight. The ends of his once vibrant brown locks now appeared dry and brittle. Perhaps he was right, and the fever had never truly left him. He looked tired, drained of the vitality that had once propelled him. Still, he had noticed something amiss with Razin well enough.

Could it have been the princess—the *beast* he had unwittingly unleashed—that had killed the inhabitants of the forest? Razin's pride had been wounded after the trickery in the grove, but when he saw the lifeless bodies, he should have said something. Why hadn't he?

"We need to cross the sea," said Dietmar softly, his voice like an empty breath. "If we are to cross the sea, we will need a ship."

"Perhaps."

"They will have a port," Dietmar continued. "And knowledge of the Sandmouth and these 'Daughters'. I cannot think of another way."

Arcadius clapped his meaty hands together. "It's settled then," he said, already clambering back onto his cart.

Razin nodded and turned back to stare at the city. Black waves crashed behind it. The storm clouds flashed green as lightning split the sky. If this strange city did not consume them, then they would need a ship and a captain brave enough to sail through the storm.

***

The gates to the city—a pair of steel-framed wooden monstrosities as tall as trees—were wide open. A column of people and carts moved steadily through them, trundling along the road between two of the canals. Figures in gold and turquoise robes, fine chainmail shirts and long spears watched on from the gate's barbican. They had the look of all city watchmen in places where the rule of law had won out over man's baser instincts: restive, slightly overweight but not fat, and smug. Theirs was a station of privilege and power, which they exercised at every possible opportunity.

Razin had seen men like these strolling through the streets of Baghdad, taking bribes to look the other way and blackening eyes in the name of justice when their moods soured. You could find them in Jerusalem, harassing the Jews beneath David's Tower, or in Damascus, fleecing the merchants in the bazaar.

It was best not to trifle with such men, whom boredom turned callous and cruel.

Razin held his breath when they reached the back of the line, drawing up behind a two-wheeled tumbrel cart. A hemp sack covered its contents, but Razin was sure he heard something scratching about inside. The driver, a dark-haired man with swarthy skin and a drooping nose, acknowledged their arrival with a slow nod. He eyed the axe resting across Arcadius's lap and then turned back to face the gate.

Razin exhaled slowly, exchanging wary glances with the others. Levi had swapped places with the girl… with 'Tanit', in case they were questioned at the gates. That was assuming the denizens of the city spoke Aramaic like Teoma had.

If not… Well, they were running out of options.

Razin found his eyes fixed on the canvas cover at the back of the tumbrel as the line inched forward. When the cart moved, the canvas parted slightly, revealing iron bars underneath.

A cage.

Something stirred inside, retreating from the light. He caught a glimpse of a long neck and feathers before a hand swiftly pulled the flap closed again.

"*Aka da kug?*" The driver had turned around on his seat and sat with his feet now dangling over the cage. He smiled at Razin expectantly.

"Shit," said Levi from behind him. "It's not Aramaic."

The driver's gaze snapped to Levi, then he waved his hand and looked back at Razin. "If you want to see *Al Anqa'a*, you must pay, huh." The words were choppy, a second or third language at best, but they were enough to break the tension.

The merchant raised his hand, rubbing his fingers together and smiling back at them. "*Kug.*"

"We've seen enough of your beasts,' said Arcadius from his cart. "You'd have to pay me to look at whatever you've got locked up in that cage. Then you'd have to pay me more not to kill it."

The man knitted his brow, his vocabulary clearly limited to the words that earned his way. "You pay me," he said, shaking his head. "I show you Al Anqa'a."

"Keep your filthy Anqa," said Amice, leaning forward in his saddle. He wagged his finger at the man in a gesture universal to all vendors and shook his head. "No pay. You understand? No *kug*."

The man muttered something to himself, then tugged the canvas down hard one last time and turned back in his seat.

"There's no need for rudeness," said the Lady Marie quietly.

Amice looked like he might reply, but a low warning growl from Arcadius made him hold his tongue.

By the time they reached the gates, the line behind them had grown. First, an elderly man and his son, their heads covered even in the heat. Then, a group of clucking women stooped with age, gripping their walking canes tightly. Razin was immediately suspicious, remembering the figure of Teoma and the concealed limbs beneath his robes. But the old women appeared intact. They carried large empty sacks over their shoulders and smaller leather pouches at their waists.

When one of the old crones saw Razin staring, she shooed him away and barked at him in her tongue. The other women cackled loudly, clucking their tongues and stomping their feet until it sounded like a chicken hock behind them.

Their laughter ceased when one of the guards whistled down from the barbican, motioning for silence. Another guard patrolled the road near the gate, a broad man with dark, oily curls and a beard protruding from his open-faced helm.

He paused by each of the would-be entrants long enough for a few questions and then waved them through before moving to the next in line.

After briefly inspecting the contents of the cage on the vendor's cart, the guard came to a halt in front of Razin.

He spoke quickly, spraying spittle with each word. He paused when he saw Razin's expression and glanced at the carts parked behind him. His eyes swept over Arcadius and Levi and settled briefly on Tomas and Adelman.

He raised an eyebrow, then spoke to them in perfect Greek. "If you are here for the market, you will be required to pay a tax on your sales on the way out. What goods have you to declare? No point lying, Gavā will check your carts when you set up your stalls."

"No stalls," said Razin, seeing no reason to lie. "We are here for the port. We hope to secure safe passage."

The guard raised his other eyebrow. "There won't be many willing to risk passage during the *Ida*. We've been monitoring the waves all day—they'll reach the clouds soon enough. Where are you headed?"

Razin hesitated.

"Antioch," said Dietmar before the pause could grow uncomfortable.

The guard eyed them steadily, his gaze moving from Razin to Dietmar and then back again. He shrugged. "Never heard of it." Then, he pointed over his shoulder and began walking toward the old man and his son. "Go on, go on," he called back to them. "And welcome to Ubar."

***

The city hated them.

Razin could feel it the moment they crossed through its gates. There was an anxious sense of impending violence, barely restrained but with a certain inevitability to it. The smallest thing might set it off, then the city would ignite like an oil lamp smashed against the walls, consuming all within its angry, hateful blaze.

Some places were just like that, more dark than light. Man's faults and foibles had seeped into the earth, his sweat and blood and anger leaked out into the world only to concentrate in those densely populated areas. All great cities had places like it: slums where lust and violence held sway over truth and order, certain streets where man acted unchecked by the self-control that governed civil relations.

You couldn't fix such places. They had to be destroyed.

Which is exactly what had happened to Ubar.

At least, that's what Razin had thought until a few moments ago.

Ubar. Iram. The City of Pillars. The City God had Destroyed.

But the seething pit of humanity displayed before his eyes said otherwise. Everywhere he looked, sweating bodies with skin the every shade of humanity jostled beside one another. Men with the dark skin of Moors bickered with raven-haired Easterners and blue-eyed North men, adding a hundred languages to the tumult.

And tumult it was.

A wall of noise greeted them as they entered the city. The hustle and bustle of merchants pushing their wares, angry drivers trying to navigate the narrow streets with their carts, watchmen breaking up fights, the hollow barking of dogs echoing off the walls, and in the distance, faint but constant, the roar of the sea.

The gates opened into a vast plaza surrounded by towering, multi-storied buildings. Columns of stone and glass with spiralling walkways stretched above them, as straight as needles. They were connected by spidering rope bridges that swayed gently in the wind. Terraces extended from the higher levels of the spires, and Razin could make out tiny figures traversing them, no bigger than ants from where he stood. They crossed the terraces and walkways like crabs scuttling along a reef.

It was like nothing he had ever seen before—none of the vaulted arches of the Franks, the round columns and symmetry of the Romans and Greeks, the intricate tilework and smooth domes of the *Mocárabe* or *Ahoopāy*, nor the competing grandeur of churches and minarets. The complicated coalescence of East and West was… absent. And with it, everything that formed in his mind when he pictured a city.

Yet here Ubar stood, as much—more—a city than any he'd ever seen. It rose with a mesmerising blend of glass and steel, towers of bronze and rust reaching toward the heavens like the antennae of colossal insects. The ribbed tents of a thousand pavilions hung from the rooftops of buildings one hundred feet tall, somehow kept aloft by rigging and posts lying horizontal against the glass. Lanterns, already lit against the coming night, floated beneath the rope bridges like luminous jellyfish beneath the sea.

Ubar's progression had been unique, untouched by the influences of conquering Romans, the Church, or Islam. It was simultaneously awe-inspiring and shocking. Though there was something about the jagged structures and bulbous tents, the crooked steel ribbed towers and swinging bridges, that brought to mind the carapace and scuttling legs of a crab. And by the stink, a dead one.

Packs of golden-yellow monkeys raced across the rooftops, swinging out from under the rope bridges and clambering up the steel rickets of the spires. They moved in troops, bickering and fighting, swarming one another to steal their food and territory. City watchmen hurled stones at them, swearing when they came close enough to kick. The golden horde would retreat, beaten back, only to regroup like a shoal of fish once the threat had passed.

Darker shapes roamed the city streets, long-haired rats the size of small dogs with teeth like rusted nails. They competed with the tribes of monkeys for scraps, snapping at the gibbering beasts when their tails were yanked and they were flung bodily into the streets. But sometimes, the rats proved swifter, and their jagged yellow teeth would find skin, filling the streets with the screams of panicked monkeys when one of their kin was dragged off into whatever dark recess the rats called home.

Razin felt his head start to ache as he took in all the sights and sounds... and smells. It stunk like a festering corpse rotting in the sun. But more than that, garish colours paired, as if by a sultan's blind wife, had been painted upon every visible brick and stone, sparing only the road. Bright pinks rested beside lurid greens, imperial purple and shocking orange.

Rolls of vermilion silk hung from the windows of the building blocks, adding to the carnage.

"Ugly *cunting* place, isn't it?" said Geoff as they followed the tumbrel cart onto the plaza.

"Looks like they let the whores decorate it," said Amice. "All that's missing is the stink of their perfume to hide the smell of shit."

Geoff chuckled.

"We're just not used to their palette," said the Lady Marie. She was resting on her knees behind Levi on the cart. "They would probably say the same thing about our cities. Besides, it's not like Jerusalem smells any better in the summer."

Razin resisted the urge to raise his keffiyeh over his mouth and nose.

He'd smelt something like it once before, in the caves above Damascus while hunting with his uncle. They had heard a noise in the dark and glimpsed shapes moving within. When Mushrie had raised his torch, it had revealed the very human figures hiding in the depths, draped in soiled, yellowed shawls. Mushrie had shouted at him then, screamed at him to get out. Later, his uncle had explained that they had stumbled upon a leper colony.

But Razin saw no signs of sickness here, and the people crossing the plaza seemed unbothered by the stink.

The last thing he wanted was to stand out, so he left his keffiyeh wrapped around his neck and prayed he would get used to the smell.

As his eyes adjusted to the shock of colours, other sights unveiled themselves. A street occupied each corner of the plaza. He hadn't spotted the small grey buildings flanking each of the roads on his first scan of the square, but they appeared to be the only things other than the road to have survived Ubar's clashing style.

"Temples," called Dietmar, following Razin's gaze. He had dismounted Theseus to walk alongside Tomas and Adelman.

Razin nodded, considering the nearest of the temples. Its design resembled the old Roman colosseums—round in shape, with smooth marble steps leading to the lower entrance. A balcony extended over the patio, and Razin could see more doorways leading into the shadows behind it. Though unpainted, the walls of the structure were adorned with markings: images and text, he thought, though he was too far away to be sure. A pair of golden statues flanked the doors to the lower floor. The first was in the shape of a giant snake, its wicked fangs bared.

The second statue was of a man standing with two fingers raised to the sky, the fingers of his other hand pointed toward the earth.

Razin had seen him depicted before: first, in the temple, and then later, the bridge.

"Pagans?" Tomas said softly, looking to see if anyone outside of their group had heard him.

Arcadius chuckled. "It's not the Christ they worship here. Not in buildings like that."

"Then who?" Tomas wrinkled his brow, staring at the nearest temple.

"Why don't you go ask one of those priests for us and find out?"

Figures emerged from the temple's doors, clad in white robes and wielding long staves with coiling black serpents hanging from them. A gong resounded from within, and another priest appeared. He wore only a scrap of cloth to cover his loins and a belt around his waist. He waved a steel pot on the end of a chain and slowly passed the line of waiting priests. Smoke billowed from the censer, causing the snakes to writhe when he approached. The man halted at the top of the marble stairs, raising his hand toward the sky, mirroring the statue behind him. Then, he turned and walked back into the temple, completing the peculiar ceremony.

"I won't be going near there," said Tomas. He shuddered, shaking his head.

Arcadius grunted, no longer smiling.

They left the plaza soon after, following the trail of slowly moving bodies down the widest of the three streets, hoping it would lead them to the docks.

The garish spires gave way suddenly to rows of ramshackle dwellings that had been carved into the stone of what must have been a small mountain hidden beneath all the buildings. These structures appeared ancient, their single doors and windows rudimentarily carved, as if shaped by the forces of wind and rain as much as human hands.

Desolate figures sat on the steps, watching the road with eyes that shone in the fading light. Some spoke quietly among themselves, inhaling smoky air from pipes with curved bowls, but mostly they just watched. Their skins were as varied in shades as those in the plaza. Some were scarified with strange designs; others inked in fading tattoos. But their robes were all the same dull grey, and their faces shared the same grim expressions—indentured slaves or labourers. Razin had seen the same hard stares in the eyes of the servile class of Jerusalem.

Every so often, the slums would give way to shadowy alleyways barely wide enough for a person to walk through. Water ran down their walls, filling gutters and flowing past the dwellings where naked children with bulbous bellies splashed in the puddles.

In one of these alleys, Razin caught sight of a courtyard at the other end. The soft glow of a lantern, then shadows moving past a small statue in the centre. It resembled a whale or some mighty sea creature, its primitive carving obscuring its exact form. Then, a figure stepped into the mouth of the alley and doused the light so that he saw only darkness.

The slums eventually gave way to the tall domed buildings they had observed from outside the city. Golden roofs capped them, swallowing up the last beams of sun filtering in from between the buildings. More priests strolled across their steps, walking between the pillars and statues on the small, forward-facing plazas of each temple.

Below them thrived a market as vast and pungent as Malcuisinat in January. Merchants waved fruits and vegetables plucked from the canals while strange meat skewers from animals with elongated limbs and horse-sized fish sprawled across the tables.

But it was the trinkets that captured Razin's attention. Every third table or so was crowded by them and manned by men who looked like priests themselves.

His gaze lingered on the nearest as he guided Riba by the reins for a closer look. Small clay tablets lay beside painted effigies and stone statuettes. Dried fish husks, preserved with some mix of salt and glue, had been threaded through fine necklaces of bone, wood and silver. Similar markings to those he'd seen on the temple walls covered the fish skin.

The merchant behind the table pointed at the fish and then gestured to the rest of his stock. The man spoke rapidly while he wiped his sweaty bald head with a cloth. It took Razin a moment before he realised the man was talking to him in more than one language—rolling through tongues with the speed of a skilled linguist from a Baghdad *madrasah*.

"What are these?" Razin said in Arabic, pointing to the fish necklaces when the man paused for breath.

The merchant clapped his hands together, his smile broadening now that he had a language with which to make a sale.

"My friend, these are fish from the belly of Bahamut, vomited up with the tide and then blessed by the priests of Addir-Melek in the temple on the hill."

"Why would I wear one?"

The merchant blinked, his façade breaking for just a fraction of a second, but he was too experienced to let his smile waver. "They say that those who wear the spoils of Bahamut's gift will be the first to see the new world when the black waters take this one."

"Who says that?"

The man jabbed a thumb over his shoulder in the direction of the priests. "They do."

"And it will happen soon?"

The merchant snorted. "Very soon, my friend. Where are you from? Not the city, no?"

Razin shrugged, tugging at Riba's reins and walking on. He could still feel the merchant's eyes staring into his back when he crossed the road to join the others around a fountain opposite the stalls.

"We need provisions," said Dietmar, guiding Theseus to drink. "Enough food and water to sustain us for the journey across the sea and beyond."

"Will they take our coin?" asked Tomas, coming down from his cart with an empty waterskin.

Dietmar shrugged, glancing back. "They'll take silver."

"Never met a man who wouldn't," said Geoff, leading his own mare to the fountain.

Razin prodded Riba forward to join them, staring at the motifs carved into the stone tiers above the basin. It reminded him of the cosmographers' maps he'd seen in the *Ummayad* Mosque in Damascus growing up. Trees covered the top tier, oaks and palms with oversized birds and strange lizards intermingled between them. The second tier was shaped into the horns and shoulders of a bull, with round eyes that covered half the surface of the stone. The lowest of the tiers was the simplest: uniform waves with jagged rocks standing like pillars in the sea.

The black waters, he thought.

"That's all fine and well," said Arcadius, helping the Lady Marie down from the second cart. "But we'll need a ship too." He gazed up at the sky, peering past the buildings and into the green and grey clouds heaving not far in the distance. They couldn't see the ocean from where they stood, but Razin thought he could hear its growling waves smash against the walls even above the clamour of the market.

Arcadius looked sceptical. "Any captain'd have to be mad to sail during this… What did the guard call it?"

"*Ida*," said Razin.

Arcadius washed his hands in the fountain, still staring at the clouds. "How long does it last?"

"We'll find out once we've booked passage across," said Dietmar, stroking Theseus's flank. He glanced at Geoff, who nodded back at him.

"Geoff and I will make for the port and find ourselves a reliable captain to take us across."

"If there is such a captain as that here," said Arcadius.

"Or as close to *reliable* as we can find," Dietmar added, turning to the market. "We'll meet you back here before nightfall when we've found board upon a ship and rooms for the night."

"We should come with," said Tomas.

"There's no point us all trailing into the docks to get thieved and beaten," said Geoff.

"Aye," Dietmar agreed, tilting his head toward a pair of turquoise-caped figures idling through the market. "I'd rather leave you and the carts where the city watch can keep an eye on you."

"Fill those waterskins while we're gone," said Geoff.

"And see what you can pick up in the market: meat, bread, fresh fruit." Dietmar turned to Adelman. "You have enough coin?"

The old man nodded once, reaching into his tunic to retrieve a small pouch. "I have silver pieces if they'll take them."

"They will," said Dietmar, tugging at Theseus's reins and then passing them to Razin. His eyes were cloudy, red-rimmed like he'd been drinking. "Keep an eye on them while we're gone," he said. Then he clicked his tongue and started walking, not waiting for Geoff to follow.

***

The market street, crowded by day, took on an altogether different façade by night. Many of the vendors had rolled up their stalls and packed them onto their carts to make room for the mammoth iron pots and rotating spits, where assorted meats slowly cooked over blazing firepits.

Street performers weaved through the throngs, entertaining a willing audience with dazzling feats of skill and daring. A fire-breather, stripped to his waist and glistening with sweat, scaled the post of a remaining stall and unleashed a fiery torrent over the heads of the onlookers. Dancers spun on crates, their colourful trestles and painted bodies like ethereal forms in the flickering light of the fires. They moved to the deep, thumping rhythm of troubadours seated on cushions nearby.

Dark-haired beauties with kohled eyes and near-transparent silks stalked through the crowds, their gentle smiles enough to draw the gazes of even the most chaste men. They whispered in the ears of those who caught their attention and then led them toward a line of tents that had sprung up beneath the temples. Burly men with stern expressions guarded the entrance, extending their hands to halt the incoming men. The exchange of silver or gold followed suit, and then the tent flaps opened.

Tomas noticed Razin watching a pair disappear into the tents and inclined his head. "Is it so different from Jerusalem, with its secret brothel houses that everyone knows about?"

"There is shame in that," replied Razin, looking away from the tents. "Or, at least, the pretence of it. Here they conduct their sins in the open, beneath the watchful eyes of their idols and fellow man."

Arcadius sat down on the back of the cart beside Tomas. He peeled off a boot and rubbed at his swollen ankle, grinding his teeth. He looked up at Razin. "What difference does it make if everyone is doing it anyway?"

"Perhaps it makes no difference."

"So then?"

Razin dipped his cloth into the fountain, wringing it out before dipping it again until it was clean. "You feel shame because you know you have acted foolishly or transgressed in some way. That shame is an incentive not to do so again."

"Or not to get caught the next time," said Tomas with a chuckle.

"Yes, indeed. But to be *caught* implies transgression. It means that there is a rule, some moral law. Look around you… Here, there are no rules, only vulgar displays of excess. They are little more than animals fulfilling their wants and needs."

Arcadius stared back at the tents and then at the men drinking and laughing on the pillows in front of them. "It looks like a good time to me."

"Old Rome before its fall would have appeared good to some men too, for a time." Razin wiped his forehead with the now damp and cool cloth. "If this is how they behave in the open, imagine what acts they think too shameful to carry out in public."

"It sounds to me that it is less that they don't have rules and more that you don't like the rules they do have."

"Perhaps," Razin conceded. "But is that not the way with all people and their rules?"

Arcadius grunted again but didn't reply.

After a while, Razin got to his feet and motioned to Tomas. "Come," he said. "Let's see that Adelman hasn't lost the last of Dietmar's coin."

Ubar glowed at night, ablaze with the light of a thousand oil lamps and fires. It added to the phosphorene glow that hung over their heads, the eerie green veins of light rippling beneath the clouds.

Even at night, the city was stiflingly warm. Humid, like the forest—made worse by the hundreds of bodies crammed into the streets, breathing in each other's heat, sweating into each other's skins.

Razin walked alongside Tomas, his eyes watching the crowd as they pushed their way through. The restless tension he had felt upon entering the city was stronger here, concentrated around the laughing, dancing, drunk celebrants.

He wanted to leave.

"There he is," said Tomas, pointing above the heads of the revellers.

Razin followed his hand past a pair of acrobats using each other as climbing posts. Their bodies were painted jet black, with only the whites of their eyes showing.

Adelman stood in a short line in front of one of the roasting pits, his attention divided between the acrobats' performance and his place in the queue.

Razin attempted to squeeze past the onlookers and get closer to the assembly of ramshackle stalls erected to the side of the road. He gave up after a string of growled complaints and settled down to watch the rest of the performance.

The acrobats were a duo—a man and a woman, both with the coarse hair of the Moors. Razin hid his disgust when he realised they were naked, their bodies barely concealed by a thin layer of black paint.

He looked away when the man grasped his partner's breasts, fondling her as she clambered down his waist. This was a wretch's show, he thought, his eyes passing briefly over the faces of the watching crowd. Leering men and women surrounded him, enrapt by the performance. Some whistled and laughed, while others clapped and urged the acrobats on in their harsh tongue.

He was about to try push his way through again when he felt a hand tug at his sleeve. Glancing down, he saw a grubby-faced boy with dark hair and skin but bright blue eyes that looked the fit of someone twice his age.

The boy wore a rope around his neck.

"Go away," said Razin, yanking his arm back before the boy could pull at him again.

"Don't mind him," came a voice.

Razin looked up and saw a man standing behind the boy, his hand resting on the child's shoulder. A priest, he thought at first, taking in the man's attire. The man wore long dark robes that trailed in the dirt and a *ghutra* wrapped around his head. Markings inked his cheeks above a beard that had been oiled and curled in the same fashion as the guard captain at the gates. The man met Razin's eyes and smiled.

"Sagar is harmless but infinitely curious. And he sees in you something, I think, that doesn't belong."

Razin glanced at Sagar, then followed the rope around his neck with his eyes. It was fastened to the base of a bronze idol perched on the ledge of an alcove behind the tables. Incense burned in the pots beside the figure, alongside the oily white tendons of a hundred candles. Bowls of fruit and flowers covered the ground before it—offerings from the devout or perhaps the fearful? Razin's brow knitted as he took in the bronze figure. It was the same man he had seen depicted throughout this plane, with a corded beard and fingers raised to the heavens. His legs were crossed beneath him, though in place of the serpentine plate, he wore a simple tunic.

"Addir-Melek," said the man, watching him. "The last prophet."

Razin turned to walk away but felt the boy's hand tugging at the hem of his burnous. He swiped the hand again, scowling.

"Prophet of what?" he said, looking from the boy to the priest.

"Sagar's instincts were right then, yes? You are not from here." The tattoos on the man's cheeks creased with his smile until the lines looked like waves above his mouth.

"No," said Razin glancing back over his shoulder. Tomas stood a few feet away, his attention fixed on the performance. "And I do not know your prophet."

The man laughed, drawing Razin's gaze back to him. "Perhaps that is why you have been brought to me, why little Sagar picked you out of the crowd. And on the eve of Ida! Surely *Neruk* has ordained our meeting."

Razin blinked. "Neruk?"

"Ah," the man let out a breath, waving a hand. "You may know him by a different name: *Elil, Nergal, al-Lat…The Destroying Flame*. But everywhere, he is the same. Addir-Melek is his prophet."

"And what divine revelation is this Addir-Melek the messenger of?"

"Many things," the priest replied. "To share them all would take a seven-night, and I would prefer to celebrate the Ida with my brothers and sisters. But… it is the truth of death and renewal, and the wisdom of Neruk's Daughters."

Razin tensed. "Daughters?"

"Oh yes." The man nodded. "The goddesses, three."

"My friend." It was Razin's turn to smile now, though he knew he shouldn't provoke this pagan in a city where he was a stranger. "I think you must be mistaken. Allah has no daughters. Divinity cannot be shared. This is as true for the Christians with their Holy Trinity as it is for al-Lat or your Neruk. Let me ask you, who would be worthy of carrying the seed of God if such a thing were even possible? Who would be His consort?"

"His wife," said the priest, no longer smiling.

Razin laughed. "God's wife! And she a God too, then? No, my friend, as I said before, you are mistaken! Confused about the nature of God, I think. But let me help you: there is only one God, and Muhammed is His messenger. His *final* prophet."

"I see now that Sagar has made a mistake." The priest's eyes darkened, and the boy whimpered softly as the man's fingers dug into his shoulder. "You are not a man open to the many faces of God."

"Many faces..." Razin shook his head. He was annoyed now, the condescending tone of this pagan was getting under his skin. "Tell me, friend. Can the wife of Neruk create? Can their daughters create? Can they intercede against Neruk or Allah on your behalf?"

"Do not be foolish."

"So you see? Then why do you worship them? They are not gods!"

The priest bristled, and Razin noticed that people around them had turned to watch their exchange instead of the acrobats' performance.

"There was another who spoke as you do now a long time ago." The priest's voice grew louder, aware of the audience. "He condemned us, the sons of ʿĀd, and blasphemed against our gods—the gods of our fathers. He cared not for the legacy of our ancestors, the inherited wisdom and truth passed down. He was a disruptor, an apostate, and a heretic, concerned only with breaking down our traditions. His name was Hud."

"I know the story," Razin replied quietly. "He tried to save you."

"Save us?" The priest bared his teeth. Markings like those on his cheeks had been etched into them, inked black. "He was an atheist!"

"He preached Tawhid," Razin said, shaking his head. More of the crowd were turning to watch the exchange. They did not look welcoming, but Razin continued stubbornly. "He was not an atheist but a believer in a single God: Allah."

"He denied our gods," the priest spat. "That makes him an atheist. We suffered him for too long, we ʿĀdites. We were too tolerant of his lies and were punished for it. That is why we are here, in this place where the black waters grow deep and the veil between us and Bahamut grows thin. A storm took the city, damning us for our weakness. And here we shall remain until we prove ourselves again."

"The Sandmouth," Razin breathed. He frowned. The story was inverted. "It was because you would not give up your pagan beliefs that Ubar was destroyed."

"Destroyed?" The priest cackled, waving his hand dismissively. His knuckles bore dark, tattooed marks. "See, my little atheist. Does it look like we were destroyed? This great city that dwarfed those of the Sumerians, and Babylonians, and your cities too, I think, yes?"

"Enough," whispered a voice near Razin's ear. Tomas stood beside him, and a nervous-looking Adelman was just a step behind. "Let's go, please."

"And this? More atheists in our city?" The priest turned to address the crowd, their attentions now fully divided between the acrobats and the argument unfolding in their midst. "Have we learned nothing from the trials of Hud? And on this sacred day of Ida, when Bahamut will show himself to the city before returning to the deep." The priest shook his head, tapping Sagar's shoulder with his hand. "Perhaps the boy's instincts were right after all, but I misunderstood his purpose in finding you."

Sagar flinched beneath the weight of the man's hand, but when he realised he was no longer in trouble, he nodded fervently.

"He meant no offence," said Tomas, trying to defuse the mood. "*Tell him*," he hissed, glancing at Razin.

Razin hesitated, his eyes flicking to the watching crowd. Unfriendly faces met his gaze. He could feel it, the hate rising off of their sweating bodies like it were a tangible thing.

"Forgive me," Razin said with a soft bow to the priest. "As you said, I am a stranger in this place. It was not my intention to question your beliefs."

"He just likes to argue," Tomas added. "He means nothing by it."

The man pursed his lips, contemplating Tomas. His eyes flickered with a mix of azure-green and gold beneath the light of the clouds. They seemed to hold the tension, the imminent violence that Razin had sensed since entering the city. Violence, he thought, that might now be directed toward them.

Fool, he thought to himself, cursing his own arrogance and hubris.

The priest looked up at a voice from the crowd—a woman with kohled eyes and braided hair, her lips coloured a deep sea blue. There seemed to be some disagreement. The priest shook his head while listening to her words, then raised his hand to silence her.

"It is the prophet who preserves us, who keeps Bahamut beneath the black waters."

Another man spoke, in Greek this time, stroking his long beard as he wagged a finger at the priest. "It is the prophet who *calls* Bahamut to wash clean the world. Addir-Melek was only a man; he cannot keep a god beneath the waves."

Nods of approval came from those around him while the priest scowled in response.

"Noahites! I should have guessed," the priest exclaimed. He made a motion as if to reply but paused and then grinned. "Look how easily the atheists divide us. Is this not what Hud did before Ubar fell out of favour with the gods?"

Razin flinched when he felt a gentle grip on his arm.

"Do not turn around," a voice whispered urgently. "It was foolish of you to attract the attentions of a priest of ʿĀd. Very foolish."

"He found me," whispered Razin from the corner of his mouth.

The grip tightened. "*Quiet!* You must come with me before the mob turns on you. Now, while the priest still fights with the Noahites."

Razin glanced at Tomas and saw another man wearing a heavy cowl whispering in his ear. He caught Tomas's eyes and nodded.

"Let's go," said the voice, pulling him. "Quickly!"

Razin didn't resist as the hand led him away from the crowd. Another man slipped into the spot he had been standing in, filling the gap before his disappearance could be noticed by the busy priest.

He glanced past the man and saw the boy, Sagar, still watching him, a thin smile on his dirty lips.

24

The city has us now, Razin thought as they hurried through narrow streets and dark corridors. They followed their guides out of the crowded market and down a set of steps so steep Razin and Tomas had to walk with Adelman between them, his arms locked with theirs.

She is bringing us up to her breast, and she will never let us go.

The two figures who had pulled them away from the mob were as much stinking beggars as they were wily sewer rats. Their clothes, little more than rags, were plain, with none of the clashing colours so fashionable in the rest of the city. Servants then, Razin thought. They moved through the street like spiders, hunched deep in their hoods and scuttling. Their long robes were stained with filth up to their knees.

They soon found out why.

"Down here, please," said one of the dirty-robed figures, a hand pointed to a niche in the wall. Razin hesitated.

The second figure was a woman.

"To shit with this," said Tomas, staring down the steps. Water sloshed about inside, nearly coming up to the street. "Why can't we go back the way we came?"

"They will be looking for you," the woman explained. Her voice was shrill, but she spoke with an air of authority. *Perhaps not a servant, then.*

She noted Tomas's reluctance and sighed. "It's not that much further. Come on."

"We have friends," said Razin as the woman splashed into the passage. "We left them in the market. They're waiting for us."

He didn't mention Dietmar and Geoff.

The woman paused, glancing back at Razin. Her face was surprisingly clean and not the scarred, pustule-riddled visage he'd half-expected, though she was no great beauty either. Her face was broad, centred by a short, stubby nose that gave her a slightly porcine appearance. She had a weak chin.

"Where?"

"By the fountain opposite the fish vendors."

"Hashur will find them," she said, nodding toward her companion.

"And the mules." Adelman raised a trembling hand, casting an anxious glance between the woman and Hashur. "Balaam and Silensus. Please, you must bring them too."

The woman pinched the bridge of her nose and let out another breathy sigh. Then she shrugged and nodded to her companion.

Hashur grumbled something beneath his breath but turned quickly on his heel to jog back up the steps in the direction of the market.

"Now, please," said the woman, waving her hand toward the passage. "Follow me."

Razin and Tomas watched as the woman waded into the watery tunnel. They could run for it, leave this woman in the sewers and disappear into the streets. But their choice was made for them when Adelman followed her down the steps.

***

They splashed through ankle-high water down a long corridor until they found themselves in a large cavern. A forest of columns surrounded them, like the stone pillars of the great mosque of Damascus. They disappeared into the darkness ahead.

The belly of the city.

Their guide pulled a torch from the wall, pausing only long enough to motion at Razin to do the same.

Then she was moving again, sloshing through the water with her torch raised above her head.

"The caverns will flood again with the next tide," she said, holding her torch up to the nearest column. It glistened under the light, still wet from the last time the cavern was filled. "We must move quickly, or they will only find our bodies in the morning."

"Where are you taking us?" asked Tomas. He held his robes bunched up in his hands, showing his skinny white knees. They were already covered in slime.

"To meet the *šubur*," said the woman. "He will know what to do with you."

"Why couldn't you just leave us be?" Adelman groaned, limping a step behind Tomas. He was looking more dishevelled by the minute, and his few remaining grey curls stood out like strands of wire behind his ears.

The woman glanced back, her sharp stare enough to make Adelman pause.

"You don't know what they do to monists here," she said softly, her voice a near whisper. "Adites and the Sons of Noah will put aside their differences for that. Trust me. You do not want to find out. Now come, I won't drown in here with you when the black waters come."

They followed the woman across the cavern, splashing through the brackish pools until the waters finally receded, and they found themselves walking up a gentle incline.

The passage ahead of them narrowed, and they gradually left the towering pillars behind. They ventured along a serpentine passageway, winding their way amidst the grey walls that Razin thought might have been a part of the mountain itself. A tender zephyr whispered its welcome as they stepped out from the tunnel and onto the paved steps of an open courtyard beneath the clouds.

The yard clung to a terraced ledge that jutted out defiantly from the mountainside. It ringed the stone, tracing its contours along the summit's circumference, spiralling upward into the lofty empyrean. Glass and iron gleamed from between the rock, reflecting sinuously between the rugged crevices and soaring spires that protruded like insectoid feelers above the city.

Razin let his eyes linger on the peaks and then turned to stare at the clouds. They blossomed with a green light, shimmering with an iridescent opalescence that brought to mind the inside of a seashell. He drew his gaze from the clouds and looked around. They were on the rooftop of one of the spires they'd seen coming into the city—whether it was built into the mountain or formed from a part of it, Razin couldn't tell, but the feat of engineering was astonishing either way. They must have stood a thousand feet over the city walls. Higher, dwarfing even the most ambitious of Frankish and Syrian structures he'd seen.

The sky growled like something alive, thunder booming from within the green-tinged clouds. Rain came down in thick sheets over the sea, but the city itself remained as dry as the humidity allowed. He stared past the glowing radiance of the dwellings below, his eyes fixed on the heaving mass beyond its walls. Waves as high as mountains rose and fell, reaching toward the clouds before coming back down, crashing against the city boundaries. If there were ships down there, they would be battered and broken, wrecks left to lie at the bottom of Ubar's port. Nothing could survive swells like that.

"Urshal!" The woman called, dropping her torch into a brazier and striding across the courtyard. "Rouse yourself. We have guests. Or are you drunk again?"

A bleary face appeared from behind the curtains of a pavilion on the opposite side of the yard. He was young, in his early twenties at most. He wore his curls combed back, sleeked with wax. His thin, aquiline face and large eyes made Razin think of a praying mantis. He stepped out onto the stone paving and paused, seeing Razin and the others behind him for the first time.

"Hud's breath, Zua," he said, looking back at the woman. "Who are they?"

"Travellers," said Zua, unwrapping her dirty robes and hood to reveal a much cleaner but no less plain chemise beneath. Her hair was tied tight against her head, braided into a single long weave that hung down her neck. She deposited the robes into Urshal's waiting hands and snapped her fingers. "Go, go, food and drink for our guests. I shall inform the master of their arrival."

"He's *not* going to be pleased, Zua. Hud's spit, what were you thinking? All right, all right, I'll go summon the old crag then, shall I? Be it on your head!" Urshal made to move back behind the curtain but then raised a wrinkled brow, his brown eyes darting from face to face. "Where is Hashur?"

Zua scowled. "He will be with us shortly." She clicked her fingers again, motioning to the empty stone table in the middle of the courtyard. "For once in your life, will you just do as you're told? And without the complaining?"

Urshal winced but nodded.

"Enough for…" Zua glanced at Razin, who had moved to sit on one of the benches around the table.

"Five more," said Tomas.

Urshal blanched. "Five more! Gizzal is going to—"

"*Without* the complaint, if you'd please. I'll deal with Gizzal."

The wiry man sighed, then blinked one last time at the guests and disappeared behind the curtains.

"He's right," said Zua when he was gone. She tidied up her crinkled chemise and straightened her back. "He's going to kill me for bringing you back." With that, she followed Urshal into the pavilion and through a door on the other side.

Razin and Tomas exchanged a glance. Adelman muttered something about his mules.

Above them, the clouds boomed.

Gizzal announced himself with a string of curse words that made Razin flinch and Tomas chuckle.

"You *bloody fool*, Zua!" His voice was dulled by the thick curtains, but every angry word still echoed across the courtyard, growing louder like the thunder above their heads. "What foolishness possessed you to bring them here? *Here*, of all places? And on the eve of the Ida, no less? You foolish girl! By Hud, if I hadn't—"

Then the drapes parted, and he was on the patio, his sandals clicking as he walked toward the table, his hand extended outward.

"Friends!" he exclaimed, his anger seemingly forgotten. "Sit, sit, don't get up for me, please! You must be tired from your journey. Zua tells me you had an encounter with Bezal in the market? God rot his bastard skin! I imagine you saw his little familiar then too?" Razin felt his hand clasped firmly, then shaken like a piece of straw in the wind. "Sagar, I think his name was? That boy never ages. Like a little impish fiend with those strange blue eyes. I swear he can read your mind with just a glance. I've instructed Hashur to deal with him should he ever get the chance, but Bezal keeps him on a tight leash, quite literally, too!"

Gizzal was thin and wiry, like Urshal, but where the servant was only thin, Gizzal's arms were knotted with muscle. He walked with the grace of a swordsman or dancer, though his bearing spoke of the authority and easy arrogance of nobility. What gave Razin pause, however, was the long curling scar that drew from his left ear to the corner of his mouth. It stuck out like a seam.

So, this is the šubur.

He must have been in his late forties at the youngest. His hair was hidden beneath a maroon headwrap, fastened with a golden clip, but his beard—cut short and neat, was heavily streaked with grey.

His eyes creased, and he met Razin's gaze with a smile.

"You are lucky we found you when we did," he said. "Bezal and his zealots would have eaten you alive and cast your bones to the sea for their God to feast upon."

"Rot his bastard skin," Urshal repeated, returning with a tray filled with fresh fruit and carafes of water.

Gizzal rested down on a cushioned seat and took a cup from the tray. Taking a deep draught, his gaze swept across his guests before finally settling on Razin. More scars marked the corners of his eyes, thin straight lines that looked like rays of hieroglyphic light. Torture? Razin wondered. *Punishment for some crime? Or was this an act of fashion peculiar to the aristocracy of the city?* A wretched, degenerative practice either way.

Gizzal wiped his mouth with a finger and carefully returned his cup to the tray. Then, with an officious flourish, he motioned to his guests.

"You have come at a poor time, my friends, as I am sure my little birds have told you. It is the eve before Revelation for many in the city. I am sad to say that they become like beasts with the prospect of seeing their

God manifested, their faith proven to them if no one else. It is a dangerous time for strangers. Particularly for those who do not know our ways. You were brought by the storm, yes?"

Gizzal searched Razin's face and then nodded. "I imagine you have questions then. I will answer what I can."

Razin nearly laughed in his face. *Questions? In a city thought destroyed by God? In a land where ifrits and half-men eat their own?*

"Yes, I have *questions*."

"Who the hell are you?" said Tomas. He'd picked up a strange-looking fruit covered in thin purplish petals and was eyeing it sceptically.

"And where are my mules?" said Adelman softly.

Gizzal raised a brow and turned to the old man.

"Hush now," said Tomas, gently patting Adelman on the knee and placing the fruit back on the tray. "Hashur is bringing them with the others, isn't he?" Tomas glanced at Zua, who was busy lighting paper lamps along the terrace.

She shrugged.

"My name," said Gizzal, leaning back in his seat and resting a foot over his one knee. "Is Gizzal dumu Bazi. And I am the šubur of the *Hursaĝ* Towers, an allotment of the *Kura-Agal* in Great Ubar, the City of Pillars, of the Sands, Omanum of the Desert, Iram, the Jewel of *Eden-ne*. Your new home."

"We're not staying," said Razin.

"Šubur?" asked Tomas. "Hersag?"

"*Hursaĝ*." Gizzal waved a hand. "The towers north of the *Ama-i-de Gate*. I am the elected servant of the people who live in the tallest spires of the Kura-Agal."

"He's very important," said Urshal, leaning over the table to refill the carafe.

"Don't you have something better to do?" Zua blew out the taper and shook away the whisper of smoke. "There's *şalvar* that need mending before the Ida Parade. Go on, off with you."

Urshal rolled his eyes but didn't argue, taking the jug and stalking back toward the pavilion. Razin watched him pull back the curtains and saw a small candle-lit study with walls filled with books and a dark corridor beyond.

"Why are we here?" Razin turned back to the šubur.

"In my quarters?" Gizzal ran a finger along the side of his mouth, tracing the scar with his nail. "Because my dear Zua has a soft spot for strays. One day she will bring back something rabid, I think. But try telling her that."

Zua snorted.

"Or do you mean here in Eden-ne, in these wind-cursed sand-hills where monsters walk amongst men? That answer is more complicated." Gizzal steepled his fingers and watched his guests from over his interlocking hands. He sat like that for what felt like an age, appraising each of them in turn, measuring them with each slow blink of his scarred eyes. Thunder rolled in the clouds above.

Gizzal's fingers, Razin saw, were stained dark like the pagan priest's—Bezal.

No, not like Bezal's, he realised. The dark splotches marking their host's skin were not tattoos but ink. A scholar, then.

Gizzal pursed his lips, unfurling his fingers to stroke the scar on his mouth. He did so with the familiarity of longstanding habit. Then he sighed. "You are not the first travellers to be spat out by *Me-anesi*, but few make it to the City of Spires after falling out from the Mouth of God. In that, you are fortunate. Or perhaps blessed by God? But not so blessed that you avoided this place, eh."

"What is this *place*?" said Razin, staring meaningfully at Gizzal. He was done with abstractions and vague, meaningless allusions. If Gizzal had answers, he would have them.

"On a map?" The šubur rolled his fingers over his wrist and shook his head. "There are no maps that can show us Ubar. Not now. Of course, some have tried. I myself have made some humble attempts—little more than an amateur's efforts at cartography, you understand. They are vulgar things. Half-finished imaginings of ideas I barely grasped, exploratory works at best." Gizzal let out a weary sigh, waving his hand dismissively. "I leave the scribbling to my colleagues in the temples now. My talents are better served elsewhere. In theory and hypothesis, where the rigour of method and form can illuminate the *apocalyptic*—the hidden. I mean this in the revelatory sense, you see." He leaned forward in his seat, his eyes suddenly aglow. "Now, some people understand that word to denote something purely theological: *Apocalyptic*. Ah, the occult! Ethereal! The spiritual and numinous. And they are not quite wrong—theirs is simply one of the ways of seeing necessary to understand. Men such as them might be satisfied with a geographer's representation of Eden-ne. The lands from *Imud* to the *Gu-be Straits* are grand indeed. But such landscapes are of little interest to you, I think. Those maps will never reveal the secrets that lie within every shadow, the veils upon veils that conceal and hide from us the truth. To see that, you must ask a different question: where is this place *in relation to where you came from*. From *Ukum-Sila*—the Levant, yes?"

Razin nodded his head slowly, trying to make sense of what Gizzal was saying. The man was talking in abstraction and allegory, referring to places he'd never heard of, things he'd never seen. He was finding it hard to keep up, and by Tomas and Adelman's bewildered expressions, he wasn't the only one.

Gizzal pursed his lips, perhaps sensing the perplexity of his guests. "From where we sit, Ukum-Sila is nowhere. It does not exist."

"Now, wait just a second," said Tomas, frowning. "Of course, it exists. It's where we came from."

"It doesn't exist in any material way," said Gizzal, still smiling. "Not in a form that can be drawn on a map. At least, not in a conventional sense. But…" Gizzal raised a stained finger to silence Tomas's protestations. "That is not to say that it does not exist *somewhere*. It is just not visible on the plane we currently occupy. Perhaps it will be easier if I show you, yes? Urshal!" Gizzal snapped his fingers, calling out to the pavilion. "My instruments, if you please."

There was a grumbling noise from behind the curtains, the sound of chairs being moved around and drawers rattling open, then Urshal elbowed his way out from the pavilion and marched across the patio. He held a thin wooden box in his hands, no thicker than his thumbs but as wide as his chest. The dark polished wood looked like it came from oak or cedar or even one of those strange dead trees they'd come across by the river. It was sealed shut by a simple bronze clasp.

Urshal deposited the box gently on the table in a space Zua had cleared for him and then stepped back to hover behind the benches.

"Now," said Gizzal, leaning forward and flipping open the clasp. "Let it not be said that engineers are not capable of great feats of art. It may not be as poetic a life as that of the scribblers and scribes in their austere temples, but…" He lifted the lid of the box slowly, with the sort of reverence Razin associated with the sacred, with the holy. It was the same manner in which Nicolo had treated the relic in his care.

But he had feared it, Razin thought.

He had called it a cursed thing. Maybe it hadn't been reverence that he'd noticed at all, but fear? Fear of the profane?

The thought settled uneasily on Razin's shoulders as he remembered how Dietmar had appeared the last time he had seen him, the hand still secured in a pouch at his side. His friend had appeared haggard and tired, his skin taut around his cheeks, like a man taken by the grips of some great malady.

Razin knitted his brow, half expecting to see the same rotting appendage revealed to him, the anaemic white hand resting on a bed of velvet. Instead, the interior contained a pile of paper-thin sheets of glass, each neatly slotted into the ribbed walls of the box. The glass slide at the top of the stack was covered in delicate lines, forming intricate patterns across its surface. Whorls of colour had been mixed into the glass, creating striations in a dozen shades. The light of the lamps reflected off of it, turning the shimmering surface into a ruptured firmament, like a slice of colour spilling from the heavens.

Razin could just make out a second pane beneath the first, more lines and colours in a jumble of incomprehensible patterns.

Gizzal removed the first slide from its slot and held it up to stare at. A smile made its way across his face, and he looked past the glass to Razin. "Such marvels require more than just an artist's eye. Anyone can muddle around with a little paint or stone for sculpting. For this… *this* requires mathematics, geometry, physics. But not even the material sciences are enough! Here we are moving into theology and *Kispuology*, ritual. The luminous, you see? Such an artisan must, perhaps, even be familiar with thaumaturgy—how else could one reveal the hidden?"

"What is it?" said Tomas, eying the glass sceptically.

"A triptych," said Razin. He had seen one before, in the chamber of the *Ulamā* of the madrasa in Baghdad. He had spent a week there with his uncle listening to scholars and poets, mathematicians and physicians, astrologers and astronomers, philosophers and alchemists, theologians and imams. Learned men from all across Islam. When the Ulamā had heard they had travelled from Damascus to listen to the lectures, he had invited them to his chambers and entertained them for an evening.

His rooms had been filled with discoveries, with trinkets from further east, ticking time-keepers from beyond the Urals, wind-up puppets that moved in jarring, shuddering steps, and the triptych.

The simple three-glass panelled device had fascinated Razin at first. Each of its panes was inscribed with a different set of reliefs: the constellations, a starry firmament made of holes that pierced the glass; the half-moon, rendered so as to highlight its crescent; and a plain of trees and rolling hills. When viewed in the right light and from a certain angle, the effect was dazzling. Razin had stared in wonder at the images superimposed over whatever he directed it at, creating an alternative reality when viewed through the lens. His interest with the device had lasted until, at his age, rather predictably, Mushrie had introduced him to the wind-up puppets.

"Almost," said Gizzal, still smiling. He placed the slide into a row of slots in the roof of the box. It slid in vertically so that its surface was still fully visible. Then, he retrieved another slide and repeated the process until all twelve of the glass panels contained within the box had been placed upright in their grooves.

"This is an *Igi-dañal-na*. An Occularis Box. It is, I think you will agree, a great deal more compelling than a triptych—a mere children's toy." Gizzal pulled at a small wooden panel to the side of the lid. A roof tray sprung up, elevating the glass slides over the rest of the box. "It works with refracted light, which travels internally within each slide, away from the light source. Once the light reaches the patterns cut into the glass, it is disrupted—its journey altered. Of course, some of this light seeps out of the panels and disappears. Some of it illuminates the fissures and markings, but the rest of it flows through the panel to shine upon the next slide. The light that completes its trajectory exits the final panel in every direction, spilling out from the translucent edges like water from an overfilled trough. As the light passes through each slide, it leaves behind a non-physical form: an imprint in the lines carved into the glass. Are you following?"

Gizzal looked up at the eyes blinking back at him and then gestured to the box, ploughing on. "The pattern from the previous pane is rendered on the subsequent one via refraction, creating a silhouette of pure light. As you add more layers, the image becomes increasingly sophisticated, until spatially, this non-physical rendering appears as a distinct and fully formed dimensional object." Gizzal felt along the floor of the box, retrieving three smaller mirror panels which connected together with a satisfying click.

"Now, anyone with a rudimentary understanding of the principles can piece together a refraction box. The real skill is getting the colour washed into the glass to reflect with the light. We tried mirrors"—he pointed down at the trifecta in front of the box—"silver shards, glass infused with salt. We even mixed flax oil in with the pigments. But, if any of that could possibly work, it'd take someone a damn sight more skilled than me and my tinkerers to figure it out. The only thing that resulted in any success, that created a strong enough beam for our purposes, was converting the inside of each glass slide into a prism. See, look here…" Gizzal lifted one of the slides, holding it up horizontally for them all to see. "There's just enough room in the glass for the three sides, which are placed in the glass before it's sealed up. Painful work, but the result… Diamonds." Gizzal returned the panel to its box. "Quite dazzling, but you'll see. Zua, if you'd be so kind as to hand me one of those lamps. Yes, that one will be fine, thank you."

The šubur pushed away the tray of fruit and empty goblets before sliding the Occularis into the centre of the table. Then he placed the lamp Zua handed him in front of the box and adjusted its wheel until it burned at its brightest. Plumes of oily smoke rose from the glass opening above the wick as Gizzal fiddled with its steel back plate. He removed it after a few less-than-gentle tugs.

"This usually works better in daytime," said Gizzal conversationally. He sat the backplate on the table and retrieved the mirrored panels. "But this ought to give you some idea of the reality I am describing." He clicked the mirrored panels into place behind the lamp, where the backplate had rested, and blinked away at the focused ray of light that suddenly shone out from the front of the lamp.

He angled it away from his face, directing the light to shine directly at the front pane of the Occularis. The box flickered, the light spasming momentarily as it adjusted to its new course, guided by the intricate cuts, lines and panels. Gradually, the twelve glass slides started to illuminate, casting light from their sides and allowing it to pass through, carrying the shapes carved into their surfaces to each subsequent pane.

Gizzal grinned as the beam flooded through the last pane, pouring out the other side in a coruscating whirl of colour and light that reached a few feet onto the patio beyond the benches. The light swirled and danced like a shimmering pool of green and blue and umber, red, gold and yellow, in all manner of hues and contrasts.

Razin heard Tomas gasp as the waves of light settled, and he had to subdue his own surprise as a form gradually materialised from the undulating waves of light.

"*Rub' al-Khali,*" said Gizzal as a peak formed from the wash of light. It was like watching a tower loom out from the mist or the tide slowly ebb away to reveal some monolithic edifice beneath. Abstract streaks of gold and brass combined in hundreds of gently oscillating lines to form the bastions of a great ruin. Fully shaped windows and stairwells were rendered in a near-physical form. Walls followed, and then thin lines in garish pink and blue. The fields of light created the impression of rooftops and arching temples. Pillars of stone appeared from the glowing pool. And in the blink of an eye, a whole city had been conjured from the light.

"It's like a mirage," breathed Razin, unable to move his eyes from the spectacle. "Just... *more.*"

"The principle is the same," said Gizzal with a subtle tilt of his head. "As the light traverses through fluctuating air temperatures, it mimics the panel effect of the Occularis, albeit to a lesser extent."

The stream of light swelled again, striations of colour twining and blending with one another to maintain the shape of the cityscape. More peaks bloomed from the lines, towers as tall as the Kura-Agal, with slat terraces that covered their walls like ribs. And in the space above, stars appeared, shining aspects that trailed light like dust.

Razin finally pulled his gaze away from the rendering to stare back down at the box on the table. Each of the panes shone with its own peculiar luminance. The patterns inscribed on each piece of glass glowed like iron left in the fire too long.

He tried to make sense of the markings, the lines and holes cut into the panes and how they translated into the depiction before them, but he couldn't decipher any order to their arrangement.

"Each pane is like an artist's brushstroke," said Gizzal, watching him. He pointed to the first slide. The glass flickered, streams of amaranth and velvet light coursing across the patterns on its surface. "And each marking on the glass is a bristle: quite unique on its own, but it is *together* that they become remarkable. Without one another, they would not be able to produce *our* mirage, you see? But, notice when you look at the aspect created by the Occularis, you cannot see the individual layers. Like a master painter, the brushstrokes are concealed. Hidden! We are only capable of seeing one aspect at a time. But look what happens to the mirage when you alter its inputs—the many layers it is built from."

Gizzal removed the first slide, his ink-stained fingers basking in the afterglow of the Occularis, and pointed to the render.

Rub' al-Khali disappeared, its spires and walls and shuttered windows, its rows of rooftops and temples, all swallowed up by the undulating light. Another cityscape appeared in its place. Squat and ruinous, with low walls and twisted architecture. Wooden watchtowers dotted the walls. They were like those that abutted the gate to Ladah, spindly things with caved-in rooves and rickety ladders.

What resemblance there was to the scene before it was thin, perhaps the rooftops and tiled windows, but little else. There was a sense of uncanniness to the image, of shapes and angles that didn't quite fit. Jagged pillars stuck out like bent nails. Stairways leading to nowhere rose beside doorwells with no buildings behind them. Balconies hung from the empty wall faces, window shutters without windows.

"What is that?" said Tomas softly, his eyes flicking over the façade.

"Something that's always been there but hidden." Gizzal removed the next slide, replacing the hunched cityscape with an empty plain. He let it sit briefly while the light retraced to match the slides, then he removed that too. "These are the layers that make up the whole—the bones and meat and organs, hidden by the skin. Our world is not so different from what the Occularis shows us, I think. We simply do not see it, do not *want* to see it."

The next panel showed a crowded treeline beneath hills that disappeared into the distance, gleaming stars above.

But no moon.

Gizzal placed the unused slides down on the table and sat back on his bench. "Whether by our own minds or by God's will, we are only able to see one state at a time. But they are there, resting just out of sight. The physical and non-physical. Material and immaterial. The spiritual and the profane." He let out a breath, exhausted, though his eyes still gleamed with excitement. "Our whole reality is built from them."

Razin stared into the sculpture of light, tracing the subtle beam of the hills back to the lens of the Occularis while he considered Gizzal's words. His immediate impulse was to reject everything the šubur had said. Surely, these were the ramblings of madness? Of a man so caught up inside his own head that he had lost sight of reason.

Is that not the same thing?

But what was reason in a place like this?

The moment he put any rigorous thought into what he had seen and experienced, he was forced to leave reason behind. He had seen *too much* to dismiss Gizzal's theory out of hand; he knew that now. He had already resigned himself to the fact that they were no longer in the Levant. For that to be true, there would need to be a reason *why*. Their host's theory offered as good a solution as any he had considered.

Unless, of course, they were truly in Jannah with the damned… He hadn't fully dismissed that notion either.

Then he remembered Paul of Balata, the brigand in the pillocks whose body they'd found in the basin, rotting amongst the reeds. Had the man they'd spoken to been a mere aspect? A reflection or an *echo*, as Gizzal had called it. Razin thought back to what he'd told Dietmar. Paul was a qareen. A vision from another plane—a spiritual double that occupied an immaterial place. Was that not consistent with Gizzal's theory?

"What you propose is an ontological dead end," he said, meeting Gizzal's eyes. The šubur had not looked away from him since removing the first slide. "You are suggesting things that cannot be observed or studied to test your theory against."

"Not quite," said Gizzal, smirking. "There are places here where the lines between states become thin. Where, like the light, you can see echoes of the other aspects reflected in our own. Places like the Dead Oceans of

Ud, where all the colour runs out of the world. Or the Moonhead Towers, where no sound can ever be heard to pass… And sometimes, in those places, the aspects tear."

"What happens when they tear?" asked Tomas.

"How do you think you got here?"

"The… Me-anesi? You called it the Mouth of God?"

"Surely all things are by His design," said Gizzal. "Even this." He chortled and leaned forward to pick up his cup. "Zua tells me there are more of you still? For so many of you to make the passage, now that is a surprise."

"There were others," Tomas muttered, crossing himself before picking up another fruit from the tray. "They've all been stabbed, eaten, torn up, dragged to whatever *poxxing* Hell there is by demons and half-men."

"Half-men?" Gizzal rubbed his beard. "You have encountered the *Maštur* of Ladah then?"

Tomas nodded hesitantly.

"That is a bad place," Gizzal said, his voice filled with unease. He reached out to the lamp, adjusting the brass pin at its side to dim the light, causing the oily smoke to disperse. The effect was immediate. The glowing aspect blinked once and then disappeared, the source of its existence too weak now to traverse each of the remaining slides and sustain its illumination. It left the space on the patio dark and empty, and Razin feeling strangely empty with it.

"I have petitioned the Viziers to cleanse the lands from the *Duta* Hills to the Imud River," said Gizzal. "But my pleas have fallen on deaf ears. They think the savages who dwell there have been touched by their blood-thirsty Gods and will not move against them. The fools."

Tomas shifted in his seat, looking uncomfortable. "What are they?"

"The beast men?" Gizzal frowned, scratching the grey in his beard as he looked at Tomas. "Scions of the gods, if you'd believe Bezal and his kin.

The result of some degenerate breeding with their most devoted acolytes. That's the thing with these pagans: they think the gods are either there to fuck them or to eat them. Sometimes both. They crave that feeling of fear on the horizon of desire."

Razin tensed, resisting the urge to flinch at the memory of the beasts of Ladah and their engorged phalluses. Their hunger had driven their lust, the prospect of violence so stimulating that they could not help but be aroused by it.

"You have another explanation?" Razin shook away the image, staring at the empty spot where the aspect had floated just a moment ago.

"Of course." Gizzal motioned to the now-defunct Occularis. "In the places where the boundaries are thinnest, the lines between order and chaos have become blurred. The natural order is undone, or its laws suspended at the very least. There are no doubt things that occupy those other spaces that we would rather not see. Things that do not conform to our understanding of the world. Where the boundaries blur, we are granted glimpses of them. We see distorted aspects of man and creature, their trajectories warped by exposure to the other."

"Like the glass panes," said Razin, thinking of the way the patterns in the slides altered the light's passage.

"Just so." Gizzal nodded. "When conflicting laws of nature converge, they result in aberrations and absurdities. And so you have the beast men and their shepherd, the Maštur. Or perhaps the Adites and their beliefs hold true, and it *is* the gods. All I have are mere inklings and my theories."

"That little goat-bastard told us of a way home," said Tomas. "Before he tried to eat us."

Gizzal blinked. "Oh?"

"North, beyond the 'Daughters'. Does that mean anything to you?"

"Hmm," The šubur mused, thumbing his lip. "The only daughters I am aware of are Neruk's brood. However, it might be the mountains of *Igisi*... Igisi's Pass. There are three peaks—"

"Three daughters?" Tomas questioned.

"Perhaps." Gizzal shrugged. "But why he would point you that way, I do not know. It is an empty place, filled only with creatures not even the trackers will risk hunting. There are some places you simply do not go."

"What about the temple in the forest," Razin asked quietly. Tomas stiffened at the mention of the place, and Razin found himself clenching his own jaw, his knuckles going white around his cup.

Thunder boomed again, deep, like the ifrit's voice in that tomb of bones.

Gizzal and Zua exchanged a look, and some silent communication passed between them before Gizzal leaned forward, his eyes shining, unable to mask his enthusiasm.

"You have been into the lion-mouth's temple and come out? But how?"

"The hand saved us," said Tomas.

"The hand? What hand?" Gizzal looked from face to face, his excitement mounting.

Razin shook his head, silencing Tomas with a stare and then glanced back at their host.

"First, tell us about this Me-anesi—the Sandmouth. You said others have crossed it before us. How? Why?"

The šubur hesitated, reluctant to move away from the topic of the temple. But when he saw Razin's unflinching stare, he sighed and leaned back into the cushions.

"Zua," he said, licking his lips. "I will need something stronger if I am to speak of such things. And I think they will too. Something from *Nemur*, I think, yes. Dark and rich. The *nar-wine* will do."

Zua nodded and slipped back into the pavilion, reappearing a moment later with a clay jug and silver goblets covered in yellow gemstones. She placed a goblet down in front of each of them and filled them up to the rim with the dark red wine. Razin waved her away before she could fill his.

"*Me-anesi*," he repeated. "Please."

Gizzal took a quick sip from his goblet, swilling the wine in his mouth before swallowing. Then he began.

"No doubt you have heard tales of Ubar. Every traveller who passes through the sandstorm and finds themselves before the city gates has heard some version of it: that in some forgotten past, the city sank into the earth, was consumed by fire and ashes by the divine, was taken by a tempest... but the city arrived here just like you: through the Mouth of God."

"Why?" asked Razin.

Gizzal took another lingering sip. Then he placed the goblet on the table and stared across the patio, at the shadowy expanse beyond the city walls.

"The bastard Bezal told you of his God, Neruk?"

Razin nodded, but Gizzal's eyes flicked to Tomas and Adelman's blank expressions. "The Sons of Noah and the Adites—those who claim lineage to the eponymous ʿĀd—once stood as allies. That was before the beast they call Bahamut appeared in the waters and the words of its herald—this so-called *prophet*—with it. Now they fight over Addir-Melek and the seven tomes of nonsense he left behind. Did you know that some think he disappeared into the Me-anesi himself? Oh yes, to spread his revelations. That's what the more fanatical of the sects believe, anyway. Others say he was swallowed by the Godfish in his attempt to restrain it."

Gizzal paused, meeting each of their eyes in turn before continuing.

"The Sons of Noah believe that even now he stands somewhere upon the coast, summoning Bahamut to bring an end to this age and usher in a new one. But not before drowning us all in a black tide that would sweep clean the world."

When Hud appeared to preach of a single God, the pagans rejected him outright. They called him blasphemer, iconoclast, daemon, worse things. The old fathers believe that was why the city was condemned. Plucked from its rightful place as the jewel of the east, and placed here to slowly rot and whither away, like a whale washed up on the shore for the scavengers to pick at until only bones remain."

"But you do not think so?" Razin had noted a change in Gizzal's tone recounting the hypothesis, something he recognised from his own voice when dealing with dubious claims: it was contempt.

"It is… plausible," said Gizzal. He fingered the top of his scar and shrugged. "But it does not explain why so many men and women—faithful believers in one God are so often found wandering the *rakalama*. Bezal and his ilk believe we are here as punishment for the leniency of our ancestors, for humouring Hud and his false message against the gods. But as many believers of *Ashur* and *Enlil* have walked through the gates of Ama-i-de as any other. It is a simple theory, satisfactory, I think, for some…"

"But not to you," Tomas finished.

Gizzal smiled thinly, lifting his goblet and swilling its contents. He brought the drink up to his nose and inhaled deeply, then let out a satisfied sigh. "Nar-wine is made from hardy stock, adapted and bred to survive the dry months of Eden-ne. During the hot months, the vines shrivel on their posts until one might mistake them for dead. And then, when Ida brings the rainy season, they blossom again. Alive. *Thriving*. The winemakers in Nemur were here before us, clearing their fields to the east of the *Ki-sur* Hills while Ubar was still a den of squalor in old Rub' al-Khali, trading rocks with *Sabeans* and *Nabateans*.

North of Nemur, beyond Igisi's Pass, lie the ruins of the Kingdom of Jabulsa—a civilisation that rose and fell before ours even came to be. It rests in the shadow of Mount Qaf, a mountain of peridot and green emerald that glows in the night. The things that dwell there now... I did not believe it until I saw them for myself. Only the bravest of merchant trappers dare its slopes to hunt the creatures beneath the green sky. Those that survive the hunt become rich men... but there are few that do."

"The beasts they bring back seldom live long—the ones our trappers can catch are weak and old, but more than that... It is as if they are not built for this place. I have seen the skulls and skins of sea creatures found in the desert, huge monolithic beasts with shaggy winter furs and thick blubbery skin, beings made for colder climes than ours, and yet they are here. Those that are brought back alive often starve rather than eat our food, and when they finally do, it is as if they have been poisoned. I do not need to tell you that it is a terrible thing to watch a beast wither away only to spew out its insides when it finally eats."

"They are... not a hardy stock?" Razin asked, an idea of where Gizzal was going forming.

"Just so."

Gizzal tapped a finger against his goblet, his silver ring clicking softly.

"It is not only beasts we find..." His voice faded, and Razin found himself leaning forward in his seat, listening.

"Across the *Abzu-kurgal*, beyond the Gu-be Straits, there are a people who claim friendship with those who live on the islands of the Ennu-Spine."

He took a long sip of his wine, his brow furrowing.

"They say the inhabitants of those islands are something between ape and lizard. More than beast, yes, but not men. They have language and the written word, perhaps primitive to our eyes and ears, but so is the *galka* tongue of the people in the Gu-be Straits—who are little more than fishermen and shepherds, clinging to the edges of the map like barnacles."

"I have not had the chance to speak to one of the *Ennu* peoples from the Spine, and I am still not sure that they are even real. But if the stories are to be believed, they are not from here."

"And they are not from our home either," said Razin.

"Just so," Gizzal repeated. "From my understanding, they have their own explanations for their appearance here—to do with transgression, crazed magi and maguses—the sort of stories you'd expect from lesser cultures. But..."

"The Sandmouth," guessed Tomas.

"It is present in their tales, too, yes. A storm of red and brown, a dark horizon, and then... this place."

Tomas started peeling the leathery fruit he still clutched with a thumb. "Could it not be God's punishment too? From what you say, they are pagans, surely?"

The šubur snorted dismissively. "They worship the sand and rocks. They had not even heard of the one God before encountering the tribes of men in the north. But..." Gizzal traced the rim of his goblet with his ring finger, his lips drawn into a thin line. "If ignorance is their only sin, then this is a punishment most severe, don't you think? And one their children and children's children must suffer too? No, I think not. Our presence here is not some divine punishment but a mistake in the universe, a fracture we all fell through, one way or another."

"What of the Falak?" said Razin, looking up.

Gizzal creased his brow. It was his turn to look bemused.

"The black serpent we found in the pools of an oasis about five days' ride from here. It emerged from the waters to swallow the dead... and the living."

"It ate Comus," whimpered Adelman, his eyes suddenly wide. He looked around, staring. Tomas placed a comforting hand on his shoulder and spoke to him in a soothing tone until he calmed.

"*Mušmaḫḫū*," spat Gizzal. "Bezal and his brood worship that wretched thing like it was a God itself. They believe it guided their prophet through the desert, providing shade to Addir-Melek from the scorching sun. That is why its coils are charred black. It still slithers through the caverns beneath the city, where they… they sustain it."

Razin blinked. "Sustain it with what, exactly?"

"The descendants of Hud." Gizzal wrinkled his mouth in distaste. "There are few of us left now, but we have grown wise and cunning. Still, every so often, one of us is found out. Then, it is to the serpent's mouth… or worse."

"Damn that devil," said Tomas, shaking his head. "Why don't you leave?"

"And go where?" Gizzal showed his teeth in a sad smile. "North, to live among the savage tribes of the Abzu-kurgal? To toil out an existence beneath a sun that never sets, eating what root we can scavenge from between the rocks and dead soil? Or perhaps we could move south to live amongst the Maštur and his hyena-kin? How long do you think we would last there, I wonder? No, my friend. This is our home. In any case, we are not so helpless as you might think. Many of us have risen high in the ranks of the city—to become šuburs, as I have, and higher still. There are… plans."

"*Gizzal!*" Zua hissed, shaking her head.

"Yes, yes." Gizzal waved his hand and took another sip of wine.

"Zua thinks I am too trusting," he said, placing the empty goblet on the table. "That, perhaps, I might be the target of some complicated scheme, the intrigues of the Patriarch's Court and their spies. Hah! Let us not forget who brought you here… who pulled you off the street and into my quarters unannounced."

Zua rolled her eyes, refilling his goblet.

Razin shook his head when she offered to fill his again and turned to Gizzal. "The black serpent the mušrikūn worship, this… familiar of the prophet's—"

"Mušmaḫḫū."

Razin nodded. "Before the Sandmouth took us, we heard of its appearance in our world—that it had been spotted at the bottom of a well in Samaria. The man who told us of the creature tried killing it with poison. He failed, but the basin we found the beast in when we arrived was putrid, its waters killing any who drank from it. Perhaps…"

Gizzal scratched his chin, listening intently and then nodding. "It sounds like Addir-Melek's pet has found another bridge between states. I have known of the Me-anesi, but this…" He clapped his hands together suddenly, making Zua flinch. "I must write to Tabira and Amah with news of your discovery. You will show us where you found the snake, yes? This oasis?"

Razin hesitated, remembering the path they had taken… the ashen steppes and black river, the mountains with their ruins and that feeling of emptiness when they had passed it, then the bodies in the forest and the stinking, scuttling thing he had unleashed upon the world. Then there was Teoma and his pack to consider.

"We will be quite safe," said Gizzal, noticing his reluctance. "A šubur of the Kura-Agal does not travel with less than one-hundred spears. Besides, the other inhabitants of Eden-ne have learned not to trifle with Ubarian blades lest we turn our attention to them." The šubur paused, then cocked his head and turned to look down the passage they'd emerged from earlier that evening. "You can discuss our expedition amongst yourselves, of course. It sounds like Hashur has returned with the rest of your companions."

Razin glanced back at the corridor, listening to the soft echo of boots on stone. Zua moved across the terrace to greet the new arrivals but hesitated mid-way.

"Something's wrong," she said, raising a hand. She clicked her fingers, turning to the pavilion. "Urshal, bring the guards! And *quickly!*"

Razin tensed at a low moan from the passageway. There was a muffled cursing, then the scuffing of boots on concrete.

A wide-eyed face appeared from the darkness, with bloodied lips and a swollen eye. Razin identified him as the man from the sewers. Hashur. He was propping up a figure with his shoulder, struggling beneath the weight of the gigantic frame.

Another shadow burst from the corridor, helping Hashur with the man.

Razin's breath caught when he recognised the wounded figure, blood streaming from the grooves of his lamellar plate.

It was Arcadius.

"We've been discovered," gasped Hashur.

Then he crumpled beneath Arcadius's weight.

25

The crowded market streets fell away, replaced by wide thoroughfares that resonated with the booming calls of guildsmen and labourers toiling in the yards along the way.

Even at this hour, the city buzzed with ceaseless activity, a bustling hive. Teams of drivers led carts laden with wood and briquettes of coal, steel girders and nails, rope and glass into the open yards of squat buildings nestled between low-slung structures. Rough-hewn men with hard stares scurried to unload the carts once they arrived, forming lines that vanished into the cavernous recesses of the buildings, like ants disappearing into their anthills.

Bone-thin posts of steel and brass arched overhead, their sinewy forms interlaced with cords of rope that suspended a multitude of lanterns to illume the workshops below. They glowed a soft yellow, casting an otherworldly luminescence upon the bustling streets where traders, merchants, crewmen, and labourers scuttled, their movements all falling into the single harmonious rhythm of commerce.

Dietmar and Geoff followed the road between the workshops, passing beneath towering statues of granite and marble, depictions of heroes or gods, Dietmar couldn't tell.

Sometimes he caught sight of litters, their long curtains drawn, being escorted through the streets. Armoured figures with golden beak helms and long spears cleared the road ahead of them. Those in the street moved quickly aside, letting the litter through with little complaint—already well acquainted with the privileges of Ubar's elite or else familiar enough with the blunt end of their guard's spears to move out of the way.

Other times, he saw hooded figures, like the priests from the plaza, in slow-moving processions. They mingled with the crowds, shouting out in their coarse tongue. Their staves—mercifully empty of the serpents that had covered them in the plaza—were held above their heads.

The streets to either side of the thoroughfare disappeared into a tangled weave of boroughs—a warren of brick and stone and stained walls.

Smaller workshops with dwellings perched precariously on top of them formed looming edifices that hung out over the lanes. Tumbledown buildings with chimneys puffing black smoke sat beside crowded workshops, gangs of men working the night shift.

In the distance, hemmed in by the city walls and protected from the storm, the masts of hundreds of ships split the near horizon.

An impenetrable nest of ropes and rungs, fluttering pennants and hooded topsails, their sails drawn in tight against the coming storm. Above them, fastened to ropes and spindly steel chains, bulbous canvas sheets hung in the air, somehow suspended atop the masts of the ships and portside buildings.

Dietmar watched them for a moment, seeing figures moving in the baskets beneath. They were backlit by a soft amber light which spluttered out from under the canvas bag. The air around them rippled like oil on water, creasing under the stress of the heat from the glow.

As he watched, the baskets began their descent, returning to the earth before the storm could pluck them from the sky and scramble their occupants. Light flared from the nearest of the floating baskets, then it slowly dimmed until it was little more than a flickering candle so that the basket and bag could return to the earth like a deflated lung. A rung ladder was thrown over the side before it touched the ground, and figures clambered down onto the platform, aided by the waiting crewmen below.

The thought of hanging in the air, hundreds of feet above the ground, made Dietmar's stomach churn. And yet… he had never seen such marvels before. To float above the teeming streets of a city in little more than a wooden box, propelled by some arcane technology, was beyond even the wildest imaginations of the learned men back home. He stared at the passengers descending the gently swaying ladders with unabashed wonder, his wide-eyed expression shared by Geoff beside him.

"You won't catch me in one of those," said the mercenary captain once the last of the passengers had disembarked. He looked away from the platform and shook his head. "Not for a bag full of coin and a flagon of wine. And for what? To see the heads of your fellows bobbing in the dirt beneath you? Before they take their turn on the floating box? Nah!"

"You wouldn't like to see the world from the clouds?"

Geoff laughed. "I doubt I'd see much. I'd have to drink my fill just to climb the ladder. I'd spend the way up spilling my guts out over the side. You're telling me you'd go up there? Willingly?"

Dietmar glanced at him, his face twitching. His teeth had started to ache again, and he could feel another in the back of his mouth coming loose. He tried not to fiddle with it, but his tongue seemed to move around of its own accord.

Geoff's voice faded into the background as the presence nestled alongside his mind began to stir.

—resourceful heathens, aren't they? To have built all this…

Dietmar growled under his breath and walked ahead, forcing Geoff to hurry after him. He tried ignoring the voice—*that bastard voice*—focusing on the paved street beneath him. The voice of the Saint, or Devil, or whatever he was, had become near incessant. A constant dirge of chatter that sublimated his thoughts. He had tried pushing it back like before, but the presence had grown stronger and wouldn't shift.

Now he just ignored it, mostly. Though an uncomfortable idea had made itself felt: what happened when the voice grew too loud to ignore? When its foul words slipped into his thoughts as if they were his own, that slimy execrable presence's tendrils seeping into his consciousness until they were one… until there was nothing left of him.

He rubbed his jaw, trying to soothe the ache.

Another pressing thought made itself felt: would he live that long? He felt like he was falling apart, piece by piece, his body surrendering to whatever malady or *maladies* he had picked up from the hand.

He glanced down at the pouch by his side.

That cursed fucking thing, he thought angrily. He considered, briefly, throwing it away, leaving it in the gutters for the rats to gnaw on. But the thought passed quickly. It always did. He couldn't let this all have been for nought—all the death and misery, fear and doubt. More than that, he couldn't give up on his son. Not if there was even the slightest chance he could drag him out of the dark and into God's light.

God's light… another thought was conjured into life in the back of his mind, and he wasn't sure if it was his own or one spawned by the resident who now occupied that corridor beside him. Was it truly his God who had created such a place? Such beings as those they had encountered? He let the thought linger for a moment, testing it like a weaver might their yarn, searching for impurities in the thread.

Then he extinguished the idea, discarding it before it could unravel him.

Spindly treadmill cranes rose alongside the thoroughfare, their pallets lifting blocks of stone and building materials above the scaffolding of new constructions. Half-built edifices of bronze and stone, with stained glass windows that made the Aachen Cathedral back home look like a stables.

—it must feel strange to be the savage for once, beholding wonders he cannot truly fathom. And all this, built to the glory of pagan gods! It makes you wonder, doesn't it? No? Perhaps it is just me, then

Ephium laughed, his leathery voice evoking a lurching, shuddering feeling in the pit of Dietmar's stomach.

His mouth tasted like rot.

He moved aside as a bronze-encased litter carried by a dozen porters appeared on the road ahead. Oil lamps hung from the load-bearing poles resting on the porters' shoulders. They sweated in the dull afterglow, gritting their teeth under the strain as they passed. Dietmar glimpsed a masked figure lying upon a bed of cushions inside the litter, a tattooed hand holding the mask in place, painted nails.

He blinked as a lumbering shape filled his vision, obscuring his view of the litter. A man, monstrously tall, but with reams of fat hanging in rolls from his waist. His thick chin was like a bullfrog's throat beneath an oily beard. The man lifted a hand, uncoiling the whip he carried and motioning to Dietmar before gurgling out an incomprehensible command.

Dietmar didn't have to understand the words to know what they meant:

Piss off, scum.

He obliged, lowering his gaze to an appreciative grunt from the guard. The man stared at him a moment longer and then trailed after the litter, his whip still dangling from his hand.

"Everywhere the same, eh?" commented Geoff. He saw the bemused look on Dietmar's face and laughed. "Of course, how could I forget? Where we're from, people got out of *your* way, knight. Ah, well, there's a change that'll take some getting used to. From lounging about on your back through the streets of Jerusalem to being spat at by a pig-man in this stinking pit! Hah!"

Dietmar watched the litter disappear, the crowd reforming around it like water in a disturbed pond. Then he turned back to Geoff and smirked. "The only time I spent on my back in Jerusalem was after taking a Turkic spear between the ribs." He walked ahead and then called back over his shoulder. "And then only for a day!"

Geoff chuckled, muttering under his breath before taking a swig from his flask. He wiped his mouth and then followed Dietmar through the crowd. He could already smell the salt and stink of the docks.

***

The smell got worse when they departed from the thoroughfare and walked out onto the long piers of the harbour. It stunk like kelp and fish and brine and… something else, rotting away beneath the ebb and flow of the harbour current.

Ships sprawled out as far as they could see, leagues long to either side. Mighty hulks rested beside stub-nosed cogs and sturdy galleys with hundreds of shining windows, their oars stowed, anchor and rope keeping them from barging into each other with each swell that rippled through the harbour.

But the swells were relatively gentle, never reaching the top of the concrete slabs of the pier—the reason why was soon apparent. The walls of the city had been built into the sea, forming a cave-like opening at the mouth of the harbour. Ubar's engineers had created an artificial barrier to protect the bay from the crushing black waves that broke against the city walls.

Water gushed through the opening, foaming gouts that hissed and sprayed before receding, leaving a coiling mist in its wake. The bay glowed luminously, a soft green light reflected from the clouds. This close to the open ocean, the hammering waves and growl of thunder should have been near deafening, but the thick walls muted the worst of the storm.

Life thrived in the protected waters. Forests of kelp swayed gently with the swells, and wispy shadows darted between them. Dietmar saw a shoal of long fish with bulbous heads, their tails flickering bright yellows and gold as they raced through the shallows. There was a soft splash as something dived off the pier, a furry grey body that could have been an otter but for its leathery reptilian skin and the strange eel-like tail that whipped out behind it as it swam. It chased after the shoal, singling out the slowest and separating it from the school. The two creatures, predator and prey, played out their aquatic dance. They swirled through the dark waters, sliding through hidey-holes and past nests of sea anemones and large pustule-like urchins, until, finally, a patch of water turned red, and chunks of cartilage drifted up to the surface. Scavenger birds swooped down on the remains, their hooked beaks snatching what they could before they disappeared back into the rigging of the ships around them.

Dietmar and Geoff came to a rest at the neck of one of the piers, which stuck out some way onto the water like a finger, ships moored to either side.

A little way ahead, corps of engineers swarmed over the metal shell of a vessel that looked like something between a crab and a blowfish. It rested half-submerged in the water, suspended by a complicated rig. The steel rope it was attached to unspooled from a slowly turning wheel. The vessel sunk further into the water with each revolution, the large glass cap to the front of the construct blurring and distorting as water rose to fill its frame, obscuring the shadows moving within.

Shadows, Dietmar realised with some discomfort, of people.

The sea around the strange engine frothed foamy white, and a haze of mist followed the last of the engineers as they clambered off its hull.

The ropes tethering the vessel were detached at a pull of a lever from the rigging platform.

The construct shuddered. And then it was gone, slipping beneath the surface, leaving only displaced water and bubbles in its wake.

Dietmar watched as the shadow crept across the harbour floor, making for the harbour mouth. He exchanged a look with Geoff, both in silent agreement that they *would not* be booking passage in one of those.

They moved further up the pier, looking hopefully at the hulls of the galleys moored there. Skeleton crews scuttled along their rigging, lighting lamps and torches and shooing away the little packs of monkeys that seemed to inhabit every corner of the city.

The pier itself was empty but for a pair of fishmongers bargaining with ships' accountants, a city watchman on patrol, and off-duty crewmen sitting on crates in front of their vessels, passing the time with dice and glass bottles of smoky brown liquid.

Dietmar called to the crewmen, inquiring about passage across the sea in French, German, Greek, and broken Arabic. He held his coin purse out before him, using it to bridge any misunderstanding. But they weren't interested.

They spoke to captains on clippers, seamen on vast, low-resting ships with names like *Anunitu* and *Ninlil*. They showed their coin to cabin boys and second mates, hoping to bribe their way aboard the officious-looking galleys and speak to their captains, but nobody would hear it. They shook their heads, waving them away, pointing toward the next ship along the line… until there were no more ships on the pier, and they still hadn't found passage.

Dietmar was about to call it a day and return to the market to find the others when he spotted a vessel they hadn't yet tried. It sat inconspicuously between two of the pompous-looking galleys, its own dull lights barely enough to keep the shadows at bay.

The ship rested low in the water, bobbing gently with the tide. It was not a galley or a hulk or a cog or any other vessel Dietmar recognised. It was tall and narrow, with three mast towers, spindly thin but long. Glass windows stared down from all along the forecastle, candles flicking within. A grotesque figurehead leered down at them as they approached, with sharp teeth like those of a shark caught in a rictus grin, her seraphic features contorted in a siren's scream.

"Ho there!" called Dietmar to a figure sitting above the forecastle, his bare feet dangling over the side.

"Let me handle this one," said Geoff. "Time for a fresh approach, I say. A bit of a captain's luck when talking to these sea dogs, eh?"

Dietmar shrugged, and the mercenary stepped forward, calling up at the figure on the ship. "How'd you do, son?"

A pair of white eyes blinked down at him, then the feet disappeared.

"Bugger," said Geoff, looking back at Dietmar. "Maybe—"

"What's your business?" boomed a voice from the deck. A barrel-chested man in a thin linen shirt appeared above the railing, his arms folded to rest on the wood. He stared at Geoff and Dietmar, his face wreathed in shadows.

"Passage," said Dietmar before Geoff could reply. "Across the Black Waters."

The man leaned forward, revealing a shaven head and thick eyebrows that looked like arrowheads above his steady gaze. "When?"

"Tomorrow… tonight?"

The man's laugh burst from his chest like a wild animal sprung from its cage. "Have you not seen the currents? Nobody sails on Ida. Not the night before and not the day of. You'd have to be desperate or insane."

The man uncrossed his arms and gestured to something at his feet. A shadow leapt up from the railing to become a ball of golden fur that clambered up his arm and came to a rest on his shoulder. The monkey chirped and clicked happily into the man's ear and then started grooming his beard.

"Which is it?" asked the captain. "What should I tell my crew we're to risk the wrath of the Godfish for?" He opened his arms and laughed as the clouds finally broke above the city, unleashing a deluge of warm water in a torrential baptism.

Dietmar held up his coin purse, spilling gold and silver into the palm of his hand.

"How about for rich men?" he shouted over the rain. "Looking for passage to the Daughters?"

The captain smiled, and in the half-light beneath the flickering oil lamp on the deck, it looked like the golden monkey was smiling too.

26

After a long threatening pause, the storm finally hit. Hot winds tore through the spires, whistling as they passed between the glass windows and brass fittings, rattling steel filaments and tugging at anything left loose. The bulbous tents that clung to the towers like grotesque growths whipped and flittered about until they looked like the sails of ships being dragged across a tempestuous sea. The once-tethered rope bridges connecting the peaks had been untied from their anchors, now tightly fastened against the spires to prevent them from snapping and crashing against the glass stained-windows.

The rain blasted Ubar.

It came in a tepid squall, cascading down the walls and washing away the year's accumulated dust and grime. The gutters overflowed, water spilling out onto the streets to fill every crack and crevice between the paving stones of the city. The sewers were quickly inundated, forcing their miserable occupants to seek refuge above ground. A scurrying mass of grey-brown refugees emerged from the flooded depths, clambering onto the pavements in search of shelter.

Tarpaulins and the scaffolding in the now abandoned yards offered a brief respite from the deluge.

Their rivals, the golden horde, watched on from protected alcoves, from their terraces and niches hidden deep within the arching spires of Kura-Agal.

The warm waters scoured the city, replenishing its pools and reservoirs, washing clean the stains that covered it like scars, and was greeted with open arms.

The people of Ubar took to the streets with the first drops. They pounded their feet in the dust, churning it beneath their heels, between their toes, as the rain turned it to mud. Men and women stripped to their waists, drinking in the warmth of Ida with their skins. Tattooed and scarified flesh dripped with sweat and oil and water as they danced in the storm, an ethereal mosaic, barely silhouettes in the guttering torches.

Their pounding feet, a chaotic, frenzied tempo, found a rhythm in the madness until the whole city seemed to shake beneath the thundering percussion of skin on stone.

Mouths found each other in the dark, tongues slipped past lips, hands and fingers enmeshed as the fevered tempo raced to some unknown crescendo. Engorged members were guided by slippery fingers in the dark as the ecstasy overcame some, but not all.

Not most.

A roar to match the pounding feet and pounding flesh rose from the streets, as if from the very depths of the city, from the underground chambers beneath their feet—Ubar's cavernous belly. It grew louder with each thundering syllable, until it was too loud for some to bear. They fled from the streets, their ears covered, even with those words still on their lips.

Bahamut! Bahamut! Bahamut!

And in the depths of the black waters, beyond the city walls, in a darkness so deep and old that no light had ever penetrated it, something stirred.

***

"God fuck me," Arcadius roared, falling in a heap atop Hashur, his hands clutching at his side. Levi and the Lady Marie appeared beside him, trying to lift his heavy frame out from the tangle of limbs. But he wouldn't budge.

Gizzal snapped to his feet, motioning Zua forward and clicking his fingers at the guards emerging from his pavilion.

Razin got to Arcadius first. He gripped the Greek by the forearm and slowly helped him up before extending a hand to Hashur. The guide scrambled to his feet without his help and made straight for Gizzal and Zua. He spoke to them in a hurried whisper, pointing back toward the passageway, jabbing the air urgently with his fingers.

"What happened?" Razin asked, casting a quick glance at the wound on Arcadius's side before peering into the dim corridor, listening for any signs of pursuit.

Arcadius gritted his teeth and drew a deep, ragged breath. "It was that bastard Amice," he replied. "He shoved that knife he's always toying with between my ribs and fucked off before I could grab him."

Razin looked back at him, wide-eyed. The nodding heads of Levi and the Lady Marie confirmed it.

"That filthy, treacherous rag," spat Tomas.

"Why?" asked Razin, his voice calmer than he felt. The tension between Arcadius and Dietmar's former squire had been palpable, but for it to spill over like this, to manifest as an act of blatant violence… He'd come to think the Greek would be the first to snap if either of them ever did. But not here, in this strange city. He had hoped for cooler heads than that.

"Does he need a reason?" Arcadius grunted, opening his hand to stare at his side. The plate beneath his breast, between his seventh and eighth rib, had been punctured, leaving a clean wound amidst the already bruised skin. Blood spilt out to cover Arcadius's fingers, though the flow weakened as Razin watched.

A good sign, Razin thought.

It meant the wound wasn't deep enough to be fatal, though it might pose other challenges to the ageing Greek.

"It was because of me." The Lady Marie held a strip of cloth she'd torn from her dress out for Arcadius. He moved his hand aside again and let her press it against the wound while she explained to Razin.

"He followed me through the market. I didn't see him at first—he's always sneaking around. But then he was beside me, talking to me like he knew me. Like I was… his." She shook her head, and her lips drew tight. "He said he wanted to show me something. Something I'd like, he told me. But he got angry when I wouldn't come. He took my knife and tried to drag me with him. Nobody stopped him. Nobody cared. It's like these people…" The Lady Marie wiped her nose against her sleeve, blinking back the moisture in her eyes.

For a moment, she was just a scared young girl. Desperate and afraid. But her resolve hardened and was reflected in her stony stare. "*Somebody* did hear me, though." She looked up at Arcadius. "My bear."

"I'll tear his head off." Tomas cursed. "Where is he?"

"I shouldn't have let you go wandering off on your own," said Arcadius, still looking at his ward. He groaned again and then let his weight fall onto the arms of Gizzal's guards, who had just crossed the courtyard.

The two men gripped him gently, pausing only long enough to be ushered back toward the pavilion by Zua. She clucked like a protective hen as she directed them.

Gizzal remained in the middle of the courtyard, absorbed by Hashur's report. He rubbed the corners of his eyes as he listened, his fingers tracing the scar tissue in a slow, rhythmic pattern. After a brief exchange with

Hashur, he strode purposefully toward the pavilion, leading the way for Arcadius and the guards.

Levi and his daughter trailed after, and Razin waited for them at the entrance to the pavilion. He looked past them, back toward the corridor and frowned. "Where is the girl?" he asked. "Tanit?"

Levi shrugged. "She disappeared after Amice made his mess, and the city guard started stirring. She's probably more at home here than with us anyway. For all we know, this *is* her home."

Razin didn't disagree. In truth, he wasn't sad to see the back of Tanit. There was an untamed quality to her, an intensity in her gaze that unsettled him. It reminded him of a caged lion, pacing restlessly, fixating on its prey—them.

"And Amice?" Razin lifted the curtain with a hand, letting Sara in ahead of him.

Levi shook his head and sighed. "Gone," he said. "He was so quick with that blade of his. You should have seen him. He hit Arcadius before he even knew to look out. Then he disappeared into the city, cackling like a jackal. Evil little shit." He made to cover Sara's ears, but the words had already been said, and she brushed his hands away.

"He poked him quick," said Levi, meeting Razin's gaze. "But not so deep, I think."

Razin followed them into the pavilion, across the small study behind the curtains toward the doorway on the other side. It smelt like pine and sandalwood beneath the canopy, and Razin saw a small ceramic thurible smoking peacefully on the desk before he stepped into the passage and through the doorway beyond.

Thunder boomed across the night sky, and the rain that had threatened for so long came down in sweeping sheets, a torrential downpour across the city.

The corridor led to a large, round chamber with a high ceiling and open windows that he hadn't seen from the outside. Oil lamps flickered from the walls, casting shadows that danced and writhed with the wind coming through the windows. The lamps revealed a sturdy shelf filled with books on one side of the room. And on the other… Razin paused, his breath caught in his chest.

The wall opposite the bookshelf had been replaced by a long strip of glass, with the curvature to fit the room. The pane was about a foot tall, set in the stone just beneath the windows. But instead of the lights of the city blinking back from the darkness—the torches and oil lamps, the fire pits and amber glow of streets—Razin saw only an inky blackness.

Indeed, the light coming from the room itself seemed to disappear behind those murky panels, absorbed as if by some ceoptic force, swallowing the light from this plane only for it to be reflected on the other side, beyond their view. Razin briefly wondered if that was the case, if this Gizzal would be so foolish, so foolhardy.

Then he saw a flicker of something moving in the murk. A shape—no more than a shadow—darting past the window.

It took him a moment to realise that he was looking at water.

A tank, built into the walls, filled with water as dark as pitch.

Zua strode across the carpeted floor, holding up a pole with a brass hook on its end to close the windows. Arcadius was gently helped down onto a long *suffah* bench, his lamellar plate now a discarded pile on the carpeted floor. He swore as he settled onto the plush seating, crimson droplets of blood staining the cushion beneath him.

Urshal appeared with a bowl of water and clean cloth for bandaging, but Zua shook her head at him. "He will need stitches first. Go, bring a physician."

Urshal nodded, leaving the water and bandages with Zua and crossing the study.

"Wait," said Gizzal. He sat perched on the edge of a desk in the corner of the room. Hashur stood nearby, leaning in to speak softly into his ear, but Gizzal dismissed him with a wave of his hand and turned to Urshal. "None of those black-lipped *Asipus*, please. They ask too many questions. Find an Asu from the towers. They charge more but keep their silence."

Urshal nodded again and disappeared through a dark niche beside the shelves.

"Now," declared Gizzal, rising from the desk. He exchanged a meaningful look with Hashur before scanning the room. "My secretary has informed me that there are watchmen searching the spires, even now. They will be here soon. When they arrive, not even the privileges of a šubur will prevent them from searching my chambers."

"What are they looking for?" Adelman asked, helping Tomas gather up Arcadius's plate and wiping the blood from it with old rags from his pocket.

Gizzal arched an eyebrow. "Why, you, of course. Did you think your arrival went unnoticed?" He twirled at a braid in his beard, staring at the glass panes and murky depths beyond. "I had hoped for more time. Time to learn, to understand. There is so much... but that's not important now." His voice lowered so that Razin had to strain his ears. Gizzal sighed. "We could have done without your encounter with Bezal. That's what triggered the search, I imagine, and on the eve of Ida, no less! They will be ecstatic, I'm sure—unbelievers within the city!"

Hashur leaned in to murmur in his ear, motioning with his hands as he spoke. Gizzal's brow furrowed deeply, and he blinked, shifting his gaze to Arcadius, who still groaned on the suffah while the Lady Marie fussed over him.

"We will need to disappear him," Gizzal said. "He cannot travel like this."

"You're not disappearing anyone," the Lady Marie retorted, whipping her head around to face Gizzal. "Wherever he goes, I'm going too."

"You can't stay here," said Zua. There was a note of urgency in her voice. "If they catch you, they will—"

"Enough, Zua," said Gizzal firmly. He nodded to Hashur.

The secretary bowed softly and then followed Urshal's path from the chambers.

"They do not need to know the details of Bezal and his kind's debauchery… but it is true. You cannot stay here. My men will escort you from the Kura-Agal into the low city, where you can disappear until after Ida. Tempers will cool, and the religious fervour will… dissipate somewhat. These people grow mad when they are given sight of their God," Gizzal explained.

Razin looked at him, uncertain. His eyes drifted to the desk's contents. He saw sheaves of paper scattered beneath the šubur. Old notes and scribblings, words and symbols in the unfamiliar language of the Ubarians. Some pages were adorned with sketches, depicting figures and shapes, the form of which he recognised, if not the substance: cosmographic charts and maps, drawings of foreign lands, and the ocean—oceans and tundra with scribbled calculations that might have been numbers beside them. One of the pages contained a crowded series of illustrations, overlapping like a palimpsest. Each diagram depicted a detailed landscape compressed into a thin layer, creating a bewildering mesh of cross-hatched lines.

This must be Gizzal's work, he thought, tilting his head curiously.

Embedded within the layers, bleeding through the slabs, was a roughly sketched shape. At first, Razin mistook it for a mountain, but upon closer inspection, he realised its true nature. A fin—long and protruding, scaled like the appendage of a reptile—stretched across the domains like the root of a colossal tree. It pierced through each realm before emerging from the firmament beneath the fluffy clouds at the top of the page.

"Yes," Gizzal affirmed, seeing Razin's mesmerised gaze. "Their God, Bahamut. That is what they yearn to see, what they *will* see with the arrival of the Ida storms."

"And if we don't move swiftly," said Hashur, his voice like gravel on stone. "They will feed you to it—to the Godfish."

***

Arcadius howled and thrashed while Gizzal's Asu administered to him, snapping his teeth at the physician as he sutured his wound. The physician continued quite unperturbed, chattering conversationally to Zua and Urshal while they held the Greek down. He wielded his tools expertly, sealing up Arcadius's side with small silver pins from a device that clicked and whined in his hands. Once the suturing was complete, he applied a creamy white balm to the wound and carefully wrapped Arcadius's waist with bandages.

Afterwards, the Asu packed away his assortment of tools: the steel and silver utensils, the glass cylinders that emitted gentle ticking sounds, bags of sand and powder, as well as the clamps and stapling tool he'd used to seal the wound. Zua placed a bag of coin into his waiting hand, but before the Asu could tuck it away within his robes, she held up another larger coin purse and nodded to Arcadius, still lying supine on the suffah.

A few moments of tense negotiating followed, with Zua hissing through her teeth and holding up the purse, adding a handful more coins from a concealed pouch in her sleeves. The physician grinned, taking the coins and purse and barking instructions to his aides. The boys, more skin and bone than anything else, swiftly fashioned a makeshift stretcher and bundled the semi-conscious Arcadius onto it, then marched out of the chamber and into the rain. The Lady Marie hastened to follow, waving her goodbyes and trailing behind them through the pavilion.

When the Asu noticed the Lady Marie, he shook his head and motioned for her to stay back. But the girl ignored him, and after a sharp word from Zua, the physician relented.

"He will hide them away with his other patients," Zua told Tomas as they watched their departure down the passage. She saw his look and added, "Or I'll toss the Asu from the tallest spire for his boys to clean up off the street."

***

The sewers spat them out into the warm rain like dead things.

They'd crossed beneath the cavernous chambers of Ubar's guts, sloshing through the quickly filling halls and tunnels before the stone floor had undulated and risen slowly into a steep incline. Then the tunnels had grown narrower, the ceiling lower, until they were finally standing in the doorway of a small niche cut out of the city walls.

Hashur was waiting for them in the rain, his grey eyes peering out from under a thin hood. They were somewhere east of the Kura-Agal spires, Razin thought, stepping out into the downpour. The streets around them were narrow and dark, crowded by ramshackle dwellings like those they had passed after leaving the plaza, not long after entering Ubar.

There was nobody about, the servants or slaves or indentured labourers all hiding behind their dirty windows as the heavens broke above them. Despite the emptiness, the night was far from quiet. Atonal voices called out from nearby, blending in an almost rhythmic hum. The sound was amplified by the narrow roads and squat, tumbledown architecture of the Quarter.

Úr-Dul, Gizzal had called it as he bid his guests farewell—*The Mound*. Razin could understand why. The structures here consisted mainly of sand and clay, with water cascading from their flat roofs in dirty torrents.

The simple gutters lining the streets had already flooded, forming shallow pools for them to traverse.

Shadows flittered across the mouth of the road, disappearing into the warren of muddy houses on the slope.

The susurration of voices in the city grew louder, like jackdaws crooning in their nests. Razin flinched at a cry from behind him and turned to see Adelman stumbling toward a pair of hunched figures in the rain. Balaam and Silensus—the mules—greeted him with a bray, nuzzling against him as if they were long-lost friends.

Razin exchanged a questioning look with Hashur, receiving only a shrug in reply.

"It was the stable boys," Hashur explained when Razin didn't look away. "They told me the other horses did not take well to their presence. Perhaps they don't like mules, or perhaps it is something else… The šubur is precious with his mounts. Some of them were sired by…" The secretary snorted, shaking his head as he stepped out of the little sheltered alcove and into the rain. "It does not matter either. The mules will join you in the rooms Gizzal has prepared. Come, it is not far."

They followed Hashur through winding alleys, passing sealed windows and wooden walkways that connected the scrappy houses, crisscrossing the gaps above their heads but providing little shelter from the storm.

A pattern slowly emerged to the tumbledown streets and alleyways, though it was nothing like the urban sprawl of city centres like Jerusalem or Damascus, with their inherited Greco-Roman grids and tidy blocks. No, The Mound—perhaps Ubar as a whole—resembled a wheel, with broken spokes that lined the city, passageways and hidden corridors all racing toward the hub of spires at its centre.

Razin paused as the street started to slope, the mud oozing out between the old cobblestones beneath his feet. He gazed over the flat roofs, streaked and stained, attempting to catch a glimpse of the glass and iron of

Kura-Ugal. He moved aside for Tomas and Adelman, leading the mules behind Hashur while Levi and his daughter huddled together against the rain.

The sky flickered with fluorescent life, the thick, velvety underbelly of the clouds tinged by an octarine glow. They swelled and transformed with the storm, rolling with the warm updrafts coming in from the sea, trapping in the humid air like a hermetic seal.

In the distance, the Kura-Agal spires dominated their surrounds. Glass and steel windows, bronzed terraces, and brass-capped peaks shimmered with the light of the clouds until they appeared as pyres of luminous green on the horizon. Beyond them, a darkness had settled. In the north, a tempestuous abyss of roiling clouds and tumultuous waves brooded behind the city walls. It was too dark to see anything, and still, Razin thought, in that swirling morass of night, that something was moving, rising from the sea.

He blinked away the water from his eyes, staring at the empty skyline, and then trudged after Levi and Sara.

"What's that noise?" Tomas tugged the bit of the mule he was leading, his head cocked to listen. The droning burble of sound grew louder, almost drowning out the hiss of rain on mud and flesh and stone.

They were nearing the edge of The Mound, where the buildings grew more prominent and less like the hunched backs of vultures crowding over the streets. Rusty iron gates guarded cavernous doorways and stained-glass windows with intricate patterns. Rain washed off the sloping rooves with piscine ease.

"They are celebrating the rains," Hashur said softly. There was a hesitancy in his voice, and his eyes darted nervously up and down the narrow lane they stood in.

"And?" said Tomas, picking up on his discomfort.

Hashur furrowed his brow, the lines on his face folding together with practised ease. "I think they have found someone."

Figures splashed through the water at the neck of the road, where it opened up to the larger market streets. Giddy laughter followed them, voices raised in excitement. Razin followed them with his eyes until they disappeared around the bend.

"Found who?" he asked, his thoughts immediately jumping to Dietmar. Or perhaps Arcadius and the Lady Marie had been discovered, betrayed by the Asa for a higher price. Any man who could be bought once could be bought twice.

Hashur shrugged, flinching as another roar of noise reverberated through the streets. It sounded like a crowd was gathering in the market up ahead, pounding their feet to the rain, their individual voices lost to the roar. Hashur sighed. "It's best we do not know." He caught Razin's gaze and shook his head. "You can do nothing for whoever they have found. Not now. They will throw them to the Black Waters as tribute or take them into the tunnels for Mušmaḫḫū to feed upon."

More figures darted across the streets, flashes of colour moving through the haze of rain. One of the figures spotted them in the lane and paused to stare. A boy, Razin thought as the indistinct outline became a crouching silhouette, rolling back on his haunches. The boy called out, ignoring Hashur's attempts to wave him away and curse at him.

"Street rat," Hashur growled, picking up a stone from the road and weighing it in his palm. He threw it at the boy, who snatched it out of the air and barked something back, showing his teeth. His one hand fidgeted with something around his neck.

Razin suddenly recognised the boy.

It was Sagar.

"It's Bezal's imp!" Hashur barked, realising the same. "We must go another way, *quickly*, before he—"

But it was too late. The boy let out an excited yell and scuttled back into the haze, his arm jabbing the air in their direction. More figures appeared behind him, men and women stepping out of the grey like *sílā* spirits.

They were stripped to their waists, their skin daubed with paint and dark ochre, gleaming. The scarified flesh on their bodies rippled as they moved, shimmering with the water that cascaded off them.

Adelman let out a startled yelp, stumbling backwards against his mule. He kicked out with his sandals at the flooded gutters by his feet, and dirty hands emerged, grasping the empty air through the sluicing holes. Razin blinked in disbelief. No one could survive down there, not with the rising tide flooding the tunnels. They would surely drown.

He looked closer, his eyes narrowing as he realised that it was not dirt that covered the clasping hands, but scales—tiny slivers of silver scute adorned their abnormally long fingers. The gaps between them, he saw, were dark and webbed. One of the hands caught hold of Adelman's leg and pulled.

Then Balaam was stomping down on the drain, crushing skin and bones, sending black ichor spuming across the gutters from the ichthyic limbs. Razin fought back the urge to gag, holding his nose as he knelt to help Adelman up. A putrid stench rose from the pools of water where the blood had spilt, like salt and fish and rotting octopods.

"What was that?" Adelman whimpered, his eyes wide and white, still staring at the gutters.

"*Sereine*," Levi cursed, pulling his daughter close.

"They come with the Ida rains," said Hashur. His eyes darted between the approaching figures on the opposite side of the road and Adelman. Razin could read his thoughts clearly on his face. They wouldn't be able to outrun Sagar, not with the old man and his mules. Hashur's lip curled as he surveyed the various side alleys and passages that converged on the market street and plaza. He made up his mind. "They slip into the sewers when they flood with the tide. Sometimes we find the waste from their meals. Animals, mostly. But sometimes…" He shook his head, his disgust evident.

A whooping yell from the street brought his attention back to the present, and he gestured toward one of the roads branching from their path, leading toward the market.

"We might be able to lose them in the crowd." He motioned for the others to follow as he darted across the street.

Adelman hurried after him, half-leaning, half-dragging his mule through the puddles. He kept to the middle of the street this time, away from the gutters.

Razin guided Levi and his daughter behind him, stealing another glance at the slimy, ichor-coated drains as he hurried toward the plaza. He pictured dark things with gills and prehensile forms; flat dead eyes and sloping skulls; cold, wet tongues and jagged teeth.

And then they were in the market, surrounded by a sea of heaving, stomping bodies. When Razin turned to face the crowd, he saw who it was they'd found.

It was Amice.

"Let me go, you filthy fucking savages!" Amice bared his teeth, the cords in his neck pulling taut as he screamed into the crowd. He stood naked in the plaza square, his hands bound and a chain connecting his one foot to a towering stone post. He had been cut a dozen times, and shallow welts covered his chest and stomach in horizontal lines of varying width and length.

Amice spat and cursed, pulling at the chain that bound him as he floundered around the post. His invective gradually turned into pleas, his voice wracked by sobs as he begged for mercy. A heaving mass of bodies ebbed outside the range of his chains, like the sea around an island.

And like the sea, they were deaf to his appeals for mercy.

Poor, monstrous fool, Razin thought.

He pitied him. Yes, cutthroat that he was. Whatever spectacle he was about to become party to, he deserved and no doubt more. Arcadius had been lucky, but there were likely others who had not been spared his administrations, bodies who had ended up at the end of his dagger and at the bottom of a pit somewhere. If anyone's past was littered with the dead, it was Amice's.

And not just the murdered. Razin remembered the way the squire had looked at the young maids when he had still been in Dietmar's employ.

There is something wretched inside that boy, Razin had thought. *A poisonous, vile thing that no amount of lecturing or beatings can ever dispel.*

He had known then that the boy's fate would be a violent one, one way or another. Had he ever had a choice? Could anyone have been any different with such a wretched soul? That was why he pitied him: there was a sense of inevitability about his transgressions and fate, perhaps not all his own to decide. Still, he had done enough wrong to enough people to justify this, whatever it was.

The onlookers filled every inch of the plaza, hanging from balconies and clinging to pillars and guardrails. They watched from the temples and towers, the bronze and silver domes, and glass posts with hooked terraces of rope and steel.

Gold and turquoise banners drooped limply from the rain-soaked façades. Figures jostled for space between the pillars, making room on the steps of the overlooking temples. Barely clothed, the masses stood breathing in the stifling heat, exhaling hot moisture into the air.

Animals roamed freely through the square, unattended sheep and goats, a bridled horse without a rider, and… other things. A beast with a long neck and scales, bony knubs jutting out from its back where… *wings* had been removed? The creature's long lips reminded Razin of a camel as it chewed on something fed to it by its owner, who held its reins.

Razin squeezed his way between the bodies, following in the wake of Adelman and the mules like a string of ships searching for a berth. A few disgruntled voices rose above the chorus of sounds—their chants and curses unintelligible to his ears, but the complaints were short-lived. Everyone was preoccupied with the figure in the centre of the plaza.

"We must not linger here," a voice whispered beside Razin's. He flinched and saw Hashur appear beside him. The secretary wore a dour expression, his eyes constantly scanning the crowd for potential threats. Hashur tugged his hood down further over his head, revealing tattooed knuckles resembling Bezal, the priest's hands.

"Come on," he said, turning into the crowd. Razin followed, seeing the secretary in a new light.

He was once a pagan, too, he thought, ignoring the hands shoving him as he navigated the plaza. He wondered if Hashur's teeth had been cut and inked like Bezal's or if that was a practice reserved for the priestly class.

And Gizzal?

The scars on his mouth looked more like punishment than ritual scarification to Razin's eyes. Had Hashur played some part in that before switching allegiances? He imagined a whole world of politicking and backstabbing, rival sects and religious wars, all festering in the shadow of Kura-Agal.

Razin hesitated as he noticed the sudden silence that had fallen over the plaza.

Looking around, he saw that everywhere it was the same: the brown tide of humanity around him had settled, every face turned toward the pitiful figure of Amice. His pleas had grown hoarse, little more than desperate exhalations.

As if on cue, the rain that had battered Ubar since nightfall finally subsided, leaving behind a haze that hung like steam above their heads.

Razin saw Hashur still wading through the crowd ahead and made to follow him but halted mid-step. There was a shifting sensation beneath his feet, as if the very ground was moving. He gazed at the plaza floor, briefly wondering if Ubar suffered earthquakes and what would become of the towering spires if it did. The notion was dispelled by a sibilant sigh that rose above the grinding, shifting, scraping noise beneath him.

A hiss, like hot air spilling out from a pot brought to boil, filled the plaza, growing louder.

Something was sliding through the tunnels.

"Mušmaḫḫū," Hashur uttered, turning to face Razin, his eyes wide with alarm.

People started moving ahead, scrambling away from the post where Amice had been chained. They cleared the area beneath the temple's steps, revealing a bulwark of stone that formed a tier upon which the temples stood. As the crowd surged away from the post, Razin was able to make out for the first time what had been built into the wall. Vast and cavernous, water pooling at its entrance, was the mouth of the sewers.

Amice appeared to have realised what was about to transpire, and his cries for help grew more intense. A slopping sound echoed from the tunnel, accompanied by a sickly smell that Razin recognised from when they'd first entered the city. He had managed to get used to the stink, but here it became overpowering.

He tried not to gag and stumbled after Hashur in the direction of the bobbing heads of Adelman's mules. They were moving against the tide, but nobody seemed to care, and they managed to get to the other side of the plaza, skirting around the tunnel mouth with relative ease. It was only when Razin helped Adelman with his mule up the steps that he managed a glance back over the heads of the throng.

Amice was a pale spectre beneath the post, his hands desperately pulling at the chain still binding his foot. He'd given up on mercy and was focusing his efforts on yanking his foot out of the shackles. The skin around the limb was a seeping, bloody mess, but it looked like he'd managed to twist it at a crooked angle, partially freeing it from the irons. He leaned down on it, letting his weight fall fully on the foot and was rewarded with a loud *crack*.

Silence briefly enveloped the square before Amice's scream shattered it, soon fading into a pitiful whimper as he cradled his broken limb. He continued whimpering as the shadows in the sewer mouth lengthened, deepening until the crevice resembled a black hole from which nothing good could come.

And then nothing good did come.

Blooming tendrils of smoke preceded its arrival as it stretched across the mouth of the tunnel. The opening suddenly filled with a form that Razin recognised, causing him to recoil even as he acknowledged it. Black coils unfurled, revealing sharp serrated ridges rippling over muscular contours. A long, flickering tongue tasted the air as the serpent quivered, unveiling itself. The Falak blinked its crimson eyes, billowing smoke from its mouth like an upturned waterfall.

Amice screamed.

And then, somehow, impossibly, he caught Razin's eye across the crowd.

The terror on his face transformed, first into recognition, and then into something more sinister. Razin looked away, but it was too late. Amice made his final desperate move, calling out and shouting at those nearest him while pointing at the stairs.

"Treacherous dog," Razin snarled, urging Adelman up the steps, all thoughts of pity forgotten. The boy would give them all up out of spite, even if it meant he still shared the same fate.

"Rot him," said Tomas, leaning down the steps to offer Adelman a hand. The old man moaned as he was pulled up the first step, leaning bodily, his arm wrapped around Balaam's neck as he ascended.

Beyond the plaza, vertiginous temples lined the way, illuminated by the crackling clouds and rows of coloured lanterns hanging from string and hooks along the walls. The lanterns sputtered, more than half their number already extinguished by the rains. Those remaining revealed a tangled network of passages and side routes between the temples. The sloping grey walls gave way to gaudy streets a little further in, where pools of eddying darkness mixed with the coal-smoke-stained walls of the workshops.

Amice's yells and gesticulations were starting to gain attention, and Razin felt curious eyes turn to them as they summited the plaza steps. He glanced back over the heads of the crowd, iridescent in the strange glow of the clouds and the sheen of water and sweat. Amice hobbled behind the mass, his naked form hunched and crooked, his foot dragging behind him. The chain rattled as he tugged at it. He hadn't managed to get loose.

Behind him, the Falak's vast head bobbed from side to side. Its forked tongue tasted the air as it began to emerge from the tunnel, like a maggot from a wound. The peculiar appendage hanging from its back—a malformed wing—fluttered as it moved, swivelling in slight peristaltic motions.

A useless thing, Razin thought.

Too small and weak to aid the movement of so large a beast.

But then he thought of the waters flooding the tunnels and the sea straddling the city walls, filling the caverns beneath with each rising tide. He could imagine the tattered wing springing to life beneath the currents, giving those subtle motions as much purpose as a fin or tail.

The serpent's gaze finally settled on Amice, its whole body going as still as stone as it considered him. Amice whimpered, trying to put the post he was bound to between himself and the creature, slipping on the wet flagstones as he dragged himself across them.

"Sagar!" said Hashur suddenly, dragging Razin's eyes from the spectacle.

There was a ripple of movement, a swell of bodies wading through the centre of the plaza. Voices boomed in officious tones, demanding obedience from men who expected it. The crowd parted, making space for the figures to pass through.

Sagar, followed by the tall and looming shape of the priest Bezal. Beak-helmed men in turquoise robes materialised beside them, brandishing short swords and spears at anyone who didn't move aside quickly enough.

"This way!" called Hashur, bounding up the last steps and slipping into the crowd like an eel through water. He disappeared into the press, headed for the smoke-textured walls of buildings beyond. Tomas made to follow, dragging Silensus by the reins and pushing his way past the last few people on the steps. Razin traced his path, mindful of Levi and his daughter moving in his shadow and the old man and his mule to his right.

Something shifted in the throng. A subtle change from passive audience to active participant, driven by the appearance of Bezal and his men. Their desultory trance broken, they heaved forward, sweeping across the plaza toward the steps in a roaring wave.

Men and women slipped on the wet stone, tumbling to the uneven grots only to be absorbed by the tide of bodies, trampled or pulled back to their feet—their fates hidden by the undulating throng. Others raced up the steps, their outstretched hands reaching for Levi and Sara, only to be pushed aside by others eager to catch them first.

In the midst of the commotion, Razin felt a hand on his back and lashed out instinctively. He slammed his elbow into something soft and fleshy and was rewarded with a satisfying crunch. Whoever had been behind him fell away with a bathetic cry. Razin didn't pause to look. He drew his sword, guiding Levi and Sara ahead of him up the last steps.

Bezal's furious voice echoed behind them, growing louder as he approached. Suddenly, a face appeared in Razin's path. It belonged to a coarse-haired man with long dirty braids adorned by colourful beads and cheap jewels. The man's bare chest bore stains of various ochre hues and paint, washed away by the rain. He leered at Razin.

Razin didn't hesitate. He slashed out at the man's outstretched hand with his sword, splicing air and skin in one swift, ergonomic motion. Blood followed the path of his blade, spraying across the steps in a violet plume, mingling with the man's dark skin and staining Razin's robes. The yowling man was sent sprawling with a forceful kick to the belly. Razin brandished his sword at the figures behind him, and they came more cautiously than before.

Adelman cried out as a ragged band of street urchins swarmed around him. They tugged at Balaam's reins and jabbed their dirty fingers at the old man's ribs. Whether they were trying to help Bezal or merely taking advantage of the situation, it was impossible to tell. But Razin saw their quick fingers latching onto Adelman's coin purse before Tomas appeared to shove them away.

Coins spilt from the leather pouch, bursting from the seams as it was torn open, little bits of silver and bronze and nickel rolling onto the floor, bouncing from the steps like apples from a cart.

Chaos followed.

The little gang flung themselves at the steps, scooping up the coins and obstructing the path of those coming up, forming a bottleneck on the stairs. Amidst the commotion, one of the street rats hung back from the rest, watching them fight over the coins before turning to stare at Tomas and Adelman. She had a dirty face with bright yellow eyes and a torn lip, split just beneath her nose.

It was Tanit.

Tomas called to her, coaxing her like a stray cat. For a moment, it looked like she might ignore him, and she turned her head back to stare at the band of squabbling urchins. But then the girl hurried across the road, acknowledging Tomas's smile with a subtle tilt of her head. She didn't stop once she reached him but moved up the road and motioned down one of the adjacent side alleys.

"She wants us to follow?" said Tomas, staring down the passage.

"May as well," said Levi, squinting into the dimly lit corridor. He glanced back at Razin. "Hashur has already abandoned us anyway. Scampered off the first chance he got, looks like."

Bezal's booming voice came again, and Razin caught a glimpse of his hooded figure moving through the crowd, cursing at anyone who got in his way.

A scream erupted from the plaza, drawing Razin's attention in time to witness the red ocular pits of the Falak glow like burning oil and wash the square in a surge of oscillating light. With a hiss that sounded like hot coals spilling out over flesh, the serpent snapped forward.

Its sleek aquiline head smashed through the pillar like a hammer, sending shards of stone and mortar careening into the crowd. The post's capital bludgeoned one of the strange animals trapped on the plaza, causing its rusine head to shatter like a melon.

The Falak twisted with preternatural speed, jack-knifing after the tumbling naked figure behind the ruined post. Those still standing in range of its unwinding coils were pulverised, reduced to ruddy smears on the wet floor.

Amice somehow managed to regain his footing, dragging his now slack chain with him, only to be thrown back to the ground, narrowly avoiding the serpent's smouldering jaws as it shot past him.

The plaza descended into chaos. Those around the sewer entrance scrambled to escape, their earlier euphoria and awe at the sight of the Falak now forgotten as panic took hold.

Razin caught sight of Bezal's corpulent figure forcing his way through the throng, attempting to restore order with his guard, but to no avail. Razin looked back at the sewer mouth, searching for Amice amongst the pit of fleeing bodies, but the boy was gone, either into the belly of the serpent or vanished amongst the crowd, swallowed once more by the depths of Ubar.

The city can have him, Razin thought, turning his back on the plaza. He couldn't think of a more fitting fate for both of them.

They followed the girl down the narrow streets, through dirty, flooded warrens and across rickety bridges that looked like splintered limbs. She guided them away from the temple district, passing through deserted market stalls and into a labyrinth of workshops and courtyards.

Tomas tried asking Tanit where she was taking them, but his questions were met with a blank stare or an impatient growl, and he eventually stopped asking.

Not long after, they figured it out for themselves—when the stink of salt and fish and sour air grew impossible to ignore, and masts loomed before them like jutting bones in the dark.

27

Darkness.

Wind lashing.

Rain falling in a tepid squall that stung the skin and tasted like oil.

Thunder booming from behind variegated clouds, accenting the howling chaos with each stroke. Punctuated violence from the eddying firmament.

Dietmar's vision extended only as far as the pilings that anchored the *Ishkur*, with everything beyond obscured by shadows and enveloped in coiling darkness. The night, as black as pitch, spread like an inky stain wherever his gaze landed. Occasionally, movements flickered within the obscurity—whether they were people, monkeys, rats and birds, or the things that hunted them all... he could not tell. At that moment, anything that lurked behind the veil of rain and night was unknown and unknowable.

So, this was the fathomless void that had confronted Noah with the world's unmaking. This was the countenance of the deep from which the ordered cosmos emerged, bringing light forth from its primaeval depths—the darkness of Genesis from which God had forged all creation.

In that warm, dark night, it was easy to believe.

Though, there was something else… a feeling that lingered in Dietmar's mind. He had heard a story once from an unorthodox scholar, a scribe in the employ of a noble family's estate in Darmstadt—though the scholar had never disclosed which family. The man had recounted an intriguing anomaly he had stumbled upon during his studies—a contradiction, as he called it.

It concerned the Bible.

Dietmar had listened with rapt attention as Cuno—he was willing to divulge his name at least, but only after Dietmar offered to cover his drinks—explained that the creation story documented in Genesis might not be as straightforward as it seemed.

In the beginning, God created the heavens and the earth. Now the earth was formless and empty, darkness was over the surface of the deep, and the Spirit of God was hovering over the waters.

According to Cuno, the passage carried a deeper meaning, perhaps truer than most people understood. In the Hebrew translation from which subsequent translations were derived, the Hebrew word for "deep" was *Tehom*, which traced its origins back to the Sumerian word *Tiamat*.

Cuno explained that Tiamat was not merely "the deep" from which God commenced creation. Tiamat was a God. After some research, the little scholar had discovered that Tiamat was the personification of the primordial sea in Babylonian cosmology, and it was from her that all the gods were born.

If his retranslation was correct, it gave new meaning to Genesis. This formless void from which all creation emerged was not just an inert, oleaginous chasm but a primordial entity—a deity as old as God Himself, perhaps. And she had been subdued, reshaped, and moulded by Yahweh to breathe life into the universe.

When Cuno had noticed the look on Dietmar's face, he had raised his hands, a thin smile on his lips. "I know, I know. It must sound strange," he had said. "But there is more… more that connects our own cosmology with… something else…

And from his lips came fire, his words a storm to all who heard… In his right hand, he held the sun, and in his left, the stars. A gleaming sword sprouted from his mouth, an impossible blade. His eyes perceived all, and all were perceived."

"John?" asked Dietmar, recognising something of the scripture in Cuno's words. He thought the scholar was describing an angel.

"No," the scholar had replied, his eyes gleaming with excitement. "That is from the *Enuma Elish*. It is a description of *Marduk*, their creator God. The one who subdued Tiamat and brought order to her cosmic seas."

Dietmar had entertained the little man's theories long enough to finish his own drink, but he recognised heresy when he heard it. The unorthodox scholar was venturing into dangerous territory with ideas that could get him in trouble if the wrong ears caught wind of them. And Dietmar, already heavily indebted to the Church, wanted to avoid any further attention from them.

He had made his excuses, paid for Cuno's cups, and then disappeared into the depths of the drinking house to ruminate over the hand God had dealt him. Soon enough, he forgot about the scholar and his theories.

But now, standing amidst the wash of night beneath effluent clouds, his teeth aching and his eyes nearly sealed shut by the wind, he found himself wondering. God had fashioned order from chaos, but had that chaos ever been dispelled? Subdued, yes… but it lurked just on the edge of things. What would happen if it ever had the chance to break free again? What reality would unveil itself upon creation, displacing the careful order of things with its own chaotic energy? Dietmar thought what he had seen since passing through the Sandmouth was a good approximation of it.

This wasn't Hell; even Hell had an order to it, perhaps not one he fully understood, but it was there: the Seven Circles, a pit for every vice; a hierarchy of Barons and Lords—devils to be sure, but *structured*. One might even begrudgingly respect such a place. But this? If there was a tether to the chaos, Dietmar had yet to see it.

"Dear sweet Paul's Arse!" a voice cried out over the wind. Geoff, undoubtedly. Dietmar hadn't heard such casual blasphemy from anyone but Tomas in his time in Jerusalem, and Tomas was safely ensconced in the lower decks with Levi and the girls.

They'd appeared on the dock as mere outlines against the storm, hunched against the rain, casting furtive glances back the way they'd come.

Malah had taken one look at the skittish mules making their way up the narrow gangplank and immediately raised his fee, demanding surety against any damage the frightened equines might cause during their journey. When Arcadius, the Lady Marie, and Amice failed to materialise with the others, the captain agreed to the initial price, with the added promise that if either Balaam or Silensus bit one of his crew, they'd be added to the ship's stew.

"This storm's going to sink us the moment we hit the open sea," Geoff exclaimed, looming out from the darkness. Water streamed down his face, and his hair was drenched, clinging to his head like a skull cap. "What's the great hurry anyway? We could shore up here a while, keep our heads out of it until the wind dies down. It might give me a chance to find that boy and bop his head in for being a backstabbing cunt."

"You heard what Razin said," Dietmar replied, looking past Geoff, at a bauble of light approaching along the railings. He squinted until he could make out Kal, Malah's first mate, making his way across the deck with an oil lamp in hand.

"They're looking for us," Dietmar said. Other figures moved in the shadows, flittering across the forecastle as the crew prepared the ship for departure. They worked in near darkness, hauling in the gangway, stowing away cargo nets, and sealing the hold. Stevedores scuttled along the pier, their hooded heads shrouded by the downpour as they dismantled cranes and trolleys used to load the ship.

"Aye, this Bezal and his cult," Geoff remarked, joining Dietmar by the railing. He leaned against it and spat over the side, watching his saliva disappear in the downpour. "So, we're stuck with the choice of being fed to a giant serpent or being dashed against the rocks by the sea, is that it?"

Dietmar shrugged. "Malah says he's sailed through this storm before. He knows how to navigate it and keep us in one piece."

"He's a smuggler." Geoff made to reach for his flask but stopped and cursed. He'd tossed it aside when he'd finished the last of its contents that morning.

"So are we," Dietmar reminded him. His hand moved instinctively to the pouch at his side, feeling the weight of its contents secured against his hip. "Amalric would have taken our heads if he'd caught us moving this out of the city."

"And that might've been a damn sight better than what most of my lads got." Geoff spat again, shaking his head as he rubbed his mouth. "I don't trust him, this Malah. A whole *cunting* city full of heathens eager to cut our throats, and he's just willing to risk his life and his crew's to see us safe?"

Dietmar snorted, looking away from Geoff and peering into the darkness of the city. Somewhere in that tangled warren of glass and stone, hidden by the night, were Arcadius and the Lady Marie… and perhaps Amice too, if he'd survived. When he had heard what had transpired, he'd suggested going back into the city to search for the Greek and his ward, but a glance from Razin and the terrified expressions on the faces of the others had quickly dissuaded him. Still, the thought of abandoning them to the city did not sit well with him—this place in-between, a purgatory of sorts, between the demons of the plains and their own world.

But was that not to be their fate anyway, Purgatory? The idea wormed its way to the fore, burrowing through his mind, refusing to be dislodged. The voice had told him… the Lady Marie, born of the seed of sin. And Arcadius, her father, the sinner.

Dietmar forced the thought aside and peered deeper into the downpour. Only the girl, Tanit, appeared unfazed by the events Razin had described.

Considering what she must have seen and lived through as a slave in Ladah, Dietmar couldn't say he was surprised. She'd disappeared below deck with the rest of them, her relief to be out of the rain the first genuine emotion he'd seen from her.

"It's not our safety he cares about," said Dietmar. "The only thing men like him are interested in is what's in it for them: the last of my coin and an excuse to get a head start over the other captains and crews in the harbour."

"I wager he's as zealous as the rest of them," said Geoff, lowering his voice as Kal approached. "This ship is covered in rotting idols to their sea god. Little craven things hanging from every mast. Makes my skin crawl."

"Sailors' superstition," Dietmar whispered back. "Even the ships of Christendom are filled with it. A good captain knows when to turn a blind eye."

Dietmar had noticed the effigies too. Strange unions of wood and flesh, with fish tails and fins attached to crude humanoid sculptures, rotting pieces of silver scales exogenously affixed. The sight of them had given him pause when coming aboard the ship. Malah had seen his expression and dismissed them casually, claiming they kept the crew content. And if they were happy, he was happy.

That was before Razin and the others had arrived—led, somehow, by Tanit, who must have followed Geoff and him to the port. How else could she have known the location of the ship? That aside, mere sailors' superstition was one thing, but from what Razin had told him, anyone in the city who did not worship their many gods was not safe. His friend had promised to speak of it more once they'd left the city.

"Believe what you want," said Geoff. "I won't be sleeping a wink while we're aboard." He scowled at Kal, who was making his approach, and then stomped off across the forecastle, taking the steps down to the main deck and disappearing into the hold.

Kal watched him leave, his weathered face as unreadable as the lettering inked into his skin. It covered his neck and hands like tessera on a bath-house's walls. He nodded at Dietmar and then lifted his lamp above the rails, peering into the swirling stygian night.

"Crew'll be pulling in the lines soon," he said, turning to Dietmar. "You'll want to be beneath the deck when the fore-line sings and we spring from the harbour. Cap'n likes to pop out of the harbour mouth like a ray-fin, 'specially when we're racing Ida."

"You've done this often?" Dietmar asked, feeling a sense of relief that they weren't sailing into certain doom, only probable.

"On occasion," Kal replied. He blinked at Dietmar, revealing the epi-canthic folds in the corners of his eyes. His skin was as pale as a haddock's, and in the flickering lamplight, the veins beneath showed like inky black worms, vessels of chthonic darkness that had taken root in the seaman's flesh, never to be removed.

Kal looked away, and Dietmar blinked back the thought. He was the one who had an unwanted guest taking root, not Kal. Even now, he could feel Ephium relishing in his discomfort, taking in every sight, and sound, and thought in his mind.

—*he looks like his water god's children,* came the voice, as he knew it would. —*ask him if he hatched from an egg or was he shat out like the rest of us? If he has many brothers and sisters? Thousands, I imagine, a whole brood. A great bitch like her would pump out enough eggs to satisfy even the hunger of the Kyivan Rus and their black tongues*

Dietmar shifted aside as a pair of towering figures in oilskins emerged on the forecastle, bellowing commands to the phantoms moving about the deck. The crew began pulling in the bow and stern lines. Hunched over the ropes, they sang tunelessly in the language of salt or Ubarian or some other godforsaken tongue.

Dietmar felt rather than saw something move behind him. He spun around, flinching at the red-eyed visage that met his stare. Malah's golden monkey chittered at him with a hint of malicious glee. It bared its tiny, razor-sharp teeth and then slipped down from the railing, disappearing into the maze of rigging to find its master.

"I'll take you below deck," Kal offered, hoisting his lamp. "Cap'n kill me if anything happened to you that wasn't meant to."

Dietmar lingered on those words as he followed the second mate down the stairs, descending into the dark maw of the hold, into the belly of the ship.

***

The Ishkur was something between a hulk, with its twin castles at the bow and stern, and a Roman dromon galley, with three lateen sails wrapped up in their sail yards. A pair of rounded ship's boats, equipped with a single mast and capable of accommodating a small crew, were fastened to the railings to either side of the weather deck.

Spools of rope and netting covered the deck between the foremast and mainmast, wound up tight around the cylindrical iron posts nailed into the floorboards. What purpose they served, Dietmar could only guess at, but the racks of harpoons and spears that lined the walls below deck suggested that they were on a vessel that did more than just transport cargo across the black waters. They were hunters, too.

In size, the Ishkur dwarfed any vessel Dietmar had ever seen. The cog he had crossed the Middle Sea in had been little more than a fishing vessel, in comparison. The windows he had glimpsed from the pier belonged to about a dozen small cabins located beneath the forecastle. These cramped rooms contained a single cot facing the door and mounted window desks that looked out over the figurehead protruding from the Ishkur's prow like a hooked nose.

Dietmar sat in one of these cabins, watching the water parting for the ship's prow as she made for the harbour mouth. Voices and movements echoed from the neighbouring cabins: Levi and his daughter bickering over their cot, Razin pacing slowly across the creaking floorboards. Somewhere below, Adelman and Tomas were seeing to the mules. Adelman, in particular, had grown anxious when the animals were taken out of sight and insisted on remaining with them, with Tomas agreeing to keep an eye on him.

He hadn't seen Geoff since their conversation on the deck. The mercenary had been sour since the news of Amice, or perhaps it was due to running out of alcohol. He was probably snooping around the ship's kitchens in search of a drink.

Dietmar had, rather begrudgingly, taken a liking to the uncouth mercenary. Geoff was blunt and to the point and didn't bother hiding his thoughts behind a veneer of vague allusion. And he was easy to read, which Dietmar found reassuring amidst the chaos that had followed them from Old Samaria.

He thought of Razin then. By all accounts, the opposite of Geoff. His friend was reserved by nature, but his quiet thoughtfulness had taken on a new quality over the last few days. The mask he wore had become more serious, and Dietmar wondered what it would reveal when it finally slipped.

Razin had seen something in the forests before Ubar. Whatever it was had made him more aloof, colder. He wouldn't talk about it, of course, choosing to bottle it up like all his other doubts and feelings until only the most sanitised emotions made it to the surface. He had been like this before, after Galilee, where Dietmar and Razin had fought alongside a minor baron against a coalition of apostate Turks and Christians. They had uncovered an alliance of Christian and Muslim nobles aiming to carve out their own fiefdom from the back of Outremer's waning power. A kingdom free from the clutches of Nur ad-Din and Amalric's rule.

Razin had known one of the apostate faris knights, Ibn al-Hasan. They had known each other since childhood and rode together from Damascus to join the muster at Krak des Chevaliers. They shared victories against the Franks in raids along the Jordan River, as well as the disappointment at the state of Nur ad-Din's camp. Their final hopes were shattered when Amalric and his motley band of Latins, Frenchmen, and Cilicians wiped the field with them at the battle of al-Buqaia.

Ibn al-Hasan's appearance among the renegades had deeply shaken Razin. He had come up with excuses for his friend, believing that he had been tricked or fooled into joining the league of bandits and traitors—that there had been some mistake.

But when he finally spoke to al-Hasan, his friend had denied nothing. *How could I deny the truth?* he had asked Razin before branding him a naïve fool, too guarded to see the truth of the world. There was only power. The power of kings and sultans. Everyone else was just playing at games.

Razin had left al-Hasan's cell a colder man, the first tessera of his mask firmly in place.

Dietmar leaned back in the small cradle chair in front of the desk and gazed upward at a stain of azure light breaking upon the horizon, illuminating the harbour mouth as the Ishkur tacked toward it.

Is Razin's way really so different to my own?

He watched the stain spread, a growing patina beneath the clouds. He had his own façade. A mask he wore to hide his shame and fear, his sense of ineptitude and despair. He was just better at hiding things than Razin. What face would he show the world when his mask slipped?

The floorboards beneath his feet started to hum as Malah swung the ship eastward, bow-side, to take full advantage of the wind. Then, with a swift tack back toward the gate, the ship surged forward, propelled by the slipstream. The Ishkur strained under the pressure, shuddering as Malah bent her to his will.

She raced toward the wall now, on a course that would bring her smashing against the mortar and stone that protected Ubar from the storm. Her pace increased, her nose bobbing in and out of the waves as the tri-lateen sails caught the wind.

Dietmar clung to the desk, jolting forward as Malah made course corrections, dangling the Ishkur's snout toward the harbour mouth, even as she trembled and groaned beneath the stress. Dietmar moaned, already regretting the prow. He felt like he was perched on the tip of a wobbling arrowhead in the clutches of a first-time archer, swaying back and forth in front of the intended target.

If this was what the protected harbour was like, how would they possibly survive the open sea?

Any chance he might have had to change his mind was long gone, and he watched, white-knuckled, as the Ishkur zipped past the last of the piers and straightened out to be received by the gate.

He thought they must look like a sea-spider in their tall ship and narrow hull, scuttling from left to right across the harbour. Yet, despite the Ishkur's imposing size, it paled in comparison to the vertiginous walls of the Ubar Gate. The walls resembled weathered bones in the gloom, femurs that had been fashioned into curving arches that rose as high as the tallest spires in the city. Water gushed from the grooves where the pillars met the wall, forming cascading waterfalls that enveloped the harbour mouth in a gaudy mist.

The mist swirled in the wind, an amorphous haze that rippled beneath the surging storm. Dietmar's eyes fixed on the stone arches, tracing their embowed forms with his eyes as far up as the vaulted roof, then back down to stare at the columns as they crossed between them.

"Even their sea gate bears the mark of their gods."

Dietmar snapped his head around, staring into the room. Razin was standing a step behind him, looking out of the windows.

He hadn't heard the cabin door open or his friend's footsteps across the floorboards.

Razin steadied himself against the desk as the Ishkur shuddered. The ship's violent spasms had subsided now that Malah had caught the wind, but the faint keening sound of the hull lingered.

"They call it Mušmaḫḫū," said Razin, his hand sketching a line in the air, his eyes still fixed on the walls of the sea gate.

Dietmar tilted his head, craning his neck to peer up into the passing stone.

"They believe it accompanied their prophet across the desert, shielding him from harm," Razin continued, his voice carrying a hint of awe. Finally, Dietmar's eyes found what had captured his friend's attention.

The stone blocks lining the inner walls of the gate had been cut into geometric tiles arranged in an overlapping sequence that resembled the scales of a snake. Even in the dim light, they gleamed, awash with a corposant glow, the source of which Dietmar could not identify.

He blinked away from the tessellation and turned back to Razin. His friend's face was vacant—another mask.

"It slips between the world-edifice, through the layers of existence, appearing and disappearing as it pleases. That is how Paul of Balata came to see it in Nablus. It can traverse all aspects of the terrestrial plane."

"That is what this Gizzal told you?"

Razin nodded. "I thought Paul was a qareen. Perhaps he was. Perhaps that is what a qareen truly is—an echo occupying the liminal spaces. He must have been present when the Falak burrowed between places, peeling back the layers like skin from bone."

"To what end?" Dietmar asked, trying to follow Razin's explanation. They had briefly discussed Gizzal's theory upon Razin's arrival on the ship—the šubur and his light box, the layered world; an enigmatic palimpsest that Razin had seen on Gizzal's tabletop. It was a strange panoply of ideas Razin had left him with before disappearing into his cabin. "From what you told me, the people here already feed it, worship it. Why did it come to Nablus?"

Razin turned away from the glass. "I believe it is searching for something."

"What?" Dietmar pressed.

"Its master. Their prophet." Razin met Dietmar's gaze, his expression giving away nothing of his thoughts. "Some of the mušrikūn believe that Addir-Melek took passage through the Sandmouth to spread his message: the word of Neruk, his god."

"What do the others believe? Those who think he stayed?"

"That he perished, or that he is still here, raising the beast from the depths of this ocean to transgress the many aspects and flood existence with its being. Bahamut. The other face of God."

Another flood, Dietmar thought, thinking again to the words of the heretical scholar all those years ago. He envisioned a seething, churning chasm of oily water—the primordial state. But was it merely that? Or was it chaos, the embodiment of some ancient god from which existence had been moulded? When he looked out of the cabin window, he saw the same image manifesting before him—endless black waves rising and cresting, never breaking—an eddying darkness of immutable energy.

His breath escaped him, leaving behind a growing sense of unease that spread from the pit of his stomach. They couldn't hope to cross those waters. It was suicide.

A memory of something lost stirred within him, dislodging itself from a wall he couldn't remember constructing. He glimpsed cracked lips, a pale face quickly concealed by a white veil. Then, despair. Utterly. The memory was fleeting, swept away by the anguish that coursed through him, like the waves around them, leaving him trembling in his seat.

Razin was suddenly kneeling beside him. There was concern in his eyes as he dropped his inscrutable façade, genuinely worried for his friend. "Are you unwell, German? Are you sick?" Razin examined Dietmar, searching for the cause of his shaking limbs. "Should I fetch the ship's physician? I am not sure I would trust a man who keeps such company, but—"

Dietmar shook his head, waving his friend's concerns away as the shakes subsided, fading away so that only the sense of despair remained. It was a void inside of him. A hole that could not be filled, and he did not know where it came from. It was not a new thing, this hollow. He could not help but be aware of that fact as the hopelessness that had threatened to overpower him ebbed back—suppressed once again. Hidden, but not gone.

"It's the sea," he breathed, the words sounding more like a half-truth in his own ears. There *was* something of the coursing void present, both in how he felt and in what he could see breaking beyond the sea gate. Maybe the ocean had awakened it in him, alerting him to the emptiness he had long ignored—but for how long? He thought of his dream then, in the forest with Enneleyn… the glade… the empty hole in the ground.

That had been different, though. Something foul and rotten had stirred between the trees, had taken hold of Enneleyn and possessed her in his dreams. Or was it something in his head, twisting his thoughts like a putrid maggot that would not be dislodged, distorting his memories until even the profane was tainted by its oil? Ephium, the *saint*.

But the despair that had flooded through him had not felt rotten or tainted either. It had just *been*. Merely. But all-encompassing.

He could feel Ephium's presence beside his own, like a figure standing just behind him but never reaching out to grab him, even as he tensed in preparation. The saint didn't speak, content simply to watch as Dietmar's thoughts raced, desperately trying to fill the gap in his mind and make sense of the emptiness he felt.

His silence unsettled him.

"What did you see that night by the river?" Dietmar said, searching for a distraction and finding it in his friend.

The Ishkur rocked as the slipstream Malah had found crossed into the turbulent waters. They were nearly out of the sea gate.

"By the river?" Razin replied, the tone in his voice telling Dietmar he knew exactly what he was referring to.

"You know what I'm talking about." Dietmar let out a breath. His shoulders slumped as the last of the shudders left him. He looked at his friend. The concern from a moment ago was gone, a guarded look now in its place. "The night Amice witnessed… the night Amice thought he saw the hand move."

Razin's gaze flickered toward the pouch at Dietmar's waist, his eyes narrowing. "It is a strange thing you carry, this hand of a dead man."

Dietmar showed his teeth and let out a weary laugh, his dry lips cracking. "You're trying to change the subject."

"Did it move?" Razin rose from his knees, and Dietmar could feel his friend appraising him, his eyes moving from the pouch to his hands, to his yellowing nails and pale skin, to the welts slowly pressing up on Dietmar's neck—boils that would need lancing. More of them covered his back and chest, mercifully hidden from view by his hauberk and padded shirt.

"It didn't move," Dietmar replied as Razin's eyes settled on his face. A face, he knew, that had grown gaunt and thin. His cheekbones jutted out beneath his eyes like jagged peaks, and his dark eye sockets resembled crags beneath his brow.

"The boy was… *is*, if he made it out of that cursed plaza, full of more stories than are good for him. It was dark. It didn't move. How could it? It is a dead thing."

It hadn't, had it?

He couldn't remember. He'd been dreaming, caught between Enneleyn and his father on that bridge before the tomb. He hadn't felt it move, but still, he couldn't remember removing it from its pouch to hold either.

The soft susurrus of dry skin behind his ears, deep within his skull, made him think the saint was laughing. He ignored it.

"Now, what did you see?" Dietmar blinked away from Razin's stare, too penetrating for him to maintain in his current mood.

"Nothing," Razin replied but then sighed, relenting. "A woman, as if from a dream. Perhaps it was a dream, and I truly saw nothing. But I fear it was not. She tricked me."

Dietmar raised a brow. Razin was not someone easily beguiled by a woman's charms. "She tricked you?"

"I was not myself."

"How did she trick you?"

"With her words… her lips." Razin seemed unashamed by the admission, as if he were recounting events that had happened around him, to him, as a mere observer. "As I said, I was not myself. And…" He hesitated, searching for the words. "…And I suspect the woman was not as she appeared either. There are no noble daughters here."

"No," Dietmar agreed.

Razin leaned forward, his hands resting on the desk as the Ishkur ploughed forward. "In the morning, we came upon the massacre in the woods. A village undone by some woeful savagery." Razin had to speak louder now to be heard, the noise of the heaving ocean spilling in through the open mouth of the harbour as they passed through it. "I let something free in that forest, between those trees that smelt of jasmine and honeycomb. I should not have, but I did."

Dietmar stared at his friend, his mind racing to process the horrifying revelation. What had Razin let loose? Something ungodly had slithered out from those trees and struck that village. The state of the bodies they'd found… the sap that covered them like webbing… His friend's face was pensive. He knew the same questions occupied his mind, complicated further by the shame he felt.

"You could not have known," said Dietmar.

Razin shook his head. "A better man would not have been so easily deceived. There is no innocence to be found in this place. I was a fool, and others have paid the price."

Waves as large as cliffs broke against the sea gate, showering the ship's prow with spray. Smaller waves erupted in misty fountains around the sun-washed embrasures that encircled the base of the walls. The towering waves surged over one another, sweeping back and forth between the stone blocks, converging to create a tumultuous shoal that the Ishkur would have to pass through if it were to reach the open waters.

Razin's words were matter-of-fact, but Dietmar knew his friend well enough to read the shame writ between them. It manifested in the stiffness of his posture, the tension in his back and shoulders, the clenched jaw and resolute gaze, and the shadow that lurked in his eyes. Razin wore a mask, but to those who knew the signs, it was clear to tell that Razin carried a burden for what had happened.

Dietmar scratched at the sleeve of his mail, rubbing at another welt forming on his wrist. "Who's to say those villagers were not as the beasts of Ladah? Hyena-men who would have fallen upon us but for your maiden in the woods."

Razin scowled, dismissing the notion. "An evil act that spares us from another evil does not become good for that reason. No, my friend. I appreciate your sentiment, but I must bear this burden just as you must bear your own." He turned his head, his gaze flicking to the pouch at Dietmar's belt. "Both of us, until the end, whatever it may be."

They crossed out from beneath the vaulted gates of Ubar's harbour, leaving what shelter its great walls provided in exchange for the frenzied sea. Titanic waves, midnight black, swelled like mountains, their steep inclines threatening to capsize the Ishkur. Foaming crests rippled like steaming torrents, engulfing the ship and pulling it this way and that as Malah set his will against the ocean. The horizon vanished, taken by the sea—a black void, the thin skein beneath which infinity surely waited.

Water leaked through the iron-framed windows, spilling in from the deck to flood the corridors and passages below and filling Dietmar's cabin with the brackish stench of the sea. But he didn't care. Nor did Razin. Their eyes were fixed on a shape rising from the waves—an imposing pillar, what must have been the peak of a great mountain submerged beneath the sea.

Dietmar's mind desperately clung to the explanation, hooking onto it to understand something so impossibly large. It rose higher than the walls and spires of Ubar, surpassing even the dark clouds that obscured the sky. The waves crashed around it, water spraying off its slick surface and converging at its base in ferocious swells that threatened to tear the Ishkur apart.

Dietmar followed the gentle curve of the edifice into the dark, his eyes hovering on the bone-like striations running up its side and the rubbery texture of the whorls of gleaming black. It was growing larger by the moment, a hardened carapace emerging from the black waters.

Dietmar could hear his own breath in his ears, even above the billowing wind and crashing waves. Short, panicked inhalations in time to the rhythm of his pounding heart, growing more rapid even as his mind tried to reject what he was seeing. But, already, he knew.

Bahamut was rising. The Godfish.

28

We are sinking, we are sinking! Silensus kicked at the post with his hind legs, straining against the limits of the rope tethered around his neck.

"We are *not* sinking," said Adelman, trying to placate the panicked mules. They had been on edge since coming aboard, and the cramped, leaking hull had only worsened their nerves. Neither of them had ever been at sea before.

Balaam *hawed* gruffly, shaking his large grey head from side to side. *We are to be left here, punished like dear poor Nicolo, bless his soul.*

Bless him.

"Bless him indeed," Adelman murmured.

Like Jonah in his boat, with only the fish to keep us while we drown. Balaam let out another miserable *haw* and dropped his head.

"I am not leaving you anywhere." Adelman rolled his eyes, scratched Balaam's side while he wrapped a comforting arm around Silensus's neck. "Honestly, you two. Did you think I brought you this far just to abandon you on some leaky ship?"

Silensus flicked his ears indifferently.

There's a lot of water, Balaam commented, leaning into Adelman's soothing scratches.

"All ships leak, especially in a storm." Adelman surveyed the dimly lit hold, where the wooden hull of the ship had become more like a sieve. Balaam was right: there was a lot of water, even for a storm.

The brackish water had seeped in through a dozen cracks and holes, spilling in from the decks above and through the passages into the hold. It was knee-high now and rising.

Adelman's gaze settled on a figure slumped over a spool of fishing nets in the corner of the hold, their sandalled feet resting on crates just above the waterline. How can he sleep at a time like this? he wondered, with something close to awe.

Tomas had clambered onto the crates not long after they'd left the harbour and had dozed off. He'd managed to sleep through the creaking ship's bones, the groaning floorboards, and the roar of the storm. He'd even managed to sleep through Silensus's frantic braying.

Adelman peered deeper into the gloomy hold beyond his sleeping friend. A single oil lamp hung from the mast post in the centre of the space. Its light flickered as the ship shuddered, threatening to go out with each jerk and pull of the Ishkur. More crates filled the cavernous space, housing fishing baskets and rusty iron cages. Most of them were empty, though, in others, Adelman could just make out the incongruous shapes of wet things, long slippery bodies writhing behind the bars of slattern boxes.

Bait, Adelman thought, recalling the harpoons and nets that littered the deck. But for what?

When Adelman turned around, he found both mules watching him quietly.

"What is it?" he asked, stroking the spot between Balaam's ears affectionately.

Silensus pressed his head against Adelman's open hand, nuzzling him with his snout, then he blinked his large brown eyes meaningfully. *There is something you must do.*

It is important, added Balaam.

And dangerous.

"Tell me," said Adelman.

Balaam and Silensus drew their heads back from the old man's hands, their ears going flat against their heads like those of anxious dogs.

"You're scaring me," Adelman confessed nervously. He'd never seen them like this, not even after their master fell victim to the demon.

You must not be afraid. Balaam's great ears twitched, and the mule looked up at Adelman, meeting his eyes with its own gentle stare. *But you must do this if you are to save our souls.*

Damnation, damnation! Silensus brayed in distress.

Adelman straightened, standing taller in the face of Balaam's proclamation. This was important—a task only he could accomplish.

"Are you angels?" he asked softly, his breath catching in his throat. He had pondered the possibility since he first witnessed them in prayer, but he hadn't dared to ask, afraid of what the answer might be.

Silensus brayed in that laugh of his, his blocky teeth showing from beneath his upper lip. *Not angels, no, no.*

Angels have wings, said Balaam. *And aren't afraid of water.*

"Then what are you?" asked Adelman. "How do you know so much?"

The mules exchanged a look, and what passed for a shrug rippled through Silensus's dusty mane.

A moment passed, filled only with the ship's groans and the sound of dripping water.

We hear a voice, Balaam eventually replied, turning back to face Adelman.

Silensus's tail swished nervously behind him. *In our heads.*

Adelman's brow furrowed. "The hand?"

No, no. Silensus's head swung from side to side. *That is a bad thing. Foul.*

We hear that too. Balaam stomped a hoof, spraying them with murky water and then looking at Adelman apologetically. *A rasping, rotten thing that talks into the night, singing its songs and telling its lies. But this voice comes from another place. It is truth and beauty and grace.*

"Where does it come from? This other voice?"

Balaam blinked at him slowly, as if the answer were obvious. *From God.*

"God?" Adelman echoed in surprise.

The mules bobbed their heads in unison.

Adelman couldn't help but smile at that. *My saintly mules. Messengers from God! Of course, of course. How did I not see it before? How else could they speak? And to me! Me, of all people! Why, that puts me close to saintliness myself. And perhaps... Yes, Saint Adelman!*

He beamed with newfound understanding. "What does the Lord wish of me?"

They told him.

***

The steps from the hold were slippery wet, and steep, like those of Mount Moriah. Adelman had stopped visiting the temple at the top after his knees failed him for the second time. He had always preferred the quiet reverence of the Church of St. Anne in the Syrian Quarter anyway.

Gripping the rotting rail, Adelman pressed himself up against it as another tranche of water cascaded down the stairwell, threatening to dislodge him. The old man held on grimly, his head bowed against the spray. Chaos roared through the corridor, the sound of crashing waves and resounding thunder. He tilted his head as the ship rocked. There was another sound, low and resonant. He could feel it through the railing and the floorboards beneath him. It resembled a billowing horn, attenuated and slightly ululating.

Adelman blinked.

It wasn't just coming from above but also from below.

"I am going mad," he muttered, glancing up as the wash of sea spray subsided. He unfurled the lantern from the folds of his oilskin coat and lifted it to stare at the steps. Water pooled on each of the slattern planks, glistening ominously beneath the light. He could just make out the opening at the top of the stairway, a doorway leading out into the stormy night.

Another thunderous roar reverberated from above, and he quickly covered the lantern before a torrent of water surged down the corridor.

Adelman waited for it to pass and then continued his ascension.

***

As he stumbled from the hold, a wave swept across the deck, nearly taking him with it. He cried out, clutching onto the doorframe, cursing himself for a fool when his mouth filled with salt water, and then crying out again when the lantern was pulled from his grasp. He watched its light blink out as the lantern disappeared, doused by the sea.

"You fool, you fool," he moaned, bracing himself as another wave broke against the ship. *My angels have sent me to my death.*

But the wave passed, and he was still there when it did. Still alive, breathing. Not just another piece of flotsam in those dark waters. He crossed himself and looked at the deck, taking deep breaths while his aching limbs settled.

Suddenly, a shape materialised before him, a hand held out like some lurching cadaver. Adelman recoiled, almost tumbling back down the stairs, but managed to steady himself at the last moment.

A face emerged from behind the hand, with yellow eyes and thick lips. The crewman scowled something at Adelman, motioning back toward the hold.

"I need to cross!" Adelman shouted, his voice carried away with the howling wind.

The crewman stared at him, tapping his ear and shaking his head.

"Across!" Adelman repeated, pointing toward the looming forecastle on the other side. "I need to get—"

The crewman barked something, in Greek perhaps, but he couldn't make it out. Then, a sneer formed on the man's face, and Adelman thought he glimpsed a thin sheen of white skin covering the crewman's eyes, flickering beneath heavy lids. The motion was so swift that Adelman couldn't be sure he'd seen it at all. The crewman shook his head again and turned away, lumbering back into the haze.

Not your problem, am I? Adelman thought, watching the figure vanish into the shadows. *If a silly old man wants to drown himself, so be it, eh?* He chortled to himself, unable to contain the giddy sensation welling up inside of him. He'd never done anything like this before. Not in all his years of ink and ledger, stylus, and ruler. Numbers had been where he had felt safest. There was a certainty to them, an irrevocable order to rely on.

They did what they were supposed to do.

Even in his later years, when the figures had started to blur before his eyes, he had still found solace in his books. It hadn't been the numbers failing, after all, but his own frail body… and, later, his mind. But he didn't like to dwell on that.

He could have taken Dietmar's pension and retired to a small plot on the estate—for however long that lasted. But what would he have done with himself then? Withered away with the passing seasons until nothing remained? No, no, he wasn't some old fool to be pitied. He had a *purpose*. More than that, he had his angels now!

His resolve fortified, he stepped out onto the deck.

A rope rail had been rigged between the main and forward masts. He stumbled a few steps toward it and latched onto the rope, like a barnacle clinging to a ship's hull. It pulsed gently beneath his weight, sending vibrations rippling through the darkness.

I am going mad, he thought as he watched a figure dart over the rail, disappearing into the rigging of the main mast like a scuttling spider. Adelman was sure he'd seen something hanging from the crewman's rear—a slithering tail. He caught another flash of movement from the corner of his eye and swung his head around in time to see something vanishing over the ship's side. He glimpsed leathery skin, glistening scales, a smooth and aquiline head, and pale eyes—an impression of something from the depths. Chthonic.

Then he remembered the creature that had grabbed him from the sewers, attempting to pull him into their dark watery abyss until Balaam had dropped his hooves on them.

"No, no, no," he moaned, pulling himself along the rope rail.

More shapes appeared from the shadows, moving swiftly across the deck as another wave washed over them. Hunched-back crewmen, driving against the rain; agile bowmen scaling the rails to secure the sails, but there were other things too.

Adelman squinted into the gloom, clinging tightly to the rope. He thought he saw something slithering ahead between the strange iron cylinders affixed to the ship's floorboards.

He decided he'd rather not know and put his head down to carry along the railing. As he leaned more heavily on the rope, his arms started to strain. He was tired, yes, and his muscles ached. Still, it felt like he was moving up an incline.

Adelman paused to catch his breath and closed his eyes as water sprayed over him. When he opened them again, he blinked and looked over the side of the ship for the first time. The sight almost made him let go of the rope.

The Ishkur was nearly vertical, her prow digging into the black waters as she rode a towering wave as steep as a mountain cliff. Clouds of ocean spray washed over the prow and forecastle, drenching Adelman again as they sloshed from port to bow.

He could hear the ship groaning beneath the roar, timber creaking under the strain, on the verge of cracking. If she broke, they would all be cast into the rupturing chasm, sinking beneath the black waves into a watery tomb. He knew he shouldn't, but the urge to look back behind him was overpowering. He turned his head over his shoulder and immediately regretted it.

A massive wall of water rose behind them, steep and menacing. Its surface rippled, coursing upward in a spray of mist and white-capped froth on an inky-black mantle. Adelman was certain he saw movement in the Ishkur's wake—grey heads bobbing in and out of the water like limestone tusks in a rapid.

Adelman stood still, momentarily frozen by panic. He wanted to turn around, to retreat back into the hold, and hide away from the world with his mules. Tomas would be awake by now, searching for him in the darkness. Surely even he couldn't sleep through this.

No, no, no going back. What would the mules think of him if he failed? Perhaps they wouldn't speak to him again, leaving him empty and alone. The thought sent shivers down his spine.

He wiped his eyes.

No going back.

He dragged himself forward, one hand over the other, until the forecastle reared over him like a fortress emerging from the mist. A sharp clicking sound caught his attention to the left. The cylinders nailed to the deck had started spinning, their rope lines disappearing into the water. They spun faster and faster, gyrating on their posts until all Adelman could see was a blur of grey rope and iron.

The whole ship shuddered, as if it had scraped against the tip of some great edifice beneath the sea—a shoal or reef. Then, quite suddenly and all at once, the cylinders stopped spinning.

Adelman hesitated, staring at the iron tubes, then he peered over the side of the ship into the murky waters. There was something there, a shape, or form or matter beneath the towering wave.

The deep, reverberating boom sounded again. It was the one from before, like a resonant bullhorn. The sound stirred something within Adelman.

He was frightened, yes. He hadn't stopped being frightened since they'd left Jerusalem. Since before then, if he was honest with himself. But now there was something else, something he hadn't felt in a long, long time. It felt like awe.

The Ishkur began to veer to one side, moving across the wave's surface, away from the protruding object beneath the water. Adelman stood still, breathing quickly, as he watched the wave part from the thing beneath.

A dark shape emerged from the ocean, rising like a jagged peak from some benthic trench long hidden. Water cascaded from its denuding surface, enveloping the ship in a misty gauze. Adelman tried to speak, but only garbled disbelief, fear, or nothing at all escaped his lips as he staggered.

His words were carried away by the wind, snatched up by the roar of the world coming undone. Again, that sound from the deep. A bellow—hollow, like the wind through a cave, low and undulating. Blaring. So loud it would have drowned out even the cacophony of Hell.

Adelman stared with gaping astonishment at the ascending belemnite tusk. Its dark, textured surface glistened as his eyes followed its arching curve into the clouds. Organic folds and bony striations adorned its skin, creating deep grooves in the surface—in the *skin* of this crag from the sea. It trembled and convulsed, pulsating gently as its immense circumference extended into the sky.

The sense was of an unfurling. An opening of some vast crease of skin and bone and scale and hide, unsheathing itself from the chaotic sea like the fin of some ancient colossus. The entire surface vibrated, oscillating in a thousand minute movements too subtle for the eye to fully perceive. Its outline blurred, buffeted by the emanations.

Adelman's face collapsed in on itself. His eyes itched, and a tingling sensation spread across his skin, like on those hot days in Jerusalem before lightning rent the air.

Was this Leviathan? The unmaking of things?

This was only a part of it, he realised with a start.

The fin, the monster's back bared to creation from the void. Adelman fell to his knees, a scream welling within him, yet unable to escape. The breath wouldn't come, so he just watched, fixated on the swirling dark and shimmering flesh—black and purple and midnight, like cold shadows rippling over a skein of impossible muscle.

Suddenly, something tugged at the rope in his hands. He spun on his knees, coming face to face with Malah's golden monkey.

The creature bared its yellow teeth, shrieking over the wind and bellowing sounds of the beast like an enraged parrot.

"Get away from here!" Adelman yelled, flinching as the monkey advanced along the rail. It rocked on the rope, putting its forearms into the motion as if to dislodge him.

Adelman cried out, slumping over the rail as it trembled. His hands dug into the fibrous knot he'd been clinging to, and he gasped but managed to hold on.

"Away with you!" This time, he leaned forward and swiped at the creature, but his balance faltered, and his hand found only empty air.

The monkey's little red eyes gleamed with malice, and it redoubled its efforts. Adelman was sure it was grinning.

"Blast you to hell!" Adelman yelled, relinquishing the rail and lunging at the beast.

The monkey's eyes widened in surprise, and it just had time for one panicked screech before Adelman seized its neck and pulled it from the rail.

The creature's greasy fur felt repulsive to the touch, and Adelman caught a whiff of its rich stink—a mixture of musk and salt—as he dragged it away. Its little fingers scrabbled at his skin, its sharp, filthy nails digging into his hands and fingers. He nearly let go when it yanked at his thumb, tearing the skin from the nail to the ridge of his knuckle.

"Begone, demon!" Adelman cried out, heaving the monkey toward the broiling sea and finally letting go. The little monstrous beast shrieked as it spun overboard, its arms outstretched, desperately looking for something to clasp onto.

Adelman slumped over the rail, his heart pounding in his chest as he watched the creature vanish into the water. Just before it disappeared, he was sure he saw it turn to face the water, its arms extended like a diver's. In that fleeting moment, its tail appeared too long and supine. Its wet fur shone like a constellation of silver pieces. Something protruded from its back, little bony knubs, like wings.

Adelman stayed there for a moment, searching the dark water for any sign of the beast. But when nothing was forthcoming, he pulled himself back to his feet.

The forecastle loomed ahead of him.

No going back.

29

The night had brought rain, a gentle drizzle that exposed the flaws in Tobias's hasty repair work. The room now carried a scent of dampness and decay, with faint watermarks etched on the walls like greasy snail trails. Dietmar couldn't help but feel that Enneleyn was too lenient with Tobias. If the son aspired to inherit his father's position one day, he would need to excel beyond leaky roofs.

Dietmar sighed. He'd have to have words with the boy as soon as he was done with…

He blinked.

Timo was standing in front of him, wringing his hands pensively. Timo wore a simple robe, the hood pulled back to show his square face. The jaw of a soldier, Dietmar had always thought. Yet Timo's touch was gentle, and his eyes held a softness that could never entertain violence.

The old physician spoke slowly, pausing to blink and hold Dietmar's eyes. "It was the fall, sire. From that height… Well, it would have been painless: a quick snap of the… She wouldn't have suffered. I believe she may have slipped on the rain-soaked steps… Though how she ended up in the middle of the courtyard, well…" Timo hesitated, his thick brows wedging together like two hairy grey caterpillars. "Perhaps the wind caught her off guard. Although, I don't recall there being more than a breeze last night. To have fallen such a distance from the steps… It's puzzling."

Timo's words faded into the background as Dietmar looked past him to the bed nestled in the corner beneath the window. A shadow lay across it, cold with the promise of a truth Dietmar had almost forgotten. His eyes traced the silhouette beneath the funeral cloth, the contours of lips and a nose, like mountains against the linen sheet.

This isn't her room. Why had he put her in here? It wasn't right.

"…the girl claims she witnessed it," Timo was saying. "She was in quite the state, understandably so. Nevertheless, she says she saw it happen."

Dietmar said something in reply, though the words escaped his hearing. Timo nodded and turned to the door, addressing the silhouette standing beside it. "Fetch Else, please. She's with Beate and the kitchen staff."

The guard nodded before vanishing through the door while Timo returned his attention to Dietmar. "They'll be fussing over her like the hens they are, poor girl." He winced, waving a hand. "Of course, what she is going through is nothing… compared to…"

A sound emerged from the corner of the room, capturing Dietmar's attention. For the first time, he noticed a figure seated beside the bed, little more than a shadow. Prominent cheekbones protruded from beneath a ridged brow, and wet, yellowed eyes blinked incessantly, fluttering like the wings of a fly. The figure wore a long, white gown draped across its bony knees. Its arms and hands remained hidden beneath the fabric. Dietmar couldn't tell if it were a man or a woman, its cadaverous features defying such categories.

Death, he thought briefly, but Timo seemed oblivious to the silent observer.

“Father Sander was here earlier,” Timo said, fidgeting with his hands. “He spoke to the girl before leaving. I believe… you will need to speak to him soon.”

Dietmar looked away from the strange figure, turning to Timo instead. “What did the girl tell him?”

“Only what I have told you,” Timo replied. “That she fell. That, from the break… from the angle.” He hesitated, picking at the skin around his nails with a finger. “She must have slipped, but sire, I must speak frankly: to have fallen so far from the stairs, she was either pushed or…”

“She fell,” said Dietmar, iron in his voice.

Timo bowed his head and didn’t lift it again until voices filled the doorway behind him, and the girl, Else, emerged. Beate, the cook, stood beside her, holding onto her shoulder with a pudgy hand, like a worried midwife.

“Come in, Else,” Timo said, offering her a reassuring smile. He motioned for Beate to wait outside. “If you’d wait outside, Frau Beate. We won’t be long. Thank you.”

The cook gave Timo a stern look before glancing at Dietmar. Her expression softened as she murmured something, her portly face wilting into a sorrowful frown.

“Thank you,” Dietmar found himself saying, though it didn’t feel like his own words. There was a noise that filled the gaps between them, a clangorous roar from a great distance away. He looked around but couldn’t identify its source, and then it was gone.

Beate bowed gently and then ushered Else into the room, closing the door behind her.

The girl stared at Timo and Dietmar, blinking as she glanced into the corner of the room where the figure on the bed resided. Else’s eyes were red from crying, her long blonde hair damp and greasy, tied back in a tight weave behind her neck. There was a soft intake of breath, and Dietmar wondered if she'd seen the figure beside the bed. But the moment passed, and her eyes dropped to the floor before her.

"Don't look so frightened, Else," Timo spoke gently. "You're not in any trouble."

"Yes, m'lord," Else murmured.

"And I'm not a Lord."

Else blinked, briefly looking up before her gaze returned to her feet.

Timo gave Dietmar a sidelong glance and cleared his throat. "You were outside the kitchens last night during the storm?"

"Yes, m'l—yes. The stable boys needed their supper, and I was the one to take it to them. Onion stew and a wedge of bread. Beate found some leftover radish and leek pie for their…" Else's voice faded off.

"Yes, yes." Timo waved his hand dismissively. "Tell us what you saw, what you told Father Sander."

"Father Sander?"

Timo nodded.

Dietmar felt something shift behind him, as if a curtain were being drawn across an open window. Only, instead of silencing the undulating roar outside, it grew louder.

"The same thing I told you, ser. It was dark, and I couldn't see well."

Dietmar glanced back over his shoulder as she spoke, staring into the growing pool of shadows in the corner of the room. The stained walls seemed to darken, the watermarks deepening so that long, thick striations covered their length, like the ribs of some emaciated boar.

Now, the figure lying supine on the bed was veiled by shadows, the contours of the face beneath the funeral cloth little more than ruffles in the fabric, like the creases left on the bed he shared with Enneleyn.

"I heard a sound coming from the stairs," Else continued. "At first, I thought it was one of Tobias's kittens. You know how they've started exploring and all. But when I got closer, I realised it was a voice."

"What did it say, this voice?" Timo pressed.

"I couldn't tell you. Those words weren't meant for me," Else hesitated, her own voice growing softer. "I believe it was a prayer. I called out, hoping it might be one of the stable boys playing about, trying to trick me like they always do..."

"Go on," Timo urged.

Dietmar's eyes followed the stains from the bed to the window. It lay open, its raw-bone frame vibrating softly as the sound from outside swelled.

"What is that?" Dietmar heard himself say, but the girl kept speaking. He knew that sound. He'd heard it before. But where?

"When I called out again, I saw something move at the top of the stairs." Else's voice quivered. "It was fleeting, and I wasn't sure I'd seen anything at all."

Dietmar took a step toward the window, turning to face it fully. The air felt close, the scent of damp clawing at his nostrils like a noxious taint. He was vaguely aware of the figure beside the bed staring at him again, the folds of its jaundiced face taking on an almost mycoidal aspect. Like an intruding spectre.

He ignored it.

Streaks of wispy cirrus clouds laced the sky beyond the window, embroidering the russet-coloured firmament like a quilted brocade. Something stirred beneath the heavens, as if the slumbering hills had awakened, rising like giants from their rest.

The window began to rattle as the roar grew louder, the glass dancing in its frame.

Not hills, Dietmar realised as he edged forward. *Waves. I am looking at waves.*

The ocean surged against the room's walls, spilling in through the leaks that permeated the roof like holes in a rotting hull. The coarse sky shimmered, swallowing up the thin clouds as it transformed into a swirling haze, a miasma of corposant colours above the turbulent sea.

"She must not have heard me," Else continued, undeterred. "She was standing near the edge of the stairs, her head tilted to one side, like she was listening to something. I… I…"

Dietmar blinked into the storm. Something was breeching in those waters, rioting in that vast expanse: a variegated form, a husk, a prodigious appendage—both colourless and somehow suffused with a shimmering sheen, like oil and midnight.

Dietmar strained to catch the girl's voice, her shrill words barely audible amidst the deafening void pouring in through the window.

"…She was gone so quickly," Else said, her voice trembling. "Before I could reach out to her… to grab her…"

"She slipped, didn't she?" said Timo. "That's what you told Father Sander, isn't it?"

There was a pause. A moment of quiet, uninterrupted by the chasm opening outside of the four walls they stood in. It lasted as long as a breath, a fleeting instance. Then, it shattered, with a roar like stones tumbling into the sea, an undulating horn resounding from the deep. Dietmar's body shook as he stared into the night, transfixed by the extraplanar fin rising from the sea.

He couldn't look away.

"That is what you told him, isn't it, Else?" Timo's voice cut through the inchoate roar, bringing Dietmar back to the room. "That is what you told him, Else?"

There was a susurrating hiss, like steel being unsheathed, like a dry scab being pulled from dead skin.

The figure in the corner of the room stirred, rising to its feet.

It seemed to occupy more space than it should have, its tattered white robes billowing as it moved. The motions were jagged, too fast and then too slow, uncoordinated and imbalanced. Dietmar caught a glimpse of gold where its fingers should have been, but it vanished, concealed beneath the swirling robes.

Dietmar's eyes flicked from the window to the aspect, giving it his full attention.

Why hadn't they noticed? he wondered as he watched its mouth open.

Else and Timo stood frozen beside him, unmoving. Their voices echoed around him, like distant reverberations in a cave.

"Speak, girl!" Timo demanded, his voice coming from far away.

The figure's mouth was an empty hole now, its jaws widening as it crossed the stone—*no, the wooden floorboards*. Water seeped through them. From the sea? The figure moved in front of the window, its elongated jaw extending further, until Dietmar found himself staring down its throat.

Grey teeth and a grey tongue collapsed inward, parting like the walls of a tunnel until he could see right to the back of the aspect's throat, and through the other side, to where the window stood.

Walls of black water surged in the darkness, enveloping the fin of a God rising from the depths. They would crash upon his home and sweep the land clean and then the world. Only then, when nothing was left, could something new be created. Something *better*.

Dietmar stared. He could no longer hear Else's stammering voice amidst the thunderous booms and call of the storm, but he already knew what she was saying. For within those vertiginous waves that bloomed like the folds of leathery wings spreading for the first time, he saw a truth long forgotten.

Enneleyn hadn't slipped.

She had jumped.

***

Dietmar awoke with a roar, his chest heaving beneath his sweat-stained gambeson. The sounds from his dreams followed him out, mingling with the waking world before dissipating, leaving him alone with his laboured breaths.

He tongued at his gums, feeling another tooth come loose in the back of his mouth. It was the third one in as many days. His spit tasted like iron and salt and faintly of something rotten. A blister on his tongue stung as he pressed it against the loose tooth.

He must have collapsed onto the cot sometime during the night. When the storm began to subside, Razin had departed for his own cabin, and then… Dietmar had sat staring from his window into the wash of salt and sea. How long he had remained there, he wasn't sure. Minutes? Hours?

The details of his dream came slowly back to him as he propped himself up on his elbows in the cot. Timo and Else, that small room and the figure on the bed. It had been a dark day. The roof had leaked the previous night. The past reeled in, opening to him as the wall he'd erected in his mind crumbled. That… *thing*, the tusk, the pillar of meat and bone emerging from the sea, had been there, pouring through the cracks in the walls. And Enneleyn…

Memory flooded through him, like the black waters through the window of his dream. They had found her in the courtyard, broken. Devoid of the spirit that had given him purpose, that had kept him going after Rudi's death.

When Adelman and Timo had knocked on his door in the early hours, Dietmar had awoken to find the bed beside him cold and empty. Even before he rose to open the door, he sensed that something was amiss. The world felt out of sync, like a dissonant note beneath a troubadour's chords—a moment of dislocation accompanied by a prickling unease on his skin. Yet, when Adelman and Timo had told him that his wife was dead, he hadn't believed them. How could he? To accept such a thing in that moment was to make it real. If he just hid from it, if he closed his eyes, went back to sleep… she'd be there when he awoke. But she hadn't returned, and Timo and Adelman hadn't left his side. Even with them standing there, uttering words of comfort, he had felt alone.

Dietmar became dimly aware of the presence beside him, slowly unfurling. It stretched, unwinding like rope from its tether. Though he couldn't see it, he sensed its gaunt visage—decayed and cadaverous. An emaciated spectre. The aspect from his dream.

She hadn't tripped.

The thought struck him like a hammer to the back of his head, causing him to shudder as if from a physical blow. She hadn't slipped in the rain or been dragged over the balustrade by the wind.

She'd jumped. She'd chosen death. Chosen it over him. But worse. He recalled Timo's agitated fidgeting, the nervous revelation that Father Sander had already come and gone.

She had damned herself.

Dietmar lurched upright in his cot, his brain tingling with an inexplicable itch. He rubbed his face. Ephium was still there, watching him in that unnerving way of his—quietly, a presence lurking just on the edge of his vision. He hated the feeling. He hated the taste in his mouth and the unctuous oiliness that now seemed as much a part of his skin as the fine hairs that covered his arms.

"What do you want?" Dietmar growled, forcing himself to focus and clear the rings from his eyes. A small oil lamp cast a flickering glow from a hook in the corner of the cabin. It made fitful impressions in the dark, its dirty light giving the room a monochrome hue, elongating the room's dimensions so that it appeared oblong, as if the threshold to the door had been pushed back while he slept.

He felt a sense of unease as something prickled across his skin, crawling like nails.

Ephium tensed as if to speak but faltered—a feeling like muscle being pulled tight and then relaxing. That putrid form nestled deeper into the folds of his mind, leeching into his thoughts like a mucal worm.

Disgusting parasitic thing.

Ephium leered.

Dietmar stifled a curse at a noise from the other side of his cot. Something had moved within the room—was *in* the room with him. He blinked into the dim light, slowly sliding his legs off the cot and reaching for his sword. His movements felt sluggish, as if he was moving through a mire. His muscles ached, and his arms felt heavy to lift. The dark clung to him like mud.

The floorboards creaked, hinting at the corporeal nature of his interloper.

Not a spectre, then, he thought.

Not some shadow leaking out from his dreams. He caught a glimpse of a slender figure beneath the lamp, cloaked in black, with hunched shoulders, a swivelling head and bloodshot eyes.

Dietmar lurched to his feet with a billowing groan, brandishing his sword at the figure. If he was going to get mugged by Malah's crew, he'd give a good accounting of himself before they got the rest of his coin.

"Show yourself!" he hissed, his breath like fire in his lungs.

There was a gasp, and the skulking figure stumbled back, waving its hands like a startled bird. It fell into the light, revealing a balding head and wrinkled grey skin, wide eyes and a mouth set in a determined line.

"Adelman?" Dietmar lowered his sword, his tone incredulous despite his relief. "What the Hell are you doing here, sneaking up on me like that?"

The old man hopped from foot to foot, the remnants of his grey hair plastered to his head, drenched with water.

"Christ's bones," Dietmar swore, leaning his sword against the cot's frame. "I could have run you through. What were you thinking?"

"I… I'm sorry," Adelman murmured.

Dietmar nodded slowly and then cocked his head, looking past his friend. The roar of the sea had diminished. There was still a savage groan echoing through the creaking bones of the ship, but it had lost the deafening ululation from before. Either the storm had passed, or they had passed through it and survived. Somehow.

Dietmar glanced about the room, to the open door and the briny water sloshing about the floor. He turned his gaze back to Adelman. The old man's eyes were hooded, his stare fixed on his feet.

"You still haven't told me what you're doing here," Dietmar stated, suddenly aware that he hadn't been alone with the bookkeep since they'd left Jerusalem. In fact, even before that. Seeing Adelman now, quivering in the dirty wash of light, his thin frame barely more than skin and bones beneath the oilskin he wore… The old man had been his constant companion, but also served as a reminder. From Germany through Middle Europe to the cities of the eastern empire, across the sea to Antioch, and finally, Jaffa and Jerusalem. Razin and Tomas carried their pasts hidden, their truths gradually revealed over the years. But with Adelman, there was no curtain to draw between past and present. Every moment between them was coloured by history. It was intoxicating, like being thrown back into that room, feeling every emotion batter against him over and over until he was raw.

He hated it. And he loathed himself for it. What had the old man done to deserve any of this?

—stole from you, lied to you… Worse, much worse

"What happened to your hand?" said Dietmar, noticing the red lines that covered the skin of Adelman's fingers. It looked like he'd been scratched or bitten. Adelman briefly glanced at his hand, turning it over before hiding it behind his back, a strange look on his face. He murmured something under his breath, finally meeting Dietmar's eyes.

"Demon?" said Dietmar, not sure he'd heard correctly. "On Malah's ship?"

Adelman nodded, stepping further into the room. His eyes were clouded grey. They moved slowly from Dietmar's face to his side, to the pouch still fastened at his belt.

"What is it?" Dietmar frowned, a sense of unease stirring in the pit of his stomach.

"The mules… They told me… God," Adelman murmured. He stared up at Dietmar, his voice petering out. Pain flickered across his features, then his eyes narrowed, his face hardening. "The hand!" he suddenly cried out, springing forward.

Dietmar's limbs felt as heavy as stone as he staggered back, just out of Adelman's reach. The old man howled, his face contorted. "Give it to me! Now, give it to me!"

Dietmar gasped as Adelman's nails scraped across his wrist, just below the sleeve of his gambeson. The skin tore like rotten fruit under the assault. A noxious stink filled the room, and Dietmar's head spun. He barely managed to compose himself and swat away Adelman's second attempt. He drew back another step and found his strength, grabbing onto Adelman's flailing arms, gripping them tightly, like a wrestler.

"What's wrong with you?" he growled as the old man writhed in his grasp. Jutting elbows dug into Dietmar's belly, and sharp heels stamped against his feet. But even in his weakened state, Dietmar was no match for the bookkeep.

"The hand…" Adelman paused his struggle, reaching for the pouch at Dietmar's belt. "It is the Devil's own! I swear it! The Devil's!"

Adelman grunted, wringing his wrist after Dietmar swatted it away. "It would see us in Hell. It drags us there to be whole again with its master. *Don't you see?*"

"Who told you this? Who is filling your head with this nonsense?" Dietmar's grip slackened, allowing the old man to spill from his arms, collapsing to the floor like a bag of bones. Adelman whimpered, wiping his nose with a dirty sleeve as he looked up at Dietmar.

"Speak, damn you!" Dietmar's fists clenched and unclenched at his sides. Waves of anger surged through him, turning his words into a thundering roar. It took him a moment to realise that he wasn't angry because Adelman had tried to steal from him. It was because what the old man said was true.

The cadaverous face from his dream flickered before him, those folds and folds of skin and a mouth that caved in on itself.

It could only be the Devil.

"Speak," he said again. But this time, his words weren't just for Adelman.

The voice stirred from deep within him, now intertwined with his blood and bones, his very being—a prison of flesh. But Dietmar was the prisoner here. The voice, his captor.

—what comes but once, a beginning without end. He is I, and I am that

"What? Enough with your oneiric riddles. Tell me what you are, damn you!"

Adelman stared at him wide-eyed, the whites of his eyes showing as he shook his head, not privy to the words in Dietmar's head. "It was the angels… the angels told me… They hear it too… You have been touched by the… by the Devil himself."

Ephium chuckled. There was a nightmarish quality to the sound, like a dried-up cadaver being peeled open.

—not even the Devil would touch you now. He might get some of you on his hands, the cowardly cretin

Adelman's gaze flickered to the pouch by Dietmar's side before meeting his eyes again. "Cast it overboard. Into the sea. Before it's too late."

—and see your son's soul lost for all time. A beginning without end

Adelman shuffled forward on his knees, his hands open before him. "Would you reduce an old man to begging? *Think*, Dietmar! Please! Before the hand, we saw none of the demons that now walk beside us. We have damned ourselves with its presence. We must… get rid of it or lose ourselves in this place forever."

Dietmar blinked at him, then ran his hands over his face and sighed. "The hand did not lead us here," he said softly. "We… slipped between places. Razin told me of this šubur and his theories—"

"I was there," Adelman snapped, a trace of his former self returning. "It is nothing more than a pagan trying to rationalise his own damnation. No, it is the hand. Believe me, you must. The angels—"

"*What angels?*" said Dietmar suddenly. It didn't feel like his words. It hadn't even sounded like his voice. He furrowed his brow in confusion.

"*The* angels," Adelman replied, wiping his nose and sniffing, then glancing past Dietmar to the door. There were footsteps approaching from the passageway. "They speak to me. They're lonely and sad since their master passed… but now they have me."

Dietmar shook his head, not understanding, but Ephium's sniggering voice sounded between his ears.

—the donkeys! Those asses! Haw, haw! Never met an angel that wasn't an ass

"Balaam?" Dietmar muttered. "Silensus?"

Adelman nodded. "They spoke to me that night amidst the rocks when the demons sang. They told me things."

"What things?"

The bookkeep rubbed his nose again, blowing it into his sleeve. "That you are sick," he said. "That… that you hear things. A voice. They hear it too."

Ephium's sniggering presence fell silent, and Dietmar could feel him staring out at Adelman from beside him.

The footsteps grew louder, hurrying along the corridor toward them. Dietmar turned as he heard his name, finding Razin's figure in the doorway. His friend's face bore a hardened expression, his eyes wide with urgency.

"Come," he hissed, gesturing to Dietmar with outstretched fingers.

"What is it?"

Razin showed his teeth, his lips curling back in a grimace. He looked past Dietmar, briefly acknowledging Adelman rising to his feet behind him, but did not blink.

"The crew," he said softly. "They're gone."

30

"I knew there was something wrong with those *cunting* searats," Geoff roared. "You can't trust them on a good day. And here? Where in Christ's name did they even go?"

Razin pointed across the deck, walking between Dietmar and Geoff toward the main mast. "They took the ship's boats. There were four of them."

"But that wouldn't be enough for the entire crew," said Dietmar. "One hundred men on four small boats? They must be here, somewhere. Have you checked the hold?"

"You're not listening," Adelman moaned, hurrying after them. "I saw them. They were *changing*. Turning into something else in the storm."

"Into what?" Geoff glanced over his shoulder at Adelman. "More beast men, is it?" He gave Dietmar a nervous look, and his hand moved to his sword.

"No, no," Adelman replied, skirting around the mast to get ahead of them. "Well, yes. But of the sea, with tails and fins and watery eyes."

"And you *saw* this?" Geoff asked.

"I… I think so, yes."

"Not so easily dismissed," said Razin gently. "Considering what we have seen these past days."

"Aye," Geoff nodded. "Still, why would they leave us here with their ship? To what end?"

Dietmar came to a halt beside the rope rail still suspended between the masts. The world around them had quieted, the undulating waves and deep booming rolls of thunder now absent. He gazed at the horizon, into the swelling patina, the chiaroscuro of cloud and mist that hung where the sky met the sea. As he watched, flickering lightning bloomed from within the distant storm. For a brief moment, he felt that feeling of dislocation once more, as if time was moving both backwards and forward simultaneously. He searched the shadows for that great appendage but saw no sign of it.

"A sacrifice," Razin spoke solemnly.

Dietmar turned around to look at him.

"What greater way to pay homage to their God of the sea than this?" Razin ran a hand along the rail, staring up at the tightly bound masts above. Dietmar followed his eyes.

Strange things hung from the ship's boom, nailed to the wood or swinging from rope and strings. Pulpy fish-things with octopoidal limbs, etiolated by a life in the deep, had been fastened to crudely hewn effigies—more of those humanoid statuettes with elongated skulls and swollen limbs. They swayed from the rigging like apples in an orchard, by the dozen. It seemed more of them had been strung up during the storm while they were below deck.

"Christ's nails," Geoff muttered, crossing himself. "A sailor's superstition, huh?" He turned to Dietmar and spat on the deck. "Bunch of heathen fish worshippers, that's what. And now they've left us here. For what?"

"Best rouse Levi and his girl," said Dietmar, glancing at Razin. "I'll go find Tomas and see if I can't find Tanit."

"Hunting rats in the dark, no doubt." Geoff barked, but his face was grim.

They all turned to the hold at a shout coming from the bowels of the ship. Moments later, Tomas's red hair appeared from the dark slit beneath the mast, his face flush, and his robes bunched up in his hands. He had lost a sandal.

He took a deep breath and steadied himself before pointing back down the way he'd come.

"Water… in the hold," he gasped. "We're sinking!"

***

"Those bastards scuttled us?" Geoff spat again, this time not bothering to wipe the spittle hanging from his mouth.

"Show me," Dietmar instructed Tomas. He quickly crossed the remainder of the deck to stand beside the Englishman. Together, they peered down the dark passageway, into the depths of the hold. Razin and Geoff joined them a moment later, with Adelman hobbling behind.

"I thought it was just the leaks," Tomas began, taking the first steps into the hold. "But the water kept coming. It just kept coming, until it was to my damn knees."

"The crew is gone," said Geoff bluntly.

"What?"

Dietmar nodded grimly. "It's just us now."

Tomas gave him a wide-eyed stare, his face disappearing into the shadows and then reemerging under the illumination of Razin's lit lamp.

Dietmar gestured toward the steps. "Show me," he said again quietly.

Tomas guided them down the steep stairs, into the belly of the Ishkur. The darkness seemed to swell here, breeching in the corners, spooling out from between the crooked beams and floorboards like the black coils of a rope, as if the ship itself was inhaling shadows. They retreated from the feeble light of Razin's lamp, slinking back into the dark places of the vessel to pool just a few steps away.

A desultory breeze coursed through the corridor, whistling through the cracks like a breath through broken teeth.

Dietmar's gaze traced the lines on the ceiling as they descended. The aged hardwood was marked by deep grooves. Ridges ran across its width, bringing to mind the walls of a serpent's throat. Each gust of warm wind felt like a breath from its belly.

He shuddered but pressed forward, reaching the floor of the hold just behind Tomas. Water gushed in from about a dozen small holes in the ship's hull, but they were mere pinpricks compared to the massive rupture in the stern. The sea fountained through it in an unwavering seam. The water had already risen to the third step of the stairway.

"Shit," muttered Geoff.

"Shit," Dietmar agreed.

Adelman pushed past them, wading into the hold and making for the two grey outlines standing hunched over the water. One of them *hawed*.

"We'll need a hammer and nails," said Dietmar. "And any scraps of wood we can find. We'll take them from the ship if needs be and seal these holes."

"Don't bother," said Razin. He gestured toward the other side of the hull.

Tomas let out a low moan.

A second hole had been carved into the Ishkur's hull, nearly as large as the first. Oily black water poured through it like a river mouth.

"What are we going to do?" Tomas was on the verge of panic. He stared around the hold, then looked up at Dietmar.

"Get off this ship," said Dietmar. They wouldn't be able to close those holes. Not before she'd taken on too much water. They'd have to take their chances on the open sea.

The ship groaned.

"Come on," said Dietmar. "We don't have much time. They've taken all the boats—"

Tomas moaned again.

"But we'll make do," Dietmar finished.

Adelman called out to them, waving an arm. He was pulling at Balaam's reins, but the dusty grey mule wouldn't move.

"He needs our help with the mules," said Tomas, dropping the last few steps into the water.

"Go on, then," said Dietmar, exchanging glances with Geoff and Razin.

There wouldn't be enough space for the mules.

***

Dawn found the Ishkur in tranquil waters, her prow leaning forward drunkenly, slowly succumbing to the sea. What waves there were lapped gently against the ship's keel, like delicate fingers beckoning her down into the watery depths.

A grey haze hung over them, a crude smog clinging to the lateen sails and spreading above the water. The sun bloomed dimly from behind the veil, its weak light fading as it passed through the unctuous air.

A somnolent wind rustled through the masts while they worked. Dietmar drove the last of his nails into a piece of wood salvaged from the ship's rails, then passed the mallet into Levi's waiting hand. They'd managed to cobble together something serviceable, he thought, stepping back to consider their work.

They'd gathered an assortment of flotsam: dismantled doors, slattern ribs from their cots, rail posts, broken panels from the floating crates in the hold, and even a make-do mast. The makeshift raft spread out over the deck, its frame reaching out over the Ishkur's starboard side. Once the ship began her final descent, they were going to push the ramshackle raft out into the open. Any earlier, and they risked rolling the raft as it slid into the sea, or worse, her frame snapping as she went overboard. It would need to be eased in, though they risked being dragged back by the Ishkur's wake.

Dietmar looked away from the raft, drawn to a string of curses emanating from the hold. Geoff appeared a moment later, struggling with the reins of one of the mules. The stubborn beast strained against his attempts, pulling back and stomping its hooves against the wooden floor.

"Blasted thing!" Geoff cried. "Come on, get out of there, you stupid donkey, or I'll leave you for the fishes."

The mule stopped just short of rearing up on its hind-legs but continued tugging at the reins, braying as it pounded its hooves against the splintered floorboards. Adelman hurried out from the shadows behind them, wiping his sweaty forehead and shaking his head at Geoff.

"All right. Then you do it," Geoff grumbled, thrusting the reins into Adelman's hands and stepping away from the hold. He glanced at Dietmar. "What's the point, anyway?" he said, but stopped when he saw the look Dietmar gave him.

The mule calmed under Adelman's gentle touch and allowed itself to be led onto the deck, where it was secured to the main mast. Adelman whispered a few quiet words in its ear before returning to the hold to help Tomas with the second mule.

Dietmar's eyes lingered on the mule, watching its grey head sway from side to side.

What does it understand of what it has seen? he wondered.

It had witnessed the great serpent in the basin, the wolf men of Ladah, strange chthonian limbs, and a city of glass and iron. Did it understand that things were not as they should be? Or was its perception limited to hunger and fear?

As if sensing Dietmar's scrutiny, the mule raised its large brown eyes to meet his gaze. Dirt clung to the fur beneath its eyes, and dried stains streaked its face like rivulets. It looked like the mule had been crying, its face stained like the statue of the Holy Mother in one of those fabled churches.

Dietmar found himself unable to match Balaam's unblinking stare and looked away, suddenly uncomfortable.

"There's something in the water." Razin's voice broke the silence, carefully modulated so as not to alarm the others.

He stood against the ship's railings—those that hadn't been cannibalised for their raft—and glanced at Dietmar before turning back to the sea.

Dietmar dusted off his hands and rose to his feet.

"Of course there is," he said, coming to stand beside his friend. "It wouldn't be our luck if there wasn't."

He peered over the rails, gazing at the undulating tide. White-mantled peaks crested the waves, like rippling fringes of fire.

He used to think the ocean was like the forests back home—vast and unknowable. Immense expanses you could never truly comprehend, leaving you with only glimpses of its true nature to satisfy your curiosity. But this sea was different. It was a smear upon existence. A stain spreading across the world's surface like a festering wound. He didn't *want* to know what resided beneath its waves, calm now as they were. He'd already seen enough.

He thought of that jutting fin then, that colossal flesh column rising, rising. A god, or demon, or both. He shook his head and stared into the water.

"There!" Razin pointed over the railing. "They ride the waves, drawing nearer the ship and then break beneath the surface to wait for the next wave to carry them in."

A flash of silver slipped under the nearest wave just as Dietmar caught sight of it. He leaned forward, tracking the shadow's path until it vanished beneath the murky tide. The wave broke against the Ishkur, and Dietmar's eyes followed the next swell. Shapes glided through the crest of the wave like serpents, their bodies graceful and sleek.

Chitinous heads bobbed in and out of the water, bone-white against the ocean.

"What are they?" Dietmar asked, watching a tail disappear beneath the wave. His hand moved to his sword instinctively, but the creatures slipped away before getting too close to the sinking vessel. They didn't need to come to the ship; its occupants would soon join them.

Razin stood in silence, watching the silhouettes dance beneath the waves. He seemed unbothered by their presence. But then again, he always seemed that way.

"They have been following us since the storm," Razin said, his brow knitting as his gaze flickered between Dietmar and the sea. "Perhaps this isn't the first time Malah has played this trick. They know a sinking ship means food."

"Everything here wants to eat us."

"Yes."

"But not their god… What we saw in the storm, it could have swallowed this ship whole."

Razin kept his eyes fixed on the ocean, but Dietmar saw his brow twitch. What they had seen had deeply affected Razin too.

"It was… We are…" Razin shook his head, rubbing the bridge of his nose. He let out a frustrated sigh. "We are beneath the notice of such a thing as that. Less than ants. If it hungers for anything at all, it is not us."

"*Bahamut*," Dietmar breathed. The word felt different on his tongue now that he had seen the entity that bore its name, sounded different in his ears.

"It is no god," said Razin, snapping his eyes to look at Dietmar.

"Then what is it? How can something… something so vast be anything but a god?"

His friend leaned forward on the railing, picking at the wood with a nail. "You have your Leviathan, your Behemoth. Do you think they are any less? No, my friend. And yet they still fit within the natural order of things."

"Order?" Dietmar couldn't help but laugh. "You think God had a hand in making these things? The beast men? Your black snake? Bahamut? What about Lamassu?"

Razin's frown deepened. "Where did you hear that name?"

—tell him

Dietmar hesitated, the words on the tip of his tongue. Was it Ephium that stopped him, or something else? He suppressed a cold shiver. The justifications rose unbidden, pushed forward by the spectre in his mind or by his own unconscious thoughts: *Save Rudi! Save the Hand! Save Rudi!* Until it felt like a single unbroken thought repeating itself.

Shaking his head, Dietmar leaned against the rail next to his friend. He nodded toward the waves. "You saw that storm, didn't you? Did it not seem to you an ancient thing, like something from Creation? A question that survives its answers."

Razin's searching gaze met Dietmar's unwavering eyes. After a moment, Razin nodded. "Perhaps," he said simply, looking back to the sea, "We Muslims, but you Christians too, understand that if it exists in creation, it is by Allah's hand. There is no God but Allah."

"I know your words."

Razin snorted. "But they are more than just words. If we attribute the power of creation to another entity, it undermines the concept of God itself. God, by His nature, is supreme. It cannot be that there is another God, as it would also need to be supreme! And if it is not supreme but subordinate to another, then it is not God. Do you understand? There is only one God because there can be no other way."

"Or perhaps there are no gods at all."

Razin smiled thinly. "It would take a brave man to think thusly."

The Ishkur groaned and shuddered, leaning further into the waves. Her creaking bow was now fully submerged, and the lower decks were flooded. Dietmar glanced over his shoulder and saw Geoff and Levi securing the last of the cannibalised boards to their rickety vessel. It looked like they'd broken off the doors to the cabins too.

"We'll need those harpoons," said Dietmar, his eyes returning to the shapes in the water. He turned away from the railing, making for the lower decks, but paused, looking back at his friend.

Razin hadn't moved.

"Bahamut," Dietmar said softly. The word hung in the air, and for a moment, he wondered if its mere utterance could summon the colossus from the waves again.

Razin blinked, his reverie broken.

"It is written about in the *Lives of the Prophet*," Razin began. "And in the great cosmologies. *Lutīyā*, *Balhūt*… Bahamut. They say that the universe, all of creation, rides upon its back in a vast sea that spans the length and breadth of time itself."

"These people worship it as a God."

"It is not a god."

Dietmar looked past his friend, his gaze fixed on the grey skies behind him. "What happens when it breaches? When it emerges from the cosmic sea to gaze upon the world on its back?"

Razin hesitated, caught off guard by the question. "I… It would be…"

"An end of things," Dietmar finished.

Razin nodded silently and turned back to watch the sea.

Dietmar left him to his thoughts.

***

"I found her lurking about the kitchens," Geoff announced, emerging from below deck. He pulled Tanit ahead of him while balancing a bundle of harpoons cradled in his arms. "She nearly got away from me. Would have, if I hadn't been catching street kids since afore she was even a kitten, eh, girl?"

Tanit hissed at Geoff as she climbed the last steps onto the main deck.

"Cheeky thing," grinned Geoff. "Doesn't know what's good for her neither. Do you understand, girl? *You will drown here, yes?*"

"She's a mute, not a fool," said Tomas, motioning for her to come closer. He placed a folded blanket on the floor next to him and smiled warmly.

Tanit's golden-green eyes glanced at the blanket and then at Tomas before she made her way to the other side of the deck to join Levi and his daughter, leaving wet footprints behind.

"Maybe she does know what's good for her," Geoff barked. His laughter faded as the Ishkur growled beneath them, her hold and lower decks straining as they bore the weight of the sea pouring in. The deck shuddered and creaked as the Ishkur slipped further beneath the waves and then went still, her passage suspended by some hidden air pocket still to be swallowed up by the water.

"Not long now," Geoff declared. He lowered the pile of harpoons onto their ramshackle vessel before climbing aboard himself. "Might do to offer a prayer to one of those sea gods you mentioned about now."

Dietmar followed Geoff's gesture, his gaze landing on the effigies nailed into the Ishkur's rigging. They baked in the weak light, the silver scales that covered their bodies turning into lamina in the sun. They must have been freshly made, just in time for their arrival aboard the Ishkur.

Dietmar snarled, thinking of Malah's betrayal. The captain had taken half his coin too. If he ever saw that sea dog again… But deep down, he knew that he would never see Malah and his crew again. They had likely retreated to the safety of Ubar's harbour, leaving Dietmar and his companions to their fate. The most Dietmar could hope for was that they would be drawn back into the storm, their tiny ship's boats swallowed up by their god's berthing.

"Do you think that's what's in the water?" asked Tomas, his voice soft. He was staring at the nearest fish-thing nailed into the railing by their raft. They had chosen to leave the post behind, not wanting to invite any further misfortune.

One of the mules *hawed* from where Adelman was attending to them near the forecastle. Dietmar hadn't the heart to tell the old man that they wouldn't be coming with, but by the sombre look on Adelman's face, he already knew.

"I haven't had a proper look at them," said Geoff, scratching his chin. He crouched down beside Tomas, taking the blanket meant for Tanit. "But if I had to guess…"

"Yes," Dietmar replied simply. He let his eyes linger on the craven shape. In the light, it was no less repulsive. Its mouth stretched wide, devoid of teeth—an empty void. Human lips and eyes, too large for the face, only added to the strange sense of *wrongness* emanating from the idol.

Dietmar blinked, his attention drawn to Razin's voice. His friend appeared, ascending the steps a moment later. His face was hard-set, his eyes grim.

"It's time," Razin announced, motioning to the raft. The ship groaned once more, a low rutting sound as her lower decks succumbed to the sea. There was a splintering sound from below and then glass breaking as water flooded the cabins.

"Slowly and then all at once," said Geoff, getting to his feet. "Right, help me push."

The raft was splayed out between the front and main masts, resting on three round timber shafts that Geoff had cut from the deck to use as rollers. A single cruciform mast rose from its centre, securely fastened to the planks and further reinforced with ropes extending to each corner of the vessel. A patchwork sail was folded across its top yard, the fruit of Tomas's fishing through the crates in the hold.

Dietmar leaned against the raft, making room for Levi to squeeze in beside him. Geoff and Razin pulled from up front, standing where the rails once stood, overlooking the sea. Tomas threw his own weight in behind Dietmar, groaning as his muscles strained.

"Once it's over, don't wait around!" Dietmar shouted. Anyone caught off the raft would be dragged back into the swell of the ship, sucked under with her. He'd seen it once before, coming into the harbour of Otranto after a storm. A cog had become ensnared on the reef, scraping her hull open. The quicker crewmen had managed to scramble overboard before she went under, but the cabin boy and cook had been swallowed by the sea. They'd been no more than a hundred yards from the shore.

The raft started to move. A crack, like a tree being pulled from its roots, echoed from somewhere beneath their feet. Dietmar lurched forward as the raft slid, gaining momentum as the Ishkur tilted toward the sea.

"Get on!" he yelled, waving at Tanit. She stood frozen, staring at the ocean with wide eyes. In a moment of panic, she turned her head to face Dietmar, her eyes darting around like a trapped animal. Then Tomas was by her side, pulling her onto the raft.

Dietmar glanced back at the panicked mules. They were throwing their hooves against the deck, their distressed brays echoing in ragged breaths. He looked back at the raft, counting Razin and Geoff, still pulling it forward, Levi climbing in beside his girl, and Tomas clinging on to Tanit while she watched the sea with mounting alarm.

"Where's Adelman?" he heard himself say.

He scanned the deck, searching for the old man, calling out his name.

The Ishkur was nearly at ninety degrees, with rope and netting from her rigging stretching out like a spider's web across the deck. The strange iron cylinders started spinning, the dark ropes unspooling like a weaver's web, their ends already cast out into the sea.

Where is he? The doddering old fool.

He thought he glimpsed a figure moving along the rope rail, a wiry frame clad in an oilskin coat.

"Adelman!" Tomas called, adding his voice to Dietmar's. "What is he thinking? He'll be dragged down with the ship."

Tomas made to get up from his seat, but Dietmar waved him down. "I'll get him," he said, turning from the raft.

He picked his way across the deck, holding onto the rope rail as he navigated the space between the two masts.

Something splashed in the water to his left.

He stared across the slowly flooding deck, searching for the source of the sound, but could only see tangled ropes and nets being carried away by the waves.

Razin called to him, his voice urgent.

But… *there*. A figure moving along the rails.

"Adelman!" Dietmar bellowed, pulling himself forward, his hands aching from the strain. He could feel his skin tearing against the rope, splitting open like ripe fruit and bringing that rotten stench with it. He tried not to breathe it in.

Water was sweeping across the deck now, Razin's voice growing more urgent.

One of the mules kicked out at something up ahead, a shape moving in the corner of his eye. There was a garbled cry, like air escaping a deflating wineskin. Then Dietmar saw a form slipping back into the water, leaving a trail of ichor in its wake.

"I won't leave them!" Adelman cried, appearing from behind one of the iron spandrels further ahead. He stood beside the rope rail, his one hand clutching the reins of the grey mule. "They won't... They *can't...*" His voice faltered, his eyes darting between Dietmar and the mule. Some internal conflict played out on the old man's face, turning it into a fluid thing, like molten wax, never settling.

Then Adelman pointed a trembling finger at the pouch by Dietmar's side, his eyes hardening like flint. "They hear it. They hear the thing that speaks to you. That *lies* and fills your ears with filth, like spores and rotting, rotting, *rotting!*"

Dietmar felt his hand move over the pouch protectively, and something, something deep within the recesses of his mind, stirred.

"What are you talking about, you old fool? We need to go *now!*"

Adelman shook his head, stabbing the air with his fingers toward the pouch. "It is leading us to Hell, don't you see?" He wiped his nose with a dirty sleeve and leaned heavily against the mule.

Balaam, Dietmar thought.

The mule's panicked braying had ceased. It simply stood there now beside its master.

Staring at Dietmar.

"It wants to be with its master!" Adelman's voice rose in pitch, his words tumbling out in a frantic babble. "The angels... *my* angels. They told me. The hand, it wants to be whole again!"

There was a hiss, but not from the rising sea or even from the Ishkur's creaking bones. It emanated from the depths of Dietmar's blood and flesh.

—*lies*, came the voice, in something close to a moan—an obscene gasp.

Balaam flicked his ears back and stomped a hoof, its mane bristling.

Could it be? Had it heard the Saint's voice in his ears? The mule stomped its front hoof again, sending splinters across the deck.

Adelman glanced at the distressed mule, his eyes narrowing.

"It is speaking to you now, isn't it? Telling you horrible things. About us. About the world. About… me?" Adelman's expression softened suddenly, his grey brows unfurling like the wings of an owl.

"What does it say about me?"

"We must go, please," Dietmar pleaded. "Adelman, you're not making any sense."

Another voice hissed beneath his own.

—*leave him. He is not worth the breath you have wasted getting here. Or have you forgotten what he did?*

"Tell me what it says?" Adelman's eyes widened, his nose now running freely. "It's poisoned you against me, hasn't it?"

Dietmar shook his head. "No."

—*no Christian burial for your wife and son, no, no… But where did the coin go? Into those greasy little palms, lost between his ink-stained fingers. Little thief! He takes and takes! He stole from you for years. You are not your father. And look at you now. Seven of your years lost because he couldn't keep his hands off your coin!*

Dietmar growled under his breath, willing the voice to silence while wondering if it wasn't all true.

"I can see it in your eyes," Adelman cried. "It has, it has!"

Dietmar tried taking a step forward, but Balaam brayed loudly and shook his head from side to side. It watched him with its keen, brown eyes, too canny for those of a mere dumb animal.

The ship moaned again, longer this time, like a mournful ululating cry from the deep. Its death rattle.

Something broke beneath their feet, giving way to the ocean, like ribs being pried open by a massive watery hand.

"Adelman, please!" Dietmar ignored the braying mule, desperate now for his friend to follow him back to the raft. He could hear Razin and Tomas shouting. It wouldn't be long before they risked themselves too.

"I can't leave them," Adelman muttered, blinking his wet eyes. "My angels… No, no, I can't. I won't." He threw an arm around Balaam's neck, hugging it tightly as Dietmar crept cautiously forward.

"Listen to me!" said Adelman suddenly, causing Dietmar to pause, one hand hanging onto the rope rail and the other pressed against the mast.

Adelman's voice was barely audible over the ship's groaning and the clamour of his companion's shouts. Dietmar leaned closer against the rail, straining to hear.

"The hand," Adelman whispered. "You must do away with it… cast it into the sea! Please, I beg of you. Do it now before it's too late."

"Come with me," Dietmar implored, opening his hand and reaching out to Adelman. "We can talk about it once we're all off this damn sinking ship."

Adelman blinked, his thick brows wedged together. He took a hesitant step forward, still clinging to Balaam's neck.

"That's right," Dietmar encouraged. "Just a few more steps, then we'll get off this thing, safe and sound."

Adelman took another step but then froze, his gaze fixed on something behind Dietmar.

—Silensus

Too late, Dietmar registered the creak of wood beneath heavy hooves and the musky scent of the second mule. He spun around, leaning back against the rail, and cried out as Silensus reared over him, lashing out with its hooves.

"No, don't!" Adelman screamed, lunging forward.

Dietmar glimpsed block teeth and a fleeting russet blur.

The air was knocked out of him as the hooves found his chest, sending him spinning across the deck. He bounced off the main mast and came to a stop against one of the iron cylinders. He gasped, just managing to pull his arm away from the unspooling rope before it entangled him.

Dietmar tried to get up but found that he couldn't. His legs wouldn't obey him, feeling numb and lifeless beneath him. The mule had broken at least two of his ribs. He tasted blood in his mouth. Another tooth came loose against his tongue. Streaks of midnight ran across his vision, darkness encroaching from the periphery like a rolling fog.

"Why did you do that?" Adelman cried, staring at the mule. "You said you wouldn't hurt him."

Silensus brayed back, placing himself between Dietmar and the old man.

Water was coming up to his boots now, spilling over the Ishkur in a rising swell. He heard footsteps approaching, Tomas's voice cursing, Razin issuing urgent instructions. Then, he felt strong hands grip him, pulling him through the water.

He looked up, blinking into the pale light just as his vision started to blur.

Tomas called out to Adelman, pleading with the old man to join them.

He wouldn't come.

The last thing Dietmar saw before he was dragged aboard the raft was the old man standing in the middle of the sinking deck. He stood between his two mules, their heads resting on his shoulders, their ears pressed back, waiting for the sea to claim them.

Then his vision swam, and he closed his eyes.

31

Dietmar lay somewhere between sleep and death, his consciousness adrift like the raft upon the black waters as fever consumed him. When he dreamed, he dreamed of Enneleyn. Of her hand resting upon the small of his back, of her quiet words when he said something wrong or acted carelessly. He had marvelled at her ability to bring him back in line after a churlish comment or brash action with just a whisper. She had been so small beside him, but her presence had been greater than that of any faris or Frankish knight he'd faced down.

Between his dreams, he caught glimpses of the world around him.

He saw his friends from behind his fluttering eyelids. Worried faces staring down at him. They prayed for him, cursed Malah and his crew, fought and bickered among themselves… and then went quiet.

But the quiet didn't last long.

A scream shattered the stillness, followed by the sound of a splash and a menacing roar. The raft beneath him swayed as frantic limbs scurried across its surface. There was a smell: salt and kelp and old fish, an effluvia that filled his nostrils and made him gag. A mellifluous susurration accompanied the stink, a singsong murmur that sounded like voices echoing from beneath the waves, keening and cooing as they approached the raft.

Dietmar forced his eyes open, wiping away the perspiration and drowsiness. Through his blurred vision, he saw Geoff lunge beneath the mast, brandishing a harpoon like a knight's lance. Razin stood beside him, swinging his scimitar in elliptical arcs, striking at the gaping pale faces thrashing in the water around the raft. Dietmar blinked again, wincing at the sharpness of the pain at his side. Then he stared.

A white, gelatinous creature was dragging itself onto the raft, its long, slimy limbs reaching out. Translucent appendages wrapped around one of the posts, pulling and straining against the rails that held their floating refuge together. Geoff unleashed a curse and attacked the creature, driving the harpoon into its writhing, gooey flesh. His yell turned into a roar of triumph as the harpoon broke through the creature's skin, spraying the deck with spumes of oily black blood. The roar became a gasp when a squirming tentacle plucked the weapon from his hands and sent him careening across the raft. Geoff barely managed to stay aboard, fending off the grasping hands that reached for him from the water and rolling away from their clutches.

Dietmar struggled to sit up and nearly blacked out from the effort. His ribs were like hot needles in his side, swollen and throbbing. He reached out, his hand groping blindly for his sword, patting the empty planks beside him, unable to turn his head to search properly.

"Where are… you…" he grunted through shallow breaths. "You worm… bastard."

He could *feel* Ephium watching his every move, coiled tight, tense and… Was that a sense of nervousness exuding from the cadaverous spectre, the grey snake inside his mind? Dietmar could hardly distinguish his own emotions from Ephium's anymore. But there, amidst the murky folds of his mind, a tiny white stain of cowardice: uncertainty. Fear. The Saint was scared. Dietmar smiled.

A shadow moved over him as he made another attempt to rise. He felt a hand on his shoulder, a firm touch, then the outline of the girl appeared in front of him. Tanit. She hissed at something out of sight, then lunged forward. Frantic scrambling ensued, accompanied by rending noises, a muffled cry, and the sound of a splash.

The girl appeared, hovering over Dietmar once more. Her mouth and hands were smeared with a black watery substance. She spat something over the side of the raft and grinned at Dietmar, her teeth glinting in the wan light.

Dietmar's head started to swim again, and this time he let the darkness take him.

Day had turned from light to dark and then to light again by the time Dietmar was fully awake. He rose with caution, mindful of his tender ribs, as he pulled himself into a sitting position. Someone had removed his hauberk and gambeson while he had slept and tried their best to bandage his waist. He recognised the strips of cloth from Tomas's robes and the light blue fabric of Razin's keffiyeh.

He looked up and saw the girl observing him. She sat perched on the edge of the raft, her arms folded over her legs, resting her chin on her knees. Her two front teeth showed from behind her cleft lip. They were stained dark.

"Water," Dietmar rasped. His lips cracked with the word, and he tried not to wince.

Tanit tilted her head but didn't move.

"Here," Razin offered, walking carefully across the boards. He extended a waterskin toward Dietmar, crouching down beside him.

"Thank you," Dietmar croaked. He took a few short sips, rinsing his mouth, and then a larger pull before feeling Razin's hand on his shoulder.

"We don't have much," Razin murmured softly.

Dietmar nodded, corking the skin and returning it to Razin. He remembered waking up on his back after the sandstorm had hit, not knowing where he was. Razin had appeared beside him to coax him into wakefulness then too. It had barely been more than a week since that fateful day. To his body, it felt like years.

He glanced down at his scabby skin, a shock of red now after lying in the sun. He'd lost both fat and muscle. His arms looked thin and feeble, barely thicker than his bony wrists. Boils covered his chest and shoulders like the leather folds of a lizard's hide. He spotted another of those peculiar growths emerging beneath his collarbone. It was the same size as the others, a three-sided shape as long as his thumb, its narrow tip pointing toward his belly. He considered it for a moment before shifting his gaze to the open sores that had formed around his right nipple.

He could only wonder at what might be waiting for him beneath the bandages.

Dietmar let out a sigh, catching Razin's expression as he glanced back up. His friend couldn't hide the worry in his eyes.

"Adelman?" Dietmar asked before Razin could speak.

His friend shook his head slowly. "We waited for as long as we could, but he wouldn't come. Tomas tried to grab him, but..."

"The mules?"

"They wouldn't let us near him. It was... a strange thing..."

"We have seen many strange things," Dietmar murmured, his gaze fixed on his lap, his lips moving in a silent prayer for his friend. When he looked back up, Razin was eyeing the boils on his chest.

"It is getting worse, whatever ails you."

"Aye."

"It is not..." Razin hesitated, glancing over his shoulder to ensure Tomas and the others weren't within earshot. "...It is not plague that has caused this?"

Dietmar shook his head.

"Then it is something else." Razin paused again, giving Dietmar time to fill the gap. But when he was not forthcoming, Razin wrinkled his brow. "You will be in my duas, my friend." He rose to his feet. "Now rest, regain your strength. We will need your arms for the oars soon. Levi thought he saw something on the horizon—a smudge. Perhaps it is the storm again, and we are not long for this world. Or..."

"Land," said Dietmar.

Razin touched his shoulder gently. "We shall see. But for now, I will pray for your health and for the wind." He offered Dietmar a thin smile before returning to the others by the long wooden planks they used as oars. Razin sat down beside Tomas, who glanced Dietmar's way but didn't meet his stare.

"Aye, I'm still here," said Dietmar, seeing Tanit staring at him. "I'm not going anywhere anytime soon."

He groaned, placing a tentative hand on his side. When he didn't black out from the pain, he fingered the offending ribs gingerly. Two of them, broken for sure. That would make things difficult if they ever managed to get off this damned sea.

"What's out there?" he asked aloud, leaning back on his elbows and looking out over the water. Something felt different about the ocean, he thought. It was dark, yes, but no darker than the wintry seas back home. It no longer held that antagonistic tension, that promise of secrets unveiled, of violence and unmaking. Now it was just an ocean like any other.

His eyes came to rest on a thin smudge on the horizon, little more than a shadow—a hair's width and length.

"You know that place?" he asked, looking to the girl.

She unfurled her legs, rolling onto her belly to lie on the edge of the raft. Her one hand hovered over the water, skimming its surface as she stared into its depths.

"No, then," said Dietmar lazily. The warm sun was making him sleepy again, and he lay back down. "Just more things that want to eat us. But not me. I'm just skin and bones. I wouldn't fill a plate."

He blinked his eyes back open at a sound—a soft laughter.

"So you do understand me after all," he said.

She turned her head to stare at him with those leonine eyes of hers and then looked back into the water, submerging her hand beneath the waves.

"Fair enough," said Dietmar. "Wake me when we find land or if something tries to eat me—even if it is just old Tomas."

The girl laughed again, and Dietmar couldn't help but smile as he closed his eyes.

***

Dietmar awoke, still caught in the throes of memory—dreams of his past that blurred with his nightmares. Visions of the sinking ship appeared before him—the haunting image of Adelman and his mules, the dark waters rising, rising. From those depths, insalubrious shapes appeared, slopping onto the ship like fleshy maggots with great anaemic wings and pulsating veins. Adelman and his mules glowed with light, enough to make his eyes flicker, but they remained closed.

He saw the pages of an impossible map, layers of images overlapping in an endless cascade of colour and contorting patterns—an impossible tapestry. As he watched, more lines appeared on the pages, inky tendrils that formed an intricate weave. It branched out in every direction, spilling out into the world like an enormous web. Through the web, he saw the pages turn to ash and then water, unfurling across the dream in a relentless wave—a vast and timeless ocean of making and unmaking.

Within it, something stirred—a shifting shadow beneath the tide.

He gasped, opening his eyes.

The surge had subsided, but the ocean remained.

"Are you with us, German?" Razin's voice reached Dietmar's ears, prompting him to lift his head and take in his surrounds. Choppy waves battered their raft, making it buck and heave like an unbroken horse beneath them. The distant skyline had taken on a gossamer glow, blending seamlessly with the sea in an unearthly kiss as the day leaked out its last.

Razin stood a short distance away, leaning over the raft's edge with his sword in his hands. He was staring into the water.

"They will try again before we reach the shore," Razin murmured, briefly glancing at Dietmar before returning his attention to the watery expanse. "Can you stand? We will need your strength if we are to hold them off."

Dietmar rubbed his face and sat up properly. His skin had started to itch again, and bits of it came off in dry, flaky scabs beneath his fingers.

"Shore?" he murmured. His eyes widened slowly, and he looked past the hunched figures of Geoff and Tomas rowing beneath the mast.

In the half-light, Dietmar made out a stretch of land emerging from the waves ahead. A grey beach adorned with protruding tusks of stone and blooming kelp came into view. Jagged spires of rock rose from the shallow waters before the beach, sculpted by the wind and sea. They caged the coastline like limestone bars, their lacerated surfaces awash with ocean spray. The murky waters around them teemed with coiled shapes—fields of kelp and skeins of sand, swirling with the rhythm of the tides.

Beyond the beach, sandy dunes extended into the distance, merging with the deepening shadows of the encroaching night. Vague outlines of hazy peaks bestrode the shadowy horizon. Three sprawling mountains stood like stooped old women, their heads lost to the firmament above.

Could it be? Dietmar wondered.

Have we found the Daughters at last?

Hope swelled in his breast, but it was a fleeting thing, and he quickly quelled the emotion. This was not a place for hope.

Dietmar took a deep breath and leaned unsteadily on his hands. His side throbbed in protest, but he was committed now and slowly straightened to his full height. Razin saw the piteous look on his face and took a step toward him, extending a hand, but Dietmar waved him away.

"I'm fine," he gritted through clenched teeth. "Or, I will be. Just… give me a moment."

Razin nodded and returned to his position at the edge of the raft. He balanced on its edge, his eyes shifting between Dietmar and the choppy seas.

"There!" called Tomas, pointing frantically at something in the waves. He raised his oar, careful not to lose balance, while Geoff leaned over the raft beside him, a second harpoon levelled at the water.

Dietmar cast a quick look around the raft, searching for his sword. His eyes skimmed over the other occupants as he hobbled toward the mast, eventually spotting the cruciform hilt. Levi crouched down in front of his girl, gripping the ends of a tangled net in each hand. Tanit was crouched a few paces away from Tomas and Geoff, weaponless—her dirty nails curling like talons by her side.

But where is Adelman?

Dietmar felt himself deflate as he remembered the old man's fate. Why hadn't he listened? Why hadn't he come with?

The hand, he thought bitterly.

This cursed fucking thing. I should throw it into the sea and be done with it.

But would that change anything? Would the voice stop whispering, chittering like a mad simian in the back of his mind? Or was it lodged there now, as much a part of him as his skin and bones?

He yanked his sword out from the bundle of rags containing their scant possessions: a few waterskins, bread loaves, dried meat salvaged from the Ishkur's kitchens, a half-empty oil lamp, and a handful of rolled-up blankets. That was it. That was all that remained of their company's supplies from their departure in Jerusalem all those weeks ago.

And that fucking hand.

Dietmar looked around, his gaze sweeping over the rolling tide that carried them closer to the beach. With the oars no longer needed, a gentle breeze caught the sails, causing them to billow like pale leathery wings.

Geoff lowered his harpoon, still poised over the ocean.

"There's nothing there… not anymore," he murmured. His eyes fixed on a wave coming in, his body tensing as he searched for any signs of movement beneath the surface. But when the wave passed without event, he shook his head and signalled to Tomas. "Come on, let's bring her into shore. We'll need to keep those peaks at bay with our oars, or we're getting smashed to splinters in the bay."

"It was right there," said Tomas, still gripping his oar. His voice was subdued and tired. He blinked away from the sea and saw Dietmar watching him. He shrugged. "A long grey tentacle, I thought…"

"Or maybe kelp," said Geoff, dropping his harpoon onto the deck and picking up a makeshift oar. He nodded toward the nearest rock spire, which now loomed ominously over them, its jagged edifice like the scorched walls of a lava pit. "We'll deal with the fish-men again when they come, but we won't stand a chance if we're bobbing in the sea like seals without a raft."

"Geoff's right," said Dietmar. He took a slow step toward the mast, his arm pressed against his swollen side. He motioned toward the blossoming sail, wincing at the movement. "Let's wrap up the sail and bring her in by oar alone. Given the tide, we'll have little control near the beach without the wind complicating things further."

"What about those *things?*" said Sara. It was the first time Dietmar had heard her speak aloud since Ladah. Her voice was firmer than he remembered, than he would have expected after what she'd seen.

"Sereine," said Levi, putting an arm around her shoulder. "They're gone now. You don't have to worry." He stared up at Dietmar, imploring him with a look.

"They don't like the coast," said Razin from behind him. Whether that was true or not, Dietmar didn't know, but he nodded all the same. The girl needed reassuring.

They all did.

He turned his attention to the nearest rocky spires, squinting in the fading light as the towering sea-masts grew closer. The waves crashed against their sides, frothing in a configuration of mist and ocean where the currents converged. Crude stone formations jutted out from the base of the spires, encircling them like an uneven crown of variegated rock. Dietmar eyed the sharp peaks sticking out of the water with unease. There was no way of knowing if more of them lurked in the gap between the spires, waiting just beneath the surface to tear the raft apart as they passed.

Geoff turned to Dietmar, a humourless smile twisting his lips. "That little cunt, Gelmiro, is going to get it when this is all said and done." He hawked and spat over the raft, then turned to face the spires.

"Slowly does it," he called as the roar of waves breaking against rocks grew louder.

Dietmar reached up toward the mast, helping Tomas with the sail. His friend's eyes darted nervously with each collision of the waves. Together, they carefully rolled up the fabric, stowing it against the creaking beam.

The raft shuddered violently as it scraped against something sharp and jagged. There was a groan and the sound of wood splintering. Dietmar held his breath, locking eyes with Tomas, both of them bracing against the mast, waiting for the planks beneath them to give way like they had on the Ishkur, like the world had… but the raft held.

"It's going to be close!" Geoff's voice boomed. He held onto the rope securing the mast to the corner of the raft and pushed with his oar. It cut through the water, nearly disappearing as Geoff's arm strained beneath its weight. The mercenary bared his teeth, cursing as he pulled the oar out of the water to fend off the impending rocks.

Dietmar could only watch as they raced toward the tallest of the two spires, pulled closer by the relentless force of the slipstream between the rocks.

A yell erupted from behind him, and Dietmar turned his head to see Razin slashing at the water beneath the raft. Gripping the rope, Dietmar pulled himself across the swaying vessel, grunting with each step as the rope pressed against his side.

Razin was hacking at a flailing limb, his sword slicing through mounds of sticky flesh from an oozing appendage as it tried to straddle the raft. Another tentacle rose from the water, its anaemic skin striated by pulsing black veins. It hovered in the air above Razin, twisting like an antenna, as if sensing the world around it, tracking its prey. It quivered for an infinitesimal moment, and then it shot down toward the raft.

Razin cried out as the whorling barb slammed into his shoulder, sending him spinning across the deck like a ragdoll. He came to a rest at Dietmar's feet, clutching his injured shoulder. The mail beneath his burnous had been cut clean through, the skin beneath punctured by the creature. Blood streamed from a ragged fold of skin, and Dietmar glimpsed the white of bone between Razin's trembling fingers.

The creature writhed onto the deck, hissing and screeching in some foul register that made Dietmar's skin crawl. Pulsing ocular sockets emerged from beneath the beast's octopoidal limbs, attaching themselves to the raft. It screeched again, the sound spat out from a slowly widening concavity at the base of its flailing limbs. A distended maw appeared, a dark slit expanding inexorably.

"Kill that fucking thing!" Geoff bellowed. He stood at the edge of the raft, leaning perilously over the water, tightly gripping the rope as he pushed away the rocks. He whipped his head around, his eyes filled with fear and rage, and locked onto Dietmar. "Kill it! Before it drags us under!"

Dietmar broke free from his momentary torpor, pushing off from the mast and drawing his sword. He could hear Ephium chattering in the depths of his mind, agitated and alarmed.

It knew what he was going to do and didn't approve. He ignored the rictus thing and stumbled forward, reaching for the mast's rope. His hand found its grip, and he pulled himself up against it, wedging the rope beneath him while he regained his balance.

He was vaguely aware of Razin calling to him from somewhere behind and Tomas's silhouette in the corner of his eye. His friend was holding something—an oar… No, a harpoon.

The creature contorted its body, growing larger as more of its grotesque form emerged from the water. The skin around its mouth trembled, rippling in an oscillating pattern as the opening expanded further. Bilious exudations streamed from the hole, releasing a putrid stench like the fumes from some stygian pit.

Dietmar hesitated, momentarily awed by the monstrosity rising before him. The creature's mouth-cavity flared, widening like the swollen lips of a labia, pregnant with the promise of something within.

But his awe was quickly replaced by atavistic disgust, propelling him forward. With a wide arc, he swung his sword before him, aiming it at the heart of the abomination.

A clutch of tentacles thrashed through the air, lashing across the deck with unnatural speed. At the same moment, Tomas leapt forward, hurling his harpoon at the noxious creature's quivering core. The harpoon glanced off one of the writhing appendages, slicing through a constellation of pursing suckers before embedding itself in the limb's trunk. Ichor splattered across the deck, coating it in a viscous, repulsive discharge.

The beast went berserk.

A tentacled growth swung at Tomas, its rows of vestigial feelers lacerating his flesh as it coiled around him. Tomas cried out, his arms pinned against his sides as the grip tightened.

Dietmar inhaled to yell, scrambling across the deck to his friend. Instinct guided his actions, and he hacked at the pale, veiny limbs bearing down on him. The onslaught of violence drenched him with the organic effluent pouring from the creature's ruptured appendages.

But his strength was waning. The surge of adrenaline fuelled a vicious outburst, but his weakened body hindered his efforts. His ribs throbbed, and his muscles burned with exhaustion.

A horrifying sound filled the air as the creature vomited a ball of gory ooze onto the deck. The gelatinous excretion steamed and seeped into the wooden floorboards. Inside the fibrous agglutination, long stalks like roots or veins pulsed rhythmically. Dietmar baulked when he noticed a shadow pass beneath the fleshy sac—a tiny replica of the beast before him.

Its spawn.

Dietmar fought off another string of flickering feelers, but his blows were quickly losing their impetus, and he found himself moving back toward the mast, away from Tomas.

He tried desperately to rally, calling to Razin and Geoff for aid, but from the shouts behind him, they were in the midst of their own struggle. Another tentacle slithered across the deck, winding itself around Tomas's legs with a lascivious flourish.

Horror gripped Dietmar as he watched the creature drag his friend across the deck with its massive limbs. The coiling tendrils rippled in peristaltic motions as they drew the Englishman toward the creature's slit.

"*No*," Dietmar gasped, slashing at another chimeric limb. He wouldn't watch another friend die. He couldn't.

Tomas's eyes rolled back, his head lolling to the side. Blood and slime coated his body from the glabrous appendages. A stream of mucal spit spewed forth from the creature's widening orifice. Segmented rows of teeth unfolded from within, their sharp edges gleaming beneath the bituminous saliva.

Suddenly, the creature flinched, its panoply of limbs pivoting like the heads of predatory birds, all facing the stone spire. They twitched with agitation, shuddering like hunting hounds who had caught the scent of bear. Something had captured the monstrous hulk's attention.

Dietmar didn't wait for another chance. He stumbled the last few steps toward Tomas and hacked into the writhing appendage that held his friend captive. Nearly losing his footing, he carved deep into the fleshy limb. The appendage recoiled, unravelling without resistance. Then the tentacle wrapped around Tomas's legs began to retreat, dragging itself back toward the etiolated mass on the edge of the raft.

Dietmar caught Tomas as he fell, nearly buckling under the weight of his friend. His arms burned, but his side had gone numb. There was that, at least. The pain would come later, he knew.

It was only after another long moment that Dietmar realised the creature was ignoring them. Its long, sinuous limbs propelled it back into the water, its serrated teeth chattering in what looked like fear. Dietmar glanced to the front of the raft, allowing Tomas to lean against him while he surveyed the scene.

Razin and Geoff were busy pushing a pale, chitinous body over the side to let it sink beneath the rolling waves. The discarded figure looked a lot like one of the effigies aboard Malah's ship, Dietmar thought dully. He blinked, following Razin's stare.

At first, he thought the closest spire was collapsing into the sea, its walls crumbling in a thunderous rockfall. But then, amidst the cascading debris, he saw a slithering form, and then another, and another, until the whole edifice was nothing but oily black bodies sliding into the water.

Serpents. Thousands of them.

The sea-beast spat out another high-pitched, gibbering sound as it detached itself from the raft. It moved in a shifting, inelegant motion, its glutinous body buoyed by the waves as it swam away from the raft, making for the open water.

Dietmar looked down.

The water beneath them had transformed into a clouded sepia, teeming with the backs of countless serpentine forms undulating in a fluid, coiling mass toward the ineffable thing that had attacked them. They were hunting it, Dietmar realised. And it was terrified.

Dietmar tightened his grip on the mast's rope and watched as the chittering beast attempted to submerge. Its eddying limbs thrust deep into the water, like a swimmer's arms, propelling it deeper into the waves with each stroke. Just as its amorphous back was fading from sight, the water around the creature began to froth, transforming into a maelstrom of white spray and frenetic motion.

Dietmar stared in astonishment as the sea was whipped into a seething cauldron, thousands of writhing black bodies turning the surface iridescent with their sheen. The serpents moved in winding sinusoidal motions, their tails flicking with powerful thrusts, propelling them onward. Though fleeting, Dietmar caught glimpses of their features as they streamed past the raft. He saw distended bellies, strange and protruding against the sleek black bodies, then long fins extending toward the tip of the serpent's tail, and flat, piscine eyes staring up blindly from arrow-shaped heads. Snapping jaws with teeth like the blocky stones of a ruined temple jutted out from their eel-like faces.

The flailing sea-monster slipped in and out of sight, the one moment a storm of lashing limbs and shuddering flesh, the next, hidden beneath the waves and by the swarming reptiles. As Dietmar watched, he saw the creature's flesh being punctured by the snapping teeth of countless snakes. Ichor sprayed from numerous wounds, horrific gouts of vile discharge pouring into the sea. The titan screeched in its piercing two-tone grate, shaking from side to side in an effort to dislodge its assailants. The waters around it churned with foulness as the silhouettes of flickering shapes surged relentlessly to tear into the monster.

Dietmar spun around at a cry from Sara and saw a snake entangled in her hair, having fallen onto the raft instead of the water as they passed beneath the spire. Levi stood over her, grappling with the hissing serpent, shielding his daughter's face from its snapping jaws.

Tanit appeared beside him and swiftly snatched the writhing snake. Dietmar barely registered the motion as she pulled the snake from Sara's hair, inadvertently taking strands of her dark locks with it, disregarding Sara's yelps. Gripping the snake beneath its neck while its tail thrashed in the air, Tanit held it at arm's length. The serpent hissed, its mouth opening and closing in futile aggression, revealing a vast grey tongue behind its square teeth, licking the air hungrily.

Tanit hissed back at the snake, then flung it out over the raft. It twined in the air before splashing down amongst its kin, disappearing amongst their writhing forms.

The monstrous battle raged on. The octopoidal creature struggled to break free from the swarm of snakes. Each time it submerged, a hundred slavering jaws bit into its flesh, dragging it back to the surface. By the indolent swipes of its feelers, the loss of blood and open wounds were taking their toll.

"Let's go," said Razin, limping across the deck. His shoulder was a mess of ragged skin, and more cuts covered his arms. He knelt beside the mast and hefted an oar with his good arm. His eyes never left the battle. "Now, before this brood of serpents seeks easier prey."

Dietmar glanced at the water. The stream of serpents had dwindled to a trickle, leaving only the slow and malformed ones still moving alongside the raft.

Dietmar stood still for a moment, then snapped his gaze around to fix on the gently pulsing sack resting on the raft. Spidering limbs twitched within its confines. Overwhelmed by sudden revulsion, he stepped toward it, his lips curling back in disgust. With a swift kick, he tore through the fleshy shell with his boot, spilling its contents across the deck—something white and pale wriggled within the ooze, resembling a mollusc basking in the sun. Dietmar stomped on it forcefully until it stopped moving.

He thought he heard a roar from the open waters, a mournful cry from the creature, as if it had sensed the fate of its offspring, aware of its demise even while it faced its own.

"God's fucking nails and be damned," swore Geoff, recoiling from the stench that accompanied the cracking of the egg.

Dietmar tried not to gag and covered his mouth and nose with a hand. The pulpy mess on the deck split apart, like a piece of squashed fruit. Inside, Dietmar saw the pale segmented limbs of the creature. It was covered in a hard, chitinous manifold of bone and hardened skin that looked like lamellar plate. Dietmar prodded it with the tip of his sword and then flicked the remains into the sea.

There was a soughing sound as the sea snakes snapped at the foetal excrement, devouring the sack and the thing inside in an orgy of carnivorous violence.

"Come on," said Dietmar, reaching out to help Tomas to his feet. His friend gave him a blank stare, his eyes darting around, their whites exposed. Slime and ichor covered his robes, and the skin around his neck was red and blistered from where the creature had held him.

"Poxxing thing," Tomas muttered, his tired voice barely audible over the waves. He attempted a smile but winced instead, leaning on Dietmar's shoulder for support.

Slowly, carefully, they navigated their way between the stone spires. Their passage was marked by the haunting, undulating death cries of the beast.

Dietmar wasn't sure if the creature was dead, if it had managed to escape the serpent's nest, or if it was simply too distant to be heard anymore. But, by the time they reached the beach, the air had fallen silent, a profound stillness settling after all the violence.

Dietmar waded through the shallows, pulling the raft behind him as they crawled toward the grey sand. The gentle ebb and flow of the sea aided their escape from its cold embrace, propelling the raft forward with waist-high waves, spilling them onto the coast like drenched sea-rats.

The sun's strength was waning, its last anaemic rays stretching across the beach. Dietmar helped Tomas out of the shallows, hauling his friend and his heavy, sodden robes onto the sand. Tomas collapsed in a heap the moment his feet touched dry land, gasping for breath while Dietmar looked over the strange coast they found themselves upon.

Stone tusks littered the beach, like saplings in fresh soil. Each stood as tall as a man, wide and curving, with gentle slopes that culminated in sharp, conical tips.

Like fangs.

Forests of kelp lay discarded across the sand, rotting under the pale light. Swarms of gnats and flies hovered over them, filling the air with a low-pitched, buzzing whine. The kelp forest stretched out ahead, receding as the beach veered steeply, becoming the dunes that bordered the shore.

"Don't wander far," Dietmar called to Tanit, watching her stalk between the tusks.

He left Tomas wheezing on the beach to help Razin and Geoff drag their battered vessel from the waves. He didn't fancy the idea of getting back aboard the raft, but it wouldn't do to let it get pulled out by the tide if they needed it later.

Finally, the raft secured and their last remaining things safely on dry land, Dietmar slumped down beside Tomas to examine his friend's injuries. White circular markings covered Tomas's neck where the creature's tentacles had grasped him, leaving welts about the size of a thumbnail. They would heal.

Dietmar glanced up as Geoff approached and followed the mercenary's gaze toward the dunes. Footsteps ran in a jagged line along the beach, disappearing up one of the inclines. Dietmar frowned, searching for the girl amongst the tusks.

"Where's Tanit?" said Geoff.

32

Tomas swore beneath his breath as he dragged himself up the dune. His face hurt. His neck hurt. His bones hurt. His skin was bruised and blistered where the sea-beast had grabbed him, and his wet robes made ascending the slope a hellish endeavour.

"God, forgive me whatever of my sins has brought me to this," he whispered, "and I will try to live the life of an honest, sober man. Just take us away from this place. Send us home."

"He won't," said Geoff, stepping beside him. The mercenary had removed his mail coat, slinging it over his shoulder like a shepherd might a lamb. His once-white jerkin was stained and soaked with sweat. He gave Tomas a nasty look. "He doesn't care about us."

"Believe what you want," Tomas replied.

"I will."

"But if the Lord can't—"

"Won't," Geoff corrected.

"*Won't* save us, then we are truly lost."

"Aye, That we are."

Tomas paused to adjust his robes, clutching them tightly to keep them from dragging in the sand.

"You can't truly believe that," he said as Geoff turned to wait for him.

"You just said I should believe what I want."

"I know what I said," Tomas snapped, growing more irritable. "But that doesn't mean you're right."

"Oh? You think not?" Geoff hawked and spat onto the sand. "Each of my bastards had it coming. Amice, Eudes, Liso, Odilo… all of them. They were rotten cunts. And you know what? So am I. So, if you're here with me, maybe you are too, eh?"

"We are *not* the same," Tomas said softly.

Geoff laughed. "Of course we fucking are. We all are. Greedy, rotten, self-serving—"

"Not him," said Tomas, nodding toward Dietmar. His friend was limping up the slope beside Levi and his daughter, his own mail coat hanging loosely from his gaunt body like sagging skin. Dietmar's worn and faded tabard, already in tatters before their journey began, was now little more than a rag. Blood, dirt, and foul discharge from that godless creature in the water covered the fraying sigil at the centre of his chest—the proud wolf. It seemed somehow thinner and more craven now, reduced to a scavenging jackal, like the man who wore it.

"Are you so sure?" said Geoff, following Tomas's gaze. "You've heard him in his sleep. Muttering, cursing, talking to who knows which gods… as if they're listening. Innocent men don't sleep like that… I wonder if that bastard boy Amice wasn't right after all."

Tomas stared at him. "What do you mean?"

"The hand."

"It saved us from the demon."

"Did it?"

"You saw it with your own eyes," Tomas insisted.

Geoff licked his stained teeth and slowly shook his head. "I don't know what I saw, Tomas. All I know is that the keeper of that rotting thing told us it was cursed, that it was evil. And now your friend carries it by his side… sleeps with it close to his chest. And if Amice spoke the truth—and he was a lying bastard, I won't deny it—but if he *did* speak honest, then there's something going on with that wretched thing."

Geoff fell silent as Razin passed between them, taking the lead alongside the girl's path away from the beach. If he'd overheard their conversation, he kept his silence, barely acknowledging them as he continued his ascent.

"Look at him," Geoff muttered beneath his breath, glancing back at Dietmar. "Do you think that's a man unencumbered by sin? By burden? He carries something. Either that hand is cursed, or he is. *Look at him.*"

Tomas opened his mouth and closed it again.

"He has pits for eyes." Geoff rubbed his face, shaking his head slowly. "God's grace doesn't look like that, does it? All skin and rotting bone… No, no."

"Men have been tested before," Tomas offered, his words sounding hollow even to himself. He cleared his throat and glanced back at Dietmar, avoiding Geoff's stare.

His friend had paused halfway up the dune, his cadaverous chest heaving from the exertion. His beard, once lush and thick, had grown wiry and unkempt. Sunburn covered his skin, but where it hadn't turned red, it had taken on a sickly yellow hue. Patches of his hair had fallen out, leaving only dry rat-tails behind.

"I better be sainted after all this testing, then." Geoff made a derisive snort.

Dietmar looked up and waved.

Tomas hesitated for a moment and then waved back. If this was a test, it was one that Dietmar might not survive.

"It is a marid," Razin's voice broke the silence. He stood a few paces ahead, his gaze fixed on Dietmar.

"Or a *shedim,*" he continued.

"What?" Geoff growled.

"A powerful ifrit among the jinn," Razin explained. "It lives to torment man, to lead him astray. I believe that is what haunts our friend."

"More heathen falseness," said Geoff, though his heart wasn't in it. How could it be, after all they'd seen? He licked his cracked lips and watched Razin before asking, "So, another of your Sons of Adam, then?"

"And Hawah," Razin affirmed with a curt nod. "But there were others before the first man. Elemental beings who lived between Heaven and Hell, but… they were different from us. To say their true names, to even bear their memories, grants them strength."

"Shedim," Tomas whispered, his voice barely audible.

Razin muttered something under his breath, briefly closing his eyes.

A prayer, Tomas thought.

"That is what the Jews named it," Razin's eyes blinked back open. "They have had their own encounters with this thing, I think."

Geoff looked unconvinced. "Too evil to name but not too evil to fuck, is that right?"

Razin looked at him.

"You told us Adam and Haw—and Eve bred with them, didn't you say that?"

Razin nodded slowly.

"Well then," Geoff continued. "Do you see my point?"

A strange expression crossed Razin's face. His brow twitched as his eyes took on a distant look. "Not all forms of evil are so obvious," he said quietly. "It is only when she draws near that we can truly perceive her for what she is."

"She?" said Tomas. "It is a she-demon, then?"

Razin pursed his lips momentarily, then his expression returned to its usual enigmatic state. "Perhaps."

Tomas and Geoff exchanged a bemused look.

"Did you not wonder why the mules feared him so?" asked Razin.

"The mules?" said Tomas while Geoff shook his head.

"There is a story," Razin continued, "from the time of *'Abd el Ghâfar*, when the servant Noah was sent to warn mankind of the Flood and construct the ark. He was mocked and beaten, even by his own wife; the unbeliever, Canaan, and his son—the giant, Og. They doubted him and the word of God. So, when the Flood burst from the *tannûr*, only Noah and his companions, and the animals that Allah had caused to enter the ark, were saved."

"Including an ass," said Geoff.

Razin nodded. "An ass under whose tail Iblis hid, disguised as a fly. But the donkey sensed the ill intentions of its clandestine passenger and refused to enter the ark, unwilling to carry the Evil One. It resisted, kicking and braying like Adelman's stubborn mules until Noah was forced to drive it onto the ark with blows from his fists. As a reward for its suffering, it was decreed that one of its descendants would be granted entry to Paradise."

"How had it known?" Tomas asked. "If Iblis was in disguise."

Razin shrugged. "Perhaps they have a sense about them that we lack?"

"And you think that's what those two felt?" Geoff remained unconvinced. "You think Dietmar carries this Iblis with him?"

"Not Iblis," said Razin, "But he has undoubtedly been touched by… something. That much is certain."

"How do we stop it?" asked Tomas. He pushed his robes across his knees and started trudging up the incline.

Razin stared at him in silence.

"Don't tell me you don't know," said Geoff, shaking his head. "Goddamn it. Are we just supposed to leave him to rot, then?"

Tomas turned to gaze back at the path they had travelled. The strange rock formations that crowded the beach looked like the stubby remains of a forest after the woodsmen had been at it.

"There must be something we can do," Tomas murmured, almost to himself. That's if Razin was right at all about what afflicted Dietmar. The šubur in Ubar had spoken of distortions, of places where the borders between natural and unnatural grew thin. When Tomas had tried to follow Gizzal's complex web of thoughts, he had only grown more bewildered. Yet, those places… those layers… were they Hell? Or something else entirely? Was the hand and whatever was contained within it made stronger where those borders grew weak? But Nicolo had said it was cursed before they'd even left Samaria…

Tomas groaned, feeling more lost than ever.

"You can pray," said Razin, turning in the sand and resuming his march up the dune.

Geoff shrugged unhappily. "Like that's done us any bit of good so far."

***

"I'm not going in there," Geoff declared firmly.

Razin crouched down beside Tanit's tracks and looked up, tracing their path across the sandy ground. "That's where the trail leads."

"And I'm not following it." Geoff shook his head, a look of distaste crossing his face. "Why do we care what happens to that street-rat anyway? Given the chance, she'd gouge our eyes out. We all saw her fighting off those fish bastards. She's a savage."

"She led us to the Ishkur," Tomas explained patiently. "Without her, we would still be trapped in that city, likely dead. Fed to that snake-thing of theirs, or worse."

"Worse?" scoffed Geoff. "Not me. I would have left you sorry lot behind and cut out on my own."

"And then what? Where would you have gone?"

Geoff fell silent.

"That's why we have to find her." Tomas looked over Razin's shoulder at the spoor, tracing its path down the slope. He glanced at Geoff and added. "We are *not* the same."

The mercenary grumbled something under his breath but didn't respond. And when they made their slow descent from the dune, he reluctantly followed them toward the thing jutting out of the sand.

Toward the tower.

The grey sand gave way to hardy soil, with gorse thickets and long grass sprouting near the base of the dune. Thick succulents and weeds punctuated the scrubland, while large boulders littered the flat basin. They were surrounded by twisted trees and bushes that rose as high as a man on his horse.

But nothing came close to rivalling the tower.

It stood like some monolithic obelisk of grey stone and concrete. A solitary bastion upon the flat plain. Its shadow stretched over the scrubland, enveloping the twisted trees that desperately reached for the last glimmering rays of sunlight.

Tomas appraised the tower with a furrowed brow. It appeared well-maintained, with the slat tiles of its conical roof in decent repair and the grey stone blocks forming the spire free from any signs of decay. It resembled a Frankish outpost, similar to the ones that scattered the borders of Outremer, keeping a watchful eye on the movements of Nur ad-Din and Saladin.

A single window peered out from the top of the tower, just beneath its roof. Tomas's frown deepened as he heard something emanating within.

It sounded like singing.

"It's those demons again," Levi said, scrambling down the slope with his daughter, joining Tomas and Razin in the bushes.

Tomas shook his head slowly, listening to the voice from the tower. The Sumerian demons' song had been mournful, filled with a sorrowful melody that had made him want to cry.

But this… this was different. Ugly. Vulgar, in comparison. The voice sang in a guttural gurgle, closer to a nasal shout than any semblance of singing. It sounded human.

Dietmar caught Tomas's attention, gesturing from behind a boulder where he and Geoff knelt, signalling them to move forward.

"We're going closer?" Levi whispered, pulling Sara down when she peered over the bushes. She shrugged him off but remained low.

"That's where the girl went." Razin pointed to the ground, at the footprints that led a short distance ahead before vanishing amidst the grass and hardier, darker sand.

"Haven't we learned by now?" said Levi heavily. "We should stay away from this place."

Tomas opened his mouth to speak, but Levi waved a finger at him.

"Yes, I know," Levi began. "The girl. A stranger to us all. Not a Christian. Not a Mohammedan, and certainly not a Jew."

"Does that matter?" asked Tomas.

"Damn it, but it might." Levi pointed toward the tower, where the baritone voice still boomed from the window. "Let the knight and his Arab go and fetch her. I've done my part and more… and I've lost because of it."

"Abba." Sara reached for her father's hand, gently clasping it in her own.

"I've already seen one flower plucked from my grasp." Levi's voice trembled, but his eyes were set. "I won't see another."

"Do not let your pain cow you." Razin shifted on his knees, dusting sand from his palms as he turned to face Levi. "We have all suffered losses, but it must not prevent us from doing what is right."

Tomas's thoughts drifted to Adelman then. Dear, foolish old Adelman and his mules. He remembered watching them as they pushed away from the ship, leaving them behind. They hadn't had a choice… but maybe he could have been stronger? Could have pushed past the kicking Balaam or Silensus or whichever of the pair got in his way… Maybe he could have saved him? He groaned inwardly, knowing it wasn't true. They would have all perished on that ship. Adelman had gone mad in the end. Or they had.

"What if it were her in there," said Tomas quietly, looking from Levi to the girl by his knees.

The dyer shook his head irritably, but Sara was now staring at him as well.

"You would ask us to risk ourselves to save her, wouldn't you? And Tanit would have helped us, wouldn't she?"

Levi shook his head again, annoyed.

"She needs our help," Tomas finished.

"*Ben zona,*" swore Levi. "We should have stayed in Ubar with that Greek. At least there, we knew what wanted to kill us."

"Everything," said Tomas with a subdued smile.

"Right." Levi sighed miserably. He looked up, wincing as the singer reached a ragged crescendo, his voice struggling to grasp the desired notes and settling somewhere in between instead.

"What's he singing about?" Sara asked, risking another peak over the bushes. Levi dragged her back down, shaking his head. "It's not any words I know," he replied when she settled.

"He sounds… happy." Sara brushed away her father's hands and tilted her head.

Tomas couldn't help but agree. There was a satisfied lilt to the man's gravelly voice, unpleasant as it was.

"Happy in a place like this," he muttered. He couldn't fathom such a thing.

"It must be lonely up there," said Sara.

"Perhaps that is why he is singing," Razin suggested. "He has found company. The girl."

"He's about to have more guests." Levi pointed toward Dietmar and Geoff, who were rising to their feet, abandoning any pretence of stealth and moving out into the open.

"Let's go," said Razin, getting to his own feet.

***

Tomas hurried to catch up with Dietmar and Geoff as they marched across the scrubland. He'd long since discarded his remaining sandal, having lost its sibling aboard the Ishkur during the mad scramble to escape. He could feel the transition from warm sand to dirt and grass between his toes.

Pale, sinuous roots grew in thick clumps across their path, scattered throughout the soil like worms. Hardy grey bushes, like the dense foliage of Old Samaria, grew thick in places, and Tomas found himself flinching at the flickering shadows they cast, silently praying there was nothing lurking within them.

When they reached the base of the tower, Dietmar signalled for them to halt. He craned his neck, staring up at the window. For all the tower's height—and it was tall, bringing to mind the belltower of *Le Trappe* in Normandy, where Tomas had spent a rambunctious pair of nights drinking and gambling before setting off for Alençon—it was not very wide. Tomas wondered how comfortable a living could be made inside its thick walls. He wouldn't have survived long in Le Trappe, nor Alençon, for that matter. The wine flowed too freely there, and the women with it.

The splitting headache he woke up with on the first morning was nothing compared to the clanging bells that had roused him.

The singing continued unfalteringly. If whoever resided within the tower had spotted their approach, they seemed unfazed by their presence. That fact made Tomas nervous.

"Ho there!" Dietmar called, cupping his hands to his mouth.

The singing stopped mid-crescendo, leaving silence in its place. It was quickly replaced by the sound of shifting stones and a croaky voice muttering.

"I don't see a door," said Geoff, cautiously circling the base of the tower. He kicked aside a knot of dead roots and frowned, shaking his head before glancing back at the others. "No ladder either, and that's a steep climb."

"So how did anyone get…" Levi never finished his thought, the words fading on his lips as the tower's occupant finally appeared at the window.

"Thank God," Tomas silently mouthed, feeling a slight sense of relief despite his lingering caution. They had been tricked before, but for now, the small, grey-haired man staring down at them didn't appear to pose much of a threat.

He wore a simple brown robe, not dissimilar to Tomas's own, with a wide hood draped behind his head and billowing sleeves. From where he stood, Tomas couldn't make out his features clearly, but he had a vague impression of thin lips and smiling eyes.

"My apologies!" Dietmar yelled up. "For interrupting your song, but we are in need of your help if you are willing?"

The small man rested his elbows on the windowsill and leaned forward.

Dietmar took that as an invitation to continue and nodded his thanks.

"We are looking for one of our companions, a girl. You might have seen her come this way?"

Silence.

Tomas shifted on his feet, watching the little man at the window stare at them. Now he was certain of it—the hermit was smiling.

"Do you understand?" Dietmar exchanged glances with Razin and Geoff before taking another step forward.

The hermit remained silent as Dietmar approached, though he watched him closely, leaning further out the window to track his route.

"Enough of this," growled Geoff, striding across the grass to stand beside Dietmar.

"Her tracks led us here," he shouted, pointing back the way they'd come, toward the grey sands and rising dunes. "Is that little urchin here or not? If you have her, send her down, and we'll be on our way."

Again, that harsh scraping of stone against stone filled the air, like a team of unseen masons were pushing great blocks of mortar together.

Tomas looked down from the window, tracing the sound along the neck of the tower. Then, abruptly, it ceased, just as suddenly as it had started.

Levi stepped back nervously, gripping Sara's arm. "This thing isn't going to collapse on us, is it?"

"Strong as David's Tower," Geoff replied without a backward glance, though he, too, took a cautious step backwards.

"Maybe he's sworn to silence," Tomas mused, returning his gaze to the window. He couldn't tell if it was the fading light or the encroaching shadows that enveloped the old man, but his skin appeared an unusual shade of grey—more akin to that of a corpse than to the complexion of a Frank or an Arab.

"A strange sort of vow," said Dietmar. "To sing but not to talk, don't you think?"

"Aye," Geoff scoffed. "If you can call that singing." He waved a hand at the little man. "Come down," he called out. "We want to talk to you."

The hermit remained unmoved.

Geoff showed his teeth and spat at the sand. "Else, we're coming up there to see what you've got in that room. How'd you like that?"

The hermit showed his own teeth in return, his smile widening.

Dietmar chuckled. "It looks like he'd like that very much."

"The little bastard." Geoff sighed, glancing back at the tower's base. "I suppose one of us could scale it? Won't be me, though. We could take some rope from the raft and hoist… Well…" He looked at Razin, his eyes settling on his tattered arm, then to Dietmar, his eyes quickly moving away from the German's gaunt visage. He shook his head at Levi, staring pointedly at the dyer's ample belly. Finally, his eyes landed on Tomas, and he smiled.

Before Tomas could protest, a voice echoed from above, rough as granite and as ugly as sin.

My eyes doth see beyond the now,
To fates that lie ahead, somehow,
But when guests come knocking, daft and bold,
My heart's surprised, its beats unfold,
For destiny's surprises ne'er grow old!

Tomas winced at the hermit's ragged pentameter.

"Daft indeed," muttered Geoff before raising his voice to address the hermit. "You can keep your songs, tower-keep. We just want to know if you've seen our girl around. Tall, bony little shite with a crooked lip and sharp claws. You can't miss her."

The man seemed to ponder his words for a moment and then opened his lungs again in song.

"Fuck's sake!" yelled Geoff over the singing, but the hermit would not relent.

No maidens near this tower to see,
But creatures lurking stealthily,
Amidst the shadows, they reside,
Their presence felt, I cannot hide,
Though still no mortal girl beside!

"You might need to get a rope just so that we can gag him," Dietmar suggested, unblocking his ears as the last note faded. There was a pained look on his face, and Tomas knew that he bore it too.

"Another madman." Razin mouthed a short prayer, then looked up. The hermit was watching them, his head cocked to the side like a curious hound.

Tomas shook his head, already anticipating what would follow but asking anyway: "Why are you here? And no, don't give us another of your—"

Through tangled webs I glimpsed my plight,
Punished now, my fate is blight,
In this tower, I shall stay!

Tomas stared at the block of stone ahead of them, hearing something stirring within the tower's walls. It was like coarse, dry skin brushing against rock and stone bricks. Tomas took a hesitant step backwards, exchanging a glance with Dietmar. His companion had heard it, too, and slowly drew his sword from its sheath at his side.

The noise was getting louder.

To etch history's tales before the last day,
A scribe of time, until I wither away!

"We're wasting our time here," said Geoff. "We should move on, before nightfall. I don't much like the look that little cunt is giving me."

"What is it, Razin?" Dietmar nodded at his friend, who stood with his head tilted, staring at the figure in the window.

"He says he is being punished," Razin said after a brief pause.

"Punished for what?" Tomas watched the grey-skinned man, searching his creased face for answers without wanting to vocalise the question. He didn't want to trigger another chorus from the tower.

"A crime against fate," said Razin, not taking his eyes off the window. "And now he is condemned to this tower to write the history of the world. He may not leave until it is complete."

"But that means… forever." Tomas frowned.

"No, not forever." Dietmar leaned his sword against his leg, its tip resting in the dirt. His hand fidgeted with the pouch by his side, but he stopped when Tomas caught his gaze. Dietmar's eyes shifted from Tomas to the leather sack, his mouth twitching involuntarily. "It means until the world… ends," he finished.

"Washed away by the black waters and Bahamut," Razin added, scratching his beard. "He must have committed a great crime to be awarded thusly."

Dietmar frowned. "He claimed to be able to see both the past and the future?"

Razin shrugged. "Don't all men who write history?"

"Or perhaps that is his crime," Dietmar pondered. "To be able to look into the future and change his own fate." He blinked slowly, his eyes taking on a faraway look as he no doubt thought of his own past and the future that could have been. "What man wouldn't transgress against their gods if given such an ability?"

"Oh no," moaned Tomas as the little man leaned back and opened his mouth obscenely wide.

He who forges ruin, his blaspheming ways,
A dirge for the world, a twilight haze,
A relentless soul, to challenge the divine!
An end he beckons, the warnings malign!
In shadows he stands, fate's tapestry unwinds!

Tomas swore beneath his breath, cursing the little man and the gods who had punished him but spared his tongue. He took another look up at the tower before squatting down to sit on the grass beside Levi and his daughter. His neck was sore from craning, and his legs felt stiff from traversing the dunes. The sting on his skin from the sea-beast's tentacles still lingered, and he absentmindedly rubbed at it in irritation.

"Shall we leave?" said Geoff, eyeing the darkening skyline.

"And go where?" asked Dietmar, sitting down beside Tomas.

"Anywhere. I don't know."

"She came here once. Maybe she'll come back."

"Or maybe she's still here, stuck in that tower with that cretin."

Dietmar stopped fiddling with the pouch and looked at Geoff. "If she hasn't returned by morning, *you* can go up there and get her."

Geoff scowled something about not getting caught dead up there and wandered off to take a slow circuit around the basin.

"Better get comfortable," said Dietmar as the little man above them opened his arms to sing again.

Tomas blocked his ears.

***

Sometime after nightfall, their host sang his last note and retired to the room behind the window. They heard him moving around inside, muttering loudly as he shifted through what could only have been sheaves of paper, great tomes, and scrolls. He was evidently looking for something amidst his recorded histories. Soon, a warm glow emanated within the room, casting the hermit's shadow on the wall behind him. He sat hunched over something—his writing desk or table, and there he remained.

Dietmar reclined with his back propped up against his bedroll. He had removed his hauberk and gambeson, finding the night air cool but not uncomfortably cold. A gentle breeze wafted in from the dunes, and with the hermit's singing now concluded, the distant roar of the sea reached their ears. Waves crashed against the dark spires that adorned the shoreline, resembling the spikes of a thorny crown.

Carefully, Dietmar unwrapped the binding around his waist and stared down at his swollen side. A dark bruise had spread across his skin, forming in layers like the growth rings of a tree. It grew lighter the closer it neared the centre. Welts covered the skin around the bruise, a mini-archipelago of scars and scabs that disappeared beneath the folds of his bandages. Another of the triangular protrusions had emerged, the fourth of its kind, resting just beneath his sternum. He traced its outline with a gentle finger before pressing against it. Solid. Like bone. He would need to lance the growths like boils. He'd been putting it off but couldn't delay much longer.

He let the wrap fall back across his ribs and settled down against his mat to listen to Geoff discuss the blunter points of theology with Razin. The two were gathered around a growing pile of kindling, attempting to start a fire and cook the meagre scraps they'd managed to salvage from the Ishkur.

"But if he were a giant," Geoff was saying, "how did he... *you know?*"

Razin held a flint over the kindling, raising an eyebrow in response to Geoff's question.

"How did he *breed*, man? If he was as big as you say, it sounds like that might have posed a certain kind of problem, yeah?"

Razin struck the flint, cupping the small flame against the wind with his hand. "He had no children," he said, leaning closer to the faintly glowing embers. He blew them gently, coaxing them into life.

Geoff tossed a handful of dry grass onto the pile of kindling, his expression incredulous as he looked at Razin. "But he must have sheathed his sword in something, right? No lady giants wandering about?"

Razin shook his head.

"God." Geoff chuckled. "No wonder he was such a miserable shit then. I would have been, too, with only my hand for company. Less bastards to worry about, though. I suppose feeding one mouth is hard enough when you've got a belly that big. How tall did you say he was?"

"When he lay down, he stretched from Banias to Lake Merom. He could cross from Mount Hermon over El-Beka'a in a single stride."

"How did he die then? Don't tell me he tripped…" Geoff cackled, spraying the small fire with spit. "A fall like that would take a week to finish. It would leave a horrible mess, too, wouldn't it?"

Razin poked at the flames with a stick, then settled back, placing his sword across his lap. "They say Og met his end at the hands of Mûsa—your Moses. The giant had intended to destroy the Israelites with a great rock he had unearthed. It was large enough to obliterate the entire tribe of Israel." Razin retrieved a cloth from the folds of his burnous and began the process of cleaning the blade. The edges were still stained from his encounter with the pale, white-skinned apparition from the sea, and he scraped at the marks fastidiously while he recounted the tale. "Og carried the rock on his head, planning to drop it over the Israelite camp. But when the time came, Allah sent a bird that pecked a hole in the rock, causing it to slip down over the giant's head and onto his shoulders. He became trapped inside, his arms raised and his eyes covered by the enormous boulder. Moses saw the giant and divined his plans, so he leapt the height of ten dra'as and struck Og's ankle hard enough to make him fall. The fall, as you have already guessed, proved fatal."

Geoff grunted, satisfied with the tale of Og's demise. He watched Razin wiping the gore from the base of his hilt, and the mirth in his eyes faded. When he spoke again, his voice carried a sombre and apprehensive tone, as if he regretted the question but couldn't resist asking it.

"What stories have you of that beast in the temple?"

Razin looked up from his sword, and a sense of disquiet stirred within Dietmar. Ephium had been silent since their arrival, ever since the pale, white creature emerged from the waves only to be met by the horde of slippery black and brown bodies from the rocks. Silent, but not absent. Its presence lingered, like an unfulfilled promise, waiting and watching.

—Lamassu

The name came as a whisper, like some forbidden thing better left lost to the black depths of that Roman temple.

He frowned. Razin and Geoff stared at him across the crackling fire.

He had spoken the word aloud.

A moment passed. Razin's brow creased, his eyes narrowing, the sword in his lap forgotten.

"How did you come by that name?" he asked for the second time.

A heavy silence settled between them, and Dietmar became aware of Geoff's eyes darting back and forth between him and Razin.

"Tell me," Razin insisted.

"I heard it."

"Where?"

Dietmar shook his head slowly, then more vigorously, as the thing inside of him began to laugh.

—tell him, Ephium chortled. *—oh, but look, he already knows! The clever Mohammedan*

Razin's gaze flickered to the pouch at Dietmar's lap, his lips pressed into a thin line.

"It's that thing, isn't it?" said Geoff, noticing Razin's stare. He motioned to the pouch. "That old scriniarius was right. It's cursed."

Dietmar nodded wordlessly. There was no use denying it. He wore the curse on his skin, in the rotting teeth inside his mouth, and the boils that marked his hands and chest.

"We should burn it," said Geoff, rising to his feet. "Right here, right now. Throw it into the fire and be done with it."

"What's going on?" Tomas asked, walking over from where he'd been sitting with Levi and Sara. He saw the looks on Geoff and Razin's faces and halted in his tracks. "What happened?"

"The Arab was right, after all." Geoff nodded toward Razin before shifting his gaze back to Dietmar. "That hand has done something to him."

Razin tossed the dirty rag he'd been using to clean his sword into the fire and watched Dietmar.

"How long?" he asked.

"Since the temple," Dietmar replied. "After I touched it."

"It… speaks to you?"

Dietmar nodded.

"Christ's teeth," Geoff snarled. "And you've just been carrying it around with you? You didn't think to throw it into the sand? Or the sea? Or… anywhere would have done."

Tomas crossed himself, staring wide-eyed at Dietmar.

"It's killing you, isn't it?"

"Give it to me," said Geoff, striding across the camp with an outstretched hand. "I'll get rid of it if you won't."

"I'll die," said Dietmar plainly.

—*yes*, echoed Ephium, the voice dry and softly spoken.

Geoff halted, standing over Dietmar with his hand still extended to take the pouch. He hesitated, his hand lowering slightly.

"But it is *killing you*," Tomas whimpered.

"Yes," Dietmar said, echoing Ephium. An image of the white spectre, the ghoul that haunted Enneleyn in his dreams, flashed before his eyes.

Is that what I am to become? he wondered.

Dead... but not dead? Trapped in a state between life and death... A vessel for the soul harbouring beside my own.

"But that will kill me even quicker," Dietmar continued, shaking off the vision. "And then I'll lose the chance... What chance I have left..." He let the words trail off.

The fire crackled, finally catching hold of the dead roots and grass that Geoff had fed it.

"Your boy," Tomas murmured, understanding dawning.

"His mother," Dietmar said, his gaze fixed on the dancing flames.

Surprise flickered across Tomas's face. "But I thought—"

Dietmar's shaking head cut Tomas's words short.

He sat there for a moment, motionless. To speak the word would make it true, shifting Enneleyn from that liminal space in his mind to the void, but deep down, he knew she was already there. There was no more point pretending. He'd pretended long enough.

"She took her own life," said Dietmar. "I... I had forgotten somehow. Or perhaps I didn't want to remember. I pushed the memory away like a coward." He had been a fool, spared the truth by his own mind's instinct to protect him. But he had no more spoken Enneleyn's fate into existence than his ignoring it had brought her back... or redeemed her soul. "I remember now." He turned to face Tomas. "Do you understand what I must do?"

"I'm sorry," Tomas said, his gaze filled with sadness and pity. "I didn't know."

"Can it be done?" Geoff asked. "Can you bargain for her soul like that? I understand with the boy, but a suicide… Surely…" The burly mercenary fell silent, his face a knotted visage of doubt and uncertainty.

"I can only try," Dietmar replied quietly.

What other choice did he have? Leave her to her fate? To burn. To be ravaged by the fires of Hell. He thought of Rudi, then. His boy. If he succeeded, Rudi would remain outside of God's light. He had left that part unspoken, hoping his companions would do the same. The choice he had to make had been clear from the moment the memories resurfaced: his wife's soul or his son's… One damned, the other left out in the cold. What man should ever be forced to make such a decision? What father…

In his desperate moments considering the problem, he had thought it might not be a choice at all. The answer was, in some ways, obvious. Enneleyn *suffered*. Whatever pain he had endured, however dark the realm of Limbo where his Rudi resided, Enneleyn's immortal soul was damned. She suffered the same punishment as Christ's betrayer… his beloved Enneleyn.

But she had taken no pieces of silver, betrayed no one. He could reason through this, he knew. There must be a *right* choice to make. But that was just the thing. Enneleyn had made her choice. She had chosen to leave this world, not out of rejection of the Christ but because she could no longer face it.

That choice was more than Rudi had ever been given.

Dietmar buried his face in his hands and cried. He hadn't meant to, but the tears streamed from his face and wouldn't stop. All of his losses, his failings—Enneleyn and Rudi and Adelman, the things he had witnessed and done—came rushing back to him with those tears. He was broken, and he would never be whole again. That certainty echoed within him, as strong as his impending death. Yet, perhaps… Just maybe, he could accomplish one last thing before his time came.

He wiped away the tears with the back of his hand, feeling the boils and scabs that riddled his skin, and breathed out a long sigh. The sound was like a death rattle in his ears.

He looked up when he felt a hand on his shoulder. Tomas was crouched beside him, his oily hair hanging over his red-rimmed eyes. The touch of his friend's hand made him think of Enneleyn again, the warmth of her presence by his side. He wanted Tomas to stop, to shed the pity and let him wallow in his grief. But he didn't want that feeling to disappear either.

"Just tell us what you need," Tomas said. "We're with you."

Geoff mumbled something under his breath but fell silent when Tomas snapped his head around to glare at him. The mercenary shrugged and then nodded.

"Aye," he grunted. "What he said. We're with you."

Dietmar patted Tomas's hand and dried his face. He attempted a smile at his friend, but his lips hurt, so the grimace would have to do.

"You don't owe me anything," he said.

Tomas gently squeezed his shoulder and stood up. "If you hadn't taken me in, I would have ended up in the gutters like my father. I owe you my life. If you think that getting that rotten relic to the Church will help you and yours, then I'm with you."

Tomas turned his gaze back to the fire, peering beyond it at Razin. "Isn't that right?"

Razin blinked. He hadn't taken his eyes off Dietmar since the revelation. Then, slowly, he sheathed the scimitar resting on his lap and rose from his mat.

The quiet breathed, only to be filled by the soft crackle of the fire and the distant, dull boom of waves crashing against stone. Just when Dietmar thought Razin would remain silent, he spoke.

"There is another way," he said. Then, he turned from the fire and stalked into the shadows beyond the camp.

33

The wind soughed through the dunes, a lascivious moan that made Razin think of the temptress in the forest, where he had been so easily beguiled. She had been the embodiment of his desires—pristine, untouched, with eyes that promised much and lips that hid delicate, delicious secrets from the world. His thoughts wandered to her almond eyes and the dimple on her chin, the smell of honeycomb and lavender that lingered with her touch. The feeling of her soft skin pressed against his own.

His manhood stirred, and Razin recoiled in disgust, shaking his head at his own weakness. A servant of Al-Jann had found him wanting, but it would not happen a second time.

It is this place, he thought, staring up at the dark sky. The first stars had just begun to emerge, but there was no moon. Never a moon.

This troubled him more than the unfamiliar stars or the vicious things that roamed the land. On the Day of Judgment, the moon would be cleft in two… but what did it mean for there to be no moon at all? Had Allah's guidance been withdrawn from those beneath these stars? The only sign of God he had seen here was in the devils unleashed upon this place. This Eden-ne. For surely even they had come by God's hand?

And now, his friend was in the clutches of another of Hawah's offspring. Razin didn't even know if Dietmar could be saved. His body was a festering ruin. Bones protruded from beneath the skin of his cheeks like the arms of a ship's mast, pulling the flesh taut. His eyes were deep holes, cadaverous chambers from which two pale yellow orbs blinked slowly. The movements were sluggish, like those of an old man. When Razin helped ease Dietmar down beside the fire, he felt as though he was cradling a child—so light and frail.

"Will this work?" Tomas asked, his voice mirroring Razin's doubts and fears. He sat beside Dietmar, his legs folded beneath him, one hand resting on his friend's shoulder. The tower loomed behind them, silent, its presence indicated only by the flickering light emanating from within. Shadows enveloped the dunes, smothering the slopes and twisted trees in a darkness as dense as mud.

Razin remained silent, studying Tomas, Geoff, and Levi with his eyes, one by one. Then he nodded, turning to Geoff.

"Water," he commanded, taking the cloth from his belt and passing it to Tomas.

"We don't have much—"

Geoff saw the expression on Razin's face and unfastened the leather skin on his belt. He shook his head belligerently but passed the flask to Tomas anyway.

"Clean his face," Razin instructed.

Tomas wet the cloth carefully, using no more than a mouthful to soak the fabric. He leaned over Dietmar and gently wiped his face. Thin lines of clean skin emerged beneath the layers of dust and grime, nearly pink beside the dirt.

We must all look like this, Razin thought—*caked in dirt and salt and sand and death.*

"Now what?" Tomas asked, the soiled rag still clutched in his fingers.

Dietmar stared up at the sky, his head cradled in Tomas's lap, his face a pallid mask. Small cuts and abrasions lined the corners of his mouth, once hidden by the dirt but now impossible to miss. A sheen of sweat had already formed on his brow, trickling down between his eyebrows despite Tomas's efforts with the cloth.

"Now, the hand," Razin said, motioning toward the pouch still hanging from Dietmar's side. The soft leather had moulded to the shape of the object inside so that he could almost make out the individual digits.

Dietmar snapped his head to look at Razin, an awkward motion in Tomas's lap. Panic stirred in the dark clefts that held his eyes.

"You said—"

"Be calm. It is only temporary. You must not have the object of your affliction on your person when I perform *al-'asm.*"

Dietmar shook his head.

"It will distract you," Razin explained patiently. It was crucial that the cursed thing was not on Dietmar's person if this was to succeed. And even then... he had seen the al-'asm performed only once before, and that was by a *raqi*. At the time, he had thought it a mere spectacle, a trick to entertain the audience. But those performers had been earnest, and even his uncle had held his breath while the al-'asm was conducted.

An image of the little alleyway appeared in Razin's mind's eye. A queue of people had formed, craning their necks to catch a glimpse.

Mushrie had laughed with him, mocking the crowd's foolishness. People from all over *Bab Sharqi* had gathered to watch from the doorway of the small Damascene dwelling just a street away from the bazaar.

The raqi had demanded a modest fee from the observers before commencing, passing his keffiyeh around to collect their contributions. When he was satisfied, he ordered the curtains closed, leaving only a single oil lamp and the faint light filtering in through the door. Mushrie and Razin exchanged glances, and his uncle began to speak, but the raqi silenced him with a sweep of his arms. The edges of his khalat billowed behind him, like the flare of a cobra's hood.

After that, his uncle fell silent, and they waited in hushed anticipation.

The air inside the room grew stale and suffocating, filled with the heat of a dozen bodies tightly packed together, inhaling one another's sweat and breath. A low murmuring started somewhere in the back, threatening to escalate as the raqi's audience grew impatient.

Then, just as the atmosphere threatened to tip into unpleasantness, she emerged. The timing was perfect, only furthering Razin's suspicions that he was about to witness nothing more than a performance.

Two men escorted a feeble elderly woman out from a room in the rear. The raqi's aides, Razin thought at first, but the care by which they held her and their expressions of fear and nervousness dispelled that notion. They were family—her sons, perhaps, or neighbours.

They guided the frail figure to the centre of the dimly lit room and, at a nod from the raqi, joined the rest of the audience. The raqi, an old man himself, circled the woman, moving with a serpentine grace. After the third rotation, he began to speak.

His voice was low and warm, but clear. The voice of a performer. He recited the Throne Verse: the *Ayat Al-Kursi*, followed by the *Surah al-Nas*, while the elderly woman watched, her eyes shifting from the raqi's face and the faces of her sons or neighbours behind him.

Razin had just started to grow bored when he noticed a change in the woman's face.

He saw a glimpse, nothing more. In that moment, her nervous, anxious eyes had been replaced by something ancient and cold. Red-rimmed and dark, they stared at the raqi with such contempt that Razin was sure he'd heard the man stumble over the final words of the Surah al-Nas.

Razin glanced at his uncle to see if he had noticed it too. Mushrie's expression was grave, his smile was gone. Then, the raqi shouted out in triumph, and when Razin snapped his eyes back to the woman, her face had returned to its previous state of anxiousness.

The raqi declared that the *Aamar*, the affliction, had been banished by the power of the *al-baqarah* and the will of Allah. When Razin looked at the old woman again, he noticed that many of the lines etched on her face had vanished. She appeared rejuvenated, standing taller now that the raqi's al-'asm had been completed.

A great trick, both Razin and Mushrie had agreed. But when they exited the little domicile and found that night had already fallen, they had hurried home quickly without talking, their eyes twitching nervously at the shadows.

Afterwards, neither of them had broached the subject of al-'asm again.

That was a long time ago, Razin thought, catching Dietmar's eye. His friend's upper lips hung over a nearly toothless mouth, making it look as if it had caved in on itself. Whatever plagued Dietmar ran deep, far more advanced than the red spirit that had tormented the elderly woman in Damascus. He looked again at the protrusions on Dietmar's chest, the strange leaf-like shapes nestled beneath his skin.

Like little arrowheads, he thought, counting their number. He saw four on Dietmar's chest and what looked like a fifth pushing against the skin beneath his pelvis.

Some sort of boils? But no, he saw no heads to the growths, just the elongated bodies of the triangular protrusions. Perhaps, when this was done, they would drain and cauterise them.

"Trust me," he said, looking up at Dietmar's face.

His friend grunted in response, and Razin gave Geoff a brisk nod.

"Don't let it touch your skin," Tomas warned. He dabbed at Dietmar's brow once more before squeezing out the last of the moisture from the cloth.

"I'm not stupid," Geoff snapped, clicking his teeth. His gaze shifted from Razin to the pouch, then to Dietmar. He let out a resigned sigh, cursed his luck, and crouched beside Dietmar, gesturing toward the pouch.

"Come on," he said. "Let's get this over with so we can all get some sleep."

Dietmar untied the string securing the pouch to his belt, careful not to loosen its opening. He held the leather bag in his hands, gazing down at it while propped up against Tomas's knees. Razin thought he might reconsider. He tensed, ready to snatch it from Dietmar's grasp, but the moment passed, and Dietmar handed the pouch to Geoff.

"I'll keep it safe," said the mercenary, holding the relic by the drawstrings. He stared at it with visible disgust and rose to his feet, holding the pouch away from his body while he walked, as if he had caught a rat sneaking about his chambers and sought a place to dispose of it.

Sara watched from a few yards away. Her father had insisted she not be a part of the proceedings, but out in the scrubland, there was nowhere else to go. She sat with her knees drawn up to her chest, her eyes mere pinpricks in the darkness.

Razin let out a quiet breath. He could sense Tomas and Geoff watching him expectantly, waiting for him as he had once waited for the raqi years ago.

He looked down at Dietmar, taking in his friend's emaciated form, marked by bruises, welts, and the abrasions covering his bare chest. He placed a hand on Dietmar's shoulder and nodded toward Tomas.

"Now we begin."

He started with the Throne Verse, the Ayat Al-Kursi, just as the raqi in Damascus had done. According to hadith, the Throne Verse was regarded as the greatest verse in the Quran. The Prophet himself had declared it the most significant verse and a powerful protection against evil spirits. It was one of the first verses Razin had committed to memory as a young boy, performing it under the watchful eye of Mushrie.

"'al-lāhu lā 'ilāha 'il-lā hūwa," he recited.

Allah! None has the right to be worshipped but He

"al-ḥay-yu l-qay-yūmu,"

the Ever Living, the One Who sustains and protects all that exists

"Lā tākhudhuhū sinatun w-walā nawmun,"

Neither slumber, nor sleep overtake Him

Razin heard Geoff grumble something, shifting uncomfortably where he sat. But he didn't interrupt or object to Razin's "heathen" words. After all, God was God.

Razin focused, clearing his mind of all distractions. He could feel Dietmar twitching beneath his hands, his shoulders tensing in response to the aya.

It's working.

Razin continued, barely pausing to take a breath between lines.

"Lahū mā fi s-samāwāti wamā fi larḍi."

To Him belongs whatever is in the heavens and whatever is on earth

He would draw the marid out of Dietmar, leaving it without a host so that it would starve and wither away, deprived of a vessel to sustain it.

Dietmar flinched, his eyes opening wide to stare. If the entity inside him had been oblivious to its fate, it was fully aware now.

Sweat flowed freely from Dietmar's face, despite Tomas's futile attempts to wipe his brow. The Englishman's own face glistened with a silvery sheen in the flickering firelight.

Suddenly, Dietmar kicked out, his shoulders convulsing as he struggled to sit up, pushing against Razin's restraining hand. He possessed more strength than his appearance suggested, and Razin recalled something the raqi had mentioned—that the possessed often manifested enhanced abilities bestowed by the possessing entity, even as it drained the life from them.

"Help me hold him down!" Tomas cried, casting a desperate glance over his shoulder at Geoff and Levi. Razin motioned to them without breaking the rhythm of his recitation. His voice grew louder as his confidence swelled.

It is working.

Geoff and Levi crouched on either side of Dietmar, lending their strength to Tomas as they grappled with the thrashing German. Levi let out a yelp as Dietmar's nails dug into his wrist, hastily retracting his arm and inspecting the skin where a nail remained embedded.

"Hold him!" Geoff barked, his eyes fixed on Levi.

Dietmar gasped out a moan, writhing against his friends' restraining grips. He lashed out with an arm, a wiry, pale limb that momentarily looked like a flickering appendage. The boils on his skin rippled in the fire's glow, like dozens of tiny mouths—*the suction cups of a tentacle.* Geoff swiftly pulled the arm back down, securing it at Dietmar's side.

Razin blinked.

It was just an arm.

"Say the damn words," Geoff growled, glaring at him.

With a start, Razin realised he had faltered, pausing somewhere between the fifth and eighth lines of the verse.

"Hush," Tomas crooned, stroking Dietmar's brow. Dietmar writhed beneath him, his chest rising and falling with ragged breaths. If he could hear them at all, he gave no indication.

Tomas looked at Razin, silently pleading for him to continue.

Razin stumbled through the remaining lines, "Walā ya'ūduhū ḥifẓuhumā." Dietmar's face contorted in a mask of twisted muscles. His brow formed a crooked V, reaching the bridge of his nose. His lips curled into a vicious sneer, revealing toothless gums. He sucked in a deep breath.

"Wahuwa l-'aliy-yu l-'aẓīmu," said Razin, finishing the Ayat Al-Kursi breathlessly. He looked instinctively to the sky above, searching for the moon for solace before realising his mistake.

A memory stirred, a story his uncle had shared about the ancient cosmologies. When the moon was at its fullest, the light would sometimes fall upon that part of the great ocean where Bahamut resided. When it did, the colossal creature would open its mouth and seize the moon—only to spit it out in fear of Allah.

Razin thought of that towering fin rising from the ocean and the inky black skies above. *What happens when the beast no longer fears God?*

"Allah grant us refuge," he murmured, looking back down at Dietmar.

His friend's face was caught in a rictus grin, the veins on his neck protruding like inky black snakes beneath his etiolated skin as he strained against Geoff, Levi, and Tomas.

Then, with a dry breath like sand scraping against stone, Dietmar's body went limp.

"Christ in heaven," Geoff exhaled, a wry smile beginning to form on his lips, "I thought he was gonna—"

"Quiet!" Razin snapped, leaning forward to stare at Dietmar's face.

Something was wrong. Razin had yet to recite the Sura Al-Nas or confront the marid that had latched onto Dietmar.

The fire flickered, growing dim so that Razin was forced to squint. He sensed a change in the air before he felt the tiny pinpricks all along his skin, as if something was tugging at his flesh, causing goosebumps to ripple across his arms.

What is this?

A shadow passed over Dietmar's face, like an oily wave.

Tomas gasped.

Not a shadow, but something moving *inside* his friend, beneath the skin. It pressed against his cheeks, shifted beneath his lips, and moved toward his eyes.

Eyes, Razin saw, that had glazed over. They stared up at the night sky blindly, white and empty.

"What's happening to him?!" Tomas cried, desperately searching Razin's face for answers.

Geoff teetered between a curse and a prayer, withdrawing his hands from Dietmar, watching the shadow on his face ripple across his cheeks.

Razin remained motionless, his eyes narrowing further as he tried to make out his friend's features. He blinked. In the space of that blink, he thought he saw something—a shape emerging from the shadows. It flickered, and he wiped at his eyes with his palms.

There it was again—an oily blur, a stain leaking from Dietmar's mouth. It forced its way out between his lips, flowing out from the empty gaps in his gums like tendrils of trailing smoke.

"It's working!" He looked at Tomas to see if he had seen it too, and then at Geoff and Levi. Their faces were fixed masks of concentration, but by their bemused expressions, he could tell that they had not.

More of the oily black smoke spilt from Dietmar's mouth, now emerging from his eyes and nose, causing him to cough and gag. In the darkness, a shape began to materialise. Something solid taking form amidst the black smoke.

A figure, Razin thought, attached to Dietmar's mouth by the lips.

It is not a jinn.

Razin felt panic surge inside him. The smoke was *solidifying*, transforming before his eyes, unveiling some inhuman form. He tried to speak, to call out to his friends, but his lips moved soundlessly.

He trembled, battling the urge to flee.

Finally, he managed to recite the words of the sura. His voice wavered as the fire flickered, diminishing even as Geoff hurried to add more fuel.

"Bismi l-lāhi—"

The fire flared as if doused in oil, flooding the campsite with a blinding light. All the colour vanished, swallowed up by the harsh radiance, leaving only shades of grey and black in its wake and that shrouded *thing* emerging from Dietmar.

Then, the fire blinked.

And went out.

Razin yelled in alarm, drawing his sword as he struggled to rise. He blinked rapidly, urging his eyes to adjust as he stumbled to his feet. Tomas was shouting. Levi called out for Sara. Had they seen it too?

Something stirred in front of him, unfurling in the darkness. He could just make out an outline—a quivering presence unfolding from where Dietmar lay.

Razin swallowed hard.

Blearily, unclearly at first, he saw the thing looming over his friend. It was a naked, grey-skinned creature of vaguely humanoid proportions, straddling Dietmar's chest with its thighs. It sat over him like a lover, its bony shoulders hunched, its concave chest pressed tightly against its abdomen. It leaned down to reach Dietmar's face with its own.

A glistening sheen of milky white sweat dripped from its skin folds, staining Dietmar's bandages with its foul residue.

Razin watched the creature's throat ripple, throbbing with a peristaltic motion as it sucked on Dietmar's mouth. It looked like it was drinking.

Razin closed his eyes, hoping that when he opened them again, the apparition would have vanished.

The night snapped back into focus, revealing the cadaverous form still present, pinning Dietmar down. An image superimposed.

Horned dog, snapping teeth, befouled fur.

Razin took a step forward, raising his sword, but then hesitated… No mortal blade could dislodge this thing. Tomas's voice reached him from a distance. He hadn't moved; he hadn't witnessed the wretched creature draining their friend. How had he not seen it?

"…What is it? Razin? Can you hear me?"

"Do you not *see* it?" he hissed back.

Tomas hesitated, frowning in the dark. Then he followed Razin's gaze to the space above Dietmar's chest. Slowly, he shook his head.

"See what?" growled Geoff, kneeling amidst the ashes of the extinguished fire.

Razin didn't reply.

Slowly, in jerking choleric movements, the creature turned to look at him.

It is not a jinn, he thought again, certain of it now.

Sweat covered the creature's face, like a mucal slime. Its gaunt features resembled the countenance of a bat, with flaring nostrils in the shape of leaf-like folds and a small, narrow mouth. Sparse strands of oily hair dangled from an otherwise bald head, creased and spotted with age. The creature considered him through two black holes inside its skull—empty orbs, bereft of life. *Hackles raised, gaping maw.*

Then it spoke.

"Finish your song, Mohammedan." A slatherous black tongue emerged from its lips, flickering behind square teeth that looked like rotting stumps. "It has been so long since I was honoured in this way. Sing, Mohammedan. *Sing!*"

The voice was like an empty breath, an exhaling susurration of dry skin and wet lungs. An echo followed each word, repeating them half a second after they were spoken in an agonised moan.

Razin's eyes swivelled to the source of the echo.

Dietmar's mouth hung slack, his eyes glazed and white. Tomas and Geoff stared at him. They still couldn't see the creature, Razin thought.

They'd only heard its words repeated.

"The sura is not to honour you, shayāṭīn." Razin brought his eyes back to bear on the hunched figure. He took a deep breath, searching for his courage.

And finding it.

"It is to ward off you and your kind, son of Iblis."

The creature's lips parted, glistening with moisture, and formed a slavering smile. "*To Him belongs whatever is in the heavens and whatever is on earth.* Are these not your words?"

Razin felt a chill race down his spine. To hear the Throne Verse repeated, uttered by such profane lips.

"Impossible," he murmured.

The creature's laugh was like a whooping hyena, its wet echo amplifying the sound moments later. Its slobbering tongue writhed within its mouth as it shifted on Dietmar's chest, repositioning itself to face Razin better.

"I am *Him*."

Razin hissed. "Liar!"

The dark orbs welled, two empty cave mouths—the tombs of Cain and Abel, of Adam and Hawah. The creature sniggered. "Doubt has ever been your burden, Mohammedan—doubt about your friends, yourself… and your faith. Tell me… how did *Anak* taste? I can still smell that daughter of Adam on you. She is delicious, isn't she?"

Razin flinched, his cheeks burning with shame. *How did it know? (Consort to Barqan, teeth gleaming.)*

The creature licked its lips lasciviously, its black tongue unspooling. "Did you fill her womb with your seed? Yesss, you did, or you wish you did. I can give her to you. Speak the word, and she will be yours. Sweet Anak, her succulent fruit ready for your harvest."

"What is he talking about?" Tomas shook Dietmar's shoulders, trying to rouse him from his stupor. "Who is Anak?"

"Don't listen to him," said Razin, not averting his gaze from the creature. "The Devil speaks through him."

"The Devil," the creature hissed, the sound turning into a dry cackle.

"If not the Devil, then who? Name yourself, shayāṭīn!"

"Name myself, name myself," the creature crooned. *He saw a hyena dripping in blood, a leonine carcass at its feet.* It leaned forward, folding its limbs to rest on Dietmar's chest. His eyes shifted to the long nails curving like talons from one hand. He frowned. The other arm ended in a flat stump above the wrist.

"*Neither slumber, nor sleep overtake Him,*" the creature sang in its lilting, gravelly voice, "*the Ever Living, none has the right to be worshipped but He.*"

"Silence!" Razin roared. "You dare mock the words of the Prophet?" He turned to Tomas, who still stared wide-eyed at the space above Dietmar's chest.

"Cover his mouth," Razin commanded, motioning with his sword. "It cannot speak without him."

The creature laughed again, the sound moist from Dietmar's mouth. "Clever Mohammedan. Always so clever. Until your loins stir and hot blood fills your veins, is that it?"

Tomas scrambled forward on his knees, using his hands to close Dietmar's mouth. "Help me!" he cried, turning to Geoff as Dietmar started to thrash against him.

"What do you want?" Razin watched the creature's hand gently rubbing one of the arrowhead-like growths on Dietmar's chest in a disturbingly tender manner. The motion, so at odds with the creature's coarse words and pallid wet skin, set Razin's teeth on edge.

"Want?" I already possess what I desire. And with each passing moment, I grow more satisfied by it." The creature's dark, empty orbs gazed down at Dietmar before returning to Razin. "What is it you want, Mohammedan?"

To be free. To see this place behind me.

There had been a subtle pause before the question. Enough to make Razin hesitate.

He shook his head slowly. *It is a trick.* The spirit sought to ensnare him in some accursed bargain and see him undone. He would not be lured into it.

"Qula 'ūdhu birabbi n-nāsi," he uttered instead, reciting from the Al-Naas. If it had revealed the spirit to him, perhaps the sura could dispel it too. If not… His mind reeled, slattening down at the thought of there being any truth in the creature's words. He pushed the notion aside and shook his head. *That way lies despair.*

Geoff swore in the dark, yanking his fingers from Dietmar's mouth and shaking his injured hand. "The bloody fool bit me!"

The creature's greasy lips parted, its fleshy tongue lolling within its mouth.

"Do you know me yet, Mohammedan?"

Razin ignored the question, motioning to Geoff and Tomas to keep trying while he recited the sura.

"The humble would sheer their heads for me," said the creature conversationally. "My faithful flock, making offerings of their locks."

Geoff grappled with Dietmar's jaw, narrowly avoiding his snapping teeth with a pained grimace.

"And in return," the creature traced the contours of the growth beneath Dietmar's sternum, its gaze fixed on Tomas, watching the Englishman while he struggled with Dietmar's mouth, blind to the apparition mere inches away.

"And in return, I would grant them guidance… until the Pretender arrived and cast me out. You speak his words now. He knew me."

Razin shook his head, trying to block out the haggard thing's blasphemous words.

It chuckled, its neck moving in that jagged motion once more as it turned to face him. "Tell me, Mohammedan. Do you know to whom your prophet's life was dedicated?"

"Who are you?" Razin growled. "Not Allah. Not *God*."

The creature's elongated limbs unfurled, extending like the segmented legs of a spider. Again, that black tongue. *An image of a wolven head, great jaws snapping shut around him.* "I am He of the Quraysh and of the waxing moon. Of El-Lat and of Hit. Of Petra and the waning crescent. Worshipped in all places from Pozzuli to Ka'ba. I am the one before Him, from whom your God came, and to whom your prophet was dedicated."

"*Say your name!*"

"Dushara."

"No."

"He of Baal."

Razin shook his head. *No, no.* He saw an old man, his hair streaked with grey, standing over a be'er. The walls of Ka'ba rose behind him. He was leaning forward to stare into the cistern. There was something inside that wanted to come out.

"Do you know me yet, Mohammedan?" The creature repeated softly.

A seated figure, crown of bones, hyenas by his feet, long tongues lolling.

Razin nodded.

"So, name me."

"Hubal," said Razin.

The creature smiled.

34

"I recognise that look," Mushrie said, taking the seat opposite Razin within the shade of the cupola. "It's the same look you used to get when working through your sums. I know it means you're thinking whenever I see it—not often enough!"

Razin attempted to match his uncle's smile but quickly gave up.

"That serious?" Mushrie plucked a date from Razin's bowl and popped it into his mouth, chewing thoughtfully as he considered his nephew. "Is it that girl again? Shuhadah? Has that Al-Azm boy finally taken her away? I told you nothing good would come from that, little lion. But perhaps it is better to feel such things now rather than later, while the heart is still young and can heal."

"It is not that," Razin replied, shaking his head. Although his brief entanglement with Shuhadah *had* come to an end, he had always known that it would. Haqqi came from a wealthy family and had relatives in the Emir's own household. He would rise high and perhaps even have the Emir's ear himself one day. Razin's prospects were fewer in Damascus, and his future was less certain… if he chose to stay. He had already toyed with the idea of answering Nur ad-Din's call and joining the Jihad against the Ifranj, but that conversation with his uncle was for another time.

"Oh?" Mushrie's brows knitted together, the flecks of grey like salt on *Baharat* spice, as he scratched his round chin. "A matter of the mind, perhaps, rather than the heart?" He relished such discussions, using them as an opportunity to both teach and challenge his nephew. But when it came to rumour and superstition, the gossip of the common fellahin, Razin knew to be cautious. Mushrie didn't place much value in the wisdom of such things nor in the folk tales of the wandering *Bedû* who frequented the city. They lacked the epistemic quality of the hadith and relied too heavily on pagan traditions, where many of them found their origins—that they had been updated and now passed from the lips of the *Khataibs* and others of El Islam mattered not.

Mostly, Razin ignored such matters as well. But this one troubled him.

He averted his gaze from his uncle's stare, instead turning to watch the streets through the oriel window of their *mashrabiya*. The old road, the *Al-Aftāris*, would soon fill with people when the *ʿaṣr* prayer ended. A young man in thick *sirwâl* trousers, too warm for the summer, hurried past their balcony, making for the Great Mosque at the end of the street. The imam would scold him for his tardiness, and worse if he interrupted *takbir*.

"It is a matter of the soul, uncle," Razin finally turned back to meet his uncle's stare.

"Which is fed by the mind," Mushrie replied, still smiling.

Once, Mushrie's stubborn ability to have an answer for everything would have frustrated him, but now he found comfort in it. Such certainty was reassuring when it came to questions of the mind and soul. Razin picked a date from the bowl, took a sip of water to wash it down, and then told his uncle what he had heard.

"There is a story, amongst the followers of *Ruh' Allah*—"

"And how did you come to hear of it?"

"From 'Iweyz."

“’Iweyz again?” Mushrie spread his hands, already looking exasperated. “How you have the patience to listen to those women, I will never understand. You know the guests the Emir allows to visit are so eager to impress them that it’d be a wonder if any truth passes through their lips at all, and then there is the matter of—”

“*Uncle.*”

Mushrie paused and tilted his head, raising a hand in apology while snatching up a date with his other. “Go on. Tell me what story from the Christians has the Emir’s harem wagging their tongues and my favourite nephew so troubled.”

Razin snorted. As far as he was aware, he was Mushrie’s *only* nephew. But he ignored the well-meaning quip and turned serious.

“A *tajir* from Galilee, who trades silks and spices in Kedesh, told ’Iweyz that the priests there believe El Islam is as pagan as the beliefs of the old tribes. They claim that our assertion of one God is false… This tajir said that we are like the mušrikūn to the Christians—that we may claim Tawhid, but practice shirk.”

Mushrie watched him quietly. He had listened to enough of Razin’s puzzles and philosophical musings over the years to know that something as simple as the Franks’ derision—a common enough thing—was not enough to unsettle Razin’s mind. There would be more.

Razin folded his hands neatly, resting his wrists against the edge of the small round table as he contemplated his next words. Like his uncle, he wasn’t one to put much stock in the gossip of Unur’s harem, but something in ’Iweyz’s words had alerted him to the fact that what she had heard and relayed was more than the mere ramblings of a merchant seeking admiration.

Mushrie inclined his head, motioning for Razin to continue.

Razin obliged.

"They say that even the polytheists used 'Allah': it is simply a term used to refer to the chosen deity of the old tribes. It is not a name, not a proper noun. Somehow—the priests did not explain how—'Allah' became the substitute for the name of the God of our tribe. The Christians believe that we have been deceived, tricked into worshipping a deity that claims supremacy but is just one among many and that we have forgotten this fact. They…" Razin hesitated, glancing down at his hands and then back at Mushrie. "They say we worship a moon god. One of three."

His uncle rapped the table with the back of his hand, his knuckles bouncing off the wood once… twice… a third time.

Eventually, he tugged the sleeves of his thin *furweh* up to his elbows and placed his large hands in his lap.

"So typical," he said, "of the Christians to accuse us of the very thing they themselves are guilty of. I wonder if it is not to deflect attention from the nature of their Trinity that they accuse us of shirk? Or is it simply ignorance? What evidence did this merchant supply for these allegations?"

Though his smile remained, something cold had made its way into Mushrie's eyes.

"Speculation, only," Razin murmured softly, already regretting bringing up the topic. "Theory masqueraded as fact. Surely it is as you say, and they wish to deflect attention from their own… ambiguity."

Mushrie saw through his nephew's reluctance and dismissed his words with a wave of his hand. "Enough to trouble you. Let me hear it, if only to dispel the idea and put your mind at ease."

Razin sighed. He recognised the determined look in his uncle's eyes. It usually preceded Mushrie getting his way.

"They claim that the 'Allah' we call upon is simply the name we use to refer to our God—one who shares its origins with the 'Allah' of the mušrikūn, who are mistaken and believe that His divinity can be shared."

"They do not know God."

"No." Razin nodded. "But that is how the Christians compare us. According to 'Iweyz, they equate this moon god with Allah, suggesting that we have forgotten while the mušrikūn remember. It is for this reason that the mušrikūn argue Allah has children and a consort... that He belongs to a pantheon that has faded from the memory of us Muslims."

"But the Christians claim to know?" Mushrie turned to watch the street, his eyes wandering over the sun-baked cobblestones of Al-Aftāris. A gentle sirocco wind rustled the pine and jasmine bushes in the garden below, stirring a pair of nightjars that made their home there. They hopped from branch to branch, exchanging warbling birdsongs, before taking flight and disappearing into the *kakhli* sky.

"And how would they come to possess such knowledge?" Mushrie asked, shifting his gaze back to his nephew. "I have heard something of the strange theories they entertain... But this?"

Razin picked at a date distractedly. It was the same question he had posed to 'Iweyz after she had recounted the tajir's story. She had been vague in her details, more captivated by the taboo nature of what she had heard than concerned with whether it was true. She had grown irritated by his questions and snapped at him before sharing what she could remember to satisfy Razin's curiosity.

"They claim to possess a text," he began, pushing the bowl away. "Something from Ras Shamra, they say. A cuneiform alphabet that speaks of Allah and another entity in the same breath. It recounts their victories over Yammu and Mâtu... it describes the consort 'Anatu and his daughter... and it refers to them as the Trinity of the Moon."

"The moon," Mushrie growled. "And when was the last time 'Iweyz spoke to the Emir's son, I wonder?"

Razin frowned.

Faruk had vanished after Nur ad-Din's lieutenants had exposed the cult operating within the city. The Emir himself had disowned him and been compelled to negotiate with Nur ad-Din to safeguard his position as rumours spread throughout Damascus.

"Perhaps there is no tajir," Mushrie pondered aloud, continuing his train of thought. "Perhaps it is Faruk who speaks through 'Iweyz, sowing the seeds of his cult in the minds of the impressionable. After all, he was close with 'Iweyz, wasn't he?"

"He was."

"So, you see?"

"I had not thought to look at it like that, uncle."

Mushrie splayed his hands and motioned toward the bowl, taking a handful of dates between his large fingers. "This other entity," he spoke while chewing. "What name did Faruk give it? Who is this second face of Allah that we seem to have forgotten?"

Razin looked up as the call to prayer resounded from the minaret of the Grand Mosque, filling the air with the melodic voice of the muezzin.

"Well?" Mushrie rapped his knuckles against the table to get Razin's attention.

Once… twice… a third time.

Razin glanced at his uncle's hands and then back at his face. "'Iweyz would not say. But when she grew tired of my questions, she told me it was not one named by the Prophet. That he railed against al-Lat, Manat, and al-'Uzza, but there is no polemic in the Quran against *Him* because…"

"Because he is *He*," Mushrie finished.

Razin nodded.

"So, she makes an argument from silence. Or perhaps it is Faruk who does." Mushrie smiled thinly. "If we were to accept that every pretender not explicitly denied by the Prophet had some claim to Godhood, how many contenders would there be, do you think?"

"Many," Razin readily agreed. 'Iweyz's words now seemed naïve to him, and he felt foolish for even bringing up the matter with his uncle. It would take more pages than there was ink to fill them if the Prophet had declared every false god for what they were.

"Indeed, many," Mushrie repeated. He retrieved a pip from his mouth and dropped it into the bowl alongside the others. "Doubt has a way of clouding the mind, my young lion. It is through doubt that individuals like Faruk and his moon cult attract followers—through negation. But, like their false gods, their trinity of the moon, they offer no evidence for their beliefs. That is why they remain in the shadows while we bask in the light. Think of Faruk, who must deceive foolish girls to spread the lies of his god while he hides in some cave, dirty and hungry. He is worse than a dog! Yet, even a dog might attain Paradise or an ass… just as the Ass of 'Ozair did."

Mushrie leaned back in his seat, exasperated, though his eyes glowed with excitement.

Razin took a sip from his water, parsing his thoughts. Mushrie had dispelled any lingering doubts he harboured, as he so often did. Still, something niggled at him, a thought not yet fully formed, but given enough time, he knew, the seed of doubt.

"Uncle," he said, drawing Mushrie's gaze away from the street. Al-Aftāris was filling again, the afternoon prayers now concluded.

"Hmm?"

"What was the name of the god in Faruk's moon cult?"

Mushrie waved his hand dismissively. "One of the old Meccan idols. What does it matter?"

"Which one?" Razin pressed, already suspecting the answer.

Mushrie's indefatigable smile slipped.

"It was Hubal."

***

Razin stumbled back, his uncle's words vivid in him. The memory of that afternoon above Al-Aftāris reeled out in his mind's eye, unfolding like the images from Gizzal's Occularis Box. He could see the sunlight filtering in through the square panes of the mashrabiya, feel the warmth against his skin, and taste the water from his cup on his lips.

They do not know God.

His uncle's words rang inside his head. That smile—so certain—suddenly wavering as a shadow passed across his face. Had there been doubt in his eyes at the end? Razin tried to remember his uncle's words to him. What had he said next? But the memory began to fade, the strands of their conversation winding down on themselves until he felt like a spider caught in the depths of his own unravelling web.

Hubal.

A sudden wave of nausea overcame him, and he gasped for breath. *How could a name affect him so? A name, a name, that was all.* But even as he thought the words, he knew it wasn't true. The name was a symbol, a neat heuristic for a weave of complex contradictions. It wasn't the name itself that made him reel or caused his uncle's smile to falter; it was what it symbolised.

He blinked, staring into the gloat of shadows, bringing himself back to the present.

And then, Hubal moved.

The action was disjointed, inorganic. The creature's limbs shifted in short, staggered motions, dislocating as it rose on Dietmar's chest to squat over him like a *shibeh* scavenger over its prey. *Stumpy teeth, chattering jaws, a hyena's laugh.* It was larger than he'd first thought. Or had it grown within a matter of moments? Its black tongue slithered out from between its grey jaws, like rotten meat falling through a butcher's grate. The empty space of its eyes swelled, a darkness so absolute that no light could ever live there.

Two cave mouths into which the sons and daughters of Hawah walked, cast to live amongst the nightdirt and fallen things.

Razin found himself staring into those orbs, his thoughts numbing until they were little more than an empty drone, penetrated by motes of silence and then something else—a sonorous utterance of

A-la-la

The words came in a percussive roll, a squall of one hundred voices in the distance; at once, the bark of a rabid dog echoing from the walls of Al-Aftāris, then as something forbidden, whispered in a lover's ear.

Hubal extended his intact hand, the fingers opening like the petals of a rotten flower, pointing at Razin.

"You know my name, Mohammedan. And so you know me."

A-la-la

"I do not know you," Razin murmured, his voice breathless in his ears.

"I am the question that survives its answers," said Hubal. "But to *ask at all* is to know me."

Negation. Razin blinked, feeling his mind reel. Was this madness? Had he touched upon the chaos that would unravel him? Was doubt alone enough to see him undone? But doubt in what? In himself? In his faith? *In God.* How many years had it been since that first question—and every question since? He floundered. The darkness in the orbs was growing, itself an offer: a promise of an answer.

A-la-la

He did not want it.

"No!" Razin cried out, tearing his eyes away from the thing's gaze. "You are Shayāṭīn! Jinn! You ape the language of God, but it is as mockery. You hold dominion over nothing!"

Hubal scraped its jagged nail against the stump of its hand, its lips parting in a smile.

"I am He, brother to El-Lat."

"God has no brother."

"The conqueror of Mâtu and Yammu."

"Allah conquered all."

"'Anatu was my consort."

"There is none equal to He."

"I was favoured by Abdul Mutallib, father to Abdullah, father to Muhammad. He knew me. He heard me."

Razin snarled. *It lingers in the darkness because it cannot face the light.* "You are a deceiver, that is all. No more than a jinn. Beneath Adam."

Hubal's laughter echoed, shattering the errant drone that clouded Razin's mind. The nebulous holes in its skull flickered like swollen lids, blinking open and closed. It gestured toward Razin with its stump, lips parting once more.

But it did not speak.

The creature snapped its head upward to stare at the coned roof of the tower. A strange look contorted its gaunt features. Its twisted bat's nose creased and wrinkled, folds and folds of skin shimmering as if sniffing the air.

Then, it spat out a word—a curse, a stolen word from a forgotten tongue—and its face folded in on itself.

Fear.

Razin spun around, his eyes drawn to the tower. Something was descending from the window, their silhouette a dark figure against the illuminated room beyond.

The hermit? Razin wondered. But the figure's movements were lithe, nearly feline in nature. *The girl!*

With astonishing speed, she scaled the wall, using only her fingers and nails to navigate the surface, scuttling over the cracks and grooves she was using as handholds. Suddenly, a shadow loomed behind her, blotting out the light of the room, swaddling them in darkness once more.

At first, it looked like a coil of smoke, a single long plume protruding lengthways from the window. But as Razin watched, it grew, lengthening as it unfurled.

Then the shape solidified. Imposed itself upon the world.

Silvery white scales, anaemic in the faint starlight, rippling muscle that quivered beneath the reptilian layers. Substantiality emerged from the wisp of smoke, the weight of the thing's presence like a splinter in existence. A face appeared from within the coils, grey hair and thin lips, a mouth parting to reveal fangs as long as arms.

Geoff let out a roar of warning, and Sara screamed.

This they can see, at least.

Behind Razin, someone coughed violently, choking and gasping in a horrific wracking manner. He snapped his gaze around in time to see the last of the wretched thing that was Hubal disappearing back down Dietmar's throat. Its bilious limbs, long feet the length of a human arm, squeezed impossibly through the small hole. Dietmar's eyes flickered open as he dragged in a breath, confusion clouding his wet eyes. Vomit covered his mouth and chin, dripping onto his bare chest.

The campfire blinked back into life, illuminating the camp.

Hubal was gone.

***

The world came back to Dietmar in a flood of agony. He retched, crying out at the pain in his throat and chest. It felt like someone had tried to flay his skin with boiling water. He tried to swallow, but something pressed back in his throat, forcing him to gag. In that breathless moment, he felt torn in two, dislocated, like he had upon the Ishkur when the truth he had banished for so long had come looking for him. This was the same. Only, this pain held no truth.

He remembered a voice. *Razin?* And then another: the lecherous thing inside his head. He had nearly succumbed to that voice, slipping away into a silent void to be at peace at last. A part of him yearned for it—no more violence, no more anger, no more heartbreak… no more pain. An emptiness reserved for him, if only he would let go.

Ephium smiled, and Dietmar felt his own lips parting to mirror the motion through no action of his own. He was losing control to… Not Ephium. No, that wasn't his name. He was… something else.

Shapes emerged from the shadows around him. A face hovered above, red brows arched, eyes wide. Panic and fear and desperation all competing for a place and agreeing to take it in turns.

Tomas.

He was saying something, something important by the intensity of his gaze, but Dietmar wasn't listening. His eyes had fixed on the canvas of night sky behind Tomas's head. The air was creased, wrinkled like old skin dried out by the sun and wind. Colours began to bleed into it, with long, iridescent streaks staining the sky like bruises. The firmament shimmered, awash with the glow of a strange patina.

Dietmar stared, his eyes alighting on something within the celestial expanse.

A shadow moved beyond the stars.

It stood out against the luminescent canvas, a void in the midst of colour. Revelation, he thought, watching the great tendril looming in the darkness.

Not in the darkness, but of the darkness.

Delirium washed over him, mingling with exhaustion, fear, and sickness. Nausea rolled in relentless waves as he continued to gaze at the sky. Yet, even in his disorientated state, a sense of awe settled upon his scarred skin. It was the primordial thing, the tusk from which the sea of chaos was nourished and existence fashioned. And it was breaching, rising up from the primaeval sea—*Tiamat*. That is what that mad little scholar had called it.

Dietmar wanted to laugh as his head swam.

He saw Razin, his friend's face flickering before him. A memory? Yes, from before, when the thing inside him had become untethered. When it had *used* him, usurping their positions in their relationship in an instant. It had stripped him of autonomy. Did that mean he had none at all? Razin's mask had been replaced by a look of anger, and then... *A hyena's face, blood coated.*

Dietmar flinched at the empty holes that were its eyes. They widened until they were the size of cave mouths. Servile teeth encircled them, gnashing together in hypnotic asymmetry. The nose resembled a withered leaf, folding and folding until it concealed the entirety of the creature's face.

And then, it vanished.

Dietmar felt hands upon him, and loud, urgent words barked in his ear. He tore his gaze away from the sky and locked eyes with Tomas.

The world got loud again.

"*Demon!*" Tomas screamed, spittle flying from his mouth. "In the tower!"

The Englishman shook his shoulders so hard he thought they might come off, only stopping when he cried out.

He cried out again when he looked past his friend and saw the thing descending from the tower. Its skin was grey and nearly translucent, ribbed like a worm and covered in miasmic welts. The impression of something ancient and vulgar insinuated itself into the meaty grooves of his mind, and he shuddered in revulsion. He felt his gorge rise when he saw the face appended to what must have been the head of the creature. It was stretched too wide and flat to be a human's. And yet the face staring down at them *had* been human once.

Tattered flesh hung in strips where the skin had ruptured. Bulbous eyes protruded, glazed over in an empty stare.

And behind it, pools of red glowed like smouldering coals.

The serpentine body wore the hermit's face like a mask, pulled taut over its sinusoidal form. The old man's lifeless arms dangled at his sides, his body ending abruptly at the waist, merging seamlessly with the creature beneath.

The creature's red eyes shifted away from Dietmar, fixing on the figure scrambling down the walls below.

"Tanit," Dietmar mouthed, forming the words with his tongue and lips but not hearing them in his ears. His lungs felt like they were on fire.

The hermit's face stretched wide, the skin peeling back to reveal a fleshy pink hole. Rings of spiky barbs bristled inside. Long, needle-like shafts akin to those of a porcupine quivered, shifting in minute waves.

The serpent lunged forward, its body unravelling with incredible speed toward the girl. Dietmar thought it would catch her, engulfing her head with its maw. But she moved like an acrobat, kicking off from the wall and folding in the air. Her legs rotated above her head, and she landed gracefully on her feet, quickly springing up before the creature could adjust its course.

And then she ran.

She skipped past Dietmar and Tomas, leaving them gawping up at the beast in stunned disbelief. Geoff's face appeared, aglow in the light of the rekindled fire. He herded Levi and Sara in front of him, holding his sword out behind him in the direction of the serpent.

"What are you waiting for?!" He cast a quick glance over his shoulder and motioned to Dietmar and Tomas. "Unless you want to see your faces stretched like that fucking thing, come on!"

Dietmar hobbled forward, moving into a slow limp after Geoff. He winced as he felt Razin's hand under his arm, offering support and urging him to move forward.

He risked a glance over his shoulder and saw the serpent rearing up, exposing its belly as more of its monstrous form spilt from the tower. The white flesh of its underside was stained a bright sickly orange, like some kind of fungal growth or rot had set it. *The rust of ages.* His eyes widened at the sight of two slender arms dangling from the creature's chest. The arms had small, infantile hands with short stubby fingers that twitched and grasped at empty air.

For some reason, that was the worst thing about it.

The grating sound resurfaced, like grinding rocks. It was coming from the tower's neck, spilling out of the window with the serpent's coils.

It's not stone on stone, he realised. The whole tower was filled with the creature's writhing body, pouring into the night. A waxen oil coated its scales, aiding its rapid movements as it coiled around the tower's peak. Finally, the end of its tail emerged, near glowing with the sickly orange rot that covered it. It curved vertically, tapering to a point like a crocodile's. It was adorned by twin rows of serrated spines culminating in a trigon spike, as sharp as any arbalest's shaft.

The creature peered down at them from the rooftop, following the girl's flight from behind its contorted skin mask.

"It *ate* the Hermit," Tomas moaned.

"No," Dietmar said, feeling the eyes of the beast turn to him. His voice was feeble, and it hurt to speak, but he *could* speak now and felt some small relief at that, if nothing else. "There was never any hermit. It lured us here to boast to, and then to hunt and eat."

"But... the songs?" Tomas shook his head, his brow knotting as he parsed through the possibilities. "That mouth. How?"

"What does it matter?" Dietmar croaked, trying not to trip as they hobbled away. "It could come from its arse for all I care. Let's go."

When Dietmar looked back again, he saw that the serpent had begun to move. Its head swayed from side to side as it descended, slithering across the stone with coarse scales. The skin mask mimicked life, with the hermit's arms flapping in a grotesque imitation, like a rotting puppet. The creature's reptilian hide rippled as it picked up speed, revealing more of the white barbs rising along its back, like a crest.

Dietmar turned away from the thing, setting his mind to the task of putting one foot in front of the other. A voice urged him onward—Ephium? No. *Hubal.* Had there ever been an Ephium? A benevolent saint who healed the sick? Or was it always just this *thing*. It didn't want to die here either. *Could it die?* The thought was doused before he could properly consider it when Sara started to cry up ahead. Her father whispered reassurances as they loped past the fire but to no avail. Geoff shouted at her, and she only cried louder.

And then, when the serpent began to sing, Dietmar thought that he might cry too.

Regretful hunter, bound by des-s-stiny
Perhaps now, you s-shall be s-s-set free

He felt for his sword, drawing it clumsily, while Razin and Tomas dragged him through the sand.

My fangs-s-seek life
Yet I mourn with every bite

The grating sound stopped, and Dietmar knew that the creature had moved onto the sand and was now gliding quietly over it. It would eat them and skin them and wear them like masks for eternity.

Come to me, my s-s-sweet-s-s

A figure darted out from the shadows ahead, moving swiftly over the dirt. But not into the darkness beyond the tower. It was running *toward* the serpent.

The girl.

She sprinted over the sand, her lips parted in a feral snarl.

Dietmar's foot caught on something in the dirt, and he stumbled, then fell, bringing Razin and Tomas down with him in a tangled heap of limbs and muffled curses.

He glanced up, ignoring Razin's muffled protestations as he tried to get back on his knees. Tomas struggled in his robes beside him, yelping as panic threatened to take him.

"It's coming, it's coming!" he cried.

Dietmar cursed and told him to be quiet. In the midst of the chaos, he caught a glimpse of the girl within the flickering glow of the fire. She was hunched over it, dragging a branch from the smouldering embers. The serpent slithered through the sand, flattening what gorse and shrubbery remained in its path.

He could see it clearer now. A flat, toad-like skull pressed against a man's skin. Bony ridges protruded where the creature's face was at odds with the hermit's, turning the skin white from the tension, creating a strange asymmetry that only added to its horrifying appearance. The torn, ragged mask clung to the hermit's face, held in place by a fan of white quills.

How did I ever mistake this for a man?

Advancing steadily, the serpent locked its gaze on the girl. The hermit's face opened at the mouth, stretching impossibly wide to show the rows of spiny teeth. Flakes of skin sloughed off, shedding in motes of dry flesh. The quills stuck out of it like tent pegs, pressing against it in strange ways, contorting and warping the expression on the face even as they tore through it.

The girl stood undaunted in the face of the beast. Then, just when it seemed she would remain rooted to the ground until it was upon her, she leapt forward, gripping the burning branch tightly. She swung it with both her hands and launched it high, over the serpent's head.

Dietmar watched its curling arc against the night sky. Sparks trailed it like the tail of a shooting star, flittering out as the dry leaves caught alight and lived and died in that moment. The girl's throw was good, and the branch spun once before vanishing through the tower window.

"Away, girl!" Tomas cried, helping Dietmar to his feet.

But the serpent had paused, coming to a shuddering halt just a few paces away from Tanit. Its monstrous head turned toward the tower, fixating on the window.

There was a soft hiss—from the creature or from the window, Dietmar wasn't sure.

Then, the glow from the tower room swelled, streaks of orange licking the air like fiery tongues, casting dancing shadows upon the walls. Smoke billowed out from the window as the fire took hold.

The serpent snapped its head around, its prickly mouth quivering in a nervous undulation. It seemed uncertain, torn between the girl and the fire burning its way through its room.

Through the history of the world, Dietmar thought. *Perhaps that much was true if nothing else about the demon?*

The creature reared up again, its crest splayed and fluttering, but it didn't lunge forward to swallow Tanit whole. Instead, it pivoted on the sand, carving a path back toward the tower. Its head bobbed rhythmically as it moved, coiling its long body around the stone walls, while the hermit's lifeless form mimicked the movement, arms swinging limply from side to side. Each winding motion brought the hermit's hands together, producing a resounding clapping sound that echoed across the camp.

As Dietmar turned to run, a thought crossed his mind—it seemed as though the dead hermit was applauding.

35

They fled the hermit's tower in silence, their retreat through the scrubland unmarked by curses or prayers or questions without answers. And what comfort could be found in the sound of each other's voices anyway? What words of reassurance could bridge the unsettling void that engulfed their hearts?

Even when dawn broke ahead of them, and they had put enough distance between themselves and the tower to slow, they spoke little. A few words to pass the time while they rationed out the water, a curious comment at the sight of strange birds flocking above, or a simple question and its answer. But anything of substance, anything that might broach the subject of what they had seen or disrupt the soporific numbness that had enveloped them, was left unspoken.

In truth, the only thing that kept them going was the sight of the growing peaks in the distance. They straddled the horizon, each peak as towering and vast as the Carpathians or the Turkic mountains, where so many Franks had gone to die.

The Daughters.

Their sheer size made the rest of the world appear flat in comparison. The once soaring hills diminished to mere mounds, while rugged gorges appeared as faint lines against the backdrop of their unearthly grandeur.

The *Jebel Kâf*, Razin called them. The World End Mountains.

When Tomas pressed him for more, Razin fell silent, his knitted brow fixed upon the looming range, until Tomas gave up asking. But he had said all he needed to. The meaning was clear: they were nearing the edge of the world.

They pressed on through the dawn, traversing from dry scrubland to dunes and back to scrubland again. As the day progressed, they found themselves following a path of sorts amidst spindly bushes devoid of leaves and short, stunted trees. The path meandered gently along a rocky escarpment that might have once been a riverbed. Now, it lay barren and desolate, with only unsightly weeds sprouting between the grey stones that littered its surface.

"A goat's path?" Tomas asked as they followed the trail.

Dietmar grunted and then furrowed his brow. *What goats could survive such a place?*

"Don't ask questions you don't want to know the answers to," said Levi, trudging along the hardened sand. He kept his head low, his shoulders hunched, with Sara never more than a few yards away.

Tomas cast a nervous glance up the slope and then back down toward the empty riverbed but kept any further questions to himself.

At noon, Geoff pointed out a fourth peak rising in the distance, separate from the Jebel Kâf. The air around it carried a faintly green gossamer glow, like colours reflected through morning dew on a spider's web. As they picked their way through the chaparral, the glow grew brighter until it was like a second sunrise to the east. Dietmar rubbed his eyes and looked away but noticed Razin still staring at it.

"That is where the *daevas* dwell." Dietmar's mouth formed the words, and he spoke them, but they were not his own. "Wait," he said, shaking his head. "I didn't say that."

Razin blinked, finally tearing his gaze away from the emerald peak to regard his friend.

"That wasn't me," Dietmar whispered, panic welling in his breast.

I am losing control.

The realisation sank in—it wouldn't be long until there was nothing left of him, just his rotting body, a vessel for the demon that was killing him.

Razin snarled. "It is that thing within you, the ghul, that claims godhood. It recognises its home—that is Mount Qaf. There are jinn there, and… other things."

—*other things*, Hubal echoed, and Dietmar fought the urge not to repeat the words. He looked back at the glacial rock on the horizon, shimmering like glass, its roof concealed by the haze of clouds and dust.

"It will grow more animated the closer we get." Razin reached out to gently touch his shoulder before striding ahead. He said, "You must ignore it, German. Soon, we will put this place behind us."

Would they? Dietmar wondered.

All they had was the word of a man-eating hyena shepherd that their path home lay beyond the mountain range before them. What reason did that treacherous little bastard have to tell the truth? He had wondered at that before, concluding that Teoma had no reason to lie either. Still, from what Razin had said of the jinn, their natural state lay closer to dishonesty than to truth. But, like so many other things, Dietmar kept his concerns to himself. If their path proved false, they had nothing.

He followed after Razin, quickening his pace at Geoff's alarmed cry up ahead.

Geoff stood on the edge of a small ridge, staring up at the branches of a leafy tree pinioned between two boulders on the slope.

"What *is* it?" he asked as the others trudged up to join him.

Dietmar scanned the branches for a moment, not immediately sure of what had caught the mercenary's attention. Then he gasped, his pulse quickening as his eyes settled on it.

A human face was watching them from the tree.

"Not again," Tomas moaned, stepping behind Razin.

"It's not a mask," Geoff said quickly, waving at him to calm down. "Or at least, I don't think it is."

Dietmar fiddled nervously with his hilt, not taking his eyes off the tree, half-expecting to see the hermit's white coils and flaring spines at any moment. But Geoff was right. The face watching them was not a mask, or if it was, it was exquisitely crafted, devoid of the puncture marks and tattered edges of the face in the tower.

The creature moved slowly, taking them all in with its large eyes. Its motion was smooth, accentuated by a subtle bob that brought to mind the curious head movements of a barn owl. The leaves parted slightly, revealing a long-feathered neck and a broad plumage-covered chest. There was a seraphic beauty about the creature's face and its slow, elegant movements, and Dietmar wondered if it might not be an angel.

"Fuck off!" yelled Geoff, reaching for a stone.

"Wait!" Razin stepped in front of him and raised a hand.

Geoff gave him a bemused look and cocked his arm. "You think that thing doesn't want to eat us? Look where you are, man. *Everything* wants to eat us. That pretty little thing too. Best we scare it off before it grows bolder and takes one of our legs, no?"

"Not this," said Razin, glancing back at the tree before locking eyes with Geoff. A warning laced his voice as he said, "Leave it be."

The creature had shifted forward on its branch, tilting its head to observe the events unfolding on the slope. Dietmar couldn't see anything in its alien stare to indicate a threat, not that that meant much.

"Leave it," he said when Geoff turned to him for guidance.

The mercenary grunted and quickly dropped the stone without further protest. By the look on his face, he wasn't keen on pelting the beast anymore anyway.

"Why does it look like us?" Sara asked, taking a few steps toward the tree before Levi grabbed her by the arm and guided her back.

"Or us like it," Dietmar mused. He caught Razin's eye. "Can it talk?"

"I don't know."

"But you know what it is? Enough to know it won't harm us?"

Razin shrugged, earning a snort from Geoff, who was fingering the hilt of his sword.

"We have encountered one before," said Razin, ignoring the mercenary. "A captive in Ubar. At the time, I wasn't certain, but now I am sure."

Dietmar considered this and then recalled the trader who had been ahead of them in the line at the city gates. There had been a shadow within his cart, a vague impression of something long and avian, before the vendor had closed the back flap and tried to barter with them.

"An anqa?" he recalled the trader's words.

Razin nodded.

"So, we saved ourselves a couple of kug," Geoff said, visibly relaxing. If that slimy trader had managed to capture one, then it couldn't be so dangerous after all.

"They dwell in the Jebel Kâf," said Razin. "It is said that they can live to be hundreds of years old and possess greater wisdom than mankind."

"Not wise enough to *evade* man though." Geoff chuckled, but his laughter sounded forced. When Dietmar glanced at him, his features were shadowed and sombre.

A sad look crossed Razin's face. "They do not see the malice in man because they possess none in themselves. Such creatures should not be confined to cages. We only expose our own wickedness by doing so."

"I don't think the fine folk of Ubar give much of a fuck about that," said Geoff, absentmindedly scratching at a pimple.

"No," agreed Razin. He stared at the anqa for a moment longer and then continued on his path along the ridge, moving past the tree with a single nod toward its occupant.

After seeing Razin pass unharmed, the others followed suit, with Dietmar being the last to pass by. As he approached, the creature shifted farther along the branch, revealing a long, drooping tail adorned with vibrant, flaring colours. He counted four wings neatly folded against the anqa's almond-shaped body and marvelled at the intricate patterns purloining its chest.

But Dietmar couldn't fully appreciate the ethereal beauty of the creature. He was too busy trying to suppress the voice whispering in the depths of his mind, urging him to

Kill it, kill it, kill it.

***

As the afternoon wore on, a hot wind picked up, drying their lips and eyes and scouring their skins raw until they were forced to walk with their heads bowed and their faces covered. Dark clouds trailed the wind, their bellies swollen and ominous with the promise of a storm. They billowed forth from the Jebel Kâf and would be over them by nightfall.

Dietmar risked a glance upward, observing the perpetually green glow that now shrouded the sky. He gestured for the others to climb up the side of a steep hillock, leading them away from the path and toward the refuge of an overhang nestled against its side.

The stone lip concealed a shallow hollow within the rock, just large enough for them to squeeze into, and they settled in, away from the wind.

"I'll start a fire," said Geoff, squatting on his haunches to bundle together what slivers of dry wood and grass he found on the floor. After a moment, he ducked out of the hollow to search for more.

Dietmar unrolled his sleeping sack and folded it into a makeshift cushion before sitting down and looking around. A single spear of light was all that made its way through the opening, illuminating the sandstone wall to the back of the hollow. A hairline crack split the wall in two, and he followed its passage out of the light and into the gloom. The crack widened, culminating in a hole large enough for a small person to crawl through near the floor. Levi and Sara sat to either side of the pit, watching it nervously until Razin covered it with his own sleeping sack.

When Geoff came back, they lit a modest fire from rags, dead leaves, and branches and listened to the wind howl over their little recess.

"At least we'll have water," Tomas remarked, prodding the fire with a stick before glancing up at Dietmar. "How are you feeling?"

"Like shit," Dietmar replied, stifling a laugh that threatened to turn into a cough. It hurt when he coughed, like his lungs were riddled with tiny wooden splinters. Come to think of it, even breathing hurt.

Tomas nodded, a sad look in his eyes that lingered too long. Dietmar pictured himself in Tomas's eyes: a skeletal figure with pale flesh hanging off him like an old hessian sack. His back was fixed in a permanent crooked hunch now. It wouldn't straighten no matter how hard he tried, and he wasn't sure if he had enough teeth left to eat, even if they did manage to forage up some food.

Tomas tossed the stick into the fire and folded his hands in his lap, where he fidgeted with them while watching Dietmar.

"Can you hear it?" he asked. "The… Saint?"

Dietmar shook his head and then nodded. What hushed conversation among the others ceased, and he felt their gazes turn to him, except for the girl, who hadn't taken her eyes off Razin's sleeping sack since he'd covered the hole with it.

"It never *stops* talking," Dietmar confessed, looking over the fire at Tomas. "But if it was ever the voice of Ephium, it has long since been corrupted. If there was even a saint to begin with."

Tomas frowned. "You think Gelmiro tricked us and then betrayed us too?"

Dietmar hesitated, then shrugged. "I do not know what I think anymore. But this voice…even in my sleep, I hear it. Sometimes it speaks to me directly. Sometimes I think I'm only hearing its thoughts. It hears mine, too. It knows things… things I had forgotten." He could hear it now, crooning in the dark place behind his thoughts, growing louder, nearly impossible to ignore.

"Your… wife?" said Razin. He sat on the sand floor next to Tanit, carefully slicing pieces from a wooden block he had found.

"Her, and other things."

"What other things?" Tomas leaned forward, his hands warming by the fire. He looked up as the shard of light coming from outside vanished. The clouds were above them now.

Dietmar shrugged. "Stories, mostly. When they're not outright lies, they're close enough to them."

Tomas stared at him, waiting for him to continue.

"Simple things," said Dietmar before taking a sip from the flask being passed around. He wiped his lips on the back of his hand, wincing as he felt the boils against his skin. His very breath was a reminder of what was happening to his body. He fortified himself, not letting self-pity flood his thoughts, and continued. "The Lady Marie and Arcadius, for instance… It told me that they were kin, that Arcadius had sired her after coupling with the Lady Chiva, her mother. I doubt even Arcadius knows, if it's true."

Geoff snorted. "That Greek dog."

"They shared a chin," commented Razin, not looking up from his carving.

"What else?" asked Tomas.

"Things about me. Things about you." Dietmar waved his hand vaguely. "Things about all of us."

"Blasphemous, treacherous things, no doubt," said Levi, taking the flask.

"About… me?" Tomas watched Dietmar intently.

Profligate, philanderer, drunkard, sodomite.

"Oi," spat Geoff. "What did the Jew tell you about asking questions you don't want to hear the answers to? What good could a demon's words possibly bring to you or us, eh?"

Dietmar looked at him.

Murderer, traitor, blasphemer, rapist.

"Fuck that *cunting* thing, I say," Geoff continued, throwing more wood onto the fire. "I don't want to know what it thinks."

"It lies," said Razin, turning the carving over in his hands and then blinking up at Dietmar.

Coward.

"That is its purpose: to lead us astray, to turn man against man. It envies us. That we are favoured by God drives it to an anger we cannot even comprehend."

Dietmar could feel Hubal's consciousness intertwining with his own—silent, listening. It hardly needed to articulate its thoughts anymore, the vocalisations of before a poor substitute for the flow between them of now. He sensed Hubal's emotions, reading them like he knew it was reading his own. But there was no jealousy or rage within him, only contempt… and perhaps a thinly veiled delight at Dietmar's misery.

"It told me that Adelman had stolen from me," he said suddenly, almost to himself. He sighed. *How can I believe that?* A little part of him—the dark part where Hubal now resided—had felt a twinge of relief when the old man had died. He had become a burden, incapable of surviving in this place. He was a reminder of a time Dietmar wished to forget, of emotions he wished to bury. The excuses had lined up. Or perhaps it was because he had seen the thing within Dietmar before anyone else, recognising it for what it was, that he had felt relief when Adelman was gone? Him and those mules that had seen too much and listened too well. But that feeling… it had never really gone away.

What did that make him, then?

Callous. Bastard.

He glanced at Razin, looking for some sort of reassurance. He'd managed the books about as much as Adelman near the end. But his friend simply shrugged and returned to his carving.

Dietmar had noticed Razin's reluctance to meet his gaze since the events of the previous night. Did he fear him now too?

"What about her?" asked Geoff, with a nod to Tanit. "What does your demon say about our little savage?"

"We'd all be dead without her," said Tomas, some paternal instinct stirring within him.

"Aye, maybe," Geoff replied.

"She saved us." Tomas pulled his sleeping sack over his knees and settled into a more comfortable position. "If she hadn't thrown that branch through the tower window, that flayed thing would have eaten us all. But no, it chose to save its histories, so here we are."

"Do you really believe that?" Geoff briefly glanced to the opening where water splashed beyond the overhang, turning the world outside into a grey haze. "The history of the world," he said, turning back to Tomas with a toothy grin. "And how did that beast pen its history then?"

"With *its hands*," Tomas said, ignoring the sarcasm in Geoff's voice.

"I saw them too," said Sara, her voice meek amidst the sound of rain. Levi nodded in agreement, causing Geoff to hesitate.

"What was she doing in the tower anyway?" Tomas asked, staring at the girl.

"Not reading, I reckon." Geoff sneered. "Can you read, girl? Do they teach you your letters in shitholes like Ladah?"

Tanit blinked at him.

"Thought not," said Geoff with an ugly laugh. He yawned, showing his teeth again, and then turned to Dietmar. "You never answered my question."

"What?" Dietmar shook his head, distracted.

"Your demon." Geoff pointed at the girl. "What did it say about her?"

Razin wiped the statuette down with his fingers and then tossed it to Tanit, who plucked it out of the air without even looking. Her eyes were still fixed on Geoff.

"I don't know," Dietmar replied vaguely, staring at the carving in the girl's hands. "It hasn't said anything about her." He realised that was true. Hubal had been silent about Tanit. Even now, he was mercifully quiet. Dietmar tilted his head to get a better look at the little wooden figure Razin had carved.

It was a small cat.

Tanit smiled.

***

They slept poorly that night, plagued by dreams that mirrored their waking thoughts and fears. They were jolted awake by strange sounds. At first, Dietmar thought it was coming from outside, but when he peered out into the rain-lashed night, he heard nothing. Then he saw the girl sitting in front of the hole between Levi and Sara. Her back was lit by the faint glow of the fire's last embers, the muscles in her shoulders tense. The covering over the pit had been removed.

The girl turned her head slightly to acknowledge Dietmar with a slow blink before resuming her watch, fixated on the dark void of the hole.

The sound, the one that had disturbed Dietmar earlier, returned. A scraping sound, as if someone were dragging themselves over stone. Like their legs didn't work, and they had to rely solely on their upper-body strength to move forward.

It was coming from the hole.

"Get away from there," said Dietmar, stepping forward.

Levi stirred from his slumber, groaning as he opened his eyes and disentangled himself from his sleeping bag. The girl cocked her head but didn't move.

The sound came again. Louder this time. Dietmar instinctively reached for his sword, only to realise that he had left it on the ground where he had slept.

He thought he could hear breathing now, uneven inhalations unaccompanied by any exhalations.

"Tanit?" Tomas said, looking nervously at the girl. "What is it?"

"It's just the wind," Levi said, the quiver in his voice betraying his disbelief.

"The fuck it is," said Geoff, crouching over his own sack, his sword resting on his knees. Dietmar noticed the pouch at Geoff's side, still untouched. Geoff gestured toward the hole. "It's that snake come to finish us off."

"The hole is too small," said Dietmar, picturing the hermit's stretched face struggling to force its way into the hollow.

It's something else.

He shifted to make room for Razin by the fire. His friend stared at the hole for a moment, then poked at the dying coals in front of them with his sword. Carefully, Razin scooped up an ember with the tip of his blade, balancing it as he moved closer. He settled onto his haunches, his sword held in front of him and launched the ember into the hole.

The coal spun into the darkness, flaring bright orange light that left a trail of shimmering ash in its wake. It didn't stop falling, even though its trajectory was perfectly horizontal.

A play of light? Dietmar wondered. *Some trick of the eye?*

Or had the coal's flight altered, finding a concealed curve within the hole and falling, falling. But if that were the case, shouldn't it have vanished from sight?

Then, without warning, the ember stopped moving. It flickered, its little light growing dimmer.

That sound again, like breathing.

The ember started to expand. At first, Dietmar thought that something was stoking it back into life, but then...

Tomas gasped. "Is it—"

"Coming back up," Dietmar finished, transfixed by the light even as he stepped back.

It was gaining speed, ascending quicker than when Razin had first flicked it into the hole. Dietmar thought about retrieving his sword, to have something to beat back whatever was propelling the coal to the surface, but he couldn't take his eyes away from it.

"It's *coming!*" Tomas's voice was coloured by fear, but he hadn't moved either.

Then, when the light became so bright that it caused Dietmar's eyes to sting, Tanit stepped over the hole and dragged Razin's sleeping sack to cover its mouth.

The sound stopped.

Dietmar braced, waiting for the coal to burst through the sack or the thing that had dragged it back up from the depths to plunge into the hollow.

But there was nothing.

Silence.

The girl moved away from the hole, stretching languidly before curling up in her corner. She blinked at Dietmar once, then closed her eyes.

"Try to get some sleep," said Dietmar to the others, his eyes still fixed on the canvas concealing the hole.

But none of them did.

***

The next morning, they departed from the hollow and the hole that may have led to Hell. But the landscape they found themselves in now was vastly different from the scrubland they had left behind.

Dietmar paused, coming to a stop on the slope above their narrow 'goat's path' and gazed across the transformed landscape. Where only dust and grey had previously prevailed, little more than a desert cappuchilia, now there was life. It bloomed in all the prismatic colours of a palace garden, and Dietmar thought this might be what the world looked like after the Flood.

The stunted bushes and sparse trees had swelled with the nourishing rain, their thick leaves and petals still glistening from the previous night's storm. Stalks had burst from the ground, growing in hearty clumps amidst broad-leafed creepers that stretched over the rock and soil. When Dietmar looked down at the escarpment, he saw that the dry riverbed now flowed with a rushing current, disappearing beyond the hill's slope.

Strange birds, creatures that had not known the refuge of the Ark, inhabited the trees lining the river. They darted into the water, using their hooked beaks that looked like hands to snatch stranger-looking fish. Dark shadows moved beneath the water's surface, tracking the birds. Dietmar watched as a large reptilian creature seized one of the hunters, pulling it beneath the water when it got too close. The bird's companions raised the alarm, squawking like monkeys on their perches while their compatriot struggled, thrashing madly against the ragged jaws of the shadowy predator. In a brief moment of respite, it managed to escape, shaking off the creature's teeth. Its wings were drenched in its own blood. The other birds created a cacophony of noise, flapping their wings and bobbing in the trees as they witnessed a second shadow hurtling toward the injured bird, still struggling to soar more than a foot above the water's surface. But the bird was too slow. It lurched into the air, flapped its injured wings once, twice, and then disappeared when a long, spiny body plunged it back into the river.

The birds in the trees lamented their loss, emitting shrill, panicked calls that cut through the air like a bittern's mournful song. Gradually, their cries subsided, and silence returned. Before long, they ventured back into the water, braving the depths to search for fish and avoid the lurking shadows.

There was an element of the Spring back home, Dietmar thought as they resumed their journey along the path. He had always found something disturbing about those early days when the tranquil stillness of Winter was stripped away, and life—vibrant, sweeping, fecund, and lascivious—erupted in its place. The change was *violent*, and if it weren't for the ensuing beauty of the days that followed, Dietmar doubted he would find anything redeeming about Spring's arrival.

That feeling of violence was everywhere here—an essence of revolution, of apocalypse. The creation of the new from the old, overturning it again and again. A part of Dietmar revelled in this primal force, but he knew that wasn't truly him. It was the thing inside him that recognised something of itself in this place—a reflection of the revolution it was performing on Dietmar's body and mind. The two coexisted in parallel… but from the scrubland, a verdant paradise had emerged, and Dietmar wondered what might flourish in his place once Hubal's rot succeeded. He thought of the spectre from his dreams again, the white, lifeless visage—a mere husk.

The sense of despair that accompanied such thoughts threatened to overwhelm him. All this, just to become the empty vessel for some craven thing that dared to compare itself to God? Again, what did that make of him?

He added *blasphemer* to his list of faults. *Iconoclast*, too. Because no holy man could carry such a curse or be damned to such a fate. If it weren't for the thought of Enneleyn and his son, Dietmar would have crumbled, surrendering himself to the riverbank for the birds to peck at.

But how long would that resolve last? How long could the memory of the dead keep him grounded before it, too, withered away, leaving his mind untethered from the world?

As long as it has to, he thought, slogging forward grimly.

The distant peaks loomed, their cold hues of blue growing closer with each step. That was all he could do—press on, one foot in front of the other.

When they judged the waters safe enough, free from the predatory shadows that stalked the birds, they paused to fill their flasks, taking it in turns while the others watched the river.

Razin was the last to kneel by the riverbank. After washing his hands and splashing his face with the cold stream, he stood up to find the girl standing before him. He arched an inquisitive brow, and she extended her hand toward him, concealing something small and white between her fingers.

"Take it," Levi said, passing by Razin and ascending the riverbank. "She is thanking you for your gift with one of her own. Take it!"

Razin cautiously opened a hand to receive Tanit's offering.

Her lips curved into a crooked smile before she dropped the gift into his palm. Then she followed Levi back up to the trail, leaving Razin to stare into his hand.

"What is it?" asked Dietmar, leaning over his friend's shoulder to see.

Razin closed his fingers before he could get a proper look and shook his head. He said something that sounded like *Isfahan* and pocketed the gift.

"Isfahan?" asked Tomas, emerging from the bushes and adjusting his robe's belt. "Did I hear that right? What's Isfahan?"

Razin turned in the sand, staring after the departing girl.

"It is the name of the serpent who smuggled Iblis into Paradise."

Dietmar frowned. "What did she give you?"

"This," Razin replied, retrieving Tanit's gift from the folds of his burnous. Resting in the centre of his palm was a fang, about the length of a finger, hollowed out as if the bone had been scooped out.

"Why's it hollow?" asked Tomas, moving closer to inspect it.

"Where do you think Iblis hid when the serpent carried him?" Razin closed his hand around the fang and stalked after the girl.

"He can't be serious," Tomas muttered, watching him leave. He glanced at Dietmar. "Can he?"

Dietmar shrugged.

"But that would make this Paradise," said Tomas.

"Eden," said Dietmar. He shrugged once more and followed Razin up the slope. Tomas muttered under his breath, shaking his head in disbelief, then glanced back at the shadows stirring in the water before hurrying after Dietmar.

***

Geoff died sometime after midday.

The sun had begun its slow descent, casting a different shade of green across the sky, as if smoky vapours were seeping out from the heavens.

It was not a good death.

He didn't meet his demise at the hands of a nightmarish creature or torn apart by a demon or jinn like the others before him. Still, it was not a good death nor a clean one.

It was the wet that undid him. A misjudged step on the slope sent him tumbling, sliding off the rocks like a bundle of old bones. He'd barked out a shocked laugh, but that had quickly turned into a scream as his legs collided with the first boulder, propelling him toward the ravine.

He hadn't stopped screaming.

Not until Razin had knelt beside him, silencing his agony with the same knife he had used for carving the night before. It had been a mercy. The way his neck had been bent, there was only pain left for him. Geoff had deserved mercy at the end, even if he had been a bastard. Even if he'd never offered mercy to another living soul in his mean, hard life.

And now he was dead, buried in the rich soil beneath a beautiful tree whose branches spread like a peacock in display. Geoff would have hated that, Dietmar thought. But how many could boast of a grave in Paradise? Not he. Someone had to be alive to bury the others. Someone's bones would have to be left to bleach under the sun and that green sky, to rot away in Paradise.

They may as well be his.

36

Tomas was the first to notice that they were being followed. He caught a glimpse of movement, a flicker of gold and brown among the trees lining the river. Each time he turned his head to look directly, it vanished into the dense foliage above, reappearing only when his gaze shifted away.

Another damn demon on the road to Hell, he thought, swiftly turning his head to catch sight of it in the open. A branch rustled, leaves fluttered to the ground, but of the elusive golden spectre, he saw nothing.

Could a demon dwell in Paradise? Tomas wondered, slowing on the path behind Levi to stare. Their trail had descended from the lofty slopes where Geoff had met his end, and now they walked amidst reeds, following the river at a distance no greater than a stone's throw.

There have been demons here before, he thought, scanning the branches for any sign of movement. Razin's 'Iblis' was a demon, was it not? *The* demon, from what Tomas understood of his friend's beliefs. Iblis and the Morningstar were mirrors of one another; the one, a jinn, resentful toward man for the pride of place God gave him. The other, an angel. That was… before the Fall.

And Iblis *had* snuck into Paradise. Perhaps he had lingered after tempting Eve, and it was him traversing the trees, chasing after the descendants of those he had first come to despise.

Chased by the damned Devil himself. Tomas shuddered, coming to a halt, his gaze fixed on the thicket.

"What is it?" Dietmar asked, limping up behind him. His cheeks were gaunt and hollow, like the stone peaks they endlessly marched toward. He followed Tomas's gaze, his hand trembling slightly as he touched one of the new sores forming on his lips.

"There's something following us," said Tomas.

"What did you see?" asked Levi, turning back on the trail to face him.

"A demon," Tomas replied, not looking away from the trees.

Dietmar stiffened, his hand going to his sword. "Are you sure?"

"No," Tomas confessed. "But something *is* following us. It moves when we move. It's quick, too quick for me to catch out in the open when I look. I only see glimpses: flashes of gold, like old coins… I think it is the Devil."

"A golden Devil."

To Tomas's annoyance, Dietmar relaxed a little, dropping his hand from his sword. Always the fool, Tomas thought bitterly. *Even in Hell, they will doubt that I saw demons.*

"It's there," Tomas said sharply, standing in Dietmar's way. He looked past Levi to Razin, who was retracing his steps to investigate the delay.

"He's still here, isn't he?" called Tomas.

Razin showed his palms, uncertain. He glanced at Dietmar.

"Don't look at him," snarled Tomas. "*I'm* the one who's asking. He's still here, isn't he? In Paradise!"

"Who is?" asked Dietmar. "Who are you talking about?"

"The Devil," Tomas growled, exasperated. "Iblis! Where did he go after tempting Eve? He didn't just disappear." He pointed at the girl still walking up ahead. "She found his hiding place, didn't she? This is Paradise, and the Devil is—"

"Cast out," Razin said before he could finish. "Flung from the Gate of Malediction to land face-first in Akabah. He is not here, my friend."

"Even if this is Paradise," said Levi, rubbing his chin. He'd lost weight since they first met in the desert after Samaria. Unlike Dietmar, he wasn't sick and still far from skin and bones. But the days without food and the meagre rations when there was anything to be found had taken their toll. "Which it's not," Levi finished firmly, as if the certainty of his words alone was enough to dispel the idea.

"Oh?" said Tomas, growing more agitated. "Look around you, all of you! We've all seen the slopes of the Kidron Valley after the rains, but this?" He snapped a reed, holding up the broken tip for all to see. "*Nothing* grows like this overnight. Trees don't burst from the ground after one storm, do you understand?"

"Why don't you just relax," said Dietmar softly.

"Relax?" Tomas laughed. "Am I the only one who sees what's happening here? There's a *demon inside of you*, and you're sceptical that I saw one following us? And now you want me to relax? Am I the poxxing fool, or are you? Which is it, eh?!"

"It's a monkey," said Sara, pushing past Levi.

"Huh?" Tomas shook his head, quite lost.

"A monkey," Sara repeated, motioning toward the trees. "Look!"

Tomas turned to stare and found that she was right. A golden monkey had descended from the branches and was hovering near the base of one of the trees.

It was watching them.

Tomas groaned. "Is that… Malah's monkey?" Memories of the Ishkur and the black waters flooded through him, along with images of the captain's flinty, treacherous eyes.

"I don't think so," said Dietmar, suddenly alert. He swept the treeline with his gaze, searching for signs of the captain and his crew.

Sara brushed the curls from her eyes and shook her head. "This one looks different. It's bigger."

Tomas had to agree. Where Malah's wretched beast had been sleek and lithe, spindly even, perfect for moving quickly up and down the masts of a ship, the creature watching them had a far more muscular physique. Squatting on its haunches, it looked, even from a distance, like it could reach up to Tomas's waist. Its features were different, too: its snout more pronounced, with a long, straight muzzle that reminded Tomas of a dog's. Its eyes lay hidden in the shadow of a brow as prominent as any Greeks' Tomas had ever encountered.

"It's a baboon," said Razin.

"Ugly thing," said Tomas with a nod. He'd seen one before, in Jerusalem. It had performed as part of a mummer's show, dancing and clapping at the urging of its master—a Muslim from Cairo. He had told the crowd that baboons were spectres of the dead. Ghosts sent by God to do man's bidding. Then the baboon had leaned back lazily and fiddled with its balls.

Tomas shivered, remembering the size of the creature's teeth when it had yawned.

"What's it doing here?" he asked.

Razin snorted. "Following us."

***

The baboon trailed behind them for a while, sometimes walking on foot, sometimes clambering through the trees, but never far from sight. Then, when the river and its fence of trees peeled away from their trail, the baboon loped ahead of the little band, gifting them with the sight of its purple bottom before vanishing into the reeds.

"It's probably laying traps for us," said Tomas. He'd been distracted since its appearance and had needed to be pulled from the reeds more than once after slipping on the rocky path.

"Baboons don't set traps," stated Levi. "They're scavengers, when they eat meat at all."

"So are hyenas," Tomas replied darkly. "And we know how that turned out, don't we?" The words were hardly out of his mouth when he realised his mistake. He raised a hand, flapping it in the air as if to retrieve the words before Levi could hear them.

The dyer scowled at him, his face a potent blend of hurt and anger—the look of a grieving father. He pushed past Razin, leaving Tomas stuttering an apology in his wake.

"I didn't mean it," Tomas babbled to no one in particular. Levi snapped something at Sara, who was staring back at him. She shook her head and hurried after her father.

"Bugger," Tomas muttered, pausing on the path to gather himself. "I never know when to keep my mouth shut, do I?" He'd had a habit of putting his foot in it since childhood, but usually, it'd been deliberate. When he'd grown tired of working in the Moors' churchyard, he'd asked the Abbot about the young woman he'd seen the clergyman carousing with in secret; when he'd tired of toiling for his keep in the sewers of Alençon, he'd commented on the steward's predilection for dice-throwing. There was no surer way of seeing yourself put out on your arse in the streets in his experience. It had been self-destructive, he knew. He'd given up a good thing each time: the safety of certainty, the security of a warm bed and a full belly each night. But each time he had known it was time to go—the east was calling. The longer he put it off, the more frustrated he felt, which only served to sour his mood and sharpen his tongue.

What I wouldn't give for my old room in Alençon, he thought wearily, trudging after Levi. He'd need to make his apologies and hope Levi didn't hold a grudge like he himself often did.

The sun was lowering when they saw the baboon again. Its golden fur shone in the fading light, capturing the last shards of light so that it glowed where it sat, motes of dust and dirt suspended in the air like a heavenly aura. A scattering of trees occupied the plain behind the creature, their tall, skeletal flames looked like they had survived the aftermath of a recent fire. Long, empty branches stretched like shadows from their heights, devoid of leaves. The trees stood as ashen husks, their bark gone grey and, in some places, pustule-yellow, bearing the marks of a sweeping malady that had plagued the woods.

The end of Paradise, Tomas thought as they left the reed path behind. Their route would bring them in close proximity to the baboon, and they all watched warily, mindful of its powerful jaws and canines that would put a hound's to shame.

The baboon eyed them in turn, grooming its coat and shifting lazily as it basked in the last of the sun. As they neared, Tomas noticed a glint of silver around the creature's neck. A collar. His thoughts briefly turned to Sagar in Ubar, the young boy with knowing eyes who had pointed them out to the priest, Bezal. He wondered if the boy had been transformed into this beast by some enchantment and if Bezal might appear at any moment to torment them.

But the man who stepped out onto the path from behind a tree was not Bezal. He was thin and delicate and altogether different from the priest who had wanted them dead. The stranger greeted them with open arms, like the Christ, and offered a warm smile. It was only then that Tomas noticed the bandages wrapped around the man's eyes. He was blind.

The golden baboon stirred at the man's arrival, rising from its haunches to stand at his side.

"We want no trouble," said Dietmar, coming to a halt just before the petrified forest. "Just to follow the path, that's all."

"No trouble," the man replied, raising his hands further. He wore simple travel attire—a lightweight cotton cloak over a shirt and sandals. His hair was concealed beneath a faded turban. "We are following the path, too, although our journey leads us in a different direction. Fortuitous, I think, for if we were headed the same way, our paths might not have crossed. We cannot disregard God's providence. I am Laurus the Blind." Laurus offered a slight bow before straightening, his hand moving to stroke the golden head of the baboon at his feet. The creature leaned into the touch, its leg kicking playfully like that of a dog.

"That yours?" Tomas asked, gesturing toward the baboon.

Laurus nodded.

"*We?*" Dietmar questioned. "You mean you and your beast? This is no place for a blind man and his pet. There are dangers here, both behind and ahead. Go home."

The man laughed, and even that possessed a delicate and beautiful quality, thought Tomas.

Then the stranger motioned toward the trees behind him, and suddenly, the path teemed with golden-brown figures. They poured out from the lifeless woods like a pack of famished wolves. Their coats radiated an autumnal hue, forming a carpet of furry bodies to replace the fallen leaves absent from the forest floor. At first, Tomas thought it was only baboons that had emerged—an entire troop of these muscular simian creatures, each adorned with the same silver collar as the first. But when he looked closer, he counted other men and women among them, all dressed in simple traveller's cloaks and sandals. They carried long staffs fashioned from a dark material that Tomas did not recognise. He thought it looked like stone. Strange patterns adorned the length of the canes, asymmetrical lines punctuated by letters in an alien alphabet. Each staff ended with a simple almond-shaped eye at the tip.

But, more curious still: all of the travellers were blind.

"What happened to your eyes?" Tomas blurted out before he could stop himself.

The man tilted his head, turning to face him with unerring accuracy. "They were removed to preserve the purity of our souls," he said, still smiling. "It is a simple procedure, quite painless… but necessary. Your companion is correct: this is a dangerous path, but its true perils lie not in its threats to the flesh—though they are plentiful—but in the perils of the soul! We have taken the necessary precautions."

"All of you?" Tomas glanced past the man, counting six others standing amidst the baboons—two women and the rest men. They followed the conversation with subtle movements of their heads, tilting them back and forth in unison, giving them the appearance of a synchronised troupe. Tomas found it unsettling and looked away.

"We are all pure," Laurus replied, bringing his bandaged eyes back to Tomas with a gesture that felt oddly familiar. Tomas wracked his memory, attempting to recall where he had seen that movement before.

"Then who leads you?" asked Razin.

"Our troop, of course," the man replied, sweeping his hand in a grand movement that encompassed the golden figures surrounding them. "They are our guides, companions, and friends. And when circumstances demand it, our protectors. Noble warriors, each of them. We began our journey with one hundred, but now we are left with only a dozen."

Tomas furrowed his brow. "What happened to the others?"

"They were killed. By the spirits that haunt this path… and by us. We must eat, after all."

"But they're—"

"Quite delicious, I assure you."

Tomas made a face, glancing at the nearest baboon. It rested on its haunches, casually picking its belly while it watched its master. If it knew its fate, it appeared unbothered by it.

"And… what do they eat?" Tomas asked cautiously.

The stranger's smile deepened.

"Disgusting," Levi growled, voicing Tomas's own thoughts.

"It is the price of our journey," the man said. His smile remained unwavering, and Tomas felt his own lips involuntarily mirroring the expression. He fought the urge and hoped the man hadn't noticed.

Fool, he thought, nearly laughing despite himself. *How could a blind man notice such a thing?*

"Your journey from where?" Razin asked, offering his hand to one of the baboons as it sauntered over to inspect him. It sniffed at his outstretched limb and then tried to grab it with its own hand. Razin swiftly withdrew his fingers and took a step back.

"We are from *Es-Sanawineh*," said the man.

Razin pushed the baboon back when it came too close again and shook his head at the stranger. "You lie."

"Lie? Come here, Babi." Laurus beckoned to the baboon. He somehow sensed the nuisance it was causing without being able to witness it himself. The baboon bared its teeth at Razin, and for a moment, Tomas thought it might leap toward him. But the moment passed, and the creature closed its mouth before returning to its master.

"To lie would be impure," the man said, opening his palm to the baboon. It clasped his hand and sat beside him, holding onto it as a child might cling to a parent.

They eat them, Tomas thought, his own disgust rising. *They eat each other.*

"What's wrong with this Es-Sana?" Dietmar asked, casting a glance at Razin.

Razin looked unsettled, his habitual frown returning. "It is another place that shouldn't be."

"Like Ubar?"

"Yes."

"What happened to it?" Tomas was becoming increasingly unnerved.

"Nothing," said the man, and Tomas was sure he saw the baboon beside him nod.

"It was destroyed by God," said Razin. "Because the people who lived there were *too foolish to live.* They took guidance from animals—ate raw meat, built their homes to mimic those of birds, and walked on all fours like dogs. Foolish, foolish people. One night, when the moon was slow to rise, they believed it had been stolen by a neighbouring village and rode out to slaughter them. It was only upon reaching the first hill that they realised their mistake, seeing the moon rise in the distance."

The man chuckled. "Yes, they did that, indeed. But that was before my time with them. When I found them, they were in need of guidance, it's true. But destroyed? No, no. Es-Sanawineh was there when we departed, and it will be there upon our return."

"Where are you going?" Tomas asked, eyeing the baboon. Its long snout twitched, and its lips rippled. Then, it exposed its long fangs in a smile that made Tomas want to leave the forest behind.

The stranger dropped the creature's hand, ignoring its grasping fingers and pitiful grunts. He raised an arm and pointed eastward toward the emerald peak.

"There is nothing for you there," Razin stated, a shadow darkening his eyes.

"Yet, we are going."

"Why?" Tomas asked, his gaze shifting from the baboon.

"To fetch our king."

Again, that familiar hand motion—each finger unfurling, beating against his palm in a deliberate rhythm.

Tomas's eyes narrowed. "You said you joined them? Where are *you* from?"

The stranger tilted his head, and Tomas felt like he was being scrutinised, considered, truly seen by this man who lacked sight.

"The same place as you," he said slowly. He watched Tomas for a moment before turning his head toward the others and spreading his hands. "The same place as all of you,"

"The Levant?" said Dietmar.

But to Tomas, it seemed as if the previous words were meant solely for him.

Could it be? He reconsidered the stranger in a new light, scrutinising each subtle movement, each wave of his hands and gentle tilt of his head. It had been so long, and all he truly remembered were those hands. They did bear resemblance—scarred from toiling in the fields or from the scorching heat of the Holy Land? He couldn't be certain. And that gesture, that habitual flick of the fingers and the gentle beat against his palm, reminiscent of a drumskin. A nervous tic. He had seen it before, as a child. A gesture, fingers unfurling, beckoning him to follow.

"What king is this?" Razin asked. "That mountain is home of those children of Adam and Hawah who were cast out of the light. There are things there that would tear through your remaining beasts and annihilate you within moments. It is not a place for kings or men."

"Perhaps. Perhaps not. Come with me, and I will show you." The stranger's words were meant for everyone to hear, but for some reason, Tomas knew that the invitation was meant for him alone.

The man turned his smile to Tomas and addressed him directly. "You wish to see the king, do you not?"

"Our paths take us a different way," said Dietmar before Tomas could respond.

The man's empty stare remained fixed on Tomas as he spoke. "The king will be most disappointed. He always looks forward to receiving guests."

Razin shooed away a second baboon, slapping its hand when it reached for his sword. The creature barked at him, feigning outrage, cradling its arm as its eyes widened. Its thick brow raised in an expression remarkably close to human shock.

Razin ignored it and pressed the stranger. "What is the name of this 'king'?"

Laurus laughed, but it was a cold sound, not like the laughter of before. "The human mouth cannot form the shapes required to utter his name. To hear it said at all is to risk the maddening of the mind, for we are not made to comprehend such sounds. No, to us, he simply *is*."

"*Is* what?" Levi shook his head, muttering to himself. "The maddening of the mind? Sounds like it has already taken hold here, eh?"

Dietmar waved at Levi, urging him to be silent before he could offend the stranger and his entourage. Blind or not, Laurus's escort looked strong enough to tear a man limb from limb.

Tomas blinked, considering the stranger's words. A king, he'd said. He wondered if it could be the lost king of the Orient, the mythical Christian monarch said to wield an emerald sceptre and be descended from the Three Magi. But then…

"The… human mouth?" Tomas mumbled. "What kind of mouth is it meant for then, this name?"

"None that we'd like to see, you can bet on that," Levi growled. One of the baboons had taken a keen interest in Sara's long hair and was attempting to reach for her curls without incurring her father's wrath.

"Another reason for our blindness," the stranger explained, motioning to his bandaged eyes. "The sight of our king alone would blind us if it were not already so. Now we may stand in his presence without distraction. It is a small price to pay for such a privilege."

"And once you bring him back to Es-Sanawineh?" asked Dietmar. "What fate awaits the people in your village?"

"Oh, they will need to be purified too."

"Blinded, you mean," said Dietmar.

That smile. The gentle rhythm of his fingers against his palm.

"I believe it is time for us to continue on our way." Dietmar motioned to Razin, stepping aside from the path. Tomas noticed his hand resting on his sword and Razin's as well. They were anticipating a fight, or at least prepared for one.

But the stranger simply nodded, his smile only wavering when he looked at Tomas. "The offer stands, should you desire to meet the king. All you need do is follow the path."

"There'll be no following," said Levi hoarsely, growing impatient. He kicked at the baboon bothering Sara, losing his temper with the creature. "Now take your monkeys and leave us, or I'll see to it that there's none left to guide you to your mountain. Then it truly will be the blind leading the blind, and the stupid."

"As you wish," said the stranger, not rising to the threat or insult. He clapped his hands together once, producing a loud crack that echoed through the trees. The baboons sprang to their feet, suddenly alert. The stranger clapped again, and Tomas felt a strong, hairy hand push him out of the way.

The baboons had begun their march.

Laurus allowed Bibi to hold his hand once more and was slowly led along the path. The baboon moved in an awkward bipedal gait, unwilling to release its master's hand now that it had regained it. The other human companions were nudged gently in the right direction. How the baboons knew where they were going, Tomas never thought to ask, as the peculiar caravan departed from the trees, leaving him and his companions behind.

Tomas watched them leave, his gaze fixed on the shape of the tall, slender man as he vanished into the dense reeds. He continued staring long after he had disappeared from sight, lost in contemplation. It was only when Dietmar called his name that Tomas finally tore his gaze away from the fading trail.

37

They spent the night camped on the edge of the forest, choosing the cold open space over the meagre shelter the woods could provide. The unsettling aura of the forest had grown stronger the longer they stayed near it, and a gnawing silence accompanied their footsteps beneath the crooked limbs of the burned and scarred trees.

With a quiet sense of relief, they found themselves on the eastern edge of the forest. The gradual slope swiftly transformed into a steep incline, leading to a sheer drop beyond the rocky rim of the gorge. The river flowed somewhere below, its constant roar bringing solace after the eerie silence within the woods. They set up camp overlooking the shadowy gorge, taking turns to keep watch throughout the night before breaking camp at first light.

The next morning, they moved briskly through the remaining stretch of the forest, only stopping to examine the remains of what must have been Laurus's camp the previous night. Baboon droppings covered the floor, and the foul stench of animals and shit filled the air. But it was the sight of the bones that made Dietmar pause. The carcass lay a short distance away from the ashes of a fire at the centre of the camp. Its ribcage had been forcefully pried open so that it resembled the splayed legs of a dead spider on its back. The bones had been picked clean.

"Truly, we are among savages," Levi said, his lips curled in disgust.

"What's the difference?" said Tomas, staring at the carcass. "We eat sheep and cow, don't we? Why does it bother you if they eat their baboons?"

Levi shot him a sharp look. "Sheep and cows do not look like men. That's why."

Tomas shrugged in response but didn't offer any further arguments. While Dietmar understood the logic in his words, he found himself siding with Levi. He knew his agreement stemmed more from revulsion than any sort of reason, but he had come to understand that such feelings were often rooted in some primordial instinct that had proven useful enough to survive mankind's growth from mere woodsmen to a sprawling civilisation.

It was wrong to eat man, and so it was wrong to eat things that looked like man.

Abiding by the second rule ensured the preservation of the first. Once that disgust was gone, once you made normal something so close to the sacrilegious, it was only a tiny step to the violation of the sacred itself. Sometimes, it was wiser to side with instinct.

Dietmar kept a watchful eye on Tomas as they pressed on past the abandoned camp. His friend remained tense, like a tightly drawn bowstring, ever since their encounter with Laurus and his golden guides. Tomas lingered at the rear, frequently glancing over his shoulder, pausing to gaze into the gaps between the trees, and then hurrying to catch up. A night's rest hadn't seemed to alleviate his unease. Even after they emerged from the other side of the forest, his eyes would snap back to the receding treeline.

His face bore a mix of hope and fear yet always settled into an expression of disappointment. What was it he hoped to see? A golden silhouette? Laurus? The Englishman seemed to shrink into himself, growing smaller with each step away from the lifeless trees. Dietmar observed him on more than one occasion, staring into his own hands, mimicking the gestures of the stranger, and muttering to himself.

When Dietmar finally tired of Tomas's antics, he slowed his pace to walk beside him and asked what was on his mind.

Tomas hesitated for a moment before letting out a sigh. "I know that man."

"Laurus? From where?"

"I'm… not entirely sure. But I have seen him before."

"Are you certain?"

Tomas seemed on the verge of saying something more, but he shook his head and fell silent. His sudden silence only heightened Dietmar's concern. The little Englishman had always been the most open and forthcoming among them—not wont to retreat into his own thoughts, like Razin; or to devolve into befuddled musings, as had been Adelman's custom, even before his mind had started to deteriorate. Where Razin and Dietmar's friendship had developed at a slow, awkward gait, Tomas had felt like an old friend within a matter of days. He had a way of settling into people's lives, crossing boundaries in a manner that only someone who had known one for years possibly could and still get away with it. It fooled you into thinking he *was* an old friend, that the familiarity you were feeling was earned. But now he appeared distant, evasive when questioned, and reluctant to do what he had excelled at: conversation.

Something Laurus had said had gotten to him. But what?

Dietmar sifted through the memory of their encounter, trying to identify the source of his friend's unease. Had Laurus recognised Tomas as well? It seemed improbable that a blind man from a lost village would know his friend. And yet, at times during their conversation, Dietmar had felt like a mere bystander, an eavesdropper on their exchange. And the way

Laurus had worded his invitation… Had it been meant for all of them or for Tomas alone?

He resolved to quiz his friend further on it later and kept a careful eye on him while they walked. Maybe he'd get more out of him once they were safely clear of the forest and Tomas had let his guard down a little.

But Tomas's shrunken shoulders never straightened, and his fingers drummed incessantly against his palm as they walked.

Beyond the forest, the land devolved into a series of shallow gorges flanked by rocky outcrops and impassable ravines. The verdant vegetation of Paradise gave way to short, hardy plants and tufts of coarse drybrush. Eventually, even these meagre plants disappeared, leaving them to traverse an empty plain with only the shadows of distant hills on the horizon.

And in the distance, the peaks of their destination loomed.

The earth had taken on a reddish hue, and even the stone protruding from the hardened sand resembled stained bones in shades of violet and pink. The tint was not restricted to the soil and stones, however. In every direction they looked, a velvety haze hung over the horizon—dust and sand and shards of light reflecting off the plain. It created the impression of a second layer, a gauzy reflection that floated above the first. This ethereal veil, mingled with the verdigris glow emanating from Mount Qaf to the east, resulted in a luminous wash of colour, like stains of oil seeping into the ocean. Russet dust fingers stretched upwards, tenderly reaching toward the iridescent sky, only to be dispersed by the wind and reduced to a lingering haze just above the ground.

Strange patterns formed along that second plane, figures standing in the distance only to dissolve as they approached, then reemerging further ahead. Low clouds of dirt and sand formed whirling currents that swept across the horizon. But no matter how high these clouds rose, they could never obstruct the view of the Three Daughters.

Dietmar had begun making out the details from their silhouttes, dividing the homogenous blur beneath the peaks into three distinct mountains. The shortest of the three sat like a hunched crone, her shoulders sagging beneath a pointed crown. The second towered over the first like a raptor on its perch, surveying the plain. Or perhaps it was closer to a vulture, scanning for bones within the sand. The third mountain was the tallest of them all, sat between the other two like a venerable patriarch—proud, rigid, and ancient. Its vertiginous brown slopes soared, forming nearly sheer cliffs in places. Imposing. Insurmountable. Even from a distance, Dietmar could tell that the mountain face of the tallest of the three was barren. No signs of life adorned those desolate slopes and empty stone cliffs.

How will we ever get past that, Dietmar wondered. He stole a glance at Razin, who walked beside him, but his friend's eyes were fixed on something—or rather, someone—else.

The girl.

While Dietmar's attention had been fixed on Tomas and his inner turmoil, Razin's gaze had hardly strayed from Tanit since their encounter at the hermit tower. She came from hardy stock, they had all agreed—how else could one survive in such a place? But even then… even granting the strength it would have required to reach adolescence in this place, her actions had been remarkable. There was no denying that she had saved them from the cadaver snake, but Dietmar began to wonder if she had also rescued them from the hollow. They had all stood frozen, paralysed by the sight of something scuttling toward them from the darkness. Would they still be alive if she hadn't sealed the opening? And earlier, she had led them to Malah's ship, liberating them from Bezal and his Falak.

Dietmar remembered her glistening black smile as he lay recovering on the raft, her mouth still dripping with the ichor of some sea creature she'd torn apart with her bare hands and teeth. The look in her eyes had etched itself into his memory—a pure, unadulterated delight in the violence she had unleashed.

If they ever made it back to Outremer, he would need to think about what to do with her. He could well imagine her thriving in the forests of his estate, hunting alongside wolves and facing off against bears, but it was the *getting there* that posed a problem. A pagan girl with a crooked mouth and eyes like the sun would undoubtedly raise eyebrows, and that was assuming she behaved herself.

That was assuming he lived long enough to make it home. Every bone in Dietmar's body ached, and he could feel the skin of his gums giving way in his mouth. Soon, he would struggle to talk, and after that? A distressing image appeared in his mind, his comrades dragging his lifeless body up one of the mountains, his mouth agape and arms hanging limply at his sides. He swiftly pushed that thought aside. He couldn't allow it to come to that.

Dietmar watched the girl moving ahead of them, navigating the red soil with her bare feet. She was still as lithe as she had been when they found her hiding in Ladah's fishing hut, hissing like a cornered cat. Tanit must have felt his eyes on her because she turned to look at him, her mouth fixed in a perpetual smile. He thought he saw her grin widen before she turned back to the path.

It was Sara who first noticed the distortions.

It was their second day on the plain, shortly after breaking camp. They'd slept under the stars that night without a fire. The sand had retained its warmth from baking in the sun all day, and besides, they had nothing to cook.

They were making for the nearest hill with its rocky outcrop, hoping to find some shade to rest in before striking out once the sun began to wane. The desert pan had started to simmer, and without any covering, the heat would take its toll on all of them.

A few miles from the hill, Sara cried out so loudly that Dietmar had thought she'd taken a fall or been bitten by something lurking hidden beneath the sand. He swung around to face her, only to find her gazing upwards at the sky, her mouth hanging slack in astonishment.

He craned his neck, following her gaze, and then his own mouth dropped open.

A colossal boulder hung suspended in the air above their heads. It was about as wide as ten men standing lengthways and stood just as tall. Lifeless roots dangled from its sides, swaying gently in the breeze. He spotted another boulder beyond it, then more scattered further above. Dozens of rocks floated like clouds—resembling the leather-skinned vessels they had encountered in Ubar. Only, the grey rocks lacked any discernible means of propulsion. There were no visible cables, wires, or other mechanisms holding them fixed in the air. Clumps of dry sand clung to the underside of the nearest boulder, remnants of soil upturned during its ascent.

Dietmar scanned their surroundings, suddenly nervous that they might find themselves plucked from the ground and suspended in the air by whatever contrivance had done the same to the rocks. But he didn't see any holes in the flat plain, nothing to suggest that the rocks had originated from nearby.

Levi cursed as he caught sight of the levitating stones, and soon Tomas noticed them too. Tomas made a clumsy attempt at crossing himself before settling on the ground to stare in disbelief.

Only Razin seemed unperturbed by the levitations. He and the girl, who barely acknowledged their presence.

She's seen them before, Dietmar thought. *She's been here before.*

"Gizzal told us this would happen," said Razin, blinking up at the sky. He shaded his eyes with a hand and carefully considered each of the rocks in turn.

"He did?" Tomas patted his sweaty brow and shook his head. "I'm sure I would remember him mentioning something like this. Stones *floating above our heads* seems like something that'd stick in my mind."

Razin waved his hand irritably. "It is the distortions he spoke of. Do you remember that, or were you too deep in your wine to pay attention to his words?"

"Aye," Tomas grunted. "I might recall something about that amidst all the other nonsense he shared with us. He said something about the air thinning, didn't he?"

"The boundaries." Razin replied, lowering his hand and shifting his gaze to the ground. He scanned the sand around his feet, searching for something. After a moment, he retrieved a small red stone and tested its weight. Satisfied, he cocked his arm and hurled it toward the floating boulders above. Dietmar tracked its course as it spun through the air, striking the nearest boulder and causing a shower of loose red sand to descend, only to remain suspended in the sky like a blossoming flower. Then, when Dietmar thought the stone would come tumbling back to the ground, it abruptly halted.

"See," said Razin. "The natural laws are broken here. Gizzal told us that there are places where the boundaries grow thin, where the natural order between two layers converges and undermines one another. He said his theory remained untested, but this must be one of those places."

Now the stone hung in the air like the others, gently rotating on its axis from the momentum that had propelled it skyward. Eventually, that stopped too.

"What does it mean?" Dietmar asked, taking his eyes off the stone.

Razin had resumed walking but briefly glanced back at his friend. "It means that we are close. Close to home."

***

The sun had long since passed its peak by the time they trudged into the foothills beneath the mountains. The skin of Dietmar's hands and face was burnt again, and he could feel the blisters forming on his scalp where his hair had fallen out.

He limped noticeably now, from his boots no longer fitting tightly around his ankles and from the throbbing pain in his toenails as they loosened with each step, exposing raw skin against the unforgiving leather. He would have to bandage his feet soon.

A sixth protrusion had appeared on his chest, pushing against the skin beneath his left nipple. It had hardened overnight, pressing tightly enough to whiten the surrounding area and leave thin stretch marks. He wanted to cut it out, to lance each growth and purge whatever vile substance had caused them to appear.

To his mind, the growths on his skin and the boils that riddled his body were both cause and effect of the parasitic presence gnawing at his brain. If he could just clean himself of the maladies that affected him physically, the malady that occupied him spiritually would depart too. But when those thoughts came, he quickly dismissed them.

It couldn't be as simple as that, he thought.

Like cutting the meat from his bones would be easy. If he didn't die from the procedure, he'd probably die from the festering wounds soon after. Besides, if Razin's al-'asm hadn't been enough to do it, then scorching his skin clean of the vulgar marks was unlikely to fare any better.

"Stop that," Dietmar growled, glaring at Levi as they clambered up the slope.

The Jew had started to whistle.

As if they hadn't just buried a friend and seen another lost to the sea. As if his daughter hadn't been plucked from his hands, from Levi's very hands, while he screamed futilely. As if there wasn't a demon inside Dietmar's head.

Levi opened his mouth and closed it again. His face reddened. He didn't whistle again.

A little while later, Razin pointed out a crumbling pile of stone on the other side of the slope. It appeared to have been a structure once. But all that was left of it now was a grey mound and the remnants of an ancient doorway. Nestled between a hill and a rocky outcrop at the base of the slope, it had likely been an outpost before falling into ruin.

They walked past the remains, taking turns to stare through the empty doorway. But it was dark, and there was nothing inside.

Then, when they reached the top of the next slope, they found the keep.

***

"We should leave this place," said Levi. "Move on into the outcrop or back onto the plain. Something about these ruins doesn't sit well with me. There will be mazzikin here, or worse."

"In a moment," said Dietmar, waving away Levi's concerns. There was something familiar about the square towers and rectangular walls before him. The outer wall had been built low so that he could see the inner enclosure, still intact within. A rusted iron portcullis hung partially open at the entrance to the keep. The stone sloped at a gentle angle, culminating in the crenellated teeth of the battlement. He counted four machicolations between the corbels on the parapet and loopholes at every corner of stone.

Dietmar's eyes traced the embrasures and then shifted to the towers looming over the gatehouse. With a full garrison manning it, the stronghold would have proven a difficult nut to crack, and any would-be attacker would have had to think very carefully about whether it was worth it.

A memory stirred of a castle built in the style of the old Roman *castrums*—a concentric design with two walls, one higher and one lower, to better defend from. Behind the rectangular outer wall stood the keep itself, a square bastion with four corner towers and another jutting out from its western-facing wall.

Dietmar took a step forward, tilting his head to peer around the corner of the crumbling stone tower. There it was—the gatehouse, exactly where he remembered it.

He had been here before.

"It is the Keep of *Kawkab al-Hawa*," said Razin, joining Dietmar's side. "The last time we laid eyes on it was after crushing the rebellion of Ibn al-Hasan."

"How is this possible?" Dietmar shook his head in disbelief, his eyes coming to a rest on the tallest of the collapsed towers. "These ruins have the look of ages about them. But Gilbert of Assailly was still building his castle when we departed Galilee."

"It has been many years," Razin replied quietly.

"Not so long that this could have happened."

Razin remained quiet, and Dietmar turned to face him. "This doesn't make any sense."

"There's a garden!" called Tomas, who had moved ahead with Sara and Tanit, peering over one of the low outer walls. "I see rosemary and sage, there's even some peppermint, and could that be… wild garlic! There are mushrooms, too!"

Before Dietmar could shout at Tomas to wait, he disappeared through a gap in the wall, followed closely by Sara and Tanit.

"Come on," Levi urged, hurrying past Dietmar. "I'll face a mazzikin spirit over something to eat and two of them if there's a chance of a potage.

Just don't touch the mushrooms!" He shouted. "Let me check them first, you hear?!"

Dietmar and Razin trudged wearily after them, their minds on the past as they entered the gates of Kawkab al-Hawah.

The sun was just beginning to set.

They found Tomas and the others in the herb garden, chewing on fennel and tansy stalks while digging through the soil.

"Onions," Tomas declared, pointing to a cluster of dirty bulbs lying on the ground beside him. The girl reached out for one, but he swatted her hand away. "Not yet," he warned, wagging his finger. "Here, this'll subdue the hunger pangs until dinner." He tore a handful of green stems with purple flowers and offered them to her. "It's bitter, but you'll feel better for it."

The girl eyed the leaves sceptically, then snatched them from his fingers and shoved them into her mouth. She chewed once and then spat them on the ground, making a face at Tomas.

"I told you they were bitter," said Tomas, barely concealing a smile. He plucked white flowers from a yarrow stem and offered them to the girl. "Try this."

His spirits seemed to have lifted since the morning, and he appeared closer to his old self again. Though his smile never quite reached his eyes. None of theirs did, not truly. They had grown numb, responding out of habit with hollow gestures and expressions, simulacrums of their former selves. Like actors in a play, a mimicry of real life. It was the only way to deal with what they had seen and felt, with the doubt and fear that occupied their minds.

But in moments like this, when the horrors of the world faded into the background, vestiges of their true selves emerged. They could smile and laugh, shedding the guarded skins they wore, if only for a fleeting moment.

Dietmar watched Levi as he identified the various herbs in the garden, naming them for his daughter and nodding as she repeated them back, offering corrections when needed, his smile reflecting his approval. He felt a stab of shame and regret for snapping at the dyer earlier. They all had their coping mechanisms, ways to distance themselves from the relentless onslaught they had endured since departing the Levant. Levi had suffered more than most, and Dietmar had barked at him for the subtlest infringement on his frayed nerves.

He thought about joining them amongst the weeds, rooting about in the dirt for bulbs. But he knew his presence served as a sickly reminder of where they were. He could see it in their eyes—pity, yes. But at times, when they caught sight of him unprepared, he noticed their lips curl, the winces, the looks of disgust that quickly transformed into forced neutrality. He didn't blame them for that. They couldn't help it any more than he could help the state of his own body.

So, he left them to fill their pockets with flowers and bulbs while they laughed among themselves and turned to survey the ruins.

The herb garden nestled in the corner of the southernmost wall, in front of one of the vaulted storerooms that had once served as a granary for the keep. The storeroom extended to become a turret beyond the first floor, and through the gaps in the crumbling wall, he could glimpse the steps leading up to the tower. A row of shelves lined the back, swathed in darkness. Only dust filled them now.

Dietmar turned away from the storeroom and made his way toward the grand structure at the heart of the castle—the keep itself. It appeared just as he remembered, though in a level of disrepair Gilbert of Assailly would never have allowed. The once-fine glass panes, crafted by skilled artisans from Galilee, were absent from the empty window frames. Somewhere along its history, the magnificent wooden doors that once barred the keep had been reduced to splinters, their remnants scattered across the floor, good for firewood now and nothing else.

The second tower above the gatehouse sagged precariously, a far cry from the once-proud turrets Dietmar had seen when he first came to al-Hawa.

Pennants had fluttered from the towers alongside the flag of Galilee and the banners of House Assailly. Silver-helmed warriors and men donning the red and blue of Assailly's household guard had met him at the gates. And then, Gilbert himself had emerged, enveloping Dietmar in a bearlike embrace.

"Now we have the numbers!" Gilbert had roared, his voice resonating like the clash of swords against shields. His eyes had taken in the men Dietmar had brought with him—fellow knights and auxiliaries from Jerusalem and Antioch—pausing only briefly on Razin, who stood patiently behind Dietmar.

Gilbert had clapped his hands together in a thunderous gesture, his eyes alight with the prospect of what was to come. Then he had waved them into his home, into Beauvoir Castle.

The campaign that followed had been long and bloody, claiming the lives of half their company. Death had not been discerning, taking those who fought for God and those who fought for coin in equal measure.

Dietmar trudged along the inner walls of the keep until he reached an open yard littered with broken tiles. Once, a fountain had graced its centre, water flowing as they shared meals and joked about each other's mothers. But now, like most of the men who had accompanied him, it was gone.

He limped across the yard, then took the stairs to the rampart, pausing midway to catch his breath.

Another of Gizzal's distortions, he thought.

It must be.

But this was more than mere rock defying its nature—this was a ripple in time. How else could Gilbert's keep have aged a century and fallen into ruin? Dietmar wondered if he wasn't being afforded a glimpse into the future, a time after Nur ad-Din and Saladin's armies had run riot through the Holy Land, finally unseating the Franks from the east. What would remain? It was the reason the Church was scrambling to secure its relics. Papal rats fleeing a sinking ship, but not without their cheese.

He took another shaky step and then another.

He had lost friends within these walls and pieces of himself on the blood-soaked sands they'd fought over. But it was Razin who had come away from Beauvoir a changed man. When Ibn al-Hasan had been clasped in irons and declared guilty of violating the peace between Nur ad-Din and Amalric, it had been Razin who had led him to the executioner's block, hearing his final words. From what Razin had told him, they had been like brothers in their youth.

He had never really recovered from the loss.

Dietmar summited the last of the steps and hobbled onto the rampart, taking in the fading sun as he made his way toward the weathered brown-stone balustrade. From here, he could see Tomas and the others still busy in the garden, picking their way through the weeds under Razin's watchful gaze. His eyes lingered upon the patch of life, feeling a well of emotions stir: love for his friends, fear for their future, and sorrow for all they had endured. They had suffered greatly with him, *for* him. If he had refused Gelmiro's offer, none of this would have happened. They would have boarded a ship in Jaffa and found themselves in some safe port a few days later, drinking wine and celebrating putting their backs to the Holy Land.

Would I have done otherwise? he wondered. If he had known what they would face, would he have rejected Gelmiro's offer? Was there anything he wouldn't have risked for a chance at salvation for his son and wife?

He blinked and continued along the rampart, casting his gaze northward. The question was too terrible to consider.

He came to rest beneath the slouching turret he had seen from the yard and leaned his elbows on the battlement, staring out across the desolate plain between them and the Three Daughters. Sand and rock, leafless trees and dry riverbeds, cracked earth, and sun-scorched wilderness met his eyes. And beyond that, the mountains themselves.

They dominated the entire horizon, their massive and unyielding presence stealing his breath away. Steep slopes and barren ridges; vulgar, empty places that his eyes struggled to focus on; black walls of impenetrable rock; and the peaks that thrust toward the sky like fists in a challenge to the Heavens themselves.

Dietmar felt despair.

We will never summit those.

We will never find the Mouth of God.

Then his eyes settled on a shadow at the base of the tallest of the Three.

He leaned forward, making out the details of a ravine or canyon, sloping walls that parted between the rock.

An opening into the mountains.

Their path home.

***

That night, they made a small fire inside Gilbert's hall and ate mushroom and onion soup infused with garlic and more herbs than Dietmar could count. They laughed and spoke about life before Ladah.

Tomas regaled them with tales of talking bones beneath the crypt of Seeon and how the priests had thought the alcoves were haunted by spirits before one of their number discovered Tomas hiding in a recess, whispering in the dark and moving the bones of some poor sap's skull with a stick and string.

Levi spoke of home, a smallholding near the sea of Galilee, and the dishes of *itri* and *levivot* his wife would have waiting for them upon their return. Even Razin opened up that night.

He told them of his uncle, who had raised him in Damascus after his father's passing. Razin recounted the tales he had been told growing up—stories of clever fellahin outwitting sultans, of a faithful old mule who waited for his master until he starved, only to find himself welcomed at the gates of Paradise as a reward for his unwavering loyalty. He told them of an impartial judge more interested in finding guilt than serving justice and of wily dervishes and arrogant sheyks.

They washed down their soup with cool mint water, continuing their stories well into the night. It was the best meal Dietmar could remember having, and as it came to an end, something close to contentment stirred within him. If this were to be one of his last nights, he couldn't have asked for better companions to share it with.

38

Razin was dreaming.

He knew it was a dream because his uncle appeared exactly as he had remembered him from his childhood. His beard had only just started to grey, his eyes were sharp and lively, and the stoop that had occupied his later years was absent. He stood tall and proud, his strong hands at his side.

He motioned to Razin.

They stood within an interior courtyard, surrounded by white walls adorned with intricate *zellij* tiles in shades of green and blue, white and yellow. Similar tessellations extended across the floor, the mosaic forming a radiant star beneath their feet. Mushrie led him through the courtyard, passing beneath four stone arches embellished with calligraphy bands in Kufic script and into the vaulted corridors beyond.

Daylight filtered through the windows they passed, casting little slivers of light rendered as shards, splinters of the sun scattered across the tiled floor. Curious, Razin attempted to peer through the nearest window, but the yellow latticework of the mashrabiya obscured his view, leaving him with only a vague impression of crenellated façades and tall spires in shades of turquoise and gold.

Then he noticed his uncle's attire. He wore a white *ridā'* draped over his shoulders, with an *izār* flowing down to his sandaled feet. Razin looked down at himself and found he was dressed in the same manner. He wore the clothing of *ihram*—of pilgrimage.

"Uncle," he called, looking up. "What is this? Where are we?"

Mushrie glanced back over his shoulder, a small smile playing on his lips, but he remained silent, leading Razin further through the corridor.

Eventually, they came to a halt in front of a pair of grand doors adorned with golden floriations of Kufic script. Perfectly straight letter strokes rendered the *takbir*, the *Shahadah*, and sacred names: God, the Ever Living, and the Prophet. The words scrawled across the glazed wood, forming geometric patterns that made Razin's head spin. In some places, the letters overlapped, creating new words unintended by the reed pen that had recorded them. The Ever Living became the Undying, the Prophet intertwined with Gabriel, becoming Tiamat. Other unfamiliar words, names, and titles emerged before Razin's eyes, as if a hidden hand was at work in the shadows, etching out the words before his eyes: *Mooneater, Son of Adam, Qoselah, Al-ilah, God of mnkw.*

The inscriptions swirled before his eyes until Razin blinked and looked away.

Mushrie was watching him.

"Uncle?"

"Do you not remember?" Mushrie replied. "It is the *Dhu al-Hijja*. Come, we are not yet too late."

Mushrie pushed open the doors and stepped out into the sun.

Razin followed.

He found himself within a vaulted, three-sided hall decorated with glazed tiles and more bands of Kufic script. He ignored the calligraphy, fearing the discombobulation from before, and stood beside his uncle, gazing out from the *pishtaq*.

Flat roofed dwellings stretched out before them, coloured in the grey and brown hues of coral stone and silt clay. High-windowed *maqads* overlooked the narrow roads of the city, streets that ran like the threads of a *tiraz*, each corner embellished by mashrabiyas and colourful screened windows.

Minarets soared above the domiciles, their white spires culminating in gentle peaks capped with the golden sigil of the crescent moon. Red-domed rooves squatted beneath them, and Razin counted two of the canonical schools of law within his line of sight; the others were hidden behind the structure dominating the centre of his view.

The *Masjid al-Haram*.

The Grand Mosque.

Its ashen white walls towered over the surrounding dwellings, serving as the focal point toward which all structures in the holy city were oriented. Tiered walls bore the markings of numerous caliphs and sultans—rulers who had renovated it in the trappings of their times. Countless windows punctuated the walls, like alcoves lined side by side. Above them, the balconies and galleries of one hundred rooms adorned with mosaics and gold and marble.

Razin's eyes lingered on the Masjid al-Haram before shifting to the streets below the mosque. The narrow roads should have been filled with pilgrims, the lifeblood of the city, all converging on the Ka'ba. A chorus of ululating merchants and bickering traders, the calls of the devout mingling with those of the opportunistic. Laughter and joy and anguish, all in the city of God's final prophet. But the streets were empty.

The city was empty.

"Come, nephew," Mushrie said, placing a hand on Razin's shoulder and guiding him toward the steps below the pishtaq. "There is something you must see."

Razin let himself be led away from the *iwan*, staring with wonder at the empty streets and houses. Only in a dream could ancient Mecca be empty.

He followed his uncle onto the main thoroughfare, the *Ibrahim al-Khalil*, which passed by the *Masjid al-Jinn*—a mosque where the Prophet was said to have recited the Quran to a gathering of jinn. According to the tale, after hearing his words, the jinn were so moved that they swore a *bay'ah* to the Prophet and converted to Islam on the spot.

Razin considered the Mosque of the Jinn. If this was a dream, then it was a strange one. The walls of the mosque were covered in a white, viscous substance that cascaded from the balcony of its minaret to the sloping dome roof of its entrance gate below. The strands glimmered in the sunlight, glistening like a shoal of fish in water.

As he looked up at the solitary window facing the road, Razin caught sight of a shadow moving within.

They were being watched.

"*Anak*," he breathed. The name felt like profanity in such a sacred place. Memories of the forest flooded his mind—the dead hanging from trees like rotting fruit and their smell, the fragrant stink of grave things.

"Uncle, it's not safe here." He reached instinctively for his sword, too late remembering the ihram garb he wore. He grabbed his uncle's arm instead, hoping to usher him away from the nest.

Mushrie shooed him off, pulling his arm back with a strength he had not had when Razin saw him last.

"Be at peace, nephew," he said irritably. "She will not bother us here."

"She? You know this *thing?* How?"

"We are all children of Adam."

"But she is a beast, uncle. A monster."

Mushrie tilted his head. That thin smile again. "She is misguided, perhaps. But in her heart, she means well. Leave her be, and with time, you will come to understand."

Razin frowned. "Uncle…"

"But, come!" Mushrie exclaimed, opening his hands and placing one on Razin's shoulder. "That is not what I have brought you here to see. They will be waiting for us already. We must hurry."

"Who?" Razin asked. "Who is waiting for us?"

Mushrie's smile grew, showing all of his teeth. Razin thought of a wolf then, of a scavenger in the desert with its hackles raised, empty eyes.

Cold.

He shivered.

"It's not far," Mushrie assured him, the warmth returning to his face. And soon enough, Razin found his legs moving, taking him toward the Masjid al-Haram.

"I know that look," Mushrie said as they walked past Al-Mu'allaa Cemetery, staring at the grey tombstones scattered across the field. The slopes of Mount Arafat sprawled in the distance.

"You wear your thoughts on your brow, nephew. Perhaps you hide them from others, but not from me. I have seen too many years and had you under my roof for enough of them to know when something weighs on your mind. What troubles you?"

Razin hesitated, his eyes caught on the ridge of Mount Arafat, the site of Adam and Hawah's reunion after being expelled from the gates of Paradise. By then, their spawn already covered half the earth—ifrits and marids, the jinn who would grow to hate man. Were they to blame for the ensuing evil? What could they have known of the darkness they were procreating?

He thought of Anak and the brood of Adam. Their resentment toward man was rooted in their placement beneath him by God. It was not so strange a thing to harbour hatred toward those who forced you into the dark corners of the world and who claimed dominion over all, leaving you and your kin to dwell in the shadows. If God was the father of all, then man was the favoured child, spoiled by His love.

Razin glanced at Mushrie and saw him waiting patiently for his reply. He knew he could rely on his uncle for reassurance, for words to stay his mind and thoughtful answers to complex problems.

Taking a deep breath, Razin began, "Do you recall Faruk's moon cult? The one Nur ad-Din uncovered in Damascus during the siege?"

Mushrie scratched his chin in thought. "I might. What about it?"

Razin continued, "What were they attempting to achieve?"

"To achieve?" Mushrie glanced at him. "What do all fanatics desire? To grow in numbers, to influence others, to grasp at the reins of power. They seek *legitimacy*, but to attain it, they need to attract powerful benefactors. The moon cult was too impulsive, too naïve. They sought spectacle when wisdom demanded patience. Faruk's own recklessness led to their discovery. Foolish boy. He was caught on the Baradā, naked as a newborn, shouting at the river."

"Shouting at the Baradā? Why?"

"He thought he could raise the beast from its waters—an aspect of their god from the primordial ocean. This beast… they believe it will swallow the moon and thus prevent Allah's day of Final Judgment. Such an idea! To suspend the judgment of the Surah Al-Qamar…"

"Is it possible?"

"Perhaps. If judgment is said to begin with the cleaving of the moon, and there is no moon… Well! It is plausible, if not a little dogmatic for my tastes—and it is from me that you're hearing that said!" Mushrie chuckled, then appraised Razin with a keen glance. "Why do you ask, nephew?"

"And did Faruk succeed? Did he accomplish his goal?"

Mushrie laughed. "We are here, aren't we?"

No, uncle, we are not.

Mushrie halted abruptly in his stride, giving Razin a curious look. "Perhaps you would like to tell me what this is all about?"

Razin slowed his pace. He could see the balconies and windows of the Masjid al-Haram up ahead. Shadows danced amidst them, flickering forms that defied tangible shape. They flittered from window to window like a swarm of flies, lacking the physical presence that manifested them. Razin watched the shadows move like a swirling cloud across the mosque.

"Nephew?" Mushrie called, and Razin turned to find his uncle waiting expectantly.

Perhaps even a dream can offer me answers.

He considered his uncle for a moment and then said, "I have seen a place that has no moon, where men eat men and devils walk the earth without fear. They do not need to hide in the shadows here. Instead, it is man who must hide. I fear this place is… without God."

Mushrie shook his head. "Come, nephew. There is no place that is without God! If you look closely enough, you will find one of His many faces in all things."

Razin tilted his head, narrowing his eyes. *The many faces of God.* He had heard those words said once before, spoken by a pagan.

"Uncle, there is only one face of God."

Mushrie smiled and nodded. "Of course."

"Then, why…" Razin's voice trailed off, doubt casting a shadow over his mind. "Uncle, how did you come to know so much about Faruk's cult?"

Mushrie's smile did not waver.

Wolven jaws, slobbering.

Razin blinked, taking a step back.

"Look!" said Mushrie, suddenly pointing toward the end of the street. "See, they have grown impatient with our dawdling and have come to meet us!"

Razin swung around to follow his uncle's gesture and gasped.

Two figures stood beneath the balcony of the Masjid al-Haram.

He recognised them both.

'Iweyz and Ibn al-Hasan.

Like his uncle, 'Iweyz appeared just as he remembered her as a boy in Damascus. Her long dark hair hung in an intricate braid behind her head, adorned with gold and silver brooches in the style of a Damascene princess. She wore a simple yellow jellaba, its sleeves reaching just above her wrist.

"Razi!" she cried, foregoing etiquette for a hug. She smelled of jasmine and myrrh, of flowers in bloom.

Razin gasped as she squeezed him tightly and laughed along with her when she finally released him, holding his hands in hers and assessing him from head to toe.

"You've grown," she said. "Soon, you'll put your uncle in your shadow. He'll love that."

Razin grinned, then looked past 'Iweyz to Hasan, who remained standing where he had first appeared beneath the balcony.

"Salam Alaikum, brother," Razin greeted with a subtle nod.

Hasan inclined his head in turn. "Wa alaikum-salaam."

While Mushrie and 'Iweyz appeared as he remembered them, Hasan had changed. His once proud features—his aquiline nose, and arched brows, the sharp cheekbones that bestowed an air of imperiousness—were now subdued, creased by age and overshadowed by a thin layer of fat that Hasan had never carried in his youth. His once lustrous hair was cropped short, barely reaching his ears. But it was in his eyes that Razin found the greatest change. The sharp hazel eyes that were once so quick to find fault now appeared glazed and bloodshot, darting about nervously like a dog used to being kicked.

Hasan bore the look of a haunted man.

"It has been too long," said Razin, meaning it. Memories of the last words Hasan had spoken to him resurfaced in his mind.

You are a fool, Razin. A naïve fool.

"To me, it has only been a moment," Hasan replied with a tepid smile, his cracked and yellowed teeth on display. "But it is good to see you too, old friend. We have... much to discuss."

'Iweyz touched Hasan's shoulder lightly, still beaming at Razin. "He has been waiting here with us, haven't you, Hasan? Keeping me company so that Abdul Mushrie doesn't talk my ear off. Sometimes, if we are lucky, Hasan shares a tale of his own with us. Oh, but he tells the most wonderful tales, Razi! You wouldn't believe the things he has seen since leaving Kawkab al-Hawa.

Razin glanced at 'Iweyz and then back at Hasan. "Since... leaving?"

But you died there.

He had walked Hasan through the crowded yard. He remembered the stares of disapproval he had received for knowing Hasan and those separate glares and words directed at him for being a Syriano like Hasan. The doubt and mistrust in the eyes of the Franks he had fought alongside, even after all those months. They could never fully trust him. Even as he led his brother to the butcher's block, they doubted him.

But it was not to appease the Franks that he had declined to object to Hasan's sentence. For apostasy, there was no other possible verdict.

"You, too, have seen much, I think," Hasan said, stepping forward to stand beside Razin, deftly moving out of 'Iweyz's grasp, Razin noticed. "I wonder if we might not exchange stories. Just you and I, as we used to. *Wake up, brother.*"

"What?" Razin blinked, unsure he had heard correctly.

A pained expression briefly contorted Hasan's features, a fleeting moment of desperation before his noble countenance returned to passive disinterest.

"There will be time for stories later," said Mushrie, placing a hand on each of their shoulders. "First, we must pay our respects." He nodded toward the doors of the mosque and guided them inside.

"What is this?" Razin moaned, stepping through the arched doors of the Masjid al-Haram. The floors were littered with animal droppings and discarded fruit peels, obscuring the mosaic tiles beneath. Dust covered the marble pillars, and their once-golden capitals were tarnished from years of neglect. He covered his nose, repulsed by the stench. "Who is responsible for this? Where are the Keepers of the Ka'ba?"

Movement caught Razin's attention behind one of the pillars, and he swiftly turned to look, again regretting the swordless belt around his waist.

His eyes widened in disbelief.

A monkey sat at the foot of the pillar, watching him intently. It gnawed on small fleshy seeds that looked like raisins in one hand while gripping a tall and wide carved wooden object with its other. It was an idol, a statue.

Razin yelled, breaking into a sprint toward the monkey with his arms outstretched. "Get out! Get out!"

"Wait, nephew!" his uncle called from behind, but his blood was up now, his anger propelling him forward, ignited by his fury at the sight of the desecration.

The monkey took one look at him and fled, cradling the wooden statue awkwardly as it disappeared into the shadows of the mosque's corridors. Razin watched it vanish, stepping over the rotting fruit and droppings that coated the floor where it had sat.

"*Disgusting beast*," he hissed. "In this holy place. How is this possible? Where are the Bani Shaiba?"

Mushrie came panting up beside him.

He sucked in a breath, leaning against the pillar, and wiped his lips with his hand. "One morning… they were gone… and…" He exhaled slowly, raising a hand while he gathered himself. "And the next day, the monkeys came and took up residence. I tried to drive them out, but they multiply with each passing day. Pay them no heed, nephew."

"It is a punishment," Hasan stated, kneeling beside the pillar and clearing away the dirt to reveal the shining mosaic beneath. He smiled before looking up at Razin's bemused expression. "*Qirada*. Just as those from the town by the sea were transformed into apes for transgressing, so too have the Bani Shaiba been transformed."

"Nonsense," said Mushrie, glaring at Hasan. "The Bani Shaiba were *chosen* to look after this holy place. Al-ilah would not punish them. He only rewards the loyal." He lowered his hand and moved off the pillar, offering to help 'Iweyz as she navigated through the filth.

"Why were they punished?" said Razin softly so that only Hasan could hear.

"They are the tribe of Quraysh."

"And so?"

"You know who it is they worship. The Life-eater."

Razin cast a quick glance at Mushrie and 'Iweyz, who were engaged in hushed conversation, their smiles never faltering.

"They were converted by the Prophet himself," said Razin, looking back to Hasan. "You must be mistaken."

Mushrie clapped his hands together loudly. "Come, you two. We have tarried here enough. It is time to pay our dues."

Hasan rose from his knees and walked toward Mushrie. As he passed Razin, he lightly touched the sleeve of his ridā', whispering without moving his lips.

"*Wake up.*"

Razin removed his now-dirty sandals, soiled from the floors of the anterior halls of the Masjid al-Haram, and stepped onto the white stone of the *Mataf*. The marble was cool beneath his feet, and he felt a calm wash over him, dousing the last of the anger he had felt before.

Once he had completed the *Tawaf* and *Sa'ee*, he would find a way to deal with those monkeys. Perhaps 'Iweyz could begin cleaning the mosque while they hunted? He smiled to himself, imagining the Emir's favourite scrubbing floors. He would never hear the end of it.

Mushrie stepped out onto the Mataf ahead of him, motioning at them all to follow.

Together they approached the holy Ka'ba.

They passed by the Zamzam well, where Gabriel had cracked the earth to provide Hajar and Isma'il, the wife and child of Ibrahim, with water to quench their thirst. Razin thought of the vision he had experienced when confronted by the spirit that called itself Hubal. He had seen an old man gazing into the well, his hair streaked silver. It has been Abdul Mutallib, the Prophet's grandfather.

According to the story, Abdul Mutallib had discovered gold and armour in the depths of the well. But the other inhabitants of Mecca—the Quraysh and those living near the Ka'ba—made a claim to the find as well. To resolve the matter, Abdul decided to submit the matter to sacred lot. He fashioned seven arrows, splitting them equally between himself, the Quraysh, and the Ka'ba. The seventh arrow was dedicated to the statue of Hubal, who would oversee the drawing of lots.

But in Razin's vision, there had been no armour or gold in Zamzam. Something else had waited for Abdul Mutallib at the bottom of the well.

A God.

He shook his head, startled at the unbidden blasphemy that had appeared in his mind.

And in sacred Mecca, before holy Ka'ba.

He whispered the Shahada under his breath and looked to the Ka'ba itself, finding reassurance in its presence.

The four-walled structure was hidden beneath the *Kiswa*, the black cloth that was replaced every year in a tradition going back to a time before the Prophet, though it was Muhammad who had introduced the practice to Islam.

When he had conquered Mecca, dislodging the polytheists from the sacred city, he had found the Ka'ba veiled. The Prophet left the original Kiswa undisturbed, only replacing it after a fire burned through it.

Even the pagans had known this was a sacred place, Razin thought, trailing behind 'Iweyz and Mushrie. Hasan lingered a step behind him, almost breathing down Razin's neck.

He watched Mushrie as he approached the Black Stone on the eastern corner of the Ka'ba, offering a dua as he embarked on his Tawaf. He reached out with a hand, gently touching the Black Stone, before moving aside for 'Iweyz to do the same. Then, together they began to walk the route around the Ka'ba, commencing the first of the seven circuits known as *Shawt*.

But when Razin finished his prayer and reached for the Black Stone, he felt Hasan's hand pulling him back. He turned, angry at the interruption, but his words froze when he saw Hasan's wide-eyed stare.

"*Do not touch the Black Stone*," Hasan hissed, looking to see where Mushrie and 'Iweyz were on their circuit. They had just past the *Maqam Ibrahim* and did not appear to have noticed Hasan's interference.

They're going the wrong way, Razin thought dimly. The Tawaf was meant to be performed from right to left, but his uncle and 'Iweyz were walking in the opposite direction.

Hasan glanced back at Razin, beseeching him with his eyes as he stepped forward to take his place in front of the stone.

"*Wake up, brother. Do you know where you are?*"

"Tell me."

But Hasan fell silent and then closed his eyes to perform the *Vitr* prayer himself. He raised a hand toward the stone but did not touch it either.

Shadows shifted within the gallery above the Mataf, and Razin watched monkeys emerging from between the arches, clutching little wooden carvings, idols and statues like the first intruder he had seen inside the mosque. They perched on the arcade ledges and settled down to watch the figures down below.

"We have an audience," said Mushrie, clasping his hands together as he concluded the circuit. "They have grown bolder now that the Daughters are near, don't you think, 'Iweyz?" He laughed, but the sound became a haggard bark.

Razin blinked. His uncle's face was a wolf's face now—silver and grey, with a mouth full of razor-sharp teeth and a slavering tongue.

"They want to hear another of Hasan's stories." 'Iweyz's head was that of a hyena. It rested heavily on her shoulders, too large for her thin, elegant neck.

She laughed, and the sound was like a child's cry.

"Uncle," Razin mouthed, taking a step back. He spared Hasan a glance and saw that his head had fallen from his shoulders, cut where Gilbert's executioner had brought down his blade. It lay motionless on the white marble of the Mataf.

"Where am I?" Razin whispered, his voice caught in his throat.

He wanted to scream.

Jahannam.

This is Hell.

Hasan's head twitched on the ground, his mouth moving in a futile attempt to speak. He formed the shapes with his lips and tongue, but without the breath from his lungs, there was only silence.

Hasan had died an apostate.

He had turned away from the Faith to serve himself.

He was in Hell.

A monkey scuttled across the stone floor, coming to a stop beside the fallen head. Hasan blinked, his mouth contorting with rage as the monkey tugged at his hair. Then it dragged him from the ground, lifting the head up and hurrying back toward the gallery before Razin could think to stop it.

"You have not completed your Tawaf." Mushrie's words were distorted and growing louder. "*HURRY*," he howled, worms cascading from his mouth. "*YOU MUST TOUCH THE BLACK STONE.*"

The thing that had once been 'Iweyz giggled beside him, her crooked ears twitching as she advanced toward Razin.

'Iweyz… what had become of poor 'Iweyz, who had taken her lover's words to heart and believed the lies of Faruk and his cult until they turned her soul black.

She smiled at him.

Teeth like tombstones, rotten spines.

Then she inclined her head toward the Black Stone.

There was a sound behind Razin.

Hasan's headless body finally collapsed to the ground. But there was another sound, one he had heard before.

"Don't mind them." 'Iweyz sniggered. "The Keepers like to sing."

"*COME, NEPHEW*," the wolf-head growled, its hands open, gesturing toward the Ka'ba. The Black Stone stood before Razin, shimmering from between the curtains of the wall.

A-la-la

Razin glanced up at the gallery. The monkeys were clambering down from the walls now, slowly making their way onto the stone floor below while they sang. He saw Hasan's head being tossed around, a monkey chewing at his ear, another up to its elbows in his open neck, while Hasan's mouth gasped in futile silence.

A-la-la

When Razin looked back down, he was standing in front of the Black Stone, his hand extended toward it.

'Iweyz giggled again, her snout by his ear. "Touch it."

"*GO ON*," the wolf-head growled.

Razin felt the words of the Shahadah forming on his lips.

"*There is no God but God; There is no God but God…*" he repeated them over and over, but even as he spoke the words, his hand drew closer to the stone.

The rock had been polished smooth by countless hands, by pilgrims reaching out toward it just as he was now.

He realised that deep inside, he *wanted* to touch it. What did Hasan know? Why should his warning be heeded? *He was damned, and he would damn me too.*

A-la-la

The surface of the stone rippled, the polished marks gleaming like a glass mosaic, twisting in the light.

His hand was almost upon it, his fingers reaching for the first stone of the House of God. But it had been here since before the Prophet… since before Allah. It was like a shard from the deep, from the substance of creation. From it, all had come. But it was not an empty thing—it was power and wrath and fear and… and… hunger.

He pushed aside the thoughts, frowning as he stared into the miasmic skein beneath his fingertips. It was like staring into the ocean, into the primordial waters from which Bahamut had risen and from which all creation had sprung. Gasping, he saw a flicker of movement within the stone. There was something inside. It was moving, pushing up against the rock.

It wanted to come out.

Razin screamed, yanking his hand away from the Black Stone.

Then, darkness.

He was standing in darkness, his hand extended before him. The Ka'ba had vanished, as had the walls of the Masjid al-Haram. As his eyes adjusted to the gloom, he found that he was staring at the rusted iron bars of a cell. His hand hovered over its handle.

Water dripped from somewhere nearby.

He could not see inside the cell, but he felt something watching him from the shadows. A heavy presence, ancient. It smelt like salt and fish, of the dampness in the dark. Sweat covered his face, and he wiped it with a hand. It smelt of iron.

Footsteps approached from the shadows. He flinched, stepping back, pulling his hand away from the handle. He had nearly let it out, this dark thing veiled by shadows.

He grew afraid.

And then he heard Dietmar's piercing scream.

***

Dietmar was sitting up in his sleeping sack, still screaming, when Razin found him. His voice had become a choppy, broken hiss, his eyes rolled back into his head.

"It was a dream!" Razin told him, shaking him awake. "Only a dream!"

Dietmar's gambeson was dark, soaked through with sweat.

Then, Razin saw the knife in Dietmar's hand.

"*What have you done?*" Razin moaned, glancing down at Dietmar's chest. He had cut through the wool of his undervest and into his own flesh, hacking at it as if it were a block of mutton. Bits of bone protruded through the holes in his sternum, blood congealing in tepid clots in some places while flowing freely in others.

"Tomas!" Razin cried, wresting the knife from Dietmar's grasp. He looked around the hall, where Levi and Sara still lay before the hearth.

How had they slept through this?

His eyes shifted to the figure sitting in the corner. Tanit. Her yellow eyes gleamed in the flickering firelight, but she did not move to help him.

"Tomas!" Razin called again, searching the hall. "I need you. Tomas—"

"I saw him," Dietmar gasped, his body trembling.

"Tomas?" Razin looked back down at his friend, cradling his back with a hand. He was so light now, just bone beneath his fingers. "Where is he?"

"No, no." Dietmar shook his head. It was too large for his body, ungainly like

'Iweyz's hyena face.

Suppressing a shudder, Razin peeled back pieces of Dietmar's gambeson to inspect the wounds he had inflicted upon himself. Two of the growths he had counted before were gone, leaving mushroom-like cavities in their place.

"It was Hubal," Dietmar groaned. "I was him. I… *am* him." His breath came in shallow gasps, but his voice began to calm.

"I saw the world through his eyes."

"It was a dream."

"No. It was… a memory. Or… or something else. The serpent was there. The Falak. It guided me through the desert, nourishing me, shielding me from the sun… Sometimes, it carried me in its mouth. I lived that way for days, then weeks, maybe years—I know it wasn't truly me, but I still felt the passage of time, every single minute of it. I had no fear of the creature. I loved it. I believe it loved me too. It led me across the desert to the Black Waters, where the waves rose like mountains, and you cannot see the sky for the stars. I stood on its shores and raised my arms, calling to the soul of the deep.

"And something answered. Something responded to my call."

Razin shifted uncomfortably, listening intently to Dietmar's words. His wounds had stopped bleeding, and Razin saw something clutched between the fingers of Dietmar's left hand.

"I left this place then," Dietmar continued, his gaze growing distant. "I followed the Falak through one of its tunnels—you were right, my friend. It traverses the world plane, weaving through a maze of burrows, a network of interconnected tunnels, like a web stretching across places and unplaces. Some parts of the tapestry have yet to be woven, while others have long been dead, and there are only empty spaces left behind."

Razin focused, trying to keep track of what his friend was telling him. And still, his thoughts went to the šubur resting on his cushions in Ubar.

Another being had left this place once before.

The Adite prophet, Addir-Melek.

"What did you see?" Razin asked, his voice a low whisper.

"Home," Dietmar replied, smiling—smiling with a toothless mouth. "But it was before… before you or I. Before the Prophet… I believe, even before Christ. I sat within a four-sided temple, and people flocked to me in droves. They asked about the past, about the present…"

"About the future."

Dietmar nodded. "I humoured their requests, passing the time as I parsed their fates, through stone, coins, and then from my tools. But that wasn't why I was there. I was waiting for something. Waiting for the right time.

"I had come too early."

"Too early for what? Why were you there?"

Dietmar winced, lifting his hand from his lap and opening his fingers to reveal the objects he had cut from his own skin. Two bloody arrowheads rested in the centre of his palm.

"To raise Bahamut," he said, looking from his hand to Razin. "To rouse Leviathan."

39

Levi and Sara never awoke from their slumber. Their cold bodies lay motionless before the barren hearth, their vacant stares fixed upon the ceiling of Gilbert's hall until Razin covered them. They bore no wounds, Razin said—self-inflicted or otherwise. Whatever had taken their lives had come from their dreams.

Perhaps it was the mazzakin, after all, claiming them in their sleep, extinguishing their lives while Dietmar screamed into the night. If they had made any sounds, he hadn't heard them amidst the echoes of his own tormented cries.

And Tomas was gone.

At first, Dietmar thought he'd been taken, swallowed up by whatever spirit occupied Beauvoir Castle. He scoured the great hall, calling out for Tomas, and explored the corridors, kitchen, and garden, but when he found the stairs leading to the bowels of the keep, Razin halted his search.

"There's nothing for us down there," Razin stated, placing a gentle yet firm hand on his shoulder.

Dietmar stared past him at the stone steps and sloping walls that spiralled into the ground. He could hear the sound of water dripping somewhere below.

"But… Tomas."

"He's not here," said Razin quietly. "He must have slipped out sometime during the night."

"But… why?"

—Laurus

Razin blinked at him, then nodded slowly.

He must have voiced the name aloud. Again, like the time beneath the hermit's tower. Hubal was slowly squeezing him out.

"Something stirred in Tomas when we came upon Laurus and his flock." Razin helped Dietmar onto one of the steps leading to the gallery above and adjusted the hastily applied bandages around Dietmar's chest. "When Laurus appeared, it was as if we didn't exist. He was only interested in Tomas. I knew then that he would leave us."

"You could have stopped him."

Razin hesitated, his gaze shifting toward the staircase below—it was more a recess, with small narrow steps and barely enough room for a grown man to stand. A darkness hung there. The sort that no torch or candle could dispel.

"I was… preoccupied."

Dietmar saw Razin's face then, properly for the first time since he'd woken. His thick black hair, usually hidden beneath the folds of his keffiyeh, hung over his brow, obscuring—but barely—the dark circles beneath his eyes. Streaks of grey he'd not noticed before lined his beard and eyebrows. His skin had lost some of its colour, despite the blistering sun the previous day. It didn't look like he'd slept.

"What's down there?" Dietmar tilted his head toward the recess, catching a faint sound, like wind through wheat, like the after-breath of a door slamming shut.

"An *'aduwallah,*" said Razin softly, his voice barely more than a whisper. "The spirit of this place. It does not like that we are here."

"Could Tomas not have—"

"He is gone!" Razin snapped, his eyes darting from the recess to Dietmar. His hands were shaking. "Please, Dietmar. He is not down there. I would have seen him. There is a single cell. It is… empty."

"There's something else," said Dietmar, sensing the weight of the spaces between the words left unspoken. "What did you see?"

"An enemy of God." Razin rose to his feet, concealing his hands within the folds of his burnous. "It tried to break me."

Then he went silent and would say no more.

***

They laid Levi and Sara to rest in the garden beneath the wall. Neither of them knew the burial rites of Levi's people, so Dietmar spoke a few solemn words while Razin shovelled earth into their graves.

Dietmar had wanted to bury them beyond the walls, away from the place that had seen their last. It felt wrong to inter them so close to the spirit—this *'aduwallah*. But the sand outside the walls was hard as rock, and the spade Razin had found in the storeroom was not up to the task. So, Dietmar had contented himself with the only place in Beauvoir Castle where life could still be found, beneath the onion bulbs and garlic, the stalks of fennel and tansy, where the mushrooms grew.

The girl watched them from the steps of the keep.

When the burial was complete, Razin offered a prayer of his own—a dua to protect their graves from any disturbance by restless spirits. Dietmar stared sadly at the now flattened soil of the herb bed while Razin recited the prayer. Until last night, he had thought the worst behind them. Now that the mountains were in sight and a passage through them, they might be given some respite from the horrors that had dogged their path.

And now, the last of their party were being interred in the ground.

Who would tell Levi's wife what had become of her husband and children—that they were eaten by hyena-men and killed by mazzikin spirits. How could any wife believe such a thing?

And Tomas was gone.

Fled into the night, leaving them behind. Dietmar had refused to believe it until they discovered his tracks past the gates, headed east. And he had not been alone. A vaguely humanoid set of prints had paired with his own, vanishing into the hills toward Mount Qaf. A guide. One of Laurus's golden baboons.

Dietmar had argued with Razin over the trail. Tomas could not have gotten far, he'd said. They could still find him—bring him back to safety. But Razin had shaken his head and waved at Dietmar's bound chest and ribs. He was in no condition to go marching back into the desert. And even if they could catch up with Tomas, what then? They had both witnessed the connection between Tomas and Laurus. This had not been a stranger to Tomas, as it had to them. He had *known* the man and decided to follow him.

He had made his choice.

So it was that only three of the six that had entered Beauvoir Castle left that morning. They headed north toward the Daughters.

And home.

***

Dietmar walked in a daze, staring blankly at the world around him as they wandered north, always north.

At times they navigated the path together, helping each other cross deep chasms filled with jagged stones and empty holes that breathed hot plumes of smoke, like Old Tirus beneath the Dead Sea.

Where are you going, Chevalier? He heard that mad Frenchman's mocking voice in his head again and again, over and over. *Where are you going? Where?*

Home, he thought. *I'm going home.*

Occasionally, they would drift apart, the distance between them growing until Dietmar had to shout to be heard by Razin.

He could barely distinguish his own thoughts from those of the thing inside him anymore. Memories surged forth. They came in waves, images from the past, from places he knew and didn't, words he had spoken in anger and in pain. Some, he had come to regret, others he did not. Memories that were not his own emerged as well. He saw the Black Waters once more, a figure standing on its shores, gazing out at the sea, heralding a great and terrible thing—an end, but not *the* end.

He saw Ennelyn, too, standing in the sand of a desert he did not recognise, a brown tomb behind her.

Sometimes, as they walked, he caught glimpses of her amidst the plains, draped in the shroud he had last seen her in. He called out to her the first time she appeared, startling Razin, but she did not reply. Eventually, he ceased his calls.

Dietmar became dimly aware of a strangeness to the vast plain they had descended upon. Shadows of trees stretched across the stone and sand where there were no forests, disembodied voices echoed from deep cracks in the ground—long fissures resembling pressure lines in wood—whispering in unfamiliar tongues. When the girl stood over one of the cracks to stare down into the empty place within, Dietmar was sure he'd seen a hand, long fingers reaching toward the girl standing above it. Razin swiftly pulled her away, and the hand disappeared beneath the sand.

They kept their distance from the fissures after that.

There were the animals, too.

Slippery beasts that swam through the sand like water, vanishing the moment Dietmar caught a glimpse of them. Reptiles with sun fins resting on the rocks, their watchful gazes following the travellers as they passed. Each creature was the size of a small horse, possessing jaws that appeared capable of rending through chainmail. Dietmar breathed easier when he saw one of the creatures peacefully chewing clumps of leaves from thick-limbed bushes. Its mouth moved in slow, lazy motions, bringing to mind the great grinding jaws of a tortoise.

And then there were the birds.

They circled the sky above them like vultures. And, indeed, some of them did look like the great raptors. But for every curved beak and scythe-like talons, other features emerged—a cacophony of monkey-like mouths and hands. Silvery scales adorned their bodies instead of feathers, save for their leathery wings that resembled those of a bat, ending in sharp, nail-like appendages. Their silvery tails swirled in the air as they bobbed and weaved above, forcing them to duck until the girl plucked one of them from the air and swiftly broke its neck.

After that, the birds kept to a safe distance, content to watch them from afar. They were scavengers, not hunters, but their presence alone was enough to worry Dietmar. He became more vigilant as they ventured further into the shadow of the mountains.

"How's your chest?" asked Razin, crouched over a bundle of dry kindling, attempting to spark a fire. The bird the girl had caught lay neatly skewered at his feet, ready to be roasted.

"Feels like someone's been at it with a knife," said Dietmar, offering a thin smile.

Razin snorted, looking up from his flint. "If you had cut any deeper, I would have needed to dig a third hole this morning. I am tired of digging holes for friends."

"No more holes," Dietmar agreed. He thought of the glade where he had buried Enneleyn and Rudi in… of the hole in his dreams. Empty. He remembered now. Father Sander had denied them Christian burials, condemning Rudi for the sin that was not his own and Enneleyn for hers, which was.

He had thought his troubling choice was between the two of them, if there was even a chance he could secure salvation for one of them. But Hubal's thoughts, those glimpses of the creature's mind, had shown him another possibility, another future that might arise if he continued on his path.

Hubal sought passage through the world-edifice, and he had found a vessel Dietmar.

But to what end?

He already knew. He had seen the black ocean in his dreams. Hubal had tried it once before, in the guise of a prophet. But he had not gone to spread the word of some God like Razin had suggested when they first contemplated the passage of Addir-Melek. It had been to raise one. To summon Bahamut from the primordial sea and unleash chaos upon creation.

He failed then. Perhaps he will fail again?

Dietmar wanted to scoff at his own selfish thoughts and foolish hopes. To choose between Enneleyn and Rudi, to face an impossible decision, only to lose them both—was this his test as a father and husband? He feared he was failing.

Razin stared at him, his eyes shifting between Dietmar's face and his ragged chest. It wasn't pity or sadness he saw in Razins expression but wariness, perhaps even fear. Then Razin returned to his flint, and soon a small fire crackled to life.

They had made camp in the open. With no trees or hills to provide shelter on the plain, they simply settled where they stood as the shadows lengthened and the sky darkened.

Dietmar's limbs ached, reducing his limp to a slow shuffle by late afternoon. He knew he couldn't go much further without rest, even if Razin believed they could reach the mountain path by walking through the night.

They shared a flask of mint water and chewed on herbs they'd plucked from the garden while Razin slowly turned the bird over the fire. The girl sat at the edge of the camp, her legs crossed, staring at the dark shapes ahead.

The mountains now covered half the sky, concealing the horizon behind their imposing slopes. Iridescent streaks of green and yellow creased the firmament, flowing from the east where the fourth peak lay—the path that Tomas had taken.

It was Tomas who usually cooked for them. He was not a skilled fighter like Dietmar or Razin, not a numbers man like Adelman, so he had made himself useful as their cook whenever they had something to throw onto the fire. He hadn't been very good at that either, but it made him feel useful, so Dietmar and Razin withheld their complaints—leaving only poor Adelman to moan about their overcooked meat and burnt eggs.

"He's really gone, isn't he?" said Dietmar.

Razin lifted the spit from the fire, poking at the bird with his knife before returning it to the flames. He glanced at Dietmar and nodded. "He made his—"

"Choice. Yes, I know. To follow a blind man into the wilderness. But to leave us… for that?"

Razin shrugged, settling on his haunches near the fire. "I cannot tell you what motivates Tomas. But has it not seemed as if he were searching for something? He was lost even before we came here. Perhaps with Laurus, he will find what he is looking for?"

"A demon king?" Dietmar muttered with disbelief.

Razin shook his head slowly. "Not all who inhabit the slopes of Mount Qaf harbour ill intentions. Jinn are… complex beings."

"Ill intentions?" Dietmar scratched gingerly at his chest, feeling the itch of his wounds. He took a sip from his flask, trying to ease his dry throat.

"They bear us more than that, my friend," he said. "They want to

—eat us. They hunger for us and our bones

Dietmar coughed, blinking at the fire. His throat was starting to chafe. He took another sip from his flask.

Razin stared at him, a peculiar expression on his face.

"And what about the people here?" Dietmar continued, wiping his lips. He could feel his empty gums against his hand and knew that his words now carried a subtle lisp, a hiss. "They would feed us to their gods—the snake, the hyena-men, the mouths of the sea

—to that bitch Lamassu

The girl was staring at him too now, her lips curling to reveal her teeth.

"Dietmar," Razin spoke softly, pleading with his eyes.

—And you, you let him go! You could have stopped him, should have stopped him! Now he's in the mouth of a king with eyes and eyes and a voice like the chasm and the void. He followed, he followed, hoping to find the man who shot him from his seed. But now he has abandoned us, like his father before him. His life, a circle, now at a close

Razin left the spit on the coals and raised his hands. "Please, my friend. You are not yourself."

—Do you not like what you hear, Mohammedan?

Dietmar reeled as Hubal's presence surged in his mind. He felt him permeating every corridor, every vessel within him. He could vanish now and be truly lost as Hubal exerted control. The arrowheads on his chest burned so hot that he could smell the scent of his own flesh cooking. He closed his eyes. Or Hubal did.

He sought refuge from those lecherous tendrils, retreating deeper into himself, searching for a place untouched by Hubal's grip, those life-eating appendages that had sunk so deep into his consciousness.

But Hubal followed.

As vast territories of his mind fell under Hubal's sway, memories slipped away—words, feelings, expressions, ideas—all lost. The gates were open now, and Dietmar wondered if he could ever close them again.

Then a voice called out to him.

He saw a face—Enneleyn. He clung to the image, fighting not to forget, even as the deafening roar filled his ears.

The creature, this demon or jinn or God, spoke to him and through him, using his mouth and lips to shape words he would never utter. But Dietmar ignored them, anchoring himself to the memory of his wife.

A sea rose around Enneleyn, with towering waves and inky waters, yet Dietmar refused to let them claim her. She became his raft in that abyss until the roar subsided and only silence remained.

From a distance, he heard his name being spoken—by a voice he recognised and loved. There was fear in that voice, a rising panic. Dietmar opened his eyes.

Razin stood over him, a hand resting gently on his shoulder. It was the third time his friend had woken him thusly.

Dietmar blinked, slowly sitting up on his sleeping sack. His eyes settled on the knife in Razin's hand.

"I thought you were gone," Razin said, returning the blade to its sheath. He didn't comment on why it had been in his hand. They both knew, implicitly understood, the nature of Dietmar's malignancy. If it came to it, he trusted Razin wouldn't hesitate.

"Not yet." Dietmar released a slow breath, the taste of bile lingering in his mouth. He looked up to see Razin and the girl still watching him. He mustered a faint smile.

It wasn't far, now. He could still make it.

But was that what he wanted anymore?

Razin studied him for another moment, making certain the fit had passed and Hubal wasn't lurking, ready to resurface. Then he turned his attention back to the fire and removed the spit from the coals.

The bird was burnt, just as Tomas would have prepared it.

The raptor tasted closer to fish than to chicken, Dietmar thought. Naturally salty and with a certain sourness that reminded him of… something he'd eaten as a child. Pickled herring? The details eluded him. That part of his mind was sealed off to him now, along with all the memories attached to it.

"…they are not all Godless spirits." Razin's voice broke through Dietmar's thoughts. He gnawed on a charred thigh, using his fingers to strip away the remaining bits of bone. "Some recognise the Prophet and accept man's dominion over them. Others… the lion-mouth is… complicated. I do not believe she sees us in a manner much different to how we view ants."

Dietmar furrowed his brow, puzzled. "The lion-mouth?" Then, with the realisation: "Lamassu?"

Razin nodded, flicking the bones into the fire. Tanit had already finished hers and now cast a hungry gaze toward the remnants of Dietmar's meal. He had to cut the meat into fine slivers to spare his mouth and found that his hunger had waned after the initial few bites.

"Here," he said, passing his leftovers to Tanit. "You caught it. It's only fair."

Tanit snatched the wing from his hand with lightning speed, the same swiftness with which she had captured the bird. She crouched by the fire, devouring the meat while keeping her eyes fixed on Dietmar.

She is a savage, Dietmar thought, and then another thought played about his mind before vanishing.

"It comes from an old religion to the north," Razin said. "There are still stone statues of it near the *Naqš-e Rustam*, in Persepolis. We call them the *aladlammû*—protective spirits." He turned his gaze at the dark mass of towering peaks behind them. The gossamer light cast its silhouette in a spectral chiaroscuro, long shadows stretching over ridges and gorges, making them appear larger, closer. Razin brought his eyes back to Dietmar. "The aladlammû are guardians of the gate. I thought it was an ifrit at first, but… Lamassu. It is no ifrit."

"Guardian," Dietmar repeated, thinking of the winged beast with its rows of teeth and funeral breath. It had toyed with them, then it had eaten half their number. "That thing killed Aimery and Nicolo. It tore through our guards like a hell-fiend."

"Like a dog that finally catches the mouse it's been chasing," Razin replied. "It doesn't know what to do with it when it does."

"It knew," said Dietmar firmly. To be reduced to the mere plaything of a demon, to have his fear and anger, along with all those lives, dismissed so easily. And what difference did it make if the so-called "guardian" bore them no ill will? It had consumed them all the same.

"You must understand that we mean nothing to such a being." Razin added more kindling to the fire, the last of the dry brush they had gathered during their march across the plain. "Trapped within that vault, we would have been nothing more than sustenance. How long do you think it had waited there, between those pillars? When was its last meal?"

"It played games with us," Dietmar muttered.

Razin glanced up from the fire, meeting his gaze. "It found us in its lair. You saw those bones, the chains, the stone altars. Someone had been feeding it."

"Priests."

"And then we came… another meal."

Dietmar watched Tanit as she devoured the bird and casually dropped the remains on the ground at her feet. Her mouth glistened with fat as she smiled at him.

"If I falter," said Dietmar suddenly, "you will finish what I set out to do, won't you? You will take the hand to Naples?"

He thought he saw Razin stiffen in response, but he eventually nodded once.

"Try to get some sleep," said Razin, stretching out on his sleeping sack.

"Soon," said Dietmar, still watching the girl.

But the embers had long since turned cold by the time he closed his eyes.

He dreamed of chains and of wings beating in the dark.

***

Razin woke early, completing his morning prayers before the others stirred from their slumber. Like all the mornings before in this place, he did not know in which direction *Qiblah* lay, so he faced northeast, in the direction it would have been had they not slipped between the layers of the world.

It would suffice, he knew. His prayer would be valid. He would not need to repeat it, as he had no way of knowing in which direction to perform the *Fajr*.

Once he finished, Razin gently prodded Dietmar awake. For the briefest of moments, he hoped his friend wouldn't stir, that this corpse before him had finally given its last, releasing Razin from the dread that had been growing with each passing minute.

This is the al-Dajjāl.

The end of things.

El Kharrûb.

The Destroyer.

Razin thought about the knife at his belt and the twisted, contorted presence that had manifested beneath Dietmar's face the night before when Hubal had spoken through him. He should have put an end to it then, but he couldn't bring himself to do it. He lacked the courage to carry out what needed to be done.

He was a coward, he knew. He always had been.

"Forgive me, my friend," Razin said as Dietmar's watery eyes opened.

"For what?"

"My failings."

Dietmar sat up stiffly, shaking his head. "Then there is nothing to forgive. You have done no wrong in my eyes. Now come, help me up."

Dietmar's frail arms felt like bones in Razin's hands, and he tried not to recoil from the weeping wounds beneath his touch. Dietmar had discarded his hauberk, finding it too loose and heavy for his emaciated frame. He now wore only the remnants of his tattered gambeson and tabard. Barely anything of the wolf from his sigil remained, and the once vibrant yellow had faded, leaving behind a washed-out white. The holes in Dietmar's chest were now blackened clots, filled with pus and dirt. They would be infected soon if they weren't already. Perhaps the infection would do what he could not and release his friend from his misery.

He felt his face flush at the thought and looked away before Dietmar could see his shame and read the thoughts in his eyes.

"We will reach the mountains today," Razin said, shifting his focus to the shadowed cleft that split the stone walls ahead. He could just make out the outlines of a passage running through it—a mouth of a ravine. The air above it appeared darker, staining the slopes of the mountain behind it. The haze swirled as he watched, twisting like a cloud of birds in a hypnotic murmuration.

Dietmar noticed it too.

"The sandstorm that brought us here."

Razin nodded, watching the scar throb and shift. It rippled, gathering more sand and dirt, but it did not move beyond the confines of the gorge. It hung there, suspended by some unseen force that prevented it from sweeping across the plain.

The Mouth of God, Razin thought. *And we are to walk down its throat.*

Razin noticed the change in Dietmar sometime after noon.

His strides had lengthened, no longer hindered by the painful limp that had plagued them during their journey across the plain. He stood taller, his bony shoulders squared and his hunched back straightened. There was something different about his voice, too. The lisp, born from the loss of his teeth, had vanished, and he spoke with renewed vigour.

He laughed too.

A loud, barking laugh that made Razin flinch.

At times, when Dietmar spoke, Razin caught glimpses of a second tongue flickering in his mouth, scraping against the ridges of his empty gums. A grey stump of flesh entwined with Dietmar's own tongue so that it looked like two serpents coupling in his mouth. Razin thought of Iblis then and how he had tricked the serpent into carrying him into Paradise.

Could such a trick work twice?

His hand hovered near the hilt of his sword.

I walk beside the Devil.

My friend.

But then Dietmar had looked at him, and his eyes were his own. Any resolve Razin had wavered and crumbled. He couldn't do it.

Not here.

Not now.

When there is nothing left of him, he thought miserably, withdrawing his hand from his hilt.

When it is easier for me.

Coward.

He would do it before they crossed. He couldn't allow Dietmar to bring whatever was in him home.

If Dietmar noticed the inner conflict raging in Razin or the near-draw of his sword, he didn't comment, and they made good progress across the plain.

As they reached the passage through the mountains, the resolve that Razin had been slowly building finally left him.

A hot wind blasted out from the ravine, forcing Razin to squint against the grains of sand it brought with it. He hunched over, leaning into the gust. A dull roar emanated from deeper within. Razin caught a glimpse of a spiralling sand cloud. It was the same cloud he had seen spilling over Mount Ebal all those weeks ago. It whipped across the opening of the passage, fluctuating like the patterns on watered steel, fresh from a Damascene forge.

Dietmar stood ahead, unbowed by the wind, his gaze fixed upon the stone walls of the ravine. Razin followed his line of sight, squinting against the gusts of sand, and then he saw what had captured Dietmar's attention.

"The Daughters!" Dietmar called over the howling wind. He raised his hand, pointing. "We had it all wrong. It's not the mountains! It never was!"

Carved into the face of the ravine were three colossal stone figures. They covered the entire surface of the rock, standing as tall as the *'Amud*

El-Sawari, the giant Corinthian he had seen in Egypt, or perhaps even as tall as Tancred's Temple, the *Qasr Julad* in Jerusalem.

Each statue depicted a feminine figure with pronounced hips and slender waists. They wore the loose robes of an *abaya* or Roman *stola*, draping down to their sandalled feet. Their hands were raised in the same pose as the figure they had seen on the pillars in the temple and again crossing the bridge to Ladah and in Ubar. It was the pose of the prophet, Addir-Melek.

A hand raised in a fist, two fingers extended toward the heavens, while the other pointed toward the earth.

A sense of unease stirred within Razin as his eyes scanned the statues, eventually resting upon the face of the nearest one.

A wolf.

Then, the next.

A monkey.

Then, finally.

A hyena, tongue lolling.

"Their names are written beneath their feet," Dietmar called out, advancing closer. The wind pulled at his words, snatching pieces of them from the air. *Their names… are… written.*

He stopped beneath the wolf-head, peering down at the script carved into the stone at its feet.

"This one is Manat," Dietmar called back.

Razin's frown deepened, his unease growing with each passing moment. He did not recognise the language etched in the stone. The symbols Dietmar was reading were meaningless to him.

"And this is al-'Uzza!"

Each name sounded like a question on Dietmar's lips, one which evinced an answer to Razin's ears. He knew these names. He had heard them spoken by Gizzal and Bezal, by pagans and believers alike. These names were blasphemy. God had no daughters.

"I do not think that wise!" Razin shouted, now hurrying toward his friend. He hunched against a sudden gust of wind that nearly blew him over. When he looked up, Dietmar was striding toward the third statue, larger than the others. Its elongated snout jutted from the rockface like a bridge to nowhere. Its ears were wide and dark, and Razin wondered briefly if they were hollow, like cave mouths. He buried the thought, hastening his steps to reach Dietmar.

His friend knelt over the markings etched into the stone beneath the hyena-face. He brushed away the sand that had gathered in the grooves of the symbols and locked eyes with Razin.

He smiled.

His mouth was filled with thick, blocky teeth that were not his own.

"No!" Razin cried, certain now that the names should never be spoken aloud. He drew his sword, regretting his hesitation earlier and hoping there was still time.

A grey tongue flickered behind Dietmar's alien teeth, then rolled out of his mouth to lick his lips lasciviously. When he spoke again, it was not Dietmar's voice that emerged from that twisted mouth.

"The Third," he said, his voice a hissing serpent. "al-Lat."

Razin raised his sword, poised to land the killing blow. He was just a few paces away now.

And then the impossible happened.

The Goddesses began to move.

40

Razin fell to his knees.

The world around him dissolved into a swirling abyss of black and grey. The sandstorm roared, a tempest of chaos and dread, unshackled by the emergence of the...

Stone moved over his head in great grinding motions that made his mind reel. He fought against the notion, rejecting it with every fibre of his being, but it could not be ignored.

They are not real.

There is no Manat, al-'Uzza, and al-Lat.

I have dreamed of them before...

...but this is not a dream.

The statues moved like rope puppets, each ponderous motion a jagged sequence of disconnected smaller motions. al-Lat, the largest of them, pushed herself away from the wall, shedding her stony exterior in a cataclysmic cascade that shook the very ground beneath Razin's feet.

Razin saw dark, scarified flesh. Hands, with elongated fingers and a stained Kafan shroud draped over her shoulders.

Razin's vision blurred as the sandstorm intensified, forcing him to squint against the onslaught of sand. He watched as the wolf-head shrugged off the last of her shell. A giant, like Og.

But not a god.

He emptied the contents of his stomach on the dirt. After a moment, he tried vomiting again, but there was nothing left within him.

He looked up.

This is Hell.

I am in Hell.

Dietmar walked toward him, his arms open wide like the symbol of his faith. His face shimmered and rippled, twisting as something shifted beneath his skin, struggling to break free.

Shadows writhed behind him in the dirt, barely discernible forms that howled and yelped in the wind. Razin saw the outline of wings and hooves, the impression of a serpentine body unfurling within the storm. He heard bestial grunts, gibbering calls, the sound of rutting bovines, and strange birds. The shadows flickered, still caught within the veil of sand, a vision from this place and another.

The layers of reality were colliding.

Dietmar's voice pierced through the raging storm, dissonant and jarring.

"You are still here, Mohammedan." His mouth moved in a way that did not match the words—too fast and then too slow before stretching into a cadaverous smile. "You will bear witness then, perceive as I have perceived. Many will witness, but you will be the First."

"I will bear no witness to your deeds, Shayāṭīn. *Destroyer.*" He tried to rise to his feet and found that he could not. He was transfixed there, held down by some impossible force.

"Destroyer?" Hubal laughed, and the sound was the opening of a tomb. "No, no, my little Mohammedan. At first… perhaps. But I am here to *create*. To build anew from the void I bring."

Razin blinked, baring his teeth.

"You cannot create," he declared, his voice resolute.

I must kill this thing.

"Oh?"

The air around Dietmar's body shimmered like Gizzal's lightbox. For a fleeting moment, another image was superimposed over his form. Razin saw a fiery mouth, a gleaming sword pushing out from between his lips. In his hands, he held orbs of light and dark—the sun and moon.

But when Razin blinked, it was gone.

Then, Hubal extended a hand toward the Daughter towering above them.

The wolf-head snapped her jaws, gnashing at the swirling dirt and dust. After a moment, her hand came to rest on her belly, her scarred fingers pressed tight against the dirty fabric. The monkey-head started gibbering behind her, clasping at its own stomach. Then the hyena-head erupted in laughter.

al-Lat's womb swelled as Razin watched, straining against the Kafan she wore so that he could see the outline of the thing within, spines, and horns, and bones pressing against her dark skin. He looked past al-Lat, to Manat and al-Uzza and saw the same thing repeated.

The Daughters were pregnant.

Hubal lowered his hand, a triumphant smile spreading across Dietmar's twisted face. But Dietmar was gone. What little bit of him that remained had finally disappeared, leaving only his body behind. Hubal's nose twitched and unfolded, the skin creasing and uncreasing, remoulding itself until it resembled the leaf-like protrusion Razin had seen during the al-'asm.

Dietmar's eyes darkened, his pupils receding into the cavernous chambers beneath his brow.

"You would deny your own eyes?" Hubal gestured toward al-Lat.

"My senses can be tricked," said Razin, refusing to look at the wolf-head.

She will birth a mockery of creation, a foul mimicry, a pale reflection. It will not be real. None of this is real.

A dark light blossomed from the heart of the sandstorm, casting oily rays across the ravine. The monkey-head screeched, her mouth opening and closing as something like pain passed over her face. Sweat matted her golden hair, and her eyes rolled back. With faltering steps, she advanced, clutching her swollen belly.

Razin felt something tear inside of him, his uncle's words ringing mockingly in his mind.

Only a fool takes the word of the many over his own senses.

The hyena-head sniggered—a wretched barking laugh that reverberated off the ravine walls, blending with the howling wind.

Amidst the swirling sand and dirt, Razin discerned another form, like a wave crashing against Ubar's sea wall.

The wolf-head suddenly howled, and the sound was madness. She shuddered again.

And again.

Water spilt from her womb.

Black and coursing.

It spilt onto the sandy ground, forming rivers that twisted through the ravine. Within the water, shapes emerged, silver-backed with fins. They writhed and slithered, only to be devoured by the shadows in the storm.

Hubal stood over him now, his eyes little more than pinpricks in his face. He exhaled deeply.

It smelt like the ocean.

Razin stared past him, his eyes locking on Manat and al-Uzza.

They were both squatting now, joining their sibling, giving birth to an ocean where they stood.

Chaos.

The ocean of existence.

It would spill through the Sandmouth, flooding the places and unplaces, the web of tunnels between the terrestrial plane. The layers of the world would become one.

And Bahamut would rise.

Razin saw himself in Mecca again, standing before the Ka'ba.

It was a dream.

But it was more than a dream. It was a dream interwoven with the spirit of Kawkab al-Hawa, where the order of things had been undone, unmade, and fashioned anew.

The rippling stone held a revelation. There was something inside of it. It belonged in these waters. It came from the ocean, and the ocean came from it.

"I see your doubts, friend." Hubal's voice was Dietmar's, his careful tone and inflection. The hiss that had once marked his words was gone. "When was it that you lost your faith? Was it in Nur ad-Din's foul camp, amongst the whores and revelling of your equals? Or was it in Capharleth, when your sword could not distinguish between man or woman, the young and old? No, no, even that wasn't enough to sway you. It was in al-Hawa when you killed your friend. A man you had called brother and been called brother in return."

"I did not kill Hasan."

"You did not wield the sword, but you did not stop it either. And 'Iweyz... you have seen what has become of her, I think."

"No." Razin shook his head, catching sight of the hyena-head. *That is not her fate.*

"She did not long survive your absence," said Hubal. "A foolish girl. One wonders what path she might have taken if you had stayed. Would you like me to tell you?"

Hubal pulled at the collar of his tabard, exposing the scarred skin of his chest. The blisters and boils that had covered it were gone, leaving smooth, pale white flesh in its place, with the exception of the arrowhead growths. Those remained.

Hubal ran a hand over the growth above his sternum, his long fingers gently caressing it. Then he squeezed it like a boil, pressing it with both hands. Puss erupted from the growth, followed by a gout of blood and a silver tip. He plucked the arrowhead from the wound, letting it settle in his palm before repeating the process until five bloody arrowheads rested between his fingers.

Then he opened his mouth, stretching it wide before reaching into it with the other hand to retrieve two more arrowheads.

Hubal held them in his hand, shaking them like dice before tossing them into the air above his head in a glimmer of silver and blood.

But they did not fall.

Instead, the arrowheads hung suspended in mid-air, mirroring the rocks they had seen upon the open plain. Hubal considered them for a moment, his gaze shifting between the shards of iron to Razin. Behind him, water sprayed across the dirt floor of the ravine, vanishing into the veil of sand—the Me-anesi.

Amidst the churning waters, Razin thought he glimpsed a leathery fin moving in the undulating S-pattern of a serpent. But as quickly as it appeared, it vanished, submerging into the sand wall.

He looked away, his gaze coming to a rest on the seven spinning arrowheads above Hubal. Each rotated slowly on its axis while their master read them.

"You might have saved her," Hubal remarked, nudging the closest arrowhead with a gentle touch and smiling. "But perhaps not. Some fates are like rivers, and their course cannot be altered no matter how we try. And others, others are like the ocean, and they drag you along with them."

But Razin was no longer listening. His eyes had settled on the pouch at Hubal's waist.

The hand.

The water had reached them now, trickling past his knees and wetting his sirwâl trousers.

Another sound boomed from the sand—deep and thunderous. He had heard it before, aboard the Ishkur. Flinching at the resounding boom, Razin thought he saw a monstrous shape moving behind the veil of sand.

"And what of Hasan?" Hubal flicked a hand at the arrowheads, turning them over with a gesture. "If you had not abandoned him. If you had not left him to pursue your own selfish desires, what would have become of him?" Hubal shook his head, unable to conceal his mirth. "My little Mohammedan, where has that brought you?"

Here.

Now.

Razin lunged forward, almost toppling toward Hubal from his knees. He reached out, desperately grasping…

…And felt the hard leather of the pouch between his fingers. He yanked at it, and the string came loose, away from Dietmar-who-was-Hubal's belt.

Then something struck him on the side of the head, sending him sprawling across the wet dirt and water. His arm moved hard in a direction it couldn't and then made a sound it shouldn't, too. Gasping for breath, his vision flickering, he came to a stop in the shallow waters, where Manat had once stood, and lay there, motionless.

"It's too late for that," barked Hubal, striding toward him.

Razin stirred, gazing down at his body. His left arm hung limply by his side, causing a soft moan to escape his lips when he attempted to lift it. Left with no choice, he left it where it lay, partially submerged by the rising waters. Then, he looked into his other hand and saw his fingers still tightly wrapped around the neck of the pouch.

Hubal splashed through the shallows, reaching out for Razin. "Perhaps if you had listened to that foolish old man, but not now. No, no. *Give it to me.*"

Razin tried to crawl, kicking his legs in the sand and water, desperately trying to distance himself from the approaching figure. He rolled onto his stomach, crying out when his arm hit the sand.

I will die here.

I am in Hell.

And I will die here.

What happened to a soul already lost to Jahannam when its bearer passed? What would become of the *naf*—the self—if he were to meet his end in such a place?

Would he see the gates of Jannah? Would he cross the bridge of as-Sirāt?

What if this is my punishment?

What if we died there in those winds of Old Samaria, and this is our judgment?

He scrambled through the filth, his elbows caked in mud. Water seeped through his burnous and chainmail, caressing his skin. He saw shapes darting in the shallows before him—like tadpoles but growing and changing as he watched. A fishy mouth appeared in the pool, and then another. He ignored them, dragging himself out from the mud and onto drier dirt.

He looked up and saw the stone plinth where Manat had stood. Her name was written in a blocky script he did not recognise.

Then Hubal was standing over him.

"I did not think it would be you here at the end." Hubal crouched down on his knees and regarded Razin. His eyes were empty now. Black pits of pooling darkness that made Razin's skin crawl to look into. "Perhaps the old man, yes. But those mules... Or Tomas, loyal to a fault, or so I had thought. He will be close now, walking blindly with his kin, guided by the Shepherd. Perhaps this time, the King will finally eat his fill? He has many mouths but only one belly, after all. But not you, no. I had thought you would be the first to fall. That doubt would be enough to break you. It is a strange thing to see the contradictions, as you surely do, and yet to embrace them all the same. Why is that, I wonder? And don't tell me it's your *faith*."

Hubal laughed, and in it, Razin heard the sound of his own despair.

"Perhaps it is good that it was you at the end," Hubal continued, reaching out toward him, his fingers unfurling like the wings of a bat. He motioned for the pouch. "I do not think the others would understand. Do you, Mohammedan? Do you understand?"

An oily light spilt around them, causing Razin to blink. He clutched the pouch tightly, keeping it out of Hubal's grasp, but Hubal crept closer, crouching on his haunches. The arrowheads remained suspended above his head, floating in mid-air.

I cannot stop him.

He saw the thing inside the Black Stone flex, an unending ripple of motion as it stirred—a shard of the void, transfixed. Soon it would break free.

"It matters not," said Hubal, though he sounded disappointed. "There will be time for understanding later. There will be time for many things later. But first—"

Hubal paused, his head tilting as he looked at something past Razin. The darkness within his eyes swelled, and he rose to his feet.

Razin heard footsteps approaching from behind him and strained to catch a glimpse. He saw a shadow moving in the gloom, half-hidden by the veil of sand.

Something from beyond? His mind turned to the forsaken entities Gizzal had mentioned, those that lurked where the boundaries between realms were thinnest.

But no, this was different.

Hubal scowled. "*Apsasû.*"

A leonine mouth, wicked fangs, and curved wings beating in the dark.

And then he remembered the girl. How could he have forgotten about her?

Tanit stalked across the sand, stepping over the rivulets of water spilling onto the dirt floor. Snapping shadows flitted behind her, bull-horned beasts and long-snouted mouths forming and reforming like a swarm of locusts. They watched her path, careful not to get too close.

Razin shivered when he saw her eyes. They glowed with a feral hunger, an inferno burning deep within her skull.

"Your sister is not here, little lion-mouth," Hubal addressed the girl, his palms open and his long nails dangling like talons from his fingers. "Her brain has long since rotted away in that wretched tomb she calls a home. You should go to her. See what has become of that bitch Lamassu."

Lion-mouth. Lamassu.

This savage girl couldn't possibly be one of the aladlammû.

Tanit came to a stop a few paces from Razin's feet.

"You are too late, anyway," Hubal declared, gesturing toward the Daughters standing behind him. They arched their backs like bridges, their upper bodies supported by their hands as water streamed between their legs. Three cascades of water flowed into the swirling sandstorm, transforming the dust into a frothing maelstrom, a tempestuous whirlwind. Razin glimpsed that fin again, spread out like a bat's wing as it glided through the water.

"Long have they waited for me to return and awaken them from their slumber, to fill their wombs so that they may empty them. And long have I waited to return to them!"

The air shimmered where the girl stood, and Razin thought he heard the faint sound of wings beating—once, twice…

She moved too quickly for him to see, a blur of colour within the storm.

Then, a crack reverberated through the air, like thunder, and the storm began to unravel—or rather, it parted. The sand and water split like curtains, splashing against the walls of the ravine.

Razin smelt smoke.

Ash and fire.

He wanted to run.

A monstrous figure emerged from the darkness, its crimson eyes leaving a trail of shimmering colour in its wake.

Razin found himself on his knees.

My sword!

He swiftly wedged the lip of the pouch between his belt and waistband, drawing his sword with a determined grip.

Now?

He looked up and saw the girl ensnared within the unspooling coils of the Falak. The creature had snatched her from the air before she could reach Hubal. Desperately, she fought against it, tearing into its obsidian scales with her nails until blood and gore crusted her hands and fingers.

I must help her.

He stumbled to his feet, his one arm hanging useless and the other clutching his scimitar. He pointed it toward the Falak.

He heard Hubal's laughter behind him. "Where are you going, Mohammedan?"

He retched but pressed on, refusing to falter. If he stopped now, he might never move again.

The girl was clawing at the serpent's skin, pulling great chunks of meat from it with hands that looked like claws. The Falak snapped at her with its sulphurous maw, but it couldn't close its jaws around her. It couldn't consume her.

The girl occupied more space than should have been possible. The Falak writhed and thrashed against her, not noticing as Razin made his approach.

And why would it care?

What could I do?

He swung his sword against the creature's side, slicing through wispy tendrils that covered its coarse hide. He stabbed again, piercing the hardened scales and then staggered back, gagging. Smoke and searing heat poured from the wound, reeking of putrid eggs and death, causing his eyes to water. His vision blurred, but still, he hacked.

The snake thing shuddered.

Had it felt me? Could I have hurt this thing that spews smoke and fire and promises the end of the world?

But no.

The girl had it now, between her teeth. Her mouth was too small, and yet she had it. She tore meat from between the razor-sharp spines, digging her fingers into the dense mass of fat and muscle at the base of its leathery fin.

The creature screamed, its flanks quivering and twisting as it struggled to dislodge Tanit from its back.

Kill it! Kill it!

Razin lurched forward, driven by a surge of determination, only to be sent sprawling once more as the Falak's tail slammed into his side. He hit the ground hard and fell face-first into the storm waters. A wall of pressure hit him, spinning him beneath the surface.

I will drown here.

He gasped, inhaling water.

I will drown here, and then the world will drown.

His sword slipped from his grasp, and in a moment of panic and desperation, he reached out, searching for something to hold onto.

And found stone.

His fingers slipped into the grooves like a climber's grip, and he held on. Things bit at his hands and feet, burning things and barbed things, and things with more limbs than he had fingers.

But he refused to let go. With a tremendous effort, he began to pull himself out of the water.

The biting things left him, leaving him crawling in misery upon the goddess's plinth. He spat water across the stone and lay there, gasping.

I have to help her.

He got up and waded back through the shallows, searching for his sword but not finding it.

The Falak screamed again in rage and pain. The girl was hurting it, disassembling it scale by scale, spine by spine.

Lion-mouth.

Apsasû.

He thought of the creature lurking beneath the pillars, the shackles and stone and its mad wretched games. The creature there had stunk of decay and misery. It was savage and wild, but they were not the same.

Razin found a spine in the water, sharp and black and as long as his leg. He dragged it from the mud and tucked it under his arm like a lance, stumbling toward the chaotic frenzy of blood and dirt and black scales. He nearly fell into the water again but managed to regain his balance. He would not get out a second time.

Then he saw Hubal.

Hubal roared at the serpent, urging it to dispense with the girl clinging to its fin, even as she ate through its back. Shaking his head, Hubal's arrowheads formed a halo-like fan around him. Then he turned his attention to the Daughters, shouting words that Razin couldn't discern over the howling wind.

But al-Uzza had heard.

The hyena-head moved like a spider, her arms acting as hind legs as she scuttled across the floor of the ravine. She was making for Tanit.

I have to help her.

How?

Razin glanced at the spine-lance cradled under his arm and then at Hubal.

He broke into a run.

The oily light danced ahead of Razin as he sprinted along the shore of the newly formed river. The light came from *within* the sandstorm, beyond the veil the Me-anesi had lifted.

Even before he drew near, Razin knew what it was.

The moon.

From another place.

Not here. That moon was long gone, swallowed by the beast.

This moon comes from home.

Razin set his jaw and quickened his pace, moving from a loping run to a full-fledged sprint as he bared down on Hubal.

On Dietmar.

He flinched at an ear-splitting screech from behind him, followed by the sound of sinewy skin unfurling, muscles tensing, and fangs snapping. The girl and the beast continued their tumultuous conflict.

He was close enough to see Hubal's tools now—the seven arrowheads whirling above his head. They gleamed in the moonlight, their crimson and silver hues like diamonds.

al-Uzza scuttled past, bringing with her a flood of still-coursing water. But Razin ignored the giant. His eyes were fixed on Hubal.

I can do this.

"Can you?"

Hubal turned and smiled, his eyeless face contorting, his nostrils flaring. The arrowheads above his head spun toward Razin.

They moved so fast.

He barely saw them.

But he felt them.

They hit him like the spikes of a mailed fist, tearing through his robes and mail coat and into his flesh. Blood sprayed from new wounds and old ones as the vicious barbs reopened his arm.

He cried out but didn't drop the lance.

I can't.

But Razin was too slow. Momentum lost, the element of surprise vanished.

Hubal seized him by the broken arm and yanked, pulling him to his knees and sending the lance sliding over the dirt. Then he pulled again, and Razin saw black and white but somehow managed to remain conscious.

"ENOUGH!" Hubal roared.

And there was quiet.

Only, it was the quiet of the catacombs when there should have been the roar of titans—of the Falak and Apsasû locked in mortal combat.

Then, wings, beating in the dark.

Hubal spun around, dragging Razin along with him. The arrowheads darted out once more, and something—not a human something—but something ancient and old moved within Hubal, like a mouth opening to scream.

There was a bestial stink, like wet fur and animal, of the wild places and the wind.

Talons like knives and nails extended, and teeth that were the same.

Razin caught a glimpse of golden eyes, wide and hungry. Then he fell away, pushed aside like a child by a monstrous strength that could have killed him but did not.

Hubal howled as Apsasû sank her teeth into his flesh, tearing through his shoulder. Her talons pierced his arms, trapping him within her grip.

Her paws.

She began to drag him closer, pulling the struggling Hubal toward her gaping maw, her unhinged jaw and rows of razor-sharp teeth.

But he would not go.

A blazing fire erupted from his mouth, a celestial blade forged from stars and shards of stolen moonlight. It scorched Apsasû's hair and singed her coat, saturating the air with her scent. She released her hold on his arms, relinquishing her grip.

Now it was Hubal lunging forward, his sword striking Apsasû's flank, while the arrowheads darted in and out, puncturing her tough hide. Apsasû roared with rage.

Razin tried to get up.

He could feel the earth shuddering beneath him.

al-Uzza was coming.

He looked up and saw her gnashing teeth and long slavering tongue, her mouth opening to consume them all. Then, her eyes widened.

And shock, and fear, and pain covered her face.

A sigh, like the sound of tearing fabric, resonated from behind Razin. He turned and saw Apsasû had finally caught hold of Hubal again. The air behind her wavered as she pumped the wings now hanging from her back.

Hubal screamed, straining against her grip.

Then she pulled and pulled again.

Hubal stopped screaming, and for a moment, he was Dietmar again. Relief glistened in his eyes.

He saw Razin and smiled.

And then Apsasû pulled him apart.

Razin cried out for his friend, whose death he had already mourned and would mourn again. His voice was lost, first to the wind and then to the shrieks and cries coming from above.

al-Uzza cried first and loudest, but then al-Lat and Mannat joined her cacophony. They screamed and screamed, at the sky, then at the figures on the ground beneath their feet. And then at each other.

Manat's head burst open as a rock hurled by al-Lat collided with her skull. Then al-Uzza struck her sister in the face, and both tumbled into the ravine, making the earth shudder a final time.

Razin rose to his feet.

Rock was falling all around him, the walls of the ravine collapsing as al-Lat and al-Uzza beat each other to death. He stepped aside as a boulder large enough to crack the walls of Jerusalem landed in front of him.

He felt unmoored, lost as the sand and wind and screaming daughters filled the world around him. His mind faltered, his limbs growing numb. He became aware of the blood that covered his arms and chest from half a dozen wounds.

They might kill him.

They might not.

Then he became aware of another thing.

The black waters were receding, dissipating into the earth as the goddesses closed their legs, ending the torrent that had surged through the Sandmouth. Dead things lay where the water had flowed—snakes with shells and many heads, snapping fish with hairy tails gasping their final breaths.

Razin looked up from the riverbed and saw the pale light again. A single ray arcing out from the walls of dark sand.

Movement caught his eye to the left.

The girl.

Apsasû.

Her eyes no longer gleamed. She was just a girl now.

As Razin began to limp toward her, she shook her head, stepping back.

He stared at her, watching as she moved into the shadows.

Not here. This place is not for you, her silent message conveyed.

With a slight tilt of her head, she vanished into the swirling veil of sand.

Razin blinked as more light shone out from the storm. It was growing brighter as the Me-anesi moved along the ridge of the ruined ravine.

The wind tugged at him as he walked, growing louder as he approached the centre of the howling sand.

He followed the moon.

He roamed the sands without a name and without a memory of having had a name.

He became a *šabaḥiyy*, a spirit dwelling in the foothills.

Days passed like that, and then weeks.

Gradually, his physical wounds began to heal. Although the scars on his soul remained, they would take longer to heal, if they healed at all.

He drew his water from a well the goat herders used and begged for bread, meat, and olives from pilgrims traveling along the road.

What interaction he had with others was done by way of hand gestures alone, and he soon forgot the sound of his own voice.

Those that saw him thought him mad. A lost fellahin who had given up on the world. But he had not given up. He had simply forgotten. It was remembering that threatened to plunge him into madness.

Some days he prayed. Others, he did not.

In moments of doubt, he asked himself how faith could endure what he had seen. Yet, in the depths of his doubt, he found solace in a counterquestion:

How could it not?

Each night, he buried the leather pouch containing the hand, intending to leave it entombed. But with the morning light, he would unearth it once again, unable to abandon it completely.

There was something he had to do: a promise made to a man who had been his brother. But the memory only offered itself in glimpses, and understanding eluded him.

He had opened the pouch once to look inside, hoping to stir his mind. His body had gone suddenly stiff and cold, a fragmented past stirring deep within his mind. His breath caught in fearful gasps as he peered into the bag.

But it was only a hand.

Nothing more.

One day, he wandered northward, straying farther than he had had since awaking in the hills. North meant lights and people, and he did not want those. Yet on that particular day, something stirred within him, compelling him to walk toward the distant twin peaks.

Their names had once danced on his tongue.

He knew their slopes.

Perhaps, he thought, when he got closer, he would remember their names again.

As night descended and weariness settled in, he gathered twigs and kindled a modest fire, patiently awaiting the veil of darkness.

He ate the dry bread he had begged from a group of Franks headed for Nazareth and chewed on a stalk of fennel. He thought of a garden then and laughing friends. But he did not know their names either.

He slept a while beneath the bushes. He stayed away from the caves. He didn't like those.

When he awoke, someone was watching him.

He added kindling to his fire, coaxing the coals back into life, and went about his business as usual, pretending not to notice the presence lingering in the darkness.

If they were bandits, he had nothing of value to offer. If it were anyone else, he would offer them space by his fire and leave them to it. He was not in the mood for company.

Perhaps this would be his end, he thought, killed by some bloodthirsty Frank who mistook him for a spy. A spy in tattered rags, devoid of weapons or sustenance.

Razin snorted to himself and looked up at the sound that emerged from the bushes. It was a sound he recognised, one that had annoyed him in the past. He squinted into the gloom and saw the faint outline of a horned figure approaching.

His heart skipped a beat, ready to run, but something held him back.

Not horns, he realised.

They were long, sharp ears sprouting from a narrow face above a pair of warm brown eyes.

He knew that face. He had seen it before, but it should have been gone… gone… lost to the seas in a place that shouldn't be.

"…Balaam?" he said, his voice barely more than a croak.

The mule's ears twitched, and it stepped out into the light, revealing itself fully.

"But you died," Razin muttered in disbelief.

Balaam shook his russet head once, affirming his presence, and Razin's gaze shifted to a second figure behind him, still in shadows.

"Silensus, too?"

A soft bray answered his question.

"There is space by the fire, but I have no food."

I am mad, truly.

Balaam stomped his hoof and turned in the sand, then craned his neck back to look at Razin.

His ears twitched impatiently.

You want me to follow?

"In the morning—"

Haw!

"Now I remember why I didn't like you."

Balaam stomped his hoof again and started walking back the way he'd come.

"Wait!" Razin cried out, his voice filled with a sudden sense of urgency. He didn't want to be left alone. "I'll come. Just wait!"

He hurriedly got to his feet and extinguished the fire. Then he turned back to retrieve the pouch from the sand near where he had been sleeping.

He needed that; he'd promised. He thought of Dietmar then and caught his breath, his memories flooding back with a bittersweet intensity. He waited for them to pass and then wiped his eyes.

He could see the mules walking ahead, their long heads swaying from side to side as they trudged up the slope. More hills loomed before them, and lights twinkled in the distance.

A town.

Its name was Nablus.

The moon had just started to rise.

For all their help with this book, my love and thanks go to my mom and dad—first readers, always. My tireless editor and friend, Scott Miller; Stephen Spinas, who listened and shared his wisdom while we plowed through the cheap bottles, and then the expensive ones; Maxine, who suffered us; Justin and Dev, who listened to my mad ramblings and then somehow managed the patience to read through them too (Justin, anyway); and Dylan, who didn't read it but heard all about it. Brett Allen-White, who wrote this book's first mini-review and, hopefully, many a tasty lick for *God is in the Rot.* Lisa Fillmore, who should be done with the book soon, hopefully. Then, to Alasca and her Arab Spring. Thank you to Hussein, who sat through my naive questions with patience and compassion.

Ultimately, 'Pilgrim' is a work of fiction, but it would not have been made possible without the work and research of Ahmed al-Rawi, J. E. Hanauer, Patricia Crone, Dan Gibson, The Organisation for Islamic Awareness, Adrian J. Boas, Wim Raven, H. Radau, Brandon R. Grafius, John W. Morehead, Dan Jones, Peter Frankopan, Simon Sebag Montefiore, Matt Cardin, and Timothy K. Beal, to name but a few. Any historical inaccuracies or poorly wrought depictions are, of course, my own, but there are undoubtedly fewer of them thanks to the above authors and their works.

Finally, thanks must go to those who took a chance and read 'Pilgrim' while it was still in its infant stages—strangers who owed me nothing and yet took the time to patiently comb through this sizeable manuscript, to point out errors and inconsistencies, their likes and dislikes. My warm thanks to Evan Noren, Graham Wilcox from 'Old Moon Quarterly,' and to Zach Rosenberg. Perhaps this is not quite the book you were looking for; nonetheless, it has been made far better by your insight and thoughtful comments.

Mitchell Lüthi is a writer and producer based in Cape Town, South Africa. He has written a number of scripts, short stories, and radio plays. "Pilgrim" is his first full-length novel.

In addition to his writing, Lüthi produces and scores the Sentinel Creatives Podcast. His short stories, "The Bone Fields" and "The Breeding Mound", received honorable mentions in the 2020 and 2022 L. Ron Hubbard Writers of the Future Competitions.

Made in the USA
Coppell, TX
20 June 2025

50958695R00402